# GARDEN OF LIES

## Eileen Goudge

## CORGI BOOKS

# GARDEN OF LIES

Originally published in Great Britain by Bantam Press, a division of Transworld Publishers Ltd.

PRINTING HISTORY
Bantam Press edition published 1989
Corgi edition published 1990

Copyright © Eileen Goudge Zuckerman 1989

This book is set in 10/11 pt English Times
by Colset Private Limited, Singapore.

Corgi Books are published by Transworld Publishers Ltd., 61–63 Uxbridge Road, Ealing, London W5 5SA, in Australia by Transworld Publishers (Australia) Pty. Ltd., 15–23 Helles Avenue, Moorebank, NSW 2170, and in New Zealand by Transworld Publishers (N.Z.) Ltd., Cnr. Moselle and Waipareira Avenues, Henderson, Auckland.

Printed and bound in Great Britain by
BPCC Hazell Books
Aylesbury, Bucks, England
Member of BPCC Ltd.

Eileen Goudge is a descendant of the
novelist Elizabeth Goudge. She lives with
her husband in New York City.

*To my mother and father,
who made it possible
to dream*

# Acknowledgements

One of the best reasons for writing a book, I think, is the opportunity it gives to live other lives. For this vicarious thrill, and their generous assistance, I would like to thank the following professionals: Fred Queller, for giving me a day in the life of a trial attorney, and providing his valuable time and transcripts. John Freedman, for vetting the book for legal accuracy (and staying up late to do so). Dr Paul Wilson, for his medical expertise and thoughtful editorial comments. John Robinson (formerly First Lieutenant, 1st Battalion, Third Marines) both for helping me through the dark days of computer meltdown and for sharing his Vietnam experiences (he asks a rather unique favor – if anyone traveling to Vietnam should climb to the top of Dong Ha Mountain, please look for his class ring, which he lost in battle there twenty years ago: Cranbrook School, Class '63, silver with blue stone). My dear friend Brenda Preston, whose roses have given me such pleasure through the years, and who provided useful information about them. Susan Ginsburg, for her guidance and for believing in me in the first place. Pamela Dorman, my editor at Viking, for her help in 'fine-tuning' the book.

And last, but far from least, my wonderful husband and agent, Al Zuckerman, who is all my heroes rolled into one, and who provided the glue that holds it (and me) together. Without him, this book truly would not have been possible.

# Prologue

*A poor widow once lived in a little cottage with a garden in front of it in which grew two rose trees, one bearing white roses, the other red. She had two daughters, who were just like the two rose trees; one was called Snow-white and the other Rose-red ...*
Grimm's Fairy Tales

Sylvie Rosenthal stood before the tall gilt-framed mirror in the millinery department at Bergdorf's.

'I don't know,' she said to the saleswoman hovering behind her. Sylvie straightened the brim of the green straw cartwheel. 'You don't think perhaps it's a bit too much?'

'I saw Eleanor Roosevelt wearing one just like it, in a newsreel just last week,' the plump saleswoman offered. 'Of course, she wasn't . . . ah, *expecting*.' She dropped her voice to a funereal hush.

Sylvie felt a flash of irritation. Why was *everyone* always reminding her? Dear God, couldn't they let her *forget* just once?

She fingered the straw brim with its ruching of apple-green tulle, her annoyance at the woman lost in a wave of self-doubt. *Oh dear, if only Gerald were here. I never know what to choose. And I'll feel so awful if he doesn't like it.*

She took the hat off, and peered at her reflection, feeling, as she had so many times in the eight years since her marriage, puzzled, unworthy even. *When he says I'm beautiful, God knows what he sees.*

She saw a long, thin face, ordinary except for the eyes. They were wide, a champagne-bottle green, and her lashes and eyebrows were so pale, they were almost invisible. Her eyes seemed somehow to look perpetually astonished.

Sylvie remembered Gerald once telling her she reminded him of a Tenniel engraving of *Alice*. She smiled to herself. *Yes, perhaps he's right about that. I do think I'm in Wonderland sometimes.*

She glanced around her. Shopping here at Bergdorf's

11

was incredible, a secret paradise seemingly untouched by the war. The stone urns erupting in sprays of tiger lilies and orchids. The delicate French tables and bow-front vitrines filled with lovely hand-blown perfume bottles – even if these days the perfume itself was ersatz. The enormous crystal chandelier suspended from the marble rotunda. How far she'd come from the days she'd picked over the sale table at Ohrbachs, when paying more than five dollars for a hat would have been unthinkable. *Yes*, she thought, *I have tumbled right down the hole into Wonderland*.

Tomorrow, the Golds' annual Fourth of July lawn party, and pregnant or not, she was looking forward to it. The red-white-and-blue striped tents; the smoky mouth-watering barbecue smells; then dancing to Lester Lanin on an enormous platform ringed with Japanese lanterns. Except no Japanese lanterns this year, Evelyn had told her. Evelyn's kid brother, shot down near Okinawa. Japanese lanterns were the last thing in the world she wanted at her party.

Sylvie carefully took off the green hat, and surrendered it to the saleswoman.

Perhaps the navy Lilly Daché with its red ribbon would be more appropriate, Sylvie pondered. And with its military brim, more in keeping with the times. She so wanted Evelyn to—

Sylvie froze.

Low in her abdomen, she felt a sudden heaviness, as if inside her the baby had plunged downward. No, was actually *pushing* down. A hot pressure. And, oh God, *it wasn't letting up*. The ache in her lower back that had been bothering her all morning now became a fistful of needles jamming into the base of her spine.

*It's not happening*, she thought. *It can't be. I won't let it*. But she knew it was.

Deep inside her she felt a snap, like a piece of elastic giving way. Warm liquid, what felt like a river of it, gushed between her thighs.

Sylvie staggered as if someone had struck her. She felt her

heart bump up into her throat. Then she stared down, horrified at the spreading, darkening stain on the beige carpet. Her water had broken. Dear God! She felt as ashamed as when she'd wet herself as a child in school.

Icy dread sluiced through her.

This was it, no more pretending to be delighted, over-joyed even, reassuring herself the baby was Gerald's, *had* to be Gerald's. Now the truth. Fear closed about her heart like a cold fist. *It might not be Gerald's.* And, oh God in heaven, if it wasn't . . . if it looked like Nikos? Eyes black, with his coffee skin and springy black hair . . .

No, she had to shut that out, slam the door on it.

Sylvie, struggling to calm herself, peered into the mirror. This time she saw not Alice, but a puffy, blurred face floating above a grossly misshapen body. She felt strangely detached, as if she were gazing at some exotic specimen of marine life in an aquarium. Or a drowned woman, her face a watery gray-green, filaments of red-blond hair drifting about her pale neck like seaweed.

'Madame . . . are you all right?' An anxious voice reached through the green depths to her.

Sylvie turned to find the henna-haired salesclerk gaping at her, eyes boggling behind cat's-eye glasses, the clown spots of orange rouge on her sagging cheeks now a dark blood red.

Yes, that's where she was. Bergdorf's, Hats. The green or the blue? She lifted the blue hat from its stand on the glass countertop, fingering its veil. Cunning, the way little beads of jet had been sewn into the netting to make it sparkle . . .

'*Madame?*' Plump fingers gripped her arm.

Sylvie, forcing herself, managed to resist the current that kept pulling at her.

She opened her mouth to say she was fine, please don't make a fuss.

Then in the pit of her stomach she felt a thump that spiraled up into a wave of dizziness. No, she was *not* all right. No, definitely not.

13

Her knees began to buckle. She clutched the edge of the counter, steadying herself, and was confronted by a row of dummy heads, each sporting a different hat. Their smooth eyeless faces sent a chill through her. They seemed to be accusing her, a jury rendering a verdict: guilty.

*If only Gerald were here!* He would know what to do. He could summon a maître d'just by raising his eyebrow. A flick of his finger and like magic a taxi would materialize from snarling traffic. A single *look* from Gerald at the bank could bring clerks, cashiers, loan officers scurrying.

But no, wrong, Gerald must not know. Thank God he'd still be in Boston until tomorrow . . . bank business . . . about war bonds or something.

Sylvie covered her mouth, one hand clapped over the other as hysterical laughter bubbled to her lips. The one person she needed, depended on . . . now, when she needed him most, she dared not turn to him.

How could she have done this to him? *How?*

Gerald was so good. Always. Her headaches – when she had one, even the slightest little noise set off an avalanche inside her skull and, God bless him, Gerald made sure that he and the help moved about the house silent as shadows.

Sylvie thought of the days when not just her head, but her feet, her whole body had constantly ached, when a cab ride seemed the most heavenly luxury. Standing all day passing money through the grille of her teller's cage, stampeded in the subway, and then home, climbing the cabbage-smelling stairs, six never-ending flights, every blessed night.

Exhausted, wondering how much longer she could manage to stand on her feet, Sylvie felt as if she'd just now climbed those stairs. She shivered. Why was it so cold? The hottest day of the year, the radio had said, and yet the store felt like an icebox.

'Should I call a doctor?' The salesclerk's shrill voice broke in on her.

'No, I . . .'

14

The ache in the small of her back was spreading, like a tight band wrapping about her middle, as if she were wearing a girdle that was too small. Pain slammed through her in icy waves.

*God, God, get me to the hospital. Any minute, they'll have to carry me out of here on my back, in my stained dress. Everybody staring. God, no, I'd rather die.*

She shook free and pushed past the perfume counters, their mixture of fragrances cloying, making her stomach heave. Somehow she made it outside, through the heavy glass exit door, wrenching her way to the curb through air so thick it was like syrup.

'Lenox Hill Hospital,' she gasped, sagging into the back of a cab.

She cranked the window down, letting in a blast of hot air, a soup of exhaust fumes and baking sidewalks. Still, she couldn't stop shivering.

The elderly cabbie began humming 'While We're Young.' Sylvie wanted him to stop, but felt too wretched to speak, and too guilty.

'Wadda ya say, now that we got those Nazi bastards pushed outta Egypt, ya think Ike'll invade Italy?'

Plainly, he was the talkative type. She stared at the little roll of fat bulging over the back of his collar. It was an angry boiled-red color, scribbled with wiry black hairs.

Sylvie wanted to be polite and answer, but just then she felt nausea rolling up her middle in a slow greasy wave.

As the taxi lurched up Park Avenue, she got that tight feeling again, starting in her lower back and spreading around her abdomen like pincers. Tighter and tighter, until it became a red-hot shaft driving straight through her. *God!* Sylvie stiffened, arching her back, feeling the springs of the caved-in seat digging into her buttocks. To keep from screaming, she bit the inside of her mouth.

Sylvie longed for her mother so intensely that for a minute she could feel Mama's firm plump arms about her, smell the sharp eucalyptus scent of the Vick's VapoRub she always massaged into Sylvie's chest when her asthma

15

was bad. *Don't cry, shainenke*, Mama's voice soothed inside her head. *I'm here. I won't leave you.*

She could see her mama's sleep-puffy face, the frayed gray rope of her braid twisting down one shoulder of her worn flannel wrapper. And in her watery blue eyes, the ghost of the little girl who had played croquet on the lawn of her papa's great house in Leipzig before she'd had to flee to America.

Mama, abandoned by her weak husband, selling postcards and catalogues in the Frick Museum for twenty-eight dollars a week, foolishly dreaming of that better life she had left behind.

It had embarrassed Sylvie to hear how she spoke of the museum, as if she owned it, as if every painting were theirs.

*Tomorrow after school you'll visit me at the museum, and I'll show you the new Rembrandt. Think of it, Sylvie. Such beauty, to own such beauty!*

*We owned nothing!* Sylvie cried out to herself, struggling against the claws of pain that drove into her now. Only a few sticks of furniture. And the hand-me-downs that Mama's sister, Aunt Willie, whose husband had built up a big business in fox collars and stoles, sent over in the gold-colored boxes meant for his merchandise.

*Mama always said we had something better than Aunt Willie's big house on Ditmas Avenue. We had each other.*

But that wasn't true, Sylvie thought with a pang. *Mama left me, didn't she?*

The pain in Sylvie's belly seemed to snake up into her throat. *Mama . . . oh Mama, why did you have to die?*

She closed her eyes, felt tears burning behind her lids slip out the corners, slide down her cheeks. She thought of that day, prissy Mr Harmon calling her from her teller's cage into his office. *Your mother . . . I'm sorry . . . a stroke.* Everything had gone fuzzy and gray, then black. And then, waking up, she was riding in a limousine. Leather seats smooth as melted butter, deep cushions and carpeting under her feet, a window separating the back

16

seat from the front, with a gray-capped driver. How strange, a whole other world!

Beside her, an arm around her shoulders giving her support, was a man. *Why, it was Mr Rosenthal himself, the boss of the whole bank!* She felt alternately hot and cold, alarmed and thrilled. She thought she'd seen him looking at her, though he'd never actually spoken to her. The other girls gossiped about him over coffee and sandwiches at the luncheonette – his wife had died more than twenty years ago, leaving no children, and they all wondered why he hadn't married again. She'd thought perhaps other women were too much in awe of him to get close. Sylvie recalled how intimidating he always looked, striding through to his office, his suits always perfectly pressed, gold cuff links winking at monogrammed cuffs, issuing orders in a quiet but commanding tone.

But here he didn't seem at all frightening. She saw kind blue eyes caught in a fine net of wrinkles, older than she would have guessed, at least fifty, silver-blond hair so fine the white ridge of his scalp gleamed through it. He was taking her to the hospital, he'd told her. To her mother. Hearing him, Sylvie could feel the calm strength radiating from him, flowing into her.

Then, afterwards, taking care of Mama's hospital bill, making all the funeral arrangements, then looking after her when she was so sick she couldn't get out of bed. Never once, not *once*, being forward, trying to take advantage, until he'd asked her to marry him. Him wanting to marry her, oh the miracle of it! She'd done nothing to deserve it.

And, oh God, look how she had repaid him.

The memory of Nikos chafed like a pebble in a shoe. For a whole year, each morning when she woke up, it was there, sometimes more irritating and sometimes less, but always there. It lodged in her throat when she tried to eat. It tormented her sleep. It mocked her fierce yearning that the baby growing inside her would look like Gerald.

Sylvie laced her fingers over the hard mound of her belly. The tightness was beginning to subside, and the

17

pain. *If only*, she cried to herself, *I could have gotten pregnant before Nikos, then I would be sure*.

It wasn't for lack of trying, God knew. Taking her temperature every morning and marking it on the chart Gerald kept by the bed – three years of that! And those visits to the doctor! Lying there spread out like a chicken to be gutted. Cold steel probing inside her until she'd wanted to scream. And then being told there was nothing wrong. Give it time. What did doctors know?

She'd wept seeing the disappointment in Gerald's face each month when her period came.

Why couldn't she give him just this one thing? Look at the glorious new life he'd given her. Not her fault, three different Park Avenue specialists had told her; but Sylvie knew better.

She felt sure she could get pregnant if only she could find a way not to hate having sex with him.

How could she feel this way? Why? What husband in the whole world was ever more kind and generous?

Yet the memory of their wedding night, seeing him naked for the first time, still made her cringe. In his crisp, hand-tailored suits he'd looked large, prosperous. Naked, his belly a sagging pouch, he looked old, grotesque almost. And he had breasts, *breasts* like a girl's! To this day, Sylvie felt revulsion when he lowered himself on her, no matter how many million times she told herself she loved him and he loved her. His doughy belly pressing against her, making her gasp for breath, his *thing* inching its way into her. Then such grunting and heaving, as if he were in pain. *It'll get better*, she'd told herself over and over, *it* has *to. It's only because we're not used to each other*.

But when he announced his desire by taking off his pajamas and folding them at the foot of the bed, after eight years her flesh still shrank.

And then Nikos . . .

A flare of pain in her abdomen jerked Sylvie from her reverie. She twisted in the back seat of the cab, as if that

18

somehow would let her escape its hot punishing grip.

As the taxi jerked right and left, weaving its way through the clotted traffic, she leaned forward against the front seat, gasping, cradling her huge belly as gingerly as if it were a bomb about to explode.

'I've changed my mind,' she told the driver. 'Please take me to St Pius instead.' She gave him the address and in the rearview mirror saw him roll his eyes. He'd never get a fare back downtown from that part of the Bronx, but up there in her old neighborhood she would feel, well, safer somehow.

Just in case Gerald called, she'd leave word with Bridget that she was visiting her old friend Betty Kronsky. Later she could say that the pains had become so bad there hadn't been time to get back downtown or to call that stuffy Doctor Handler, who was Gerald's college roommate.

She knew this was crazy, hopeless really. Eventually Gerald would have to find out. But for now at least it felt easier. Back in the old neighborhood, she would feel closer to Mama, almost as if Mama were soothing her, protecting her. And maybe, well, she'd have a miracle – a baby that looked just like Gerald, or her.

Out of midtown now, the taxi picked up speed, gliding past the stately apartment houses that lined Park Avenue. Sylvie glanced at the diamond-studded Patek Philippe watch Gerald had given her last Chanukah. Past two. God, would they get there in time?

Abruptly, it seemed, the elegance of Park Avenue became the sordidness of Harlem, and they were rattling over cracked pavement, potholes, debris littering the streets. And worse. Old drunks crumpled on the sidewalks. She shut her eyes. But she couldn't shut out the stink. The smells from mounds of uncollected, rotting garbage.

Then the the humming vibration of the taxi's wheels crossing the Third Avenue Bridge into the Bronx. Sylvie opened her eyes. Turning off Bruckner Boulevard, she saw the streets were filled with children – children of all

19

sizes and colors, splashing in the gush flowing from uncapped fire hydrants, darting in and out, oblivious to the traffic, so heedless of danger. She saw a nappy-haired boy with smooth chocolate skin chasing a little girl, her long black braids whipsawing wildly at her back. Sylvie shuddered, imagining *her* child here, a wild brown thing playing hide-and-seek behind garbage cans.

The cab lurched to a halt. Sylvie paid and maneuvered her bulk out the door, her legs threatening to buckle as she stood.

She stared up at St Pius Hospital. Its brick and granite facade was so blackened with grime it made her think of an oven, one that hadn't been cleaned in years. She felt her stomach knot in dismay. It would be like an oven inside, no air-conditioning, probably no fans either.

The street noises assaulted her, children shrieking, radios blaring, voices yelling in Spanish from open windows. Fighting back waves of dizziness, she trudged up the hospital's front steps.

A deafening crack caused her to reel, her heart smashing against her rib cage. She was so startled she stumbled against the top step, and only barely kept from falling by catching the iron rail. Then she saw. Kids. They were setting off firecrackers on the sidewalk. Of course, tomorrow was the Fourth of July. She'd forgotten.

Glancing up past the kids to the tenement window above, Sylvie saw a pregnant woman in a faded print duster, her enormous stomach sagging over the sill, following Sylvie's progress with an impassive stare while a plump brown baby squirmed at her breast. Sylvie turned back and pushed her way inside, feeling unsteady. Gray spots skated across her field of vision.

She could feel the contraction beginning to tighten. Sylvie was suddenly so dizzy she didn't trust herself to let go of the doorknob. The floor tilted sharply.

*Please . . . someone . . . help me . . .*, she opened her mouth to say as a hood of gray gauze slipped over her eyes, but no words came.

The black and white floor tiles swam toward her. Something cool and hard smacked her cheekbone. Pain rolled through her like distant thunder.

Then darkness.

Opening her eyes, Sylvie found herself in an iron bed with rails on either side. A green curtain surrounded it. Through the slit where the two ends didn't quite meet, she could see the opposite wall. A framed picture of Jesus hung between two tall windows, His eyes raised heavenward, palms extended to show puncture wounds dripping blood.

Sylvie hoisted herself on to her elbows. The effort sent hammers of pain smashing into her temples, causing her to cry out. Her face felt stiff. She touched her nose, her fingers meeting coarse adhesive.

With a clattering of metal rings, the curtain was yanked back. A woman in a white uniform, with a short white wimple covering her head, stood over her. The overhead fluorescent light reflected off her eyeglasses, giving her an odd expressionless look. Her face was as white and rubbery-smooth as a boiled egg.

'You're lucky,' she said. 'It's not broken.'

Sylvie groaned. 'I think I'm going to throw up.'

'No, you're not.'

The stern reply so startled her Sylvie forgot how sick she felt.

'It only *feels* that way,' she kindly assured Sylvie. 'You'll be fine.'

Then the nun-nurse began rolling a tight rubber glove over her hand. From the tray she'd carried in with her, she selected a tube and smeared something white and creamy over her gloved fingers.

'I'm going to examine you to see how far you're dilated,' she said. 'My name is Sister Ignatious, by the way,' she added as she pulled back the sheet and roughly inserted two greased rubber fingers into Sylvie's vagina.

Sylvie arched backward, her whole being shriveling from

21

the invasion. A cold crampy feeling spread throughout her lower half as the fingers probed and prodded.

Sister Ignatious withdrew, and clumsily patted her arm. 'Six centimeters,' she announced. 'You've a while to go yet. Your first?'

Sylvie nodded, feeling suddenly like a very small child, scared, helpless, and so alone. Tears gathered on her lower lashes.

Sister Ignatious disappeared, returning a few minutes later carrying a basin of soapy water and a razor.

Sylvie, alarmed, asked, 'What are you going to do?'

'Now, now, let's not make a fuss,' clucked the sister. 'I'm only going to shave you. It's for your own good.'

Eyes squeezed shut, Sylvie submitted to having her gown raised once again. A rough wet washcloth scraped over her abdomen, moving lower. Water dribbled uncomfortably between her legs. An icy hand was placed across her stomach. How could anyone's hand be so cold in this heat?

Sylvie was ordered to hold still. 'Never mind your contraction, dear.' While the razor scraped over her pubis like a small animal, pinching and clawing, the rest of her body rippled with great thundering waves of pain. She struggled not to cry out or move. She wanted to be good, to do what she was told.

And what else *could* she do?

Finally Sister Ignatious straightened up, removing the basin and lowering Sylvie's gown. 'Dr Phillips will be in to see you shortly,' she said. With a clatter of metal curtain rings, she was gone.

The next hours were agony beyond anything Sylvie would ever have thought possible. In her torture, she forgot about Gerald, and Nikos, even the baby inside her struggling to be born.

There was only the pain.

It no longer was coming in waves, with lulls in between, but had become a never-ending surge.

White-gowned figures flitted in and out of her vision. A

gum-smacking girl with a clipboard took her name and asked questions about insurance. Then a tall gray-haired man wearing a green smock who introduced himself as Dr Phillips and asked her to open her knees so he could examine her. She felt no embarrassment, as normally she would have. Only discomfort. She cried out. Sweat dribbled down her face. Her skin prickled as if it were on fire. Gentle hands placed a cool wet cloth over her forehead.

Sylvie heard a scream, which seemed an echo of her own. She realized dimly that there was a bed beyond her curtain that must be occupied by another woman who was also in labor.

She could feel the baby moving lower, becoming a fiery pressure. Sylvie instinctively bore down against it, grunting and heaving. It seemed to shift. Could this horrible pain inside her be dislodged? Could she *push* it out?

'Don't push yet,' a voice commanded.

Through the red veil of her pain, she forced herself to focus on the face hovering above her. Sister Ignatious. 'I have to,' Sylvie whimpered in protest.

'Wait until we get you into Delivery,' the nun said.

Sylvie was resisting the urge to push, but it felt unbearable. She felt as helpless as if she were being strangled, and could do nothing to save herself. But it wasn't only her neck being squeezed to death, it was her whole body. She'd never survive this without being torn in half.

How in God's name did women get through this, and live? And not once, but several times. How could *anyone* choose to go through this again once they knew what it was like?

She wouldn't. Never. Not for Gerald. Not for any man.

Strong hands lifted her from the bed on to a gurney. Sylvie shivered, even though it was so hot she was gasping for breath. Her body was drenched with sweat, her hospital gown twisted underneath her like a wrung-out rag. She tried to clamp her knees together, to keep the pressure from tearing her apart, but her knees would not stay together. She clutched herself between her legs, humiliated at being seen doing this, yet desperate to relieve the horrible burning pressure.

She was dimly aware of being rolled down a corridor, rubber wheels bumping over uneven linoleum. A new room. Sudden, blinding brightness. Light from a huge lamp in the center bouncing off shiny green tiles. Stainless steel everywhere.

Sylvie groaned, twisting helplessly. Panic inched its way up her throat, blocking her air, causing her to fear she might choke to death. This cold awful place, like a public bathroom – nothing could be brought to life in this place.

She was hoisted on to a table. Her legs spread apart, feet strapped into high metal stirrups.

'Relax, Sylvia. It's going to be all right. You're doing just fine.' Dr Phillips's voice behind that mask. Kind blue eyes, and a shaggy gray hedge of eyebrows.

But who was Sylvia? Then she remembered. *She* was. The girl with the clipboard hadn't gotten her name right.

She began to push. It was terrible. Pushing was almost as bad as not pushing, but she couldn't stop herself. She heard gobbling animal sounds escape her. She couldn't stop those, either. She no longer had any control of her body. *It* was controlling her.

Voices filtered through the roaring of blood in her ears, telling her push. PUSH.

A black rubber mask was clamped over her nose and mouth. Sylvie fought it, trying to push it away in panic, afraid she would be suffocated, but the hand holding it only pressed down harder. A sweetish aroma enveloped her, followed by a spiraling light-headed sensation.

'I'm giving you a little gas,' Sister Ignatious said. 'Breathe in. It'll help.'

Just when she could feel her body about to split open, Sylvie felt the pressure abruptly ease. Something small and wet – far smaller than the gigantic thing inside that had caused her so much pain – slithered free.

She heard a tiny gurgled cry.

24

Sylvie sobbed, this time from relief. She felt as if a crushing boulder had been rolled off her. She seemed to float, weightless, at least a foot above the table.

'A girl!' she heard someone shout.

A moment later a tightly wrapped bundle was thrust into her arms.

Sylvie blinked as she stared at the tiny face peeking out from the white folds of the blanket. The vast relief she'd felt turned to crashing despair.

*It's so dark!* A mass of glistening black hair framed a tiny squashed-looking face the color of an old penny. Its eyes opened, and Sylvie saw with a shock two gleaming jet buttons. Weren't all babies' eyes supposed to be blue?

Sylvie felt her insides funneling down like sand through an hourglass. She had a falling sensation as she stared into that tiny dark crumpled face, as if she were slipping down into a black void.

Nikos's child. There could be no doubt. None.

But still, she longed to hold it. Felt her nipples stiffen painfully with the desire to clasp it to her breast.

She turned her face away, a new kind of pain welling up in her, tears sliding down her cheeks. *God, I can't. I don't want to. She's his baby, not mine and Gerald's. How can I love her? It will kill Gerald, make him stop loving* me.

'They all cry,' she heard Sister Ignatious observe knowingly to the young nurse at her side as she relieved Sylvie of her burden.

Sylvie was wheeled into another room. It looked the same as the previous one, except that her bed faced a window overlooking a brick alley. There were three beds besides hers, all occupied. Two of the women were asleep, the other one eyed her sympathetically.

'Well, it's over at least, ain't it?' She addressed Sylvie with the Bronx twang she herself would have had if Mama, thank God, hadn't constantly corrected her speech, kept her insulated with all those afternoons in the Frick, and Saturdays at the plays, concerts, dance recitals to which Mama often got free tickets.

Sylvie acknowledged her with a nod, too exhausted to speak.

'My third,' the roommate continued, unfazed. She had an open face framed by curly brown hair. Large, merry brown eyes and a smattering of freckles across her upturned nose. She sighed. 'Another girl. Dom was countin' on a boy this time. Boy, is he gonna flip! Not that he don't like girls, mind you. It's just he was kinda hopin' for a boy.'

'He doesn't know?' Sylvie had trouble forming the words. Her mouth felt stuffed full of cotton.

The girl gave a raspy laugh. 'That's the US Navy for ya. Baby wasn't due for two more weeks. They're shipping Dom home next week for the big event.' The smile faded and her expression darkened. 'His ma, I coulda called her, you know. The old bitch, excuse my French. But I figured she'd just give me a hard time like she always does. ''You shoulda waited,'' ' she mimicked in a whiny, nasal voice. ' ''Doncha think Dom's got enough on his mind being at sea without worryin' about more babies. Isn't two enough?'' Ha! She oughta talk some sense into her son when he climbs into bed. Who does she think I'm married to, the friggin' Pope? Whew! Damn good thing she's in Brooklyn. Don't see much of her since me and the girls moved up here to be with Ma . . . just until Dom gets home, that is. Ma's lookin' after Marie and Clare right now, or she'd be here.' She reached for her handbag on the metal stand beside her bed, fishing out a pack of Lucky Strikes.

'Cigarette?' Sylvie shook her head. The girl shrugged, tossing away her match. 'Name's Angie. Angelina Santini.' She squinted at Sylvie through the haze of smoke drifting from her nostrils. 'How 'bout you? Got any other kids?'

'No,' Sylvie said with a shudder, wondering again why any sane woman would go through that kind of torture more than once. Yet in some small way she felt comforted by Angie's easy confidence. As far as Angie was concerned, they were two soldiers sharing the same foxhole.

'It's rough, I know.' Angie nodded knowingly. 'Especially the first time. But you have a way of forgettin'. It's ... whatdayacallit ... human nature. You sorta blank it out ... like when your man's on shore leave and you ain't seen him for four months ...' Angie sighed wistfully, then, at the squeak of footsteps outside their door, she jerked upright and quickly stubbed out her cigarette. 'If the sisters catch me smoking in this old firetrap ... say, I didn't get your name.'

'Sylvie.' She instinctively felt that Angie was someone she could trust.

Angie flopped back on her pillow, elbow cocked, hand supporting her head. 'You look like hell, Sylvie. No offense. I know I do too. Why don't we get some shut-eye while we still can?'

Sylvie managed a weak smile. 'Yes. I am tired.' She felt half-dead, as if she could sleep for a year.

The same picture of Jesus she'd had in the other room hung on the wall opposite her bed. Bloody palms outspread. Eyes upturned in agony. A bloody welt on His chest, making her think of the purple scar above Nikos's left knee.

Drifting asleep, Sylvie thought of her lover.

She remembered that first day. She had expected the person applying for the handyman job to be elderly, or a kid like the others she'd interviewed, males not eligible for the draft. She'd opened the service door, and there was Nikos. She saw him as clearly as if he were standing before her now. It had been raining, and his boots were wet and dirty. At first, that was all she'd noticed. Those knee-high, heavy-duty work boots, so unlike the sleek black rubbers that fit neat as sealskin over Gerald's Italian shoes. And this new man was tracking muddy footprints all across her immaculate kitchen's black and white tiles. He walked with a slight limp, and she wondered if he'd been wounded in battle.

Then her gaze had traveled upward, taking in the stocky figure in a beat-up khaki mackintosh, a mass of black curls glistening with raindrops, a pair of eyes black as new moons in a face that seemed to throw off light. Tiny creases radiated from the corners of his eyes, though he couldn't have been more than thirty.

A sturdy arm thrust forward, and she had taken his hand. Huge, she remembered, the skin calloused, his wrist matted with black hair. She had stared at that hand, fascinated, unable to meet those piercing black eyes.

Then he took off his mack, and she saw the small triangle of black hair that crowned his sturdy chest, disappearing into the collar of his khaki shirt. She'd never seen so much hair on a man. Gerald's body had practically no hair, except for the sparse silvery fluff between his legs. And Gerald had small hands for a man his size, smooth and dainty as a girl's. He sometimes reminded her of the tenors in the operas he loved so, barrel-bodied men with a woman's grace, flitting about the stage like bumblebees.

'I am Nikos Alexandros,' he boomed. Then grinned, a brilliant show of teeth. 'You have work? Good! You work for me.'

She thought his broken English oddly charming.

She learned he was from Cyprus, that he'd been a seaman on a British tanker, torpedoed near Bermuda, but survived six days without food or water on a raft. He was one of the lucky ones, he explained in his halting way, though his leg had been nearly crushed. Sylvie understood, now, about the limp.

What she didn't understand was the sudden breathlessness that had come over her. Sylvie nodded, and said, 'Yes. I think you could work for us. You look very . . .' she'd been about to say *strong*, but she quickly supplied '. . . capable.'

He grinned, and pumped her hand once again. The feel of his warm calloused flesh against hers had a strange effect. She felt frightened and exhilarated at the same time, which she could remember happening only once before. When she was fourteen, alone in the house one evening, she'd spied from her window a naked man and woman entwined on a couch in the apartment across the alley. She'd quickly yanked the shade down, but she'd seen enough to make her hot and shaky, as if she had a temperature.

And through the whole year Nikos worked for them, when he was near, those feelings came creeping over her. Sylvie would watch him surreptitiously as he repaired a broken drainpipe or dug holes in the garden for her roses – his chest bare, shirt knotted about his waist, the muscles leaping in his glistening brown back – and would experience that same secret flash of shameful excitement. She'd wonder what it would be like to be kissed by him, to feel those big rough hands sliding over her. Guiltily, she tried to banish those thoughts. Women would kill for a husband like hers. How could she even *look* at another man?

Yet she couldn't control her private fantasies. Bathing, she would become aroused suddenly by a warm trickle of water between her legs, and feel impaled by a hot arrow of desire. Or napping in the afternoon, she would dream that Nikos was beside her in the big four-poster bed, his sweat soiling the stiff, hand-embroidered linen sheets Gerald imported from Ireland. Then she'd awaken to sunlight sifting through the drapes, and stare up at the tall carved bedposts, filled with a kind of dazed yearning. Sometimes, still half-dreaming, she'd give in and satisfy her desire. But afterwards she'd hate herself even more.

What was this, she would ask herself, was it love? Yet how could that be? She didn't admire him the way she admired and respected Gerald. And when she came home from the infertility specialist's office, aching all over from yet another painful test, it was always Gerald's arms she wanted about her, no-one else's.

And yet . . .

It was Nikos's muscled chest she thought of when Gerald heaved atop her. Nikos's powerful hands and full mouth. Sometimes she closed her eyes, found herself imagining that Gerald *was* Nikos, and only then would Gerald's touch bring her pleasure.

29

But the worst thing was that she thought Nikos *knew*. It was nothing he said or did; it was the way he looked at her. A sideways glance sliding out from under heavy lids as he appeared to be absorbed in the dismantled parts of a faucet. Or a long speculative gaze from atop a ladder as he paused while patching a ceiling.

Late one sticky summer night with the air so thick she felt as if she were suffocating, Sylvie had gotten out of bed, leaving Gerald asleep, snoring softly. Downstairs, out on the terrace that led off the back parlor, it was cooler, and she could breathe.

She had seen the red tip of a cigarette glowing in the darkness, and had frozen, startled first, then terrified that the shadowy form half-astride the stone balustrade might be an intruder. Then it struck her that the steps curving down to the garden led around to the basement room where Nikos slept.

He rose and came forward.

Silhouetted against the moonlit garden, he appeared somehow darker, more dangerous than an intruder.

A shiver ran up the back of her neck.

He offered her a cigarette, which she accepted even though she didn't usually smoke.

'I couldn't sleep,' she explained. 'It was so hot I thought I'd come out for some air.' She was self-conscious about the transparency of her silk robe, and fiddled with the sash, talking too fast. 'You know what I used to do when I was a little girl? I'd pull my mattress out on to the fire escape and sleep there. Mama would scold me, she was always afraid I'd fall.'

He laughed, tossing his head back. 'And now you have no fire escape.' His English had gotten better over the past year, but was still limited to short sentences. 'Too bad.'

'Yes, it is too bad, isn't it?'

A spacious brownstone overlooking Riverside and the Hudson, servants, more money than she could ever have dreamed of, but no fire escape. She laughed too, a high-strung giggle.

30

'And your mama, where is she now?'

Her laughter shriveled. 'Dead.'

Sylvie looked out at the garden, at the dark cascade of ivy obscuring the brick walls, and at her roses, gleaming in the moonlight like old and precious silver. She even loved their names. Blue Nile. Peace. Old Gold. *Her* children, probably the only ones she'd ever have. For them, she didn't mind getting dirt under her fingernails, and her hands scratched from the thorns. And when leaves curled and turned brown, a bud withered and drooped with blight, she felt a stab of grief as, surely, a mother would at a child's skinned knee, or cut finger.

She suddenly turned away, needing to run back inside to safety, to her husband's bed. 'I'd better go in. It's late.'

Somehow Nikos's hand was on her arm, burning through the thin silk of her robe. 'Wait.' He leaned close, and in the shadowy backlit glow of his cigarette, his black eyes appeared endlessly deep, a void she could tumble into and never escape.

Sylvie imagined he was going to kiss her. 'Please, don't . . .,' she whimpered, drawing back.

Then she realized. He was merely offering her a light from his cigarette. She felt so ashamed, humiliated; now he had to know her secret.

Tears welled up in her eyes.

He looked distraught. 'I have offended you?'

'No. I'm sorry, I made a mistake. I thought you—'

He remained silent. Understanding dawned in his face. Then slowly, so slowly it seemed as if she were dreaming it, he dropped his cigarette and drew her into his arms. He kissed her, tasting of nicotine and something faintly, deliciously spicy.

Sylvie felt as if all the heat of the summer night had seeped in through her pores. She could feel her insides melting, flowing downhill in a slow stuporous slide.

She had to pull away, stop this instant, run inside. She thought of Gerald, calmly sleeping, trusting her, but she couldn't move. It was as if her shame and these forbidden tastes were all part of some exquisite paralyzing drug. She'd never been kissed like this before. Slow, sweet, endless kisses, an open sea with no land in sight, and nothing to grab on to to keep herself from drowning.

She followed him, half-believing this *was* all a dream, down the curved stone steps to the garden. There, she half-stumbled, her slipper catching against an uneven brick in the path. He immediately caught her, and she grew feverish feeling the hard corded muscles in his arms. He carried her the rest of the way, despite his bad leg, as easily as if she were a child, under a trellis bowed with a profusion of Silver Moon roses, filling the air with their perfume, down the narrow flight of slate steps to his basement.

Inside, she saw a narrow bed, a dresser, a small window with the moon caught in one of its panes. Wordlessly, he set her on her feet beside the bed. He untied her sash, pushed her robe off her shoulders; it slid to the floor, a puddle of rose silk. Then he took off his own clothes, hurriedly, not bothering to fold them as Gerald always did.

Sylvie stared at him. His naked body moved toward her slowly, the long planes of his shanks, paler than the rest of him, reflecting the moonlight, tantalizing her, as if he were engaging her in some ritual dance. It was the first time Sylvie had thought of the male body as beautiful. Even the purple scar snaking from his left hip all the way down to his knee seemed thrilling, a tattoo of his ordeal.

Suddenly too weak to stand, she sank down on the bed, and he came to her. He slid his hands up her arms and took her by the shoulders, gently pressing her on to her back. He knelt on the floor before her, lowering his head as if in prayer.

There. Oh dear God, he was kissing her *there*.

Sylvie was shocked. And that somehow made it more wonderful. And so wicked. She buried her fingers in the springy moss of his curls, pressing his head closer. She was trembling so hard her legs jerked in spasm. Did people really do this? Surely *nice* people didn't.

Right now she knew she wasn't nice, and she didn't care.

32

There were only his fingers digging into her behind, his hot sweet mouth. His tongue. She couldn't stop trembling . . . couldn't stop . . .

Then he was inside her, driving into her, fiercely, their bodies slippery with sweat. Kissing her on the mouth with her own taste on his lips like some strange forbidden fruit. And she cried out again and again, her arms and legs wrapped all about him, her whole body shuddering with pleasure, with urgency, with need.

*Oh, this exquisite feeling! Is it really me, making all this noise? Could this be what Gerald's heaving and grunting is all about? Oh God . . . I don't care . . . I just don't want it to end . . . so good . . . it feels so good.*

He was plunging deeper, faster, his body tensing. Back arching, cords on his neck standing out. She dug her fingers into his buttocks, hard, loving the sculpted feel of them, the way they curved in like spoons. He was crying out too, a hoarse guttural sound, over and over.

Then, stillness, a delicious floating sensation as if she were a feather that could be picked up by the first breeze, carried off into the night.

Sylvie opened her eyes to find Nikos grinning at her. 'This time you will sleep,' he said.

She was awakened by the loud popping of firecrackers outside. She peered groggily at the window. It was dark. She didn't know how long she'd been asleep. Not long enough. Sleep was a cave she longed to crawl back into.

She felt as if she'd awakened in someone else's body. Everything hurt. She couldn't budge without something aching. Her deflated stomach felt like one gigantic bruise. Thick pads chafed between her legs.

Sylvie saw Angie stir in her sleep. One of the other women snored softly. How she envied them! They would take their babies home to joyful husbands, settle back into their old lives. They had such happiness to look forward to, playing with their baby, fondling it, showing it off to cooing grandparents, walking it in the park on sunny days.

And where would *she* be?

Sylvie felt a chill settle over her, trying to contemplate what lay ahead. She could remember seeing Gerald angry only that one time, but it had shaken her so badly she'd never forget it.

That gray, foggy afternoon, coming up from the basement after she'd been with Nikos. And there was Gerald, looking down at her from the terrace. *God, oh God.* Her insides turned to scalding water. Usually he didn't get home from the bank until dinner time, but there he was, staring, his expression stony.

Sylvie began to shiver. She had the strange disconnected feeling that this wasn't really happening, *couldn't* be happening. Dear God. *He knows I never go near the basement, that I feel suffocated in dark clammy places. What can he think except that I've been with Nikos? What excuse can I possibly give?*

But suddenly the lie was there, as instinctive as throwing a hand up to ward off a blow. 'Darling, what a surprise!' she called cheerily, her heart hammering in her throat. 'I was just bringing poor Nikos some aspirin. He's in bed with a fever, and since it was Conseulo's day off . . . But why didn't you let me know you'd be home early?'

Gerald didn't reply at first, merely continued looking at her in that odd way, as if she were someone he'd never seen before. His eyes, she saw as she came toward him, were cold as frost on a windowpane.

'I didn't know myself,' he said in his normal voice. 'I came back for some papers I left behind this morning.' When he took her arm, however, it was not in his normal, gentle way, but with the firm grasp of a parent taking hold of a wayward child. 'You look a bit feverish yourself, my dear. Your face is all flushed. Let's hope you haven't caught something from that man.'

'Gerald, I don't think—'

'You know you really can't be too careful around the servants,' he continued as if she hadn't spoken. 'There's no telling what you might pick up.'

34

'Gerald—' She wanted to tell him he was hurting her, pinching her arm, but the look on his face stopped her.

'I'm afraid I must insist you lie down in bed, my dear.'

He led her through the ground-floor terrace doors, the hollow clack of his footsteps against the polished parquet floor creating shock waves that traveled up into the pit of her stomach. The journey upstairs to their bedroom seemingly endless – and also, like a thorn digging into her, reminding her of everything she stood to lose. Gay, giddy dinners with Gerald and the Golds at Le Chambord, her precious rose, and, oh God, this wonderful house. Passing through the parlor with its arched ceilings and lovely antiques, the Waterford chandelier like a bouquet of dancing prisms, the precious Tabriz carpet, she felt as if she must memorize it, burn it into her brain so it wouldn't escape her.

Up, up the curving black marble stairs, her legs trembling with the effort, footsteps muffled by the Chinese runner, past the satin-wood calendar clock chiming the hour in a doleful tone, the Rose Medallion vases standing guard in their hollowed-out marble niches.

Then their bedroom, the most beautiful of all, only now cold and somehow implacable. The river mist that clung to the diamond-paned windows casting a gray pall over the Aubusson rug, turning its lovely autumn colors winter pale.

Then he stood there, as if he had all the time in the world, watching her undress, never taking his frostbitten gaze from her. Usually, he averted his eyes politely. Sylvie felt as if he was scrutinizing her for a telltale sign, proof of her crime. She fumbled at the hooks of her brassiere. Was it fastened properly? Dear God, there was a tear in her slip where Nikos had grown impatient tugging it off her. Had Gerald noticed?

Sylvie was nearly in tears by the time she had climbed into bed and slunk under the coverlet. She was shaking so hard she thought she must be sick after all. The tall posts at each corner of the huge bed seemed to tower over her, the carved dolphins at their peaks no longer delightful, but frozen and ghastly with their fixed sneers.

Gerald walked over to the French windows, and stood looking out over the garden. It was late October, and the apple tree was nearly barren except for a few ragged leaves and one or two wizened apples clinging to the branches like small fists.

'Oh, by the way, I've decided to let Nikos go.' He spoke softly, but each word hit her like a hammer against an iron anvil.

Sylvie felt the air squeeze from her lungs, as if the anvil were sitting on her chest, pressing down on her, yet she feigned only mild surprise. 'Oh, why?'

'Remember my missing cigarette lighter? Conseulo found it in his room. Stupid of him. It wasn't even valuable.' He slipped a hand into his pocket and took out the silver lighter, turning it over in his palm – how oddly delicate, those hands, their fingers white and tapering, with small flat seashell-pink nails, like the hands of the Meissen shepherdess on the mantel. Then very calmly, he lit one of his long thin cigars.

He was lying, the bastard. And he didn't care that she knew it. Conseulo never went near Nikos's room. Sylvie was positive, too, that the lighter had never left Gerald's pocket. This was just an excuse for Gerald to get rid of him.

Dear God, had she been so obvious? But what if she hadn't been? Perhaps he only suspected.

Yes, if Gerald knew for sure, had proof, he would toss her out like Nikos. Not so quickly maybe, but in the end wouldn't it be just the same?

Sylvie reached across the iron rail for the glass of water beside her hospital bed, thinking *and now he'll have the proof*. And, she alone, with a baby to care for, no home, perhaps penniless, she'd end up back here on Eastern Boulevard, standing in line at Home Relief.

A burst of crackling noise shattered Sylvie's forebodings. More firecrackers, only this time they sounded as if they were right outside, in the alley below her window.

Despair pressed down on her. Sylvie yearned with all her heart to fly away from here, to rub out everything that had happened and to start all over again. She glanced over at Angie, peacefully asleep. *Oh, what I would give to trade places with you.*

But her body's needs overpowered her intense longing, and Sylvie closed her eyes, and slept.

She dreamed of her wedding day.

She and Gerald standing under the silk-embroidered huppah that had been in his family for generations. He and Estelle, his first wife, had been married under it . . . but she wouldn't let even that thought spoil this wonderful moment. Gerald could not have loved Estelle as he loved her. He hadn't exactly told her so, but he'd shown it in so many ways.

Sylvie, trembling with happiness, looked over at him. Gerald stood tall in his dark tuxedo, his face filled with love as he gazed at her.

She could hear the cantor chanting, crooning, even wailing a little. And the ancient melodies soothed her, bringing her back to the little shul on Intervale Avenue where she went with Mama on Rosh Hashanah. Gerald raised her veil, bringing a cup of wine to her lips. It was thick and sweet, so sweet it burned her throat, making her gag.

Suddenly she couldn't breathe.

A horrible thickness clogged her throat, her nostrils, each breath sending a spurt of pain into her lungs.

It was hot. Suffocating. Why was it so hot?

Then she saw.

The huppah was on fire! Orange flames licked up the gilded support poles. Sparks rained from the canopy. Desperate, she reached to throw her arms around Gerald, but he'd evaporated into the smoke.

Time stopped. She couldn't move. She tried to scream, but when she opened her mouth no sound would come out.

37

Sylvie awoke with a start. Her tongue felt as if it were made of flannel. Her eyes and nose stung. The air was thick and dirty. There was a horrible smell, like burning rubber, or one of those awful chemical factories.

She pulled herself up with effort, and swung her legs over the side of the bed. The warped linoleum beneath felt warm under her feet. The air seemed to grow thicker. She coughed, lungs burning.

Air. She had to get some air. She lurched to the window, ignoring the pain between her legs, and tugged to raise it up as far as it would go. But it was stuck, wouldn't budge. The thing was ancient as the rest of the building, fossilized beneath layers of paint.

Then she saw – black smoke billowing from the floor below, a finger of orange flame shooting up. Fire! No dream, this was really happening.

Sylvie, stunned, knew she had to move, run. Had to wake the others. And get out.

She snatched the pillow from her bed and held it over her face to filter some of the choking smoke. She staggered over and shook Angie. Angie moaned groggily, but wouldn't open her eyes.

'Wake up!' Sylvie screamed. 'Fire!'

The other women were awakened by her shouts, were scrambling out of bed, hurrying as best they could into the hallway.

Sylvie gripped Angie's shoulders and shook her with as much strength as she could muster. But her roommate only uttered a deep moan and rolled back on to the pillow. Sylvie struggled to lift her and drag her out of the bed, but Angie felt like a granite block. Someone else would have to come and help.

Sylvie, half-choking, terrified, aching all over, made herself rush from the room. There was something she had to do.

The corridor was a nightmarish scene all its own. Patients in gowns pushing each other, screaming, others screaming from their beds, making Sylvie think of

Picasso's *Guernica* or some mad surrealist painting. A gurney shot past, wheeled by a white-faced nurse. Smoke clotted the air, tearing at her lungs. A fit of coughing doubled her, sent tears streaming from her stinging eyes.

She heard the faint pulsing wail of a fire engine. It sounded far away. Too far.

The nursery, she must get to the nursery.

Sylvie thought only of her baby as she staggered down the corridor, following the arrow pointing the way to the nursery. She must let nothing happen to her, no matter what.

She stumbled, a hard smacking pain in her wrists, knees, but she picked herself up, and forced her legs to move. She seemed to be moving in slow motion. So weak. And between her legs it hurt so.

There, up ahead, a glimmer through the haze of smoke. The long window looking into the nursery. She sobbed with relief. But something was wrong. It looked deserted, the rows of bassinets empty. Sylvie blinked to clear her streaming eyes. No, there was still someone. A young nun she recognized from the delivery room.

Sylvie pushed her way through the door.

The young nurse glanced up briefly, her face pinched, a mask of terror. She was frantically wrapping a squalling infant in a wet sheet. Sylvie saw the name on the bassinet: SANTINI. Angie's baby. Nearby, hers, the one marked ROSEN.

Empty. Her heart froze.

She clutched at the sister's arm. 'My baby . . .'

'The babies are safe,' the nurse rasped, coughing. 'They've all been taken down. This is the last one.'

Relief crashed through Sylvie, leaving her trembling. Then she remembered about Angie. 'Mrs Santini,' she gasped. 'I couldn't wake her. Please. You have to help her. I'll take the baby.'

'Wait.' The nurse snatched up a pair of scissors and snipped off the beaded I D bracelet about the infant's tiny ivory wrist. Beads scattered, pinging off the linoleum

39

floor. 'Porcelain,' she choked. 'Absorbs heat . . . might burn . . .'

Sylvie saw there were other beads from other bracelets scattered about the floor, the counter. One, a tiny pink cube imprinted with a black 'R,' winked up at her from a starched fold in the young sister's sleeve.

Sylvie reached out, took the damp bundle in her arms. Feeling her strength surge back with the warm weight of the infant against her breast, her palm supporting the tiny wobbly head.

Relentlessly, Sylvie fought her way back through the thickening haze, past the deserted nurse's station, toward the stairwell.

Turn the corner. There. Just ahead. She wrenched open the door marked EXIT. And threw herself back.

The stairwell was engulfed in flames. She heard a high shrill scream and realized it was hers.

*Dear God, where now?*

She remembered the windows. They opened out on to fire escape platforms, the old-fashioned kind with stairs that zigzagged down the side of the building.

Sylvie hurried into the nearest room, gently lowering the baby on to a bed. She struggled to raise the window. But it wasn't budging. Then she heard a crack – a sound like a gunshot – and the window jerked up. Sylvie, weak with relief, snatched the baby up. She pulled a chair to the sill and carefully, slowly stepped up on to it.

And looked down.

Five stories below, the street swam dizzily into view. Strange, how light it seemed, more like day than night. Insect-sized people scurrying about. Fire engines angled like toy trucks along the curb. The sidewalk a snake pit of hoses.

Everything seemed to tilt sharply, and she felt as if she were going to fall. Sylvie closed her eyes and took a deep breath.

*No. Don't look down. Just move.*

Sylvie stepped out on to the platform, the iron slats

warm and rough beneath her bare soles, and began inching her way down the stairs, gripping the iron handrail with one hand while she braced the baby with the other. The stairs seemed perilously steep, making her legs and arms go rubbery with terror.

How would she ever make it down five stories? What if she were to fall, or drop the baby?

No. No, she couldn't think that. She mustn't.

Coughing, her eyes stinging, Sylvie groped her way down, scraping and bruising her feet as she scrabbled for purchase.

She had just reached the fourth-floor platform when the air rocked with a deafening explosion, and the fire escape shook violently. Sylvie froze. She darted a glance upward and saw flames shoot from the window above her. Shattered glass rained down, pinging off the fire escape. Something glanced her shoulder with a hard, stinging blow.

Sylvie screamed, terrified and in pain. Something warm trickled down her shoulder blade. She felt her muscles go slack, her insides turn to water. Numbness crept through her. She willed herself to move, but found she couldn't. She absolutely *couldn't*.

Time seemed to stop, and the heat grew stronger, seeming to sear her through her nightgown. Oh dear God, was this the end, would they both die while she stood frozen like Lot's wife?

Then the baby stirred against her. A tiny hand thrust free of the blanket, seemed to search the air until it found her cheek. Featherlike fingers fluttered against her mouth.

Tears gathered in Sylvie's throat. *Oh, stupid body. Move, dammit. For this baby if not for yourself. MOVE!*

Somehow she forced her limbs to unlock; she forced herself to go on.

Sylvie wasn't aware she'd reached the bottom until strong hands grasped her about the waist, lifting her free. Her feet touched pavement. It felt so blessedly solid.

Voices came in a rush. Hands everywhere. Guiding her. Supporting her.

Pulsing red dome lights stabbed at her eyes. Loud voices bellowing orders through megaphones seemed to follow her as she and the men helping her wove their way past the tangle of canvas hoses and fire-fighting equipment.

She felt disconnected, unreal. Stretchers floated past, ghostlike. Firemen in grimy yellow turnouts bellowed at one another above the roar of the hydrants, their blackened faces contorted, like gargoyles'.

'. . . some damn kids playing with firecrackers . . .,' she heard one of them say.

Sylvie, alone now with the baby, made her way through the crowd. In spite of her dazed feeling, one thought stood clear. She must find her baby. But first Angie, to let her know her baby was safe. My God, the poor woman must be out of mind!

She spotted a familiar figure, shepherding two patients in wheelchairs. 'Sister! Wait!'

Sister Ignatious turned. Her white habit was torn in a dozen places, streaked with black. And there was something oddly naked about her. Then Sylvie realized it was because she wasn't wearing her wimple, and no eyeglasses. They must have fallen off in the confusion.

Sylvie, desperate to know if her child was all right, clutched at the nun's filthy sleeve. 'Sister, please, the other babies . . . '

'Safe, all safe, praise be to God.' Sister crossed herself.

Then Sylvie remembered the baby in her arms, Angie's baby.

'Where can I find Mrs Santini?' Sylvie asked.

She was about to explain, but Sister Ignatious's naked eyes clouded with tears. 'Mrs Santini is with God now.' She crossed herself again. 'The explosion. It was too late. By the time they got to the fifth floor she . . . our poor Sister Paul, too. She died trying to save Mrs Santini.'

Thinking of the warm, tough-talking woman who had occupied the bed next to hers, Sylvie felt sorrow seep through her. How Angie's brown eyes had lit up at the mention of her baby, despite her disappointment over its being a girl. Poor Angie! Sylvie felt tears well up.

Then Sylvie, for the first time, peeled back the sheet covering the tiny form asleep in her arms.

Peering up from the filthy folds was a face as exquisite as an ivory cameo. Sylvie drew her breath in. Round blue doll's eyes, a sweet little rosebud of a mouth. Light-brown hair like the fuzz on a baby duck. Not all dark and crumpled like her tiny girl's. She brushed a silken cheek with her finger, and the baby turned her head toward it, mouth working.

Sylvie's dry, burning eyes flooded with tears. In all this nightmare, a thing of wonder. She touched a miniature hand, felt it tighten about her finger with surprising strength. She marveled at the tiny fingernails, no bigger than seed pearls.

She felt Sister Ignatious's hand against her shoulder. 'God was with you. And your baby too. It's a miracle neither of you was hurt, climbing down all that way.'

Sylvie stiffened in astonishment. Sister had mistaken Angie's baby for *her* child! But, then, it was a natural mistake. She had come through hell on earth to save this infant. And who but a mother?

Splintered images spun in her mind. Nikos. The dark, briefly glimpsed face of her own baby. Gerald's pale blue eyes, watching her as she undressed.

And then her brain cleared suddenly, like a shaft of light breaking through the clouds in a medieval painting or an illuminated manuscript.

No-one would ever have to know. If she kept this child as her own, who was there to dispute her? Not Angie. Or Sister Paul.

Only perhaps Sister Ignatious, who was half out of her mind, and she'd already unknowingly bestowed her blessing. There'd be no records either. The obstetrics floors had been destroyed by the explosion.

Overwhelmed, Sylvie began to tremble. It was

43

monstrous, how could she even think such a thing? Give up her own child . . . to whom? There were such crazy people in this world. But Angie's family – they had to be nice people, like her – and they would no doubt assume the baby to be theirs.

Could she do this? Could she? Never to see her own daughter again. Never to see her grow up . . .

Then Sylvie thought of what her life, her baby's life, would be if Gerald were to divorce her. Strip her of his love, his protection. Send her off to raise her baby in shame, alone.

Alone. Without Mama. Without Gerald.

No, *worse* than alone. She would have a baby to take care of. A baby no-one would welcome, not even Nikos.

She remembered how sick she'd been after Mama died. What if she got sick now? Or died? Who would take care of her baby? Who would love it?

Still, she could not believe she was thinking what she was thinking. To give up her very own child, take another baby in its place. Why, it was beyond hateful, it was . . .

*The only thing to do. The only thing that makes sense.*

*No, no, NO, I mustn't. I mustn't even think . . .*

*And Angie's husband won't suspect a thing. Remember, he hasn't seen the baby yet. He will accept it as his own, love it unconditionally. And didn't Angie say something about other children? Yes, that's right. Two other girls. Your baby will have sisters, a family.*

. . . such a terrible thing, a sin against God . . .

*You will have Gerald. And a baby he will love, cherish, raise as his own.*

Sylvie stared down at the beautiful cameo face asleep in her arms. Tears filled her eyes, and dropped on to the dirty blanket, running into its folds. Her chest felt as if it were full of broken glass, sharp cold splinters digging into her heart.

Yes, perhaps it would be better . . .

*But how can I forget her, my own baby? Dear God, never to hold her, watch her grow up, love her . . .*

44

The choice was hers. With terrible consequences either way, she turned. And she had no time. Sister Ignatious was staring at her, waiting for her to say something. She must decide *now*.

Blinking back her tears, Sylvie raised her head to meet Sister's squinting gaze.

She had decided.

'Yes,' she said. 'It is a miracle, isn't it?'

# Part One

*I heartily detest all my sins, because of Thy just punishment, but most of all because they offend Thee, my God, who art all good and deserving of my love.*
Act of Contrition, a Catholic prayer

*I have been consumed by fire, but never so much as the heat of my desire.* Jewish prayer for Yom Kippur

# 1

BROOKLYN, 1959

'Bless me, Father, for I have sinned.'

Sixteen-year-old Rose Santini, huddled inside the dark confessional, felt her kneecaps shift painfully against the hard wooden kneeler. Familiar things, the mingled scents of beeswax and incense, the faint singsong murmur of evening vespers drifting from the sanctuary, yet she felt like she had her very first time, scared to death. Her heart thundered in her ears so loudly she was sure Father could hear it even without his hearing aid.

She thought: *I know what you're expecting, Father. The usual stuff kids tell you – I lied about finishing my homework, I ate a hot dog on Friday, I cursed my sister. Oh, if only that were all . . .*

What she had done was a million times worse. A mortal sin.

Rose clenched her fist tightly about her rosary, the beads biting into her palm. She felt flushed and hot, as if she were coming down with the flu. But she knew she wasn't sick. This felt so much worse. What were cramps and a sore throat compared to being doomed for ever?

She remembered Sister Gabrielle in first grade telling her that confession was like washing your soul. Rose had seen herself stretched out on a table while a priest stood over her, sleeves rolled up and hands soapy, scrubbing away, and then giving her Penance, a few Hail Marys and Our Fathers sprinkled on to get out her extra spots.

But today her soul had to be so black no amount of scrubbing would get it clean. The best she could hope for was a dingy gray, like on those TV commercials where they used the wrong detergent.

'. . . it's been two weeks since my last confession,' she continued in a small whisper.

Rose stared at the screen before her. She could just make out the shadowy profile of the priest on the other side. She thought of how, when she was younger, she'd believed it was God Himself in there . . . well, almost . . . more like God speaking through His messenger, sort of like a long-distance telephone call, only a lot farther away than Topeka or Minneapolis.

Now, of course, she knew it was only old Father Donahue, who wheezed his way through Sunday Mass and whose hand smelled of cigarettes when he pressed the Host on to her out-thrust tongue. But knowing it was creaky old Father still didn't take away the tight feeling in her stomach. Because somewhere it was God who was passing judgement on her. He might cripple her in a car wreck, or wipe her out entirely with cancer. Look at that poor girl Sister Perpetua had told them about, the one who lapsed in her faith and thought she was pregnant, only to be cut open at the end and found to be carrying not a child, but a hideous tumor (it even had *teeth* and *hair*, Sister said) the size of a watermelon.

And at the very least, there'd be purgatory. She imagined God recording her sins in a thick black ledger with pale lined green pages, like the book where Sister Agnes marked tardies and demerits. Purgatory had to be like school – everyone went. It was just a question of who passed and who failed.

Rose recited in a rush, 'Oh, Lord, I heartily detest all my sins, because of Thy just punishment, but most of all because they offend Thee, my God, who art all good and deserving of my love.'

She took a deep breath.

Father Donahue muttered something in Latin, then fell silent, waiting for her to continue.

Rose shifted her weight from one knee to another, and

the wood let out a loud creak. In the unbearable stillness it sounded like a pistol shot. This might kill him, she thought. Give him a heart attack. PRIEST SHOCKED TO DEATH BY TEENAGER'S CONFESSION.

A pulse throbbed on the side of her neck. Her mouth felt very dry, and she thought longingly of the half-finished roll of Lifesavers in her purse. Butter Rum, her favorite. But that was a sacrilege, too, thinking about candy at a time like this.

She tried to think of a soul-cleansing thought instead. Thick heat clamped about her like a sweaty fist, and an ooze began at her armpits, working its way into the pinched flesh around her bra, an old one Marie had given her that was at least two sizes too small. She thought of Saint Joan, roasting at the stake.

Martyrdom. Rose remembered the day Sister Perpetua had first told them about it. Fifth grade, and they'd been half-listening to Sister droning on, as they nodded over their dog-eared copies of *Lives of the Saints*.

'Girls—' Her voice dropped suddenly to a dramatic whisper. Rose's back stiffened to attention. 'I have a very rare and sacred relic to share with you. I'm going to pass it around, and you may each kiss it.'

She made the sign of the cross, then withdrew a silver locket from around her neck. It had been hidden under her black habit. What else was under there? Rose wondered. Breasts? Pubic hair? But the only picture that came to her was of a shapeless sack stuffed full of the Kleenexes Sister was forever tucking up her sleeve.

Rose, fascinated, watched as Sister pried the locket open with her thumbnail that was square as a man's. Reverently, Sister placed the locket in the dovetailed hands of Mary Margaret O'Neill, who sat at the first desk in the front row. Mary Margaret, in her white blouse with sleeves ironed to a knife's edge, red hair clipped neatly back over her ears, was the apple of Sister's eye, for she already had received the Call.

A jittery silence filled the classroom as each girl, wide-eyed, took the locket, then bent to peck it with a tightly screwed mouth. Sister explained that it was a scrap of flesh from a martyr burned at the stake in Mexico more than two hundred years ago.

Rose, waiting for it to reach her, had churned with morbid curiosity. What would it look like? Could she bring herself actually to *kiss* it?

After an eternity the relic finally was passed to her. It was horrible, far worse than she'd imagined. Black and shriveled. Like a burnt shred of pot roast picked off the side of the pan. She could almost smell the smoke, the rancid stink of scorching flesh.

And then Rose had been struck with a terrible thought: *My mother. That's how she must have looked when she died. God, oh God. And because of me. If I hadn't been born that night, she'd still be alive. That must be why Nonnie's always telling me the mark of the devil is on me.*

She couldn't kiss it. Not even with Sister and the whole class watching, waiting. She would die first.

And for weeks after that she had not been able to eat cooked meat, either. Just the thought of it made her feel like throwing up.

Rose, in the cramped darkness of the confessional, imagined now that *she* was that martyr. Burning, her body roasting slowly beneath her white blouse and pleated navy skirt. *Is that how my mother felt? Did she suffer horribly?*

The burning sensation now felt even worse. Moisture trickled between her breasts, and she caught a whiff of her own perspiration, a stink like scorched rubber. *Angelina deserved to die, that's what Nonnie said. Sinned against God, and He punished her.* Her grandmother's hateful words scuttled inside Rose's head like the mice behind the kitchen wall at night.

*No, it can't be true. I don't believe it.*

But what if it *was* true? Would that make her tainted somehow? Was she marked by her mother's sin just like the human race had been by Eve's?

52

Yes, she was marked. After what she did last week, well, now she was sure of it.

But how, *how* could she bring herself to confess it? So much worse by far than any sin she'd ever committed before.

Start with the venial sins first, she told herself. Work up to the mortal sin slowly, that way maybe it won't come as such a shock.

The first part she knew she could recite in her sleep. The same sins she'd been confessing since her First Holy Communion, but with a little variation here and there.

She swallowed hard against the dryness in her throat, and it made a clicking sound in her ears.

'I lied to my grandmother. More than once,' she said.

Inside her head the silence that followed seemed loud as thunder.

Then came Father Donahue's faint rustling voice, and yes, it *did* sound a bit like it was coming over a long-distance wire.

'What kind of lies?' he asked kindly, a lighthouse keeper guiding a lost ship through dark waters.

Rose hesitated. This was the tricky part, where the safe water ended and the rocks began. If she told Father about *all* the lies she'd told Nonnie since her last confession, she'd be in here until Easter, two weeks away. No, she'd have to pick just a few.

Rose squeezed her eyes shut, ran a sweaty palm down her pleats. This was the part she hated most – actually having to *describe* her sins. And how in heaven would she confess her mortal sin? Did priests even *know* about such things?

She took another deep breath, and let the air out slowly.

'I lied about the book,' she said.

'What book?'

'*Catcher in the Rye,* by J. D. Salinger. I checked it out of the library. But Nonnie said I couldn't read it because it was in the *Index*.'

She thought about Molly Quinn, her best friend, calling

the *Index of Forbidden Books* the 'Shit List.' A book, Molly explained, didn't have to be filthy actually to be on the list, it just had to contain four-letter words. And everyone was always consulting the *Index,* the Sisters *and* the kids, which made no sense, until one day Molly told her why.

'Go down to the public library,' Molly had said and laughed, flashing a mouthful of metal (she claimed she could get W A B C *and* W N E W on her braces) and hooking her long blond hair behind her ears. 'Go see which books are always checked out.'

Father gave a dry, polite little cough. 'And you read this book even though you knew it was against your grandmother's wishes?'

'Yes, Father.' Rose sighed.

'You committed two sins then. Failing to honor your grandmother as well as deceiving her.'

'I honestly didn't see what was so wrong with it! I mean, what Holden Caulfield was trying to say . . . well, it wasn't about *sex* really—' Rose broke off, horrified. *Holy Mother of God, did I really say that? Aren't I in enough hot water as it is without shooting my big mouth off?*

Father Donahue cleared his throat. 'You must trust in the wisdom of your elders, my child,' he admonished gently. 'And keep in mind that the dictates of the Church are not yours to question.'

'Yes, Father.'

'You may continue.'

'Uh . . . that's all I can remember, Father.' Another lie. But what was the use of explaining? Father Donahue couldn't understand what it was like for her at home.

Rose pushed her hair up in back to get some air on her neck. She remembered Nonnie braiding it for her before school when she was in kindergarten, pulling it back so tight it stretched the skin across her temples and left her with a headache. But by lunchtime, it would all be sprung loose anyway, a mass of wiry black curls corkscrewing every which way.

54

*Like a little Gypsy,* Nonnie would mutter, tight-lipped, every morning declaring war on Rose's hair. With each painful yank of the hairbrush, Rose couldn't help being reminded how different she was from everyone else in the family. A freak, with her olive skin, impossible hair, and huge black eyes.

Big, too. Not like her sisters, both dainty as Ginny dolls. None of the clothes Marie and Clare handed down to her fit properly. They strained across her chest and hips, riding up in awful-looking furrows, making her feel as big as King Kong. But what could she do? It was a sin, Nonnie said, to waste good clothing because of vanity. Besides, they were too poor to throw anything away.

Once when no-one was home, Rose had peeled off all her clothes and stood in front of the speckled chifforobe mirror in her bedroom. She knew it was a sin to look at yourself that way; Sister had said so. But she couldn't tear her eyes from her dark nakedness. Dark all over, even where the sunlight never touched her. Her heavy breasts the color of the Old English polish Nonnie rubbed over the furniture on Saturdays, with nipples big as saucers, so dark they looked almost blue. And hair. A great coarse black bush of it rising from the mound between her thighs. Darker and curlier, even, than the hair on her head.

Rose had touched herself there, feeling a dart of ashamed pleasure. Blessed Virgin, where had all of this come from? Marie and Clare had cornflower-blue eyes, and beautiful wavy hair the color of ginger ale, like their father's. Even Nonnie, withered now and freckled with liver spots, had once been blond and almost pretty in a solid, Germanic way – the proof, however unbelievable, lay in the brown-tinted photo in a pewter frame perched on the knickknack shelf over the sofa. Nonnie's parents, Rose had been told, had come from Genoa, where Teutonic blood had mingled with the Italian to give Nonnie her fair coloring and pale blue eyes.

Dizzy with a kind of horrified pleasure, Rose had gone on touching herself, exploring the moist cleft buried beneath the springy black hair, then moving her hands up to cup the weight of her heavy breasts against her palms, watching her nipples stiffen like two raisins. *Ugly. I'm so ugly. No-one will ever want to marry me, touch me like this.*

Nonnie said it was 'bad blood' that made her so dark, hinting that it had come from Rose's mother. But how could that be? Mama had been fair, with light brown hair, and – judging by an old winter coat of hers, which Marie wore now – she'd been small-boned, too.

Rose had found an old snapshot of her parents tucked in the back of Nonnie's photo album. And it was that picture – not their stiffly posed, artificially tinted wedding portrait – she carried inside her head. The fuzzy image of a young woman in an old-fashioned dress with boxy shoulders, leaning against a ship's rail, her head tilted back to look up at the tall man beside her, handsome in his sailor's uniform. Laughing, obviously in love, her gloved hand held up as a shield against the sunlight, throwing a shadow across her eyes. All you could see was her bright windblown hair, and the happy slash of her lipsticked mouth.

*Bad blood. If I didn't get it from Mama, then who?*

The gloominess of the confessional then seemed to creep in through her pores, filling her with despair. Like the nightmare she'd often had of falling through a black space full of shooting red stars, of hands that would reach out to catch her, then evaporate like mist as soon as she tumbled into them.

Then Rose remembered something. Brian telling her that all that bad-blood and evil-eye stuff was just an old wives' tale.

*He says I'm good and smart. That he never knew anyone who could do crossword puzzles and card games as good as me, or could think up things, like when I figured out a way to get free tickets for my fifth-grade class, even for Sister Perp, to see the Yankees cream the Red Sox.*

In her mind, Rose could hear Bri's admiring voice – *Jeez, Rose, who would've thought to write Casey Stengel*

*a letter saying the Yanks could use all the extra prayers*
*they could get after last season?*

'Are you certain, my child?' Father Donahue broke into
her thoughts.

She bit down on her lip. Should she tell him? Now?

The hot weight of her sin felt as if it were burning a hole
in her stomach.

'I took the name of the Lord in vain once,' she confessed, chickening out at the last moment.

'Only once?'

'Yes, Father.'

She'd lost her temper at bossy Marie – she was always
after Rose to tuck her blouse in, stop slouching, *do* something about that *hair*, and for heaven's sake, *pick up your
half of the room*.

Rose had exploded. 'If you want the room looking like a
goddam army barrack, *you* pick it up!'

Nonnie, in the kitchen, had overheard.

Rose winced at the memory of being forced to kneel on
the kitchen linoleum, saying rosaries and begging the
Blessed Virgin Mary, Jesus Christ, the Holy Ghost, and
anyone else who would listen to please forgive her most
grievous sin. God, all those hours. The pain shooting up
from her bruised knees. The humiliation. And afterwards,
not being able to stand up. But Nonnie would never see her
cry. No, that Rose would not let happen. That would have
made her humiliation unbearable. So, on her hands and
knees, she had crawled to the bathroom, locked the door,
and cried her heart out, masking her sobs with the water
rushing from the bathtub spigot.

*In nōmine patris et filiī . . .*' Father Donahue launched
into the final blessing, gently reminding her that there
were others waiting their turn to confess.

Rose panicked. Her mortal sin, she hadn't spoken one
word of it. Now God would be sure to punish her!

She took a deep breath, struggling to subdue her panic.
The confessional's mingled odors – sweat and incense and
the Sen-Sens Father chewed – felt stifling, suffocating.

'Father, I fornicated,' she blurted in a hot rush. Father Donahue's silhouette shifted, loomed.

Now would he have his heart attack? Would that be her punishment, God smiting the priest . . . just as he had her mother?

He coughed, explosively, the sound reverberating in the confined space like thunder.

'My child . . .,' he wheezed. *Do you know what you're saying?*

Thank heaven, he was still alive. Rose imagined the expression on his pink aged cherub's face, the horror he must be feeling. She so wanted to snatch back her words, erase, blot out her sin.

But it was too late now for that.

'Yes, Father,' she made herself murmur through the clenched knuckles covering her mouth.

Shame flooded through her, but it was an oddly cold shame, making her feel cleansed at the same time, like the hateful icy showers she had to take when Marie had used up all the hot water, when Rose would shiver and gasp for breath, but afterwards glow and tingle. Her heart lifted. She had done it. She had asked God's forgiveness. Now perhaps the Holy Father would select a mild punishment – a sprained ankle instead of crippling her in a car wreck, two days of awful flu but not leukemia.

'Are you absolutely *certain?*' His whispered voice rose to a strained, trembling pitch.

'Yes, Father.'

'Did you commit this . . .,' cough, '. . . *act* more than once?'

'Only once, Father.' Rose trembled. The sweat pouring off her now felt as if it might swamp the whole confessional. She had never felt so vulnerable, naked, as if one more shrill word from Father would stab her to death.

But then Father Donahue began muttering his usual litany in what sounded like a low keening moan.

Wasn't he going to ask her any more questions? Scold her at least?

His silhouette through the screen blurred as he made the sign of the cross.

Oh, Lord, thank you, everything was going to be . . . well, not so dreadful. She had to lean forward to hear the Penance he was giving her. Fifteen Hail Marys and thirty Our Fathers. By far, the most she'd ever gotten. But she wouldn't mind, not a bit, no matter how long it took her, or how bruised her knees were at the end.

'Go and sin no more,' he pronounced wearily.

It was over. She'd done it. And she was still alive. Father too.

Rose slipped from the confessional into the cool, incense-fragrant dimness of the sanctuary. The old plank flooring squeaked softly in protest as she followed the scuffed-white path up the center aisle. Genuflecting, she slid into an empty pew, sinking to her knees, and dropping her forehead on to her clenched hands. She knew she should be thinking of God, but she couldn't seem to get her mind off Brian.

She struggled to shut him away, and concentrate on the rugged miles of Penance that lay ahead.

'Hail, Mary, Mother of God, the Lord is with Thee, blessed art Thou, and blessed is the fruit of Thy womb, Jesus . . .'

But, no, she wasn't getting that penitent feeling, that good hating-what-she-was-doing-but-loving-herself-for-doing-it feeling she got when she put a whole dollar of her baby-sitting money in the collection basket on Sunday, or stuck to her promise and gave up sweets for all of Lent. She half-expected to look up and find Bri standing before the Communion rail in his old altar boy robes, tipping her a wink.

Thinking about what they'd done, she felt her heart beat fast and high in her throat.

But not because she felt ashamed or sorry. *God forgive me* . . .

All the Penance in heaven, that couldn't change the fact that she loved Brian. She would walk through fire for him. Even the fires of hell.

And deep in her heart she knew that if Bri wanted her, she would do what they'd done all over again.

*If.* The possibility that now he wouldn't want her, even as a friend, put a chill in her heart. Today was Saturday, and she hadn't seen him since Monday, the night they . . . well, they forgot they were supposed to be only best friends. Had he been purposely avoiding her? She could have gone up and knocked on his door to find out, but every time she thought about doing it her stomach turned cartwheels inside her.

'Hail, Mary, Mother of God, the Lord is with Thee, . . .
*please don't let Bri hate me . . .*
blessed art Thou, . . .
*he's all I've got . . .*
and blessed is the fruit of Thy womb, . . .
*I don't think I could make it without him, I honestly don't . . .*
Jesus.'

Rose stopped fingering her rosary, and gazed at the white-clothed altar, flanked by marble figures of Jesus and the Blessed Virgin Mary. The bank of votive candles beside the vestibule guttered and smoked in the draft, which seemed as much a part of this place as its pocked wooden pews and dog-eared missals. As Rose stared ahead, a hump-backed figure in a black dress and shapeless cardigan genuflected before the altar, then shuffled on to light one of the candles, dropping a coin into the offering box with a hollow rattle. Rose noticed that the wooden lid was gouged and the padlock on it a new one. Oh yes, she remembered Sister Boniface saying there had been a theft.

A church was supposed to be the house of God, she thought. But if God could live anywhere, Rose wondered, would He really have chosen Holy Martyrs on Coney Island Avenue and Avenue R?

She doubted it. She doubted it very much.

Rose looked up. The late afternoon sun shone grudgingly through the peaked windows, casting everything around her in a gritty gray light. The windows were striped with bird shit from the pigeons that roosted in the eaves, but no-one ever bothered to clean them. Father's heart, they said, had gone out of it two years ago when some street gang had smashed the beautiful stained-glass windows, and they had been replaced by plain safety glass, which was all the parish could afford.

Rose knew just how Father must have felt. Something dear snatched away from him. Smashed to bits. Never to be restored. Gone for ever. And it was the same for her. With her grandmother. The one dream Rose treasured, the best one, Nonnie had soiled it, ruined it, smashed it to pieces.

Her mother.

*. . . whore cheap little whore that's all she was . . .*

The memory of Nonnie's hateful words twisted in the pit of Rose's stomach. She squeezed her eyes shut. Hate rose in her, red hot and poisonous.

An even bigger sin, she knew, than the one she had committed with Brian.

*I wish she were dead. I wish the old witch had burned instead of my mother.*

Rose, struggling in vain to blot away her evil thoughts, bowed her head into her clenched hands, and prayed in a feverish whisper, 'Our Father, who art in heaven, hallowed be Thy name; Thy kingdom come; Thy will be done on earth as it is in heaven. Give us this day our daily bread; and forgive us our trespasses as we forgive those who trespass against us; and lead us not into temptation . . .'

She thought about Marie, how it had all started last week with her sister's terrible announcement.

They had been eating dinner, the kitchen stagnant with the smell of overcooked pot roast and potatoes, she and Clare and Nonnie, when Marie walked in, late as usual. Rose had sensed immediately that something was up. Something big. Marie just stood there in the middle of the kitchen, arms stiff at her sides, her jaw cocked at an angle and her blue eyes blazing with sullen defiance. She was out of breath, her chest heaving, as if she'd run up all four flights without stopping once. Wearing her tight black skirt with the rolled up waistband, pink Flame-Glo lipstick, and black patent leather flats, she stirred the stale kitchen air, somehow made it vibrate, hum with danger.

Then she dropped her A-bomb.

'Pete and I are getting married,' she announced in the same the-hell-with-you tone in which she might have said, *Pete and I robbed a bank*.

For an instant, no-one had moved. It was like a tableau, Rose later thought, a weird parody of the Last Supper tableau that Brother Paul, over at Precious Blood, where Brian had gone to school, staged every year on Holy Thursday. The three of them frozen around the chrome-legged Formica table, under the ceiling's fluorescent halo. Nonnie in her black rayon dress (the one she wore to church every Sunday and First Friday), she and Clare in their school uniforms. Their forks poised over their plates, their eyes on the Judas before them.

Rose watched Nonnie's pale blue eyes narrow as they came to rest on the bulky sweater drooped over Marie's waist. Suddenly, Rose understood. It all fell into place – the miserable retching she'd heard from behind the locked bathroom door every morning for the past week, Marie's jumpiness lately, snapping at everything Rose said. And, of course, her running off to be with Pete all hours of the day and night.

Holy Mother of God, *Marie was pregnant*.

Nonnie stopped chewing and rose slowly, palms flat against the Formica on either side of her plate, pushing herself up with her bony arms until she stood facing Marie across the table. The light winked across the lenses of Nonnie's rimless spectacles, and for a fleeting instant Rose had seen her own face reflected, no larger than a flyspeck. She sucked in air to steady herself against the sudden, dizzying plunge her stomach had taken.

Nonnie pushed her chair back, and even more slowly walked around the table to where Marie stood. She raised her hand, her bones in sharp relief against the loose mottled flesh, like a Halloween skeleton's. She slapped Marie full across the face. A cracking sound like stamping on a frozen puddle.

'Shame,' Nonnie hissed. 'For shame. You. No better than a filthy whore!'

Marie just stood there, white and frozen. Hectic stripes of color now blazed against the cottage-cheese color of her face. Her eyes glittered with angry unshed tears. But she didn't move or cry out.

It was Clare who let loose an anguished sob. With a harsh, skittering scrape of her chair, she fled the room, face buried in her hands, weeping. Watching her, her numbness gone, Rose thought evilly, *That's right, run. Run to your prayer book, like you always do. Miss Goody-Goody-Gumdrops. Or are you scared it might be catching, like a disease, and you might get pregnant too?*

Then she swung back to Marie, staring at her sister, trying to make sense of all this. Marie, almost twenty now, had worked behind the budget cosmetics counter at A & S – where she met Pete – since she'd graduated from Sacred Heart. So even though the toes of her black flats usually were scuffed, and most of the time she had a run in one of her stockings, her face was always perfect, eyebrows plucked and redrawn like Audrey Hepburn's, and lipstick the palest shade of pink. Her light brown hair ratted into a bubble, wispy bangs sprayed into a line of stiff commas across her forehead.

Marie had it all. Nothing really bad ever seemed to happen to Marie. She was the tough one. Nonnie's anger slid off her like water down a drainpipe.

Despite her anguish, Rose felt her chest swell with pride and love for her older sister. Marie was tough, sure, but she could be generous and kind, too. Rose thought of the time she had begged and begged Marie to let her wear her treasured charm bracelet. And then, coming home from school, she'd lost it somehow. She had been so sure Marie would be furious with her. And Marie *had* been angry . . . at first. Then, in typical Marie fashion, she had shrugged, and said, 'Oh, stop bawling, it's not the end of the world. I know you didn't mean it. Go on, blow your nose, and I'll take you out for an ice cream.'

'*Shaaaame*.' Nonnie's sharp voice jolted Rose from her thoughts.

Rose watched in horror as Nonnie jabbed a bony finger in Marie's face. 'Whatsa matter with you? I feed you. I put food on the table in front of you. I raise you like my own daughter. And you do this to me. For shame. You, workin' in a store, paintin' your face like no decent girl. Runnin' around at night like a alleycat with that no-good spic boyfriend of yours.'

Marie bristled. 'Pete's no spic! He's half Puerto Rican, on his mother's side. You got no right callin' him a spic!'

'He shamed you, didn't he?'

'If you mean am I gonna have a baby, the answer is yeah. Yeah, I'm gonna have a kid.' Marie took a step forward, almost menacing. Her pale pink mouth curled in disgust. 'And let me tell you, something, old lady. My kid's gonna have better than what I had.'

'Ha!' Nonnie sneered. 'You didn't do so bad. The sidewalk, that's where you'd a ended up if I hadn't taken you in after the Lord took away my Dom, God rest his soul.'

Rose stared down at the meatloaf on her plate. It was cold now; little islands of waxy gray fat had formed over it. She felt sick to her stomach. If only Marie would stop! Rose was afraid her sister might make Nonnie do or say something they'd all be sorry for.

Marie's eyes had a wild look in them. She advanced another step, shoulders hunched forward and fists clenched at her sides. 'I'm not sorry I got knocked up. You know why? I'll tell you why. 'Cause I'm finally gettin' the hell outta here. I won't have you around tellin' me I'm bad all the time. Maybe that's how come I turned out bad, with you tellin' me all the time. I feel sorry for Clare. And for you, too, Rose.' She tossed Rose a pitying glance. 'If you knew what was good for you, you'd get the hell out, too.'

'You're not good enough to speak your sister's name!' Nonnie spat. 'Clare, she's got the calling. She's gonna be a holy sister. Not in a hundred years would she shame me this way.'

'Sure, you been stuffin' Jesus down her throat for so long she'd think she had the calling if somebody said "boo". And Rose, you treat her like she was dirt under your feet.' She turned toward Rose angrily. 'How come you let her treat you that way, huh, Rose? Huh?'

'Marie, please. Don't . . .' Rose felt so stricken she could barely move her lips. She gazed up at her sister, imploring her to stop.

The kitchen seemed to be closing in on her. The yellowing walls with their faded fruit-cluster paper. The row of cabinets, once blue, now a sad dishwater gray.

'Rose.' Nonnie pronounced her name almost spitting, lips drawn back in contempt. Her small pale eyes focused on Rose with a hateful glee. '*She's* not your sister.'

Rose felt as if the suffocating air had once more come alive, buzzing like a swarm of angry wasps. *I must have heard it wrong*, she thought. *Nonnie couldn't have said that*.

Marie just looked at her grandmother. 'Are you crazy? What are you talkin' about?'

'She's not my Dom's child,' Nonnie insisted. 'She's a bastard just like what you got in your belly. Sure, I got no proof. But,' she went on as she tapped her chest, 'there's some things don't need proof. Just look at her! It was God's curse the day she was born. The first time Dom look at her, he cry. I tell him, "What you know about that fancy wife of yours with her silk stockings and fifty-dollar dresses? What you think a girl like that does with her husband off at war and not around to look after her proper?" I tell you, it was a curse your mother died in that

65

fire. A punishment sent on her from God!' Her voice rose to a shrill whine.

Rose clapped her hands over her ears, but she couldn't block it out. Each word came through like the sting of a wasp piercing into her flesh.

'NO!' Rose shot from her chair, toppling it, erupting with rage. 'You're lying! My mother wasn't like that! She was good and . . . and . . .' She couldn't find the words to fit the huge hot hurting emotion that ballooned inside her chest.

Brian. She had to find Brian. He would know, he'd help, he'd stop this and make it not hurt so much.

Rose pushed her way past Marie and Nonnie, tears spilling hot down her cheeks. She stumbled through the living room, momentarily blinded by its perpetual twilight. Then her eyes caught the gray light leaking through the tightly drawn venetian blinds, the waxy gleam of the plastic-slipcovered sofa.

Rose imagined herself a bug her grandmother wanted to crush and kill, a cockroach. She wrestled with the front-door chain, hating it, hating everything about this room, this awful apartment.

Then she was in the hall, free, pelting up the stairwell to the top floor, to Brian, praying he would be home.

The noisy confusion of the McClanahans' apartment enveloped her the moment she stepped inside. Brian's mother greeted her holding a baby braced against one generous hip, while another clung to her leg. A warm spicy odor invaded the living room, which was cluttered with kids, couch cushions on the floor, and empty baby bottles ringed with dried milk.

'Rose, you're a godsend! Will you take Kevin while I get the cake out of the oven? It's Jasper's birthday and I – oh, here.' She shoved Kevin at her, soggy diaper and all, and scooted off toward the kitchen, calling, 'Bri-an! Rose is here. If you don't take Sean out of the tub, he'll shrivel to a peanut!'

Rose swiped at her runny eyes with the heel of her hand

and sank down on the seat-sprung couch, balancing Kevin on one knee. 'Hey, buddy. You want to do the cha-cha?'

The baby broke into a huge toothless grin. His favorite game was Rose bouncing him to the rhythm of an invisible Latin band. He giggled helplessly. Rose began to feel a tiny bit better.

The messiness cheered her somehow. The huge braided rug was a shipwreck of scattered Tinker toys and Lincoln logs, alphabet blocks half-chewed by teething babies, an empty Band-Aid box, Matchbox trucks, galoshes, broken crayons, and Golden Books with the covers ripped off. Atop the nicked coffee table was a pile of clumsily wrapped birthday presents. And perched on the old plaid recliner where nightly Mr McClanahan put his feet up and read the *Post*, was two-year-old Jasper, mashing a graham cracker between his toes.

'Welcome to Pandemonium City. Have you heard? President Eisenhower just declared this place a disaster area.'

Rose looked up, and found Brian grinning at her, carrying four-year-old Sean, all rosy from his bath. The sleeves of Brian's Brooklyn College sweatshirt were rolled up over his elbows. Stray flecks of shampoo suds decorated his dark brown curls like snowflakes. Just seeing him made Rose feel almost happy.

Before she could answer, he put Sean down and sank on to the sofa beside her. The front of his sweatshirt, she saw, bore the wet imprint of Sean's little body. 'Hey Rose, you all right?' he asked softly. 'You look like you've been crying.'

Rose shook her head, clamping her throat against the fresh tears that threatened. 'I'm OK. But Kev here needs his diaper changed. I don't think either of us can hold out much longer.'

'Sean,' Brian yelled across the room, 'watch Jazzbo, willya? Don't let him near the presents, OK?'

In the shoe box of a room Brian shared with two of his brothers, Rose and he worked together to pin a clean

67

diaper on Kevin despite all his squirming. Brian propped him in his playpen with a mangled Zwieback and a ring of plastic keys.

'All quiet on the Western front,' he whispered, grabbing her hand. 'Come on, now's the time to make our getaway before the Indians get wind of our trail.'

Rose thought, with a rush of affection, *He knows. He's taking me to the fort, because he knows something is wrong.*

The fort. They hadn't been up to the fort in – how long? – a couple of years at least. Since Brian graduated from Precious Blood two years ago and enrolled at Brooklyn College. After that it had seemed sort of . . . well, babyish. She could recall, though, when it had once seemed the most exciting place in the world.

The McClanahans' apartment was on the top floor. Brian's mother had long ago installed window guards throughout the apartment. But Brian had devised a way to get into the super's locked cleaning closet off the public hall. It had a window opening to a small exterior platform. Above that there was an access ladder to the roof. The regular stairway inside the building had been sealed off to tenants since four-year-old Jimmy Storelli tumbled over the edge eight summers ago while his mother was unpinning laundry from her clothesline. The access ladder consisted of eight rusted rungs bolted to the side of the building, with nothing below but a five-story drop.

She'd been seven, Brian eight and a half, when they first discovered it. She remembered being terrified to climb out on the platform, much less actually climb up. But Brian cajoled and encouraged her, promised he'd be right behind and promised he'd catch her if she fell. He even climbed it twice all alone, scampering up like a monkey, just to show her it was no sweat.

God, had she been scared. Even now, scrabbling up behind Brian in the twilight, easily hoisting herself rung over rung, she could remember how back then the wind had torn at her corduroy jumper handed down from

Marie. How it had filled with wind like a sail, billowing one moment, then snapping in hard against the backs of her knees. Her heart playing catching with her stomach, she had thought of poor little Jimmy Storelli, and imagined herself plunging down, then hitting the sidewalk with the hollow splat of a watermelon rolling off the back of a moving truck.

Halfway up, she had frozen, her knees turning to Jell-O. 'I can't' she'd wailed.

Brian's voice had floated up to her. 'Sure, you can, Rosie. I know you can. It's not hard. I promise you won't fall. But even if you do I'll catch you.'

And she had believed him. Brian *would* catch her. Of course he would, absolutely, positively. Hadn't he always taken care of her? She remembered his walking her into the kindergarten that first day when Marie, disgusted by her crying, had left her outside in the schoolyard. Brian was already in the third grade, but he'd given her a licorice whip and walked her to the classroom. And he'd held her hand. That was the best part, even with the friends all looking, the big second-grade boys from Precious Blood, razzing him. So Rose, frozen there five floors above the sidewalk, knew without a doubt that Brian would keep his word, even though another part of her knew that if she did fall he could never catch her.

Rose smiled now as she hiked her foot over the top rung, on to the roof's warm weather-heaved tar-paper surface. She paused a moment, letting her eyes adjust to the orange-gray dusk. There, wedged in between the chimney and a ventilator shaft, was the fort. Their secret hideout. She was a little surprised to see it was still there. Years ago, they'd built it from stuff scavenged out of a construction site behind Gross's Bakery – scraps of plywood, leftover Sheetrock, a roll of fiberglass insulation, some old foam cushions, a shower curtain decorated with pink seahorses. How awed Brian had been when she showed him the system she'd devised to haul all that stuff up with ropes and pulleys. The two of them, using Mr McClanahan's toolbox – Brian with his perfect vision of what it would look like, she the careful one who made sure every board was level before they drove a nail, then that all the cracks got caulked – had worked side by side to build it.

The trouble, she realized now as she crawled in behind Brian, ducking her head to clear the board on to which Brian had burned the wavery words 'Spy-Glass Hill' (after the lookout in *Treasure Island*), was they sure had outgrown it. The scrawny kid she'd played with back then was now six feet of bone and ropey muscle. Stretched out on the foam cushions, leaning against one wall with his feet tucked up against the other, Brian looked a little ridiculous. Like Gulliver in Lilliput.

Still, Rose felt a strange peace creep over her. God, the hours they'd spent up here! They hadn't done anything all that special, really, she thought. Just hanging out. Playing cards mostly. Gin Rummy, War, and Spit. Or smoking the Winstons he'd cadged from his father. But mostly just talking, imagining different ways their lives might turn out.

Brian was going to be a writer, like Ernest Hemingway. When he was thirteen, Brian wrote a novel. It was about big-game hunting, full of scenes with the hero escaping being gored by a rhinoceros in one chapter and savaged by lions in the next. And the heroine keep fainting in the path of stampeding elephants. Parts of it made her laugh, it was so ridiculous, but she'd loved it, too.

Rose's dream wasn't nearly as big or exciting. She wanted only one thing: to get out, get away, far away. She'd spun fantasies about running away, to California maybe, where Nonnie would never find her. She dreamed of sneaking aboard a ship, or a train, going as far as it would take her.

There was only one problem. Running away would mean leaving Brian.

'A penny for your thoughts,' Brian broke into her reverie.

Rose sighed. 'Better make it a dollar.'

'That bad?'

Pulling her knees to her chest, she leaned her head back

70

against the wall. Years of rain and snow had buckled and warped it. But they'd made the wall several inches thick, and secured it to the chimney with baling wire. It could withstand a hurricane, Rose thought.

She looked over at Brian. His arms were behind his head, the back of his neck braced against his interlaced palms. In the twilight that filtered through the torn shower curtain, his face was all contours and shadows. She studied the long bony ridge of his nose. His eyes, that's what really got her. They were like the eyes of saints in devotional paintings, a sort of silvery gray, shining with a light that seemed to come out of nowhere. Brian was no saint – she thought of all the cigarettes he'd 'borrowed' from his father, and the time he'd roped Brother Paul's bumper to a fire hydrant – but he was the only truly good person Rose had ever known, the only one who really cared about her.

She looked away. She couldn't bear the thought that those eyes could ever be turned on her in disgust.

'Do you ever think about your parents . . . you know . . . doing it with people besides each other?' Rose asked.

Brian laughed. 'With seven kids? Even if they wanted to, when would they have the time?'

'I was wondering about . . . well, other people. Doing it even though they're not married to each other.' Rose picked at a chunk of dirty gray foam coming loose from a cushion. 'Marie and Pete are getting married.'

'Hey, that's great!'

'She's pregnant.'

'Oh.' He was silent for a moment. 'Is that why you were crying?'

'No. I'm happy for her. Pete's OK. It's what she wants. I just . . .' In a burst of feeling, she told him what Nonnie had said.

Brian looked at her for a long time. Then he said, in that slow, thoughtful way of his, 'Even if it was true, why would she tell you?'

'To get back at me.'

71

'For what? What did you ever do to her?'

'She thinks I killed my parents. She doesn't care about my mother. It's my father she was really crazy about.'

'Jesus, you were just a *baby*.'

'He was away, a radioman on a destroyer. After my mother . . . after I was born, he came back . . . but only for a few days. I always thought the reason he didn't hang around was because he was sad about my mother, and seeing us – Marie and Clare and me – reminded him too much of her. Then after he was killed . . . I made him into this big hero in my mind. My mother, too. I pictured her as some kind of saint, like Joan of Arc. And now Nonnie is saying—' Hot tears rose in her throat, choking off the words.

'*Forget* what she said,' Brian broke in angrily. 'It's not true. You know it's not. She's always been out to get you one way or another.'

'But what if she's right? *Look* at me, Bri. I'm not like anyone else in my family. It's like . . . like I fell out of the sky or something. *No-one* is dark like me. You know what some of the girls at Sacred Heart call me? Aunt Jemima. They say one of my ancestors must have been colored.'

Brian stiffened, his face glowing white in the twilit shadows. 'You never told me that,' he said.

'I knew you'd be mad. Anyway, I took care of *them*.' A wisp of satisfaction threaded up out of her misery. 'I wrote their names on the Interested list for the all-day bus trip to St Mary's Convent. When Sister read them off, she was so happy – and none of them had the guts to back out.'

Rose started to laugh, but her laughter caught in her throat. Suddenly she was weeping, hard gasping sobs that doubled her over in pain.

Brian crouched beside her, encircling her with his arms. 'Screw them all. It doesn't matter what they think. All that matters is *you*.'

She lifted her face, wet and swollen with tears. 'Do you think it's true, Bri? Do you think I'm a . . . a bastard like Marie's baby?'

'No, but I wouldn't care if you were.' he smoothed her

hair as she rested her face against his sweatshirt. It smelled of baby powder and shampoo and his own musky male scent. 'Anyway, what's wrong with being different? You're a thousand times smarter than any girl I know.'

'But I'm not pretty.' She realized how coy that sounded, and she quickly added, 'And I'm not fishing for compliments. It's true.'

'Says who?'

Rose felt prickly heat crawl up her neck, and was grateful he could hardly see her in the dark. 'Well, I'm just not.' She spoke more brusquely than she'd intended. 'Anyway, I don't care.'

Brian drew back, and grabbed her by shoulders. 'Rose, you *are* pretty.'

'Oh yeah?' she scoffed. 'Well, I don't see anyone else rushing to get a closer look at me.'

'Maybe they would, if you didn't make it so hard. You're so sure people won't like you you've got your chin up before they say one word to you. Hell, Rose, you gotta give people a chance.'

'You mean I should flirt more, like Georgette?'

'Don't start in on her again, Rose,' Brian warned.

'What did I say?'

'You don't like her.'

Rose felt as if she were riding the Cyclone at Coney Island. She wanted to stop, but she couldn't. There was no way to get off. Deep down, she'd been mad at Brian ever since he first started going out with Georgette. It was dumb, but she'd somehow felt she was losing him as her best friend.

'I never said I don't like her,' Rose countered. 'Anyway, it's not what I think that counts. The point is that *you* like her. Maybe you even love her. She's the type boys go after. I suppose you *do* it with Georgette.'

'It's none of your damn business!' Brian exploded. He pulled away from her with an angry wrench, throwing himself down on to the cushions.

In the quiet that followed, Rose became aware that her heart was beating very fast.

'I'm sorry, Bri,' Rose said softly, reaching out to touch his arm.

She wasn't sorry really for not liking Georgette, though. Who could like someone named Georgette, who looked like a Barbie doll, wore cashmere sweaters, and had more blond hair than a collie?

'You really have it in for her, don't you?'

'I only said she reminded me of Lassie.'

'Lassie is a *dog*.'

'So? I happen to like dogs.'

Brian laughed in spite of himself. 'Face it, Rose. It wouldn't matter if she was Grace Kelly. You just don't like her because I'm dating her. You and Ma. You're two of a kind.'

'Your mother!' Rose, furious, jumped to her feet. Smacking her head on the low roof, she was abruptly and painfully reminded that she'd grown a fair bit since the fourth grade. She sank down, rubbing her scalp. It didn't hurt as much as her ego.

His mother. Jesus. That stung. Even if he was only her best friend and not her boyfriend, it hurt to have him think of her along with his big, soft, and somehow (despite seven kids) sexless mother.

'For your information, Mr Smart-pants, I've had plenty of experience myself,' she told him. 'And not just kissing.'

'Sure you have,' Brian said matter-of-factly. She could see he was screwing his lips down to keep from smiling.

She sighed, defeated. It was no use lying. Brian could always see right through her. She remembered bragging one time that her father had been an admiral in the navy, and had torpedoed a whole fleet of slant-eyes when he was in the War.

They'd been walking to school, and Brian had stooped to pick up a blackened penny off the sidewalk. He'd studied it carefully. 'Yeah,' he said. 'My pop knew him. Said he was a great guy. He didn't even have to be an admiral to be a great guy, I'll bet.' He tucked the penny in his back pocket, when he turned to her his face was solemn, the face of someone much older than twelve. 'Rose, where'd you hear that word? Slant-eyes.'

She had stopped skipping beside him, arrested by the cool light in his gray eyes. 'From Nonnie. She says the people who killed my dad were a sneaky bunch of slant-eyed yellow bastards.'

'Well, don't say it again, OK? It's a bad word. Like the ones you see on subway station walls. You like Bobby Lee, doncha?'

'Sure, I do. He's nice.' Bobby Lee's father owned the Mandarin Garden, on Occan Avenue, and the Lees lived in their building on the third floor.

'Well, if you say that word you're calling him one, too. There's names for people like us, too. Wop. Guinea. Dago. Mick.'

Rose had felt dirty and ashamed. 'I didn't mean it like that.'

Brian had ruffled her hair. 'Aw, Rose, doncha think I know that?'

Now Rose suddenly realized exactly why she detested Brian's girlfriend. Not because of anything about *her* really. But because Georgette had crossed some sort of line with Brian. No, not a line a wall – a wall that separated kids from grown-ups, the Berlin Wall of sex.

Well, she was sick and tired of being on the other side of that wall, only *imagining* what other people were doing.

People like Brian (probably) and Marie (definitely).

'Kiss me, Bri,' she said, saying it the way she would have said, *How about a game of Hearts?*

'*What?*' He sounded as shocked as if she'd suggested he spray-paint a statue of the Blessed Virgin.

'Just a practice kiss,' she explained. 'So I won't make a complete idiot of myself when it's the real thing. You can tell me what I'm doing wrong. Isn't that what best friends are for?'

'Not exactly.' He didn't sound shocked anymore, just embarrassed. 'But, well . . . OK. I suppose it wouldn't hurt.'

'Do I sit up or lie down?' she asked, feeling suddenly nervous. Her mouth was dry as sandpaper. Would Brian notice? Oh well, she decided, what did it matter, if this was just a practice kiss?

Brian seemed alarmed. 'Stay right where you are,' he ordered. 'And if a guy ever tells you to lie down, *don't*, you hear?'

She closed her eyes and waited. Nothing happened. She opened them to find Brian staring at her, frowning.

'Not like that. You're all puckered up. Relax your lips.'

'Do I say "cheese"?'

'Not unless you want your picture taken.'

'That'd be nice. A snapshot for my memory album. My first kiss.'

'*Practice* kiss,' he corrected.

Brian leaned close. She could feel his breath against her face, warm and smelling vaguely of licorice. Then Brian's lips were moving gently against hers. Rose felt as if she were in an elevator and it had just shot down three floors.

Something soft and velvety nuzzled her teeth. The tip of Brian's tongue. She opened her lips wider, feeling a gush of warmth spill though her guts as he probed the inside of her mouth with his tongue.

When he pulled back they were both breathing hard. 'Brian,' she whispered, as dizzy as that time they'd sneaked a bottle of Gallo Red Mountain up here and drunk the whole thing. 'Oh, Brian . . .'

'God, oh Rose, I'm sorry. I didn't mean—' He cupped her face in his hands. She noticed they were trembling. 'I didn't mean for it to be like that.'

'Kiss me again,' she urged. 'Kiss me for real this time.'

This time the kiss didn't end. He drew her down on the mattress. She felt strangely heavy. And wet. Down there. As if she were getting her period. Oh, Mother of Mercy, is this how it started with Marie and Pete?

Brian moaned, almost as if in pain. 'Jesus, Rose.'

His hand moved up to cup her breast. She could feel it, hot and sweaty beneath the starched cotton of her blouse. She knew it was a sin. A sin, the Sisters had warned, even to touch yourself like that. But somehow it didn't feel wrong, not with Brian. The hand on her breast was the same one that had held hers that first day of school.

Brian was kissing her everywhere, his lips on her throat, her hair, His breath bursting against her in hot, astonished gasps. He pushed his hand under her blouse, and struggled clumsily to unhook her bra.

It struck Rose then: *He's never done it before. He doesn't know how.*

Swept with new tenderness for him, she reached up and unsnapped it for him.

Brian groaned, moving his hips against her.

He stroked her bare breasts, and Rose thought she would surely melt with the heat of his hand there. But she was scared, too. It felt *too* good. Anything that felt this good had to be a sin. She wriggled to ease her skirt down, and Brian suddenly stiffened, letting out a deep, strangled moan.

Rose felt something damp against her leg. At first she thought, stricken, that he'd somehow wet himself. Then she realized, *His stuff. The stuff that makes babies.*

She felt shame, knowing they had done something terrible, irreversible. She was just like Marie.

But then the shame faded, and there was only Brian. Holding her tight. Her best friend, her soul.

He was still for a long time, his face buried against her neck. She could feel his breath in her hair, a pulse beating wildly in his neck. Rose wanted to stay this way for ever.

Finally, he stirred, lifting his head. His long face gleamed in the darkness. Rose saw the look of misery in his eyes, and pressed a finger lightly to his lips.

'Don't,' she said. 'Don't say you're sorry.'

Rose was astonished by what she was feeling, though what exactly that was she couldn't have said right then. It

77

blasted through her with the force of a jet, burning away Nonnie's hateful words. She felt new, shining, as if she'd been reborn.

*When Sister Perpetua described getting the Call, this is how you're supposed to feel*, she thought. Except it wasn't God making her feel this way. It was Brian.

Suddenly, she understood, as if a part of her had aged a dozen years and she were looking back at herself, at the child she'd been just an hour ago, at all the things she'd felt but been unable to put a name to.

'I love you,' she said.

'Rose.' He tugged her to him and held her tightly, his words muffled by her hair. 'Something . . . happened. I'm not sure exactly what. But I . . . I think I meant it. I think I must have wanted it to happen. God help me, Rose, I think I did.'

It was those last words of his, 'God help me,' that stuck in her mind like a thorn. A terrible thought occurred to her: would God punish her for loving Brian this way? They had committed adultery, hadn't they? Sister Perpetua said adultery was any unclean thought or deed. Rose didn't feel unclean, but she knew what Sister meant by it. Sex. And that was a sin unless you were married and did it to make a baby. *Any* kind of sex.

Fear took hold of Rose's heart. She thought of dreadful things. She wouldn't get pregnant, but she could be struck down by a car while crossing the street. Or fall in front of a subway train. Or—

She stopped; the pressure on her heart was hurting now. Then she realized what the very *worst* punishment of all would be.

Losing Brian.

'. . . deliver us from evil. Amen.'

Rose completed the last Our Father. Looking up, she saw that it was dark and the church nearly empty. Her knees ached, and her stomach was growling. It had to be past dinnertime.

78

She rose stiffly and sidled from the pew, wincing as she genuflected. Then, dipping her finger in the holy water in the vestibule, and crossing herself, she went outside.

Rose walked the sidewalks quickly in the fading light. Clouds had formed overhead, and it was starting to rain. Fat tepid droplets broke against her face.

Chin tucked against her collar, she hurried down Coney Island Avenue. This time of the evening the street reminded her of a boardwalk closed for the winter. Striped awnings folded back, heavy metal shutters or accordion gates drawn across storefronts. Even the pretzel man had left his corner. She glimpsed the back of his black coat flapping as he trotted across the street, pushing his cart.

Still, the avenue teemed with life. Car horns blaring, people scurrying to get out of the rain. Rose heard a burly trucker bellow to the driver of a Plymouth who was kissing his tail and honking like crazy, 'Aaaayyyy, mistah, I'll ram ya fuckin' front end up ya nose.'

She quickened her step. Loose rubbish – leaves of newspaper, bits of Styrofoam, straw wrappers, empty cigarette packs – blew across her path. She felt lonelier than any other time she could think of.

She hadn't seen Brian since that night on the roof, a week ago. He was avoiding her. Why? Was he sorry about what had happened? Too embarrassed to face her?

Guilt gnawed at her. *It's my fault, I made him kiss me. I led him into sin, just like Eve did with Adam.*

Was this to be God's punishment . . . taking Brian away from her?

*Oh please, God, please, I'll do anything if you give him back. I'll give up meat every day of the week, not just Friday. I'll fast for forty days on Lent. I'll devote my life to serving others.*

When Rose came into the apartment, Nonnie was watching 'The Lawrence Welk Show.' She barely glanced up from her knitting.

'You're late,' she croaked. 'I left supper in the oven for you.' Since the night Marie left, Nonnie had been keeping

79

off Rose's back. Rose wondered if her grandmother was regretting her awful words.

'That's OK. I'm not hungry,' Rose said.

In the tiny dark bedroom she'd shared with Marie, the other bed was bare, sheets removed, its worn chenille spread pulled tight over the mattress. Clean circles in the dust atop the dresser marked the places where Marie's bottles of perfume and skin lotions had stood. Gone, too, the snapshots and twenty-five-cent photo-booth strips that had been tucked inside the mirror frame. In Marie's side of the closet, the empty hangers swung together with a hollow metallic ticking as Rose hung up her sweater.

It was as if Marie had died. Rose shivered and, only half-aware of what she was doing, made the sign of the cross.

Then, crouching on the floor, she peeled back a frayed edge of the mustard-brown carpeting that had come untacked. Underneath was a loose floorboard. She found the metal nail file she kept in the bottom dresser drawer, and pried up the loose board with it. Underneath was a space just big enough for an old metal Band-Aid box. Her secret place. No-one else knew about it. Not Marie. Not even Brian.

Rose opened the Band-Aid box, and shook out a lump of gray cotton. Slowly, she unwrapped it, revealing the glittering treasure hidden within.

A ruby earring, gleaming in her hand like a frozen drop of blood.

The memory came rushing back. Seven years ago – had it been that long? She saw it in her mind as clearly as if it were happening now. The elegant lady in the mink coat. Rose had seen her standing just outside the schoolyard fence one day. She didn't look like any of the mothers. More like a queen. Or a mysterious movie star, in that beautiful mink coat, and a hat with a little veil that dipped over her eyes.

Then she'd realized those mysterious eyes underneath the veil were staring at *her*. At first Rose had been sure she

80

was wrong. She'd even glanced back over her shoulder to see if there was someone behind her. But, no, the lady was looking straight at her. Her eyes big and somehow wet-looking, like the clear green marbles in her collection, the ones that were worth ten cat's eyes.

Rose cautiously drew a little closer. Sad and lost, that's how the lady looked. But it didn't make any sense. Why should she be? Someone dressed as beautiful as that had to be rich, and rich people never had worries like the grown-ups Rose knew. It was a cold day, and the lady seemed to shiver, drawing her mink coat more tightly about her. Ruby earrings twinkled in her ears. What could she want?

As Rose came through the gate amid the noisy, jostling throng of classmates, the woman took several jerky steps forward, crying out in a thin strangled voice, 'Wait!'

Startled, Rose paused, remembering that she'd been told by Nonnie and the Sisters, not once but at least fifty times, never *ever* to talk to strangers. But somehow she couldn't run away. Her saddle shoes felt as if they were struck on to the sidewalk. Her arms and legs frozen in place.

Rose waited, as if hypnotized by that beautiful, some-how haunted face, its fragile bones jutting from pale creamy skin. Soft hair, the color of autumn leaves, floated over her fur collar. Rose was reminded of a snowflake that would melt if she touched it. The woman's flowerlike mouth trembled. Her eyes brimmed with tears. She seemed on the verge of speaking, but she pulled back abruptly as if she'd changed her mind.

Instead, she reached up with a glove hand – it had been trembling, Rose remembered – and unscrewed the ruby from her right ear.

As Rose stood there, too shocked to protest, the lady pressed the tiny earring, icy cold, into her palm. Then she had run off, high heels clattering on the frozen sidewalk, ducking into a long sleek limousine that waited at the curb, disappearing as if in a puff of smoke.

Rose had been sure of it. The lady was her Guardian

Angel. Everyone had one, Sister Perpetua said. But Rose hadn't believed it was true for her . . . until that day.

And now she had the earring to prove it.

Rose held it up to the light, a ruby in the shape of a teardrop dangling from a tiny gold and diamond stud. Even in the dim room, it blazed with a light of its own, causing Rose to suck her breath in with wonder even though she'd looked at it a hundred times. Yes, magic. Heaven-sent magic.

And she needed its magic now, more than ever.

'Don't leave me, Bri,' she whispered, clenching it tightly in her fist, more passion in her heart than a thousand rosaries could have summoned. 'Please don't ever leave me.'

82

# 2

Rachel frowned at her plate, at the fried egg centered between two neat triangles of toast. Round as a daisy, and not a single bubble. Bridget, she knew, fried them inside a cookie cutter to keep the edges smooth. So they would be as perfect as everything in this house. The fork in her hand, Mama's Cartier silver, was polished to mirror brightness. She caught a distorted glimpse of her reflection in it now, round blue eyes, a scatter of light brown hair.

'I'm not going,' Rachel said, quietly answering her mother's question.

How could she? After last night with Gil? Get dressed up, flirt, pretend nothing was wrong. God, what a joke that would be.

Gil's words came back now, pricking her, '*Why don't you just admit it, Rachel? You're not so goddamn moral. That's not why you won't go all the way with me. It's because you really don't like sex. You're frigid. Or maybe it's a girl you want . . .*'

Rachel brought the tines of her fork down hard into the yolk, watching it burst, ooze across the fine Blue Willow plate, obscuring the weeping willow and the three tiny figures crossing the bridge.

She was furious at Gil – of all the pompous asses at Haverford, he took the prize! – but underneath the thought itched at her, *God, what if it's true?*

*Face it*, she told herself, *it's not just Gil who leaves you cold. Something's been missing with every guy so far.*

Twenty, and still a virgin. Not, as Gil had pointed out,

because she was so moral. No. Worse. The truth was, she just hadn't *felt* like it so far.

Rachel stared down at the ruined egg yolk, feeling slightly nauseated. Only this sickness had nothing to do with the mess on her plate, she knew, or the beers she'd drunk last night.

It all boiled down to sex, she thought. Everything. Fashions. Perfume. Magazine covers. Even those television ads for toothpaste. It seemed as if everyone in the whole world was either thinking about it, talking about it, or doing it.

*So what's wrong with me?*

Was it like learning to swim? Either you were good at it, or you sank like a rock?

Or maybe she'd been born this way. Normal on the outside. Pretty even. Rachel remembered when she was a child, Great-aunt Willie in her mink smothering her in a furry, perfumed embrace, then grabbing a handful of cheek in each gloved hand, crowing, 'Just like a little baby doll! So dainty! And those blue eyes, Sylvie, she must have gotten them from Gerald! But where did that pretty little doll's face come from? Not from you or your mama. I wonder who?'

'*The Girl with the Watering Can*,' Rachel had replied solemnly.

That was what Mama always said, anyway, that Rachel reminded her of the Renoir painting. She had showed Rachel the picture in a book, a little girl with waves of red-gold hair and bright Wedgwood-blue eyes that matched her dress, standing stiffly posed in a garden, holding a watering can.

Rachel had hated that picture, and once in a black mood had scribbled over it with a crayon. Why were people always telling her she was dainty and cute and precious? She'd longed to run through the echoing rooms of their big house, instead of walking softly as Mama always admonished, to shout at the top of her lungs, and turn cartwheels on the patterned rugs. Not be like some doll or a girl holding a stupid watering can, but like a bird or a wild creature, doing as she pleased, not caring what people thought of her.

Now she wondered if she had been worrying all that time about the wrong thing. Wishing she were tall and fierce like the Amazon women she'd read about, when all along there was something wrong with her on the *inside*. Some awful undetected deformity. Missing hormones, or a paralyzed sex drive. Or even, God forbid, something actually wrong with her *down there*.

'Rachel, what's gotten into you?' Mama's voice broke into her thoughts.

Rachel looked up. Daddy, she saw, was absorbed in his paper, but Mama was regarding her with that sad, faintly bewildered expression she always seemed to wear whenever they disagreed about something. Could she tell Mama? Mama, who surrounded herself only with beautiful things, chamber music always on the stereo, silk scarves and embroidered handkerchiefs, her precious roses. She looked like a flower herself, slim and elegant, with those wide forest-green eyes and her pale, almost white-blond hair. Eight-thirty in the morning, and she already had on lipstick, wearing her daisy-print Lilly Pulitzer housecoat to see Daddy off to the bank.

*She'd probably be so shocked. She's never talked about sex, at least not to me. I wonder if she's ever felt that way, passionate about Daddy . . . or anyone.*

'I'm just not up to it, that's all,' Rachel said. 'That calculus exam did me in; I had about twenty minutes' sleep all last week.' She sighed, and picked up a triangle of toast, dipping one corner in the gooey egg. 'When I went into pre-med, I thought I'd mostly be dissecting things like sheep's eyes and cow hearts, not integers.'

Rachel saw her mother wince. Plainly, Sylvie still hated the idea of her becoming a doctor. Rachel felt a flash of irritation toward her.

*Dammit, I* won't *be like her. Like a pair of silk stockings, lovely but perishable. Doing Good Works, but not getting my hands dirty.*

85

Then Rachel was struck by a new, disturbing thought. *Suppose I'm more like her than I realize. If Mama doesn't care much for sex – and I couldn't possibly imagine her doing It with Daddy the way Sophia Loren did It with Marcello Mastroianni in* Divorce Italian Style *– then what if a thing like that could be inherited, like the color of my eyes, or hair?*

'The party isn't for another two weeks,' Sylvie reminded her gently. Her mother smiled faintly as she poured milk from a silver creamer into her coffee, and began slowly, gracefully, to stir it, her spoon chiming against the Limoges cup. 'I was just thinking. Remembering when Mason taught you to swim – you must have been four or five. The first winter Daddy bought the place in Palm Beach. Isn't that right, Gerald?'

Daddy looked up from the *Wall Street Journal*. 'Mmm? Oh, yes, yes. You and that little boy were always up to one thing or another. Most of it no good.' He caught Rachel's eye, giving her a wink, and for an instant she felt the invisible ring that enclosed just the two of them.

Then she thought with a pang, *He looks so old*.

Rubbed smooth with age, like Mama's antique silver tea set. She saw the freckled ridge of his scalp beneath the silver hair fine as cobwebs, the rust that lightly blotched his face, and felt almost pain at the thought of how close she might be to losing him.

She remembered when he used to lift her, swinging her up, up over his head. And she, suspended in the air, looking down into his sparkling eyes, seeing his love for her, perfect and shining, had felt . . . oh, bliss.

Then she thought of sitting in his lap in the dim, leather-smelling coolness of his study listening to music, such fun because each record had a story, and Daddy would tell it, pretending to be all the different characters. Some of them so silly, and some so sad. So by her eighth birthday, she knew every libretto by heart. Then he'd taken her, just the two of them, to the Metropolitan Opera, which she'd thought was the most beautiful place in the world, and they'd seen her favorite, *The Marriage of Figaro*.

But now, damn it, he seemed not just thinner, but frail somehow, moving more cautiously, eyes somehow burning, as if there were a fire inside him, consuming him bit by bit.

She remembered with a pang that awful day three years ago, when the call came that Daddy had been rushed to the Intensive Care Unit at New York Hospital. She had dashed over from school, and, too anxious even to wait for the elevator, had bolted up the stairwell. She finally reached his room, disheveled, out of breath, panting. Looking at him, gray and shrunken under the plastic oxygen tent like some mummified creature on display, tubes and wires running out of him, she had felt a mixture of despair and rage. Why couldn't they *do* something, cure him, she – sixteen years old and just over five feet tall in her stockings – had wanted to scream at the orderlies, nurses, doctors, all of whom were doing nothing but talking to each other and scribbling notes on charts. Why weren't they *with* him, working frantically to make him better? Rachel had longed so fiercely to heal him; she'd always remember that day, the precise minute even, gripping the cold metal bedframe, forehead lowered against the scratchy sheet, promising herself, and God, that if Daddy got well, she would become a doctor. So that she would never feel so stupid and helpless and dependent on people who wouldn't do anything.

Rachel pushed that memory away. Mason. They'd been talking about Mason Gold, hadn't they? 'I remember he almost drowned me,' she said with a laugh. 'He called me a dumb old sissy-girl, and I was so mad I jumped into the deep end and sank like a rock.'

Sylvie looked up, her deep-green eyes widening, disturbed. 'You never told me *that*.'

*That's the least of it, Mama*, Rachel thought.

She shrugged. 'Would you ever have let me near that pool again if I had?'

There was a moment of silent acknowledgement, a look

87

passing between Gerald and Sylvie. Rachel became aware of house sounds, comforting in their familiarity, the clackety noises of Bridget washing up in the kitchen, the low grunt of Portia under the table as she scratched herself, the chiming of the clock on the mantel. She thought: *God, they're thinking what it would have been like if I'd drowned, if they'd lost me.*

She felt weighted down, like a huge heavy backpack strapped to her shoulder; too much love, being their only child.

How she had longed for a baby sister, or a baby brother. But though Mama had kept the crib in the nursery for the longest time, no babies ever came. And so Rachel had played instead with an endless parade of dolls – presented with great fanfare each birthday and Chanukah, in shiny boxes wrapped with big satin bows – Muffie dolls, bride dolls, a Betsy Wetsy, and Barbie – but had always lost interest when she realized that no amount of imagining could make them into a *real* baby sister she could hold and love, who would love her back.

Rachel watched her mother continue to stir her coffee while it grew cold, her long slender fingers nearly as translucent as the porcelain cup. Rachel's gaze went past Sylvie, taking in the dark glow of the Sheraton sideboard adorned with candelabra and silver serving dishes. And on the other wall, Mama's china closet with the Baccarat crystal twinkling behind the diamond panes. Lovely . . . so much a part of her, as if the seams between Mama and this house had been rubbed away with time, the two flowing together, harmonious, inseparable.

Yet what was it about Mama, the odd way she seemed to turn inward at times? Rachel couldn't remember not feeling it, that faint sadness, like a shadow falling between them. When Mama hugged her, it was too tightly, almost choking her. As if she were afraid Rachel might slip away.

Birthdays, especially, when Mama didn't know Rachel was watching, the smiles that never quite reached her eyes. Rachel would blow out the candles, wishing year after year for the same thing: *Please, let my mother be happy*.

Why on earth couldn't she be? What more could she possibly want?

Rachel remembered agonizing as a child, wondering if another baby would make Mama happy. Or was it *her* fault? If she were different, more obedient and proper, like the demure little girl with the watering can. Would Mama be happy then?

'Eat your breakfast, dear,' Sylvie admonished gently. 'It's getting cold.'

'I'm not very hungry.'

Sylvie's face tightened. 'Are you feeling all right?'

*Here we go again*. 'I'm fine, Mama. It's just that I didn't get in until almost two; then when I finally got to bed, Portia wanted to crawl in with me. I think she missed me.' She peeked under the table at the fat black semi-Labrador retriever at her feet, now snoring contentedly. She tickled Portia lightly with her big toe, feeling a rush of affection for this mongrel she'd rescued as a pup. Then, glancing back up at Sylvie, Rachel saw her mother still watching her anxiously. '*Honestly*, Mama. I'm healthy as a horse.'

*God, will she ever stop? My whole life, every skinned knee and scraped elbow; anyone would've thought it was epilepsy or cancer. Poor Mama. I'd come home bruised and scratched from climbing a tree or falling off my bike, and it would be* she *who would cry.*

Rachel found herself remembering the time she'd gotten lost outside of Saks around Christmas time. She must've been five, scarcely big enough to push the revolving door. Mama had been looking at some stuff at a front counter, and Rachel had heard bells, jingling Santa bells from outside on the street. *Just a peek*, she had thought. She'd run outside for a minute, and then back in before Mama even noticed. Except there were just too many people. She got swept up and carried along with them like a leaf on a rushing brook. She couldn't work herself free until almost a block away. And then it was snowing, fat flakes like cotton balls swirling down, making it hard to see. By the time she got back inside, her shoes were soaked right through to her socks, and Mama was nowhere in sight.

Rachel never forgot that moment, that awful sinking panic. Even at that age she wasn't scared for herself, but for Mama. She knew how frightened Mama would be that she'd disappeared. Rachel darted in and out among shoppers, holding back tears and searching up every aisle for her mother.

After she'd tried all the counters, she'd gone back outside. Maybe Mama was looking for her out there. She'd stood next to Santa for a while, watching him ring his bell, and people put money in his pot, and then a nice policeman asked if she was lost. When she told him she was, he waited there with her, and then a green and white car came, and another policeman drove her home.

Sylvie's face as they came in the front door was burned into Rachel's memory. The tissue-paper color of her skin, the puffy redness of her eyes. And how she'd trembled, dragging Rachel into her embrace, squeezing her so tightly Rachel could hardly breathe. And all the while, Mama sobbing, touching her all over, her hair, her arms, as if to make sure she really was there.

'It's OK, Mama,' Rachel had tried comforting her, crying a little herself, burying her face in the sweet silkiness of her mother's hair. 'Don't cry. Please. See, I didn't get lost. Not *really*. I found my way home too, all by myself. Well, the policeman helped, but I knew the way. Mama? Mama?'

When did she first learn that other girls' mothers weren't like hers? Odd, how they dressed like Mama, had the same hairdos, and shopped in the same stores, though most of them weren't nearly as stylish.

Mama was more fun, for one thing. She made everything they did together seem special, important. Other mothers took their little girls to the park, to puppet shows. Mama took her to museums, to mysterious tombs with gilded sarcophagi from ancient Egypt; and rooms full of wonderful paintings and artifacts, a whole Japanese village carved from a single ivory tusk, paintings of plump naked women and winged cherubs, intricate beaded purses sewn by Eskimos. And Mama, holding her hand, explaining each thing, making it all feel like a miracle.

Yet her friends' mothers were much more relaxed in a way. They applied Mercurochrome and Band-Aids to their kids' skinned knees in the same way they might butter a piece of toast. They yelled sometimes, and fretted. But if you were fifteen minutes late from school, or came home with a bloody nose, they didn't fall apart.

Yet, oddly, in a real crisis, Mama held fast. Rachel remembered, after Daddy's heart attack, when Mama found her sobbing by his hospital bed, how Mama had taken her firmly by the arm and steered her outside into the corridor. She'd been stunned to see Mama's green eyes flashing, not with tears, but anger.

'I won't have it!' Sylvie had spoken sharply to her, the first time ever. 'You carrying on like that, as if he were dying. He'll get better. He'll be *fine*. And for heaven's sake, before you go back in there go to the washroom, splash cold water on your face. I won't have Daddy wake up and think we're sitting *shivah* for him.'

Yes, Mama was a mystery in some ways. Somewhere Rachel had read that silk threads woven into the same thickness as a steel cable would be stronger. Mama was like that, stronger than anyone suspected . . . maybe even herself.

'Does it mean that much to you, me going to this party?' Rachel asked, watching Mama lift her cup to her lips, wanting so badly, even now, to please her, make that faint sadness behind her eyes disappear.

Sylvie gently put down her cup. 'Oh, Rachel, it's not for *me*. I want it for you, don't you see? When I was growing up . . .' A faraway look crept into her eyes, but she pulled herself short. 'Anyway, it wasn't so bad. Just . . . lonely. Yes, a girl your age should be involved, have young men calling on her.'

91

Rachel laughed. 'Young men don't *call* on girls anymore, Mama.' *They ball them*.

She thought of Gil, and felt cold. She saw it was raining outside, heavy drops tapping against the windowpanes. Thanksgiving was a few days away, then Chanukah. She'd bought a great scarf for Gil, cashmere, a soft heathery blue.

*Am I in love with him?* But she couldn't remember ever melting inside, the way you were supposed to, no, not even in the beginning. Charmed by him, yes, the way he laughed at her silly puns, and then came back with better ones of his own. His absentminded way of dressing, a leather bomber jacket and argyle socks, or a Brooks Brothers jacket with paint-spattered jeans and scuffy Weejuns. The clever cartoons he drew in her notebook when they studied together.

But he was so superorganized, so . . . goddamned pompous, a Haverford pre-med and he was already boning up on his specialty, thoracic surgery.

Rachel felt herself growing angry, at him, but then at herself.

*Hey, it's not his fault you're frigid.*

She thought back to when she first began dating, the summer she turned sixteen, out at the beach house in Deal. She had liked it when Buck Walker kissed her; it gave her a nice warm feeling. And sometimes when he, and then Arnie Shapiro, went further. Then, at some unknown point, it just . . . stopped. The good feelings, the warm flutters. She would be aware of the hand on her breast, or between her legs, but the feeling was ordinary, no more exciting than being rubbed by a washcloth or bar of soap. She would find herself bit by bit drawing away. Not physically at first. Mentally. As if she had stepped outside her body and were hovering overhead, a ghostly sports commentator. Howard Cosell of the seduction scene.

*And now things are really warming up, folks. He's off,* *he's running . . . he's – oh boy, look at him go – closing* *in on the goal line. He's got that bra unhooked, and he's*

*working on her zipper now. He's really breathing hard,*
*folks, he looks all done in. But, wait, something's wrong.*
*She's backing off, she's pushing his hand away . . .*
*she's – let's get a close-up of this if we can – intercepted*
*him at the goal line.' Tough break . . .*

She'd heard from boys, and from her friends, that a lot
of girls cried at the last minute. Begged off on account of
religion, morality, their period, wanting to save it for their
husband, or just plain scared. So why, with her, was it the
giggles?

She would swear to herself again and again that this
time she would not, but then the giggles would start and
she could not stop herself.

No boy, she'd discovered, could keep it up in the face of
laughter.

She thought about last night, Gil driving her home from
Bryn Mawr. He'd slipped off the turnpike, and before she
quite knew where they were, he'd parked alongside the
boathouse on Lake Carnegie in Princeton. It was dusk,
the sky mauve, the water dark and still. It was too chilly to
sit outside for long, but Gil insisted. Organized as ever,
he'd come prepared with a six-pack of Löwenbräu, a big
bag of potato chips, and an old quilted mattress pad.

Then Rachel vaguely remembered clothes getting
unbuttoned, feeling looped, wanting to pee more than
anything. Then Gil's zipper was stuck, and he got very red
in the face and started swearing. Suddenly the whole thing
seemed unbearably ludicrous, fumbling around in the
freezing cold, Gil cursing with the pain of a doubled-over
hard-on.

The giggles had just erupted, like beer fizzing over the
top of a can.

Wiping her eyes, weak and ashamed when she'd finally
managed to subdue them, she told Gil, 'I'm sorry. I don't
know what came over me.'

Gil, no longer tugging at his zipper, his lower lip edging
out in a pout, seemed transformed from the young
Gregory Peck she'd once felt attracted to, to a petulant

little boy whose favorite toy had just been snatched away.

'Oh, I think you do. I think you know very well,' he said in an injured tone. 'This isn't the first time, as we both know. And what I'd like to know, what I'd *really* like to know, is what it is about me you find so goddamn funny.'

But he looked so comical, with his face all screwed up, and his hair full of foxtails; and then the lake water lapping against the shore in the darkness, making her want to pee worse than ever. Again, she felt the urge to giggle rising in her.

'It's not you, Gil,' she gasped. 'It's me. I get this way when I'm nervous. You know, like people who laugh at funerals. I get all tied up in knots inside, and then it . . . it all just bursts out somehow.' Funeral? Oh God, she thought, what a comparison.

But his mouth went slack, his anger fading a little. 'Goddammit, Rachel. What did you think this was? A quick roll in the hay? Satisfying some itch? What are you so nervous about? I *love* you, goddammit.'

Then the giggles, with a demonic life of their own, began clawing their way up her throat. She bit her tongue to hold them.

But his declaration, thank God, had shown her a way out, clear as an exit sign flashing on in the dark.

'I'm sorry, Gil,' she managed to say, tears filling her eyes – tears of pain brought on by her throbbing tongue. 'I like you. I like you a lot. But I guess I don't love you. Not enough to . . . go all the way.'

Yes, right, and then next month or next year, as soon as she fell in love, it would be different. And then she'd feel all those things she was supposed to feel.

Then it was Gil who was laughing, bitterly, as now he tugged up his zipper. 'Love? You think that's what's holding you back? Jesus, you're even more screwed up than I thought. The truth is, you don't even like sex. Unless maybe it's a woman you want.' He began folding up the mattress pad with jerky thrust of his arms, then stopped, fixing her with a baleful glare. 'Whatever it is, I hope you

94

find it. I sincerely hope you do. Just from now on leave me the hell out of it.'

Now at the memory of it, Rachel winced. Then she thought of late last night, home at last, lying awake in bed, aching with Gil's words. Desperate to prove to herself she wasn't frigid, she had even tried masturbating.

But groping under her nightgown and rubbing herself down there struck her as even more ridiculous than the things she'd done with boys, like bumping around in the dark without a flashlight. Would she even recognize an orgasm if she had one?

Finally, she had just given up and wept. She'd end up a medical curiosity with a paragraph or two written about her in some sex scientist's monograph. A freak.

She'd have no-one to love her. No one she could love back.

A clattering noise brought her back to the breakfast table, and Rachel looked up to see Bridget's broad back disappearing into the serving pantry with a pile of dishes.

'Anyway, it's not as if I'm lonely,' she lied to Sylvie, keeping her voice light. 'I've got you and Daddy and Portia.'

Daddy glanced up from his paper again. 'Well, I'm happy to see at least that your mother and I are included with your dog. Only, I *do* wish you wouldn't feed her at the table.'

Rachel snatched her hand from under the table, where Portia was greedily licking the last of the toast crumbs from her fingers.

'That's all, you big beggar,' she scolded the scruffy Lab at her feet, then sneaked him the last of her toast.

She heard Daddy grumble into his newspaper, 'Why the devil is Kennedy going to do P R in Texas of all places? Who needs him there? He ought to get busy mending a few fences in his own backyard. I don't like the way things are heating up in Indochina. It's got the smell of Korea all over again.'

'*Gerald*,' Sylvie scolded affectionately. 'Of all things, please let's not talk about war.' She turned to Rachel, her face lighting up. 'I thought we might go shopping this afternoon or tomorrow,' Sylvie ventured cautiously. 'For a dress. A new dress for the party. Cassini has a wonderful new collection at Bendel's, just wait till you see.'

Rachel's heart sank. At least thirty dresses hung in her closet upstairs, many with the price tags still dangling from the sleeves, and Mama wanted to take her shopping of all things.

How simple and pure and easy if the only clothes in her wardrobe were what she had on – baggy fisherman's sweater, jeans worn to the softness of flannel, her old kick-about loafers. In these she felt safe, her own true self. She imagined the dress Mama would pick out. Soft silk or chiffon, pale as the dawn, with billowy sleeves and a skirt that floated about her knees. And then she'd end up going to Mason's party like a beautifully wrapped gift box but with nothing inside it.

Miserable inside, she smiled anyway, anxious not to snuff out Mama's eager look, wanting to hold on to it, even if it meant pretending for just a little while to be Mama's girl with the watering can.

'Tomorrow,' she promised. 'We'll go tomorrow, first thing.'

Two days later, Sylvie sat in the wing chair across from the library television, the images on the screen blurring as her eyes filled with tears.

In between the commentators, the condolence messages from heads of state around the world, the newsreel footage of him as a young congressman, of his marriage to Jackie, they kept reshowing the same nightmare: the motorcade, the open limousine with the President smiling and Jackie chic as ever in a pillbox hat, waving to the crowds. Then everything going a little crazy, Kennedy suddenly slumping forward, a black stain, blood on the back of his head. Jackie cradling him, then starting to climb out over the back of the car, and being held back by a Secret Service man. The limousine speeding away.

Sylvie rose, stiffly and flicked the television off. Her

eyes hurt. Nearly midnight now, and they'd kept vigil around the TV since early afternoon, she and Rachel, too stunned to do anything else. And then Gerald had closed the bank and joined them. Everything, he'd said, was closing.

She and Rachel had been trying on dresses at Bonwit's when they heard. Rachel had agreed to go to Mason Gold's party, but she was impossible to please as ever, every dress too fancy or frivolous.

Sylvie suddenly found herself remembering the day her water had broken in Bergdorf's.

Sylvie felt a dull pounding in her temples. Rachel and Gerald had gone up hours ago, but she knew that if she went up, she would only lie in bed, her mind bringing back things she couldn't bear to remember.

Sylvie crossed the darkened study full of Gerald's things, the solid furniture – so much a man's room – books, and old photographs of his parents and grandparents lining the walls, the Regency breakfront containing the librettos to every opera ever translated. The stereo, and underneath, stretching all across one wall, his record collection: All the greats. Caruso. Pinza. Callas.

She stopped at his leather-topped partner's desk, and fingered the engraved silver letter knife Rachel had given Gerald on his last birthday. Old, heavy, beautifully worked, exactly right for him. She understood him so well. The two were a perfect pair, so devoted to each other.

Sylvie felt a pain then, as if the letter opener had cut into her chest. She was all alone. Gerald would never know of the terrible choice she'd made, never share her pain. How many nights had she lain awake in anguish, weeping silently for the dark child of her own body she would never hold in her arms, never see grow up?

Yet Rachel, not to have known her, *that* also would have been terrible. Sylvie couldn't imagine life without Rachel. Impossible.

Yet sometimes she sensed a *wholeness* missing from her

love for Rachel, the feeling of something permanently torn that could never be perfectly mended. How she envied Gerald, not knowing; he had Rachel, whole, without compromise, completely his.

Looking at Rachel these days, Sylvie saw fleeting images of Angie Santini, Rachel's real mother.

That stubborn streak of Rachel's, was that Angie's too? Insisting on being a doctor, of all things, a life devoted to all that was ugly in this world – sickness, pain, death.

*I've tried so hard to make her mine, cultivated, ladylike. But she's her own person, not like me, or Gerald either. Strange how she's so small and dainty . . . and yet so willful, so independent.*

Sylvie remembered Rachel as a toddler, no more than two, an enchanting child with periwinkle-blue eyes and a cloud of soft amber curls. Sylvie had tiptoed in to see if Rachel had woken from her nap, and was stunned. Rachel had managed to climb out of the crib, and grab a clean diaper from the changing table. With her old wet diaper and rubber pants sagging around her ankles, she was struggling to pin on the clean one.

Sylvie rushed forward to rescue her, and Rachel with her tiny baby hands pushed her away, and said in a clear, almost grown-up voice, 'No, Mama, I want to do it myself.'

Since then she must have heard those words a thousand times. Rachel, five, poised on the seat of her new two-wheeler, demanding that Gerald let go of the handlebars. Her first day of kindergarten at Dalton, insisting that Sylvie leave her at the door, that she'd go up alone. The memories came to her like pictures in an old photo album.

And Sylvie thought, *Aren't I just the tiniest bit envious, too*? Rachel seemed to know exactly what she wanted from life, and how to get it. Sylvie wondered what her own life might have been if she had not married Gerald. Not that she regretted it! No, not for a minute. She adored Gerald, and her life with him. But what dragons might she have slain if not for Gerald's protective shield? What talents might she have discovered?

Oh yes, there were times – not often, but now and then – when she imagined herself out on her own. In an office, perhaps, behind a desk like this one, phones ringing, people asking *her* opinion about this or that, wanting *her* advice. Not just the wife of Gerald Rosenthal, but a woman with accomplishments of her own, and a paycheck with her name on it.

Then Sylvie slumped in despair. *Who am I to want more? I have so much already, more than I deserve. The dearest husband in the world, more luxuries than anyone could hope for. And a daughter as loving as she is headstrong.*

No, she couldn't love Rachel more if she were her own flesh and blood. She ached every time Rachel walked out the door. She wanted so much for her . . . every good thing in the world. But also she longed to give back what she'd taken from her – Rachel's sisters, her real blood ties. And she could never do that, never.

Sylvie put down the letter opener. There was only one last thing she longed for, *needed*, to fill up the empty space that moaned like a dark wind in her breast.

*To hold her. Just once. My own child. The baby I carried inside me for nine months. Daughter of my flesh. Oh, dear Lord, just to put my arms around her, kiss her. What I would give for that.*

But that was not meant to be, ever. She'd probably already risked too much, hiring that detective to find out where her daughter lived. And what had she gotten from it except more heartache? Dominic Santini was dead, she'd learned. Rose lived with her two sisters and grandmother, who was barely scraping by on Social Security and a small pension.

Sylvie had longed for a way to help Rose, to see that she was well taken care of. And then watching television one day, that old show 'The Millionaire,' she had had an idea. She would open a savings account for Rose, anonymously.

Through the detective, she found a lawyer who would do what she wanted without prying into her reasons. His

99

office, on Second Avenue and Eleventh Street, was as far removed from the mahogany-paneled 55 Water Street suite of Gerald's attorneys as an Eskimo's igloo. She'd forgotten his name, but she recalled that dismal hole-in-the-wall, the dusty rubber plant atop the filing cabinet, the dead flies dotting the windowsill. Through him, she arranged for a sum of twenty-five thousand dollars – all she could scrape together without risking Gerald's suspicion – to be deposited in a trust fund in Rose's name. Then a letter to Rose's grandmother, naming her as trustee, and informing her that the money was from a benefactor who wished to remain anonymous.

Of course, it had been foolish and risky. Suppose Rose's grandmother had gotten suspicious? Suppose she had gotten in touch with the lawyer? But Sylvie had covered her tracks, giving him a false name, paying in cash. Nothing truly bad could come of it, she had reasoned. And this way, little Rose would have something, a nest egg for later on, for college perhaps, or, God forbid, if she should ever be sick, or hurt.

And yet even the knowledge that Rose would be taken care of could not erase the longing from Sylvie's heart. The terrible need to see her, touch her. And so, years later, she had done something truly reckless; she had gone to Rose's school.

'Rose,' Sylvie whispered. It felt good just to say it, aloud for once, a small stone lifted from her heart.

Sylvie glanced up, her eyes falling on the portrait that hung over the fireplace. A younger version of herself, looking serene, and yes, even regal, in a pale blue chiffon gown, her shoulders white as Easter lilies. Her gold hair was drawn up in a French twist, her head turned to one side, revealing the ruby in her ear. She remembered when Gerald had given her those earrings, just after Rachel was born – exquisite old rubies in the shape of teardrops, set in antique gold, with tiny rose diamond studs. Rubies were Rachel's birthstone, he'd explained. And how baffled he had been by her outburst of weeping then!

100

Now, her gaze fixed on that earring, Sylvie thought how skillfully the artist had captured its deep wine glow, the way the light sparkled off it just so. And suddenly she was back on the sidewalk outside Rose's school. That freezing winter day, waiting for school to let out, for Rose to appear.

The moment she'd laid eyes on her daughter, Sylvie had seen how wrong it was, the name they'd chosen for her. Rose, after the fairest of flowers. And here she was, dark as a Gypsy, all legs and eyes, with the cheekbones of a woman, not a little girl of nine. Looking trapped in that lumpy coat she'd obviously outgrown, her wild dark hair squashed into braids.

But the moment those great dark eyes tilted up at her, Sylvie forgot her daughter's dark strangeness, and felt her heart shatter in a million pieces.

Then, against all reason, she'd wrenched the ruby from her right ear. Standing outside that frozen schoolyard, pressing that earring into Rose's small cupped palm, she'd felt it was somehow fitting, yet wished it could be more, dear God, a lifetime of a mother's love.

Sylvie brought a hand to her ear, remembering. Diamonds now, she never wore rubies anymore. And the one remaining earring she had put in a place, deep and hidden, where no-one would ever find it, and where she would not have to be reminded.

She had not seen Rose, either, since that day. A few months ago, however, she had gotten up the nerve to phone Rose's apartment. She had pretended to be with the phone company, conducting a survey. The woman who answered said she didn't know anything, she was just a neighbor checking up on Mrs Santini, who had had a stroke recently. Then she had given Sylvie Rose's work number, a 212 area code. Sylvie dialed it, staying on the line only long enough to learn it was a law firm. Rose probably worked there as a secretary. She was obviously surviving. But was she happy?

*I'll never know. Never share her thoughts, or know*

*what's in her heart. I'll never take her hand, or feel her
head against my breast. Even Rachel, love her as I do,
can't fill that hole in me.*

Sylvie, overcome, sagged into the deep leather chair at
her husband's desk, and wept.

Rachel stood at the entrance to the Ballroom of the Pierre,
taking in the spectacle of Mason Gold's twenty-first birthday party.

She watched the glitter ball rotating slowly in the middle
of the ceiling, spinning and scattering light like bright con-
fetti over the enormous room. God, Mason's parents must
have spent a fortune! Bouquets of yellow chrysanthemums
and white freesias on each of the tables, vast tables heaped
with food, and up on a platform, a band in gold-sequined
jackets, playing 'Only You' for the couples swaying
together on the dance floor.

*Well, thank God it's Mason's party, not mine*, Rachel
thought. *All this . . . this flaunting of money . . . I'd die
of embarrassment.*

She searched for a familiar face, but saw no-one she
recognized. The girls all looked pretty much alike, wearing
those short-sleeved pastel sheaths made fashionable by
Jackie Kennedy, their hair teased into seamless helmet-
shaped bouffants. The boys, too, like Ken dolls with their
identical tuxedos, winter tans, and even, white smiles. She
caught one of them, a broad-shouldered boy with a blond
crew cut, eyeing her speculatively, and her stomach felt as
if it had been dropkicked in a high punt.

*Oh God, does it show? I couldn't be that obvious, could I?*

Her heart hammering, she clutched her velvet handbag
hard against her hip, and felt the flat saucer shape of the
diaphragm inside.

She felt now as if all the guys here were looking at her.
But just because she was wearing this dress that clung to
her ass and showed half her breasts didn't mean they could
tell what she was up to. Or could they?

Rachel straightened her spine, stuck her chin out. Hell,

102

OK, so what? Let them know that tonight Rachel Rosenthal is ready and willing.

And out of all these monkey suits there had to be at least one nice horny one who wouldn't mind breaking his champagne bottle, so to speak, over her prow in honor of her maiden voyage.

Last week, she'd been so upset about Kennedy she'd realized something profound. She could die tomorrow, and then she'd never know what sex was like. Maybe the whole thing was just fear – of taking that one, irrevocable last step. But once that was over and she had done It, she could loosen up and enjoy herself.

And that had propelled her through the ordeal of the gynecologist, pretending to Dr Saperstein that she was getting engaged so he would fit her for a diaphragm. Then squatting in the bathroom at home, getting that disgusting jelly all over everything, practicing insertion until she felt raw.

All of it about as romantic as tightening a lug nut on her bicycle, and so unpleasant. She felt such a failure. And she hadn't even begun!

And now, standing here, in this clingy blue velvet Oleg Cassini sheath, her long hair gleaming, wearing makeup for the first time in ages, Rachel felt more unsure of herself than ever. And the whole idea all of a sudden seemed pointless. Getting laid almost surely would confirm what she already knew herself. That she really *was* frigid.

A deep voice startled her.

' "Of all the gin joints in all the world, you had to walk into mine." '

She whirled about, instinctively clapping her hands to her mouth, laughing through her fingers as she'd done years ago.

'Mason! God, I wouldn't have recognized you. You still do a lousy Bogie, though.' She stared up at a tall stranger with dark, curly hair, looking in his tuxedo like so many of the preppies here except for one quirky touch – a gold lamé bow tie.

He shrugged. 'Some things never change. Hey, you look pretty unrecognizable yourself. What's it been . . . five, six years?'

'Yeah, something like that. How've you been?'

'OK.' He cut his eyes away, looking suddenly awkward, making her wish more than ever that she hadn't come. Then his grin was dazzling her again. 'Well, what do you think? Great party, huh? The old man still hasn't lost his touch.'

But all Rachel could see now was the press of bodies. 'You must know a lot of people.'

He shrugged. 'I get around on campus. Lacrosse. *The Yale Daily News*. Anyway, New Haven's not such a small town, and you know how frat rats multiply when they hear the word "party." '

'I'm surprised you remembered to invite me,' she said. 'We kind of went our separate ways.'

'Tell you the truth, if you won't get offended, it was Mom's idea. I kind of doubted you'd know anybody. Plus, I guess I still had this picture in my mind of this skinny kid with a mouthful of braces whose idea of a good time was arm wrestling.'

'Mosquito Bites, you used to call me,' she said and laughed.

At that, Mason's gaze dropped to her exposed cleavage. A red flush crept up the sides of his neck, and he quickly looked up again.

Rachel felt embarrassed for both of them. She had not meant that as a come-on. Mason, after all, was . . . well, almost a cousin.

A cute cousin, she had to admit. He *had* changed. From a pimply teenager with legs like bicycle spokes to this sophisticated 1963 model standing before her. Assured, but not *too* assured. Good-Looking, if you liked the tall, dark, and Jewish type, which she did.

'And I'm not offended you didn't want to invite me,' Rachel quickly said, laughing. 'It was *my* mother who talked me into coming.'

'I'm glad she did. And I'm glad you listened.' Mason sounded sincere.

The awkwardness dissolved. Mason slipped his arm easily about her shoulders. 'Come on, I'll get you something to drink, and you can say hello to my folks. Then I want you to meet some of my friends.'

'I saw your father near the coat room when I came in. He told me Birds Eye had a recall on some frozen spinach that got sprayed with the wrong chemical. Gold Star stock went up two points in one day. He looked like he'd just won the heavyweight championship against Cassius Clay.'

'Good old Dad,' Mason said and laughed. 'King of frozen vegetables since the Flood. Wants me to come into the business the minute I graduate.'

'You could do worse.'

'Have you ever contemplated suicide by diving into a vat of creamed peas and onions? I did, every summer I worked for my old man. He put me on the assembly line. Wanted to give me a taste of what it was like to work your way up from the bottom. Can you imagine what it's like coming home every day smelling like the Jolly Green Giant?'

Rachel laughed. Being with Mason made her feel seven again, riding tandem on Mason's Flexi-Flyer, screeching down one of his Scarsdale hills.

Mason steered her over to a group sitting at one of the tables. Several of the boys looked her up and down, and she felt herself stiffening, flooding with panic as she remembered what she was supposed to be doing.

'Hi,' she said, nodding as she was introduced, not succeeding in remembering any of their names. Aware only of the sweat beginning to prickle under her arms despite two heavy coats of Secret roll-on. In her mind, Howard Cosell was at his microphone again.

*We're getting ready for the kickoff, folks. The team is in a huddle now. This is the Big One. We're gonna have to see some great plays out on the old green tonight before they carry home that trophy . . .*

Rachel felt a wild giggle rising in her throat. Aghast, she struggled to swallow it. Dear God, not *now*.

They were talking about the assassination, the grisly game the whole country was playing: Where Were You When You Heard?

'I was in the middle of an exam,' a red-haired boy said. 'The prof steps out into the hall, comes back in and announces it. A real Mount Rushmore type, never comes unglued about anything. Next thing you know, he's got his head down on the lectern and is bawling like a baby. It was unreal, I couldn't believe it was happening.' Tears shone in his eyes as he spoke.

A dark-haired girl in a low-cut white dress bowed her head as if in prayer, then said in a hushed voice, 'I was in a cab. I heard it on the radio. At first I thought, no, it's got to be some kind of put-on, like that phony invasion from Mars my mom told me about. But I could see the cabbie's face in the rearview mirror. He turned green, like he was going to throw up. Then he started moaning, and I told him to let me out. I was afraid we'd get into an accident . . .'

'I was in the shower, and I heard one my roommates scream . . .'

Rachel stopped listening. She should not have come. This whole party was wrong. And her own plan seemed petty, selfish, at a sad time like this. Tears filled her eyes, she mumbled some excuse, and rose.

She was almost to the door when she felt a hand on her shoulder, stopping her. Mason.

'Hey, wait a minute, where are you going?'

'I . . . I don't feel very well. I think I'd better go home.'

'Before we have even one dance? Hey, you might ruin my wish before I've even had a chance to blow out the candles on my cake.'

They were playing that old Presley hit, 'Love Me Tender.'

Mason dropped his eyelids and curled his upper lip like Elvis, and she couldn't help but laugh. Then suddenly there she was, moving on to the dance floor with him, submerged in rippling golden light.

He held her lightly, not clutching her as most boys did. She relaxed, enjoying the spangled light playing over his face, and felt herself moving effortlessly to the music.

Suddenly she found herself visualizing the diaphragm in her purse.

She'd seen Mason's penis once, when she was seven and he was eight. They'd been changing into their swimsuits out in the Golds' poolside cabana, and she'd asked him if she could touch it, just to see what it felt like. And he'd hesitatingly let her. Just a jab with her finger, a quick sensation of rubbery softness, and then both of them staring down fascinated as it grew, that tiny pink finger, hardening into a thing roughly the size and shape of a two-cent roll of Bazooka bubble gum. Mason, beet red, had yanked on his trunks, and from then on he'd always changed in the house.

She found herself wondering what Mason's penis was like now, then caught herself, horrified. With Mason? God, what was she thinking?

'Hungry?' Mason asked, the dance ending. 'Leave it to Pop. There's enough food here for a starving African nation.'

Rachel's gaze swept over the long tables, laden with huge platters of smoked salmon, oysters and shrimp nestled on beds of crushed ice, cold lobsters, mammoth silver bowls of glistening black caviar. And there, in a centerpiece of artfully arranged melon slices and grape clusters, a tall asparagus spear carved from ice – the Gold Star Frozen Vegetables logo.

Rachel's eyes fastened on it, and the urge to giggle swept through her again. Then in her mind, she was seeing Mason, not only undressed, but with a giant asparagus stalk sprouting between his legs.

God, what was *wrong* with her? She ought to be on a psychiatrist's couch.

'Did I say something funny?' Mason was smiling.

'Nothing, nothing.' Rachel took a deep breath, struggling to regain her self-control. 'I could use a drink, please, some soda. Ginger ale, if you have it.'

Mason, an arm slouched over her shoulders, guided her over to a bar. It was noisy, people shouting, clapping Mason's back, wishing him a happy birthday. Rachel couldn't hear the bartender, but saw him shake his head.

'Pepsi, Coke, orange, Seven-up, but no ginger ale,' she heard Mason through the din. 'How about champagne?'

She shook her head.

'Never could hold your liquor.' Mason was grinning.

She knew he was thinking about the time they'd sneaked a bottle of her father's Château Petrús down to the breakwater by their houses in Palm Beach. And gotten shitfaced, though only she threw up. God, she'd puked so much she'd thought her stomach would turn inside out. And then Mason had teased her for weeks afterwards.

'Stuff it,' she said sweetly.

'You know, my father's booked a suite. I've got something better than champagne up there. Every try grass?'

*Marijuana? God Mama would die.* Then she remembered her roommate Judy Denenburg rhapsodizing about how fantastic sex was when you were stoned.

Rachel felt herself growing warm, her face hot, tight, as if she'd been lying in the sun too long. Was he thinking the same thing she was? God.

'No,' she admitted. 'But it's your party. Wouldn't you be missed?'

Mason shrugged, grinning at the crowd all caught up in their partying. 'Like a firecracker on the fifth of July.' His hand felt warm, moist as he took hers. 'Come on, let's split.'

'Wait. My purse.' She spotted it at the table where she'd dropped it, after they'd begun dancing.

'You can come back for it later.'

'It'll only take a second. I'll meet you at the elevator.'

Taking a deep breath as the elevator rose, Rachel clamped her bag tightly under her arm.

'What have you got in there that's so important, anyway,

108

the key to your safe deposit box?' Mason teased.

Rachel smiled. 'In a way.'

Yes, this was going to be it. Mason would do as well as anyone. Better. They were old friends, after all, and they liked each other. Ironic, though. Mason no doubt thinking *he* was seducing her.

In the suite, decorated like a Parisian apartment – gilded fleur-de-lis wall medallions, gilt-framed mirrors, ormolu-adorned furniture – Mason excused himself and disappeared. A minute later, he returned holding aloft a dripping Baggie.

'I had it hidden in the toilet tank. Wouldn't want my father to get busted if the maid happened to see it lying around.'

'What if he comes up?'

'He won't. You couldn't tear him away from a party to save his life. He was born wearing a lampshade.'

Rachel thought of her father, how he would have another heart attack if he knew, and felt guilty.

Mason hunkered down in front of the cocktail table, and shook a small quantity of crumbled brown leaves on to the flimsy cigarette paper. He rolled it slowly, carefully sealing the gummed side, then twisting the ends.

Rachel watched him light it, take a deep drag, then hold in the smoke for the longest time. Then slowly he exhaled, sweetish-pungent smoke drifting from his nostrils. He passed it to her, holding the joint pinched between his thumb and forefinger.

'Slow,' he gently instructed. 'Take it in slow, and hold it in as long as you can. You'll get a faster high that way.'

Despite the trembling in her hands, and a sudden shortness of breath, Rachel managed to hold the joint to her lips and draw in some of the sweet thick smoke.

She felt a sudden sharp, hot ache deep in her lungs. A springy sensation of light-headedness. She took another drag, and another. Then things began to change. Her face felt swollen, her head huge and weightless like a balloon suspended on a string. Mason, as if she were viewing him through a rotating camera lens, seemed to recede, while other things about the room grew razor sharp and clear. The colors and motif of the Persian carpet, now bright and magical, shifting from one shape to another as in a wondrous kaleidoscope. And the walls, the gold stripes in the wallpaper seemed to jump out at her, like something in a funhouse.

'How do you feel?' Mason's voice crashed into her head.

'I don't know yet. I've never felt this way. It's weird, like I'm someone else, but I'm still me. And everything looks so strange. Like I never saw any of it before. I wonder if this is what it's like for babies just after they're born.'

'You're stoned.' Mason blew out a raspy chuckle on a stream of smoke.

Rachel took another hit, dragging deeply, feeling like an old pro. 'Maybe. Among other things.'

'What other things?'

'Oh, I don't know,' she hedged. 'Lots of things.' Could she tell him what was on her mind? No, that might be like throwing cold water over him. Or, worse, he might laugh, and make some big joke out of it. 'You know how my mother is. Well, she hates the idea of me becoming a doctor.'

'Jesus. You've got it backwards.' He was squinting at her, eyes bloodshot, through a haze of smoke. 'Jewish princesses are supposed to *marry* doctors.'

She glared at him. 'OK, wise guy, it might sound corny, but I have this crazy idea about helping people, making a difference in this world.'

'Sure, why not? You and Dr Kildare.'

She stared at him, fascinated by the green and gold specks swimming in his irises. 'When did you turn so cynical?'

Mason shrugged, a somber expression taking place of the wise-guy grin.

'A lot's changed since we were kids. I've been hearing

110

rumors, and the ROTC on campus is out there in full force like Yale is West Point all of a sudden. Friend of Pop's in the State Department says they're going to start drafting guys to fight in Indochina pretty soon. Jesus, I just hope I'm not one of them.'

'You won't be. Not if you're in law school.'

His grin was back. 'You remembered.'

'Sure. Me and Doctor Kildare. You and Perry Mason.'

'Yeah, that's me, truth, justice, and the American way.'

'I think that was Superman.'

'Well, him too. Say, you ever wonder how come he and Lois Lane never did the trick? I mean, come on, what were they waiting for?'

This was it, he was making the first move. Her heart began pounding, and she had to fight to stay cool.

'Well, maybe Lois was frigid, or maybe it was true what they said about him. You know, faster than a speeding bullet.' The words just popped out, and she sat back, both horrified and amused at herself. *God, I am stoned.*

Then she began to giggle, softly but helplessly, and she knew that if she didn't get to the bathroom fast she'd wet her pants.

Rachel kicked off her shoes and lurched to her feet, grabbing her purse as she stumbled toward the bathroom.

Alone in the salmon-tiled bathroom, she fumbled for the diaphragm. *Now*, she thought, *got to do it now, before I lose my nerve.* Through her stoned haze, she struggled to remember precisely how she was supposed to insert it. First the sperm jelly. Yes, that was it. Enough to knock those pesky little buggers out in the first round. OK, now bend it in half . . .

She was holding it that way, folded over like a taco when it slipped from her grasp, and went flying, bouncing against the shower door and landing on the floor with a wet plop. Staring down at it, lying on the pink marble at her feet like some dead sea urchin, she felt as if she had lost all touch with reality, as if any second now, Rod Serling might step out from the shower and announce, 'Rachel

111

Rosenthal is about to enter . . . the Twilight Zone.'

*God, how can I go through with this? I feel about as sexy as this rubber thing I'm putting inside me.*

*Stop carrying on*, she told herself. *Just do it, for God's sake.*

Emerging from the bathroom, Rachel felt the giggles bubble up inside her seeing Mason gape at her. It was as if she *had* stepped out of the Twilight Zone.

'Rachel, my God. Is that *you*?'

'Of course it's me. Who do you think?'

'You're . . .'

'Naked. Right.'

She nodded sagely, her head, too large, bobbing weightlessly on the string of her neck. It did feel a little funny, standing there without any clothes on, but she wasn't embarrassed. She thought of their going skinny-dipping as kids some of those hot evenings in Florida. It felt that way now, the air swirling about her body, thick and warm as heated pool water.

Rachel went over, and sat down cross-legged beside him. 'Listen, you don't have to do anything about it. I mean, I know you're not in love with me or anything. I just thought it might be a good idea.'

Mason continued to gape at her with a glassy expression, mouth drooping open. Then he winced as if in pain, and Rachel saw that the joint had burned down to his fingers. He dropped it into the ashtray, and brought his hand to his mouth, sucking his singed finger. He looked back up at Rachel, his zombie expression gone. he was grinning now, foolishly, as if he still didn't quite believe it.

'Are you kidding? Because, Jesus H. Fucking Christ, this wouldn't be very funny if you were.'

'Look, I'm perfectly serious. But if you'd rather just sit and talk about it, I'll put my clothes back on.'

'Jesus, Rachel. I've heard about grass having this effect on some people, but I never thought . . . oh Christ.' He was a tangle of movement now, throwing off his jacket,

112

ripping at his tie, fumbling with the tiny pearl studs on his tuxedo shirt, now bending over. 'Damn, my shoelace is all in knots. How does Clark Kent make this look so easy?'

'Here, let me help.' She was conscious of her breast grazing his arm as she bent to help unlace his shoe. An odd sensation, not necessarily sexy, but nice. 'OK. I got it. Hey, it's still there, that bump where you broke your toe waterskiing. Does it hurt?'

'Come here.' Tugging off his undershirt and shorts, he drew her down beside him on the carpet and kissed her on the mouth. Wet, soft, that same skinny-dipping feeling, as if she were diving underwater now. Deep warm water.

'Uh, Mason, I think there's something you should know.' She pulled back a bit, and tried to bring his blurred face into focus. 'I'm a virgin.'

'A what?'

'A virgin. But I don't see why that should make a difference, do you?'

'I don't get it. Why me?' Mason looked at her, his face a damp flushed pink, both happy and bewildered, as if he'd just realized he'd won a million dollar lottery, and didn't quite believe it.

'I don't know. Maybe because you didn't expect anything.'

Now she felt something against her leg, a hot pressure. She looked down, and a small shock rippled through her.

'It got bigger,' she said, staring down at his thing. It was no longer the size of a two-cent roll of bubble gum. More like a Rocket Pop now.

Mason laughed, cupping a breast. 'You too. I can't call you Mosquito Bites anymore.'

Rachel snuggled closer as he drew her to him, shivering, trying not to think about the thick, sour marijuana taste in her mouth. Or the itchy stubble of the carpet against her backside. Mason seemed good at this, practiced, not clumsy or rough. He was gently, tenderly stroking her thigh, her breasts, kissing her nipples. And now wasn't she supposed to start feeling turned on? Even a little bit?

113

Everyone said you didn't have to be in love for that, for heaven's sake.

But the harder she tried to will herself to be excited, the worse it got. Like trying to start a car, she thought, frantically pumping on the gas pedal after the engine's been flooded. She began to feel irritated, distracted by little things, the coldness of his fingers between her legs, his beard rough against her breast, little gobbling noises he was making in his throat.

*A fine kickoff, folks, but wait . . . the ball has been intercepted . . .*

Now he was getting up, pulling a pair of jeans out of the closet, groping in the pocket. For what? Then she saw. A rubber. Well, of course. A virgin wasn't supposed to come prepared.

She watched him kneel, red-faced, tearing impatiently at the foil packet. The irony of it struck her, and the giggles forced their way up her throat.

*It's all over now*, she told herself, stomach hurting, tears running down her cheeks, *you've blown it again.*

But Mason didn't seem to be getting angry like Gil. My God, he was laughing too. There *was* something funny about all this. And she wasn't the only one who saw it.

'Never could get one of these damn things on without looking like an idiot,' he said.

'Never mind,' she told him, 'just come here.'

And then it was happening, actually *happening*. A pain, not terrible, and he was inside. Moving gently. And she didn't mind it. It wasn't so bad. In fact it was almost . . . nice.

Mason was moaning, pumping his hips.

She began to feel warm down there, like warm water lapping between her thighs. But there was supposed to be more, wasn't there? She felt as if she were swimming toward something, and though she was straining hard, she couldn't quite reach it.

Mason gave one long gagging moan, and shuddered to a halt.

114

Then Mason's mouth, damp and hot against her ear, whispering something.

'Are you OK? I didn't hurt you, did I?'

No, not hurt. She felt stiff, awkward, a block of wood in Mason's arms. It stung a little down there, but she knew she wouldn't die from it.

What counted was what she *didn't* feel.

She'd felt none of the dizzying things she'd read about in novels, or heard her friends whisper. No music. No rockets exploding. No soaring ecstasy.

What Rachel felt was . . . cold. As if she had been pulled out of a warm pool, and plopped wet and shivering on this rug.

*It's true then. You're frigid. If this doesn't prove it to you nothing ever will.*

'I'm OK,' she whispered, 'just a little shaky. Am I bleeding much?'

He looked down. 'A little. Not bad. Don't worry, it's the same color as the carpet.'

'Mason, I . . .' She wanted to tell him she was sorry for dragging him into this. It had been a dumb idea after all. But there was a tightness in her throat, choking off the words.

Then Mason was holding her tight, rocking her back and forth on the stubbly carpet. 'I know,' he murmured, 'you don't have to say it. It was great for me too. The best. You're really something, you know that, Rachel?'

*Something,* her mind echoed. *Yes, I am something.*

The question is *what?*

Caught between tears and helpless laughter, Rachel began to hiccup.

# 3

## BROOKLYN, 1968

'I baptize you in the name of the Father, the Son, and the Holy Ghost.'

The old priest's words echoed in the empty church. Rose watched Father Donahue, like an aged leprechaun in his green and white vestments, extend a trembling hand to dip a silver ladle in the marble baptismal font, then trickle the holy water over the crown of fuzz poking from the blanket in his arms.

A lusty, outraged cry broke the hushed stillness.

Rose, standing a few feet away near the wrought-iron gates that enclosed the small baptismal vestibule, felt a tug in her chest, wanting to hold her baby nephew.

*He's right to cry. Who wouldn't, if someone woke you up by pouring cold water over your head?*

Original sin. How unfair! Every newborn tainted through no fault of its own, because thousands of years ago Adam had taken a bite from Eve's apple. Marked down like a factory second on a sale table.

The way she had been branded by the sin of her mother. And punished, not just once but her whole life. Worse now since Nonnie had gotten sick. These last months a living hell.

*God, I don't know how much more I can take.*

Quickly, Rose pushed the thought away, feeling guilty. How dare she stand here feeling sorry for herself? It was Marie who deserved her sympathy. Poor Marie, she could barely manage her two little ones at home, and now this one.

She looked at Marie, hollow-eyed, puffy ankles showing

116

beneath the uneven hem of a hideous black maternity dress. *As if this were a funeral, not a christening.*

Beside her Pete, scrawny and pathetic in a plaid jacket that was too small, looking vaguely bewildered, as if some fast-talking salesman had conned him into a bad deal before he knew what was happening.

Pete's family had moved to Detroit, so there was no-one else. Just she and Clare, Sister Benedicta now. Rose glanced at Clare, standing next to her, her round face serene under its bracket of starched white. Clare reminded her of a gray pigeon in her habit and wimple, a handful of fluff over slender hollow bones. Rose felt a coal of resentment glowing in her chest.

*What good is it, all that religion of yours, if your hands are too busy praying to do any real work?* she silently accused her sister. *Where are you when I'm breaking my back to lift Nonnie into her wheelchair? When I'm feeding her and cleaning her?*

Sudden, crashing silence jerked Rose from her thoughts. The baby had stopped wailing.

Marie was holding him now, quieting him, not with a cuddle, but an ugly brown pacifier. Sallow light from the peaked amber windows – this side vestibule still had the old leaded ones – caught her sister's face and turned it the color of old piano keys. She looked more than just tired, she looked old. An old woman at twenty-nine. Rose noticed with a tiny shock that Marie now bore a startling resemblance to their grandmother.

Rose stepped forward, her snow boots squeaking over the mosaic of cracked floor tiles.

'May I hold him?' she whispered to Marie.

Marie shrugged, handing her a cloud of blankets, which for a heart-stopping instant seemed to contain nothing but air. Then Rose felt the solid, reassuring pressure of a tiny bottom no bigger than her palm, and a round face was gazing up at her, cheeks fat as muffins. Suddenly, miraculously, the pacifier slid from his toothless gums with a tiny wet pop, and he smiled.

117

'Look!' Rose cried, delighted.

Marie peered into the blanket. 'It's only gas. Bobby didn't smile until he was three months.' She gave a rueful bark of a laugh. 'I'm not surprised. He didn't pick it up watchin' me, that's for sure. Not a whole lot to smile about, two babies and Pete out of work back then, not to mention the landlady yelling for the rent money every other minute. And now I had to go and get knocked up again.'

Rose realized, her heart sinking, that today would not be a good time to talk to her sister, as she'd planned, about Nonnie.

*I'm not asking a lot,* she wanted to say. *Just visit her once in a while, that's all. Sit with her one evening so I can get out, catch my breath. So little, yet it would help me so much.*

The memory of her grandmother's most recent stroke cut through Rose like the cold December wind outside. In May, eight months ago, but it had seemed more like winter then than now. The only blessing was that now Nonnie was silent, except for the garbled sounds she made. She sat in front of the television all day, her mouth frozen in that odd twisted smirk, as if she were laughing inside at some secret joke.

Regaining her speech would take some time, the doctor said, because the words were scrambled in her brain. Like she'd say 'door' if the phone was ringing, or 'pillow' when she needed to use the toilet. Though now at least she could hobble to the bathroom with a cane.

*Still, I'm the one who has to handle it all. Dress and feed her before I can leave her with Mrs Slatsky, then off to work without a moment to myself, an hour crammed on the subway. All day juggling the phones, taking dictation, typing for Mr Griffin. Then back at night, exhausted, wanting only to relax and close my eyes. But first Nonnie, feed her, clean her if she's had an accident, help her with her medicine. And is she the least bit grateful? Half a dozen times in the night, she pounds her cane on the wall,*

118

*waking me up. Just for the pleasure, I swear, of making me get up, come to her, see what she wants.*

Rose hated feeling resentful, but she couldn't help it. What would it would be like, she wondered with a pang of longing, if she could walk away, leave her grandmother and that dark, hot little box of an apartment which was slowly suffocating her to death?

If she could move away. And marry Brian.

She pictured it then, so clearly, the house they would live in. Airy rooms painted in pastels, windows wide open to let the sun in. And a garden, even just a strip of grass, a few tulips, a tree or two.

There would be just the two of them, Brian and her. Each morning, the miracle of waking up to find him beside her in bed, then the joy of a whole day together, not just minutes snatched here and there when she could steal away from Nonnie.

Then her sunny rooms faded into gray reality. Her heart sank.

Who would take care of Nonnie? There was scarcely enough to pay Mrs Slatsky for what little grudging help she gave, much less a full-time nurse or a convalescent home. And forget about Marie. Clare too. She remembered the time she'd called Clare, pleading, begging her to come and help.

And Clare's soft, placating voice had crooned over the long-distance connection, 'You mustn't feel you're alone in this, Rose. *God* is with you.'

And believe it or not, a few days later, a box came in the mail containing a leather-bound book of Psalms and a scapular medal that had been blessed (her note said) by the late Pope John himself.

Rose had slammed them both into the trash can. Then wept, ashamed at herself for the sacrilege she'd committed.

'Thanks, Father, I appreciate it.' Pete's voice broke into her thoughts.

And Rose knew, just looking at him, that Pete was apologizing to Father for what was inside the crumpled

119

envelope he'd just slipped him. The Church expected a minimal donation, but on Pete's salary as a clerk at Do-Rite hardware on Ocean Avenue, it was probably only a fraction of the minimum.

Rose thought guiltily: *Here I am, wallowing in self-pity, as if I'm the only one with a problem. Marie and Pete, my God, how on earth do they manage?*

She followed them outside, while Clare lingered in the vestibule, talking shop with Father Donahue. Sunlight glittered off the hoods of parked cars, off the dirty snow chunked along the curb. Rose shivered, wishing she had something better than this worn camelhair coat to keep herself warm.

The baby began to fuss, squirming against Rose. She rocked him, pretending it was her own baby she was holding, hers and Brian's. *Someday we'll be married, but it won't be like this.*

Brian, at Columbia, would be finishing his dissertation this year. So he'd be through with his assistantships, and he could land a full-time appointment at Brooklyn or even Kingsboro. Maybe then she could afford to give up her job, go to college herself. Put Nonnie in a nursing home or, dammit, just send her railway express up to Clare in Syracuse.

No matter what, as long as she had Brian, everything would turn out all right.

'Here, give him to me,' Marie was saying, her breath puffing out in a frosty white plume. 'It's time for his bottle. And don't he let you know it. A pair of lungs on this kid you wouldn't believe.'

Rose eased him into her sister's arms. 'He's beautiful, Marie. You're lucky. Three perfect kids.'

*And free, too, of Nonnie.*

For a moment the grimness left Marie's face, and her eyes lit up, moist with pride and yearning. 'Yeah, they're OK.'

While Marie fidgeted with the baby, Rose reached into her purse. A twenty, that's all she had. For groceries, and she'd intended to buy a baby gift with what was left. Well, little Gabriel wouldn't miss a rattle or a pair of booties, and Marie could use the money.

She folded the bill in half, and when Pete wasn't looking, slipped it into Marie's hand.

Marie flashed her a startled look, then quickly lowered her eyes, two bright spots of color appearing on the bleakness of her once-pretty face. She jerked her head in a sheepish nod of thanks, and Rose caught the hard glint of tears in her eyes.

The awkward moment passed, and Marie, baby balanced against one arm like a sack of groceries, was moving ahead, brisk with purpose.

'Hey listen, kiddo, I hate to run out on you and the Virgin Mary back in there, but we've gotta go. Pete had to practically beg his boss for the time off, and if he's late . . . well, you know. It took him six months just to find this job, shitty boss, weekend shift and all. Anyway, I left Bobby and Chrissie with my neighbor Kathleen, and she's got two of her own. She'll be climbin' the walls if I don't get back soon.'

'It's OK,' Rose said. 'How about stopping by next Sunday, after church? Nonnie's usually in a pretty good mood then. Besides, she hasn't seen the baby.'

Marie frowned. 'What's the point? We'd just get into a fight, like always. Nothing's changed. If anything, she's worse since she got sick. Jesus Christ, I don't know how you stand it.'

Rose wanted to scream out, *I don't know how I stand it either. It's worse than you can possibly imagine. But who else is there?*

But she held herself in. No use unloading on Marie. She shrugged, and said quietly, 'I have to.'

Rose held her sister's gaze. She stared into eyes the same odd pale blue as Nonnie's, but more human, a glimpse into the heart that lay beneath her tough brittle shell.

'I always envied you,' Marie said in a voice that was softer, more earnest than her usual one. 'You're stronger.

Smarter. Not like Clare and me. We took the easy way out.' Her hand shot out, thin cold fingers gripping Rose's wrist. 'Don't let her beat you, Rose. Don't ever give up.'

Rose drew back, thrown off balance. She was astonished. Marie? Envious of *her*?

'*Shit*.'

Pete's cry tore her attention from Marie. Rose turned, saw him staring angrily at his car, a battered green Valiant speckled with rust. A ticket flapped under one windshield wiper.

He ripped it free, then turned to deliver a savage kick to the red-tagged parking meter. 'Two minutes, those bastards. They couldna give us two more fuckin' minutes.'

'C'mon, Pete, no sense gettin' all worked up about it now,' Marie cajoled wearily. 'There's nothin' we can do.' She turned back to Rose, giving her hand a quick little squeeze. 'Hey, listen, thanks, for the . . . you know. Every little bit helps. Come see us sometime, anytime, I'm always home. Hell, where else would I be?' She jerked her head toward the church entrance. 'Say goodbye to the Blessed Virgin for me, will you? I'm not up to it. One more minute of staring into that halo of hers and I'll go blind.'

Like an alleycat landing on its feet, Marie was her old self again, leaving Rose wondering if she had imagined the other Marie of a moment ago.

Rose couldn't help but laugh. It *was* true about Clare. Yet she felt ashamed somehow, having such uncharitable thoughts right here on the steps of Holy Martyrs.

'I will,' Rose promised. She kissed Marie's cold cheek, and waved to Pete, who was already in the car, gunning the engine.

She felt torn between loving her sister, and wanting to throttle her.

Now to deal with Clare, as if she didn't already have enough to handle. Sweet, saintly, helpless Clare. She watched her sister emerge from the church, screwing her face against the harsh light like a baby, her petulant child's

122

mouth rounding in a small O of disappointment when she saw that Marie had gone.

'Marie couldn't wait,' Rose told her. 'She was in some kind of hurry.'

'Oh, my fault,' Clare answered cheerfully. 'Father and I got so caught up, we lost track of the time. I'm afraid we had a little disagreement. Father thinks it's bad for the Church, this Vatican Council of Pope John's. I didn't think so at first, but I suppose Father must be right . . . '

Rose felt a prickle of irritation. Why didn't Clare ever hold out for her own opinions? They should have taken some of the starch from her wimple and put it in her backbone.

She checked her watch. 'We have plenty of time before your bus. Why not come back to the apartment? Nonnie would like that.'

'Nonnie, yes.' Clare nodded. 'You know, Rose, I say a rosary for her every day, and I've asked Father Laughlin to include her in the daily blessing.'

A foul taste came into Rose's mouth, as if she'd eaten too many sweets. How easy it was for Clare, with her rosary beads. Rose could almost hear their gentle clicking in her head. How nice, to kneel in the cool quiet of a church, ticking off your worries one by one, while others sweated.

Rose, resentment simmering inside her, strode down the steps, up the sidewalk, not looking to see if Clare was following, not caring.

Then Clare's voice was beside her, a bit out of breath, wafting on a cloud of white steam like the Holy Ghost. 'God is with you, Rose. He hears your prayers. He won't forget you.'

Suddenly Rose felt the urge to hit her sister. 'Did you hear what happened to Buddy Mendoze?' Buddy used to live next door, an old schoolmate of Brian's.

Clare's face, pink with cold, turned a slapped-looking red. It was no secret she'd had a crush on Buddy once – until Nonnie'd found out, and put an end to it.

123

'Buddy? He . . . he went into the Army, didn't he?'

'He was in Vietnam. They shipped him home last month . . . what was left anyway. His face was blown away, I heard. And most of his brain. They keep him alive with machines.'

Rose heard the sharp intake of Clare's breath, saw her make the sign of the cross. And was instantly ashamed. She closed her eyes for a moment, feeling unbearably guilty. Ugly, that's what she was becoming. Ugly and mean, just like Nonnie.

Avenue K now. They were passing Suds 'n' Duds, where she washed Nonnie's soiled sheets every Saturday, and Eva's beauty shop next door, with its row of dusty plants in the window, where she took Nonnie for a wash and set while the laundry spun in the big blue dryers.

*God, deliver me from evil*, she prayed silently.

Then, turning up the brick pathway to their apartment building, into the dark lobby smelling of pine disinfectant.

Trudging up the long flights, Rose imagined the worst, as always, Nonnie dead, another stroke. She felt a moment of dizzying hope, followed by crashing guilt. How could she *wish* her own grandmother dead?

Rose turned her key, and held the door open to let Clare in ahead of her.

Then suddenly Clare was screaming, a shrill piping sound.

Rose pushed ahead of her into the living room, dark, lit only by the ghostly glare of the television set, a nauseating smell rising up, gagging her, like the stink of an overflowed toilet.

*Mother of God, what – ?*

Then she saw. Nonnie. Sprawled face down on the plastic runner that ran diagonally across the living-room carpet, her quilted pink robe flapped open to reveal the thin white sticks of her legs. Dead? Oh God, no. And she'd *caused* it, by wishing it.

Rose knelt, light-headed with a mixture of fear and wild hope, as she grasped the wrist that was no more than a shank of bone draped in loose, sliding flesh.

Then Nonnie stirred, moaning. The horrible swamp smell was stronger now, making Rose want to vomit.

Swallowing hard, Rose thought: *Oh Lord, she couldn't make it to the bathroom so she went in her pants. She must have fallen trying to get there. Damn Mrs Slatsky for leaving her alone.*

The squawking of the TV seemed suddenly too loud, as if the volume had been turned up all the way, making Rose's head throb. Some stupid game show. A lady in a gorilla suit jumping up and down and screaming over the refrigerator she'd won.

Rose wanted to scream too, or to laugh madly. This was *her* prize, the rubber chicken behind Door Number Three. A mean old lady lying in her own shit.

She twisted to look up at Clare. 'Help me get her up.'

But Clare just stood there, fidgeting with the rosary beads that dangled from her waist, blue eyes wide and blank. Her round baby face frozen in disgust.

'Clare!'

'Do . . . do you think we should move her?' Clare fluted anxiously. 'Suppose something's broken.'

Nonnie was stirring now, trying to sit up. Rose slid an arm under her shoulders, and managed to hoist her to her feet single-handedly. She wasn't heavy; it was like lifting a bundle of dry leaves, damp and rotting underneath. Saliva dribbled from the sunken corner of her mouth, as Nonnie wrestled with the guttural sounds in her throat, struggling to shape them into words.

Damn Clare and her rosaries. Why didn't she help?

Anger fueled Rose, made her strong. Supporting the old woman, she managed to drag Nonnie to the bathroom. She wrestled her out of her robe, and somehow got her into the tub. She cranked on the water, and reached into the cupboard for a washcloth. Now came the disgusting chore of washing her.

*Just don't think about it. Thinking makes it worse.*

Rose imagined a giant hypodermic needle filled with

125

Novocain, numbing her from head to toe. She would go through the motions, but in her mind she would be somewhere else.

With Brian. Tonight. They'd planned to spend it together, and she would let nothing interfere. Not even if Mrs Slatsky couldn't stay with Nonnie.

Brain had said he needed to talk to her about something. Something important. *Dear God, let him say he can't wait, that we should get married right away, not in a year. I need him so much.*

A horrible noise roused Rose from her longings.

'Gaaarraghhhh.'

Nonnie was trying to say something. Rose felt warm spittle spray against her cheek. Nonnie's pale eyes rolled frantically from Rose to the open doorway.

'Gaaaaarrrrraaagghhaa.'

Finally, Rose understood. Clare. Nonnie wanted Clare.

Rose stared down at her grandmother's withered, gray-white body floating in the dirty bathwater. She felt as if she'd been punched in the stomach.

Nonnie didn't give a damn for all the backbreaking times Rose had carried her, the grinding routine of feedings, and this . . . cleaning up her disgusting messes.

She only wanted Clare.

And where the hell *was* Clare?

Rose found her sister on her knees on the plastic runner where Nonnie had lain, her lips moving in silent prayer.

Rage then, so fierce, like a gale blowing through her, a roaring in her head, a burning in her chest. She wanted to slap Clare, slap her senseless right there where she knelt.

Then, as quickly as it had come, the anger drained away. 'She wants you,' Rose said, too tired to fight, sinking down on the sofa, hearing the sigh of the plastic slipcover.

Clare blinked her eyes open, and smiled, as sweet and blameless as a baby awakening from a nap. 'Yes . . . of course.' She rose, smoothing her skirt, moving soundlessly into the next room on her thick crepe-soled nun's shoes.

*Think about Brian*, Rose willed herself, dropping her

head into her clenched hands, struggling to shut out the smells and the wild shrieking laughter of the television. *Soon it'll be just us. Always . . .*

Rose was floating.

Far from her grandmother, and the hellish apartment on Avenue K. Far from anything and everything that caused her pain.

In the warm hollow their bodies made under the covers, Brian's long frame stretched loose alongside her, she felt herself drifting on the gentle swells of his breathing, the pumping of his heart. Safe. Peaceful.

Brian, sweet Brian. Her lover. How strange it had seemed in the beginning, thinking of him that way. She remembered her pleasure the first time, her sickening guilt, then bursting into tears. And Brian, distraught, thinking he'd hurt her. Each of them reassuring the other, and then somehow they were doing it all over again.

Nine years ago. Mother of God, had it really been that long?

Rose had stopped going to Confession after that. What was the use? No point in telling God she was sorry, when she knew perfectly well she was going to keep right on doing it. And how could she stop? Loving Brian was the only thing that kept her alive.

She could only hope that God, in His infinite mercy, would somehow understand and forgive her.

Rose shifted, propping herself up on her elbow so that she was facing him. Over the ridge of his shoulder, she could see out the window, a street lamp glowing in a fairy ring of mist, islands of snow dotting the South Field green. And off to the right, the brick and slate hulk of Butler Library.

How many times had she lain just so, looking out the second-floor window of Brian's Hartley Hall room? Dreaming of the day when they wouldn't have to sneak time to be with each other.

*Soon*, she promised herself. *Another year at the most.*

127

*Then we'll be together, just like we promised each other. I've waited this long, so I can wait a little longer, can't I?*

Her gaze returned to the room. A narrow closet-sized cubicle, its walls pocked with thumbtack holes, and lined with board and cinderblock bookshelves, all jammed with books. The books she herself dreamed of having the time someday to read. Hemingway, Faulkner, Fitzgerald, Joyce, Baudelaire. And in the corner, on the scarred oak desk, sat Brian's ancient Underwood, a pile of typewritten pages spilling from a box lid. The novel Brian had been writing before he got buried in the dissertation.

She had read the novel, and it was good. Better than good. Pride swelled inside her, warming her. It didn't matter that this bed sagged terribly, and neither of them had two cents. He would be famous someday, she was sure of it. His books on shelves in student rooms like this one, beside Joyce and Faulkner.

She studied his face. All planes and hollows in the shadowy half-light from the street. Sweat gleamed on his forehead, the blade of his nose. She licked a bead from his temple, savoring the salty taste on her tongue.

'Mmm. I could eat you up.' She nuzzled his neck, whispering in his ear, 'But what would I do when there was nothing left of you?'

'Rose.' Brian sat up abruptly, sheets and blankets tumbling away. The cold air rushed in. 'There's something . . . I should have told you before we . . .' He turned, his profile silhouetted against the window. 'Jesus, I hate this. I wish to God there was some way to make it easier.'

Rose shivered, crossing her arms over her stomach, holding her elbows. Something was wrong. Yes, she'd felt it. Back when Brian was making love to her even. So fierce, hurting her almost in his urgency.

'Brian, what? What is it?' She sat up, clutching the sheet to her, feeling a need to protect herself against the bad thing she felt coming.

'I should have told you before we – it's just that, God,

128

when I saw you all I could think of was holding you close to me, getting you in here.'

She cut loose in a nervous laugh. 'I know. Every altar boy's wet dream, isn't it? A nice Catholic girl. I think it's something they put in the holy water, some kind of aphrodisiac. They ought to bottle it instead of perfume. Eau de Vatican. Do you think the Pope would endorse it?' If she kept talking, she wouldn't have to hear him. 'God, do you remember those terrible attacks of conscience I used to get? I know how martyrs must have felt wearing hair shirts.'

'Rose. My draft number. It came up.'

His words fell like a wrecker's ball crashing into a stone wall. Her ears rang with the impact.

'That's impossible.' But even while she said it, her muscles were cramping, and cold fingers walked up her spine.

'It happened.'

'No!' The ringing had become a wild, clanging alarm inside her skull. 'Just tell them. It's a mistake. Somebody punched the wrong computer button. You don't have to go. You're deferred. They can't take you. My God, Brian, Vic Lucchesi *died* in Vietnam. And poor Buddy . . .' She couldn't bring herself to say it.

'Not everyone . . .,' he started to say, but she covered her ears with her fists.

'No. *No*. Not you. Not *you*, Brian.'

She could hear her voice rising, turning shrill. But it seemed to be coming from outside her, an ambulance siren in the street.

'Rose, don't make it worse.' He tried to draw her into his arms, but she resisted, holding herself stiff, afraid somehow that if she gave in to him she would be accepting this terrible thing.

'They can't make you.' She forced herself to speak quietly, whispering almost. 'You're deferred.'

'No, Rose, listen. I got the notice to go in for my physical last week. I didn't see any point in telling you, not right

129

away. You know, if it turned out I had a heart murmur or something, and they decided not to take me. But I got word today. One-A. I'm to report for Basic next week at Fort Dix.'

A terrible white static filled Rose's head. Then, as if tuning into a nightmare broadcast of the six o'clock news, she saw Brian lying in a rice paddy, blood staining his fatigues, spreading in crimson circles over the scummy surface of the water. No. Oh dear God, no.

She shut out the dreadful image.

But she couldn't shut off the cold seeping through her, as if her heart were pumping ice water instead of blood.

And this was real, not just some awful daydream.

Brain was going to Vietnam. To be shot at, maybe wounded or even killed.

'NO!' Rose shot out of bed.

'Rose—' Brian swung his legs over the edge of the mattress, holding his arms out to her, supplicating.

But she wouldn't go to him. *Damn him. He probably wants this. Big fucking hero.*

'Canada,' she pleaded. 'Remember Rory Walker? He went to Canada. Montreal, I think. Or maybe it was Toronto. You could go too. Start over. I'd come with you.'

Brian let his arms fall limp at his sides. His shadow stretched across the woven grass mat she was standing on, reaching over her like a dark premonition of death. She was shivering, all out of control, feeling as if she'd come down with a high fever. And she felt a hot pressure behind her eyes, a hammering in her temples.

'Rory's in limbo,' he said quietly. 'He can't come back, not even to visit his family. He'd be arrested.'

'There are other ways. Conscientious objector.'

'Rose, you know Pop. It would kill him. He made the landing at Anzio, fought all the way up to the Alps. My grandfather served in World War I, wounded in Verdun. I remember Grandpa had this velvet box tucked in the back of his top dresser drawer.' Brian's voice turned soft. 'He

130

never showed me what was in it until one day, when I was maybe eleven, he caught me and Kirk playing soldiers in the vacant lot behind his store. Then he took us inside, and showed us. His Bronze Star. He said maybe we were old enough now to understand what it meant. To him, anyway. He said people who thought war was all about being a hero and getting medals had bed ticking for brains. Fighting, he said, was real bad, but something that had to be done, like putting out a fire before it got out of control. Nothing to get puffed up about. You just did what had to be done.'

'You're not your grandfather,' Rose shot back desperately. 'It's a different war. No-one even knows why we're fighting it.'

Brian raised his eyes, and she couldn't help but see the light in them now, clear and shining. 'Maybe not. But a lot of guys are being sent over anyway. Guys we both grew up with. Vic and Buddy and Gus Shaw. *That* means something. I'm not sure what. But one thing I do know is that if I duck out, it just means it'll be someone else's number they'll pull. Someone else who maybe gets burned while I should've been there putting out the fire.' He paused. 'I've thought a lot about it. Even before this. I didn't tell you how guilty I felt about being deferred year after year because I knew it would upset you. But now . . .'

She thought of John Wayne in *The Green Berets*. A lot of talk about honor and duty, but the reality was, his guys really loved shooting off their guns. But Brian? No, he meant every word. God, she should have known.

A memory crept in, one she had totally forgotten. Fifth grade, Brian coming out of school, the back of his hands red and puffy, striped with welts. Brother Joseph had given him half a dozen whacks with a ruler.

'Why, Brian?' she'd asked, as shocked and hurt as if she'd been struck as well. 'What did you do to make him hit you?'

'Nothing,' he'd said with a shrug. Oh, how nonchalant he'd been! 'It was Dooley. He broke a window in the rectory. It was an accident, but he's up to his eyeballs in hot water

131

with Brother Joseph already. He would've gotten ten times as many.'

*Oh, Brian. I would go in your place if I could*, Rose thought. *Because if anything happens to you, I'll die too*.

Rose sank down, the woven jute cutting into her knees. The cramp in her belly was worse. She felt bruised all over, as if she'd been beaten up.

How foolish she'd been, worrying that God would take Brian away from her.

No, this was Brian's own doing. He was choosing this as surely as if he'd gone down to the recruiting centre and enlisted.

He was leaving her.

Anger erupted in her. Rose sprang to her feet, and grabbed the first thing before her – a jar full of pennies sitting atop the dresser. She hurled it against the wall. A jingling crash. pennies sprayed everywhere, spanging off the furniture, rolling along the floor.

'YOU SONOFABITCH! IF YOU GET YOURSELF KILLED OVER THERE I'LL NEVER FORGIVE YOU!'

Something was burning her eyes, her face. Tears like acid, scalding, wounding.

'I don't care who goes in your place!' she sobbed. 'I don't care who gets killed. I only care about you. Oh God. My stomach. It hurts. I hate you. Bri. Do you hear me. *I hate you for doing this*.'

Then his arms were around her, holding her, keeping her from flying apart. Grounding her. Warming her.

Mother of God, what was she *saying*? Of course he wouldn't die. Of course. She clutched him, weeping.

'Don't cry, Rose.' His voice was shaking, and she felt something wet against her neck. Tears. Brian's tears. 'I know a year is a long time, and I'll miss you. Christ, I miss you so much already it hurts. But I'll be OK. I promise.'

Rose clung to him harder, feeling as if her heart had been torn out, just this great aching hole in her chest.

*How am I going to bear it*? she wondered. *The waiting*.

132

*From one letter to the next. Not knowing if he's all right.*
*If he's wounded, or worse, if he's—*

She drew away from him, lifting her face to meet his fine gray eyes. The exquisite pain of her love cutting through her like glass.

'Don't promise, Brian. Promises get broken. Just come back. That's all. Just come back to me.'

# 4

'Dr Mitchell. ER. Stat. Dr Mitchell . . .'

Rachel hurried along Five West, through the swinging
steel doors that led to the Labor and Delivery Ward. She
glanced up at the clock above the glass-enclosed nurses'
station. Six-thirty-five. Late for morning rounds. Damn.
That's all she needed today, of all days.

She felt groggy, sluggish, despite two cups of coffee on
an empty stomach, and the frantic dash from her apartment in the icy rain. But at the thought of seeing David any
moment now, her heart began to pound, and her hand
slipped into the front pocket of her white doctor's coat.

She fingered the slip of paper.

Rachel could see it in her mind, the sheet of pink flimsy
from the lab, with its faint carbon type: PREGNANCY,
POSITIVE.

Even now, twelve hours old, those words seemed to
burn her fingers, and send her head reeling.

*OK, God, Destiny, whoever you are you've had your
laugh. Now what?*

She had stayed up most of last night asking herself that,
and now was no closer to an answer. All her life Mama had
told her things looked better in the morning, but this
morning Rachel thought they just might look worse.

Grace Bishop, she realized, was giving her the eye, and
she felt like she'd been caught chewing gum in the first
grade. Grace had been head nurse on L and D probably
back before Rachel was born, and took flak from no-one.
She was planted squarely in the corridor outside the
nurses' station, arms folded across a bosom the size of a
janitor's drum. She unfolded her arms to glance pointedly

at the industrial-size wristwatch strapped to her coffee-colored wrist. Each movement radiating her disapproval of every female intern who'd ever walked on to her floor.

Rachel, the youngest by far at twenty-five – having graduated high school a year ahead of her classmates, and crammed eight years of college and med school into seven – felt even younger, a child late for kindergarten with the teacher looming over her.

'Rounds have already started,' she said with her clipped Jamaican accent. 'You'd best get a move on.'

Rachel gave her a stiff nod, and thought with bitter amusement of that 'Laugh-in' gag, Dan Rowan getting slapped and saying, 'Thanks, I needed that.'

Rachel then looked at herself through Grace's eyes. The same rumpled khakis she'd had on yesterday, a coffee stain on the lapel of her white coat. Her hair caught back in a frazzled braid, her face – under the merciless high noon of the fluorescent ceiling lights – ghastly pale and hollow-eyed from lack of sleep.

For once, she couldn't blame Grace for looking askance. Suddenly the old semi-hysterical urge to giggle crept into her, along with the absurd impulse to say to Grace, *Don't worry, I'm qualified, all right. Who better to treat a woman in labor than a pregnant doctor?*

But no time to lose her cool now. She broke into a half-trot down the long green corridor toward Ward One, her heartbeat seeming to keep time with the slapping of her Adidas shoes on the linoleum tiles, while she imagined herself breaking the news to David.

*Sorry I'm late* . . . She pulls him aside and then whispers, *And by the way, I'm pregnant.*

No, not quite. Maybe OK for 'Laugh-in.' But not for real life.

*David, I know it's not what we planned . . . but we'll make it work somehow . . .*

Hadn't she seen that in a movie? Sandra Dee and Troy Donahue. Fade into sunset with couple tenderly embracing. *Darling, I love you, and that's all that matters.*

'Crap,' she swore under her breath, stepping out of the way as a gurney pushed by a harried orderly careened past, and at the same time berating herself for the tears that pricked behind her eyes.

*Grow up, why don't you? He never promised you a damn thing, and now you want it all. Valentines and violins, a box of cigars, plus the handsome doctor vowing to do the Right Thing by the girl he loves.*

Except who's to say what the Right Thing is these days? A hundred years ago, even ten, a hasty shotgun wedding. Now there were choices. Options.

*You could have an abortion.*

Rachel tried to imagine the lump inside her that was their baby, no bigger than the head of a pin, and her vision blurred with tears. She half-stumbled, catching herself against the wall with its fat red arrow pointing the way to Radiology.

It was so ironic. She'd always spoken out for abortion. She'd argued fiercely that it deserved to be as basic a right as female suffrage. And she'd been for zero population growth, too. But, dammit, this wasn't just a rise on a population graph, this was a *life* growing inside her. A baby. *Her* baby.

The idea of having it scraped out of her, flushed away in some toilet bowl, drove a bolt of pain through her stomach.

And yet, what was the alternative? Have the baby, and put aside everything she'd worked so hard for?

The years of med school, feeling as if her brain were being squeezed in a vise. The formaldehyde stink that wouldn't wash off, her sleep haunted by nightmares of half-dissected corpses coming back to life.

And yet she'd also loved it. Schwartz Lecture Hall, with its purple seats and permanent sweaty odor, the droning pathology professor who invariably put her to sleep, Dr Duberman with his endless hematology quizzes. And then her third-year clerkship, working with real patients, people needing her, *real* people, feeling for the first time what it was to be a healer.

136

And now she'd come this far, halfway through her internship.

Rachel remembered coming here for her interview. The long subway ride, almost an hour, into the heart of Brooklyn, mostly black and brown faces crammed in beside her. Coming out on to Flatbush Avenue, with its run-down stores and weary-looking people, then six blocks over cracked and dirty sidewalk to this nondescript building, fourteen stories of sooty gray stone and wire-mesh safety glass. Except for the fact that there was no fence surrounding it, it looked like a prison, hardly a place where people came to get well. But come here they did, she soon learned, in droves, Barbadians, Haitians, Puerto Ricans, Dominicans, blacks, people with no insurance and no money, who needed medical care desperately.

Which was why she'd chosen Good Shepherd, despite her father's badgering that she go to Presbyterian or Mount Sinai. And she loved it here. If they accepted her, she wanted to stay on for the OB residency. And now she was almost there, two more months, her ER rotation, and she'd be finished with her internship. So how could she possibly leave, give all that up? She couldn't.

Turning right at the far end of the corridor, Rachel spotted a huddle of figures in white lab coats outside Ward One. Faces still puffy with sleep, sipping coffee from paper cups. Others, those who had been on call through the night, drooping with exhaustion, their eyes bright and glassy. Under the fluorescent glare, they all looked cadaver gray.

But no sign of David yet, thank God. He fumed when anyone came late for rounds. And he didn't pull any punches when it came to her, either. They had agreed in the beginning, there couldn't be any special favors.

Joe Israel greeted her with a yawn. 'You missed all the excitement. Twins. Lady just walked in off the street at ten centimeters and dropped them like a litter of pups.'

Rachel looked up at Israel, tall, achingly thin, an acne-scarred face that reminded her of a pool hall dart board.

She liked Israel, but a litter of pups? Jesus.

Janet Needham gave him a withering look. 'Have you ever thought about switching to veterinary medicine, Israel?'

Janet was the only other female intern. Rachel had tried to like her. But it was hard. Janet didn't like herself. Overweight, her greasy brown hair pulled back with a rubber band, she wore a perpetual scowl, suspicious of anyone who made a friendly overture.

Israel grinned at Janet, raising his coffee cup. 'If I do, you'll be the first to know.'

'Cool it, you two,' hissed Pink. His real name was Walter Pinkham. Rachel counted five pens clipped to the breast pocket of his white coat today. He was the only intern she knew who carried a briefcase.

Then Rachel caught sight of David striding toward them. He looked so tall in his spotless white coat, glowing with purpose, stirring the air, prompting the sleepy interns to straighten their shoulders a little, stand taller themselves.

Her heart began to pound. Dear God, how did he have this effect on her? Sweaty palms, adrenaline surges, the whole bit. Years of believing she was frigid, and she was afraid now it might be just the opposite. Acute nymphomania.

Smiling to herself, she recalled what had crossed her mind at their introductory session: *Anyone that good-looking has got to be a shit.*

Perfect casting for a doctor on television, with those go-light green eyes, and the sandy hair that dipped boyishly over his forehead, JFK style. *Even, heaven help me, dimples, two on either side of his mouth and one planted smack-Cary-Grant-dab in the center of his chin.*

But little by little – and God only knows why he had chosen her – he had won her over, courting her as if she were the starchy schoolteacher heroine in a Victorian novel, bringing her a rose one day, a carnation the next, flowers no doubt salvaged from the rooms of patients who'd checked out. Even a note once or twice in her locker, just like high school.

*And now a baby*, she thought with bitter amusement.

'Good morning, doctors. Sorry I've kept you waiting. I had an emergency.' David was breezing to a stop, his gaze was skimming over her, not meeting her eyes.

Rachel, fearing she meant nothing more to him than the others, felt a cold rush. Then sanity quickly asserted itself. Stupid of her, he was just being discreet, as he had to be. Of *course* he loved her.

But she was still so tense, holding herself stiffly, as if the pink lab report in her pocket were a letter bomb that might explode if she made any sudden moves.

She fell in with the group as they followed David on to the ward. A long room, painted a sickly yellow-green, with rows of beds separated by dingy tan curtains. And hot, the old steam radiators clanking and hissing. Why hadn't anyone thought to crack a window?

David stopped at the first bed. A pale face framed by a tangle of dark hair blinked up. The sheet drawn up to her jutting collarbone, in the hollow of which a tiny gold crucifix twinkled. She looked so young it was pathetic. A mother already, and still a child herself.

David glanced at her chart, then at Gary McBride beside him. 'Yours, I believe, Dr McBride?

Gary reminded Rachel of an overgrown Tom Sawyer, with his boyish looks and freckles, his red hair complete with a cowlick. He was a good doctor, though. He cared about the patients.

Gary didn't even glance at his notes. 'Miss Ortiz. Sixteen. Primipara. She was admitted at two o'clock this morning, four centimeters dilated. Blood pressure normal. But there was some vaginal bleeding, and the fetal heart rate was slow. I consulted Dr Melrose on it, and he ordered a C-section.'

'How's our patient this morning?' David inquired.

'Blood pressure a little low. Spiking a small fever. One-oh-one-point-two. She was complaining about the pain, so I gave her Demerol.'

139

Rachel watched David peel back the sheet and lift Miss Ortiz's gown, carefully removing the square of Betadine-stained gauze covering her incision. Rachel stared at his hands, feeling such awe. God, they were beautiful. The hands of an artist, a sculptor of living flesh. Broad square palms with long, oddly delicate fingers that tapered into the flat pale half-moons of his nails. Hands capable of performing miracles. She had watched him in surgery tie off the most friable veins without shredding them, seen him draw blood from the scalp of a fetus by reaching into its mother's uterus, simply feeling his way.

And wasn't it a kind of miracle, too, what he had made her feel?

She remembered, her face growing warm, their first night. Seduction, Hollywood style. His apartment, champagne on ice and soft music (the theme song of 'A Man and a Woman' stuck in her mind), then tipping into bed, sheets smelling of English Leather aftershave. The contrivance of it exciting her, and at the same time leaving her a little cold deep down, like a TV dinner that hadn't quite thawed out in the middle.

Then, in the middle of their lovemaking, he had stopped abruptly, propping himself up on his elbows to look down at her with a bemused smile.

'You're not enjoying this very much, are you?' he had observed.

Too startled by his candor to lie, she'd replied, 'I don't know how.'

She'd been with only three men in the years since Mason Gold. And with each one she'd felt more a failure than with the last. And now this. She'd wanted to cry.

Gently, David had withdrawn and moved down on the mattress until his head was nestled between her rigid thighs. And then, oh God, the flick of his tongue. She had resisted at first, too panicked and ashamed to feel anything. Then slowly, ever so slowly, strange fluttery sensations began to creep through the walls of her defenses, sensations that were surely forbidden and yet thrilling. His

140

tongue was finding secret spots of pleasure she hadn't known existed. For hours it seemed, playing her until she quivered, singing out finally in a crescendo so warmly exquisite, she felt surely she would melt with the dazzling heat of it.

And then he was rising on to his knees, grinning down as he eased himself back into her. 'All better now?'

'*Was it that night?* she wondered now. Eight weeks would make it about right. And there was a sort of poetic justice in it, if you believed in that kind of thing. Getting knocked up the first time you discovered sex could be wonderful.

Rachel tore her gaze from David's hands. She was half-afraid she would betray herself, start having vapors, like a character in a Charlotte Brontë novel. She *did* feel a little faint, as a matter of fact. Maybe because she hadn't eaten breakfast. Or maybe it was because she was—

And then it struck her, not just a missed period, or words on a slip of pink paper, but the full hard fact of it: *Pregnant. I am pregnant.*

She watched as David palpated the scarred, deflated balloon of the patient's abdomen. But she watched with a new kind of fascination, totally unexpected. It was as if she had stepped outside of herself for an eerie moment. No longer a doctor, simply a woman, being initiated into the age-old secrets of motherhood.

Tears came to her eyes, blinding her for a second, as she imagined actually giving birth to this child in her. A tiny miraculous being formed from her own flesh, after seeing the wonder of so many belonging to others. Holding it in her arms, nursing it, her breasts heavy with sweet milk.

*Wrong, all wrong*, she told herself. She had no right wanting it. She had no place in her life for a baby. In a few years maybe. But not now.

She furiously blinked her tears away, and tried to focus on the patient, at the same time reviewing in her mind her own diagnostic presentations.

'How does that feel?' David asked the girl, who was making a face, biting her lip.

141

He beamed his brilliant emerald gaze at her, and immediately the girl grew very still, like a child in school who's been called on by the teacher.

Also part of David's magic, Rachel thought, that look. A look that inspired utter confidence. Dr Kildare and Ben Casey rolled into one. Rachel was quite certain that if David had told Miss Ortiz to get up and do fifty jumping jacks, she wouldn't have hesitated.

'Does this hurt?' David asked, pressing a little harder.

'A little,' the girl whispered.

Rachel saw that she had turned even paler, but still didn't move as David held her gaze and continued probing with his hand.

David straightened and drew her gown down in one quick movement. He turned to face his audience, addressing himself to Gary McBride.

'A little fundal tenderness there. Keep an eye on it. Could be septic. And I want a CBC stat, and again this afternoon to see what her white count is doing.' He frowned at the chart. 'I don't see the name of her attending doctor on here. Who took the patient's history?'

'I . . . I did,' Gary stammered. 'She's Doctor Gabriel's patient, but I couldn't reach—'

'I don't care if he was on the moon,' David cut in. 'I want his name on the chart, along with everything else, even if you *do* find it irrelevant. *Doctor.*' He emphasized 'doctor' sarcastically.

Rachel watched in dismay as Gary flushed bright pink, his freckles standing out in cartoon relief, and she saw in his expression how he idolized David, and how devastated he was by David's disapproval.

'I'm sorry, Dr Sloane. It . . . it was inexcusable. It won't happen again.'

Rachel ached to step in, to cry out, *No, David, not like that. You're so much gentler than that.* She knew him, a side of him the others didn't. She yearned to make them see what he was really like.

Then all at once, as if he'd read her mind, David smiled,

that brilliant smile, like the sun coming out from behind a cloud, and Rachel felt herself relax. David clapped Gary on the shoulder.

'I'm sure it won't. You followed through correctly on the rest. Good work, Doctor. Now . . .'

David was moving on to the next bed, the next patient, leaving Gary McBride grinning in his wake, his relief so obvious it was a little comical.

*Yes, that's how he'll be when I tell him*, Rachel thought. *At first he'll be surprised, upset, maybe even a little cross. But then he'll put his arms around me and hold me, tell me he loves me, and that everything will be all right.*

And it *will* be, she told herself. It's just got to be.

Rachel felt herself trembling, and quickly stuffed her hands in her pockets so no-one would see. Her fingers brushed against the paper. Now it didn't seem so terrible, so impossible to accept as something real.

*I'll tell him tonight*, she decided.

For the first time in twelve hours, since she'd found out, Rachel felt that things might turn out to be OK.


'The bastard! We had a transverse arrest on our hands, a tachy baby, and he fumbled around like a first-year med student. Christ, the man was blasted out of his skull. The whole DR stank of his breath . . .'

Rachel watched David pace furiously back and forth across the worn Bergama rug in her tiny living room. This was the latest Dr Petrakis horror story. David was right, she thought idly, head of Obstetrics or no, the man should have been fired years ago. A raging alcoholic not fit to do the job of an orderly.

But she was finding it hard to stay tuned in. She couldn't stop thinking about the baby. And how to tell David. She'd even considered writing him a letter, tucking it in his pocket as he was leaving. *Dear David: I have a patient for you. She's about eight weeks pregnant, and probably a raving psychotic . . .*

But would it be crazy, she asked herself, to keep this

143

baby? Curled on the sofa, Rachel brought her hand to rest against her abdomen. It was too soon to feel anything, of course, but she *did*. A kind of warmth, a steady glow. The way a lighted window at night lets passers-by know there's someone at home.

But would he understand? She remembered his telling her once that one of the things he admired about her most was her toughness, that she wasn't sloppily sentimental like most women. And wasn't her wanting this baby just that?

*But I didn't ask for it, dammit. He knows that.*

But as she looked at him now, eyes drawn into green slits, face harrowed with anger, working up little hills in the old rug with his furious pacing, a worm of doubt burrowed into her gut.

And how could she leave here, go live with him? She loved this crummy Village apartment, despite the five flights of stairs and the postage-stamp-size rooms. And she loved sharing it with Kay Krempel, an RN she'd gotten to know at Bellevue, who was more fun and a better friend than anyone. It had been Mama's idea – her gift, really, since she'd insisted on paying for and overseeing everything – to strip the cracked and gouged walls layered with paint dating back to the Paleozoic era down to the brick, and to burn the paint off the moldings and leave the woodwork bare. Then bring in plants in Mexican pottery tubs, inexpensive rattan furniture with madras cushions, a ceiling fan in every room. 'Early Casablanca' Rachel had dubbed it, adoring it, though she wished Mama would stop hovering.

*Are you nuts?* She then lashed into herself. *Of course you'd leave this place for David. Who wouldn't?*

'. . . the man's a goddamn maniac. Fuck malpractice suits, he ought to be arrested. If I had any clout with the Board . . .'

She watched David stride to a halt in front of the curtainless window overlooking Grove Street. In the daytime you could smell the marvelous bread in the ovens of the

144

Italian bakery down below, see old armoires being carted in and out of the antiques shop, watch couples holding hands going into Pierre's Bistro.

Now the window was dark, and all Rachel could see was the ghost of David's reflection. A tall well-built man in pressed navy slacks and light blue V-neck sweater, neat hair. Loafers without socks was as far as he'd bent to today's laid-back life-style. It was almost as if he had stepped right off a page out of *Gentleman's Quarterly*. You could almost see the caption below: PRINCETON. CLASS OF '60. VARSITY CREW. Yet somehow, seeing the contrast of his rigid face, the muscles in his neck working as he fought to bring himself under control, Rachel had the disturbing sense of there somehow being two Davids battling it out under one skin. She felt suddenly, uneasily, as if she was on the verge of discovering something she would be better off not knowing.

She cut her gaze away, looking down at their drinks nested in little pools of moisture on the small oak table. He hadn't touched his, and now the ice had melted.

Rachel uncurled her legs, and pushed herself up. 'I'll get some more ice,' she said with artificial cheeriness. 'How about something to eat while I'm at it?'

*After he's calmed down, then I'll tell him*, she promised herself.

'What's on the menu?' David called after her as she stepped around record albums scattered like playing cards in front of the stereo cabinet. She paused, smiling, and picked up the first two. 'Surrealistic Pillow' and 'Beverly Sills at Covent Garden.' There in a nutshell, the difference between her and Kay.

Rachel thought of the surreal conversation she'd had with Kay this morning before both of them had dashed off. She, huddled in a chair, puffy-eyed from crying. Kay standing at the sink, taking gulps of her instant coffee like a gunslinger knocking down whiskeys in Dodge City's Long Branch saloon. All of five feet in her Dr Scholl clogs, white nurse's pantsuit stretched taut across her plump bottom, dark hair a halo of curls.

'I can't tell you what to do,' Kay had said. 'Just whatever you decide, make sure it's what *you* want, not what David wants.' She gave Rachel a dark little smile over the rim of her coffee mug. 'You know, I've always thought there was a tombstone way down deep in each one of us where we bury our own wants under some man's. Only they can't seem to stay buried for very long, can they? We never really forget . . .'

Rachel shivered now, slipping the record albums back on to the pile. *Oh, Kay, what makes you so sure that what I want is different from what he wants?*

She watched David carefully as he came toward her, his face smoothed now into easy lines, a smile in place. She relaxed.

Stepping into the old-fashioned kitchen, Rachel peered into the refrigerator. 'Milk. Eggs. Peanut butter. Some leftover chicken lo mein. At least, that's what I think it is.' She sniffed the contents of the carton. 'Better scratch the lo mein. I'd have to carbon-date it to see how old it is.'

David circled her with his arms from behind, nuzzling her neck. 'Let's skip dinner. I'm not that hungry. I'll make us an omelette after.'

'After what?' She squirmed around to face him.

Her heart, she now realized, was beating very fast. Damn him. He was making her want him, making her wet. One touch, one kiss, and she was ready. Like an alcoholic who, with one drink, is lost.

David didn't know the half of it, half the intensity of her passion for him. She'd kept it light. On purpose. The future seemed to be a topic he wasn't comfortable with, and that was OK. She wasn't ready for marriage, either. Living together maybe, someday, when they both felt like it.

*But that was before*, she told herself. *Before the baby. You'll have to talk about the future now, we'll have to make some kind of plans . . .*

She looked at him, opened her mouth to speak, then stopped herself. He was giving her that look that turned

146

her knees to water, his eyes sleepy, gold lashes over cool green pupils, the corners of his mouth curled up faintly, suggestively. Not Dr Sloane, efficient, remote. Just David. She could see the veins cabling his neck, one thick one, the jugular, pulsing on his right side, impatient. It made her think of his penis, hard, ropey with veins, the tip soft, dewy, like rose petals.

*Oh dear Christ,* she thought. *I could probably come right now. Like this, just looking at him.*

She could feel his need, too, as he backed her up against the open refrigerator, its cold wire shelves pressing into her spine, moving his hands up her ribcage to squeeze her breasts gently.

'Nice. Ripe,' he murmured. 'Maybe I'm hungrier than I thought.'

Rachel wished she'd thought to wear something sexier, more feminine, her silk robe instead of this old tattered shirt of Kay's.

Then she realized how silly she was. It didn't matter. In a minute, she wouldn't be wearing anything at all.

Rachel pressed toward him, swinging the refrigerator shut behind her. He was already tugging at her buttons, fiercely, impatiently, ignoring one that popped from its frayed threads and clattered against the scuffy red linoleum.

'Not in here,' she said and laughed, nervous, her voice fluttering with excitement. 'Kay might get back early. Let's go in the bedroom.'

He laughed. 'I told you. I'm hungry.'

Jesus. He didn't care who saw. Would he take her right here on the floor? The thought of it both alarmed and excited her. She felt strangely weak, her breasts – heavier and more tender than usual – tight, throbbing, nipples stiff against the soft underside of her shirt. Heat funneled down through her, like hot sand in an hourglass, settling between her legs. She felt as if a warm, perspiring hand were clutching her there.

Oh Jesus, sweet Jesus, *the table*, he was guiding, now

147

lifting her on to the small round table, a little roughly. He was tugging at her pants, wresting them over her hips, peeling them off her legs, which were dangling over the edge. She felt the varnished pine surface cold against her ass, the rough straw edge of a table mat pressing into her. He was still in his clothes, except that he'd opened his pants, pushed his slacks down a little over his narrow hips.

Rachel squeezed her eyes shut, waiting, ready for the first thrust, oh so ready. Then felt something hard, bony, poking between her thighs, surprising her a little, not his cock after all, but his fingers. Pushing in and out in a hard, steady rhythm.

The table, the harsh light overhead, the pressure of David's fingers for a moment reminded her of something else, something she didn't want to think about. She felt the hotness inside her begin to cool. The gynecologist, that was it. Like a visit to the gynecologist's, a pelvic exam.

*This is what David does to pregnant women at the hospital, feeling up inside them while they lie on a table, feet in stirrups.*

*No, no, I won't let myself think about it that way. It's not the same. Just my mind playing stupid tricks. Because of the baby. Because I need him to be gentle tonight.*

But playing together like this could be good too. The fire inside her was coming back. Yes, oh yes. David knew so well just how to please her. She could come like this, any minute now. Would he let her?

No. David was pulling her over on her side, face toward him, eye level with his crotch.

'Suck me,' he said.

Rachel hesitated an instant, then took him in her mouth. It was always like this, the little shock first, feeling somehow as if it was bad to do this, depraved. But then she began to feel good, powerful almost, feeling him swell even larger, hearing his moans of pleasure, imagining she was the only woman in the world who could do this. *She* would give David what no-one else could.

*And it's not dirty*, she told herself, *not when you love someone.*

She moved her tongue along his shaft. He was thrusting against her now, grunting, she could hear the steady ticking of his zipper against the edge of the table as he pumped his hips. He kept the rhythm with his fingers too, still inside her, sliding in and out. Hot. So hot they felt as if they were on fire, burning her.

She came, like shooting up in flames, and at the same time felt David burst out too, tasted the surge of salty liquid filling her mouth. She didn't mind the taste, though she'd heard some women did. Maybe she would have with someone else, but David was the only one she'd ever done this with.

David was pulling away from her now, pulling up his pants, helping her on to unsteady legs. His face was flushed, but otherwise they might have been sitting here playing cards, Gin Rummy. Cool. Nothing ruffled him. That's what made him such a good doctor. But damn it, she wished he would hold her. She needed his arms around her so badly.

Rachel watched David walk to the sink, begin washing his hands, and the awful feeling she'd had before swept over her, of being in a doctor's office. *Well, young lady, it looks as if you're pregnant, about six weeks I'd say, but we'll run a urine test to be sure.*

'David?' she called to him softly over the pattering of the water in the old enamel sink. She sank down on a chair, not bothering to put her pants on, just pulling her shirt down over her knees. 'I'm pregnant.'

He twisted his head around, looking at her as if she'd told a bad joke, his mouth crooking at the corner as if he wasn't sure whether to laugh or sneer.

'Rachel, that's not funny, not even to joke about,' he said smiling now.

'I'm not joking.' The words seemed to rise, not from her throat, but from the aching hollow of her stomach.

She watched his face grow dark, remote. Why was he

149

looking at her like that, as if *she'd* spoiled everything, as if she was somehow attacking him?

'Christ, Rachel. Are you sure?' He caught himself, hitting the heel of his hand against his forehead. 'Dammit, of course you are. You're a doctor. How on earth could you have let something like this happen?'

*You*. Not 'we.' Like it was all her fault.

'I wasn't exactly playing solitaire when it happened,' she snapped.

Two quick strides, trailing splotches of water on the floor from his dripping hands, and he was in front of her, leaning toward her, palms smacking down on the table. Anger flashed in his green eyes.

'Holy Christ, Rachel. You're not one of those kids we see, sixteen, illiterate, knocked up because they're too dumb to know what birth control is. You told me you were using a diaphragm. Just now, I thought . . . shit, that's why I didn't, inside you, because I was too hot to wait for you to put your goddamn *diaphragm* in.'

His eyes had a queer flat look that made the blood in her veins turn to ice water. She felt his anger humming and crackling in the air like electricity seeking a ground.

She stared at his hands. She couldn't look at him. His fingers were splayed against the knotty pine tabletop, the fine golden hair below his knuckles glistening with jewel-like droplets.

Damn him. The bastard.

Rachel took a deep breath, struggling to subdue her hurt and her anger. 'I *was* using the diaphragm. They're not infallible, as you know. Maybe I took it out too soon. Or put it in too late. Or maybe little green men from Mars poked holes in it when I wasn't looking. Dammit, how should I know how it happened?'

She looked up and saw his face now was very still and cold.

'Maybe you do know. Maybe it wasn't such an accident.'

Rachel felt, more than heard, his words – like ice in the pit of her stomach. *Oh God. Did he really say that?*

150

No, he couldn't really believe that. Not really. He must know she'd never do a thing like that. She wanted to hit him, shatter that expression of cool disdain.

Then suddenly the anger went out of her, and she felt deflated, flat and empty. 'Look, let's not do this. Getting angry won't help. It's no-one's fault. It just happened.'

David straightened, driving the fingers of both hands through his thick sandy hair, and exhaled as if relieved. 'You're right. I'm sorry. No sense getting all worked up. It's not as if any real harm was done.'

'What do you mean?'

He looked at her as if she were a child, and not a very bright one. 'An abortion. You'll have one, of course. I'll arrange it.'

Shrinking away from him in her mind, Rachel felt as if she were standing at one end of a long tunnel, seeing David as a dark speck silhouetted at the other end. She felt a vast distance between them, certain as she sat here in the safety of her snug kitchen that if she stretched her arm out to touch him, it would meet only cool darkness.

David, mistaking her silence for acquiescence, was smiling now, walking around behind her to knead her shoulders, his touch sure and deft.

'Look, I know what's eating you,' he continued. 'Those girls, the ones who come in all cut up from some back-street butcher with a coat hanger. It won't be anything like that. I have a friend, from med school. He's in private practice now. OB-GYN. He owes me a few favors. It'll be done right. Safe. Easy as pulling a tooth.'

She pulled away, and turned to stare at him, a rushing sound in her ears.

Rachel thought of the baby inside her, its warm glow, and how she'd already begun imagining what it would look like, how she would feel holding it in her arms. She'd thought, too, of the cozy house she and David would live in, the room they would decorate as a nursery.

And she wouldn't have to give up medicine, she had told herself. Maybe a few months' leave, and then with

David's help, and Mama's, and a nursemaid, she could still do her residency.

But now he was telling her to get rid of it, her *child*, as if it were something nasty that had to be scraped from the bottom of her shoe.

Rachel shot to her feet, bumping the table with her hip. She heard a crash. She looked down through tears at the starburst of white crystals and broken china that had been the sugar bowl.

'No,' she said, amazed at how steady her voice was. 'I won't have an abortion.'

'Then you—'

'That's right. I'm having this baby.'

He stared at her, an instant of blank disbelief, then his handsome face began to harden, his emerald eyes narrow.

'You'd be throwing away your career,' he said coldly. 'For a clump of cells. What are you, six, eight weeks? A clump of cells no bigger than your thumbnail then. Something we studied under our microscopes in embryology, way back in pre-med. Or have you forgotten? Romanticizing it doesn't change the biological facts.'

'You bastard.' She wanted to slug him, punch his handsome, smug face as hard as she could. 'You cold bastard.'

'Did you expect me to marry you, was that part of the fantasy, too?'

'No,' she said, her voice breaking. 'I just thought you'd care.' She stared at him, a tall stranger poised against the pans that hung from hooks on the brick wall behind him. She was trying to remember why she had ever thought she loved him.

He turned away, showing his profile, like a Roman emperor on a coin. 'I care,' he said, each word separate and exquisitely wrought. 'I care about being a doctor, and I care about you. But I won't make any excuses. I never promised you anything in the beginning, and I won't now. If you have this baby. Rachel, you'll have it alone.'

Rachel stared at the shattered bowl on the floor. Whole one minute, broken beyond repair the next.

152

She felt slightly nauseated, dazed by his coldness. The thought of what they'd done on this table a few minutes ago now seemed dirty, humiliating, a locker-room joke.

And an even worse joke was that even now, in spite of all he'd said, she longed for him to take her in his arms, and make the pain go away. Pain like dull knives hacking at her insides, making her struggle to breathe.

'Go away,' she told him. 'Just go.'

'Guess what?'

Kay blew in through the front door, plump arms laden with Balducci bags, her round face flushed with excitement.

'What?' Rachel asked, curled on the couch amidst crumpled Kleenexes, feeling even worse than she had last night with David.

Rachel watched Kay plop the bags on to the pine hall table. Delicious spicy, smoky smells drifted toward her. Only now they made her stomach heave.

If this is because of some guy, Rachel thought, he must really be something. Kay, the original yenta, the Sherlock Holmes of Jewish mothers, still hadn't picked up on the fact that Rachel was lying here in the dark at two in the afternoon when she should have been at the hospital.

'I quit!' Kay threw off her coat, and did a clackety dance in her Dr Scholl clogs across the bare strip of floor. In her white uniform and gold-rim glasses, her hair crinkling in a dark cloud about her round face, she looked like a demented Orphan Annie.

'No more Valium overdoses,' Kay jabbered on. 'No more breast implants. No more nose jobs. No more Barbra Streisands who think they can look like Grace Kelly.' She gave a little hop to keep from tripping over the telephone cord, stretched across the floor. 'Rachel, would you believe, today this woman, this *kvetch*, comes hopping into the ER. Sprained her toe, now get this, on the escalator at Saks, and while she's whining and bitching, a kid with multiple stab wounds is practically bleeding to death not five feet away. I don't know what

153

happened, something in me just snapped. I told her she should take her dear little toe back to Saks and get a refund. Then I went outside for some air, and I got to thinking about Abbie Steiner. Remember her? She bailed out last summer and went to a Red Cross hospital in Vietnam. I got a letter from her. Boy, do they need help over there, nurses, doctors – like, desperately. And I'm sick of making noises about this war, and not doing anything, so I decided—' She stopped, her round face puckering in sudden concern. 'Hey, Rachel, you all right, you sick or something? What are you doing home now? I thought you were on call.'

'It's a long story.'

Rachel winced as Kay raised the blinds open, harsh winter sunlight stabbing her eyes. 'Please, not that much. A little lower. I like it dark. No, I'm not sick, just a little bit pregnant. Kay, you can't be serious.'

Dumb question, she thought. When it came to good causes, Kay was nothing if not serious. Rachel remembered the nurses' walkout that first summer of her Bellevue clerkship. When Rachel had tried to wrangle her way through the picket line, Kay, a frizzy-haired munchkin with the bellow of a longshoreman, had button-holed her, winning her over with an impassioned outpouring about how it was mostly the patients who suffered when the nurses were short-staffed and underpaid. She was so intrigued that she'd invited Kay for a cup of coffee later. They'd been friends ever since.

Kay flopped on to the sofa beside her. 'As serious as a Richard Nixon is about trying to run for President again.'

'Jesus, Kay. I can't believe you actually quit Lenox Hill. Just like that. And Vietnam? It's too much.'

'I know.' Kay gave a gravelly laugh that didn't quite hide an edge of unease. 'No place for a lady to be caught in torn underwear, as my dear ma would say. But think of it, Rachel. My God, a chance to *do* something besides sit, clucking over what a rotten waste it all is.'

Rachel smiled. 'Somehow, I just can't quite picture you ever sitting and clucking.'

154

'My mother, God forbid, when she finds out about this, she'll go to Washington, harangue Johnson and every member of Congress to stop me.'

'Oh, Kay.' Rachel rested her head against Kay's shoulder, letting her tears spill out. 'I think you're crazy. And brave. And I don't know how the hell I'm going to get through this without you.'

And for an insane instant, she thought: *I wish I were going, too. So far away from this mess I'm in.*

Then Kay was hugging her, crying a little too. 'You've told him then?'

Rachel nodded. She had fallen into an exhausted sleep last night before Kay got home, and this morning Kay was gone by time she'd dragged herself out of bed.

'He wants me to have an abortion.'

'Is that what you want?'

'No.' Rachel buried her face in her hands, the pain of last night coming back acutely. 'But it's so damn complicated. Without David, how would I manage? Give up everything I've worked for? And if I don't, how fair is that, having a baby when I'll hardly be around?'

Kay shrugged. 'Who said life was fair?'

'The crazy thing is, even knowing how hard it would be, I still want it. And for all the wrong reasons. I can't bear the thought of someone scraping it out of me. And I want to see it, see if it looks like me. But the big thing is, it's already a part of me. I feel changed by it. I can never be the same again. Kay, tell me, are those good enough reasons?'

Kay stood up, moving across the room, reaching for the packet of Salems that sat on the bamboo bookcase. She lit onc, jetting the smoke out through her nose.

She gave a harsh little laugh. 'Who's to say? Did you ask for your parents? Did I? My mother, you could eat off her kitchen floor, but she hated to cook for her family. She would push her vacuum cleaner to the North Pole and back, but try getting her to sit down for an hour and play a game of Gin Rummy with me or one of my brothers. Yet in her own meshugge way, I know she loved us. The way I

155

figure it, when you're a kid, you take what you can get from whatever parents you're stuck with, and be glad for it.' She looked at the cigarette between her fingers as if surprised to see it there, her wide, generous face falling. 'I gave them up last week. Six whole days without a smoke, and now look at me. Jesus. Maybe I ought to take up vacuuming like Ma.'

Rachel thought of Sylvie then. Did wanting this baby have something to do with Mama? All those years she'd watched Mama gazing sadly at the empty cradle in the nursery? Now there would finally be a baby to fill that cradle. A baby they would both love.

Then the rosy fantasy faded. She imagined what it would really be like. Every day she'd be pulled in two directions. She'd hear secondhand from the nursemaid, or maybe her mother, about its first smile, its first steps. She'd probably end up creating the same distance she'd felt with her own mother.

Oh, why was she making this so hard? Why couldn't she grab hold with both hands, or simply let go?

*God, oh God, what should I do?*

Staring at the drift of balled-up Kleenexes, Rachel felt a sudden self-loathing. This was not the end of the world. She wasn't the first woman to get knocked up.

She stood up. 'Come on, let's unpack these goodies you brought and eat before they get cold. My head can't take any more major news, or any more soul-searching.'

Instantly, Kay was reaching into the bags, pulling out plastic containers and foil-wrapped packages.

'I wanted it to be practically a catered affair. Wait till you see what I got. French-style chicken with grapes. Nova Scotia salmon. Pickled artichoke hearts . . . Rachel? Are you OK?'

Rachel suddenly was dashing for the bathroom. *Oh Jesus, I'm going to throw up.*

Afterwards, her stomach empty, the bathroom tile cold against her knees, head aching, she sagged against the toilet seat.

Minutes later, from what seemed like miles away, she

heard the front-door intercom, a faint droning, then the clatter of Kay's clogs as she ran to answer it.

'Rachel!' she called. 'It's your mother. She's on her way up!'

*Oh Lord, not now.* But, yes, she had told Mama sometime last week that today would be fine to drop by with those drapery samples. Mama, always trying to make everything more beautiful. *She doesn't know I'm here. I told her I'd be on call, that she could go over the samples with Kay.* Rachel looked down at her rumpled bathrobe. Now she would have to dream up some reason why she was home, looking like death warmed over.

She dashed to the sink and washed her face, blotting it with a washcloth to try to ease the swelling around her eyes. Oh, what was the use? Mama would see in an instant that she'd been crying. *If only I could tell her,* Rachel thought, *how wonderful if I could confide in her, let her help me decide.*

But she knew what Mama would say. Have the baby, have my grandchild. An abortion – she'd be shocked at the very idea. So why even involve her, drag her into this mess?

Emerging from the bathroom, Rachel found her mother at the front window, holding a swatch of fabric against the frame. 'Rachel! What a surprise. I didn't know you'd be here. Do you like this one? The blue is nice with the . . . darling, what is it? You look awful. Are you sick?'

Rachel held out a hand as if to ward off her mother's solicitousness. Anxiously, she looked around for Kay, but her roommate had faded into the kitchen. Rachel heard the splashing of water hitting the old enamel sink.

'It's nothing . . . just a bug I picked up. I'll be fine.'

'Of course you will, but right now you belong in bed! Never mind about the drapes, they can wait. You go climb right into bed, and I'll make you some hot tea. Is your stomach upset, too?'

Rachel stared at Sylvie, perfectly put together in a navy-blue rayon suit with a peplum waist and crisp white blouse. But the heady richness of her perfume, Channel N°5, was making Rachel's stomach tip like an overfull bucket. If she didn't lie down soon, she'd be sick again.

Then somehow she was in her room, and Mama was turning down the bed for her, pressing a cool washcloth to her forehead. Just like when she was little. And suddenly it was all too much. Tears welled up, then began leaking from the corners of her eyes.

*Oh, damn it all! I don't want to cry. I don't want to be weak. If only she'd leave me . . . leave right now, this very instant . . . before I start telling her things I know I'll be sorry for later . . .*

'Rachel. Oh my darling girl, what is it? Can't you tell me?'

Sylvie's forest-green eyes now also glittered with tears, as if Rachel's pain was hers, too. Her face, that skin fine and powdery pale as a moth's wing, seemed to sag. She held a cool, Chanel-smelling hand to Rachel's cheek.

'Mama, I'm pregnant.' The words came before Rachel could stop them.

Sylvie stared at her. Color rose in her pale cheeks. Her lips parted, revealing the moist pinkness beyond the line of her coral lipstick. But she wasn't melting into hysterics, thank God.

'What are you going to do?' Her voice sounded surprisingly firm.

Now Rachel felt stunned. This didn't seem like Mama, no, not like her at all. How could Mama even imagine anything other than her having and keeping this baby? But then she thought back and remembered the last time her mother had so surprised her, that day Rachel had come to Daddy in the hospital, how strong, even sharp, Mama had been then.

'I don't know,' Rachel murmured.

Mama's hand slipped from her cheek, and she looked away.

Rachel followed her gaze. There, toward the corner, was the pine dresser Mama had found at a country garage

158

sale, and had stripped and varnished. And beside it, the cheval mirror and bent-wood rocker from Rachel's child-hood bedroom. Mama had known they would look just right in this room, she had such an eye for the right thing. Could she actually consider the ugly act Rachel was contemplating now?

'Is he . . . the father, I mean . . . does he want this child?'

Rachel felt something inside her shrivel. 'No.'

'I see.' Sylvie nodded, her coral mouth drawing into a firm but comprehending line. 'How far along are you?'

'Not far. Six weeks. But, oh Mama, to me it's already *real*. A real baby.'

'A baby . . .' Sylvie's expression grew wistful, then she seemed to pull herself together, and said, 'Oh, Rachel, I wish I could tell you what to do. Or at least advise you. But how can I? The right answer for me could be the wrong one for you.'

'But Mama, what would *you* do?' Rachel cried out.

'It was different in my day. People were far less . . . accepting. For women in your position there was no right choice, just the *only* choice.'

'But if I have this baby, it will change everything. Turn my whole life upside down.'

Sylvie, looking off toward the window, smiled faintly. 'Babies always do.' Then she turned back to Rachel, still smiling, her eyes shining with tears. 'You turned mine upside down.'

'You want me to have it.' Rachel, hearing the accusing tone in her voice, hated herself. She had no right blaming Mama.

'No.' Sylvie shook her head. 'I didn't say that. Anyway, what I might want isn't important. I meant what I said, I can't advise you. But I do ache for you, my darling. If I had been in your shoes, I—' her voice cracked a little, 'well, I'm not certain what I would have done, if I'd had the choice.'

'Oh, Mama . . .' Rachel bolted upright, grabbing hold

of the blankets with both fists, clutching hard. 'I wish I knew what to do.'

'Whatever you decide, my darling, I'll be here for you. I love you. Don't ever forget that.'

Rachel felt a rush of gratitude that made her throat ache. And she felt something else, too. A new sort of admiration for her mother.

'Will you tell Daddy?' she asked fearfully.

'No.' Sylvie shook her head. 'Daddy loves you, but men don't always see these things the way we do.'

'Mama?'

'Yes?'

'Did you want me before I was born? Truly want me more than anything?'

For a long moment that seemed to tremble in the air between them, Sylvie was silent. Her cool hands came to rest against Rachel's on the blanket. And there it was – that slow, sad smile Rachel had seen so many times.

'Yes, my Rachel. More than anything.'


David was looking straight through her.

Rachel felt as if she were just another part of the antiseptic landscape of the scrub room, as anonymous as the tiled walls and stainless steel sinks. She shivered, feeling chilled, her stomach beginning to cramp up again.

*Please don't do this. For God's sake, don't ignore me.*

'Dr Petrakis asked me to assist,' she explained lamely, hating him for somehow making her feel as if she had to justify herself.

Trying to curb her anger, she stamped on the foot pedal that controlled the faucet, and thrust her hands under the scalding water.

David's eyes, when she looked up to meet them, were cool and remote, the flat green of the tiled walls.

'She's his patient,' he said with a little shrug.

*And I'm a damn fool*, Rachel thought, fighting tears as she grabbed the Betadine brush, scrubbing so hard she took the skin off her knuckles.

A week, seven awful days, and still she stood here like a moon-struck idiot, hoping, waiting for a word, a sign, some glimmer of feeling. A week of being ignored, and worse. She had caught him looking at her from time to time as if she were some bothersome loose thread left hanging from the neat fabric of his life.

Was he punishing her? Or did he really, as Rhett Butler said, just not give a damn? Either way, she would not go crawling to him. Screw him if he couldn't see what he was giving up.

Rachel thrust her dripping hands into the air, letting the water trickle from her elbows. David had just finished scrubbing at the sink beside hers, and she turned away quickly so he wouldn't see the tears in her eyes.

She pushed ahead of him through the swinging doors into the operating room. More green tiles, stainless steel, cold white ceiling lights. Towel, gloves, then the scrub nurse was tying her into a gown. Rachel nodded to the circulating nurse, a lithe copper-skinned girl named Vicki Sanchez, who was busily laying out sterilized instruments on the Mayo stand. Scalpels. Homostats. Suture needles.

Beyond Vicki, a hulking gray-haired figure in rumpled surgical greens partially blocked Rachel's view of the operating table. Dr Petrakis. He appeared to be leaning to one side. And as he slowly, with exaggerated care, turned himself around to face her, she caught sight of the fiery red suns of his eyes. A jolt of dread went through her stomach.

*Jesus, he's blasted out of his skull.*

An emergency C-section to perform on a placenta previa, and here he was, three sheets to the wind. In med school, they didn't teach you how to handle a situation like *this*.

Yet, amazingly, Petrakis seemed to be holding his own. Years of practice, she supposed. Still, she found herself murmuring a little prayer.

'Where's Henson?' growled Petrakis. 'Are we supposed to stand here and watch the patient bleed to death while that so-called anesthesiologist plays with himself upstairs?'

Coming from behind Rachel, David's voice, cool, in control. 'Henson got hung up. I called Gilchrist, he should be up any minute. Pediatrics, too. I thought the PDs should be on hand just in case. What's happening with the patient?'

Petrakis moved away, and Rachel saw her, a great beached mound of stomach rising from a swirl of green surgical drapes, her skin varnished a sickly yellow-brown with Betadine. Like the object of some grotesque pagan ritual in an H Rider Haggard novel, she couldn't help thinking.

'She's holding at eight centimeters,' Petrakis answered. 'Baby won't be going anywhere for a while. But she's lost a couple hundred cc's of blood. And I don't want to wait around much longer.'

Above the drapes, two dark eyes staring out of a white face, like cigarette holes burned in a napkin. Rachel felt a stab of pity for her. No general anesthesia in this case, bad for the baby. A light Demerol, maybe. This was one wide-awake, terrified young woman. And that raving idiot Petrakis, talking about her as if she were a Volkswagen in a garage having a new muffler put in.

Rachel moved closer, signaling reassurance with her eyes. 'It'll be over soon, Señora,' she soothed. 'You'll have your baby before you know it.'

The woman spoke, a reedy whisper Rachel had to bend close to, to hear. 'I feel it coming,' she said. 'I have to push.'

An alarm jangled in Rachel's head. No, no, with the placenta slipped down over the cervix, pushing would be the very worst thing. It could cause a hemorrhage. Possibly fatal to her, to the baby, or both.

But Petrakis had said the cervix was dilated eight centimeters. Two more to go. That usually meant hours in a primipara. Still . . .

Rachel looked up at Petrakis. 'She says she has to push.'

162

He looked annoyed, she thought. Well, tough shit. Ten weeks on OB had taught her one thing, at least. When a woman said she had to push, she meant it.

'Impossible,' Petrakis barked. 'I examined her myself not ten minutes ago.'

David looked dubious as well. But at least he wasn't ready to dismiss what the young woman had said out of hand. 'Let's examine her again.'

Then Rachel saw something that made her heart turn a sudden swift cartwheel. Knees up, the patient was pushing, face clenched in a red fist of pain. Between her legs, the baby's head was crowning. A circle of glistening dark scalp the size of a quarter.

'Shit,' Petrakis said.

There was a split second in which everything seemed frozen, a scale hanging in balance, waiting to tip. Then Rachel felt shock. Nothing was happening. Jesus Christ. Petrakis was just standing there, mouth open, feet planted wide apart, swaying slightly, like a drunk in a detox ward seeing spiders and snakes.

Then everything seemed to happen at once. Petrakis shouting something unintelligible at the nurses. David lunging forward, taking charge, hands cupping to guide forth a dark scrunched head, then in a slippery rush of blood and amniotic fluid, a tiny pink body flopping at the end of a bright turquoise cord. A boy.

Rachel rushed to take him from David while he clamped the cord, balancing the blood-streaked bundle in her hands, its matchstick arms flailing, shriveled monkey face working into a squall as she suctioned him. Everything around her seemed to fade. She saw only the miracle of this new life, feeling as if a bright, hot band had fastened about her heart. Perfect. Precious. More precious than anything in the world.

*My baby too. How could I bear not to have this?*

Then she looked up.

Something was dreadfully wrong. The mother bleeding. A torrent of blood gushing between her legs, spattering the table, the sterilized instruments neatly laid out on the Mayo stand, and forming a crimson pool on the floor.

'Nurse!' Rachel heard a deep voice shout. 'Open up the lines! Start those two units of A positive. *Stat.*'

David. He was ramming a fist between the patient's legs, into all that blood, suddenly, shockingly. *Dear God, what is he doing?*

Then Rachel understood.

And she rushed in, pressing down on an abdomen that felt like tapioca pudding, pushing hard, helping David massage the uterus, trying to force it to contract.

'Get me some Ergometrine,' he snapped over his shoulder at Vicki. 'And, for God's sake, nurse, more blood on that line or I'm going to lose her. BP's down to eighty. She's looking shocky.'

'I don't feel anything!' Rachel heard herself cry. 'She's not contracting.'

'Damn it. I'm not going to lose her.' David's green eyes above his mask flashed at her, so brilliant she felt blinded for an instant. Her heart leapt in response, her hands kneaded harder.

'Contract, damn it. *Contract*,' she muttered.

Then she felt it, tiny ripples, a tightening, oh Jesus, yes, *yes*.

'That's it,' she panted. 'Good girl. Keep it up.' Her mask felt wet. She was crying, she realized.

The bleeding was slowing. Now stopping. David looked up, met Rachel's gaze. His eyes were bright with triumph, a dark stain like a rising moon on the forehead of his surgical cap. He withdrew his fist, and she saw that his arm was covered in blood all the way to the elbow.

He reached up with bloody fingers, tore his mask off. He was grinning. Rachel felt as if she'd been lifted off the floor several feet, then dropped down again. The room spinning, her stomach up where her heart should have been.

'Oh, fuck it,' he said, hugging her to him.

*

Rachel watched David strip off his bloody gloves, tossing them into the scrub-room bin. Words came to mind, none of them large enough to contain all she was feeling.

*I saw you in there*, she wanted to say, *how you fought. And I saw the way you looked after you knew you'd won. No-one who looked that way could ever truly want to destroy a life.*

'I couldn't believe it,' she said lamely.

'What?'

'Petrakis. Doing nothing.'

She stepped around to help him untie his scrubs, mostly brown now with splotches of drying blood. She couldn't see his face, but she could feel the knotted tenseness in his shoulders.

'That man signed his own death warrant today. Too many people saw. Even Donaldson won't be able to ignore this.'

But Rachel didn't want to hear about Petrakis, or Donaldson, that popcorn-headed administrator.

'David,' she said softly. 'I've missed you.'

He turned, and suddenly he was looking at her, really *looking* at her as if she were the only thing that existed. She saw something bright flare in his eyes. Relief.

'Not here,' he said in a low voice, taking her by the wrist, gripping it hard. 'Too many people around. Let me buy you a cup of coffee.'

Two floors down in the elevator, then the cafeteria, a sea of faces, steamy smells. She saved their seats while David stood in line, returning with a laden tray.

'I brought you a sandwich,' he said. 'You look as if you haven't eaten all week.'

*As a matter of fact, David, I haven't. They call it morning sickness, but it's really morning, afternoon, and night sickness.*

She shrugged. 'Too busy, I guess. You know how it is.'

'Shit, yes. What I'd give for a decent meal and a night of uninterrupted rest.'

'That was some job you did on that girl up there.'

165

'I only wish Petrakis had been sober enough see it,' he said and laughed bitterly.

'To hell with Petrakis. You were good. And you didn't panic. If I were in that girl's place, I would be thanking G—' She stopped herself. Heat rose into her face, searing, hot tears in her eyes. *No, damn it, you're not going to cry. No-one is supposed to feel sorry for you.*

She reached for the tea she had asked for instead of coffee – coffee was bad for the baby – but David caught her hand first, pressing it between both of his. Dear God, what she'd longed for, so simple a thing, yet oh how wonderful, him touching her. Now, there was no stopping the tears.

'Rachel. God. I've missed you too. I can't believe how stupid we were, arguing like that. I feel like such a shit.'

*Then why didn't you call? Why did you avoid me? Making me feel like a goddamn leper.*

No, no. She wanted to shut off that angry voice inside her.

'I'm sorry too,' she said. 'I shouldn't have dropped it on you like that. Telling you I wanted to keep the baby before we'd even talked it over. But let's forget all that. Can we start over? Right now? Here?'

*Tell me you love me. Please. That you'll at least keep an open mind about the baby until I've explained how we can make it work.*

He squeezed her hand more tightly, almost hurting. He was smiling now, wearing the same look of triumph he'd had in the OR.

'I knew you'd come around. Christ, Rachel, there's nothing I want more. And it'll be that way again. Soon as we get this thing taken care of.'

'What do you mean, David?'

He was looking at her as if he couldn't believe she'd asked. 'Why, the abortion.'

Rachel felt as if she were sinking into a deep well, black water closing over her head, shutting off the air. And cold. So cold she was starting to feel numb. She tried to imagine herself going through with it, having the abortion. Easy in a way, only a little piece of her. And she could tell herself, *See? That wasn't so bad*. And the next time someone wanted a chunk of her soul it would be that much easier to give in, because there would be that much less of her to fight. Until in the end, there would be nothing left of her. Nothing that counted.

No. She wouldn't. She couldn't.

Rachel rose, out of her blackness, getting to her feet, pushing her chair back. And in the hard light she looked down at David, and saw what he was.

'What is it? What are you looking at me like that for?' He laughed nervously, a good-looking man in a yellow double-knit pullover with a tiny alligator sewn over the right breast, and a silver I.D. bracelet loose about his left wrist. A man with the sour look of betrayal dawning in his handsome face.

'I just thought you were someone I could count on,' she said. 'I guess I was wrong.'

Then she was walking very fast, bumping against tables, chairs, blinded by her tears, aware only of a loud noise in her head, and an awful pain in her heart.

# 5

David Sloane pushed out through the hospital's heavy plate-glass door, ducking his head as hard rain pelted him in the face. He jerked up the collar of his camelhair overcoat, hunching his shoulders, cursing his bad luck as he struck out toward Flatbush Avenue and the subway.

It was really coming down, dammit, and he hadn't thought to bring an umbrella, much less a raincoat. And forget about getting a cab, on a night like this, and in this part of Brooklyn. He was stuck with riding home soaked, alongside the dregs of the IRT.

David had a queasy feeling in the pit of his stomach. He found himself wondering if his luck – the scholarships, high marks, elections to journals, Class Councils, honor societies all through Princeton, top ten per cent of his class at Columbia, the internship and now chief residency – might somehow be turning, just a little here and there around the edges, to shit.

Not that anything really awful had happened yet. But it had been ages since he'd felt this spooked about anything. And after all those years of working his ass off, just as he was almost set to get out there and make himself a bundle, he could not afford any bad shit coming down on him. Christalmighty, not now.

And it all began last week with her, didn't it? Miss Riverside Drive, Miss Kiss-My-Ass Jew Princess.

The bitch.

Stalking out of the cafeteria as if the whole thing were his fault. Stupid, stupid female. But he'd have dealt with it. Only she had to go off the deep end. Crazy talk, about having the baby.

He'd thought she was different. But now he realized she was no better than those others after all, every coed, nurse, lab technician he'd ever screwed. Which one of them had ever been thinking about him when they were spreading their legs? Shit, a diamond ring for the third finger of their left hand was all they cared about.

But Rachel, he'd thought, was smarter than that. A woman with brains who knew how to fuck. That rare and tantalizing creature – an ice princess with legs just itching to be spread. He'd seen that in her first off, not that she herself had the remotest idea. He had an intuitive sense about women, like a smell, and right away he'd sniffed it, her whole sexual history laid bare – the high school Romeos who'd whispered love clichés in her ear while fumbling with her bra hooks, the Haverford preppies whose entire lexicon of sexual expertise you could stuff in a condom, and maybe a funny uncle tucked in somewhere, copping a feel when he thought no-one would notice. Not a virgin, but the next closest thing – a woman without a clue how to use what was between her legs because no-one had ever shown her how. A woman so frozen, the right touch would set off a flood like spring melt off a mountain. A woman ripe for the plucking.

Yet there was something else about her, something he couldn't quite put his finger on. A hard nugget at the center of that pampered innocence like an uncut diamond. She had a coolness that had sized him up and found him not good enough, like those girls with long tanned legs in tennis shorts sipping ice tea out on the porch of whatever resort he happened to be busting his hump at that particular summer – Spring Lake, Sea Girt, Deal – daughters of rich daddies shelling out big bucks for their tennis lessons, along with the occasional fuck on the side if the instructor happened to be cute. Their eyes would flick over him when he picked up their empty glasses with lipstick marks like pink kisses around the rims, then move past, reducing him to a speck in the dark mirrors of their sunglasses, while they went on talking as if he weren't there – bitching about the food, their tennis game, the lack of interesting guys.

David, ducking out of the rain to buy a newspaper at the hole-in-the-wall candy store halfway to the subway, found himself remembering Amanda Waring. One of the tanned honey-blond bitches flocked on the porch at Spring Lake. After observing the restless way she crossed and uncrossed her legs whenever a good-looking man was around, and the hard, frantic energy with which she drove balls across the net out on the tennis court, he'd made it a point to catch her eye, and hold it. *A lady in need of a good lay,* he had thought.

By that summer, with a year of Princeton under his belt, David knew a few things he hadn't before. Like how to dress so no-one would guess you were a hardluck Polack from Jersey, trying to impress the rich folk. He'd packed only some faded Levi's that clung to him like a second skin, a pair of scuffed Docksiders, two plain white shirts and a cashmere crewneck one of the rich kids had carelessly left behind last summer. So when he was out of his busboy uniform, he could have passed as one of them.

*Amanda must have thought so . . . at least for a little while,* David thought with a sweet acid taste in his mouth, as he palmed his quarter in change and glanced briefly at the headlines: ASTRONAUTS LAND SAFELY AFTER MOON ORBIT. But he was not in the least tempted to read on.

He remembered a big gazebo out on the lawn behind the main building. A lot of the kids hung out there at night, smoking and getting drunk on half-pints of Jack Daniel's and Southern Comfort. David had gone there a few times, and one night Amanda invited him to sit next to her. When the bottle was passed to him he only pretended to drink – good Christ, he had more than his share of that poison at home with Pop. He'd kept fairly quiet, too. Better they think him the shy type than make a fool of himself.

Then someone initiated a game of Truth or Dare, and suddenly there was Amanda, giggly drunk, wriggling out of her slacks and top, then streaking in her bra and panties

170

across the dew-soaked lawn toward the pool. The others were either too drunk or too bored to go after her. Only David, afraid she might do something really stupid, like jump in the pool and drown, had run after her.

He caught up with her in the moon-shade of a giant mulberry tree a hundred yards or so from the pool. Out of breath and moist with perspiration, she collapsed laughing into his arms.

He took her on the wet grass, not surprised to find she was a virgin. Not surprised, either, when she wrapped her legs about him and bit his shoulder, crying out in muffled delight.

The next day he approached her as she was strolling down the gravel path to the tennis courts, racket slung casually over her shoulder. Her thick blond hair was caught back in a ponytail, and she was wearing a pleated white tennis skirt that flipped up in back when she walked, exposing the twin crescents of her sweet white ass where her panties had ridden up.

When David moved his hand down her smooth brown arm, trying to kiss her, she pushed him away with a disgusted look.

'Look, let's just get one thing straight,' she hissed, first looking around to make sure they were alone. 'Whatever happened last night didn't happen, and if you say it did – if you breathe a word of it to *anyone* – I'll scream bloody murder and say you raped me. My father is an attorney, and a son of a bitch besides. He could get you fired and probably arrested. And I don't think you want that kind of trouble, do you?'

Without this job, he'd have no money in the fall for books, clothes, haircuts. Not to mention the risk to his scholarship if she decided to stir up trouble. Hell, he hadn't been working his butt off playing Stepin Fetchit to these rich assholes to see it all go down the drain over some stupid bitch with hot pants and a short memory. She wasn't worth it, not by a long shot.

What hurt was realizing she'd seen through him all

171

along, that he really wasn't good enough. She'd enjoyed him, briefly and a little guiltily, like a girl on a diet sneaking a candy bar. Now she was simply throwing away the wrapper.

David had taken one long last look at her, engraving his moment of humiliation in his memory so he would not forget. And he never had. Even now, with the cold rain stinging his face as he dashed to make the green light, David could recall that exact spot on the sunny gravel path where the boxwood hedge had become overgrown with honeysuckle, the lazy hum of bees, the far-off droning of a power mower. But trying now to picture her face, all he could see were the twin images of himself reflected in her sunglasses, minute, insignificant.

But that kid had been Davey Slonowicz from Jersey City. A month before going back to Princeton, he had it changed legally to David Sloane.

And David Sloane was no chump. Just the opposite. *He* chose the women, and he called the shots. And if it was time for an affair to end, goddammit, *he* would be the one ending it.

So damn Rachel Rosenthal to hell. To think he'd almost been taken in by her, almost made a real fool of himself. Yeah, she had gotten to him, scratched her way down inside him somehow. He thought of this black chick he'd been seeing, a nurse with a gorgeous pair of knockers and kinky tastes who liked it up the ass. Christ, he'd even find himself thinking about Rachel while he was fucking Charlene. And he'd never done *that* before. Shit, no wonder he was feeling so damn shaky.

David saw the light go red on him as he reached the corner before the subway entrance. Fuck it. He started crossing anyway, shrugging at the blare of horns, the glassy squeal of tires braking on wet pavement. Two running strides, and he was at the opposite curb, leaping over the lake of filthy water that fanned out from a stopped-up storm drain.

Running – David felt as if he'd always been running. At

first from his father. *Sure, you got to become a track star early when your old man is a drunk, to get out of the way fast before he slams your face in for any number of federal offenses, like forgetting to tie your sneakers, or turning the TV up too loud, or just plain being in his way. Miller time. Weekends, after a hard week behind the welding torch, was always Miller Time in our house, a case of beer chilling in the fridge, another case stashed in the front hallway closet.*

After six or seven beers – David remembered learning to count them the way a condemned man on death row counts his last minutes – Dad would go from boozy good cheer to junkyard-dog mean.

*Hey, Davey, you a fuckin' fairy or something? Nose always buried in a book. You think you're too good for your old man, that it? Huh? Well, let me show you a fuckin' thing or two you may not have learned from all those books ...*

He'd had to learn to run; his senior year in high school, he'd come in first in the statewide cross-country championship. Nearly straight A's, too. Almost 800 on his SATs. A full scholarship to Princeton. He'd had his lonely days at college, feeling like he didn't belong, but then he'd found a bunch of guys, and from then on Jersey City was ancient history. It was as if he were saying to the old man, *Now let me show you a fucking thing or two.*

And soon I'll be out of this rathole hospital as well, he thought. I'll set up in Morristown or Montclair, or maybe Short Hills, where they have bucks, and all want at least two kids, and a good OB, of course. *Their* kind, who talks nice and gives lollipops to their kids, and doesn't get annoyed when they call, with heartburn or gas, panicked they're going into labor.

Yeah, he'd be his own man at last, free. And he'd be goddamned if he'd let some cunt, even a rich cunt, tie him down for ever. Maybe in five years or ten years he'd be ready for the house with the white picket fence, but not now.

David, making his way down the steps into the bowels of

the IRT, thought of something and broke into a sweat. Suppose she really went through with it? Then he *would* be a father, whether he wanted to be or not. Somewhere out there would be a kid with his features, his blood running through its veins. It would want things he couldn't possibly give. And someday maybe it would even hate him the way he hated his old man.

David was so shaken up by the time he reached the platform, he dropped his last token before managing to fit it into the turnstile. He felt afraid of Rachel, like he used to feel afraid of his pop, a stitch in his belly, a dry cardboard taste in his mouth.

Damn her, why was he letting her do this to him? Then he was remembering the morning Rachel found a pair of black lace panties, probably Charlene's, under his bed, and said nothing about it, just smiled sweetly and disappeared into the kitchen to fix breakfast. By the time he got out of the shower, she was gone. There was a place set for him on the table, a goblet of fresh-squeezed orange juice, cloth napkin in a ring. And right on his plate, those same black lace panties spread over a toasted English muffin. The note propped beside it read 'Bon appétit.'

No, even though she'd turned on the waterworks like the rest of them, she was tough and calculating too, cool as a chilled silver fork. And what if she dragged him down no matter what he did? The way Pop had. David had wanted to move out, get away, from the time he was thirteen, earning a few bucks of his own washing dishes after school for Muldowney's. But always, whenever he came close to just packing his bag and cutting out, he found he couldn't. Pop had a secret weapon, the thing that scared David the most: the old bastard had needed him somehow.

David felt a rush of fetid air, saw deep in the tunnel the headlights of an approaching train, and it was like his father's breath in his face, those bloodshot eyes lit by a drunken fury closing in for the kill.

*Y'think you're so smart, better'n me. But you'll never get away from me, Davey. And y'know why? 'Cause I'm in you. Part of you. Every time you look in a mirror, I'll be lookin' back at you . . .*

Then there was only the thundering train, and the hard hammering of his heart.

David stepped in, sinking on to the hard plastic seat. He looked around, and saw a wino in a filthy parka slumped right across from him, asleep. Not going anywhere, just keeping off the streets, keeping warm. Disgusting.

But in a weird way, this bum made him feel good. He reminded David of how far he'd come, of how much he had accomplished. He felt stronger. Whatever curve ball Rachel threw at him, hell, he'd handle it.

'Hello, David.'

A woman's voice, greeting him from the darkness of his living room. David's heart sideslipped like a car skidding off an icy road. *Who in the he –*

'Rachel?' He fumbled for the light switch.

Christ. Rachel, yes, but he wouldn't have recognized her. She sat still and straight in the Eames chair by the fireplace, hands folded in her lap, almost primly, like a very good child in school. Another odd thing. It was the first time, come to think of it, he'd ever seen her in a dress. A pretty one, too. Some kind of soft cotton, with a swirly pastel pattern, batik maybe. Her hair, which usually floated in a soft gold-brown cloud – the color of saltwater taffy – about her shoulders, was clipped back with a barrette, leaving her neck bare, white, and slender. He felt again the way he had on the subway platform, scared, as if something bad were about to happen, and at the same time, curiously aroused.

It was her eyes that spooked him most of all. Huge and dark, yet oddly vacant, like windows with the shades drawn. Whatever she was feeling was behind there, leaving him out in the cold.

There was a bottle of Cuervo Gold on the coffee table in front of her, half empty. No glass, no ice. Christ almighty. Rachel didn't drink. A glass of wine and she was under the table. So here she should be smashed, out cold, and she looked sober as a parson.

*Watch it, buddy*, he thought. *We're skating on very thin ice, here. Just watch your ass.*

'Mind if I join you?' he said, peeling off his sopping coat and tossing it over a chair. Then he sat down on the sofa opposite her, every muscle in him tense, wary. He picked up the bottle, looked at the label. 'Would you believe this has been sitting in my cupboard since last Christmas? A gift from my father. Every year he sends me one. I don't usually drink, but it's a cold night out. A little snort might take the chill off.'

Jesus Christ, why doesn't she say something, or blink an eye at least? What the hell is going on here?

Then she stirred. He saw a shudder passing through her, and her gaze locking on to him. Cold. Sub-fucking-zero. He could feel his balls shrinking up into his crotch.

Tipping the bottle toward his mouth, David noticed his hand was shaking. And down his arms he felt goosebumps breaking out.

'Don't,' she said. Quietly. Firmly.

But it was the look she gave him that made him lower the bottle. *Oh Jesus, her eyes.* Their blankness had lifted, giving him a glimpse of something frightening inside her, something terrible, a white heat burning blue at the center.

'I don't want you drunk when you do it.' She spoke again, that same maddening tonelessness, like the flat whine of a cardiac monitor after the patient has arrested.

He slammed the bottle down on the blond-wood coffee table, and some of the amber liquor slooshed out on to his hand. He brought his knuckles to his mouth, sucking them dry, the sharp tequila taste stinging his mouth.

'Do what? Jesus, Rachel, you're scary, you know that? Sitting here in the dark like a goddam spider. You could have called, let me know you were coming. Did you think I wouldn't want to see you again?'

He had to look away when he said it. The truth was he

176

wished she were on another planet. He wished they'd never met.

'I don't care about that,' she said. 'After tonight it doesn't matter.'

'Mind letting me in on your frequency? What the fuck are you talking about?'

He wasn't so scared anymore. Now he was getting pissed off.

'I mean I don't care about us anymore. That's over. I'm here about *it,* the baby.'

*Oh Jesus. Oh Christ. Here it comes. She'll say we should get married, in name only, some bullshit like that, so it won't be a bastard.*

If he ever needed a drink, it was now. Fuck her. He tipped the bottle, letting the booze slide easy down his throat, warming him all through.

Averting his eyes from her, looking about the room, he noticed how bare, stark really, it was. He'd moved in – how long ago? – six, seven months. It had seemed like the next step up. Small, on the dark side, but fantastic location – that always impressed women. Seventieth, close to Central Park. Not exactly overlooking the park, but near enough to watch the droves of pretty girls in shorts and halter tops walk by in the summertime.

What was it that fag real-estate agent had called it? A love nest? Sickening. But he'd often thought of it since, and it was true in a way. The lobby had just been modernized, but the apartments still had some Art Nouveau detail. Like the gracefully curved bronze ceiling fixture with its milk-glass shades. And the copper panels with women's profiles on either side of the fireplace mantel. He'd hung a Mucha print over it, so people would know he understood the period, that he wasn't some cultural illiterate.

But that was about it. His books and other stuff were still mostly in cartons, stacked neatly against the wall. Except the hi-fi, of course. What was seduction without music? The Eames chair Rachel was sitting in had been left by the former tenant, another fag, who'd also sold him the Navaho rug in the center of the parquet floor.

Then it came to him why he'd never unpacked. Marking time here, that's what he'd been doing. Waiting for his real move.

And now this bitch was going to try to hold him up.

'What do you want?' he asked sullenly.

'I want an abortion.' Cold, dead. 'And I want you to do it.'

David froze. What? What had she just said? He felt the bottle slipping from his grasp. His mind, too, slipping. Like the time he'd run smack into the side of Cuyler Hall in the dark, reeling back from Houseparties. A flash of crimson behind his eyes. Then pain, mushrooming, up his neck, unfolding in dull pounding waves through his skull.

Now the awfulness of her words, coming back to him, exploding inside his head.

Jesus, she couldn't be serious.

*Cool it,* he told himself. He had to stay calm, on top of things. But Christ, his head hurt. How the hell could he manage this?

'OK,' he said. In his mind he pictured himself wearing his white coat with the blue plastic ID that read *David Sloane*, MD Yeah, that made it easier. He felt his breathing slow. 'You made the right decision. You'll see, it's for the best. And like I told you, I have every intention of seeing this through with you. Steve Kelleher just happens to be the best OB man I know. Why don't I give him a call right now, see if he—' He was already up, crossing the room, reaching for the phone.

'No, David.'

'Look, I know you don't want this to get around. But he's very discreet.'

'That's not it. I don't care how good he is, or how discreet. It's you I want.' Again, that quiet, firm tone.

Jesus, now he was sweating, like he used to watching his old man sliding into a binge, waiting for the other shoe to drop. *You can stay under that bed as long as you want,*

178

*Davey. All night if you like. But sooner or later you're gonna hafta come out, and I'll be waitin' for you when you do. Then I'm gonna show you what God gave me this good right hand for.*

*Sure, you want me,* he thought. *Like Uncle Sam would if I didn't stay a step ahead all the time. Like the Grim Reaper. Like my old man.*

'You're drunk,' he told her.

She laughed then, just once, a hollow sound, like a lonesome note on a bagpipe. 'I wish I were. Honest to God I do.'

'Rachel, listen . . .'

'No, *you* listen.' She stood up, eyes blazing, the hurt in them so bright he had to look away. 'You said it would be as easy as the dentist, like pulling a tooth. I just want you to—' her voice broke a little, then steadied, 'to know, that's all. What it is really like. What we are really doing.'

David suddenly was remembering his father kicking the shit out of his mother. *Not the baby, Hal,* she was screaming. *Please, not the baby.* At the time, he hadn't understood, but later he did. She'd been three months pregnant, and she lost the baby.

Shit, why was she making him remember all that? And his headache, Christ, he needed some Tylenol, or maybe something stronger.

Then anger swept through him, taking hold of him, making him stagger a little.

'You're out of your fucking mind, babe. How do I even know it's my kid? How do I know how many guys you been doing it with?' He heard the viciousness in his voice, and a part of him, some part that was standing back from all this, was shocked to realize he sounded just like the old man.

He saw her turn pale, the color of candle wax, and for a moment he thought she might pass out. But she just held on, tightly gripping the chair. Jesus, he had to give it to her. She was hanging in there.

Seeing the anguish on her face, he felt a moment's shame. She was not, he realized, doing this to get back at

179

him. He had a moment's crazy urge to take her in his arms, tell her anything she wanted to hear.

'It's yours,' she said. 'Ours. This baby – or whatever you want to call it – we made it together. I didn't want it any more than you did, but now it's a fact. So going for an abortion by myself, as if it were some minor procedure, well . . . it would cheapen everything. How I feel about myself, life, even about being a doctor. If this little new life doesn't matter, then what does? So, David, it has to be this way. I've thought about it, and it's the *only* way. For me. If I'm to live with it.'

Rachel sat back, hands clenched in her lap, thinking how David probably hated her right now, for wreaking some kind of twisted vengeance on him.

When you got down to it, though, it didn't really matter what he believed. Whatever they had been to each other (and she knew now it was far less than she had imagined) was over. Nothing could ever again exist between them.

But first, they still had to see this through, she and David. Their baby deserved that much. A decent burial, not an unmarked grave with no-one to mourn its brief life and nothing to mark its passing.

No, she would not anesthetize this, pretend it was nothing. Lie back while some stranger humming along to the Muzak scraped her baby out like offal from a gutted fish. She felt shame, and David had to also; or afterwards, how could she forgive herself?

But she saw now how much she had underestimated David. There was something about him like a wild animal with its leg caught in a steel trap – a creature who knew that the only way out was to chew the leg off. He stood there at the far end of the living room, his handsome face haggard, his normally perfect, blow-dried hair disheveled in damp tangles that had dribbled dark spots of wetness over the collar and shoulders of his Lacoste shirt.

The expression on his face – she had never seen it on him before. And then it dawned on her: *He's scared shitless.*

180

'No.' His mouth formed the word before the cracked sound of his voice emerged. 'It's . . . obscene. You must be crazy to think I would do that to my own—' He broke off, choking himself back.

'Your own what, David?' *Say it, dammit, at least say it.*

'Nothing.' He pulled out a handkerchief and mopped his forehead. He had never felt so panicky, not even during the most life-threatening surgery. 'Look, you can just forget about it, this macabre little scheme of yours. I'm an MD, not a fucking shrink. That's what you need, baby. Yeah. You've really gone over the edge this time.'

'Maybe,' she said. 'But that doesn't change anything. We're still in this together, one way or another.'

'What do you mean?' His eyes were narrowed, suspicious.

'I mean that if you won't perform the abortion, there won't be one. I'll have the baby.'

'Are you *threatening* me?'

'No.' And she meant that too. 'I'm just telling you what's possible for me. What choices I can live with. Having your friend Kelleher do a nice neat D and C on me isn't one of them.'

Rachel felt cold, and thought this was what being dead would be like if you could feel it. She felt scared too.

She looked at David, and thought: *You're not half the man my father is. If he were in your place, he would not have done this to my mother. He would not have made her suffer like this.*

Now David was backing away, blindly, frantically. His foot caught one leg of a bar stool, and it toppled over, thudding on to the floor. He bent to pick it up, his long frame moving in jerks like an angled crane.

Then he was straightening, staring at her with wild eyes, white rims showing all the way around his irises. He looked as if he had realized he could chew his leg off and he'd still be just as hopelessly trapped.

David sagged against some cartons, and closed his eyes, his face bleached of color.

181

'All right,' he said. 'Dammit, you win. But I don't know just what it is you think you're getting out of this obscene little horror show of yours. I hope *you* do. I hope to Christ you do.'

Rachel felt very heavy, her head spinning. She *was* drunk. She just hadn't realized it before.

She had won. She was supposed to feel good, triumphant at least. But all she felt was this cold, dead numbness inside. The important thing now, she realized, was just to hang on, get through this one way or another.

The next hour was a blur.

David, on the phone with Kelleher, explaining in a low tight voice, asking for the key to his office. Then their leaving, the silent ride down in the elevator. Outside, rain on her face, pricking her scalp. Cold. She kept shivering, even in the overheated taxi.

Only when they arrived at Kelleher's office, a half-number address tucked alongside an ivy-covered brownstone off lower Fifth Avenue, did what they were doing pierce her like a knife. When David unlocked the door and flipped on the lights, when she saw the bright waiting room with its cozy furniture and Currier and Ives prints, and the Christmas tree on a table in the corner decorated with wooden angels and tartan bows.

*I'll never see my baby. I'll never hold it in my arms.*

Then the examining room, pretty pastel curtains, a border of storks stenciled around the ceiling. And pictures. Hundreds of them it seemed. Snapshots. Stuck up on a big bulletin board with colored pushpins. Pictures of all the babies Kelleher had delivered.

A cry rose in her, blocking her windpipe so for an instant she couldn't breathe. She was being cheated, and worse, she was doing it to herself. The room blurred in a wash of tears.

*I can't fall apart now*, she thought. *Later. When it's over. But, oh dear God, I know I'll never stop seeing them. All those babies. Those sweet little babies.*

There was a little curtained-off alcove at one end of the

examining room, and a soft cotton gown folded on the white cane chair in the corner. Rachel changed as quickly as she could, but her hands were trembling; her fingers, as she fumbled with the buttons on her dress, felt like sticks of wood.

A full-length mirror was screwed into the wall opposite the chair. Dressed now in the flimsy gown that tied at the back, Rachel stood still a moment, examining her reflection. She saw a face that wasn't hers, drawn and ghastly white, with eyes sunken like thumb-print impressions in a crude clay sculpture. Even her body seemed a stranger's, breasts heavy, swollen, the dark nipples visible through the thin cotton. Her stomach gently rounded, and smooth on either side where her pelvis had jutted. She brought her hands to her belly, stroking it tenderly, eyes filming over with fresh tears.

'I'm sorry,' she whispered. 'I'm so sorry.'

The cold, dead feeling was gone, and a pain blazed in her chest. *I won't forget you, baby*.

David was ready, Rachel saw, when she emerged from behind the curtain. Scrubbed, gloved, the instruments laid out on a metal tray.

She hiked herself up on to the business end of the examining table, feeling its paper covering cold and stiff against her bare behind, reminding her of her mother, oddly enough. *You be sure, extra sure, to cover the lid before you sit down. You just don't know the kind of germs you can catch in public bathrooms*.

Rachel was torn between a sob, and an insane urge to giggle. She kept her eyes carefully averted from David's. If she looked at him, if she looked at what he was holding now in his right hand, she might scream or go crazy.

'It's not too late.' David's voice floated past her ear. 'We don't have to go through with it. I can call Steve back, tell him to come over.'

His words shocking her back to reason, as if a bucket of icy water had been dashed over her.

'No,' she said. 'Do it.'

183

Spine held stiff as a yardstick, she lowered herself on to her back, and forced her shivering legs apart. Now the cold shock of the stirrups against her bare feet. Her flesh shrank in anticipation of David's touch.

But when Rachel looked down the tunnel of her hiked legs and saw what was coming, she very nearly changed her mind.

David. His face hovering between the peaks of her knees like a ghost moon in a cold sky, light flashing off the steel instrument in his hand. A chilling premonition swept over her: *It's like a marriage, isn't it? We'll be bound by this the rest of our lives.*

And then she knew it was too late.

They had gone beyond the point of turning back.

At the first cold bite of the speculum, Rachel jammed her fist in her mouth to keep from screaming.

# 6

Manon was taking forever to die.

Sylvie shifted in her seat, vaguely annoyed at the lamenting duet, the conductor waving his baton like a madman. She wished the curtain would fall. Strange. Normally she loved being here, at the Metropolitan. Seated beside Gerald in their parterre center box, a stone's throw above the elegant crowd in the orchestra seats, and directly facing the stage, the best view in the house. Like a king and queen presiding over their court, which in a way they were. Heavens, how many functions and meetings had they attended, dinners, parties she herself had given, starting way back when it was still on Broadway and Thirty-eighth. And every one of those years Gerald's bank a Grand Leadership contributor.

But tonight she felt restless. Des Grieux, sung by an Italian tenor she'd never heard of, looked like a trussed turkey in his nineteenth-century finery, and worse, sounded as if he had a cold. And the diva, who was supposed to be a ravishing fifteen-year-old beauty, had to be at least fifty and was big as a horse. Really, it was quite a feat he could even support her expiring body in his arms.

Sylvie placed her hand on Gerald's arm. For some reason there was no-one in the dimly lit box tonight except for the two of them. But Gerald probably hadn't even noticed. He should have been restless too, in his starched collar and too-tight tuxedo he insisted still fit him perfectly, but in the amber backlit glow of the stage lights, she caught the rapt expression on his face. His head tilted back, eyes half-closed, lips silently mouthing the libretto. He was not seeing Manon's straining seams, or hearing the tenor's

185

raspiness. For Gerald, there was only Puccini's tender soaring music.

Darling Gerald. Wasn't that one of the reasons she loved him so? His talent for seeing only the good, not what was really there. The way he saw in her only beauty and loyalty. Over all these years he had remained as blind to her sins as Des Grieux to Manon's.

Sylvie groped for his hand now, and felt it fold about hers, warm and reassuring. Did he look more tired than usual? She felt a bit anxious. Or was she just imagining? It pained her to compare the picture of Gerald she carried in her mind – the elegant and energetic bank president she had married – with the stooped, white-haired man she had watched tonight inching down the stairs one by one, gripping the banister tightly for support.

*He's seventy-six,* she thought, irritable with herself. *Of course he's slowed down a bit. But he's as healthy as ever.*

Still, Sylvie couldn't ward off the shiver that slid down her spine, watching Manon die.

*Without him,* she thought, *I couldn't survive. My protector, my dearest friend.*

Not her lover anymore; they had not been together as man and wife in years. Since Gerald's last operation, he had somehow been unable to . . .

But that didn't matter. She felt closer to him now than ever. Safe and beloved. When they strolled in Riverside Park, her arm tucked in his, or just sat like this, hand in hand, she felt a closeness deeper than she had in all their years of lovemaking.

Since he had retired as chairman at Mercantile, they had been together constantly. The cold months in Palm Beach, reading novels side by side, playing two-handed bridge on the pool deck while Callas serenaded them on the stereo. And that trip to Venice last spring – how overflowing with marvelous memories! – staying in the same suite at the Gritti where they'd honeymooned nearly thirty years before.

Sylvie thought of the trip they'd planned for next

month, cruising around Bora Bora and Tahiti. She relaxed a little. *Yes, just what he needs. The sea air will do him good, and that whole Gauguin paradise put some color back into him, make his eyes sparkle.*

Now the curtain was falling, accompanied by a wave of applause, cresting in some scattered cheers of 'BRAVO. BRAVISSIMO.' Seconds later the principals were trooping out, looking a bit outlandish in their costumes, cut off from their scenic world, spotlighted now against the crimson velvet, bowing low, the fat diva lowest of all, bobbling a little as she pulled herself up.

Then the lights. Chandeliers lowered majestically, magically, at the end of brass rods from the vast dome of the ceiling, starbursts of twinkling crystal.

Below, people were starting to stand, some still applauding. Men in velvet jackets and tuxedos, and women in long gowns, silks and satins and stiff brocades, their glossy furs draped casually over the backs of their seats. Sylvie heard her mama's voice in her head as if she were in the next chair. *A real lady wears a cloth coat as if it were her best mink, and tosses her mink about as if it were cloth.* If only she could be here now, see Sylvie's own Russian sable hanging in the anteroom. Mama, with her one good black coat, relined again and again over the years.

Mama would have loved the jewels, too, Sylvie thought. Marvelous pieces winking off throats and wrists and fingers and earlobes – Bulgari, Cartier, Van Cleef & Arpels. Dazzling.

Sylvie fingered the necklace about her own throat. Beautiful old cabachon emeralds set in filigreed eighteen-carat gold, designed forty years ago by the legendary Jeanne Toussaint of Cartier's in Paris. Gerald's gift on her last birthday. They matched her eyes, he'd said, never mentioning the fortune they must have cost. And how perfectly they went with the Schiaparelli gown she was wearing now, a simple black panne velvet sheath, elegant and timeless as the emeralds for which it served as backdrop.

Sylvie rose, and moved toward the back of the box. It was

a moment before she realized Gerald wasn't beside her, holding the door open for her as he invariably did. She turned back, saw him still seated. Dear God, how tired he looked! Her heart bumped up into her throat.

Then Sylvie quickly caught herself. It was late, and such a long evening, four interminable acts, two intermissions, naturally he was tired. Who wouldn't be? Still . . .

'Gerald,' she inquired gently, 'are you feeling all right?'

He straightened his shoulders a little, and managed a weak smile. Had he looked this pale earlier in the evening?

'Nothing to worry about, my dear. Just a touch of indigestion, I think. Ate a bit too much as usual.' He winced. 'You know, I've really been thinking it's time to take off a few pounds. If my waistband gets any tighter, I won't be able to sit down.'

She knew he was trying to put her at ease by making a joke, but the nagging worry she felt was hanging on. She found herself remembering his second heart attack, so much worse than the time before, Gerald in New York Hospital, tubes running into his arm, his nose, a catheter down his leg, wires taped to his chest. A monitor beeping over his bed, recording each heartbeat. As if that spiky green electronic line were the only thing to show he was still alive.

And all those medical students, interns, residents, lab technicians, cardiologists trotting in and out, never giving him a moment's rest. Scaring her to death with their long, grave looks and their hard-to-understand explanations. In the end, she and Gerald had agreed to the pacemaker.

*But he's fine now. Before we came up from Florida, the specialist tested everything. One hundred per cent, he said. I'm overreacting as usual.*

'Why don't you rest here a bit?' she said, laying her hand lightly on him, shocked by his frailty, the padded shoulder of his jacket forming a little tent over the knob of bone where flesh had been. 'No sense rushing out until the crowd thins a bit. I'll get you something to drink, some soda from the bar?'

He sighed. 'Yes, that's it. Something to settle my stomach, then I'll be good as new. You don't mind, do you? I'd get it myself, but . . .' His voice trailed off.

'Of course I don't mind,' she said with forced cheer.

Then he startled her by saying out of the blue, 'I was just thinking about Rachel. When she was eight, that first summer she went to camp. Do you remember? We drove her up there, and all the other little girls were clinging to their parents and carrying on like it was the end of the world. And our Rachel said, "They're crying because their mommies and daddies are sad. You're sad, too. But I'm not going to cry. I'm too big for that." '

'I remember,' Sylvie said softly. In her mind she saw Rachel reflected in the rearview mirror of Gerald's Bentley, a little girl in a red-checked blouse and blue pedal pushers solemnly waving goodbye. Sylvie felt her heart wrench.

Her thoughts flew back to yesterday afternoon, the shock of Rachel confessing she was pregnant. Oh, how she had longed to soothe Rachel's pain! To help her somehow.

*Should I have advised her?* Sylvie wondered. *My own grandchild, a baby after all these years, how wonderful it could be!*

Yet she had concealed her own desire from Rachel. *Who am I to say? If she only knew how when I was pregnant I prayed for a miscarriage. How I dreaded giving birth to Nikos's child.*

*Yes,* Sylvie thought sorrowfully, *I know what it's like to carry a baby you don't want. I wouldn't wish that on Rachel, no matter how much I might want it.*

No, she must think only of what was best for Rachel. She prayed that Rachel would do what was right . . . for herself. And she thanked God that Rachel had confided in her. She knew her daughter didn't feel as close to her as she did to Gerald, but now they would share this bond. Sylvie felt a small burst of triumph: *You see, she does need me, after all.*

Tomorrow morning, first thing, she would call Rachel,

find out what she had decided, offer comfort if she could. But she must be careful not to let Gerald find out. He would be so stricken.

Gerald's voice now broke into Sylvie's thoughts: 'I asked her to come with us tonight – you know how she's always loved *Manon*. But she said she had to be at the hospital.' He chuckled softly. 'I wanted so much for Rachel, the moon and more, but now that she's out there getting it, too busy for anything else, I only want to see more of her!'

Sylvie thought of another reason Rachel might have decided not to come tonight. But she said nothing, only tightened her hand on the doorknob of the anteroom.

She looked at Gerald slumped in the chair before her, the man she had lived with and loved all these years. She felt a rush of emotion that tightened her throat.

'Gerald?' She watched him turn to look up at her with a questioning smile, his shoulders straightening a bit. 'I love you.'

She was aware that she was blushing, and felt a little foolish for it – she, a middle-aged woman carrying on like a young girl in love for the first time! It was so seldom either of them spoke those words aloud, and never in public.

Gerald's gaze fixed on her, his eyes glistening. Then he chuckled. 'Mr Puccini,' he said. 'No matter how often I see *Manon*, it affects me every time. You too, I see.'

Her heart lifted. Perhaps she *had* made the right choice all those years ago. Oh yes, maybe so.

'Your soda,' she reminded him. 'I'll be right back.'

The corridor, with its cranberry velvet walls, was jammed with people winding their way toward the wedding-cake stairs that led down to the main lobby. Outside, she knew, beyond the fountain, a long line of limousines two deep was idling, while just outside the glass doors of the main lobby, chauffeurs were in position, outfitted with oversized umbrellas to shelter their masters and mistresses from the hard rain that had been pelting the city since afternoon.

190

Sylvie edged past a tall, dark-haired woman dressed in a black velvet miniskirt and gold-sequined top who was chattering in French to her escort. Everywhere she turned, bright voices, laughter. They all seemed to be speaking a foreign language, their words gibberish to her ears.

Sylvie found herself smiling, nodding in the direction of Adeline Vanderhoff, a woman she knew slightly from the Harmonic Club. She hoped Adeline wouldn't try to talk to her. Sylvie felt a little ill herself, suffocated by the crush of furs, the mingled scents of expensive perfume.

Emerging into the parterre lobby, where the crowd was spilling down the staircase, Sylvie saw with relief that the bar had not yet closed. No-one waiting in line either; they all wanted to get home.

And that's where she and Gerald too would be in a few minutes, with Emilio waiting out there to drive them home. Then she'd see Gerald safely to bed, maybe with a glass of warm milk. Maybe they'd watch a little TV; they might still catch the late news. Gerald had mentioned that Nixon was holding a press conference today, and was hoping that this new president was going to do something momentous to kick up the economy. Sylvie pretended to share Gerald's enthusiasm for Nixon, but secretly she didn't trust him. He reminded her of one of those shifty-eyed men advertising cars on late-night TV.

'Sylvie? Is that you?'

The voice, masculine and slightly accented, startled her so that she nearly spilled the brimming glass of club soda she had just picked up from the bar.

*No, it can't be—*

Then she turned and saw that it was, and felt her heart start pounding. There he stood, gray now, and a little stocky too, but otherwise hardly changed. Liquid black eyes in a face by van Gogh, blunt and earthy; tight black curls threaded with iron.

Nikos.

Could it be? How was it possible?

More than twenty long full years had gone by. Never a

191

hint of him. She had wondered, yes, but assumed . . . what? That he was dead, or had moved far away.

Or had those been simply her hopes? So that her crime would be hidden along with him, forgotten, no forwarding address.

And now here he was.

Walking toward her with short powerful strides, the crowd melting away on either side. His old limp scarcely noticeable now.

Sylvie panicked. *I can't hide, or pretend not to know him. Oh God, what will I say?*

'Sylvie! Incredible. Still as beautiful as ever. Poor Regina, she has not aged so well, but her voice is in its prime still. Did you enjoy *Manon* tonight?'

The accent was the same, but his English was better; he sounded poised, authoritative. Nikos clearly had made something of himself. Sylvie noted the superb double-breasted suit he was wearing. And his tie, an Hermès, with a gold and onyx tiepin and cuff links to match.

Could he see the effect he was having on her? She felt faint, as if all these years had never happened, as if all over again he was offering her a cigarette on the terrace outside her parlor.

'Oh yes, very much,' she said. Incredible, how easy to say the proper things even with her heart beating like a bird trapped in her chest.

'My wife, she would so have enjoyed tonight's performance.'

*There, you see. He's married, probably a half-dozen children too, and maybe even grandchildren. So why are you standing here sweating like an escaped convict treed by bloodhounds. He couldn't possibly know about Rose.*

'A pity she couldn't come then,' Sylvie murmured.

'Yes.' His dark eyes clouded over. 'Barbara died last year.'

'Oh, I'm so sorry.' Sylvie felt awkward consoling him. Her concern for Gerald came rushing back. She had to excuse herself. But she seemed unable to move.

192

'And your husband?' Nikos was inquiring. 'He is here?'

'Oh yes. As a matter of fact, he's waiting for me now. So if you'll excuse—'

Nikos placed a hand lightly against her arm. 'It's been such a long time, surely you have another minute to spare. For an old friend.'

Sylvie stared at him, feeling as if she had been burned where he'd touched her. For a terrible instant, she was sure he *did* know about Rose, and was torturing her by pretending not to.

*Smile. Act natural.*

'Why, of *course*,' she trilled a little too brightly. 'How thoughtless of me. Here I was thinking how well you look, and I forgot to ask how you've been.'

'Very well, thank you. The gods of fortune have been kind in most respects. The work is good. Enough to keep me from sitting about brooding in an empty house.' He cupped her elbow, steering her closer to the wall, out of the flow of traffic. 'Cigarette?'

Sylvie felt heat climb up her neck, again remembering the hot, sweet night when he had first kissed her. She shook her head, and watched him pull a slim gold case from his breast pocket, and withdraw a cigarette.

'What sort of work is it you do?' she inquired, trying to sound politely friendly. Obviously he no longer was a handyman.

He amused her then by lighting his cigarette, rather crudely, by tearing a match from a book and striking it with his thumbnail. She guessed the gold cigarette case had been a gift from his late wife.

'I have my own construction company now. At the moment we're putting up some apartment houses in Brighton Beach. I hope to have them finished by September, God and the weather willing.'

Sylvie was stunned. 'That's you? *You* own Anteros Construction?'

Gerald's bank had underwritten that project. She remembered him mentioning it, saying how smart it was building up in an area like that, right on the ocean and yet accessible with one fare to the City.

Nikos shrugged, a smile curling his full lips. 'One thing I have learned, the bigger your company, the more it owns you rather than the other way around. I think your husband would agree, no?'

Sylvie laughed. 'Yes. How did you know? It's one of Gerald's favorite complaints.'

'I have always admired him, you know.' Nikos drew in on his cigarette, letting a thin curl of smoke drift from his nostrils. 'A remarkable man. Smart . . . and in ways of the heart too.' He tapped his chest.

Sylvie felt herself growing warm again. Why was he doing this? He had every reason to hate Gerald. It didn't make sense unless he was mocking her somehow.

'Yes,' she answered stiffly. 'Look, I really must—'

But Nikos seemed unaware of her discomfort. 'You know, he did me a great favor when he threw me out. If he hadn't forced me, I might never have gotten started on my own. Or the—' He stopped abruptly, as if catching himself from revealing something he hadn't intended to. He covered the awkward moment with his brilliant smile. 'But I see I am selfish, keeping you so long.'

'It's all right,' she said, hoping he wouldn't see how relieved she was. She looked down at the glass of club soda growing warm in her hand. 'But I'm afraid I'll have to replace this. It looks as if it's gone flat.'

'Allow me.' Before she could protest, he had snatched the glass from her hand and was making his way toward the bar. But the gray-haired man behind the counter was shaking his head, saying he was closed.

Sylvie watched, embarrassed, as Nikos pulled a bill from his wallet and handed it over the counter. And from the eager look on the bartender's face, she guessed it to be a large one. Nikos returned a moment later carrying a fresh glass of soda with ice in it.

'You shouldn't have done that,' she said.

Nikos shrugged again. 'Let's just say I owe your husband a debt. Consider this a small partial repayment.'

Sylvie couldn't imagine why Nikos should feel grateful to Gerald, but she heard only sincerity in his voice. Perhaps it had something to do with the bank's involvement in the Brighton Beach project.

'Thank you, in that case,' she said. She put out her free hand, and it was instantly enveloped by his huge and calloused one. 'Goodbye. It was nice seeing you again.'

She was turning to go when Nikos touched her shoulder. 'Wait. One more thing. You never told me. About your daughter. She is well?'

For one terrible instant, Sylvie thought he meant Rose. *His* child. Her heart felt as if a fist had closed about it, forcing the blood out. Slowly, she turned to face him, struggling to hold on to her composure.

'Rachel is fine,' she said. Gerald must have mentioned Rachel to Nikos. That was it. Nikos was just being polite.

*But now he must see something is wrong,* she thought, feeling desperate. *Look how his eyes are narrowing, his face hard all of a sudden.*

Sylvie leaped in to cover the awkwardness. 'You must have children of your own,' she said quickly.

'No.' Nikos shook his head regretfully. 'No children.' His cigarette had burned down to the filter, and he put it out in the tall metal ashtray on the floor beside him without seeming to be in any particular hurry. 'Barbara and I wanted children. Very much. And each time she became pregnant, we hoped that this time . . . but it wasn't meant to be, I suppose.'

'I'm sorry,' Sylvie told him. Hadn't she said that already? She couldn't remember. She felt paralyzed, her mind going around and around.

Nikos bent close then, so close she could smell the nicotine on his breath. 'Sylvie, I know,' he said quietly.

He was not acknowledging her expression of sympathy. That was a statement all its own. Panic crashed through

195

her, rocking her off balance. She felt something wet seeping through her dress. Gerald's soda. It had tipped, and some had spilled down her front.

Now her mind was reeling faster. *He knows he knows he knows* . . .

'What do you know?' she asked, pinning a smile of coquettish innocence on her face that even without a mirror she knew would fool no-one.

'I suspected it for a long time,' he said. 'You gave birth to a child nine months after you and I—'

'No,' she stopped him, taking a jerky step backwards, more liquid splashing down the front of her dress. 'You're mistaken.'

'Am I? There was a time I hoped I was, I'm ashamed to say.'

'This is insane,' she hissed. 'I won't listen to another minute of this.' But his hand was circling her wrist now like a steel bracelet. Only it was his flesh that burned, her arm that was icy cold. Tears welled in her eyes. 'Please, I must get back to Gerald. He'll be wondering what's kept me so long.'

'Sylvie, I'm not trying to hurt you. You must believe that. I want only one thing. For you to say it, just *say* it. Only that. Give me that much. I never asked before, out of respect for Barbara. Gerald too. And I swear if you say it's true, I'll leave you alone. I won't ever come near—'

Sylvie wrenched away, unable to bear it a second longer, the naked hunger in his dark eyes, knowing as she now did that she had betrayed Nikos as well as Gerald.

She ran, for once not caring how she looked, or who saw. Gerald. She must get back to him. Oh dear God, it would kill him if he found out. He must never know.

'Sylvie!' Nikos was calling out to her. 'Wait!'

Sylvie could feel her face burning, imagining people were staring, gossiping.

*Please,* she wanted to shout, *please leave me alone*.

But even as she ran along the curved parterre wall with the soda slopping over her knuckles, as she ducked through the door to their box, the sound of her heart rushing in her ears like a train inside a tunnel, she knew it wasn't really Nikos she was running from but her own self, the terrible truth.

*Rose . . .*

# 7

Rose, worming herself into the packed subway car, groped for the support handle. She teetered as the train lurched forward, bodies all around surging against her. Thank heaven, at least she was going in the right direction. Home.

She closed her eyes, imagining she was there already. Climbing up the stairs, four steep flights, slowly, slowly, so she could enjoy the anticipation. Not even knowing Nonnie would be there could spoil the delicious hope that a letter might be waiting for her – a letter from Brian.

*Please, God, this time let there be one. It's been so long, two whole months, and I've been so patient. Just one letter, a postcard, anything. I know he's not dead, because his mom and dad get letters. There has to be a good reason I haven't gotten one.*

But what if that was the reason, because he didn't love her anymore?

Rose felt herself begin to sweat, a coin of clamminess between her breasts that was spreading in a circle like a drop of water on a blotter, making her armpits soggy, sticking the back of her blouse to her shoulder blades under her thick wool coat. But at the same time in her stomach she felt an icy lump of fear. *Please . . . oh please let there be a letter this time . . .*

Then she became aware that a body wedged against her back was moving. A male body that so reeked of cigarettes she could smell it from behind was undulating against her. Dear Jesus, even through the thickness of her coat she could *feel* him, his hardness. Anger and loathing boiled up inside her.

198

She tried squirming away, but she was jammed in on all sides, and meanwhile he only pressed closer. She couldn't even turn and see who he was, dammit. *Pervert, creep, he probably makes obscene phone calls to little girls.*

Then Rose thought of the book tucked under her arm, the bound 1967 *Law Review* volume. She angled it downward, and brought her elbow back in a knifing motion, the heavy book giving the blow added weight. She felt it connect, and heard a surprised grunt. The pressure against her back abruptly eased.

Then they were jerking to a stop, doors sliding open, the conductor bawling, 'De Kalb Avenue, next stop Atlantic!' Passengers squirmed out and then even more shoved themselves in. Rose had an urge to charge between them and fling herself free out on to the platform. The next train probably wouldn't be as crowded, and at least she'd be rid of the pervert.

But no. She gritted her teeth and hung on. She had to get home. To Brian's letter. Yes, today there would be one, she was sure of it. Maybe several, a whole bunch of them, all the letters he'd have sent her, which had somehow gotten misdirected, or stuck in the wrong post office somehow.

'Just this one thing, God,' she whispered under her breath, her prayer drowned out by the clackety roar of the train. 'And for every letter I'll say a dozen rosaries. And I won't kneel on the carpet. I'll do it on the bathroom floor, where it's hard and cold. And I'll start going to Confession again . . . and First Friday Mass . . .'

Thinking of Mass soothed her, and that reminded her of something else that would make her feel good. The *Law Review* volume under her arm. It had already done good for her once this evening. She savored the thought of digging into it later on, the crackling of its stiff buckram spine, feeling the smooth freshness of its thick pages. She knew she wouldn't understand everything she read, but she loved the phrases, the rich cadence of Latin terms, and all those case summaries, dry at first glance, but if you read between the lines, used your imagination, they were like stories. Yes, it *was* a little like the feeling she got kneeling in church, reading her missal, hearing the priest's incantations.

Then she felt a pang of worry. What if he found out? Would Mr Griffin mind her borrowing this, and all the others before it? But she never took more than one at a time, and she always brought it back the following morning. Probably Mr Griffin wouldn't have noticed even if she'd kept a book for a week. But why borrow trouble? Working for him was the best of the three jobs she'd had so far – the first for an office supply wholesaler who went out of business, the second for a lawyer who wanted overtime to include bedtime – and she meant to keep this one.

No, of course he wouldn't mind. He was so nice, so unlike those other two, Walsh and then Delaney. And so energetic! Why, sometimes he made her feel like Dorothy, caught up in a tornado.

She pictured him now, pacing to and fro behind his desk, the phone receiver jammed against his ear, every now and then waving his arms or even thumping the desktop for emphasis. A big man in his forties, a bit heavy around the middle, but a good face. The face of a man you could count on, she thought. He reminded her of Brian that way, though they looked nothing alike. Mr Griffin made her think of an ex-prizefighter, but one who punched with words instead of his fists. His jacket would be tossed over the back of his chair, shirtsleeves rolled up over his forearms, and he was forever plowing his fingers through his thick tweedy-brown hair, making it stand up in spikes that made her feel oddly tender toward him, the way she did toward Brain's little brother Jason, who always had a cowlick. He smiled a lot, too – she liked that about him. And that time she'd sent the wrong letter to the Cressler Corporation, the one intended for Damon Chandler, about how old Mr Cressler's memory was getting a little foggy and he sometimes got his facts mixed up – God, what a disaster! She'd felt so terrible. But Mr Griffin had been nice about it, even though she could see he was upset. He told her it could have happened to anyone, that they'd straighten it out somehow.

Rose thought he could probably straighten out just about anything. She didn't have to listen to the coffee-kitchenette gossipers to know Max Griffin was a superb lawyer, the most admired in the firm, probably one of the best in the City. God, if she were sitting on a jury, for sure he'd win her over, and the rest of the people, too.

Monday she'd tell him about borrowing these books. Not that he'd mind, just . . . well, she felt so dumb and embarrassed. What if he laughed? What if he thought her notion of maybe someday becoming a lawyer was silly, a big joke?

At Avenue J, ten stops later, Rose got off. As she clattered down the grimy steps leading from the outdoor platform, then through the turnstile and now outside on to the street, her heart began to pound. A few blocks' walk, and she'd be home.

Rose suddenly wanted to prolong the short walk. What if she got home, and there was no letter from Brian? Today was Friday, and sometimes the postman came on Saturday, but more likely there'd be the whole long weekend and all day Monday before any more mail. And she had already waited so very long . . .

She stopped at the fruit seller's on East Fifteenth and bought six oranges, choosing each one with far more care than necessary. Then at the kosher bakery across the street, seduced by the mingled aromas of cinnamon and chocolate and rye, she bought a slice of apple strudel in addition to her usual loaf of pumpernickel. Old Mr Baumgarten, who always had a pencil perched behind his enormous ear, threw in a macaroon the way he'd been doing since she was a little girl, coming here with Nonnie.

'So, your grandmother, how is she feeling?'

'Fine,' Rose answered dutifully.

'And you, such a fine young lady now! Working all the

way in the City. So stylish, and wearing high heels!'

'I'm fine, too, Mr Baumgarten.'

Rose felt herself growing warm. If she had taken off her coat, the baker might have noticed the scorch mark on her blouse. She'd been in too much of a hurry ironing it this morning, and she had no other clean one to wear in its stead. Three good blouses in her whole wardrobe! And two nice wool skirts, which she alternated every other day. This gray one, and the navy pleated one from her old school uniform. Some stylish lady, ha!

*Well, someday,* she told herself, *I* will be. *When Brian comes home, when we're married. I'll be a professor's wife then, and then I won't ever have to feel shabby or inferior.*

*But what if he doesn't come home? . . .*

Suddenly, she felt dangerously close to tears. She thanked the baker and, snatching her white paper bag from his hands, fled from the store.

Now she was running, running, charging across Avenue J, half an eye to the traffic and ignoring the red light.

She had to get home, she had to see if today . . . oh please, God . . . today . . . let there be a letter . . .

The sidewalk seemed to pull at her, slow her down, her high heels catching now and then on the uneven pavement – *step on a crack, you break your mother's back* – and when she came to some girls playing hopscotch, she had to swerve out on to the street, darting in between two parked cars. The oranges in their plastic bag swung against her, bumping her hip as she hurried.

Then at last she was bounding up the three low steps into the vestibule of her building. Breathless, she hardly paused before pelting up the four flights to her floor. Her heart was smacking against her ribcage when she reached the landing.

*Brian, oh Brian, I miss you so. Your letters, that's all I have. They're everything.*

*Today, please, let it be today.*

Nonnie was sitting in front of the television. Mrs

202

Slatsky, who always left at six sharp, a good half hour before Rose got home, had switched on Nonnie's favorite, 'Gilligan's Island.' As Rose walked in, Nonnie barely glanced up.

'Dinner's in the oven,' she said offhandedly. 'That woman, she brought over a meatloaf.'

That woman. Jesus, Mrs Slatsky was still 'that woman' after how many years?

'Swimmin' in grease, I'll bet. She don't know how to cook, that woman, any more'n I could play first base for the Dodgers.'

One of Nonnie's good days, Rose observed. Her grandmother wasn't slurring much, and she was sitting up straight, eyes sharp and bright as cut glass. Mrs Slatsky must have washed her hair, and set it, too, though it wasn't too great a job. Still, that spared Rose from having to do it, and she felt grateful.

But never mind Mrs Slatsky. Where was today's mail? Rose looked on the oak hall stand where Slatsky usually left it after bringing it up in the afternoon. Nothing. Rose darted her eyes about the darkened living room. She didn't want to be too obvious. Nonnie mustn't catch on how much this meant to her.

'On the kitchen table,' Nonnie said, as if she'd read Rose's mind.

She looked up at her grandmother, surprised.

The frozen muscles in Nonnie's face had never really gone back to normal after her stroke, and now she was looking at Rose with that curious half-smirking expression that, even after all these months, still unnerved Rose. She saw that her grandmother was wearing the quilted pink bathrobe Clare had sent her for her birthday last month. Her hands, lying limply in her sunken lap, reminded Rose of those awful curled chicken feet the butcher gave away for soup.

Saying nothing, Rose went into the kitchen. There, on the table, next to the toaster, two letters and a postcard.

Her heart hammering, she picked up the first envelope

203

and turned it over. Her hand was trembling, her mouth dry. But it was only from Clare. The other a flyer advertising a new shopping mall that was opening in Canarsie.

The postcard was from Molly Quinn, now living in Vancouver. Molly's boyfriend had decided to leave the country rather than be drafted, and Molly had gone too.

Rose's heart sank. No letter, nothing from Brian. *No, not now . . . what if maybe not ever . . .*

Oh God, how would she keep getting up every morning, how would she live? How would she push herself through another day? Another hour even?

She put her head down on the Formica, too crushed even for tears.

Then she tried to imagine that Brian was in the next room – her favorite way of tricking herself into missing him less – that any second he would come strolling in and rumple her hair, and kid her about the law book she'd lugged home. Brian . . .

But now she couldn't believe it, it wasn't working, not even a little bit. The feel of his hand against her skin, she couldn't summon it, however hard she tried. And his smell. What did he smell like?

Smell. She sniffed. Smoke hung in the air, something was burning. She jerked upright. Mrs Slatsky's meatloaf!

Suddenly, it struck her as funny. Here she was, worrying over Brian, and all the while life just steamrollered on, subway perverts, Nonnie, burned meatloaf, and all. Yes, it *was* funny. She began to laugh. Helplessly, with tears rolling down her cheeks and a knot the size of a fist in her gut.

# 8

'Why don't you have a seat, Miss . . . ah, *Dr* Rosenthal?'

Dr Dolenz smiled, but Rachel could see it was only a reassuring smile, not a really welcoming one. His manner made her think of her father, a bit formal, yet eager to please. And this Park Avenue consulting room with its massive gleaming desk and oak filing cabinets fitted with brass, it reminded her of Daddy's office at the bank, how it had seemed to her when she was little, perched in the big leather wing chair opposite Daddy's desk, feeling swallowed up by the room's heavy dark authority, its leathery, smoky man smells. That's how she felt now, swallowed up, diminished, as she sank on to the massive sofa beneath a trio of English hunting prints.

She made herself sit very quietly, hands folded in her lap, but her heart was racing. What would the results of her X ray show? Six weeks since the abortion, and she was still not free of it . . . and maybe never would be.

Silently, she pleaded with him: *Please, if it's as bad as the plastic smile on your face, then I don't want to hear it, I don't want to know . . .*

She thought back to how sick she'd been those first days after the abortion . . . burning up with fever, even delirious at times. The flu, she'd thought at first, so much of it going around. Like an arrogant fool, she had dismissed David's offer to put her in a taxi. Six blocks she had wandered, numbly, drunkenly, in the rain until finally she sobered up . . . or wised up . . . enough to hail a cab. By the time she got home, she was drenched, shivering with cold, her teeth chattering.

Three days the fever had stayed high. She knew it

couldn't be just the flu. There was the pain in her abdomen, like surgical clamps. Kay finally had convinced her to come here.

Dr Morton Dolenz. She stared at him now, a dark man with hairy arms too long for his body, and thick features. But despite his simian appearance, he'd been surprisingly gentle. He had diagnosed it as severe pelvic inflammatory disease. Bad, he'd said, but not bad enough to require hospitalization. Oh yes, she knew about PID. How it wouldn't kill you, but it could scar you . . . inside.

He had given her ampicillin, one gram four times a day. Almost immediately, she got better. Then, a month later, he had suggested the hysterosalpingograph to see if there was scarring in her Fallopian tubes, and if so, how extensive. He made an appointment for her with a radiologist, then scribbled a prescription for morphine – they injected radioactive dye into your tubes, he told her, and there would be some pain.

Now, a week later, here he was rising from his chair, undoing the clasp on a large manila envelope, pulling out films.

'I don't believe there's any point in beating around the bush with you, Doctor,' he said. 'Why don't you have a look at these with me, and I'll show you what I mean.'

She watched him clip the films to a lightbox on the wall. Slowly she rose to join him, a pulse in her throat jumping wildly, her stomach clenched.

He pointed on the films to two grayish areas where the dye had not penetrated. 'As you can see, there's rather extensive scarring in both tubes. This would make conception . . . well, let's just say . . . unlikely. At some point in the future you might wish to consider surgery. But—' he shrugged, 'as you probably know, the results in that field have been far from promising.'

*Did he mean no children? Ever? No . . . that can't be . . . oh God, no . . .*

Rachel felt lightheaded, as if somehow she had a fever again. She stared at Dolenz, riveted by a large mole on his neck from which three stiff hairs sprouted. She had to get away from those X rays with their murky patches, and from whatever it was he was saying. So she stared at the mole, wondering why a man with the power to wipe out a whole part of her life hadn't thought to snip those disgusting hairs.

'I'm sorry,' he went on, 'I wish I could have been more encouraging. But in these cases I always find it's best to be direct . . . so as not to . . . ah, raise expectations. Then you know which cards you're holding, so to speak. You can always adopt, that is, if your husband—'

Rachel extended her hand in a brisk handshake, thanking him, putting an end to his fumbling attempts to brighten her bleak future.

She made it outside, holding herself very erect, spine stiff, chin thrust up, as if by remaining totally vertical she might somehow prevent this hotness in her chest from spilling over. Stopping only for traffic lights, she walked the sixty blocks downtown to her apartment like a zombie, not slowing even when she felt blisters forming on her heels, or when rain began pelting her. Shortly past dark, her hair in wet tangles, her coat nearly soaked through, she reached home.

She slumped down in the wicker chair in the living room, not bothering to take off her sodden coat. Now she felt cold. But dry clothes or any number of blankets, she knew, wouldn't take away this coldness, like a lump of ice in her stomach.

*No children . . . no babies . . . oh God, what have I done? . . .*

She clapped her hands over her face.

*Oh, if only Kay were here*, she thought, *she'd hug me and make me a pot of tea, and we'd talk and talk, until maybe I could find some way of dealing with this*.

But no Kay now, she was gone, three whole weeks already . . . Vietnam, a world away . . .

Rachel dropped her hands from her cheeks, curling them into fists. *Damn it, no, I will not sit here feeling sorry*

207

*for myself. All right, it happened, but I'm not dead . . .*
*Lord, how could I be? . . . not with this pain in me.*

*I have to get out of here*, she told herself. *A complete*
*change. Maybe I should be with Kay. They need doctors in*
*Vietnam. And right now Kay probably needs me as much I*
*need her. Then I could forget this, be someplace where I*
*won't have time to think about it . . .*

The phone was ringing.

Let it ring. She didn't want to talk to anyone now.
Whoever it was, let them call back tonight, tomorrow.

But the phone kept ringing, on and on and on . . .

Rachel dragged herself to her feet.

'Hello?'

'Rachel, thank goodness, I nearly gave up on you!'
Mama's voice, clear and bright, rang like crystal goblets
chiming against each other in a toast.

Hearing her silvery voice, Rachel felt suddenly so vulnerable, her misery shamefully exposed, like when she was
twelve and Mama came upon her crying because that creep
Will Sperry had torn up the valentine she'd given him at
school. Mama's sympathy had hurt her more than Will
Sperry's cruelty. No, she could not stand anyone pitying
her, and especially not Mama.

And Mama, think how she would suffer, too – no
grandchildren to baby-sit, to play with and spoil. No,
Mama was far better off not knowing. Rachel couldn't
bear the thought of her mother's misery on top of her
own.

'Sorry, I was just letting myself in,' Rachel lied. 'Listen,
Mama, can I call you back? This E R rotation keeps me on
the run all day long, and I'm really beat. What I'm really
dying to do right now is jump in the shower.'

'I'll only keep you a minute,' Sylvie chirped. 'It's about
tomorrow; we'll be sending the car for you at ten-thirty.
That should give us just enough time to get to Cold Spring
by twelve, even if there is a bit of traffic.'

What on earth? Cold Spring . . . tomorrow, at twelve?
Rachel wracked her brain to make sense of it.

'Oh dear, you haven't forgotten, have you?' Sylvie, sounding dismayed, seemed to read her mind.

'Of course not, how could I forget—' She paused, and in her consternation began to giggle.

'Mason. Mason Gold's wedding,' Mama prompted, laughing a little herself. 'Rachel, honestly, don't you think about anything but medicine these days? Now don't tell me you haven't something nice to wear or I'll pop over this very instant and kidnap you, march you straight over to Saks.'

Oh God, yes. The handwritten invitation she'd gotten last month – it had struck her as a bit weird, not the stiff formal card she would have expected. She'd been intrigued, and thought how nice it would be to see Mason again, and meet this girl he was marrying. Then she'd stuck the invitation in a drawer somewhere, and it had apparently slipped her mind. Lord, if Mama hadn't called she would have forgotten completely.

Yes, it would be great to see Mason again. Rachel winced, remembering Mason's twenty-first birthday party, and the two of them grappling clumsily on the carpet of his father's suite at the Pierre. And afterwards, how solicitous he'd been, so attentive, trying to help her get dressed, then guiding her out to the elevator as if she were a barely ambulatory elderly aunt. And tongue-tied, too, as if they were on a blind date, as if they hadn't known each other a million years. She was sure she'd lost him for ever as her friend, her childhood buddy. But then, back at the party, Rachel, in desperation, had grabbed a handful of chipped ice and stuck it down the back of his pants. Mason had yelped, danced around a bit, and called her a sneaky bitch, a brat, a rotten little creep. They'd been friends again ever since.

'. . . unless you'd rather make it Bloomingdale's,' Mama was going on.

Shopping? God, that's all she needed. No, she'd dig something out of her closet.

'Don't worry, Mama, I have the perfect outfit.'

'Ten-thirty then,' Sylvie said and sighed. 'And for heaven's sake, darling, *do* remember to wear stockings and a slip. The last time you wore a dress, I could see straight through it every time you stood with your back to the light.'

Rachel, feeling a prickle of exasperation, couldn't help wondering if this was the same Sylvie to whom she'd felt so close, so in tune, when she'd confided to her about being pregnant.

'Oh, Mama, please – yes, OK, fine, I'll wear a slip, ten slips, if that will make you happy.' Then the humor in it struck her, and she smiled. 'Well, at least you're easy to please. Mama, I know you'd die happy just so long as I always wore clean underwear, and put paper on strange toilet seats, and crossed my legs at the ankles whenever I sat down. Mama, I love you. And, Mama, listen, thanks for—'

For what? *Yes, for also knowing what really matters . . . for being with me and for me when it counts . . . when I need you.*

Sylvie had not fallen apart when Rachel told her about the abortion. No crying, or fussing, or bitter accusations. She had just hugged Rachel, crushing her almost, and said, 'I love you, darling, and I'll always love you, no matter what.'

'Thanks for what?' Sylvie asked.

A lump rose in Rachel's throat, but she swallowed it. 'Oh, nothing. Just thanks. See you tomorrow at ten-thirty.'

Mason Gold's wedding was not what Rachel had expected.

She had anticipated a synagogue smothered in lush floral arrangements, bridesmaids wearing matching chiffon dresses with puff sleeves, a bride and groom decked in white satin and tails like the ones on wedding cakes.

And here she sat with her parents, inside this big old greenhouse on top of a grassy hill overlooking the

Hudson, watching two hippies promise to love, honor, but not obey each other. Mason Gold a hippie! Unbelievable. Out of sight.

True, she hadn't seen him in a couple of years . . . but now she hardly recognized him. A tall, ponytailed stranger in a flowing white caftan and sandals. The bride wore a matching kaftan, her long straight black hair threaded with tiny wild daisies. No *huppah*. They stood instead beneath a basket of hanging begonias, its meaty white blossoms brushing the tops of their heads, a scatter of fallen petals at their feet.

Rachel smiled, and thought, *Good for you, Mason. You managed to break out of frozen food after all.*

She glanced about. Long plywood tables, laden with flats of seedlings and small plants in clay pots, had been pushed against the steamy glass walls to make room for the fifty or so folding chairs. She spotted the Golds, seated in the first row, next to a tub of zinnias. Evelyn, still Mama's closest friend, sitting ramrod straight and wearing a brave, flash-frozen smile. Rachel noticed that the heels of her pink pumps, dyed to match her pale pink suit, were muddy from the trek up the soggy slope. Her eyes looked puffy and red, as if she'd been crying. Beside her, Ira Gold, plump and bald, darted bewildered glances about as if at any moment he expected to see Alan Funt pop out from behind a tubbed tree to announce they were on 'Candid Camera.' This was not a wedding the Golds had had a hand in planning . . . or could even have dreamed of in their worst nightmares.

Rachel could easily pick out the Golds' relatives and friends . . . they all looked uncomfortable, shifting about in their chairs, studying their laps, exchanging embarrassed looks. But not Mama, so elegant in a pale blue cashmere suit – she simply looked bemused. Rachel felt proud of her for that.

Rachel strained to hear the minister, a soft-spoken bearded man who seemed sincere and was wearing, happily for the Golds' sake, a suit and tie. He was reading aloud

211

the vows Mason and Shannon – her name *was* Shannon, wasn't it? Yes, something like that – had written together. Something about love being free as an eagle . . . and circles within circles. Nice, and not *too* sappy.

Rachel felt tears welling in her eyes. God, was she really crying? Maybe it was the way Mason was looking at his bride, gazing at her with such tenderness. They were totally absorbed in each another, they could have been standing in a sinking rowboat and not have noticed. David had never once looked at her that way.

Mason's friends (who else could they be?) – long-haired boys in jeans and loose shirts – sat in a cluster near the front. The girls, four or five of them, all had long hair parted down the middle, and plain scrubbed faces. One, with straggly blond hair, reminded her of the Before pictures in those Tame Creme Rinse commercials. Several others were nodding dreamily, and looked pretty spaced out. What else did they grow up here in this greenhouse besides flowers?

Mason was slipping a ring on his bride's finger, and now, his face glowing and tremulous with emotion, he was bending down to kiss her. A boy straddling an overturned clay tub, cradling a guitar on his lap, began to play Cat Stevens' 'Moonshadow.' Rachel found herself humming along, caught up in the joy of the moment.

A few minutes later, everyone began filing out, Mason and Shannon first, their friends crowding about them, grinning, laughing, everyone hugging one another.

The older people hung back, muttering their polite, strained congratulations to the Golds. Rachel noticed that Ira Gold was scowling as another short bald man who looked like a brother or a cousin patted him sympathetically on the shoulder.

Across the chairs, Rachel's eye caught Gerald's, and they both smiled. *Daddy is enjoying this . . . Ira taken down a notch or two . . . Daddy always did think he was a bit of a showoff*.

Now she was picking her way downhill, hobbling in her

high heels around the gopher holes and rocks. How ironic that she actually had worried whether she'd be dressed up enough in this white turtleneck sweater and suede skirt.

In the funky farmhouse, refreshments were set up on a round oak table. Gallons of fresh-pressed apple cider, healthy-looking salads sprinkled with sunflower seeds and sprouts, whole-meal breads, crocks of sweet butter and farmer's cheese, crusty vegetarian casseroles.

Later, in the big old-fashioned kitchen, with its Hoosier cabinets and walk-in pantry, Rachel finally managed to corner Mason alone. 'Is all this for real?' she asked. 'I can't believe it's you. What happened to Yale, to J. Press, to the Street?'

'Ever tried celery sticks with fresh-ground peanut butter?' He grabbed one off a chipped plate on the sloping counter, and stuck it in her mouth. He grinned, watching her try to chew. 'Cheyenne makes them. At first I didn't like the stuff she eats, but she turned me around.'

Rachel forced herself to swallow the pasty, stringy lump.

'I thought her name was Shannon.'

'It used to be. She changed it.'

'You're not thinking of changing yours, are you?' The thought of having to call him something like 'Tonto' or 'Seagull' made her want to laugh.

He grinned. 'Sure. How does Acapulco grab you?'

'Funny. Very funny.' Now she was giggling in spite of herself. Still the same old Mason. She felt herself relax.

'I'm sorry, that was mean of me. What I said about Yale. I'm just not quite used to seeing you in a ponytail. But I'm happy for you, Mason, honestly.'

'No offense taken. Hey, want to see the rest of the place? Shan – Cheyenne and I have the whole top floor. Dove and Gordy share the second with Lisa and Joe. Have you met Joe? The house used to belong to Joe's grandfather, he was some kind of botanist. It was Joe's idea to hold the wedding up at the greenhouse . . .'

Rachel followed Mason up a wide staircase with a

carved oak banister and charmingly turned spindles. The third floor, where he lived, was really an attic. She followed him around the low white-washed room, ducking to avoid hitting her head on the sloping ceiling. Someone – Cheyenne probably – had sewn curtains from a madras bedspread. A queen-size mattress on the floor was the only furniture aside from a chest of drawers.

Mason sat down on the mattress, his legs crossed Indian style. He caught her somewhat dismayed look, and said, 'I know, kind of bare, but it's only temporary. Till the end of summer. Then we're moving into the city. I'm starting with the Legal Aid Society in September – did I tell you? I got fed up with corporate law, rich assholes all trying to rip each other off. You have any idea how many decent people get shipped off to penitentiaries every day because they can't afford a good lawyer? Of course you'll find a fair number of incompetents in Legal Aid, the ones who're there only because they can't get anything better. But, hey, I'm *choosing* this. I want to help.'

Rachel dropped down beside Mason, and kissed his cheek. She felt proud of him, of his courage, his commitment.

'Poor Della Street,' she said.

'What's Della Street got to do with it?'

'I was just thinking, where would Della have been if Perry Mason had gone over to Legal Aid?'

He laughed, and leaned over to dig out a plastic Baggie from under a corner of the mattress. 'Want to smoke one? For old times' sake?'

He rolled a joint, and they passed it back and forth, toking in companionable silence. It felt good, right somehow to be sharing this with Mason on his wedding day. Just what she needed to take her mind off herself, her heartache.

Then Mason asked, 'So what's with Dr Kildare these days? Too busy saving lives to fall in love and get married?'

'I was in love once,' she said. 'At least I thought so at

214

the time. Think I'll stick to saving lives from now on, starting with my own . . . Hey, you know, I'm getting used to the idea of you with a ponytail. In fact I kind of like it. I must be stoned.'

'Grew it myself.'

'The ponytail?' She giggled, feeling more and more light-headed.

'This.' He held out the joint. 'Up in the greenhouse.'

'I kind of figured.'

'Pop suspects, I think. He out and out asked me if I was up to any funny stuff. He kills me. I guess he still holds it against me, that I wouldn't go into the business.'

Rachel took a long drag, coughing on the sweetish smoke. It'd been a long time since she'd gotten stoned, probably too long. She leaned back on the mattress, supporting herself on one elbow. She could see through the low window, to where the sun was setting in a tangerine haze over the river.

'You want to hear something really radical?' she said. 'I'm thinking of going to Vietnam.'

Mason stared at her. 'Shit, Rachel, are you serious?'

'Yeah.' Until now she hadn't been sure, but somehow saying it seemed to make it real.

Mason stared at the smoldering joint pinched between his thumb and forefinger. 'Wow. I knew this homegrown stuff was good, but not *that* good.'

She laughed. 'OK, I'm a little stoned, but I *am* serious.'

'Bar none, this is the craziest idea you've ever come up with.' His brown eyes opened in exaggerated, comic-book disbelief.

'I'm not talking about joining the army or anything. I'd work for a private hospital, Catholic Relief. There's plenty of civilians being shot at, maimed, over there, as well as soldiers. I don't see that it could be any worse than working in Legal Aid.'

Mason reflected on this, squinting his eyes as the smoke rose up around his head. 'Yeah, you could be right about that. Anyway, who am I to judge? According to Pop, I've pretty well screwed up my life, so who am I to be telling you what to do? Besides, I know you well enough to know you'll do it anyway.'

Mason fished a roach clip from an ashtray on the floor near the mattress, and finished the joint in silence. Rachel thought then that if she'd had a brother, she would have wanted him to be just like Mason.

'I'll drop you a postcard,' she told him.

'Just don't write "Wish you were here." ' He tapped his chest, grinning. 'Heart murmur. Four-F. Bummer, huh?'

Rachel pulled herself to her feet, feeling heavy, tired, but also better than she had in weeks. Yes, she would go . . . that was the answer . . . put all this behind her . . .

A new life, like Mason.

'Let's go down,' she told him. 'Cheyenne might wonder what you're doing up here with another woman on your wedding day.'

'Relax, Cheyenne's not like that. She doesn't believe you can own anyone that way.' He hoisted himself off the mattress.

Rachel stared down at his sandaled feet, at the weirdly angled little toe he'd broken waterskiing one summer in Deal when they were kids. It made her feel sad somehow, as if Mason's bent toe stood for a carefree part of her life she'd lost for ever.

Then she leveled a stern gaze at Mason. 'Listen, Buster, just don't ever test her on that, you hear? If you love her, don't mess with a good thing.'

Mason saluted, one corner of his mouth twisting up. 'Not a chance. She's all I can handle, and then some. Listen, I'll tell you something I haven't even told my parents. Cheyenne and I . . . well, she's three months pregnant. I'm going to be a father. Can you dig it?'

Rachel, a searing pain in her chest, felt as if he had touched a live wire to her heart. That goofy look of happiness on Mason's face. It made her think of David, how distant he'd been, how cold. Oh God.

216

Then she pulled herself together. 'You don't waste any time, do you?'

'It's something else, isn't it? Me getting married, having a kid. You maybe going to Vietnam.' He turned to her as they were heading toward the stairs. There were little red razor nicks along his jaw, she observed. He'd shaved off his beard this morning, he told her, out of respect for his parents. It would have been too much, seeing him looking like Jesus Christ on top of everything else. 'Just don't stick your neck out too far over there.' Then he added, 'Oh, hell, why did I say that? For you, that's like saying "Don't think about elephants." '

She patted his shoulder. 'OK, I promise. I won't think about elephants.'

Out on the landing, she heard a commotion downstairs, someone crying out, a door slamming, the hammering of footsteps on the stairs below.

'Rachel? Rachel?' Mama's voice anxiously calling her. Someone hurt? She thought absurdly of those old cartoons, Bugs Bunny screeching, 'Is there a doctor in the house?'

But as the white circle of Mama's face surfaced out of the stairwell, Rachel froze. Her heart felt as if it had stopped. *Oh God, something bad . . . something bad must have happened to . . .*

'Rachel,' Mama gasped. 'It's Daddy . . .'

# 9

Sylvie sat in the old red velvet rocking chair in her bedroom, sewing a button on Gerald's shirt.

She guided the needle through the buttonhole. Such tiny buttons, and so fine, the old-fashioned kind made of polished bone, not plastic. Just like Gerald to watch over every detail. His shirts all custom-fitted by the same house on Savile Row that his father had used before him.

Sylvie glanced up briefly at the tall leaded windows and saw with some surprise that the afternoon was nearly gone.

Somewhere she heard a sound, a knocking. But so far away it had to be coming from downstairs. Oh well, let Bridget take care of it. She imagined herself laying the shirt out for Gerald, so he could wear it tomorrow, with his natty blue herringbone suit and that lovely Dior tie Rachel had given him for Father's Day last year . . .

The knocking grew louder, more persistent. Why, it wasn't downstairs at all, it was right outside her bedroom door. And she heard a voice as well.

'Mama? Are you in there? Mama!'

*Rachel? What a lovely surprise. Perhaps she'll stay for supper.*

'Come in, dear,' Sylvie called brightly. 'It's not locked. Just stuck. These old doors. Give it a hard push.'

*My Lord, how awful she looks*, Sylvie thought as her daughter came into the room. Hair stringy, flat, as if she hadn't washed it in days. Face puffy, eyes swollen. Poor child.

'Oh, Mama.'

Rachel crossed the room and kneeled at Sylvie's feet. As

she tilted her face up, a dusky sunbeam caught it and lifted it from the gloom, illuminating it like a tortured soul in a Goya painting. Something in her expression stirred Sylvie from her lethargy, and made her feel cold. A bone-deep cold that no amount of blankets could warm.

*Go away*, she thought. *Leave me be.*

Rachel pressed her face into the folds of Gerald's shirt spread across Sylvie's lap. Her voice rose, muffled and thick with tears. 'I miss him so much. It just doesn't seem possible that I won't see him again. When I walk though this house, he's in every room. Oh God, Mama, it's like he's *here*, so close I can even *smell* him. Only I can't see him or touch him.'

Rachel began to weep, shoulders jerking, hot tears soaking through the dressing gown Sylvie had not changed out of since this morning.

'Hush now.' Sylvie smoothed her hand over Rachel's head, feeling the hard curve of skull under the springy silken hair, and the tender little hollow at the nape of her neck. When Rachel was a tiny baby, Sylvie had stroked her to sleep just like this. 'Don't cry, my darling.'

Sylvie felt a wonderful sense of peace. As if she had indeed left the present behind, and were suspended in another time, a time of happiness, a baby warm in her lap, its sweet powdery fragrance filling the whole room.

Then the coldness began to seep through her again.

'Mama, I miss Daddy, but it's you I'm worried about.' Rachel's words tugged at her, forced her deeper into the cold black place she didn't want to be. 'You haven't cried once. And you won't eat. You haven't been out of this room for a whole week. Bridget called me this morning. She was in tears she was so upset.'

'There's nothing for either of you to be upset about,' Sylvie replied. 'I'm perfectly fine. I just don't seem to have much of an appetite, that's all. And much as I love Bridget's cooking, she *does* get a bit heavy-handed with the butter and eggs. She's been trying to fatten me up for years. Even sneaks cream into my coffee when I've specifically

219

asked for skim milk. It's like a war with her, you know. And she just can't accept losing.'

'Oh, Mama.' Rachel lifted her face, damp and swollen from crying. 'Can't you at least cry? I'd be so much better if you could.'

Sylvie flinched from those bruised-looking eyes. No, no, she couldn't let herself cry. If she did, she'd never be able to stop. Like an ocean wave snatching her under, drowning her.

*Oh, if only Gerald were here.*

But that was what Rachel was reminding her of, wasn't it? That Gerald was not coming back to her. Ever.

Then something cracked open inside Sylvie, pressing against her chest, hurting, forcing the air from her lungs. Tears rose up her throat in a great choking wave.

And it all came rushing back.

Gerald complaining of chest pains at Mason Gold's wedding, collapsing before she and Rachel could get him out to the car. Then the emergency room, all those doctors, nurses, paramedics swarming over him, pounding on his chest, poking him with needles, wires, tubes, trying to shock his heart into beating. But it was too late by then. Too late . . .

The funeral, two days later, was hazy in her mind. How unreal it had seemed, like a dream, or a movie she was watching. Temple Emmanuel, so crowded, Gerald's friends, his clients, employees, people from the Opera. Hundreds, all of them wanting to squeeze her hand, kiss her cheek. And Rachel, close at her side, so good, so strong, remembering names, murmuring the right words of appreciation.

Sylvie saw in her mind the cemetery glittering under a shroud of snow, that awful blanket of artificial grass, so wrong, worse than the gaping hole underneath. Someone had left a bouquet of baby-pink roses at the grave, though everyone should have known there were to be no flowers. Yes, she had almost cried then. She had wanted to bundle them in her arms, carry them away before they wilted. Those lovely, wasted roses.

Sylvie had felt herself begin to wilt, but a man's strong

220

hand was suddenly gripping her elbow, supporting her.
Nikos. And he didn't seem threatening anymore. Just an
old friend, someone being kind.

He wouldn't hurt her. Or Rachel.

Sylvie had somehow known that, even before Rachel
turned toward him, frowning slightly as if she was trying
to place him among her father's many friends and
acquaintances. Then she accepted his proffered hand.

'I'm sorry,' he'd said.

And that was all. Though he had held her hand a bit too
long, his dark eyes never leaving Rachel's face, he was letting Sylvie know he was there only to offer his condolences.

Later, when almost everyone had gone to their cars,
Nikos had lingered.

'Your husband was much admired,' Nikos said kindly,
his words a white plume in the chill air, his shoes punching
deep holes in the frozen snow as he walked back with her
to the car.

'Yes, he had many friends,' Sylvie said. 'He was . . . a
generous man.'

'I know that better than most.'

'You?' She stopped to look at him. His seamed brown
face – yes, now in the daylight she could see all the tiny
lines and fissures, like old rubbed leather – showed only
admiration.

'There is something you should know,' he began as they
made their way slowly down the narrow roadway, an aisle
between a forest of gravestones. 'I see no harm in telling
you now. And perhaps it will be of some comfort to you.'

Sylvie began to feel dizzy again, and she clutched
Nikos's arm. 'Comfort?' she choked. 'How can anything
comfort me now that he's gone?'

'We can talk another time if you wish.'

'No. Tell me.'

'He knew,' Nikos said. 'About us. You and me. All
those years ago, he knew. When he fired me, he told me he
didn't blame you. He was afraid you would leave him, an
old man with nothing to offer you but money.'

221

Part of her wanted to laugh, madly, hysterically. But suddenly she was so tired, so very tired, all she wanted to do was lie down in the snow and close her eyes. She leave Gerald? Oh, dear God, if only he'd known the awful thing she'd done, just so he wouldn't leave *her*.

Sylvie felt something cold on her face, and realized she was crying. She dug gloved fingers into her cheeks. 'He knew? All along, you mean, he knew?'

'He gave me money,' Nikos said, hanging his head. 'I had to promise that I would never see you again. Five hundred dollars. I used it to buy an old pickup that started my business, what became Anteros Construction.'

'Anteros.' It dawned on her. 'The god of cheated love.'

'Yes,' he confessed, 'I loved you. But I knew what he did not – that you would never leave him for me or any other man. So, yes, I took the money, I am ashamed to say.'

'Don't be,' she said. 'There are worse things than taking money.' *Worse than you can imagine.*

They were passing under the shadow of a huge barren elm, and Sylvie shivered, thinking of that expression, *A goose walked over my grave.*

'I didn't see him again until two years ago,' Nikos continued. 'Someone told me he might be interested in property I planned to build on. And I needed financing, so I went. But mostly, I think it was vanity. I wanted to show off, show him how well his five hundred dollars had paid off. But what I remember best about that meeting was the picture in a silver frame on his desk – of you and your daughter. That's when I realized who had gotten the best of our long-ago bargain.'

The stillness that followed Nikos's confession seemed huge and never-ending. Sylvie listened to the branches of the old elm creaking under its burden of snow, the flutter of sparrows taking flight. Somewhere nearby, she could hear the firing of car engines, and the labored droning of a grave-digging machine. The sun came out from behind a bank of clouds just then, turning the snow mirror bright,

222

winking off flecks of mica in the granite tombstones.

Sylvie just stood there, looking out over the graves, feeling that if she moved too much or too quickly she would shatter this gift Nikos had handed her, this precious glimpse into the secret heart of the man she had loved, and by whom she had so undeservedly and richly been loved.

Ever her pain felt exquisite somehow, a finely wrought thing she turned over and over, examining it from all angles, marveling at its intricacy.

*I could have told him about Rose. And he would have understood. He would have forgiven. All these years . . .*

She'd felt so humbled then by her shame and Gerald's generosity.

Now as she sat in her rocking chair with Rachel kneeling before her, a shirt Gerald would never wear spread across her lap, she thought how grateful we are when our world is falling apart for even the smallest reprieves. A gentle touch. A kind word. Forgiveness.

He really was gone. Her dear Gerald. She would no longer hear his footsteps on the staircase. Or the Puccini drifting from his study. Never look up from pruning her roses and find him smiling down at her from the terrace. Or stop in the quiet of an evening to read her aloud a passage from a book.

But she still had her daughter, she had Rachel. And Rachel was grieving, too.

'Mama,' Rachel was saying, 'I've been thinking . . . don't get upset, just *thinking* is all . . . of joining Kay in Vietnam. They so desperately need doctors and . . . well, I think it would be good for me. To get away from . . . from everything. But I won't go, Mama, if you want me to stay with you, if you need me. I know that Daddy would have wanted me to look after you.'

Sylvie felt a lightning bolt of pain strike her heart. Not Rachel, leaving her too? Dear Lord, how much more could she take?

Oh, where was Gerald? Why wasn't he here when she needed him so?

Gerald, such a good protector, like the father she had never had. He wouldn't have wanted her to be alone, surely.

But Rachel wasn't meant to be her protector. Rachel had to have her own life.

'No.' Sylvie set aside her sewing, and rose from her chair. Such a simple effort, yet how she ached, as if she'd been shut up inside a box for days. Still, good to feel her body, even if it hurt. 'I won't have you putting your life on hold for me. I won't have that responsibility.'

'Mama.' Rachel just shook her head, the light falling away, her face slipping into shadow. 'I *want* to be with you.'

'Now you do. For a few days, a few weeks maybe. And then you'll be sorry. No. I hate the idea of you leaving, being so far away. And so dangerous. But I'd hate it more if you stayed here simply on my account.'

'You mean that, Mama? Are you sure?'

Sylvie did not feel sure of anything. Except perhaps of knowing that she would make it through this night. She felt so weak, so lost without Gerald. But if she could stand up, make a decision, even the wrong one, then that meant something, didn't it? It had to mean she was not going to die, wither away like those poor roses on Gerald's grave.

*Life is full of surprises*, she thought, *and maybe I'll just surprise myself*.

Sylvie brushed away a hair that clung to Rachel's wet cheek. 'Can you stay for supper? Then we can talk about your plans. And let Bridget fatten us both up.'

224

# 10

Max Griffin awoke. Bernice was snoring, a soft gurgling sound that made him think, while still half-asleep, that the toilet needed its handle jiggled. He felt a fierce need to pee.

Logy with sleep, he edged out from under the covers. Then the shock of the cold floor against his bare soles. Christ. Slippers. He groped blindly, finally found them, not where earlier he'd kicked them off, but in front of the nightstand, lined up perfectly, toes facing out. Bernice. Sure. She always put them there so he'd find them in case he might need the john at night.

No, not from her, that word. John, head, pot, or even toilet. *Powder room*, he could hear her voice in his mind, that precise, ladylike voice as she ushered company into the living room, took people's coats. *The powder room is at the end of the hall if you'd like to wash up.* Wash up, another of her euphemisms.

Max found the door, felt for the light switch. A glare hit him in the face like a flashbulb, hard bright light backfiring off chrome, mirror, shiny pink tiles. If he hadn't been awake before, he surely was now. He could now launch into a summation to a jury, his mind felt that clear.

As he peed, he stared into the toilet. Blue. The water was a bright unnatural blue, the color of a YMCA swimming pool. And now it was turning green, a sickly yellow-green. Did Bernice know what happened when you peed in blue water? No, how could she? She'd never look, never even take a peek before flushing; just the idea of doing that would disgust her.

An old memory came to him. Coming home and finding Bernice on her hands and knees on the kitchen floor before the avocado-green Frigidaire, wearing big yellow rubber gloves that made him think of Minnie Mouse, and scrubbing underneath it with a bottle brush and a plastic tub of soapy water.

'Baby asleep?' he had asked.

She looked up at him, her red hair clipped back with a plastic barrette, a fine sheen of dampness glimmering on her pale forehead. 'She's having her bottle,' Bernice said. 'I found this new contraption, a pillow with loops you can slip the bottle into so it doesn't fall over. Just stick it in the crib when she's hungry. Really frees me up.'

Mandy had been three months old.

Aside from a few hardly visible stretch marks, being a mother had not changed Bernice, Max thought. Their daughter was just one more household item to be properly organized. One more jotted reminder over the kitchen phone on the chalkboard, its frame painted with a smiling bumblebee and the sunny yellow logo THINGS TO DO.

He shook himself off, and flushed.

Now a headache was starting, a painful pulsing in his temples that was creeping outward. Jesus, he didn't need this. Not with back-to-back court dates tomorrow.

Max stepped over to the mirrored medicine cabinet, where he had to confront the unwelcome specter of middle age: a husky man closing in on forty, eyes puffy with sleep, jaw still firm, but his rumpled brown hair shot full of gray.

He popped open the cabinet, relieved to watch his reflection slide away. Rows of bottles faced him. Few of the things usually found in medicine chests, no old pre-scriptions dating back to the hernia operation he'd had in '62. No crusty bottles of last winter's cough syrup, no rings on the glass shelves. Everything new, and precisely arranged by category, neater than a drugstore's shelves. Massengil douche. Daisy feminine spray. Four different brands of underarm deodorant. The lilac plastic dial containing Bernice's birth-control pills. He found the Tylenol next to the orange baby aspirin Bernice gave Monkey when she had a fever. He shook two into his palm. Where was the water glass? Shit, she'd confiscated it again. That hotbed of germs. Jesus. He'd have to get one from the kitchen.

Downstairs the cool emptiness soothed him. The headache ebbed. This great old house overlooking Little Neck Bay. He remembered how he'd pushed for it soon after they were married, even though the mortgage payments had seemed murderous. Bernice had had her eye on one of those pseudo-Tudor attached homes in Bayside. So much easier to keep clean, she'd argued. Not like this one, with its eighty-year-old pumpkin pine flooring, where dirt could fill the cracks, with its ocean-pitted windows and crumbled caulking. Six months spent reshingling the roof, replacing gutters and drain-pipes, stripping off layer after layer of old paint before they could move in. But when the painting, wallpapering, sealing the floors with polyurethane was finished, Bernice relented. Even she became smitten by its charms, the exposed beams, the tucked-away window seats, the stained-glass fanlight over the front door.

Max crossed to the kitchen sink without turning on the light. He could see well enough. Dusky moonlight gleamed off the flagged stone flooring. His gaze moved to the brick patio jutting out below the window. He saw that the daffodils had come up around its sides, rows of flowers like neat pickets poking up through the freshly turned earth. Max felt a little surge of happiness at this sign of new life. Then he thought, feeling blue again, *They've been up for days, maybe a week, and I didn't even notice. When I was younger, I would never have missed the first daffodils.*

Max then found himself thinking about his father, recalling one summer evening out on the back lawn with his two older brothers, playing croquet. Max had been fourteen, and Dad . . . how old had he been? He'd always seemed the same age somehow, always bald on top (except for that little thatch above his forehead he called his

227

'donkey lock'), always that generous roll of fat creeping over his belt. Of that summer evening, more than twenty years ago, each detail now came back to him, passing through some sort of mental wicket, sharp and clear as the thunk of a mallet against a wooden ball. The smell of freshly cut grass mingled with smoke from the hamburgers Dad was barbecuing, the tray of dripping ice-tea glasses Mom had set out on the porch railing, and how his wrist stung where Robbie had given him an Indian sunburn. Max, lining up his shot, remembered looking down at his grass-stained pantlegs and thinking how Mom would give him holy hell. Then Eddie had begun razzing him about all the time he'd been spending locked in the bathroom lately, and Max had looked up and seen his father, wearing a pair of saggy old Bermuda shorts and baseball cap, standing there by the barbecue pit with a long-handled spatula clutched in one hand, staring off into space with tears running down his cheeks.

Max had never seen his father cry. The shock of it had hit him almost like an earthquake. The first thought that flitted across his mind was that Dad somehow had lost his job. But Norm Griffin had taught math at Pittsfield High since Adam and Eve; there was about as much chance of him begin fired as there was of Harry Truman turning Republican. Not wanting to even *try* imagining anything worse, Max had told himself desperately, *Must be the smoke, that's it, the smoke's in his eyes . . .*

But now, all these years later, Max finally had an insight into his father. *Maybe it had just occurred to him that the train had stopped, it wasn't moving anymore, this was the last stop.*

Max found a glass in the drainer. A cracked tile over the sink caught his eye. *Have to replace that*, he thought, then remembered why he hadn't. He liked its imperfection, the fact that Bernice couldn't new-and-improve it, no matter how much she scrubbed and polished.

*Like me*, he thought. *Can't change me any more than that cracked tile. Though God knows she tries.*

Like Monkey, too. A tomboy, outspoken, full of beans. He'd begun calling his daughter that when she began to walk, scampering so fast on those two little feet, her banana-sticky fingers causing more mischief than Curious George. Now it was bicycles, skate-boards, and God knew what else. Bernice, wringing her hands, had told him just yesterday about the latest misadventure – she had caught Monkey shimmying down the rain gutter.

Upstairs, Max peeked in on Monkey. In the light that fanned across her face from the open doorway, she looked no more than four or five, a baby still, precious and soft. Then his gaze moved down to the tangle of long limbs poking out from under the covers, a scabbed knee, bitten fingernails daubed with chipped red polish. Nine going on ten, and in just a few short years she'd be a teenager. He noticed the Donovan poster on the wall above her maple child's bed. When had she gotten that? And where were the stuffed animals that had always lined her bed?

It hit him then: *She's growing up.*

His heart swelled, and Max felt a pang at the thought that she would one day leave him, go off to college; that day was soon, just around the corner.

He tiptoed over, smoothed away a wisp of hair that was stuck to her cheek. She had Bernice's thick swirly red hair, not carrot colored, the red of Titian and Rubens.

Was it his imagination, or had Monkey seemed more subdued lately? Fussy, too. Wouldn't eat half what was on her plate. And tonight when he tucked her in, she had clung to him, begging him not to leave her alone in the dark.

Bernice had dismissed it with the usual 'she's just going through a stage.' But Max had doubts. Sometimes he worried about Monkey. More than he knew was normal.

*Admit it, why don't you? You're afraid she'll grow up to be like her mother.*

And what was so terrible about that? In a way, Bernice was terrific. If there was a Miss America pageant for the perfect house-keeper/cook/hostess, Bernice would snatch the crown. Her figure, too, still as slim as when he'd married her, though she had to work a lot harder at it now. A damned attractive woman. Just last weekend he'd overheard a gas station attendant whisper to a buddy, 'I wouldn't kick her out of bed.' Max smiled to himself. There was as much likelihood of Bernice cheating on him as there was of the Statue of Liberty lifting her skirts.

Best of all, Bernice loved Monkey as much as he did. So why did he break out in a sweat imagining that Monkey would one day turn to him with her mother's cool brown eyes and say, 'For heaven's sake, can't you *ever* remember to put the toilet lid down when you're finished?'

Max tiptoed out, closing her door softly behind him. His head-ache was all but gone now. Good. Maybe now he'd even get some sleep.

But as he crawled back into bed, Bernice awoke, a warm ball unfolding at the brush of his cold feet. She sat up, blinking, worried-looking, her red hair scrambled about her shoulders. For an instant, she looked so much like Monkey he felt something in his chest stir. He remembered when they were first married, how Bernice used to sleep naked in his arms, curled up like a kitten. How he would smooth his hand down the curve of her spine, and hold one small hard buttock in the cup of his palm; how she would pretend to be still asleep but her legs would move apart ever so slightly, just enough so he could explore further.

'What's wrong?' she cried out in alarm. Poor Bernice, even in her sleep, always fearful.

'It's OK,' he soothed, patting her leg. 'Go back to sleep.'

Her nightgown had fallen open at the neck, revealing one small firm breast. Max felt himself begin to grow hard, and thought, *No, God, not now*. He hated wanting her, knowing she would give in without any real desire.

But while he was telling himself to cool off and go back to sleep, he found himself pushing his hand further up her leg, hooking one finger under the elastic of her panties.

'Now?' she muttered thickly. Then sighed and said, 'OK.' and rolled her nightgown up over her flat tummy, the way Monkey rolled up her jeans before wading into the ocean.

Max stroked her for a while, hoping for a response. Jesus, oh Jesus, why couldn't she want him too, just a little? And if she felt so totally indifferent why couldn't she at least tell him to leave her alone? This . . . taking her like this . . . while she lay quiet, hardly breathing . . . Christ, more like masturbating than making love.

'Bernice? Honey, is there anything you want me to—'

'No, you just go ahead,' she murmured politely. 'It's OK.'

*No*, he thought as he entered her, *it's not OK. Not OK at all. Oh Christ, won't you at least move some, go through the motions, pretend, just for a minute, so I won't have to feel like a dirty old man getting his jollies jacking off.*

Now he felt himself coming, a fierce burning rush, wrenched from him almost against his will. Christ, oh Christ . . .

He wrapped his arms about Bernice, hard, squeezing her so tightly she yelped. And for an instant, it felt good hurting her, making her feel *something*.

Then he was awash in shame. How sick, wanting to *hurt* her.

Then it was over.

Bernice shimmied out from underneath him. 'Be right back,' she murmured.

*No. Let me hold you*, he wanted to call after her, *at least let me do that. I know how you love the back of your neck massaged, won't you let me—*

Too late. He could hear her, the thumping of the old pipes as the tap cranked on, the medicine chest clicking open.

Max lay on his back, staring up at a light moving across the ceiling, a car passing by outside. There was a tight, hot sensation in his chest.

231

He heard the tap go off. Then, 'Oh, Max, for heaven's *sake*,' Bernice cried out in a vexed tone.

The toilet seat. He'd forgotten to put it down. Again. Max suddenly felt so angry he pictured himself smashing it down on her head.

He took a deep breath. Why get angry at Bernice? It was all him, his fault. He couldn't blame her for his being too gutless to ask for a divorce. 'Divorce,' the magic word that he didn't dare utter.

And then he thought, as he always did when he imagined leaving Bernice, of Monkey.

Tears came, hard and reluctant, squeezed from him like blood from the great stone that lay on his chest.

Late in the afternoon of the following day, Max stood at the window that spanned almost the entire east wall of his office. He looked out at the purpling sky, and the postcard view of the Brooklyn Bridge spanning the East River, its weblike girders turned to chrome by the footlights of the setting sun. Majestic, that was the only word for it. Who said the bridge wasn't for sale? He was paying for it, every day too, for this corner office with its breathtaking view and for the prestige that came with it. He was paying for it with his time, his thoughts, his expertise. And was he also paying for it with his integrity?

Jesus, he hadn't had thoughts like those since he was fresh out of law school. Lawyers weren't supposed to think this way. What was it about this case?

Max turned away from the window, and sank into the chair in front of his cluttered Georgian pedestal desk. He stared at the huge cardboard blowup, propped between two antique corner chairs, of an automobile steering column that looked like something out of Cape Kennedy.

If the plaintiff, Jorgensen, were to win, Pace Motors would be out twelve million, plus another hundred million to recall all those Cyclones and replace their steering columns. Max liked the Pace guys, had driven their cars for years, and thanked his lucky stars at least weekly for his firm's having America's most innovative automobile manufacturer as his client. So his first instinct had been to rush to Pace's defense, confident that Jorgensen had been high on something and that his claim against Pace was another attempted rip-off.

But since Monday, his meeting with Caravella, the chief engineer, who had protested much too much, with a storm of technical explanations, blueprints, and test results that said less than the sweat pouring from his face; and this Tuesday, Rooney, and the PR vice-president, flying in and working the word 'settlement' into every sentence – well, Max couldn't help but catch a whiff of something that might be rotten in Denmark.

It wasn't his place, he'd reminded himself over and over, to pass judgement on any real or imagined wrong-doing of his clients – but still, he couldn't shake this slightly sick feeling, like a bad aftertaste from something he'd eaten.

'I have those depositions you wanted, Mr Griffin.' A voice, low and sweet, drew him from the downward spiral of his thoughts. 'And your coffee.'

He looked up, and there was Rose, a tidy stack of papers tucked against her hip, searching for a clear space on his desk for the steaming mug in her other hand.

He relieved her of the coffee, placing it on a yellow legal pad scribbled with his hen pecks and already stained with today's previous coffee rings. 'Thanks.' He picked up the transcripts she had laid before him, and began leafing through them. 'How about that independent engineer's report?'

'In the Xerox room. All two hundred and eleven pages of it. Including diagrams. I'm having copies made, but it'll take a while to collate.'

Max sighed, and muttered to himself. ' "Methinks the lady doth protest too much." '

'What lady?'

'They're called whores. The expert witnesses. The doctors, shrinks, engineers who'll provide you with enough trumped-up data on paper to wipe the asses of the entire jury for a month.'

He took a slug of the black coffee, and grimaced.

'Sorry for the industrial strength,' Rose apologized with a little laugh. 'It was the last of the pot.' Then the smile dropped away, and she said softly, 'You don't believe it was, how do you say . . . *res ipsa loquitur?*'

Where had she gotten that? Obviously she'd been doing more than just typing his papers. Smart girl. Pretty too. But with everyone making such a fuss these days of women's lib, he was careful always to keep his gaze neutral.

But, hell, it was a treat, seeing a woman look so fresh so late in the afternoon. Face soap-and-water shiny, her cloud of dark hair smelling faintly of shampoo, white blouse ironed to paper crispness and tucked neatly into a plain navy sailcloth skirt. An unfashionable knee length, but it suited her better than the miniskirts the other secretaries all seemed to be wearing.

No, he couldn't imagine her in one of those, bending over at the water cooler, the lacy elastic of her panties winking out from under her hem. Anyway, she probably wore sensible white cotton underwear, the kind you bought at Sears that came in packets of two. Good Catholic underwear to go with the tiny gold crucifix at her throat.

Max felt his face begin to grow warm. Jesus, enough. He forced his mind back to Jorgensen.

'Well, in a way this whole thing does speak for itself,' he replied. 'Sure, most accidents are due to driver negligence. But do I think *this* was Jorgensen's fault?' He paused. 'No. I don't.'

He felt better, voicing his suspicions aloud. Even knowing he had no business doing so. Somehow, he felt he could trust Rose. She had the air of someone who could keep a confidence.

It's her eyes, he thought. Those great black eyes of hers, they're full of secrets.

'But you're not sure.' Rose reached over, straightening

234

one of the piles on his desk. 'And if Quent Jorgensen is telling the truth, that he wasn't drunk that night, then there might be dozens, hundreds, of other defective steering columns out there. Is that what you're getting at?'

'You'd make a good lawyer,' he said and laughed. 'Ever thought about law school?'

He could see that he'd hit a nerve, and instantly regretted his idle words. Christ, how could he have been so thoughtless? Despite the almost excruciating care Rose took with her appearance, he'd noticed the same two skirts and three or four blouses worn over and over, the same black shoes carefully resoled each season. Law school? She probably was just scraping by.

A blush had risen in her cheeks, giving her dark olive complexion a burnt sienna glow that reminded him somehow of the Tuscany hills where he'd once been stationed during the war. She covered it with a quick laugh. 'Who would baby-sit Mrs Von Hoesling's Chihuahua then?'

Max chuckled, remembering how Mrs Von Hoesling had tottered in the other day to discuss her late husband's will. In the outer office, she simply had handed over to Rose her snarling Chihuahua, as if it had been a coat or a hat. And Rose, to his eternal gratitude, had taken it without comment, her expression carefully blank, simply popping it into a file drawer in her desk along with half a Danish as soon as the old lady's back was turned.

'You have a point,' he said.

'If you had some way of knowing for sure about that steering column, would it really make things easier?' she asked, bending over to gather a few balled-up papers that had missed the wastebasket. He noticed how she dipped at the knees, swiveling to one side so that her hemline barely lifted in back. The nuns had taught her good.

He rubbed his chin, scratchy with five o'clock shadow. 'No, not necessarily. I can hardly afford to tell our biggest client I think they're liars, can I? Anyway, it's not my job. And maybe all this righteousness I'm feeling is just plain ego in disguise . . . I like having all the cards on the table, good and bad, not stumbling around in the dark. The way it stands, if what I suspect is true, and if Jorgensen's lawyer should throw me any curve balls in court . . . well, without all the facts, I could wind up looking like the king of idiots.'

'But on the other hand,' Rose quietly pointed out, 'if your suspicions were to prove unfounded, then wouldn't you feel a whole lot better? At least you wouldn't have to worry about some other poor shmuck ending up in a wheel-chair, or maybe worse.'

'You have a crystal ball handy?' he asked and smiled.

'No. Something a lot simpler.' She straightened, fixing those remarkable eyes on him. Eyes both still and bottom-less, only a flash here, a glint there, of the emotions that swam in some deep dark part of her.

'What's that?'

'The car. Why don't you take one out on the road? See for yourself.'

He grinned. 'I wish it were that easy. This glitch . . . whether it's real or I'm imagining it . . . it couldn't possibly be in every steering column, or Pace would be deluged with lawsuits by now. I suspect that's why they're not being a hundred per cent straight with me. They prob-ably don't even want to admit it to *themselves*. The defect might exist only in every hundred Cyclones, or every thou-sand. And even then, not something that would manifest itself – I'm guessing at this – except possibly at very high speeds, and only under certain driving conditions.'

'Who knows,' Rose said, 'you might get lucky.' She wasn't smiling. Goddamn, she was *serious*. What kind of a woman was this, anyway?

Max felt something inside him lift, grow buoyant for a moment. Hell, maybe she was right. Maybe it was worth a try, even if it was a long shot. He said thoughtfully, 'There's a Pace dealership not far from here. I know the manager.'

'You could say you wanted to buy one,' she put in, 'take it for a test drive.'

Max stood up, pushing away from his desk, feeling better than he had in weeks, and strangely excited.

'You're on,' he said, grinning like an idiot. 'Yes, you. It was your idea, remember? Get your coat, and let's do it.'

They braked through the last toll booth on the Sawmill and then finally hit the Thruway. When they crossed the Tappan Zee, the sun had dipped below the horizon, and was now just a mellow Cointreau glow flashing in and out of the dense poplars that lined the berm on either side of the six-lane highway.

Max couldn't remember the last time he'd felt this jacked-up, like a teenager, high on the new-car smell of virgin vinyl, stirred by the road unrolling before him.

He looked over at Rose in the driver's seat, her concentration square on the road, both hands gripping the crimson wheel, which matched the fire-engine-red exterior, one long bronze leg stretched to the pedal like a taut steel cable. Then he looked at the red needle of the speedometer, at seventy now.

She had insisted on driving. No, insisted was wrong. In the dealership lot, she simply had slid into the low bucket seat behind the steering wheel, looked up at him with the eager smile of a little kid straddling her first tricycle, and said, 'You don't mind, do you? I've always wondered what it would be like to drive one of these things.'

And drive she had, cautiously and a little nervously at first, then with increasing confidence. They had not spoken a word in half an hour, there was no need really. It felt oddly companionable. In fact, Max had almost forgotten their real purpose in doing this.

'I think I've just broken the B and B barrier,' Rose said finally, flicking him a sidelong glance, her full lips curved in a smile. It was unusually warm for April, and Max caught the faint, strangely seductive smell of her perspiration riding the air current that streamed in her open window.

'B and B?'

237

'Short for Brooklyn-Bronx. They say if you're born in either of those boroughs you never really leave. You never go any farther than the subway can take you. Even the Long Island Railroad – the way a lot of people in my neighborhood talk, you'd think it was the Orient Express.'

Max smiled. 'And what about you?'

A green and white sign reading NEW PALTZ 38 MI. flashed by on the right. They had climbed a low rise, and forests graying with the dusk spread out before them.

'I've been making believe this is my car – forget about possible defects for now – and I'm on my way to . . . wait a minute, one second . . . oh, I know . . . to this fabulous resort in the Catskills. I'm a famous actress, and sinfully rich, and . . . and I'm meeting my secret lover there for a weekend of mad frivolity. I picked that expression up from a book, mad frivolity. It sounds like something Clark Gable and Carole Lombard would do, doesn't it'

'You're right, it does. You like old movies?'

She glanced into the rearview mirror, then zipped left into the fast lane, passing a blue Buick and a yellow Opel Kadet, the last rays of the setting sun skating sideways across the sleek red hood. The speedometer jumped over the eighty hash mark. Just ahead lay a straight patch with no exit ramp in sight and, miraculously, no traffic.

'Don't tell anyone,' she said. 'People will think I'm weird, but the truth is, I don't much like anything that was made after 1940. Remember the old Shirley Temple movies – she danced with Bill Robinson in every one. And Nelson Eddie and Jeanette MacDonald in *Naughty Marietta*. I even cried at the end of *Now, Voyager*. You know, when Bette Davis says, ''Don't let's ask for the moon, we have the stars.'' Or was it the other way around?'

Max looked at her, amused and a little surprised. This was the most she'd said all in one breath since she'd first come to work for him, two years ago. It seemed they'd both fallen under this sportcar's spell.

'I don't remember,' he said and laughed. 'Just the two

cigarettes. Paul kept lighting up for him and Bette in nearly every scene. I suppose the Hays office thought lung cancer was preferable to passionate kissing.'

'Spoken like a cynic. You've just given yourself away, you know. I'm like that too. I tend to dwell on – am I going too fast for you? You look a little green.'

'No,' he lied. He *was* beginning to feel pretty soggy in the armpits. Jesus. They were really moving. And how experienced a driver was she, anyhow?

A picture flashed across his mind of Quent Jorgensen. In an exhibit he had prepared for the trial, Jorgensen's lawyer had cleverly juxtaposed a photo of his client in midair clearing a hurdle at the Olympics with a later shot of the now-crippled man slumped in his wheelchair. While Max had every reason to expect the judge would keep the photo from the jury, he nevertheless found himself hoping fervently that the alcohol found in his bloodstream after the accident meant that *he* had been out of control.

She glanced at the speedometer. 'I suppose this is what you'd call *malum prohibitum*.'

'Breaking the law without evil intent,' Max interpreted. 'Yes, I think speeding would fall under that heading. That's if you get pulled over. Under different circumstances, a doctor might have another term for it.'

'What's that?'

'D.O.A. Look, maybe you had better slow down a bit. And what's with the legalese anyway?'

'I have a confession to make. I've been taking home a few of your law books.' She glanced over at him, as if expecting him to be angry. 'Only one at a time, and I always bring them back. I'm very careful. Honest.'

She was blushing again. So he *had* been right about her having more than a passing interest in law. 'I don't mind. But you may be opening a Pandora's box. Is that really what you want?'

'I don't know what I want,' she said. Her eyes clouded over. 'I used to think . . . oh, never mind, I've probably said too much as it is.'

239

'No. Please. I . . .' He couldn't think of anything that didn't sound like a line from a bad movie, so he ended lamely with 'Maybe I can help.'

She bit her lip, as if to keep from crying. 'No, I don't think so. It's . . . sort of personal.'

'As in "boyfriend"?'

The burnt-sienna flush in her cheeks deepened, and Max felt a prick of jealousy which was completely unreasonable. *Right again. You're a regular two-gun Sam, old boy.*

'He's in the army. In Vietnam for almost four months. Three months and twenty-one days. I . . . we, that is . . . plan to get married when he gets home. But the thing is . . .' Her voice rose on a sharp tinny note, then cracked. 'Oh God, I knew this would happen, I always cry when I talk about him . . .' She brushed angrily at her eyes with the heel of her left hand. 'You see, I haven't heard from him in a while. Three months, to be exact. Only one letter . . .' She sounded as if she might start to cry again.

'You really love him, don't you?' Dumb question. That much was obvious. And what of it? Just because he didn't exactly have the market cornered on marital bliss didn't mean it was a lost cause for everyone else.

She nodded, not taking her eyes from the road. There was a hurt, angry look in them now, and a new pinched hardness to her mouth. He saw the muscles in her calf tense as her foot eased imperceptibly downward on the gas pedal. The roar of the engine turned to a high-pitched whine reminiscent of a jet airliner taxiing out for takeoff.

Then she said: 'I would die without him. I know that's an expression they use a lot in movies. But I mean it. Literally. Did you ever love anyone that much?'

Max thought of Bernice. No. Even when they were first married he couldn't honestly say he had loved her enough to die for her.

He stared at this dark windblown young woman by his side. That deep and secret intensity he had sensed on other occasions now stood revealed to him, like a deer frozen on

240

the edge of a clearing, and he was afraid that if he made any sudden moves, or spoke too quickly, it would be gone.

And then something happened. He could see somehow through the ruby-dark prism she held up to him. Suddenly he *could* imagine what it might be like to love a woman enough to die for her.

Max found himself envying this man, whoever he was.

'I feel that way about my daughter,' he said. 'When we first brought her home from the hospital, I remember standing over her crib thinking for the first time, yes, a reasonable man could commit murder. If anyone ever tried to hurt Mandy, I wouldn't hesitate to kill him.'

'She's lucky she has you.' Rose was silent a moment; there was just the high whine of the accelerating engine. 'I never knew my father. My mother either. She died in a hospital fire the night I was born. How's that for cinematic?' Her voice held a bitter twist.

'I'm sorry.'

'Oh, I don't remember any of it. I got the whole lurid story later on. About how I was carried down by one of the nurses, wrapped in a wet blanket. And how my grandmother came to get me – my father was overseas at the time – and she thought there had to have been some mistake. You see, I didn't look like my two sisters, or either of my parents. But I was the last one, you see. All the other babies had been claimed. Do you think my mother would have wanted me if she'd lived?' Rose clapped a hand over her mouth. 'God, did I really say that? I can't believe the things I'm telling you.'

'It's all right. I'm a good listener. Go ahead.'

'The rest is pretty boring. You wouldn't want to hear it.' The line of her mouth grew even harder. 'I saw this old Tarzan movie once, and there was this scene where Johnny Weismuller gets stuck in quicksand – in fact, I think he got stuck in quicksand in every picture – but as corny as it was, I knew exactly how he felt. What it was like to be trapped, slowly sinking down, and the harder you struggle to get out, the worse it gets.'

The needle had crept up past eighty-five and was hovering somewhere near ninety now. The noise of the engine a shrill whine.

'Do you know what that's like?' she said loudly.

'Yes, I know.' He thought of Bernice, and it gave him a kind of perverse pleasure imagining what his wife's reaction would be to this little escapade of his. 'Rose, I think you really had better slow down.'

'What about Quent Jorgensen?'

'I suppose killing ourselves might help his case in the end, but I wouldn't recommend it.'

'I mean, don't you want to find out if—' Abruptly she tensed, leaning forward slightly, her fingers locking about the shiny red steering wheel, knuckles showing white.

'What's wrong?' Max could feel himself go suddenly tight all over, as if his skin had shrunk several sizes.

'Holy Mother of God,' she swore. 'It's stuck. I can't . . .' She struggled with the wheel, which appeared to be locked, with only an inch or two give in either direction.

That's when Max saw it. The curve ahead. And the glut of slow-moving traffic just beyond. Rose had taken her foot off the gas, and was now pressing down on the brake, down-shifting into low gear. Her whole body rigid, face white as library paste.

Christ. She was panicking, braking too hard.

There was a horrible squeal, the stink of burning rubber, and the back end fishtailed out into a spin that sent them skidding across two lanes. The guard rail loomed, with a straight drop below. Fear struck like a sandbag hurled at his chest.

'Jesus Chri—'

The instant seemed to hang in space, irrelevant to anything past or future; there was only that looming white guard rail and rocky slope beyond, the endless shrieking of the tires.

And now Rose, a wild woman he scarcely recognized, eyes huge and black as the hot-top racing at them, let loose a high, primal yell as she fought for control.

242

Max was thrown forward against the dash, his forehead thumping painfully against the strip of chrome alongside the windshield. An explosion of white like a flashbulb popping behind his eyes, then a moment when his senses went skidding over the edge of some abyss.

Through the ringing in his ears, he thought he heard her cry out someone's name. It sounded like 'Brian.'

Now his head was clearing, and he watched Rose throw her weight against the steering wheel with every bit of strength she possessed. Then a muted noise like the tumblers inside a balky lock clicking home.

And suddenly the steering wheel was turning, Rose in control again, easing the car around, pulling off on to the shoulder, and finally, blessedly, jerking to a stop.

Max opened his mouth to say something, but no words came. He could only stare a this woman beside him, this good Catholic girl turned madwoman, her dark hair matted and tumbled about her shoulders, her blouse untucked from the waistband of her skirt, her face stamped with the high fevered color of an adrenaline rush. He was too shaken, too overwhelmed.

'My God,' he finally choked. 'My God, Rose. When did you learn to drive like that?'

'I didn't know I could,' she said, expelling her breath in a short explosive laugh even as tears of stunned relief filled her eyes. 'You see, I just got my license a couple of months ago.'

243

# 11

It was the ugliest shiner Rose could ever remember seeing, more black than blue, and puffed up almost the size of the eight ball they used to play with when they were kids, the one that told your fortune different ways depending how it was turned.

Now Rose needed no fortune-telling to read what had happened to her sister. Rose stood in the shabby hallway outside Marie's apartment and stared at the black eye peering over the door chain, anger rising in her.

'Marie, my God, your *eye*.'

'Yeah, I know, I know. Alfred Hitchcock, he'd like me to star in his next movie.' Marie gave a dry bark of a laugh as she unlatched the chain and opened the door the rest of the way to let Rose in. Even in the dim foyer, Rose could see that her sister was nothing but skin and bones under a faded duster stained with baby food, her unwashed hair pasted to her skull. 'Dumbest thing you ever saw. I walked into a door. Do you believe it?'

*No*, Rose wanted to say, *I don't*. Last time, what had it been? The stairs. Marie said she'd broken her arm falling down the stairs. And the time before that, she'd slipped on a Matchbox car and somehow broken her nose and knocked a tooth out. And, sure, it was just a coincidence that each of those times Pete had been home, and out of work.

But Rose kept her thoughts to herself. There was a hands-off look in Marie's good eye, a look that warned, *It's my business if my old man beats on me, so keep your sympathy to yourself*.

She followed Marie into the living room, a cramped

boxlike space with flaky plaster walls and the temporary look of a seedy motel room. Pete was slouched in front of the television, his fist wrapped about a can of Budweiser. Bobby and Missy were playing on the floor by the radiator.

'Is that why you called?' Rose asked, instinctively reaching up to console her sister, then letting her hand fall uselessly to her side as Marie moved a bare, almost imperceptible fraction backwards.

'This?' Marie touched her eye, wincing a little. 'No big deal. I can take care of myself. Hey, you want a cup of coffee or something? I'd ask you to stay for dinner, but it's not exactly the Waldorf. Beans and franks.'

Pete glanced up from 'The Flintstones.' 'Again? Christ, Marie. You know they give me gas. Hell, I could open up my own Mobil station with all the gas you give me.' He chortled at his own joke, then called out, 'Be my guest, Rose. I'm going out anyway. I'll grab a bite down at Tony's.' Tony's was the local beer joint.

Marie shot him a dark look, then bent to scoop up the baby. Little Gabe was howling, head thrown back, mouth open so wide Rose could see not only his four little teeth and glistening gums, but all the way back to his tonsils.

'What did you do to him?' Marie snapped at Bobby, now innocently absorbed in unraveling a long curly strand from the olive-colored carpet where it had come untacked from the floor.

Bobby stuck out his lower lip. 'He hit me first. *Hard*, too. With his bottle.'

'*I'll* hit you, next time,' Marie said. 'He's just a baby. He doesn't know what he's doing.'

Bobby shot Gabe a murderous look, and went back to his unraveling. He had dark hair like his father, and small, angry eyes.

Rose went over, and hunkered down next to him. 'Hey, Bobby. I brought you something.'

She fished a tiny paper umbrella from the pocket of her raincoat, the kind Polynesian restaurants put into mixed drinks. Mr Griffin had brought it back from a lunch at Trader Vic's. For luck, he'd said with a grin, dropping it on her desk.

And then he'd told her about his friend Sam Blankenship and the Phipps Foundation, the possibility of a scholarship for college and maybe for law school too if she wanted to go that far. What a dear man Mr Griffin was. Holy Mother, wouldn't that be something, studying philosophy and Shakespeare, and learning French maybe . . . though God knows where she'd ever use French. Still, how wonderful if she could . . .

But then her bright fantasy faded.

What difference would any of it make without Brian?

Four months, dear God, and not one letter. *Could he have forgotten me? Has he stopped caring?*

No, not true, she would not let herself believe that. There *had* to be an explanation. Rose swallowed hard against the tight, aching knot in her throat. *No more tears*, she told herself. *You've cried enough. Any more and you'll be running into a serious salt deficiency.*

Bobby was staring at the little umbrella suspiciously. 'Does Gabe and Missy get one, too?'

'Just you,' she said. 'But don't tell. It's our secret.'

He smiled then, like the sun breaking through a bank of thunderclouds. And Rose felt her heart lift a little.

'You'd make a good mother,' Marie said as they were sitting at the yellow Formica table in the kitchen, drinking their coffee. She sounded wistful, Rose thought. As if she didn't quite believe in such a thing, as if good mothers were like the tooth fairy and Santa Claus.

'Why not? Doctor, lawyer, Indian chief. I could give them all a try.'

Rose again thought of Max – he had insisted she call him Max, not Mr Griffin (it seemed a little silly, he'd said, after they'd come so close to getting killed together). She'd been worried when he summoned her into his office the following morning – after all, it had been *her* bright idea to take the Cyclone for a spin. But he hadn't said one word about it. Instead he told her he might have a bit of a surprise for her after lunch. And that afternoon, when he told her about the possibility of a scholarship, Rose had been so overwhelmed she hadn't been able to say a word except 'Thank you.'

She told Marie about it, trying to keep the great excitement she felt out of her voice.

So fierce was the expression that then came over Marie's battered face that Rose was stunned. Her sister's mouth trembled, and the slit where her left eye peeked through the ghastly swollen flesh glittered like stainless steel.

'Do it,' she hissed, leaning forward, her thin hands clutched about the coffee mug set before her. 'For Jesus' fucking sake, Rose, a chance like this won't ever come again. College. I wish to God *I* had that chance. Don't waste it like I did, Rose. Don't do anything stupid.'

A tear formed on the pale blue of her sister's good eye. A hard tear like ice that didn't fall. Rose felt a wave of sorrow for her sister, trapped in this apartment, this kitchen littered with dirty dishes and toast crumbs, the only dream within Marie's reach the marked-up Help Wanted columns of the *Times* folded out on the table next to a Bic banana.

'Nothing's for certain yet,' she said. 'Mr Griffin – Max, I mean – just had lunch with this man. It probably won't amount to anything. Besides, I'd still have to work at least part time, and if I did that, plus school, who would look after Nonnie?'

Marie slumped back in her chair, eyes dull, as if the effort of thinking back over her own missed chances had drained her. In a bitter voice, she said, 'You asked me why I called? Well, maybe when I tell you, you'll think twice about wasting your life playing Florence Nightingale to our dear Nonnie.'

'What are you talking about?'

'This, that's what.' Marie got up, yanked open a drawer full of old rubber bands, plastic baby bottle stoppers, strips of twist ties. She rummaged in back, then pulled out

247

a handful of letters, wafer-thin blue airmail envelopes tied together with grocery string.

The top one was stamped with half a dozen postmarks and addressed to her in Brian's tight, spiky scrawl.

Rose's temples began to pound thickly. There was a humming, staticky noise inside her head, and she suddenly felt quite dizzy.

She reached out with a trembling hand to take the bundle of envelopes from Marie, and the solidness of it after so many days and nights of empty longing, the cool crinkly paper against her skin, her name scrawled in Brian's hand leaping out at her, sent the dizziness spiraling up and up.

*Oh, merciful God, he didn't forget.*

'How did you get these?' she managed to ask in a shaky voice. But for one delirious instant, she didn't even care. All that mattered was the letters in her hand. Her heart was racing. *Oh, God, dear God, he loves me, he still loves me.*

Marie folded her bony arms across her chest. 'I did what you been nagging me to do all these months. I was out shopping, and I thought what the hell, OK, I'll drop in on the old lady just this once. And boy was she glad to see me. Just couldn't stop talking. The words weren't so clear, just like you said, but I got the meaning all right. She hates your guts, Rose. All she could talk about was you, how you leave her alone all day, how you ignore her when you're there, don't feed her what she likes, how you wouldn't give two Hail Marys if she fell down and broke her hip trying to make it to the bathroom.'

'I don't understand,' Rose said, the dizziness settling now, becoming something cold, hard. 'What's that got to do with Brian's letters?' She clutched them in both hands, and it seemed at that moment that if she let go of them, she would sink right into the floor.

Marie's mouth curled down in a thin sneer. 'All that time she was going on about you, I could see how scared she was. Scared you'd leave her someday, and she'd have no-one to complain about. Scared shitless of being alone. But she made one big mistake. She figured I was on her side, so she told me about the letters, even where she'd hidden them.'

The drumming in her head was so loud Rose could scarcely hear what Marie was saying. Nonnie? Letters? She felt as if she were watching Marie on TV, one of the soap operas Nonnie consumed one after another like potato chips in the darkness of her living room.

'Mrs Slatsky brings the mail up in the afternoon,' Rose heard herself responding, her voice dreamy and disconnected. 'Nonnie looks forward to it. Even the junk mail. The Rexall flyers. And those window envelopes that say you may have won a hundred thousand dollars in some sweepstakes, but you won't know until you send—' Rose dropped her face into her hands. 'Oh God, Marie, I can't believe it. She wouldn't *do* this to me.'

But even while she said it, Rose knew that Nonnie would. It all made such perfect, hideous sense.

*What an idiot I've been, hoping that someday she'd show that she really does love me. Thinking anything I did for her could ever make any difference.*

She remembered the shock she'd felt, years and years ago, seeing a photograph of her father with a cut-out space beside him, like what's left after you punch out a paper doll along the dotted lines. That horrible naked hole had been her mother. Nonnie had cut her out with a pair of scissors, as if she'd wanted to obliterate even her memory.

'What are you going to do?' asked Marie, backing away, looking a little frightened now, like a kid playing with matches who starts a fire and doesn't know how to put it out.

Rose stared down at her hands, clenched into fists on the stained Formica tabletop. She was paralyzed with anger, smashing through her like a tidal wave.

She thought of Brian, people shooting at him in some jungle on the other side of the world, and of him sending her letters, waiting for her to answer, lonely, afraid, maybe even desperate. Four months. She'd written to him at least every week, but then she'd had to stop sending her letters. She hadn't dared continue, those letters had been too full of hurt and anger. All that time, Brian no doubt wondering if *she* had forgotten, or didn't love him.

Fury surged through her, making everything black. Black as death. Black as evil. Black as the rotten heart that beat in her grandmother's withered chest.

Rose thought about killing Nonnie then, placing her hands about Nonnie's scrawny neck and choking her until that black heart of hers stopped beating.

'I'm going to do what I should have done a long time ago,' Rose said.

'. . . deliver us from evil, now and forever. Amen.'

Rose stared at the frail white-haired figure knelt in prayer on the scuffed cabbage rose linoleum beside the bed. That huge, dark, Victorian monstrosity of a bed which had given Rose nightmares as a child, gleaming dully under a sallow coat of varnish cracked and fissured with age. A single dim lamp burned on the marble-top nightstand, throwing a sulfurous glow over the narrow cell-like room. Above Nonnie's bed hung an ancient plastic crucifix, split and yellowed like the teeth of a very old dog. Below it, a framed mourning wreath under glass made from the braided gray hair of Nonnie's dead father.

Rose had spent the last few hours on one of the old-people benches that lined Ocean Parkway, reading Brian's letters over and over, laughing and crying, people staring at her as if she were a crazy bag lady, then walking until her anger had worn down to a smooth steel nugget, lodged like a cold bullet in her heart.

Now that bullet began to heat, a dull red glow in her chest.

*You sanctimonious old bitch. How dare you kneel there praying. As if you had any right to God's mercy.*

Nonnie started a little and glanced up. Her mouth puckered, as if yanked tight by a drawstring. The light

250

caught her glasses, flashing Rose's reflection back at her for an eerie second.

'So. Miss America, she finally remembered she got a home,' Nonnie croaked, her pale eyes behind the sparking lenses full of disdain. 'Come here and help me up.'

All those hours, Rose thought, working with her, helping her walk, teaching her how to speak again. I should have left her to rot.

'Help yourself up, you old bitch.' Rose was shaking now, knees rubbery, heart pumping with rapid shallow beats.

'What?' Nonnie's white head cocked to one side, birdlike. The startled rictus of her mouth hardened into a thin glistening slash. 'What did you say?'

'You heard me. Or better yet,' Rose said, clutching hold of the doorknob for support, 'why don't you ask God to help you up? All these years of praying, all those Hail Marys and Our Fathers you've been stuffing in like quarters down a parking meter, you might as well get something for it.'

'Filth!' Nonnie hissed. 'How dare you speak such filth in my house!'

Rose watched her struggle to pull herself up by the bed frame, only to collapse again on to her knees, a sound like the sharp rap of knuckles against the door of an empty house.

Rose felt cold, so cold. Even in this room, overheated, stuffy, smelling like the inside of a medicine cabinet.

'Your house,' she echoed, her voice arising cold and even from the still eye of her fury. 'Yes, that's right, Nonnie. I don't belong here. You never wanted me from the beginning, you probably wish I'd died in that fire with my mother. Marie asked me once a long time ago why I let you treat me that way, why I didn't just leave. You see, you made me feel so dirty I thought if only I could make myself clean you would love me the way you loved Clare. But the dirt wouldn't come off. And now I know why.'

She gave her grandmother a long look that was hard as

flint, then said, 'Because the dirt wasn't on me. It was on you, all along.'

Nonnie grasped the bed frame once again, hauling herself up. The massive headboard creaked and swayed, tapping out a disjointed Morse code against the plaster wall behind it.

Now she was on her feet, groping for the cane leaned up against the wall, now facing Rose, a rusty old blade of a woman, twisted and hobbled with arthritis, yet still somehow a threat.

'Slut!' she shrieked, her face strangely contorted – the stroke had left one side paralyzed – like something made of modeling clay being pulled in opposite directions. 'Trash straight outta the gutter. Yes, I know what you do behind my back . . . lying with that boy and Lord knows who else. That's where you were tonight, wasn't it? Lying with a man like a cheap slut. Jus' like your mother and your slut sister, shaming me, shaming my son's good name.'

Rose felt her hatred glowing, a ring of embers around her heart.

'So you kept Brian's letters. You hid them so I would think he didn't care about me.'

Nonnie's pale eyes glittered with malevolent triumph. 'Yes, I hid them. May God's will be done. And the Wicked shall repent of be struck down by the Righteous.'

'God, oh God.' Rose covered her face with her hands, the horror of it closing in on her, overwhelming her suddenly, like the darkness of a closet clicking shut on her. Only this time the darkness was inside her too, the black hole in her chest where her heart had once been.

And Nonnie's voice hissing on and on like some devilish serpent.

'Sure, you ask His mercy now. But it's too late. He'll punish you. Just like He punished Angie. He made her burn for her sins of fornication. Then we shall see. How the Mighty are risen and the Wicked scorned. And what good will your precious letters do you then, slut? What good, eh?'

Something snapped in Rose, as sudden and swift as a rotten footbridge giving way, hurling her into a black murderous space where there was only the red sun of her rage.

With a cry, Rose lunged forward, right arm swinging outward, elbow cocked. There was a high-pitched whining in her ears, a taste like blood in her mouth. And all she could think about was hitting Nonnie hard enough to knock the head right off her scrawny shoulders.

'Bitch! You lying evil old bitch!'

But something deeper than her hate stopped her from striking Nonnie, something sane and decent buried in the bedrock of her soul.

Instead, she reached up and snatched the crucifix from the wall, yanking its blackened nail free in a skittering hail of plaster chips. She hurled it across the room at the heavy dresser hulked like a sentinel against the wall, straight into the clutter of medicine bottles and amber pharmaceutical vials. A splintering crash. Bottles and vials crashing about, flying against the spotted mirror that hung over the dresser, spinning over the edge, bouncing and rattling off the linoleum. A bottle of Pepto-Bismol tottered on to its side, oozing a sludgy pink creek down the dresser's chipped veneer side. The reek of peppermint rising in a sweet-sick wave.

Nonnie let out a shrill yelp, and sank down on the mattress as abruptly as if her cane had been kicked out from under her.

'There's your God,' Rose cried, looking down at the shrunken old woman on the bed. Her blood sang high and wild in her head, and she felt oddly weightless, as if she'd just heaved a huge and terrible burden from her shoulders. 'Let Him take care of you now.'

April 28, 1969

Dear Brian,

I'm not sure how to begin this letter, or even how I'm going to finish it. My hand is shaking so much I can

253

hardly hold the pen. And I can't seem to stop crying. I just finished reading your letters for the fifteenth or sixteenth time. And can only hope when you receive this you will forgive me for not writing sooner. You see, I didn't get your letters until yesterday. Nonnie had hidden them from me. Does this sound like a Gothic novel by Charlotte Brontë? Well, I don't think even Charlotte Brontë could do my dear sweet grandmother justice. But if there is a bright side to all this it's that I finally got up the nerve to do what I should have done years ago: leave.

Last night after THE SCENE I packed everything I could fit in one suitcase. I'm staying with my friend April Lewis just temporarily (one of the girls at the office) until I can get my own place. It won't be much probably, on what I make, but oh Brian, just the thought of it, my own place away from Nonnie, it's like a dream. I still can't believe I'm doing it. Neither can Nonnie, I'll bet. I called Clare last night from a phone booth on my way to April's. I told her what had happened, and before she could say 'I'll pray for you' the operator broke in and told me that would be another twenty-five cents. I almost laughed then, I really did, except that I was too mad. I told Clare that if she didn't want Nonnie to starve to death or fall downstairs and break every selfish bone in her body she'd better pack her halo and climb down from whatever cloud she was on, and come take care of Nonnie herself. And you know what? I don't think God will hold it against me one bit.

You want to hear something even crazier? This morning when I got to work (I'm writing this on my lunch hour) my boss, Mr Griffin, said he had good news for me. He talked to an old friend of his who's in charge of a scholarship fund for older people (that's me!) who want to go back to school, and now it's practically all settled. I'm going to college! Yes, me! The money isn't much, just enough for tuition and that kind of thing, but Mr Griffin has promised me as much free-lance typing as I can handle, so I won't starve in the meantime. I'm very excited about all this, and also very scared. Am I smart enough? Will I be laughed out of the classroom on the very first day? I called Molly at work just now, and she says I'm being completely stupid, which I suppose means she thinks I am smart enough. God, I hope so. Otherwise I'll be the oldest, dumbest freshman at NYU.

All this must sound a little weird and radical to you, but I promise it's all for the best. When you come back, we can start all over, and it'll be just you and I, no more Holy Martyrs. No more Vietnam. Brian, I miss you so much sometimes I just don't think I can stand it another minute. Is it as bad over there as they say? You don't say much in your letters about what it's like, the conditions, the fighting. Is it because you don't want to worry me? You write that you love me and miss me, but if you're suffering and don't tell me, that separates us even more. I'd rather worry than be shut out. So please, please, tell me everything. I pray for you every day, every minute. But most of all, I pray this letter reaches you before you give up hope on me.

Love Always,
Rose
XXXXXXXOOOOOOOOOOO

P.S. I'm enclosing a Polaroid snap April took of me last night even though I look like something the cat dragged in (don't show this to any of your buddies if you can help it). And don't ask why I'm wearing only one earring. It's sort of a good-luck charm, like a four-leaf clover. Two would spoil it, don't you think? Anyway, I'm wearing it for you. I won't take it off until you come back to me.

255

# 12

'You ever think 'bout what happens after you dead?' the black kid from Alabama asked softly from behind in the darkness of the trail. 'I mean, goin' to heaven and all that kinda shit?'

'No,' Brian whispered back. He slapped at something crawling on his cheek, he couldn't see what. The rain-swept darkness of the jungle was complete. He moved guided only by the quiet squelching of Matinsky's boots just ahead.

It was long past midnight. His platoon had been marching on boonie patrol since four that afternoon, and he felt as if a hundred years had passed between now and then. Five or six kilometers back, one of the men – Reb Parker – had stepped on a Bouncing Betty mine that literally blew him in half. He died with his boots on . . . except that his legs just didn't happen to be attached to his body at the time.

No, Brian didn't believe in heaven. But he sure as shit could imagine what hell would look like: endless wet corridors of jungle, waist-high elephant grass that sliced at your hands and arms like razor blades, never-ending rain, and everywhere the death-stink of rot.

'Why not?' the kid pressed, edging up alongside him. Brian could just make out the broad brown features under his camouflage helmet, and smell his breath, acrid with chewing tobacco. 'You Catholic, ain't you? I seen you crossin' yo'self.'

'It's not a given.'

'Givin' what?'

'It means just because I'm Catholic doesn't mean I accept everything the Church tells me.'

'You believe in God, doncha?'

'I'm not sure anymore.'

'Man, don't say that. I got the willies bad enough as it is.'

'This your first boonie patrol?' Brian had been on half a dozen so far. He pulled Recon his first day in country, but Alabama had just joined the platoon.

'Man, I wish it was. I been humpin' these woods so long, I figure my number's due. This here's my third outfit. Cain't pull snake-eyes every time.'

Brian paused. 'Listen. Do you hear it? The river. We're almost there, I think. We'll be OK once we get there. That's our PZ.'

'That's just the rain you hearin', boy.' The kid, whose name Brian had forgotten, laughed softly. 'Been nothin' but rain since they shipped me up-country. Lord, I'd give my left nut for a pair of dry socks and a smoke. Any gooks out there, you ain't gonna hear 'em 'cause they don't wear no boots. They ain't so busy dreamin' 'bout dry socks they goin' get their fuckin' heads blown off.'

He chuckled softly, and the chuckles turned to a stream of hysterical giggles, muffled so it came out sounding like the high whine of tracer fire. Brian wondered if the kid was losing his mind. Christ, weren't they all, one way or another?

You think about dry socks, so you won't think about dying.

You hear the river, so you don't have to think about how far away it might still be.

Like you never hear a boonie rat say how long he's been in country, Brian thought, only how short he is, how many more months before he goes home.

*Home. Oh God, can't think about that. Home's where they send you when you're dead.* He knew of platoons where the grunts carried their own body bags, even slept in them to keep dry.

He thought back to his first day. Landing in Saigon

257

aboard a Continental jet with Glen Yarbrough spinning a sugary melody over the headphones, a pretty blond stewardess chirping, 'Welcome to Vietnam, gentlemen, I'll see you again in a year.' Then hours of standing out on the broiling tarmac, waiting along with thirty or forty other cherries to be assigned to a unit. The guys were joking around with each other, punch-drunk from the heat and from eighteen hours in the air, one kid all revved up to get assigned to a front line unit so he could 'kick some ass.' Brian hadn't been too worried. From what he'd seen so far, he figured the stories he'd heard about Nam had been mostly exaggerated.

Then a big chopper landed and its crew began tossing large bags out like so many duffels. At first he'd thought it *was* some sort of cargo, and maybe he even could have convinced himself of that . . . if it hadn't been for the dull squelching noises those bags made when they hit the tarmac. Then one burst open, and in the ghastly split second before he fainted, Brian had his real welcome to Vietnam: a lump of bloody chopped meat in the shape of what had once been a human being.

Now, as he slogged through the jungle, Brian tried instead to blank his mind, the way Trang had taught him. Maybe he really would hear the river, maybe they really were getting close.

But all he could hear was the rain. The kid – Jackson, wasn't it? – was silent, and there was only the endless drumroll of the rain, the wet slap of leaves against plastic ponchos. A cloud must have lifted because Brian, peering through the gloom, could now make out the blurred shape ahead (was it almost dawn? Christ, please, yes), the hump of Matinsky's rucksack under his poncho, the antennae of his PRC-25 poking up alongside his head. He looked like some weird insect, maybe the man-roach of Kafka's 'Metamorphosis.' And beyond Matinsky, walking point ahead of the CO, Lieutenant Gruber, Brian now caught fleeting glimpses of the reed-shadow that was Trang Li Duc, moving through the dense brush with uncanny grace.

He thought: *If there's any NVA action out there, Trang will spot it.*

Trang, a Kit Carson scout, knew this piece of jungle better than anyone, and he had the eyes and reflexes of a leopard. At fourteen, he'd been forcibly recruited by the NVA, and by the time he fled at sixteen, he'd learned such tricks as listening for enemy activity by placing a small flat piece of wood on the ground and putting his ear to it, and locating claymore tripwires at night by sweeping the darkness just ahead of him with a blade of grass.

Some of the guys weren't so sure about Trang. 'Once a gook, always a gook' was Matinsky's expression. But it had been Trang, not Matinsky, who'd saved Brian's ass on a boonie patrol like this less than a month ago. They'd been humping the hills above Tien Sung, Brian walking point that time, exhausted after hours of trying to hold to a straight line on the steep ridge. By dawn, Brian was so beat he would have stretched out in a rice paddy full of leeches if it meant getting some shut-eye.

They came upon the village just as the sun was casting its first red blaze above the trees. A sleepy little village tucked way high into the hillside with rice paddies like stair risers leading up to it. Smoke curling above the thatched huts, water buffalo, the whole pastoral bit. They had stopped for a good long time, checking it out, no sign of VC, just old men and mama-sans and little kids. One old mama-san was cooking a big pot of rice. Nothing unusual there. She gave Brian a toothless smile and wrapped some in a banana leaf for him. He was reaching out to take it when Trang suddenly grabbed him, shoving him to one side. A split second later a burst of sapper fire tore up the ground where Brian had stood. Two guys bought it before they could make it to cover.

'How did you know we were walking into an ambush?' Brian asked Trang later.

Trang looked at him with those flat, oddly expressionless black eyes and said, 'Rice. She cook too much rice for one village.'

But now Brian's aching body made it hard to think about Trang, or anything but his own misery. He wanted a pair of dry socks as bad as Jackson. Inside his boots, his feet felt like a couple of rotting sponges. They hurt, too. They hurt in a way that made him afraid of what he'd see when finally he got to undo the laces and pry off these damn boots.

But nothing he could do about it now. You could no more get away from jungle rot than you could the bugs and the leeches and the rain. But, Christ, wasn't there ever going to be any end to it? The mud seemed to suck at him, drag him down a little bit farther with each step he took.

A rustling sound deep in the bush caused him to break stride, cocking an ear. The river? He couldn't really tell. Probably not yet. Dickson back there with the funny papers had said two, maybe three klicks more to go before they hit the water. But that had been more than an hour ago, hadn't it?

'Wish I had me one of them Starlight scopes,' Brian heard a voice behind him mutter. 'You could see a snake taking a piss in the dark two miles away with one of them suckers.'

Another, wearier voice, 'Oh, man, I just wish I was home.'

Then no-one spoke. Just the slapping of leaves, the squelch of boots pulling away from mud, the faint fuzzy static of Matinsky's radio.

*Home*, Brian thought. An image of Rose formed in his mind. He felt as if he'd swallowed a heat tab. A flame that crawled up from his gut and settled in just above his Adam's apple. He saw her in his room at Columbia kneeling on the floor spangled with pennies, naked, her face wet with tears. He saw himself hunkering down, gathering her in his arms, making love to her right there on the floor. The image was so vivid he could almost feel each sensation, even the pennies pressing cool circles into his flesh, the furious heat between those long legs wrapped about his. *Don't leave me, Bri, don't ever leave me . . .*

Then it vanished. He was back in the jungle. The rain pelting against his helmet, slithering off his poncho. The sound of the river just a whisper in the back of his head now. Brian felt like crying. If only he could have held on to her, just for a little while longer, until they made it to the river.

*Wise up, man, she's forgotten all about you.*

No, he wouldn't believe that. He *couldn't*. But face it, it had been months since he'd gotten a letter. She could have met someone else. Maybe she did. No, it didn't make sense. Another girl, it could happen, not Rose. But what *did* make sense anymore? Out here in these jungles, he had seen things, monstrosities, that before he never would have thought possible. Now he could believe just about anything.

Disneyland West. That was grunt lingo for Nam. A make-believe place. But here, now, Nam was as real as something he'd swallowed, something hard and cold settled deep in the pit of his stomach. It was home that didn't seem real anymore. Brian could hardly remember what it felt like to walk on a sidewalk, to lie in a bed with clean white sheets, to go through a whole day without looking over his shoulder expecting someone to try to shoot him.

Even Rose seemed not quite real. When she did come to him, it was usually in the morning, those first few seconds before coming fully awake. In that gray DMZ between sleep and alertness, he would feel her breath warm against his cheek, certain that when he opened his eyes he would find her asleep beside him, a tumble of dark curls against his pillow, one long golden-skinned arm stretched across his belly. Then someone would flop over in the bunk above his, or start banging on the corrugated metal side of the hootch, and her image would evaporate like faint morning haze.

In the real world guys got dumped all the time. That poor bastard O'Reilly, boasting nonstop about how his wife could never get enough of him. Then just last week come the divorce papers. Not even a dear John letter.

Jesus Christ. If only Rose would write. Just one letter. That's all he was asking.

Brian felt himself shivering. The rain had leaked through his poncho, soaking his fatigues. He thought about the notebook carefully wrapped in oilcloth at the bottom of his rucksack. The journal he'd been keeping since day one of this nightmare. If he ever made it out of here, he'd need that journal, if only to convince himself all this had really happened.

A sudden noise. Brian froze in his tracks. A rustling, but louder and closer than before. Farther up the trail, he glimpsed Trang sink into a crouch, his M-16 swing into position.

Brian dropped to his belly, hammered the bolt back on his own M-16, chambered a round, as if a switch had been pulled in his head. Beside him, Jackson did the same. Ahead, Matinsky broke clumsily for cover, a big slow-footed Nebraska farmboy, the radio on his back lurching and bobbing.

Brian heard popping sounds, like a string of fire-crackers going off, and Matinsky toppled, crashing into the brush like a downed chopper.

Then all hell broke loose.

More popping of automatic rifles, then the darkness exploded in a deafening blast of orange fire. *Mortars, oh Jesus, they're shelling us.* For one hellish instant, night switched to day, and the jungle seemed to leap out at Brian in a Technicolor blaze. Branches and vines twined together like snakes, veiled in mist and silhouetted by the Halloween afterglow of mortars. No sign of the enemy – but, God, it sounded like hundreds, those popping rifles, spitting fire from every bush, every goddamn tree. Chunks of red clay flying, stinging his face. A crater the size of a freshly dug grave not ten yards to his left, naked tree roots clawing their way to the surface like huge skeletal fingers. Farther down the line, men were screaming. Wounded. some probably dying. Others already dead. He heard their gunner, Dale Short, open up on the brush with a round of Quad-50 fire.

262

Brian's mind spun like an empty gunbarrel. A numbing terror seized him.

*They were lying in for us. The river. We're never going to make it to the river.*

He heard a high gurgled scream, saw Jackson buckle to his knees as if in prayer.

One whole side of Jackson's skull was blown away.

*Oh holy Christ, no . . . no . . . no . . .*

A thin film of gray came scudding across Brian's vision. His ears were ringing. His rifle suddenly felt as if it weighed a hundred pounds. Everything seemed to be taking place in slow motion. As if in a nightmare. Making sense only as dreams do, with a kind of existentialist rationale.

*Where the fuck is Lieutenant Gruber? Why isn't he giving orders?*

Another blinding orange-red mortar blast, and he heard the crackle of Matinsky's radio, and a voice not Matinsky's booming into it, 'Delta Bravo, come in, come in, do you read me? Delta Echo here. We're hit. Looks like they've got us flanked on all perimeters. We're gonna need a medevac in here, and pronto. Coordinates are VD 15 – oh . . . Holy sh—'

The voice was cut off.

*Surrounded on all perimeters.* Christ, if only he could *see* them. Brian let off a round of M-16 fire into the bush. Beneath him he felt the earth convulse with the impact of the enemy's AK-47s. He tried not to think about the body leaking its brain into the mud beside him. He was afraid he might be sick.

The he *was* sick, vomiting up the stink of cordite, blood, and scorched flesh. *Sweet Jesus, they're picking us off like ducks in a shooting gallery.*

Digging his elbows in, Brian belly-crawled into the bush, a tangle of vines and elephant grass. He stopped, bile rising in his throat again. A pair of sightless eyes stared up at the sky not two meters away. Gruber. Oh God. The rain was falling against his staring eyes, pooling in the sockets.

Brian felt a scream gathering force in his solar plexus. A scream that would rip the roof right off what remained of his sanity.

But something was gripping his shoulder, forcing him down. Brian twisted his head around, and was confronted by a sharp Oriental face streaked with orange mud, a pair of impenetrable black eyes. A face like a rusty ax blade. Trang.

*'Mau len!'* Trang hissed, motioning off into the thicket of bamboo that lay to their left, two, maybe three dozen yards away. 'River this way. Follow me.'

Brian looked back. In the hellish glow, he saw their perimeters seemed to have dissolved. No visible line of support, no voice of authority calling out flanking maneuvers. Gruber dead. The Prick-25 strapped to Matinsky's back shot to hell, a gut-sprung tangle of copper wires, circuit boards, buckled plastic casing. Sergeant Starkey lying dead beside it in a puddle of blood, the handset clutched in his frozen grip. Shot before he could radio in their coordinates.

The river. Yeah. If he and Trang could make it to the river. There was a sandspit on the opposite bank where a chopper could land, Dickson had said. If he could sit still long enough to pop open a heat tab and scoop a hole in the ground for it, the chopper's infrared might pick them out.

Brian yanked a frag grenade from his belt, popped its pin, and lobbed it into the brush to clear their way. A strobe flash of white boiling up into red smoke, a split second later a thunderous boom.

In the heartbeat of quiet that followed the grenade explosion, he heard it, the sweet sound of rushing water. So close. Not more than a hundred yards. But it might just as well be a hundred miles. They might make it to the river, all right. But in one piece?

Nevertheless, he followed Trang, now crawling low and silent as a lizard, cutting a diagonal path through the brush. Ahead lay the dense thicket of bamboo, a crosshatch of shadows tantalizing as a mirage.

Pop. A bullet whined past his ear. Brian kept low, his belly to the ground, taking the impact of each exploding mortar like a dull kick in the pit of his stomach. He used his knees and elbows to propel himself forward, foot by painful foot, branches and roots clawing at his face, the gritty taste of dirt in his mouth.

*Don't think about dying. Don't think about heaven or hell, or anything except getting out of here.*

He kept his eyes trained on the dark lizard shape of Trang ahead, hardly daring to blink for fear of losing sight of him. *Just a little bit farther. Please, God. Just a few feet more.*

Now tiny razor-edged leaves slicing, stabbing his face. Slender stalks of bamboo glinting like polished jade, falling away on either side with a dry rattle. His knees sank into slimy river mud rank with the smell of decomposition. The sound of rushing water swelled in his ears, the sweetest sound in the world.

Through the bamboo, he could see it, moonlight gleaming on black satin, oh Jesus, the river. His heart leapt. On the other side stretched a long spit of sand, wide enough for a helicopter to land.

Like a prayer answered in a miracle, Brian heard the distant whumping of rotor blades overhead. *They're looking for us.* Relief backfired through him. He fumbled inside his flak jacket for a heat tab.

His hands were trembling as he tore open the foil packet, and frantically pawed a hole in the sludgy earth. The enemy wouldn't see it, but the infra-red on Spooky could pick it up.

Just then Trang's slender form unfolded from the ground into a crouch, moving like soil skimming the surface of water to the river's edge.

Suddenly the bamboo exploded in a corona of red fire. Brian felt something slam into him, a train going a hundred fifty miles an hour.

Then a huge whistling blackness, falling like a guillotine's blade, severing him from consciousness.

265

When he came to, it felt like a huge red-hot stake had been driven through his stomach, pinning him to the earth. He tried to scream, but there didn't seem to be any air in his lungs. There was only this vast burning gulf of agony he had somehow tumbled into.

His mind skated to the grey edge of unconsciousness once again. Dimly, he heard noises. Men shouting. The strafe of Gatling guns.

Slowly, agonizingly, fighting the gray tide that pulled at his brain, Brian managed to drag himself into a sitting position. He stared down at the shredded remains of his poncho. Oh Jesus, he was hit bad. Blood. There was a lot of blood. He wondered if he was going to die.

He had never been so scared. He didn't want to die. Most of all he didn't want to die here, in this godforsaken shithole, a leftover going putrid on a dirty plate.

*I promised Rose I would come back. I promised –*

Brian heard an agonized moan, and his eyes searched the darkness. Then he saw. Trang. Face down in the slime, a shank of splintered bone sticking out where his right foot had been.

*Oh Jesus . . . a mine. He tripped a mine.*

Ignoring the white heat gnawing and twisting in his gut, Brian crawled over and hooked an arm under Trang's slender shoulders. Kneeling, he pulled Trang up so his head rested against his thighs.

'Gotta get out of here, buddy,' he gasped. 'Gotta get to the other side.'

Brian peered up at the sky. He saw the red lights of a Cobra assault helicopter swing in a wide arc, then bank, followed by an explosion, huge white and orange blossoms of fire unfurling over the trees like some beautiful poisonous flower out of Rappacini's garden.

*'Didi mau! Didi mau!'* Trang was shaking his head, his face an ashen circle in the semi-darkness.

'No,' Brian panted, 'no way I'm ditching you.' Trang had saved his life once. Brian had not forgotten.

Brian clamped his arm tighter about Trang, and felt the

stake in his gut give a savage twist. He went faint, a high-pitched whine in his head like a swarm of jungle mosquitoes. He steeled himself against it.

*Later, man, you can't lose it now. You're too close. Nobody quits on the finish line.*

The river, the river.

*Gotta make it to the other side.*

His right arm hooked under Trang's armpits, using his left elbow as leverage, Brian began the slow dragging crawl through the muck and bamboo to the water's edge less than five yards away.

The pain rose, poised on a crystal-shattering note. His mind looped in and out of delirium.

*Christ . . . He walked on water, turned it to wine . . . Old Man River, he just keeps rolling . . . rolling . . .*

Trang was heavy, so heavy . . . how could that be . . . a sliver of a kid like him?

Then his knees were sinking in deep sludge, and water filled his mouth, his nostrils. Brian pulled his head up, choking, coughing. The gray mist behind his eyes rolled away, and he saw that he was waist deep in water.

The water folded its wings about him, lifted him up, and it was all he could do to keep the limp weight of Trang from being dragged off by the sluggish current. He struggled to keep them both afloat, straining his head back as the black water crept up over his mouth, leaking into his nostrils.

Staring straight up, he saw that the clouds were breaking up. The sky underneath the color of a fading bruise, yellow and pink, a few stars poking through like splinters of bone. Almost morning.

He began to cry. So close. And he wasn't going to make it. He could feel the last of his strength ebbing downstream with the current. And the pain rising, huge and terrible, a mountain made of broken glass he must climb on bare hands and knees.

Then he heard a voice, distant but clear as an echo at the end of a long corridor, Rose's voice.

267

*You promised, Brian. You promised me you would come back. You promised . . .*

But his promise didn't count anymore. It had been so long since he had held Rose. Somewhere in that endless corridor of time he had lost her. Or she had lost him.

She had stopped loving him . . .

And now it was time to let go.

He *wanted* to let go. Let go of this burning agony, and just drift, peaceful, borne weightless as a twig or a blade of grass along the slow-moving current.

Then he felt Trang struggle weakly in his arms, and knew he couldn't let go, not yet. For Trang's sake, at least.

Brian, summoning a strength he didn't possess, his heart nearly bursting with the effort of keeping the both of them afloat, began to swim.

# 13

*The corpses were stacked like cordwood against the concrete wall of the operating room. Their olive-drab fatigues stiff with dried blood, their sightless eyes fixed on the ceiling with blank milky stares. Rachel drew close, and saw that one of the bodies on top was still alive. She froze with horror. His eyes were rolling in a face that wasn't a face at all, but a mask of caked blood. Now she was reaching out, her arms made of elastic, stretching on and on for ever before her hands finally closed about his shoulders. She struggled desperately to pull him free. Maybe she could still save him, maybe there was still time. Then tears began spilling from his eyes, cutting in muddy creeks down the ruined wasteland of his face. His mouth fell open, and he cried: 'Why did you let me die? I am your son. Why did you—'*

Rachel came awake with a sudden bolt. She shot upright in her narrow iron cot, bathed in cold sweat, heart lodged like a dry stone in her throat. She scrubbed at her eyes with sticky, trembling hands.

*A nightmare, just a stupid nightmare*, she told herself. But, oh God, so *real*. And that face. That bloody mask. She knew him.

The boy she had killed.

*He called himself my . . . but no, I won't think about that. If I start thinking about the abortion again on top of all this, I'll go crazy.*

A rattling sound now. Someone hammering at the door.

'Dr Rosenthal!' a woman's voice called. The hammering stopped, and the door cracked open a few inches, a head silhouetted in the crack. Delicate features, straight hair pulled back in a knot. One of the Vietnamese nurses. 'Doctor . . . please, you must come!'

'Wha . . . that you, Lily?' Rachel felt groggy, disoriented. Her body leaden, as if shot full of Novocain. Tonight was the first time she'd been off her feet in forty-eight hours. She felt as if she hadn't truly slept since arriving in Vietnam six weeks ago.

In the dark, she batted aside mosquito netting, and swung her legs over the side of the cot, fumbling into a pair of khaki trousers crumpled on the floor, yanking them over the man's T-shirt that hung down almost to her knees.

'It's me. Medevac chopper just came in,' Lily answered, sounding a little out of breath. 'Eight wounded. Most are in bad shape. Doctor MacDougal needs you in Triage.'

'How bad is bad?' Rachel asked.

She stood up, tugged on the chain that connected to a single overhead bulb. Bright light slapped her awake, and she looked around the concrete room she shared with Kay. Small, austere as a prison cell, but oddly, it suited her. Two iron cots tented in mosquito netting, and a single rickety dresser. Wooden louvers in place of windows. Walls bare except for the cracked mirror over the dresser, and a Grateful Dead poster Kay had Scotch-taped over her cot. She saw that Kay's cot was empty. Still on shift. Good. She would need Kay. Lily, too.

She turned her gaze to Lily, poised in the doorway, dressed in wrinkled, bloodstained nurse's whites. Tiny, fragile-seeming, as exquisitely wrought as an ivory figurine . . . yet she had the stamina of a water buffalo. She could keep going for days without sleep, and not seem to tire, and Rachel once had seen her wrestle to the ground a two-hundred-pound Marine strung out on heroin.

'Their platoon walked into an ambush,' Lily said. Her English was perfect. Her father had been a high-ranking official in the government before the war. 'Five were killed.' She paused, and added softly, 'From the looks of it, those were the lucky ones.'

270

Rachel thought about the young Marine who had died yesterday because of her mistake. The boy in her dream.

A paralyzing helplessness swept over her.

She thought: *I can't go out there. I can't let that happen again.*

But she knew she would go. Panic was a luxury. And there was no time for luxuries.

'Tell Mac I'm on my way,' Rachel told her. Lily nodded, and hurried off, leaving the door ajar.

Rachel stuffed her bare feet into a pair of thongs made of old rubber tire tread with strips of canvas sewn across the top. She'd bought them from a street vendor in Da Nang for thirty-five piasters. The expensive boots she'd brought from New York had fallen apart after two weeks of mucking about in the Tien Sung monsoon mud.

She paused in front of the mirror to bundle the loose gold-brown waves that tumbled down her back into a single thick hank, twisting it up in a loose knot, and skewering it with a small pointed stick that fitted into a strip of perforated cowhide to form a barrette.

She stared at herself in the cracked mirror for one long second, at her pale face, the purple hollows under her eyes. *God. I look like a missionary straight out of a melodrama, battling plague and killer ants in the deepest heart of Africa. Leora in Arrowsmith.*

She felt a flicker of morose satisfaction, followed by shame. *You're punishing yourself, aren't you? The 'Sackcloth and Ashes Hour,' starring Rachel Rosenthal. What will it be next, hair shirt or self-flagellation?*

Yeah, OK, maybe that's how it *had* started. Coming here probably had been a way of punishing herself for David and the baby. But not now, not anymore. Now she *wanted* to help, to make a difference, however small.

Rachel turned and gave an impatient shove to the half-open door, striding out on to a covered walkway that ran in a straight line the length of the barracks-style concrete building. Morning, she saw, had blinked its bloodshot eye open. Sunlight backfired off the jumble of corrugated tin

271

roofs below. The village was beginning to stir, even at this hour. She spotted a handful of conical straw hats bobbing among the tall stalks in the rice paddies. She could hear the mournful lowing of water buffalo, the wheels of an ox cart creaking along some rutted road. And another sound, jarring, out of tune, the whiffle of a helicopter's blades scything the sluggish air.

Reminding her of why she was here.

She ran at a half-trot, her heels slapping against the concrete with muffled clocking sounds. The walkway ended abruptly in a dirt pathway that led through a grove of palm trees to the hospital, fifty or so yards away. Rachel stepped down, sinking into mud up to her ankles.

'Shit,' she swore softly.

In the milky light, she slopped her way on to a makeshift boardwalk of two-by-four planks caked with mud. Damn the monsoons, she'd take New York City slush any day over this. She picked her way along the planks, fighting the urge to run.

At last the shadowy hospital building took shape. Two stories of crumbling vanilla stucco festooned with crimson bougainvillaea and liana vines thick as a man's wrist. Old, charming, as French as anything found in the heart of Paris . . . and the last place in the world any sane person would want to walk into.

Rounding the east wall, where the landing pad faced on the entrance to the courtyard, Rachel saw the chopper, a big transport Chinook, rotary blades cutting lazy arcs against the strawberry-milk sky, its cargo hold gaping open. Medics in green uniforms, white armbands, were unloading something on a stretcher.

Something swathed in bloody bandages.

A memory came swooping out of left field. Sixth grade. Her class had gone on a day trip to the wholesale food markets in lower Manhattan. She remembered seeing the rows of butchered beef dangling from hooks, bloody, stripped of their hides, veins and tendons exposed, and how she'd whoopsed her snack of milk and Oreos right

272

there on the sawdust-sprinkled floor. What lay on that stretcher bore a sickening resemblance to one of those bloody carcasses.

A wave of panic swept through her.

*What if it happens again. What if I cause another man to die. What if –*

No, she had to push the thought from her mind.

And run.

*Don't think, don't feel. Just get your frigging ass in gear*.

Rachel could hear Kay's throaty voice in her head: *It's like venetian blinds. You pull the cord, and see only what you have to see, block out the rest. Otherwise you'll go crazy*.

Except compared to Triage, going crazy seemed easy. Triage was a scene out of Dante's *Inferno*.

Rachel took a gulp of air, and entered. The room looked more like a factory than an ER. The triage facilities makeshift, in the style of the army surgical units for which Corpus Christi, this civilian Catholic Relief hospital, served as backup. Sawhorses to set the stretchers on, wire strung overhead to hook the blood and IVs on in a hurry. And in the corner, below the supply shelves, fifty-gallon drums full of water where the bloodied strips of gauze were soaked, and when the fat and flesh rose to the surface, laundered and used again. No sophisticated equipment, no crash carts. The only nod to the twentieth century, the electricity fueled by a balky old generator, whose faint whine she could hear above the shouting of doctors and nurses, and the screams of men dying in agony.

Wounded soldiers filled Triage, spilling over into the screened-off ER, some screaming, delirious with pain. Blood was everywhere, staining bandages and mud-caked fatigues, squirting from arterial wounds, pooling on the concrete floor.

Rachel spotted Ian MacDougal, in the corner, big shoulders hunched with weariness, his graying rusty mop bent over a double AK amp, both legs shot off at the knees. The kid, his face the color of curdled milk, looked no older than seventeen. He was twisting in agony, crying out: 'Mommy! Mommy!'

Rachel felt something give way in her chest, like soft dirt crumbling down a steep slope. *So young, dear God, I'll never get used to it. They're just kids . . .*

'Give me a hand over here,' Mac called to her in his thick Scottish burr. He sounded whipped. 'Clamp that bleeder. Good. Hold it while I debride. There now, a cleaner AK I couldn't have done m'self. Dana!' he called to one of the nurses. 'Start a line, take him to Pre-op marked *Delayed*'. When Rachel lifted her eyebrows in question, he remarked with his usual brusqueness, 'He'll live. Won't be kicking a football around with the boys back home, but he'll live.'

'Mommy,' the boy whimpered, clutching Rachel's hand. Her heart turned over, and for an agonizing instant she thought of her own lost baby, and of the babies she might never have. She stroked his face briefly, a knot forming in her throat, then quickly turned him over to Dana.

Rachel looked up, and saw Kay across the room, dear Kay, her stocky figure in bloodied nurse's whites, face tight beneath her mop of scrambled dark brown curls, barking out orders to the nurses and aides in her charge.

'Get those IV lines going. Don't tell me you can't find a vein . . . use a garden hose if you have to . . . but *find* it.'

She caught Rachel's eyes, flashing her a grim smile. 'Welcome to Yankee Stadium. Think we'll beat the Red Sox tonight?'

Rachel forced a grim smile. Their gallows humor wasn't much in the way of laughs, but it kept them sane.

A far cry from her first day here. Only six weeks? It seemed like a year. After two days on airplanes, she'd arrived in Da Nang, then an endless, bumpy jeep ride to Tieng Sung, only to walk straight into a scene like this one. Worse even. A nearby village had been shelled. Kids

274

blown apart, babies, pregnant women. And she'd stood there, gaping, frozen with the horror of it, paralyzed until someone shoved a pair of scissors into her hands, ordered her to cut off the two-year-old-boy's foot, hanging from his severed ankle by a tendon.

But she'd learned, and fast too. Act first, panic later. How to sort out the ones who would die from those who stood a chance. Expectants were taken behind that screen over in the corner to die a private death. Immediates were sent to Pre-op, marked *Priority* or *Delayed*.

'When we were kids,' Kay had told her that first day, 'we played doctor. Now we play God.'

*And sometimes we make mistakes,* Rachel thought, *because we're not gods, just human beings doing the best we can, but never really measuring up.*

Like that baby-faced Marine from Arkansas, just yesterday; he had begged her not to leave him, said he was going to die, and she told him not to worry. A shattered kneecap, that was all. Scheduled him for surgery behind two other Immediates, in worse shape than he, she had thought. Checking on him five minutes later, she found him dead. Cardiac arrest. Then she figured out why. Massive pulmonary embolism from the injured leg.

Remembering caused fresh pain to slice through her. *God, please, don't let me make another mistake like that.*

Rachel moved ahead to meet the stretcher being carried in. Would there be hope for this one? He was still in one piece, at least.

He was tall, that was the first thing she noticed. His mud-clotted boots dangling over the end of the stretcher. And sinewy thin, his face all bones and angles. His fatigues were wet and muddy, as if they'd found him face down in a rice paddy. The bandages that covered his midsection soaked with blood. He was unconscious, his skin waxy white, almost transparent, the color of paraffin. The color of death.

Suddenly she didn't want to know what was under those

275

bandages. She felt a chill tiptoe down her spine, as if a cold draft were blowing on the back of her neck.

She could barely find a pulse. Blood pressure eighty over twenty. Oh, this was bad all right. Classic shock. Lips blue, cyanotic. He was having trouble breathing as well. Jesus, he was slipping away, slipping right through her fingers.

'Get a line going here!' she shouted to Meredith Barnes, hovering at her elbow. 'Sixteen gauge. Draw four tubes of blood for a cross-match. He'll need at least six units. And a couple of grams of penicillin to start with.'

Rachel inserted a nasogastric tube to drain his stomach. Then, grabbing a pair of scissors, she began snipping at the bandages that covered his abdomen. Jesus. Oh Jesus. It was even worse than she'd thought. A gaping hole as if a prizefighter's glove had punched it in. The peritoneum ruptured too. Grayish-white loops of intestine bulging through.

Then she felt it, almost a certainty, like a clear, hard voice telling her he was going to die. No matter what she did, he was going to die. The best she could do for him was make him comfortable, put him behind the screen.

Then she glanced toward his face again, and her breath caught in her throat. Her body turned to stone. She couldn't move, or breathe, or swallow.

He was conscious now, looking straight at her. His eyes a clear, oddly lucent gray that shone like morning light from the hollowed sockets of his dying face.

And he was smiling.

Rachel had an odd sensation. It was as if something buried deep inside her were cracking open, and feeling its way toward the light, like a blade of grass pushing up through a sidewalk.

It was a moment before she realized what it was. It had been a long time since she had felt this.

Hope.

Hot tears flooded her eyes, spilled down her cheeks.

The wounded soldier brought his hand up, and brushed

it across her cheek, his fingertips soft as leaves. 'Rose,' he murmured. 'Don't cry, Rosie. I'm coming back. Rose . . .'

One of the medics, a burly black man, shook his head. 'Been calling that name ever since we fished him out of the river. Damnedest thing you ever saw. Stomach all shot to shit, and he's swimming out to meet us like he's Jesus Christ or somepin'. Dragging his dead buddy along for the ride.' He shook his head again. 'Looks like this one's for the GRs too.'

GR. Graves Registration. Where men were labeled, bagged, sent home to their grieving families. The coldness inside her turned fiery at the thought of this one, too, being trundled out like one more piece of luggage, dumped into a cargo hold.

'Not if I can help it,' Rachel said, galvanized by a determination so fierce all her muscles, her bones seemed to vibrate like taut wires.

She flew into action, clamping off arteries, debriding the wound, and digging out the largest pieces of shrapnel. Disinfecting with sterile gauze soaked in petrolatum.

'Mind if I have a look?' A deep voice startled her. She looked up. Doctor MacDougal was frowning, his shaggy reddish-gray brows drooping over his huge, sad, brown eyes.

His examination was quick but thorough. Afterwards, he drew Rachel aside. 'He's lost a lot of blood. And it looks like that right kidney will have to go. I see a lot of peritoneal leakage. And extensive damage to both small and large bowels. Lord, girl, this boy will need more than your hands to pull him through surgery. He'll need a bloody miracle. And even if he does pull through, with shock and peritonitis I don't have to tell you what his chances of recovery are.' He placed a broad fatherly hand on Rachel's shoulder. 'I know you hate to lose, Rachel. I never seen one so much for fightin' the odds, but the best you can do for this one is make him comfortable, let him go in peace.'

Rachel held Ian MacDougal's sad, bassett hound gaze

for a long moment, then answered, 'Please, let me try, Mac. I'll need you for this one, but I can assist. I'm not saying we can save him, but at least let's give him that chance.'

Mac dropped his eyes, and seemed to be considering her plea. Rachel held her breath. Ian was in charge. He could refuse her.

Finally he raised his gaze, fixing her with the look of an indulgent father giving in to his headstrong child against his better judgement.

'Do what you must then,' he said and sighed.

Rachel signaled to the orderlies to carry the patient into Pre-Op. Then she looked down once again into those clear eyes, that smile, and knew she could no more give up on this man than she could have turned her back on her own flesh and blood.

Rachel glanced at his dog tag, scribbled his name and ID number on a clipboard.

*Pvt. Brian McClanahan.*

'Hang in there, Brian,' she whispered, 'just hang in there for me, OK?'


Rachel woke to the sound of the rain drumming on the corrugated tin roof of her concrete shack. She opened her eyes. It was dark, but she could make out the huge beetle crawling along the wall in front of her. Still half-asleep, feeling dreamy and disconnected, she followed its meandering progress. But something was tugging at her mind . . . something she needed to remember.

Then it came to her, a rush of anxiety jolting her fully awake. Brian McClanahan. Three days since his abdominal surgery, and it was still touch and go whether he'd pull through. He could be dying right now, while she lay here . . .

Rachel pushed her thin cotton blanket aside with an impatient shove, and got up. She was halfway dressed when Kay stirred in the next cot, and sat up, rubbing her eyes. Kay yawned, and glanced at the faintly glowing dial of her wristwatch.

'You nuts?' she muttered thickly. 'It's three o'clock in the morning! First quiet night we've had in weeks. What's up?'

*She knows I wouldn't use the latrine before first light*, Rachel thought, *not when it means standing in a foot of water, surrounded by bugs and snakes.*

'Sorry I woke you,' Rachel said. 'I want to check on one of my patients. I'm a little worried about him. He was spiking a fever when I went off last night.'

Now Kay was wide awake, jumping up from her cot, snapping the light on. She scowled at Rachel, her brown eyes red-rimmed and puffy, naked-looking without her glasses. She was wearing a pair of wrinkled underpants, and a bright red T-shirt that had printed across the front: WHAT IF THEY GAVE A WAR AND NOBODY CAME?

'This patient's name wouldn't happen to be Brian McClanahan, would it?' Kay asked coldly. 'The same Brian McClanahan you've been hovering over like a mother hen ever since he came out of surgery? Dana came to me in tears last night, said you shouted at her for not telling you right away he was running a one-oh-four temp. As if my nurses have nothing to do all day but stand around taking temperatures.'

'I shouldn't have snapped at Dana that way,' Rachel apologized. 'She's a good nurse.' She *was* sorry, but damn it, Brian was special. A sort of miracle. Couldn't they see that? He'd pulled through surgery just barely, by the skin of his teeth, true, but he was alive, and she damn well intended to see that he stayed that way.

Kay's brown eyes flashed. 'Good? You bet she's good. She's terrific. All my nurses should get Congressional Medals of Honor. Instead, they get kicked in the butt. For years, we've been telling ourselves it'd be different when more women became doctors. But I'll tell you something I've learned the hard way, an asshole in a white coat is an asshole, no matter what's up front.' She paused, took a deep breath, then her anger died suddenly and she broke into a wide grin. 'Another thing, you can't go anywhere like that.'

'Like what?'

'Those pants.'

Rachel had finished pulling her clothes on, and now she looked down and saw she had put on Kay's khakis by mistake. They sagged around her hips, and her ankles stuck out below the cuffs. She sank down on the bed, and started to laugh. Then found she couldn't stop.

'I think I'm going crazy,' she said, wiping tears away with the back of her hand.

'Want to talk about it?' Kay flopped down on her mattress and lit a cigarette.

Rachel stared at the Grateful Dead poster over Kay's bed, a skeleton surrounded by flowers against a fluorescent purple background. An advertisement for a concert at the Winterland Auditorium in October of 1966.

'It's complicated,' she said. 'I'm not sure I understand it myself. I just have this feeling . . . that if I let go of him . . . I just might . . . I don't know . . . climb aboard the loony express once and for all.'

'Can't.' Rachel watched as smoke uncurled from Kay's lips, and disappeared up into the mosquito netting. 'This is the end of the line. We're *all* a little crazy here, Rosenthal.'

'This is different. It's . . . not just the war. It's me too. Everything. What happened before.'

'You did what you had to do,' Kay said, too quickly. And Rachel was reminded of how good Kay had been during the time, a rock then as she was now.

She remembered the night not too long ago when Kay had shanghaied her, hitching them a ride into Da Nang in an army ambulance. Her first taste of kim chee, in a back-alley restaurant consisting of one ancient woman, a cooking shed, and three rickety card tables. Then, on to a bar crammed with noisy Marines, and loud American music, where she'd gotten so drunk, listening to Otis Redding croon 'Dock on the Bay' and thinking about home. God, she'd been so sick afterwards! All that kim chee and vodka declaring war on her stomach. Kay, holding her hair back while she was sick in the bushes outside, then afterwards, when the tears came, lending a sympathetic shoulder.

'It seemed like the right thing to do at the time,' Rachel said, and started to laugh again. Only now it wasn't funny. The laughter caught in her throat like a piece of food that wouldn't go down. 'Now, whenever I think about it . . . well, I feel like I'm dying inside. When I was little, all I ever really wanted was a baby sister. And my mother would always tell me that someday I'd have babies of my own, as many as I wanted. It never occurred to me, not once, that I wouldn't be able to . . . to have children. Or even one child. One baby. Is that so much to ask? Is it?'

'Hey, look at me,' Kay said. 'I doubt if I'll ever find anyone weird enough to marry me, much less have a kid.' She was trying to joke Rachel out of her misery, but Rachel could see that her eyes, squinched against the smoke, were moist. 'Regrets. Shit, don't waste your time. That and a dime will buy you a phone call.'

Rachel forced a weak smile. 'Who would I call?'

'I don't know. God maybe. And, listen, when you get a hold of Him, would you tell Him something for me? Tell Him to end this war so I can stop smoking these filthy cigarettes. They're killing me.' Her voice went a little ragged, and she squashed her cigarette out in the empty sardine can on the floor beside the bed.

Rachel smiled. 'I guess we're all hooked . . . one way or another.'

'I read a story once,' Kay said, 'by O. Henry. About this girl who was real sick, she had pneumonia, I think it was. All she could do was lie in bed and stare out her window at the ivy growing on the wall outside. And this friend of hers, this artist who lives downstairs, the sick girl tells him that when the last leaf falls, that's when she'll die. It's winter, you see. And all the other leaves fall except this one last leaf. It just keeps hanging on. So she doesn't die. She gets better, in fact. And when she's well enough to get out of bed, she finds out why the last leaf never fell – it was painted on, by the artist. The irony is, he's the one who dies in the end, from staying out in the rain and cold while painting that damned leaf on the wall.'

'Don't worry,' Rachel said and laughed, slipping out of Kay's pants, then finding her own under the bed. 'I won't catch cold. Malaria, maybe. Or heatstroke. But definitely not pneumonia.'

'That's not what I was thinking. I was wondering.' Kay got up, and found a fresh pack of Salems on the dresser. Slowly, she peeled off the cellophane. 'What would have happened to the girl if that last leaf *had* fallen.' She went over, placed her hands on Rachel's shoulders, forcing Rachel to meet her gaze. 'Give it a break, kid. That heart of yours can use one, all the mileage you put on it. Take my advice, put it away for now. It won't do you any good in this place.'

The rain had stopped. But the path leading to the hospital was a sea of mud.

Rachel was picking her way along the planks that had been laid over the muddy path when she heard it: a high whistling noise cutting across the sky.

Mortars.

She hit the ground, slapping stomach down in warm mud, just as a deafening WHUUUUMP rocked the air. She brought her head up, and watched a dull, poisonous orange bloom above the trees, not a quarter of a mile away. Cold panic coiled about her heart. There had been shelling before, in the jungle surrounding the village, but never this close.

*What if they hit us? What if –*

She moaned softly, squeezing her eyes shut against the horrible orange glare, clamping her hands over her ringing ears as another mortar whistled overhead, then exploded, much closer this time from the sound of it.

Strangely, she was afraid, but not for herself. She thought of Brian stretched on his bed in ICU, unconscious, thin and white, swathed in bandages to his chin. His vital signs were still so precarious. If he suffered even

282

the slightest trauma, he would die. She had to get to him, make sure he was all right.

Rachel, shutting out her own fear of being killed, began crawling on her hands and knees, inching her way through the mud toward the hospital. The rockets were coming one on top of another now, like a Fourth of July celebration gone berserk. The air seemed to reel, punch-drunk, with their blasts. An artificial dawn painting the sky above the tree like orange and yellow and red. She tasted something bitter on her tongue. Gunpowder. *Oh Lord, they're right on top of us.*

When she got there, the lights were out in the hospital. The generator must have blown, she realized with a sinking heart. She groped her way in darkness through the archway that led across an open tiled courtyard. The ancient tiles were broken and heaved from the constant moisture, and she nearly stumbled a few times as she made her way toward the double doors that opened on to the wards.

Inside, a dark corridor, then suddenly blinding light. Someone shining a flashlight in her face. She squinted and threw a hand up. More flashlights now, cutting in wild arcs, casting a shadowy feverish light over the ward. As her eyes adjusted, she saw Lily struggling to drag a comatose patient, a man twice her size, under the bed nearest the door. His I V line had torn loose, and a bright crimson stain was slowly spreading across the bandages that covered his chest.

Rachel dove forward to help Lily, but Lily shook her head and pushed her aside. 'No time. Get the others down. Safer under the beds if we are hit.'

Rachel, pushing aside her worry about Brian for a moment, felt a burst of panic, as she wondered what would happen to these poor guys, all of them hers in a way, if the building sustained a direct hit. Or even if they were forced to evacuate, the agony they might suffer and possible damage to healing wounds. *God, please help them . . . make this stop.*

283

Thunder shook the building, and slashes of vermilion sky flared between the slats of the louvered windows. She heard distant screams, the squealing of pigs, and realized a shell must have hit the village on the hillside below. Would any of them be safe if this old building was hit?

And Brian. He had been so sick last night, running that high temp. Mac had been right about the peritonitis. Regardless of how careful she'd been to clean and debride the wounds, to pick out every tiny bit of shrapnel and dirt, contamination had been inevitable. Mac, she knew, didn't hold out much hope. In Brian's weakened condition it was touch and go under the best of circumstances, but this . . .

*Please, God, just let him be all right. Let him get through this night. I'll take care of the rest.*

She darted down the aisle separating the row of beds on either wall, skirting nurses and orderlies who were soothing some patients and wrestling with others. Brian's bed was the last one. She caught a glimpse of it in the thin, flickering light. Empty.

Burning pain exploded in her chest, as if she had been struck by a mortar.

'No!' she cried. 'NO!'

Rachel, half out of her mind, grabbed the arm of a nurse rushing past. It was Dana, her dishwater-blond hair straggling free of its bobby pins, her thin face pale and frightened. Dana held an IV bottle of Ringer's solution, and at Rachel's touch she jumped, and the bottle slithered from her grasp. A loud crash. Lukewarm liquid splashed Rachel's feet. A splinter of glass stung her ankle.

'When?' Rachel asked, gripping Dana's arm much harder than she'd intended. She heard the shrill note of hysteria in her voice. 'When did he die?'

Dana wrenched her arm free, and took a step backwards, eyeing Rachel as if she'd gone mad. Then Rachel realized how she must look, covered in mud, her hair streaming loose and wild. Like one of the whacked-out patients on the druggie ward, the ones who had smoked too many of Mama-san's opium-laced marijuana cigarettes.

284

Dana didn't have to ask who she meant. 'He's not dead . . . yet,' she said. 'Doctor Mac took him into OR. He went into cardiac arrest a minute or two before the shelling started.'

Relief pumped through Rachel, followed by an icy wave of panic. She must get to him, help him. *She* was the connection, the last leaf that was somehow keeping him alive. Didn't they understand that?

Rachel wheeled, and darted back the way she'd come. The operating theater was at the end of the corridor, not more than a few dozen yards, but it seemed as if she'd run miles by the time she got there. Her clothes were drenched in sweat, her legs trembling, rubbery. Her heart hammering crazily.

She burst in.

The operating room was long and narrow, with half a dozen operating tables. A flashlight shining at the far end cast huge horror-show shadows that curved up the wall and across the ceiling. Two shadowy figures crouched over an operating table. As she drew closer, she saw that it was Doctor Mac and Meredith Barnes. Meredith was holding the flashlight in her left hand and a hemostat in her right. Mac was bent over a long figure stretched on the table.

Brian. *Her* Brian. Rachel's heart lurched in terror.

He was intubated. They were bagging him, squeezing air into his lungs. Blood was smeared over Brian's thin, naked chest. She saw the long incision in the left fourth intercostal space just below his nipple. Mac was struggling with a pair of rib retractors.

He was going for open cardiac massage. Thank God there was still a chance. Thank God she wasn't too late.

Mac glanced up, shooting her a startled glance from under the shelf of his shaggy gray eyebrows. Rachel was already snapping on a pair of gloves. No time to scrub, this would have to do.

'Let me,' she begged. 'My hand is smaller.'

'Have you ever done this before?' Mac asked, sounding impossibly weary, too weary to argue.

285

'No. But I've seen it done. I can handle it.' She felt oddly calm, as if somehow, deep down, she had been preparing for this moment all along.

'Good. There's no time for mistakes. It's been too long already. He stopped breathing five minutes ago. I gave him CPR and six shots of intracardiac epinephrine. If this doesn't work, we've lost him.'

Rachel concentrated on remembering everything she had learned about emergency thoracotomy. Peering into the open wound in the feeble glow of the flashlight, she found the pericardium, and made a longitudinal incision with her scalpel, careful to avoid the phrenic nerve. She inserted her gloved right hand through the incision, feeling her way around the pulmonary artery and vena cava. Nothing. Not even a faint flutter. Oh God. She felt utterly still, cold as death, as if her own heart had stopped beating as well. Yet somehow, incredibly, her mind and body continued to function.

In the instant her hand closed about the still, flaccid muscle of his heart, she felt as if everything had somehow come to a standstill, this room, this hospital, the entire world. The shelling had stopped, or had she just stopped hearing it? There was only the steady throbbing of her pulse in her ears.

Gently, rhythmically, she began to squeeze. *Live, oh please live, Brian, you've got to help me, I can't do it all, oh please . . .*

Nothing.

Beads of sweat oozed from her forehead and trickled down her temples. She struggled to keep from panicking. Keep up the rhythm, that was the way to go. Steady. *God, please won't you help me*.

Every sense became heightened. She could smell the stale odor of Mac's sweat, and a flowery scent, the perfume Meredith was wearing. Blood seemed to float in the air like a fine mist, the taste of it on her tongue, bitter, coppery. The pressure of her hand about his flaccid heart matched by a rhythmic chanting in her head.

286

*Come ON. Get going. COME ON. Now. Please. NOW.*

Mac was shaking his head sorrowfully. 'Enough, child. It's no good. You did your best.'

Rachel could feel the sobs rising in her breath, choking her. 'No,' she pleaded. 'Just a little while longer. Please. I want to be sure.'

'Another minute, that's all. Others need us now.'

An eternity seemed to pass inside that minute. Rachel could feel it eating away at her control, threatening to swallow her. It wasn't just Brian she was fighting for, but herself, her own sanity.

At last, just as she had about lost all hope, a tiny spasm. Another.

A single faltering beat.

Several interminable seconds passed without another, then Brian's heart began to beat with a shallow rhythm of its own.

Rachel nearly staggered with the rush of stunned joy that hit her. Her throat unlocked, and tears streamed from her eyes, dropping from her chin on to the still, blue-tinged face lying unconscious on the operating table.

'It's going!' she shouted. 'It's beating! He's alive!'

She drew her hand out of Brian's chest cavity, and looked up at Mac, meeting his incredulous gaze. The beam from the flashlight leaped, and swung across the ceiling, as Meredith let go a whoop of triumph.

'I'll be,' Mac whispered. 'A bloody miracle, that was, if I ever saw one. You sure you're not Catholic?'

Rachel laughed, tears streaming down her cheeks. 'Not that I know of. Why?'

'For a second there, I could've sworn I saw an angel ridin' on your shoulder.'

287

# 14

Brian opened his eyes to a sea of white. White walls. White sheets. White louver shutters thrown open to let in the smell of rain, and the hot blue of a tropical sky.

*I'm dreaming this, aren't I? I'm at home, in my own bed next to Kevin's, and Mom is in the kitchen stirring oatmeal in the big enamel pot, and I –*

He shifted to make himself more comfortable, and the movement brought a blast of pain shearing up his middle, an instant of intense white-hot agony, followed by wave after thundering wave of aftershock. *No dream, oh Christ, what then?*

He was wide awake now. He moaned, tears of pain trickling from the corners of his eyes and running slowly down his temples into his hair.

Through the fog of tears, he saw the blurred outline of someone standing over him. He blinked, and the image sharpened.

A woman.

She was tiny, delicate, like Vietnamese women, but her coloring was fair, almost too pale, her hair a lovely coppery brown. She wore it pulled back at the nape of her slender neck and fastened with a barrette. Her eyes were so vividly blue, it almost hurt to look into them, like staring straight up into a blazing summer sky. Gradually, he took in the rest of her. Small, heart-shaped face. Stubborn jaw, and straight flared nose. A mouth that rescued her from conventional prettiness by being a shade too wide. She seemed tired and anxious. There were violet shadows under her eyes, and the skin around her temples and the base of her throat looked faintly bruised.

He had never seen her before, but strangely he felt as if he knew her.

'Good morning,' she said, those deep-blue eyes of hers fixed on him with complete concentration, never flickering off to one side. 'How do you feel?' He saw that she wore khaki pants, sandals, and a faded green overshirt with a stethoscope sticking out of its deep front pocket.

Was she a nurse? This was some kind of hospital, wasn't it? He was lying on a bed in a long room. Other beds – iron cots really – stretched along the whitewashed cement walls. And in each bed, a bandaged figure, some barely recognizable as human beings.

Brian's head felt light and shimmery, his mouth dry as flannel. A dream? Lately, it seemed, he'd been drifting in and out of one long dream, so he couldn't keep straight anymore what was real and what wasn't. The only thing he knew for sure was real was the pain. His entire body, from his neck down, felt as if it had been run over by a bulldozer. It hurt just to breathe.

'Like Sonny Liston after fifteen rounds with Cassius Clay,' he said, managing the tiniest of smiles.

As if she had been waiting for something from him, some sign, the tautness in her face relaxed. She smiled. A brilliant smile that seemed almost a physical touch, catching hold of him, lifting him.

'You gave the crowd its money's worth,' she said. 'We weren't sure you were going to make it, but you put up a good fight. Do you remember any of it?'

Brian shifted a fraction of an inch on the hard mattress of his iron cot. Pain flared again. He fell back, gasping. What in God's name had happened to him?

'Not much,' he answered, the pain a dull hammering now. 'How long have I been here?'

'Nearly three weeks now,' she said. 'You slept through most of it. The morphine helped.'

He closed his eyes. The light hurt him. The sight of the men in the other beds – looking as he imagined he must look to them, mummified under yards of gauze, tubes

289

sticking out everywhere – seemed to make the pain worse.

Inside his head, where it was dark and cool, her voice followed him, strangely restful. 'Maybe it would be better if you didn't try to remember everything all at once,' she said.

He knew that voice, didn't he? It was almost . . . familiar. Like something he might have dreamed. Now a small cool hand touched his brow, making the fiery pain recede a little.

Strange, disjointed fragments of memory floated up from some deep dark place inside his head. He struggled to fit them together. 'We were on bush patrol,' he said. 'Walked into an ambush. I was hit. Yes, I remember now. It was Trang . . . he stepped on a mine. The river . . .'

Brian's eyes flew open. He struggled to pull himself up, but was knocked flat by a pain so crushing it set off an explosion of red stars behind his forehead. He waited for the agony to subside a little, then asked, 'Trang? Is he . . .'

The woman shook her head. 'I'm sorry,' she said kindly. 'Please, don't try to sit up just yet. It's better if you lie flat. Can I get you anything?'

Brian felt sadness well up inside him. Anger too. He hadn't been able to save Trang after all. What was the use of even trying anymore? What was the use of any of it, all those guys dying, the war itself?

Reflexively, he made the sign of the cross. *Poor Trang. How many others besides? And why not me? Why was I spared?*

Suddenly, he didn't want to know. He was tired, so tired. His mind was beginning to float again.

He licked his lips, and tasted something salty. Blood. His lips were cracked, rough as old cardboard. 'Water,' he said. 'Are you a nurse?'

'Doctor,' she said, smiling. 'But please . . . call me Rachel. I feel as if we're old friends by now.'

She filled a paper cup from a pitcher of water on the small metal table beside his bed, and held it to his mouth, supporting his head with her hand. She was surprisingly strong for someone so small. Her long ponytail brushed his cheek, soft as a kiss, and he caught a whiff of lemony scent.

The scent brought another fragment of memory drifting to the surface. A dream, really, but maybe something like it had really happened. He had been in a dark place, a tunnel, walking toward a light at the other end. A light so intense it hurt his eyes, like looking into the sun. But he was drawn to it, as if by a magnet. The closer he got, the happier he felt. And strangely lighter, as if the pull of gravity were growing weaker with each step. He hurried, almost floating.

Then the tunnel was suddenly filled with a strong, almost overpowering fragrance. A heady scent that was a mixture of lemon blossoms, and summer grass, and the good smell of freshly ironed dresses hanging in his mother's chifforobe. There was a voice, too, a woman's voice. He couldn't hear what she was saying, but he felt her beckoning him. Pulling him back . . . away from the light. He fought it at first, but the pull was too great. And at last he surrendered to it . . .

Now, as he drank of the lukewarm water, tasting her scent, he thought: *It was her.* This tiny woman named Rachel. She had pulled him back from some brink. Death? Dear Christ, had he been as far gone as that?

Was he supposed to feel grateful to her? Yeah, probably. But right now all he felt was wasted. He just wanted to sleep . . .

When he had finished drinking, she eased his head gently back on to the pillow. 'You were wearing this when they brought you in.' She pressed something into his palm. Cool. Metallic. His Saint Christopher's medal. Rose had given it to him the day he shipped out. He had put it on, then forgotten he was wearing it. 'I saved it for you. I thought you might . . . need it.'

'Thanks,' he said, closing his fist around it. He tried to summon Rose's face, but it didn't come. The only picture

291

that came to his mind was of the snapshot he carried in his wallet. He'd taken it last winter out at Coney Island. A perfect day, he remembered. A whole day just for themselves. They had had hot dogs and fried clams at Nathan's, then walked and walked down the deserted windswept boardwalk, feeling like the only two people in the world, until their fingers were frozen inside their mittens. He had taken a picture of Rose, posed a little stiffly against the shuttered entrance to some boardwalk attraction, black hair blowing across her face, cheeks flushed, her smile tentative, as if she couldn't quite believe her happiness and half-expected that at any moment something would spoil it.

*Rose, dear Rosie, didn't you know you were safe with me? Couldn't you see that?*

'Sleep now,' Rachel said. 'I'll come back when you've rested a bit more. Don't expect too much of yourself at first. You've been through a lot.'

Suddenly, he didn't want her to leave.

'Please,' he whispered, 'will you sit with me until I fall asleep? Just a few minutes longer?'

She smiled, and sat down on the very edge of his cot, laying her fingers lightly across his wrist. His hand, he saw, was bound with gauze and adhesive tape where an IV needle was stuck into a vein just above his knuckles. But he didn't seem to mind. 'I'll stay as long as you like,' she said.

A week later, Brian was sitting up in bed. A pillow across his knees formed a makeshift desk for the battered spiral notebook over which he was bent. His hand was trembling; it had been so long since he'd held a pen, or even sat up for longer than it took to relieve himself on a bedpan. But once he began to write, the words flowed easily:

*Today is the first day of June. Bobby Childress had his trach tube out two days ago. This morning they shipped him out to the naval hospital in Okinawa. A couple of hours ago, they brought in another guy with a tube sticking out his chest, and one arm missing. Someone said he'd picked up a whore in Quang Tri, and that she left him a little present before slipping off into the night. Deke Forrester spoke for all of us when he said, 'Too bad it wasn't the clap.' That's how you get to think after a while. It's never a question of good or bad, just degrees. How bad is bad when you're lying next to a guy with a couple of oozing stumps where his legs used to be? Or a nine-year-old kid missing half his face?*

*As I'm writing this, a few of the guys are playing poker at the bed across from mine. Big John and Skeeter Lucas and Coy Mayhew. Skeeter is dealing, and someone is picking up the cards for Big John because Big John, who would have gone home to a football scholarship, is missing all but two fingers on his left hand. And the guy holding Mayhew's hand for him is kidding him about 'blind luck.' Mayhew caught a beehive round in the face, which severed his optic nerve. He'll never see again, but he considers himself extremely lucky it wasn't a lobotomy, compliments of the US of A.*

*The weirdest part about all this is, with all their left-over parts stuck together, they make a whole. No, better than that. There's a generosity of spirit . . . I don't know how to explain it . . . just that I've never seen anything like it, not even in battle. The quality of mercy, in the words of old Will Shakespeare. Yesterday I saw that quality in a paraplegic who dragged himself out of bed to spoon-feed a buddy too sick to sit up.*

*At night is when they cry. It's like the wind blowing in the trees, you get so used to it. The sound of men weeping quietly into their pillows. We all want to go home, but we're scared, too. The world is the same, but we're different. Some of us on the outside, all of us on the inside. And we're all wondering, What's it going to be like? How can we go back and pick up the pieces when none of the pieces fit anymore?*

*I'm thinking about Rose just now. What she looks like, how she felt. I have to work hard at it, like drawing a picture in my mind. That scares me. I know I love her as much as ever, but the harder I work at remembering, the farther away she seems. Does she still think about me? Will she want me back? But even if she does, I'm not sure who it is she'll be getting. Not the guy who took care of her, who's been looking out for her since she was a kid. Now I'm not sure I can even take care of myself, much less anyone else. I get scared in the night sometimes. I think about Trang, and Gruber, and Matinsky, and I cry. I cry just like a damn baby, and it scares the hell out of me. Why shouldn't it scare the hell out of Rose, too?*

*Listen, Rose, if you're out there somewhere tuned into this station, for God's sake, write to me. Say you love me. Say you'll love me no matter who you find walking around in my skin when I get back. Say –*

'Letter home?'

Brian looked up to find Rachel standing over him, wearing an oddly wistful expression. How long had she been there?

'You could call it that,' he said.

He laid his pen down on the closely written page, and felt some of the ragged tension in his muscles drain away. He was glad to see her.

*Admit it, man, you look forward to it.* Well, OK, that was true. He'd gotten into the habit of expecting her around this time of the evening. When it was quiet, as it had been these past few days, she always dropped by. It was just that he hadn't realized until this moment how much it mattered to him, how much her presence soothed him. To be honest, he was a little ashamed to admit it, even to himself.

'Hey, Doc!' Big John called over. He waved the stump of his right hand, his dark face split in a grin as wide as the Mississippi. 'I'll front you a game if you want to join us.'

294

Rachel laughed, and called back to him, 'Fat chance, not after the way you skinned me last time.'

Big John threw his head back in a booming laugh. 'Sister, if I had any aces hid up this here sleeve, you'd a been the first to know it.'

Brian knew that this was a form of respect, the teasing. They knew she cared, and they also knew she didn't put up with any bullshit. He suspected a few were probably in love with her.

Big John went back to his game. Rachel sat down on the end of Brian's cot. She was wearing her hair loose tonight, and it seemed to crackle about her face like some kind of electrical field. She had just washed it, and the red highlights stood out, winking like sparks under the hard glow of the bare bulb over his bed. He caught her clean, citrusy scent, and was grateful. He'd had enough of the rotten smell of death on this ward, and each time she visited him, bringing her smile, the brilliance of her blue eyes, her fragrance, it was like a small gift to be slowly unwrapped and savored.

Now he wished he had something to offer her in return.

'It's a journal I've been keeping,' he explained when he saw her looking curiously at the spiral-bound notebook. 'I started it at the beginning of my tour. Each day I write a little something. My short-timer stick, you could say.' Some guys carried a stick with a notch in it for each of the remaining days of their tour. And each day they sawed off another notch with their K-bar until there was nothing left but a stub and it was time to go home. A kind of talisman, he supposed. He shrugged. 'It keeps me sane.'

She nodded. He saw from her expression there was no need to explain. She understood so much. She said, 'Supplies of sanity are running short around here, so take it where you can get it. Which reminds me, I brought you something.' She reached into the pocket of her khaki shirt, and fished out a chocolate bar. Ghirardelli's Bittersweet. His mouth watered just looking at it. 'My mother sends them. She likes to pretend I'm at summer camp, just

295

like when I was ten. So welcome to Camp Loony Tunes.'
She passed it over, her gaze falling once again on the note-book. 'What will you do with it?'

'I don't know yet. Maybe just keep it around as a reminder. If I ever have a son, I'd want him to know.'

'You like kids?' She looked sad.

'Sure, I do. Six younger brothers at home, I'd better. I'd always planned on having at least a dozen myself some day.'

'Only a dozen?'

'Well, for starters.'

She joined him in laughing, but he thought her laughter seemed strained.

Suddenly it struck him that he did have something to offer her after all. 'Would you like to read it?'

'May I?' Her head snapped up, an eager expression spreading across her heart-shaped face.

Brian thought how odd it was that he didn't feel shy about revealing his most intimate thoughts to her. But then, how surprising was that really? She knew his body better than his own mother did. In a way it was as if she had given birth to him. She had brought him back to life, she had touched every part of him, cleaned his filth, fed him, nurtured him. How natural then that he should already feel connected to her.

He handed her the journal, expecting her to tuck it away in one of her pockets to read later on. But she surprised him by opening it right then and there. She began to read, and didn't stop, or even move except to turn the pages, until she had finished the very last one.

More than an hour had passed. It was past ten, the chocolate just a lingering sweetness on the back of his tongue. The poker game was breaking up, men shuffling back to their beds with the unsteady gait of old drunks. Lily was making the rounds, checking trach tubes and dressings, dispensing medication. All through the ward there was the creak of bedsprings settling, men adjusting their ravaged bodies for a position that might let them sleep.

When Rachel looked up, Brian saw that her eyes were shining with tears. 'It's good,' she said, her voice tight. 'You made me feel something, and dammit, I don't *want* to feel.'

'I know what you mean,' he said, 'about not wanting to feel. I thought about writing a book when I get home. That's why I started the journal, so I wouldn't forget any of it. But now I don't know if I could. It would be like living it all over again.'

She nodded. 'I understand. But that's all the more reason, isn't it? How else are we going to stop this craziness?'

Brian tried to think. He picked up his pen and twirled it around and around inside the circle of his thumb and index finger. He felt so exposed to her, naked not only on the outside but on the inside too. *One step at a time,* he thought. *Man, I can't handle any more than that right now.*

'Even if I did write it, who would want to read it? The public wants to crucify Lieutenant Calley for My Lai. They don't understand how such a thing could have happened. You ask the man on the street what he thinks is the worst thing that could happen to him, and he'll say "death" nine times out of ten. But that's not what he's really most afraid of. I think what we're most afraid of is ourselves, what we might do if we're pushed hard enough. Guys like Calley make us nervous because we wonder if deep down in us too there isn't a part capable of wasting a whole village.'

She looked at him a long time before speaking. Finally she said, 'You're right, of course. But if we don't make ourselves look at it, what hope do we have of ever preventing it from happening again?' She leaned forward, gripping his hand between both of hers. She had touched him many times, in many places, but always with the cool efficient hands of a doctor. Now he knew that she was touching him in a different way, and it sent a shock through him like a high voltage current. 'Write your book, Brian. It's all here. Don't even worry yet about who will read it. Just write it.'

Brian, gazing into her hot blue eyes, felt as if he'd been

snatched off his feet by an undertow, breathless, knocked out by her passion, her overpowering will. He nodded slowly. 'Maybe I will. Just maybe I will.'

Two weeks later, Brian lay in bed, needing to pee, and wondering if it was possible to die from stir-craziness. He grabbed the iron rails on either side of his bed and hauled himself up into a sitting position. He felt so weak, and even this simple effort brought pain like sharp blows from a hammer. But he'd be goddamned if he was going to lie here helpless as a newborn baby any longer. He'd piss like a man this time, standing up on his own two feet, even if it meant popping the stitches holding in his gut.

'Crutches.' He hissed the word through clenched teeth.

'This is against your doctor's advice, I want you to know.'

Rachel stood over him, arms crossed in front of her chest. She was wearing green scrubs, and sandals, her hair plaited in a single loose cable all flayed with sprung wisps. Her cheeks were flushed, eyes glittering with a mixture of apprehension and anger.

Christ, he wasn't as bad off as all that, was he? He still had legs, even if after nearly a month on his back he quite naturally felt a little weak. He forced his legs out from under the sheet. Dismay filled him as he stared down at them, drooping over the edge of the mattress like an old lady's stockings hung out to dry. Skin so pale it looked dead, shocking against the lightning slashes of scar tissue zigzagging up his thighs.

*Jesus, I couldn't support a package of marshmallows on these.*

But he had to at least *try*, didn't he?

'To hell with medical advice,' he told her. 'If I fall, you can pick me up. But I'll be damned if I'm going to have you wiping my tail like a two-year-old's anymore.'

Rachel handed him the crutches with stiff arms, her face hard. 'Well, if that's all you're worried about, I've seen more bare behinds than a men's locker-room attendant,

298

and there's nothing special about yours, believe me.'

Dawson, in the next bed, lifted his black hulk on to one elbow, and rolled the one eye that wasn't covered in thick gauze bandages. 'You wanna see sumpin' *real* special, you come check out what I got in my skivvies, Doc.'

'Thanks, Sergeant. I'll keep that in mind.' She caught Brian's gaze, and held it, hard and level as if she were looking down the barrel of an M-16. 'But you guys would be better off if you did your thinking with what's between your ears, not between your legs.'

Dawson cackled with laughter, but Brian remained grim with determination.

'Gotta get out of this bed sometime, might as well be now.'

He dragged himself to his feet, and immediately regretted his bravado. His legs buckled and shook. The latrine out back suddenly seemed as far off as Hong Kong.

He swung the crutches out, took two shuffling steps, and paused to rest.

From the neck down, he was on fire, flames dancing up his middle, licking up under his collarbone. Weak, too, so damned weak. And what he saw, catching a glimpse of himself in the glass door of the med cabinet, didn't inspire much confidence, either. *Oh Jesus, is that really me?* The watery reflection of a hollow-eyed skeleton looked back at him, reminding him of those pictures he'd seen of concentration camp survivors in Second World War histories.

A string was all that seemed to be holding him up now, a thread of determination that stretched from his mind to his limbs. And by the time he'd scuffled halfway across the ward, it felt stretched to the breaking point. Sweat trickled between his shoulder blades. He felt like an overcooked fish you could just pluck the spine right out of.

The other men – Deke, Henson, Bucholtz, Pardo – were watching him as expectantly as if he were Whitey Ford at the top of his stretch with the bases loaded. Except for Boston over there – that wasn't his name, just where he was from, but everyone called him that – he'd turned so he was facing the wall. Poor kid, both legs amputated at the knee. He would never walk anywhere.

*I'm one of the lucky ones,* Brian thought.

But at this moment he did not feel lucky. He wanted to lie down, badly. The floor would do just fine. He was so tired he just wanted to close his eyes and sleep.

Only the image of himself lying in a puddle of piss kept him going.

Brian took four more scuffling steps, the wooden armrests of the crutches cutting excruciating grooves in the flesh under his arms.

Then he glanced over his shoulder, and saw that Rachel hadn't moved. She was still standing where he'd left her, about a dozen yards behind, glowering at him.

'Don't look at me with those big cow eyes,' she said angrily. 'You're so hellbent on showing me what a man you are, you go and make it the rest of the way on your own.'

'I wasn't asking any favors,' he said, a little spurt of anger fueling him, pushing him a few more yards.

'They have a rule here; once you're ambulatory, they ship you out on the next plane to Okinawa. I hear they have air conditioning. And flush toilets.' There was a strange tightness in her voice.

'I can hardly wait.' He felt new muscles – muscles he hadn't used so long he'd forgotten they were there – spring to life.

To hell with Rachel, what did *she* care where he went? There were hundreds more where he'd come from. What was he to her, anyway, except a name and number on a dog tag? She'd saved his life, sure, but that's what doctors are supposed to do.

After he'd dragged his dead weight along a dim tiled corridor for what felt like an eternity, a nurse pointed the way to a doorway that led out back to the latrines.

Outside, he squinched his eyes against the fierce sunlight slanting over the tops of distant trees. Filtered through the red spots that danced behind his half-closed eyelids, he saw a muddy path cutting across the barren,

300

wire-fenced compound to a row of four whitewashed wooden cubicles with corrugated tin roofs. On one of them was tacked a crudely hand-painted sign that read: IF YOU CAN MAKE IT TO THE HEAD, YOU AIN'T DEAD.

Brian began to laugh helplessly. Tears streamed down his cheeks, and he trembled on the verge of collapse. How true, he thought. If you could pee on your own two feet you were man enough to take control of your own destiny. And that's what this was all about, wasn't it? Taking control. Establishing some order in an existence that lately seemed to have spun out of orbit.

Every additional day he stayed on here he felt a little more of his old life slip away. Memories of home had faded like old photographs tucked away in a bottom drawer. Worse, his loyalties had become tangled, uncertain. Each day brought him closer to Rachel, and pushed him another step from Rose.

*I'm a fool*, Brian thought. *Mistaking gratitude for –* What? Love?

No. That was ridiculous. Rachel had befriended him, that was all. He had no business turning it into something more.

The need to pee was suddenly so fierce it blotted out everything else.

Brian heard a noise behind him. He swiveled jerkily on his crutches, nearly losing his balance.

Rachel had followed him. She stopped a few steps behind him on the path, watching him as anxiously as a mother might watch a baby just learning to walk, but not moving forward to help. She looked much smaller now that he too was up on his feet, and so young, with her hair braided like that, like a schoolgirl. He imagined slipping off the rubber band at the end, slowly unwinding the thick plaits, and fanning them loose, burying his face in all that silky-clean, lemon-smelling hair.

*Damn* her for making him need her so.

'I don't need a doctor for this,' he told her stiffly. 'Last time I looked all my plumbing was in working order.'

'I know that. I just wanted to say . . .' Rachel stopped,

and he heard something click in her throat as she swallowed. Her eyes were suddenly very bright. 'Look, I'm sorry. I shouldn't have snapped at you like that.'

'Can this wait?' he said, almost pleading. 'I really have to—'

He stopped, horror washing through him as he realized he wasn't going to make it. He felt something let go inside, him, and a sudden rush of warm, stinging wetness spreading across the front of his thin cotton pajamas.

And suddenly it was all . . . just . . . just too damned much . . .

'Oh Jesus,' he moaned, and began to cry with dry, hacking sobs.

Arms enfolded him, slim and strong as cables, bracing him. *Oh yes*, he thought, sinking into her softness, *oh yes*. He rested his head against her shoulder, and let the tears come.

Then, with the hot smell of urine rising up at him, came the shame.

*Christ, what am I doing? A fucking two-year-old has more control. Standing here in my own piss crying on her shoulder.*

He tried to jerk away, but those strong arms only wrapped about him tighter. He felt her hair, warm with the sun, and soft, so soft, against his neck. The lemony scent of her drifting about him.

'You idiot,' she said, her voice choked with emotion, 'do you think I care about *that?* I watched you . . . and I hated you . . . for being so brave. I didn't want you to go, dammit.'

Brian was so stunned he couldn't think what to say except 'Why?'

'I love you,' she said simply. 'And now you're leaving.'

He felt dizzy, his head swimming, as if he'd been out in the sun too long. She was saying something important, he felt, yet her words scattered and floated away, and he was left only with this terrible empty feeling. He thought, *Oh Jesus, how can I leave her?*

302

But he couldn't find the words he wanted to say.

'I stink,' he said.

'You do. But I've smelled a lot worse.' She gave a shaky laugh 'Come on, let's get you cleaned up and into some dry things.'

She stood back a little, and gave him her arm so he wouldn't need the crutches. She supported him easily, this whip of a woman, whose strength and tenderness would never stop surprising him.

And in that instant, he knew what he had been running from.

*I love her.*

It was all at once so simple . . . yet so impossible. He was leaving. Going home to see what pieces there were to be picked up with Rose. That was what he wanted. He'd wanted it so much and for so long, it was like a litany, a prayer whose words you keep repeating long after you've forgotten their meaning.

But it was Rachel he ached for now. A need deeper than mere wanting. He needed her as much somehow as he needed to breathe and sleep and eat.

But what could he promise her? How could he take her and not betray Rose? And Rose a part of him too, even deeper in a way, like the marrow of his bones.

Brian, clinging to Rachel as they slowly made their way across the yard, thought how ironic it was that of all the things he had suffered, loving her should hurt the most of all.

Two nights later she came to him.

He could see her shadowy outline pull away from the doorway, and then she was moving toward him along the latticed corridor of moonlight between the rows of beds filled with men. Men asleep and dreaming – he hoped to God – of better places than this.

She was wearing her hair loose, and it caught the moonlight, a spill of such brightness his heart snagged in his throat at the sight of it.

Then her hand, cool against his cheek, and that summery scent wrapping around him like an embrace.

'Tomorrow,' he said, pulling himself up.

'I know. I came to say goodbye.'

She was so close, sitting beside him in the half-darkness, he could feel her breath on him, warm and sweet as her smell. And suddenly he wanted so badly to take her in his arms. Just once . . . to be able to comfort her . . . because, oh Jesus, he knew if he didn't he would lie here all night – and probably for the rest of his life – regretting it like hell.

At the same time he felt it would be wrong. It might open up wide something that should have stayed locked. He loved her, but he couldn't offer her anything besides that . . . just the fact of it, plain and useless as a spoon without a plate of food in front of it. So maybe it was better off just left alone.

A week in Okinawa, then, with luck, he would have his medical discharge, his ticket home. Home to Rose . . . if she still wanted him.

He saw her in his mind, seven years old, kneeling at the altar in her white communion dress and veil like the smallest bride in the world, so solemn, eyes scrunched shut, white-gloved hands clasped before her. A little white bride all alone. And he felt again the way he'd felt then, the longing to protect her, his poor little Rose who needed so much to be loved.

Then an ugly voice taunted him, *She's forgotten you by now. Not a single letter. She's found someone else to look after her.*

Rachel spoke, shattering his thoughts, 'I suppose you'll be going home, back to the States.'

He nodded. 'If they give me a medical discharge. I'd sure as hell hate to make a U-turn in Okinawa. What's that saying, you can trick the devil once, but not twice?'

'The devil wouldn't like it here. Too much competition. Anyway, I've recommended you be discharged. You may be back on your feet but you've still a long way to go before you'd be ready for combat.'

'Jesus, is anyone ever ready for that?'

She was silent a moment. 'Promise me something, Brian.'

'Anything you say, Doc.'

'Promise me you'll write that book. You have a wonderful gift. And something important to say. People should know. People back home . . . about this war.'

*People back home.* He thought again of Rose. No, he couldn't imagine telling her about it. How could she – or anyone who hadn't been through it – possibly understand?

Rachel knows, he thought. I don't have to explain anything to her.

'If I write it,' he said, 'it'll be just so *I* can understand. And I'm not sure if maybe even that isn't asking too much.'

She touched his hand, running her fingers lightly over the knob of bone protruding from his fleshless wrist. He felt, oh, such sadness in that touch . . . he wanted to open that locked door between them and find out what else was there . . .

'Make sure you eat enough,' she said. 'You could use some fattening up.'

'Pizza,' he said and laughed, 'till it's coming out my ears. Jesus, I think I'd trade all the rice in this damn country for a single slice of Avenue J pizza.'

'Pastrami on rye at the Carnegie Deli, that's what I dream about. With brown mustard and a big fat half-sour dill pickle. Will you do that for me, Brian, will you go there when you get home and have one for me?'

'All the way on crutches if I have to.'

'I'll miss you. Brian, I don't know how to say this but . . .'

He reached up, pressed one finger lightly to her soft mouth. 'You don't have to. I know.'

'I . . . I'll miss you,' she repeated weakly, and when he leaned forward to kiss her lightly on the cheek, he felt the wet sting of tears on his lips.

*I love you*, he longed to say.

But what he said was 'I'll write it. The book.' He would dedicate it to her, though he might never see her again.

'I'm glad,' she said.

In the moonlit darkness, he saw the fine, strong outline of her face, the proud tilt of her jaw, and he had never in his life regretted anything so much as what he had to say now.

'Goodbye, Rachel.'

306

# 15

Brian accepted the pint of Glenlivet that Dan Petrie offered him. He tipped his head back in a long swallow, the whiskey burning its way down his throat. The last ten days in Okinawa had been the longest ones of his life, and he was trying – not succeeding, but sincerely trying – to get himself through one more endless day by getting royally blasted.

'Goes down cool in a hot climate,' said the cocky little Australian and laughed. 'Last time I got pissed like this I was on a fishing boat in the Gulf of Mexico swilling black rum with Fidel Castro. If ever there was a bloke could match me dead on, drink for drink, it was that black-bearded sonofabitch. But you're not doing too badly, mate. Trouble is, I don't think it's killin' the bug you're after.'

Brian focused on the sandy-haired little fellow seated in the orange plastic chair across from him. Petrie reminded him of a small-town Little League coach. The UPI correspondent was wearing a snaggly blue terry robe, his right arm in a sling, a navy bill cap pushed back showing the stubble of his crewcut. In the half hour since they'd struck up a conversation in the lounge on Two East, Brian had taken note of the cutting edge beneath Petrie's easy banter. His sharp blue eyes looked as if they'd been bolted into his head, and he had a sly knack for appearing hardly to listen while soaking up every word that was said.

'I got the word today,' Brian said. 'They're discharging me. Less one kidney and three yards of intestine qualifies me for immediate DEROS and a Purple Heart.'

Dan tipped the bottle to his mouth, then wiped his lips

with the back of his hand. 'War'll work wonders on your perspective, but it's hell on the anatomy. You don't seem too happy about it. Home, I mean, not the bleedin' Purple Heart. Which unit did you say you were in, mate?'

'One Hundred Twenty-first Infantry,' Brian said, wiping the mouth of the bottle with the sleeve of his tartan robe before handing it back. 'We were stationed about halfway between Da Nang and a village name of Tien Sung. Firebase Alpha.'

The pint-sized Australian nodded. 'Yup, I know the place right enough. Ought to . . . I was there. Bloody hell of a mess. Looks like you got out just in time.'

Brian felt himself stiffen, his throat constricting painfully.

'You were there?' he echoed.

Petrie gestured toward the sling-supported arm with the nearly empty bottle he'd clutched in his good hand. 'That's where I picked up this souvenir. Piece of shrapnel the size of a bloody doorknocker.' He grinned. 'Cracked me elbow in half. Now I've got two funny bones instead of one. But I'll be all right.' He stopped, screwing a tight gaze on Brian. 'Christ, I'm not so sure about *you*. You look like an undertaker at your own funeral, mate.'

Brian did feel queasy, a rolling seasickness taking hold of him. The lounge they were in – an ugly windowless room filled with plastic chairs and rickety cardtables where dull-eyed men in bathrobes and pajamas sat playing desultory games of gin rummy and five-card stud – tilted abruptly off balance.

He gripped both sides of his chair, afraid for a second he might fall out of it. He was more looped than he'd realized. But not enough to keep from feeling the cold knot of fear forming in his stomach.

'What happened?' he asked, a bitter chalky taste in his mouth.

'I was in Da Nang, covering some SEATO muck-a-muck, that's when we got word of this action. Time they got me there, party was nearly over . . . Charlie'd pushed

308

your company back into the hills, infiltrated the whole area.'

Brian's throat tightened so, he couldn't swallow. 'There . . . there's a hospital. Catholic hospital. In Tien Sung. Corpus Christi. I was there before they shipped me here. Do you know if they were evacuated?'

'I haven't heard, but I doubt it. Good thing you got out when you did. Place is crawling with VC – they got all their wounded bivouacked there.'

*Oh God, let him be wrong. Just this once.* But Petrie was a top reporter. If anyone had the facts straight, surely he did.

He thought of Rachel – she hadn't been off his mind for more than a minute or two in the ten days since he'd left her. The acid burn of the whiskey backfired up his throat. He'd heard plenty about what the VC did to white women . . . Christ, what about those two French nuns, found dead, tied to trees with their tongues cut out. God, he hoped they needed her as a doctor too much to inflict the horrors running through his mind.

A small voice in the back of his mind said, *She can take care of herself. She'll get out if there's danger. Who appointed you her savior anyway?*

Suddenly Brian felt stone-cold sober. The tightness was gone from his throat. He knew what he had to do. He leaned forward, and the room abruptly righted itself.

'Petrie, I have to get back there,' he said, keeping his voice low. 'Someone I know – a doctor – I want to make sure she's all right. Get her out if she's still there.'

The journalist snorted in a half-laugh. 'You and the whole bloody Armed Services. Sorry, mate, you've been watching too many John Wayne flicks. Besides, didn't anyone tell you? – there's a bloody war on.'

Brian waited. After a minute or so the cynical grin faded from Petrie's face. Then Brian said, 'I don't have much time. And I'll need your help.'

The Australian had told him about how when covering the Six-Day War he'd been taken prisoner by Syrians at

Golan Heights, and how he'd managed to con his way out of getting his balls cut off. And even if half the tale was pure bullshit, the guy's inventiveness was worthy of Robert Louis Stevenson. If Brian could win him over he'd be one hell of a useful ally.

'Christ, who d'you think I *am*, the bloody Green Berets?'

Brian could feel his mouth forming a smile he didn't feel. The muscles in his face hurt with the effort. 'They don't give out Pulitzer prizes to Green Berets.'

He could tell from Petrie's suddenly riveted attention that now he had the man's complete attention.

'There's a helluva story in this,' Brian went on, struggling to keep riding his momentum. 'I was literally dead, and she . . . she cut me open, massaged my heart back to life. And besides that . . .' He stopped.

Besides *what*? What had he been about to say?

*Nothing you haven't thought a thousand times*, he answered himself.

Petrie waited, hat off now, running short square fingers through the stubble of his crewcut. His quick blue eyes were fixed on him as if Brian were about to deliver the Sermon on the Mount.

'. . . I'm going to get her out of that place and marry her,' Brian finished.

Was that true? He didn't know. But, Christ, it had felt good saying it. And it *would* make a helluva story.

'Shit.' Petrie slapped his knee, grinning wider than ever. 'Now, that *is* a story. Maybe even a movie. Hell, I'll bet you could even get John Wayne to star in it. She pretty, this doctor of yours?'

For a second, Brian didn't know what to say. He'd never thought of her in those terms. Pretty was a bare-shouldered girl with long tanned legs passing you on the sidewalk in her summer dress. But things like that couldn't begin to describe Rachel.

'She's like no woman you've ever seen,' Brian said.

Dan Petrie drained the last drops of whiskey. There was

310

a high flush in his cheeks, and a sparkle in his eyes.

'Take you a month of Sundays to get your orders changed, *if* they'd ever let you, which is about as likely me winning the Pulitzer,' Petrie said.

'I'll go AWOL if I have to. So never mind about me. What about you? Can I count you in on this?'

'I've been accused of being reckless, but never a bleedin' idiot. Next time it could be m'head that gets shot.'

'What about Golan Heights? That wasn't exactly a Sunday picnic.'

'That was different.'

'How?'

'At least out there in the desert, you usually see 'em coming. They're not shooting at you out of trees. That's if you even get that far. First, how you plan on getting sprung from 'ere?'

'I figure it won't be the hardest thing . . . there aren't too many of us fool enough to go AWOL *back* into that hell. It's the last place they'd think to look for me. But, dammit, I'll need your help.'

Petrie thought for a moment, pulling on his chin. 'I'd have to call in some favors. A mate of mine, works for *Stars and Stripes*, he might be able to get us in. Can't make any promises, though.'

Brian, desperate now, coaxed, 'I'll give you an exclusive on this, Petrie. Hell, I may even make you best man at my wedding. What do you say?'

*Christ*, he thought, *what am I saying? What wedding? If we can even pull this off it'll be a fucking miracle.*

But for Rachel, he knew he would have promised anything.

Petrie gave a slow nod, his expression still dubious. 'I'll see what I can do, mate.'

The boy looked no older than fourteen, fifteen maybe. But in his scarred face and slitted black eyes, Rachel saw something she'd never seen before.

Hatred. Pure and murderous.

311

She felt as if she'd just swallowed something cold on an empty stomach. An ache flared above her right eyebrow. The flesh on her arms shrank with goosebumps.

She sensed that the boy lying in the bed, staring up at her with those burning eyes, would have killed her without a moment's pause if he had the strength.

*I am the enemy. He doesn't care that without my help he'd die. He'd just as soon, than have me touch him.*

Rachel shuddered, a spasm that caused her hands to shake. The IV needle she was holding slipped from her grasp, clattering to the concrete floor.

*Get a hold of yourself*, she commanded. *You're a doctor, not a soldier. Your job is to heal. It's as simple as that.*

She tore open a cellophane packet containing a fresh needle, and grasped the boy's limp, blood-smeared wrist, searching for a vein. He might need four pints of blood, but it looked as if his wounds weren't as bad as she'd first thought. Perhaps surgery wouldn't even be necessary. She'd clean and debride, sew him up. Then—

Something wet struck her cheek.

Rachel, horror-stricken, looked up and saw he was grinning, his lips drawn back in a rictus of triumph, flecked with bloody spittle.

Shaking, Rachel grabbed a clean strip of gauze and wiped her cheek where he'd spit on her. *Oh dear God, this isn't happening, it can't be happening. I'm in control—*

There was a spiraling sensation in her head, and everything went gray and wavy, as if she were looking through dirty gauze curtains. She felt that if she didn't lie down, she would pass out. She hadn't been off her feet in twenty-four hours.

Now the boy was shouting, clearly a stream of venom aimed at her.

Rachel backed away slowly, the eighteen-gauge needle still in her hand.

Her glance caught the Viet Cong soldier who stood guard at the entrance to the ward. Something in his eyes chilled her to the bone . . . he looked at her as a snake

312

might regard a rabbit while deciding whether to make a meal of it or not.

*I was useful to them four days ago, with their wounded overflowing the ER . . . but it's tapering off now . . . and Lily said she heard their commander talking about bringing in their own doctors. So who knows how much longer before I'm expendable to them? And then what?*

Now Lily was taking over. '*Yên lang chó!*' she scolded sharply. *Silence, dog.* She plucked the needle from Rachel's grasp, and jammed it into the NVA's arm. Lily looked as exhausted as Rachel felt. Strands of oily black hair that had come loose from her bun trailed down the ivory stem of her neck. Her eyes were glassy and threaded with capillaries. The front of her uniform stiff with dried blood.

When had any of them last slept? The four days since Tieng Sung was taken seemed like three years. The village now full of VC. How could she have known it would turn out like this, when she'd volunteered to stay behind, during last week's evacuation, to care for those few too sick to be moved? Now the worst of it was over, but skirmishes still brought a trickle of wounded in every day.

She thought of Brian, and for a brief instant, she felt stronger, more alive than she had in days. Thank heaven at least he'd gotten out in time.

Then the gray despair swallowed her again. God, how she missed him. She saw him in her mind, his silvery eyes, the gaunt blade of his face. The look of infinite sadness he had given her as he was hoisted aboard the chopper to Da Nang.

Gone. And probably she'd never see him again. And, oh, that hurt. It hurt so much more than she could have imagined.

But she mustn't let herself collapse. Not now. These VC were human beings, and they needed her. And as long as she helped them . . . they surely would let her alone.

Rachel moved on to the next stretcher. '*Bác-sĩ,*' she said, by way of introduction, to a wizened little old man who gazed up at her with flat obsidian eyes. *Doctor. It means I'm here to help you, no matter how much both of us hate the idea. Get the message?*

Apparently he didn't. His eyes remained blank as spent cartridges. He looked a hundred years old, and the expression on his shrunken monkey's face said he could live another hundred and see nothing more that would surprise him.

Not badly wounded, compared to the others. A deep lateral gash in his leg, looked like a knife wound, a deep one, from knee to groin.

But that face . . .

'*Cach nao gia lok?*' she asked him in her halting Vietnamese. *How old are you?*

In a voice as flat as those eyes, he answered, '*Patombadu.*' *Nineteen.*

Oh dear Christ . . .

Rachel fought the hysterical urge to giggle. She thought that if she didn't get out of here soon, she was more likely to lose her mind than her life.


Brian clung to the edge of his seat as the jeep plunged through a pothole big enough to sink a water buffalo. He braced himself against the spine-snapping jolt. Christ. And he'd thought the main road was bad. Compared to this, that had been a freshly paved expressway.

'You sure he knows where he's going?' Brian yelled at Dan Petrie over the roar of the engine, while keeping his eyes fixed on Nguyen, on the back of their Vietnamese driver's head.

They weren't on any Rand McNally road map, that was for damn sure. They'd seen no signs of civilization for at least five kilometers. This was what Dorfmeyer, a platoon buddy, used to call Cold Sweat Country. Nothing but towering teaks and mangroves wreathed in liana vine, waist-high ferns and elephant grass. Perfect for ambush.

'Haven't the foggiest,' Dan yelled back cheerfully. 'But why worry, we'll know soon enough.'

Brian watched Nguyen steer, with remarkable agility, around another enormous pothole. The road, more of a path really, was barely wide enough for the jeep, and the swerve sent them lurching and fishtailing over the berm, leaving a trail of flattened grass and churned mud in their wake.

*Why worry.* The hundredth time he'd heard Petrie say those words over the past two days. As if they were riding the D train to Sheepshead Bay. Christ. At any moment they could be killed. But Dan Petrie, God only knew how, had gotten them this far safely.

First, the flight to Saigon. Petrie somehow had wrangled a phony set of orders passing Brian off as another reporter from his news service, and then had gotten them on a C-130 full of raw recruits. Amazing luck, until a lieutenant-colonel from Brian's division asked to see his papers. Jesus, how he had sweated blood then! But the CO, looking right at him, had passed him through. Brian realized what he must look like. He probably wouldn't have recognized *himself.* Forty pounds lighter, maybe more. The cherry he'd been six months ago must've looked as much like him now as Ho Chi Minh.

Six hours later, Petrie's buddy from *Stars and Stripes* had popped into the airport officer's lounge and led them to a Chinook chopper. Soon Da Nang, a bird's-eye view of blue water and khaki-colored beaches fringed in green, pretty as any postcard. No-one would have known that right nearby people were killing each other.

Their luck ran out, or so it seemed to Brian, when Dan tried to con a motor pool sergeant into loaning them a jeep. But Dan just pulled another rabbit out of his hat, this time in the form of some brand-new girlie magazines and a pack of opium-laced cigarettes, and the jeep was theirs.

And then hiring this driver, Nguyen, was another Petrie inspiration . . . or so Brian had thought at the time.

Back where they'd turned off the highway, Brian thought, was for sure where their luck had ended. He'd agreed with Petrie then, it would be safer taking a back

way to Tien Sung. Not so traveled or heavily patrolled.
But now he feared they'd taken the wrong route . . .

They were in Charlie territory, he could feel it. His
scalp felt tight, shrunken. And if his balls climbed any
higher, they'd be lodged in his throat.

'Second thoughts?' Petrie asked, those bolted-in blue
eyes of his peering at Brian from under the brim of his cap.

'No,' Brian answered. This might well get them all
killed, but he had to at least try and get to Rachel.

'She *must* be something then.' Petrie began whistling
the theme from *Bridge on the River Kwai*.

Brian concentrated on the narrow track ahead. Any
second they might hit a mine. Or get picked off by snipers.
Christ, he wished he had his M-16. Or even just a pistol.
But in Da Nang, Dan had insisted no weapons. Civilians –
here, he'd pushed his face in front of Brian's – that's how
they were going in. That was their protection, and their
only hope, lousy as it was. Besides, even with a couple of
rifles, against VC snipers they wouldn't have a prayer.

Petrie's words had given Brian an idea, though. There
could well be other weapons besides guns. On the afternoon of the day before they were to leave Da Nang, he had
visited a Catholic church in the heart of the city. He
recalled now how the priest, a slender Eurasian who spoke
English with a French accent, had led him through a warren of narrow stone corridors, then outside to a small
enclosed garden. Stone walls blanketed in morning glories
and honeysuckle, some kind of mossy grass that grew in
hummocks amid carefully placed rocks, a small pond
studded with water lilies set in the middle of it all like a
jewel. The loveliest garden Brian had ever seen. On a teak
bench under the shade of a hibiscus tree, Father Sebastian
served him bitter Chinese tea, and afterwards Brian knelt
with him in the soft grass and prayed. He'd felt far away
from God, but the ancient words and cadences had comforted him, as if his mother had laid her hand on his brow.
Afterwards, the priest sent him on his way with a blessing
and the thing Brian had come for . . . the thing that might

ensure their safety, he hoped. Under his jacket now. He had it hidden. Not even Petrie knew.

Throwing Brian forward against the dash, the driver braked to a sudden halt.

About thirty yards ahead, someone was blocking the road, a kid in black pajamas and thongs. He looked about sixteen, and could have been a villager on his way to the rice paddies . . . except he was carrying a rifle. A Soviet AK-47.

'*Dùng lai*!' the boy commanded.

Brian watched, feeling helpless, every muscle wound tight, as Nguyen leaped nimbly from the driver's seat and trotted over to him, mud sucking at the heels of his sandaled feet.

A burst of singsong Vietnamese followed between the two, with lots of wild gesturing back and forth.

'Don't make a move,' Dan whispered, laying a hand on Brian's arm. 'Just smile. Smile like you just got picked runner-up in the bloody Miss America pageant.'

Brian did. He smiled so hard he thought his face would forever freeze into this position. And all the while, he held the rest of himself rigid too, his muscles cramping, sweat dribbling off his forehead, terror knotting his insides.

Abruptly, Nguyen turned, and headed back to the jeep. His expression tight, eyes narrowed with scorn.

Petrie swore softly under his breath. 'It's no bloody good. He won't let us pass. We're lucky he didn't shoot us.' After a short pause, he added grimly, 'Unless maybe he's saving the best for last.'

Brian thought of Rachel. He *had* to get to her. He had to chance it.

Suddenly it was as if his every muscle had fused into one, galvanizing him into action.

He tore his arm from Dan's grip, and leapt out. Too late, he realized he should have moved more cautiously. There was a spurt of orange flame. A sound like a drop of water hitting a red-hot griddle. Brian felt a hot lick of air graze his cheek.

The warm mud stank of manure. He was on his belly,

317

arms curled protectively over his head, the still-hot mouth of the semi-automatic's barrel pressed against the side of his neck. *I'm going to die. After all this. Shot in the road like a rabbit. Jesus Christ, what a waste.*

After an excruciating time of lying still and wondering what it would feel like to die, he realized that might not happen . . . at least not immediately. He lowered his arms and raised his head. He was confronted by filthy feet wearing thongs. Slowly, Brian lifted himself on to his knees, holding his arms up, palms out, to show he meant no harm. Now, looking up into the round dusky-skinned face of his captor, he saw that the kid was as scared as he was.

Brian, taking a chance, gestured to show that he wanted to open his jacket. The boy brought up the rifle, pointing it squarely at Brian's forehead . . . then he nodded.

Brian unzipped his windbreaker.

Underneath, he was wearing a priest's black shirt and clerical collar.

He made the sign of the cross, praying with greater terror than he ever had in the hundreds of times he'd knelt before the altar of Holy Martyrs that this boy was – or at least had been – Catholic, and not Buddhist.

His heart thundered in his ears, and the sweat now was dripping off his nose, his chin. A swarm of gnats buzzed, maddening, stinging him. But he dared not brush them away. He remained perfectly still. He saw a kingfisher swoop down from a tall tree, the sun catching on its wings in a blaze of iridescent colors.

After an eternity, the boy slowly, stiffly, lowered his rifle. He gestured for Brian to stand. Cautiously, reverently even, the boy reached out and touched a forefinger to the Saint Christopher's medal that dangled over Brian's collar.

Brian lifted the chain over his head, and handed the medal to the boy, smiling to show he meant it as a gift, a peace offering. The toughness dropped away from the boy's sallow face, and he smiled.

*Maybe it's going to be OK*, Brian thought.

Relief swept over him. His legs buckled when he tried to

318

stand, and he faltered twice before finally he managed to bring himself to his feet.

Brian spoke quickly, without turning around, directing his words to Nguyen. 'Tell him I must get through to the hospital. There's a doctor . . . a lady doctor . . . we need her for . . . for a priest in Da Nang who is very sick. Tell him this priest will die if we don't take her back with us.'

Nguyen translated in rapid, high-pitched Vietnamese.

Five minutes later, their jeep was climbing the steep mountain road into Tien Sung, with the pajama-clad boy riding shotgun on the running board, looking delighted and proud of his important new role.

Dan turned to Brian, his monkey face creased in an incredulous grin. 'Jesus Christ. You've one hell of a nerve. That was the best bloody performance since the Last Supper.'

Brian grinned. 'At the Last Supper they didn't serve wedding cake.'

Rachel locked the med cabinet, then turned toward the stairs leading to the second floor, balancing a tray of fresh syringes and four ampules each of morphine and penicillin. She glanced at the Vietnamese guard leaning against the wall at the other end of the corridor, holding a rifle across his chest and watching her carefully. He no longer frightened her. She almost wished he would shoot her, and put an end to her ordeal.

She hadn't slept in three days. She was on the verge of collapse. If it hadn't been for Kay, where would she be? Kay, who also looked like death, but who seemed to be drawing strength from some deep reserve. Yet Kay, too, had her limits. Earlier today, Rachel had seen her stumble with fatigue nearly dropping a load of fresh bandages she was carrying.

If only they could get away . . .

*I'm like someone who's starving, whose body starts eating its own flesh*, she thought. *But it's my mind,*

319

*craving sleep, craving an end to all this, that must be consuming itself.*

Her thoughts circled once again around the same beaten path.

*Brian, oh my love. If only we could have loved one another openly, even for an hour, how much better than this.*

She accepted Rose. Reading Brian's journal she had come to understand his and Rose's relationship better than if he had tried to explain it. Yes, it was right that he go back to her. They would marry, have the big family Brian wanted, the children *she* probably could never give him. As it should be. But understanding still hurt. Accepting did not take away the cold emptiness in her heart.

The floor seemed to be moving, shimmering like heat rising off baking asphalt. Her head swam. At the end of the hallway now there were two guards. Engaged in some kind of furious discourse. A third Vietnamese man, unarmed, sauntered over, smiling, speaking in a friendly manner. She caught the word 'cigarettes.' Then all three disappeared through the door that led out on to the courtyard.

The guards had become more relaxed over the past day or two. With the arrival last night of two Russian doctors, they had even allowed Ian MacDougal leave yesterday to accompany a two-year-old Vietnamese boy in need of complicated surgery Ian could perform only at the hospital in Da Nang. But still, where did that leave her? Lately, she'd noticed one of the guards looking at her a certain way that turned her blood cold, and made her think he had worse things in mind than merely killing her.

Now two other men were coming in through the door, walking forward. The light was dim. All she could see was their shadowy outlines. One tall and thin, the other short and wiry.

The tall one stepped forward. A priest. What was a priest doing here?

Then she saw his face. Gaunt, hollowed by sickness, but

320

still the most beautiful face she had ever seen. At first she didn't believe it. It had to be a dream.

'Brian,' she gasped.

There was a crash. She looked down at the splintered glass at her feet. She had dropped her tray.

Then she began to run toward him.

As in dreams, her legs were heavy, clumsy, as if she were running through deep sand, each step pulling her down. She flung out her arms . . . and now she was being lifted like a kite . . . wind roaring in her ears . . . bearing her forward . . .

Then he was holding her, embracing her. She felt herself being squeezed, so hard she knew it wasn't a dream. These were Brian's hands, face, body. He'd come back to her. Brian, who had made her feel worthwhile, important, blessed, who had made her glow with love. And now, a true miracle, he'd come to rescue her.

'Brian, oh Brian.' She clung to him, burying her face in the stiff black folds of his shirt, weeping. She didn't care why he was dressed in a priest's collar, only that he'd come for her.

'Rachel,' he murmured into her hair, his voice choked. 'Rachel, thank God. Oh thank God.'

He kissed her, filthy hands cupping her face, his cheek rough with stubble, but oh, how wonderful . . .

An explosion of light printed red stars on the insides of her closed eyelids.

She blinked her eyes open, startled to see a little monkey of a man standing a few feet away, brandishing a camera, and grinning as if he'd just been handed a bronze trophy.

'Well done, mate,' he crowed. 'That kiss will be seen around the bleeding world!'

# 16

Their jeep lurched over a small ditch where the choked jungle lane forked on to the main road. Branches squealed along the hood and sides, then suddenly, miraculously it seemed, there were clouds, sky, space. Now they were bumping over a two-lane asphalt highway, cracked and studded with potholes, but here there were people, a village . . . and relative safety. Rachel spotted the tail end of an army transport truck cresting a hill off in the distance. She felt like cheering.

They had made it. All of them – she and Brian, and his funny little Australian. Kay, too, thank God. Somehow, Lord only knew how, they'd all made it.

Rachel felt Brian's arm tighten about her shoulders as they hit a bone-jolting rut and wings of muddy water spumed out from the jeep's wheels. *Yes, Brian, hold me*, she thought, *hold on to me, please, or I might fly right out of this dream . . .*

It was dusk, and they'd been crawling for an eternity on that barely marked track through the jungle. But now their driver was braking for oxen, dogs and children, and wizened mama-sans bent under enormous bundles they carried on their heads, as they began passing through the suburbs of Da Nang. Bamboo huts and rice paddies giving way to shantytowns of corrugated tin, ditches flooded with foul water, cooking fires lighting up the dusk like fireflies.

Safe, she thought. Safe from snipers, ambushes, land mines. She felt her tension ebb. This place was so dismal, so appallingly filthy, yet she rejoiced in the cacophony of sounds and voices, the bellowing of oxen. She wanted to embrace every person she saw.

322

Free, she was free. And Brian, dear God, he had come back. For her. He loved her enough to risk getting himself killed for her.

Taking in his profile, his stubbled jaw streaked with mud, the strong jutting bones, she felt such love it hurt her, an ache in her belly spreading up through her chest, clutching at her throat.

'A shower,' Kay, beside her, grunted. 'That's gonna be the first thing. God, I stink worse than a goat. No wonder those VC let me go with you. They probably were praying I'd clear out.'

Dan Petrie turned back toward them over the front seat, his blue eyes peering out from a mask of red dust, and tipped Kay a wink. 'Bloody hell they were. If it hadn't been for Father Brian here, we'd all be checking into the Hanoi Hilton. But I got to hand it to you, lady—' he patted the camera case in his lap, 'that shot of you flipping Charlie the bird will go down in history.'

'My *yenta* temper. Good thing he didn't know what it meant. The way he was smiling, he probably thought it meant good luck or something.' Kay's face, round as a Buddha's, split into a wide grin as she lifted her hand high over her head, middle finger raised. 'Well, here's luck to us all!'

And now Brian was holding Rachel with both arms, and then kissing her, kissing her fiercely. He felt and smelled like the twenty miles of bad road they'd just come over, his face and hands gritty with dried mud, his black priest's shirt soaked with sweat, but she had never known anything so sweet. She felt his hand tightly cupping the curve of her skull where her neck arched back. He was trembling.

'Marry me,' he murmured, clutching her even tighter.

But had he said that, or had she just imagined it? Hell, it didn't matter. He didn't have to say it out loud. She knew what he was feeling, just as he knew what her heart was saying to him.

'When?' she asked.

Brian drew back with a laugh, but his eyes – those

incredible slate-colored eyes that had somehow captivated her before he ever had spoken a word to her – were serious.

'Now. As soon as we get to Da Nang. Petrie knows a chaplain, a *real* chaplain,' he said and laughed. 'He says this guy owes him one. Though knowing Petrie, I'd hate to think what for.'

Rachel, her emotions reeling, felt something quiet, calm, deep inside her. Yes, this was right, this was meant to be. A force even stronger than their love for each other had somehow decided this.

'Yes,' she told him. 'Yes,' she said again, loud enough for Kay and Petrie to hear, and for the whole world. 'Yes, I'll marry you!' She was crying now, 'I'll marry you in Da Nang . . . or New York . . . or Disneyland . . . anywhere you want me!'

*Brian, I feel so different than I ever have, like I'm in another country, your country; I've crossed over some magic frontier, and I don't ever want to go back.*

Everything up until now, David . . . the abortion . . . all those dead and dying soldiers . . . the VC . . . it had happened in another world, to another Rachel.

Petrie held up two fingers in a victory sign.

Kay didn't say a word, just grabbed Rachel's hand and squeezed it hard. Her brown eyes, behind the dusty lenses of her spectacles, shone with tears.

'Looks like you get stuck being my maid of honor,' Rachel told her.

'Just one question,' Kay said. 'Do I get to take a shower first?'

Father Rourke was drunk as a skunk, but ambulatory . . . just barely.

Rachel, standing with Brian before the chaplain in his rumpled khakis, felt a little faint. His breath reeked of alcohol, and he was swaying on his feet, his hands shaking as he fumbled with the pages of his prayer book. She lifted her eyes, and stared at the road map of broken veins

324

spread across his nose and cheeks. A man probably no more than thirty, who looked more like sixty-five.

She had to engrave every detail in her memory, the ugly along with the beautiful. Someday, an old married couple, curled together in the cozy warmth of their bed, in their own solid house somewhere, they would laugh about Father Rourke and this whole scene, and it would draw them even closer to each another.

She looked around. This tiny mah-jongg den behind the bar where Petrie finally – after visiting a dozen other bars – had tracked down the chaplain, was straight out of a Charlie Chan movie. Beaded curtains, orange paper lanterns, a jangle of music and singsong voices in the background. She etched it all in her mind. She would come back to this place again and again in her memory.

She looked back up at Brian, and he smiled, sharing her amusement. Then she thought of Mason Gold's wedding, how weird she'd thought it. *If Mason could only see this!*

Brian, in a tuxedo jacket rented from a rapacious supply sergeant. It was a good four inches too short in the arms. Brian's knobby wrists stuck out so far he was keeping his hands shoved into his pockets. Kay had pinned a scarlet hibiscus blossom to his lapel a few minutes ago, and Rachel saw now to her horror that it was crawling with ants.

But, oh, his dear face, the way his head cocked a little to one side as he smiled down at her, his dark curls springing loose from the wet comb tracks. She wouldn't have traded him, no, not for anyone.

'Do you . . . Rachel . . . ah . . . ah . . . Rosenthal . . . take this man to be your . . . ah . . . lawful wuh-wedded husband? To . . .'

'I do,' she answered, too impatient to hear out the rest of it.

'And do you, Brian . . .'

Off to her right, Rachel could hear Kay honk softly into a tissue.

325

*Bless you, dear Kay*, she thought. Kay had even found her this white silk tunic split up the sides, with matching trousers – traditional Vietnamese garb. Kay herself was wearing one of red cotton, which clung to her plump curves, making Rachel think of an elf in a union suit.

'. . . for richer or poorer, in suh-suh-sickness . . . or huh-health . . . ah . . . do you take . . . no, I already said that, didn't I? . . . Let's see, um . . . yes, here . . . till death do you part?'

Brian looked into her eyes for what seemed a very long time, and she felt the love in them reach out, reach down inside her and catch hold of her heart.

*I should stop this . . . tell him now . . . before it's too late. But if he knew I couldn't give him children, would he still want to marry me? Would I be enough . . . ?*

Yes, she knew she must tell him. This very minute. While he could still change his mind if he wanted to. But the words she felt duty-bound to say would not come; they seemed stuck in her throat. She couldn't bear to stop Brian from promising to love and cherish her for ever . . . to be her husband . . .

And then she heard Brian say, 'I do.'

Suddenly Rachel was too happy to concentrate on anything but Brian embracing her, kissing her, lifting her so that her toes barely grazed the floor, his body, his mouth, fusing into hers.

Flashbulbs popped, blinding bursts of white, making red pin-pricks swarm before her eyes.

Married! She and this wonderful, brave, gentle man were married . . .

With the tip of her finger, Rachel traced the scar which criss-crossed Brian's belly like a crimson thunderbolt.

'Right now, you remind me of Flash Gordon,' she teased, wallowing in contentment as she lay naked beside him on the bed, the sheet tangled about her feet. 'I loved those old episodes on television. He was a big hero of mine, back when I was in Spanky pants and Mary Janes.'

326

'What about now?'

'Oh, I don't know. I think I prefer mad Irishmen. Brings out the Maureen O'Hara in me.'

'Maureen O'Hara?'

'Didn't you ever see her in *The Quiet Man*, that feisty redhead just asking to be put in her place by John Wayne.'

'And just what place was that, I wonder.'

Rachel grinned, feeling naughty. 'In bed, where else?'

Right now, this decrepit bed with its sag in the middle felt like the most wonderful place in all the world. And this seedy hotel room, too, with its rickety bamboo chairs and yellowing prints of the Eiffel Tower and the Arc de Triomphe.

Now, in the first light of day, it looked even more dingy than last night, when their taxi had rattled through a maze of frighteningly narrow alleyways to this hole-in-the-wall, the Hôtel Arc de Triomphe. Rachel noted the bare wood peeking through the chipped spots on a red lacquer cabinet. And the window's shutters with several slats missing, through which filtered, along with the milky light, a jangle of sounds – water slapping against the sampans in the adjacent Saigon River, the clanking of pots, a babble of singsong voices. She caught the fragrant cooking smells of ginger, steamed rice, kim chee. And underlying them, the faint stink of rotten fish and urine.

Then she remembered, and felt a surge of joy. *We're married, truly married. And tomorrow we're going home!*

Home.

Mama, God help her, would probably faint when she heard the news. No nice Jewish doctor or lawyer for a son-in-law. Instead, here she was, Sylvie's daughter, the bride of a penniless Irish Catholic. But, damn it, *she* was happy. She felt happier than she ever believed could be possible. Mama would see that, and she would come to love Brian just as much.

*And Daddy would have approved of you, Brian*, she thought, smiling. *You're strong like him, you know, and gentle.*

327

'I love you,' she said, rolling over and nestling herself against his side, her curves fitting snugly with all his hollows. 'Have I told you how much I love you?'

'Tell me again when I'm fully awake, otherwise I might think I dreamed all this.'

He held her tightly. She could feel his heart beating fast. She wished they could stay like this for ever, just the two of them; and then they'd never have to explain themselves to anyone else.

But a dream, a ridiculous dream, wasn't it? Sooner or later, they would have to face other people. And when that came, she wanted to be on firm ground.

'Tell me about Rose,' she said softly.

Rachel felt him immediately stiffen. She was struck by an awful jolt of fear. If just the mention of Rose's name still had such power over him, God, what might happen when he saw her again, as he inevitably would?

There was a long, terrible silence before Brian said, 'I grew up with her. She and I . . . I guess you could say she was the girl next door.'

'Would you . . . have married her?' And then waiting for his answer, Rachel held her breath.

Brian lay rigid as a plank of wood in her arms, silent for what felt like an hour. 'I married *you*, isn't that what matters?'

'Yes, but only if it's what you truly want. If you're sure you won't regret it someday.'

Why was she doing this? Why was she torturing herself this way?

Beside her, Brian lay without speaking. Rachel felt terror gather in her chest. Suppose he was already regretting it? Had Rose – or did she still – mean that much to him?

'Let's not talk about "someday," ' Brian said at last. 'Let's just think about now. I love you, Rachel. More than any other woman.'

*That's not good enough*, she wanted to shout. *You're not answering me, not telling me!* But at the same time, Rachel felt ashamed for wanting him so desperately to

328

reassure her. She was being a little hysterical, wasn't she? After all, he had married her, not Rose. God forbid she should ever turn into one of those wives always clinging, always begging for proof of her husband's devotion like a dog begging for scraps under the table.

*Leave it alone*, she ordered herself. *Why force him into confessing something you couldn't bear to hear?*

He stroked her breast, then cupped it, gently teasing her nipple with his thumb. 'Mrs McClanahan. Has a nice ring to it, don't you think? The last woman in my family to take that name ended up having seven kids. Think you're up for it?'

Now she felt herself grow cold, rigid. *What a hypocrite I am!* she thought. *Asking him to tell me all about Rose, while I hold back the truth about myself.*

No, she thought. A marriage had to be built on honesty, total trust. She had to tell him. He would have to know eventually. From the very beginning, back when she used to sit on his bed at Corpus Christi, reading his journal, listening to him dream aloud about the future, he'd been plain about wanting a family.

'Brian . . .' But her throat seemed to seize up.

This was such a perfect moment, perhaps the most wonderful day of their lives; it wouldn't be fair to spoil it. No, not now. It was too soon. And it was too late as well. She felt like a coward. She should have told him before, given him the chance to back out before that drunken chaplain slurred his final blessings. But everything had happened in such a blur . . . except for the one thing that stood out clearly, then and now. She could not lose him. Not again. It would shrivel her up, make her want to die.

'. . . don't stop,' she murmured instead, letting herself feel the delicious chill of his hand sliding down her belly. She opened her legs, allowing his fingers to move into her. 'Oh yes, oh God, like that, just like that . . . oh darling, if you don't stop I'm going to come.'

'Wait . . .'

Then he was inside her, *really* inside, moving on top of

her with strong, trembling thrusts of his body, each one bringing its own small burst of pleasure. She arched her spine, curving to meet him, and at the same time running her hands over his buttocks – oh, the lovely concave shape of them! – feeling the pebbly tightness of his goose-flesh and, reaching lower, the little puckered seam leading like a trail to his testicles.

*Oh Brian, if only I could give you a child someday . . . if only . . .*

She felt a hot burst of sensation, a sexy powerful rush all through her, one made all the more exquisite by the fierce intensity of her longing.

Then Brian was coming too, she could feel him spilling into her. And at that moment she felt suddenly lost, cut loose from Brian, spinning out of his orbit.

No way to start a marriage. *It's wrong*, she thought, *all wrong, deceiving Brian like this*.

*Tell him*, she commanded herself. *He'll understand. He loves you*.

She opened her mouth, tried to whisper the words, but she could not push them past her throat. For a horrid moment, she once again saw in her mind the blue-white light on the surgical steel curette in David's hand, and heard David's angry, frightened voice: *You'll regret this someday. You'll regret making me do this*.

Then the image faded. There was only the moist warmth of Brian's body enveloping her, his hands cradling her head to him – hands so big they made her think of when she was very little, her earliest memories of her father holding her, her tiny skull nestled like an egg in his hands.

She let out a muffled sob.

'What is it?' he asked.

'Nothing,' she lied. Then, her arms about the birdcage of his ribs, she squeezed so hard she could hear the sharp chuff of air leaving his lungs. 'I'm so happy, that's all. I cry when I'm happy, and when I'm upset or nervous, I laugh, really giggle like a madwoman.'

'In that case, I hope I never make you giggle.'

And what Rachel hoped with all her soul was that it would stay just like this between them. Always. And she *would* tell him about the abortion . . . soon. And he would understand. He would. Then it really would be perfect. No lies between them.

The way it had been between Mama and Daddy.

Since Brian had gone overseas, Rose had become an avid newspaper reader, sifting both the *Times* and the *News* every morning for reports of battles, bombings, any progress in peace negotiations, any scrap of information, however slight, to bolster her hope that the war might soon come to an end, that Brian might come home before his tour was over.

She had gotten through the *Times* on the subway, and now she settled in at her desk – always immaculate and clear of papers first thing in the morning, pried the lid off her coffee container, and opened the *Daily News*.

On page three, she saw a Vietnam story, and a grainy photo caught her eye – a guy in a tuxedo jacket embracing his bride. The caption read: WEDDING BELLS FOR HERO AND HIS LADY DOC.

Rose skipped the opening lines full of names and ages, and jumped into the story, skimming quickly through it. A riveting tale of a woman doctor in a combat zone, and the dying soldier whose life she saved. The same soldier who later, defying orders, went AWOL to go behind enemy lines to rescue her. A love story, a fairy tale. Rose smiled, her heart lifting a fraction. *You see, happy endings do sometimes exist. They're not impossible.*

Rose glanced up again at the first paragraph, wanting to know these people, their names, where they were from. One name jumped out at her: *Pfc. Brian McClanahan. 121st Infantry.*

The newsprint swam before Rose's eyes, the photo blurred. Not her Brian, no, this had to be another soldier with the same name. A coincidence, of course, that's all it could possibly be.

So then why was her heart burning so? Why this icy feeling in her gut? Oh Mother of God, *could* it be him?

She felt dizzy, her mind whirling madly, as if she might go insane. And yet she knew she wouldn't. Sanity was right here, all around her, this desk, her work. Yes, this was what was real, sane, this steaming paper cup on her desk, this cassette of dictated letters waiting to be typed. And in a few minutes, Max Griffin striding down this corridor, flashing her his you-and-me-against-the-world grin, and wishing her a good morning that always lifted her spirits.

But this photo, this face posing as Brian's, was choking her, opening a black abyss in her mind that she could feel herself beginning to tumble into.

Now the room was somehow tilting, her chair and the carpeted floor beneath it rolling out from under her. She grabbed the edge of her desk to steady herself, and knocked over the steaming cup by the phone. Coffee poured over the open paper, seeping through to the glass-topped desk, dripping on to her lap. And then she felt the heat, searing pain, as if a hot iron were pressing against her thighs. *Hurts . . . oh, it hurts . . . Brian . . .*

She forced herself to peer at the photo, closely this time, straining to bring it into focus. His face, oh God, it was his face. Even though now the photo was sodden and buckled, she recognized that face, its long beveled shape, those haunting eyes.

Brian. *Her* Brian.

Her worst fear of all. Brian in love with someone else. No, even more monstrous than that . . . worse than she could have imagined. He was married.

Black fury gripped her. *He should have been killed, that would have been better. At least he'd still be mine.*

Rose sat back, trembling. God, she really was losing her mind. Had she actually thought such a thing? Brian dead? No, not that . . . never that.

*This isn't happening*, she told herself. *I'm just tired after last night, that phone call from Nonnie, all her whining about how everything hurts, how no-one visits her. The old bat still thinking she can pull my strings, even from Syracuse. How could I sleep after that? No wonder I'm exhausted. Yes, this has to be some kind of hallucination, a sort of nightmare . . .*

With a fierce sweeping motion, Rose gathered the sodden newspaper up and shoved it into the wastebasket. *Nothing there now, nothing at all. Why don't I just clean up this mess? And this dress, this pretty flowered dress Brian bought me for my last birthday, I'd better soak it in cold water or it'll stain –*

Yes, that's what she should do. Go home, now, this minute. Before the stain had a chance to set. Because once it set, no amount of scrubbing would get it out, no amount of soap or spot remover. Brian's pretty dress. It might be ruined for ever.

And then that picture projected itself into her mind, and the words below.

> *. . . The young Columbia graduate was to be sent home from Okinawa with a Bronze Star . . . but forged orders to return illegally to the combat zone where he almost had been killed weeks before . . . defying virtually insurmountable odds to rescue the beautiful doctor who had saved his life . . . the woman he loved . . .*

*The woman he loved*, Rose thought. *But that's me. I'm the one Brian loves. We're going to be married. As soon as he gets home, as soon as –*

*I have to get this stain out. Damn, it's probably set by now. I must get home. I must . . .*

Then she was rising, feeling disjointed, like a marionette with its strings tangled, her arms jerking at odd angles, her legs buckling, out of control. She was reaching for her purse, her arm stretching on and on for ever, as if made of elastic, her hand at the end of it like something viewed from the wrong end of a telescope.

Now she was walking, the corridor lined with doors leading to lawyers' offices stretching before her, a tunnel that seemed endless. The carpet made of quicksand, dragging at her feet. *Keep going. Go home. Yes, got to get this stain out, so Brian can come home . . .*

The massive double doors to the elevators. A car sliding open, then another. People pouring out into the hallway, streaming past, some nodding to her. All except one man, who held back as the others headed for the office doors. A big man, not tall, but solid – she imagined him solid all the way through like a tree trunk – wearing a tan jacket, carrying a briefcase, his broad, handsome face ruddy, as if he'd dashed up the stairs instead of taking the elevator, his graying brown hair crinkling up from its comb tracks. Max Griffin.

Rose felt her confusion recede a little. This man would help her. He had before, hadn't he? With that scholarship for the fall. And his talking to her, not like a boss, but like a friend.

A corner of a paper, she observed, was sticking out from his battered leather briefcase. She saw it as if looking through a magnifying glass, his hand gripping the briefcase's worn leather handle, his powerful-looking wrist – all those appointments at the racquet-ball court – and the stainless Rolex strapped to it. The face of the watch was scratched, which he probably hadn't even noticed.

But now he was dropping the briefcase, stepping forward to grip both her elbows, seeming to support her whole weight almost.

'Rose! What is it? You're white as a ghost. Are you sick? Did you hurt yourself?'

She shook her head. Why should she be sick? And how could she have hurt herself? No . . . nothing so awful . . . just this silly stain . . .

'I spilled my coffee,' she told him. 'And now I've got it all over me, and I . . . I have to get home. My dress. I'll

335

make up the time. Please. I have to go home.' Her voice, she thought, sounded tinny, strange.

Max was looking at her oddly . . . his square prize-fighter's face seeming to grow even squarer, his blue eyes sharper.

'Come on then,' he said gently. 'I'll take you home.'

She felt boneless, unable to protest. 'Yes, home.'

He steered her into the elevator, gripping her arm hard. Then they were in a taxi, swerving through the traffic, the windows rolled down and the sticky summer air rushing at her. Yet she felt cold, so cold, as if there were snow on the ground, snow all around her, inside her, freezing her heart. White noise like a blizzard roared inside her head.

And everything was running together, all the colors of the city, the bright summer dresses of the women, the gay patchwork of magazines lining the shelves of a newsstand, the hot dog vendor's striped umbrella, all smearing together, turning muddy.

She began to shiver, her teeth chattering. She wanted to make herself stop, but she couldn't.

Max, his voice seeming to come from a great distance, through buzzing static, was saying, 'You're ill, Rose. I think I should take you to a doctor.'

A doctor? What for? There was nothing wrong with her.

She shook her head, and wrapped her arms about herself, determined to stop the shivering. 'I'm fine,' she insisted. 'This is silly. You shouldn't even be here, wasting your valuable time like this. You have to be in court in an hour.'

'Never mind court. I'll get a continuance. It's you I'm worried about, Rose. You've got to tell me what happened. You look as if someone died.'

*Yes.* A voice rose from the rushing static in her head. *Brian, he's gone. The same as dead.*

Rose brought her hands out in front of her as if to ward off a blow, as if the terrible thought was being aimed at her from outside, about to strike her.

336

'No,' she cried. 'No!'

Max held her then, pinning her arms. 'Rose, for God's sake, what is it? What happened? Tell me!'

She shook her head, violently. *Please . . . don't make me say it. If I tell you, that will only make it more real.*

'I only want to help you,' he pressed. 'But I can't unless you tell me what's wrong. Rose? Rose?'

'Nothing. Nothing's wrong.' She was struck by a sudden violent wave of nausea. 'Oh, Max, I think I'm going to be sick.'

But he only held her tighter, and she felt her nausea recede a little. Then, an interminable time later, he was helping her from the cab, supporting, no, carrying her almost up the dozens of stairs to her tiny studio.

'It's going to be OK, Rose,' Max soothed her. 'Whatever it is, it will get better. And I'm here. I'll take care of you.'

No, she wanted to cry out to him. *No.* It was Brian who was supposed to take care of her. Brian always had taken care of her, hadn't he? Only where was he now? She needed him now, more than ever before.

But she felt so weak, hardly able to move. She allowed Max to pull off her shoes, then her dress . . . her ruined dress . . . and now, in her slip, shivering in the stifling heat . . . she let him tuck her into bed as if she were a child.

The room seemed suddenly too small, too dark, this Lower East Side studio she'd been so thrilled with when she first signed the lease. Quaint, the doll-size kitchen, the deep clawfoot tub, this couch that folded out into a bed. But now she was seeing how dark it truly was; no sun ever reached her back-alley window, with its grim accordion gate. She saw that the geraniums she'd put out on the fire escape were dying, all droopy and brown. Her special place seemed now like a prison cell, gray, dangerous somehow.

'It's going to be OK,' Max was saying again. 'You don't have to talk about it. Just rest. Here, drink this.' He was pressing a glass to her lips, making her swallow something. 'I'll be here. I won't leave you.'

337

His kindness triggered something inside her, as if he'd pressed a button, releasing something awful, pain, the pain of knives piercing her, cutting her.

She couldn't move or breathe.

She would die, surely die, from this pain.

'Help me.' She found her voice. She grabbed for Max's hand, his capable hand with its smooth broad palm and strong fingers; she clutched it between both of hers as if she were drowning, hanging on for dear life.

'I'm here,' she heard him through the roaring in her ears. 'I'm here, Rose.'

# Part Two
# 1974

*It is not hard to confess our criminal acts, but the ridiculous and shameful.*
                                        Rousseau, *Confessions*

# 18

Sylvie clipped a withered rosebud. A shame, she thought, not even allowed to bloom before it dies.

She bent to examine the bush, noting the fine white filaments spun like cobwebs over some of the leaves. Spider mites, from the looks of it. Well, the whole garden would have to be sprayed, and most of the bushes cut back. It didn't seem right somehow. This glorious June day, the sun shining. Not a day for blight.

Sylvie lowered herself to her knees, clippers in hand, not moving. Just listening to the drowsy hum of insects and breathing in the lovely sun-warmed scent of roses – *like to see dear Helena bottle that if she could*! – and looking out over her garden. It had gotten a bit overgrown, the French lace laden down with rose-cream buds crowding up against the lavender Blue Nile, and the tea roses had climbed right off the trellis and were taking over the whole south wall.

She would never have let it get like this a few years ago . . . certainly not while Gerald was alive. But in the past six years so much had changed.

*She* had changed, she realized with a start. *Not a silly chicken any longer, frightened of my own shadow. No more apologizing for what I am . . . and who I'm not, what I can do and what I cannot. Why, there are even men who find me attractive, desirable even – Alan Fogherty, taking me to dinner when he's in town, sending flowers, and Dennis Corbett at the bank, just last week calling to say he had two tickets to the ballet.* And then, of course, there was Nikos . . .

Sylvie found herself growing hot, as if the sun were

341

burning through her clothing. She imagined Nikos striding about among the piled cinder blocks and steel beams of his construction site, blue work shirt rolled up over his sturdy brown forearms, a roll of blueprints curled in his fist, his black eyes flashing this way and that, already seeing the building as it would be when it was finished.

And her, did he see something more in the future with her? Did he ever think about that long-ago time when they were lovers?

*God, what's happening*, Sylvie asked herself. *Is he what I want?*

She was annoyed to find that her hands were trembling, and a little flutter had crept into her stomach.

Making herself concentrate again on her roses, Sylvie began to snip. Healthy blossoms first, that way nothing would go to waste. She held up a perfect rose cut from the blighted bush. Snowfire, one of her favorites, also a most rare one. Perfect creamy white in the center, blushing to a deep crimson around the outer edges of each petal. Exquisite, a small miracle.

And here she was, middle-aged – she'd be fifty-two, her next birthday – kneeling in the dirt, as content as a child making mud pies, that was a kind of miracle too. How strange life was!

Maybe it was just this day – after so much rain. Sylvie felt the sunshine on the back of her neck, warm and comforting as the hand of an old friend. Soon it would grow too hot, and she would start to perspire and prickle. But right now it was the loveliest feeling in the world. She felt strong and . . . as if she could do anything she set her mind to.

She snipped another blossom and set it carefully in her basket.

Her thoughts turned to Nikos again. She remembered his kindness, those dark months after Gerald's death, with Rachel off in Vietnam. Calling to see how she was, telling her a funny story to cheer her up, letting her know he was

342

there if she needed a sympathetic ear, a strong shoulder for her to cry on.

She felt a little ashamed. She'd leaned on him too much, taken undue advantage of his kindness. And yet, if not for him, where would she be now? He was the one who had encouraged her to take charge of her life, her money. Gerald would not have approved, but Gerald was no longer here to protect her, either. And so she had waded in, feeling like an explorer entering uncharted and possibly dangerous territory. And what a wilderness! A majority holding in the bank, other stocks, mutual fund shares, municipal bonds, Treasury notes, real estate syndications, not to mention the big houses in New York, Deal, and Palm Beach. Their lawyer, Packard Haimes, advised strongly that he be empowered to look after it all; and it would have been a big relief just to let him. But something – yes, probably Nikos – had made that seemingly easy way out chafe at her.

So she'd gone up to Packard's antique library-like office at 55 Water Street.

Dear old Packy. She could still see him, his pink face and twinkly eyes leaning over her, his big dry hand patting her shoulder as he seated her in the leather chair across from his desk. He reminded her of Raymond Massey, tall, florid, shaggy-browed, exuding fatherly concern.

'You really haven't a thing to worry about, my dear Sylvie. Gerald's holdings were all solid as the Rock of Gibraltar, and we and the bank can look after them and keep you in comfort for the rest of your days. So you just take care of yourself, eat a bit more, take one of those cruises . . . the South Seas or some nice spot in the Caribbean would do you a world of good, you know,' he had advised, beaming his most avuncular smile, which in the past she had always found reassuring. At that moment, however, she found it irritating.

And she remembered Nikos once saying, money is usually managed best by those who risk losing their own shirt if it's not well done. And suddenly she was saying,

'I've decided to handle my own finances from now on.'

'You can't be serious,' Packy had argued. 'What do you know about—'

'Absolutely nothing,' she cut him off. 'But I'm not stupid. I can learn, can't I?'

And so she had learned, with Nikos's help. And when the long columns of figures, the balance sheets, profit and loss statements, accounts of gains and losses began to swim before her eyes, she would dredge up Nikos's encouraging words.

'It's not so complicated,' he had told her, 'it just looks that way at first. Remember two things, always. First, never be afraid to ask questions. And second, never allow yourself to believe you cannot understand the answers.'

And the notion began to grow, like a tiny seed planted in her head, that she *could* perhaps do more than Keep Busy, as she'd always done, with gardening, shopping, lunching with Evelyn Gold, raising money for the opera and, occasionally, dinner with Rachel and Brian.

There was, after all, the bank. At first, merely the idea of showing up at the monthly board meetings – the only woman among all those men! – had sent her reeling to her bed with a sick headache.

But then, two years after Gerald died, Pelham Securities went into Chapter Eleven, owing nearly twenty million to the bank. She'd visualized all Gerald's hard work over the years withering away like the buds on these blighted roses.

And that had given her courage to act. She dug out that the bad loan had been Hutchinson Pyne's doing. A pompous old fool, she'd always detested him, and now it might be disastrous to let him continue as chairman. She could forgive him for being pompous, but not for being a fool.

For the next board meeting, she'd risen at six in the morning, starting with a long scalding bath to relax her nerves. Then breakfast, which she normally avoided, forcing down two eggs and several slivers of toast. She

344

might be tongue-tied, but at least she would not faint in front of all those men.

Sylvie remembered, too, how carefully she had dressed that morning. Real silk stockings from Paris, and that Chanel suit Gerald had loved her in – double-knit, with the white piping around the hem and jacket. Then pearls, her grandmother's, the one beautiful thing she'd had from Mama. And a hat, of course, one of those smart Halston pillboxes.

She had looked long and hard in the mirror at the final result. A bit too thin – she'd lost so much weight after Gerald died. Stringy, the way women her age seemed to get if they didn't go the other way, plump and baggy. But on the whole, nonetheless, quite elegant.

Gerald, she had thought, would have been proud . . . if a little uneasy, at what she was about to do.

Even now, as Sylvie leaned forward and pinched a mottled brown bud from the bush, careful to avoid the thorns, her stomach churned at the memory of that day, walking into the boardroom and seeing all those frowns and raised eyebrows. Remembering how she'd felt (the same as when she was twelve and had accidentally blundered into the men's room at Alexander's, seeing a row of urinals, and men holding their penises as casually as a butcher weighing out frankfurters), scared and excited both, as if she had trespassed into some secret, all-male territory.

That first time, she had simply sat through the meeting, too intimidated to speak. It was enough just that she had come. The second time too. By her third, she still didn't feel wholly comfortable, but her fear was gone. And she now could almost hear their minds dictating little labels for her: *Bored just sitting around the house, lonely, wants to feel part of something. Gives her a chance to dress up in those expensive clothes, if nothing else. She's a silly distraction, but there's really no harm in it.*

*How wrong!* Sylvie thought, chuckling to herself, remembering their stunned and outraged looks. Who would have thought Gerald's timid widow would stand up and propose, bold as brass, that they elect a new chairman, one she already had in mind, a young vice-president named Adam Cutler. He was the son of a shoe salesman in North Carolina, and had come up the hard way. On the board, Cutler plainly was not part of the 'in group,' but to Sylvie he was the only one with any real sense or brains.

The moment following her proposal was engraved in her memory. The long walnut table – so highly polished she could see their reflections, faint ghosts on the veneer. Then Pyne, his face stiff and slightly purple with concealed outrage, rising to his feet, impaling her with a steely smile.

'We . . . and I think I speak for all of us here . . . welcome the interest you have recently begun showing in our bank, Mrs Rosenthal,' he said in a voice that seemed to lower the room temperature a good twenty degrees. 'But I feel it's in *all* of our best interests to remind you that what we're dealing with here isn't organizing a cocktail party or settling an overdue charge account at Saks.'

And Sylvie had been grateful to him, yes, *grateful*, for stirring up the anger to galvanize her. Her hands, which moments ago had begun trembling, now lay still, and the men seated about the table seemed no more threatening than the handymen, chauffeurs, salesmen, and clerks she'd always dealt with at home and in stores.

'You're trying to embarrass me,' she stated bluntly. 'And it's true, what you say, that I've only recently become involved.' She had looked at those men's gray faces, one by one, forcing herself to meet their eyes. 'But the only thing I have to be embarrassed about is my not getting involved sooner. Now, let me remind you I own sixty per cent of Mercantile Trust. If you *don't* wish to take me seriously, I think it only fair to inform you that I have a buyer who has offered me a good price for my shares . . .'

'Don't see how we could be much worse off than we are now,' sniped perspiring Sol Katzman, and Sylvie watched

346

him viciously tug at his tie, yanking it from the collar of his hand-tailored shirt as if he meant to hang her with it.

'I believe several of you already know the buyer I speak about,' she continued sweetly, waiting a beat before she dropped the bomb, 'Mr Nikos Alexandros.'

There was silence; and she wanted to clap her hands with glee. She had played her cards just right. It was plain that they would rather deal with a woman than a foreigner, an outsider. And a Greek, at that, whom they no doubt feared would connive to get the best of them all.

Even before they took the vote, Sylvie knew that she had won. Then the only question was, Could she make it out of there without collapsing in the elevator?

*Well, I didn't, did I?* Sylvie interrupted her reverie to struggle to her feet, clutching a stake for support. She felt a moment's dizziness. Orange-red sunspots danced before her eyes. Her heart was beating too quickly.

Time to go in, she thought, surveying the noon shadows beneath the rosebushes and the alabaster tubs of flowering quince and mock orange bordering the brick patio. If she hurried, she'd still have time to call Manuel about spraying this garden before getting ready for her lunch date with Nikos.

He had some exciting news he'd said he wanted to share with her. What could it be? Perhaps, she thought with a sudden dart of envy, he'd met someone – a woman he wanted to marry. And why not? He was still so vital, attractive. And best of all, he was kind.

Of *course* there was no reason he shouldn't marry. It was just, well, she hadn't thought of it before. And . . . oh dear, would that mean that they'd have to stop getting together for these lunches she so looked forward to? And the opera? And the charity affairs where Nikos saved her from being seated next to some pathetic old man who had just lost his wife?

Dear Nikos. She owed him so much. Rachel, most of all. In spite of Sylvie's denials, Nikos still seemed to believe Rachel was his, yet he did not press the issue.

347

Never. Always courteous and friendly toward Rachel, and that was all. Sylvie felt so grateful she would have given him anything in return. Anything, that is, except the truth . . . about Rose.

*All those years I lied to Gerald, and now I'm lying to Nikos.* The thought stabbed her like a sharp rose thorn.

If he were to know about Rose, he'd move heaven and earth to find her. And didn't he deserve to have the child he longed for?

God knows, she had tried to tell him, and yet each time the words just wouldn't come. For there was Rachel to think of. And Rose too . . . and herself, yes.

Sylvie lifted the straw basket laden with roses – blooms in every shade of yellow and pink and red – and she was so struck by their delicacy and exquisite beauty, her eyes filled with tears.

*My poor Rose*, she thought. *You don't know me, but I think of you every day. With less anguish than I used to, it's true. The years have been kind to me in that way. But . . . oh, my dear child . . . how I wish . . .*

Sylvie pulled one deep-crimson blossom from the basket, and touched it to her cheek for one long heart-rending moment.

Then, quite suddenly, she straightened her spine, dropping the rose back into the basket. Perhaps she *had* been out in the sun too long, getting herself all worked up like this.

And she had to hurry, or she'd be late. Then she felt a flush of panic. She was afraid of Nikos's news. She didn't need any more surprises in her life right now.

'So . . . what do you think?' Nikos asked, grinning down at her from the second-floor landing of the house to which he had brought her after lunch. 'Am I a fool or a genius? A hundred thousand dollars tells me I am most probably a fool.'

Sylvie caught up with Nikos at the head of the gracefully winding flight of stairs. She had come with him here, to this derelict building near Gramercy Park, up these sagging stairs, wondering what he possibly could want to show her. Now she understood. Her gaze swept over a badly damaged and rubble-strewn room, which once had been a magnificent Edwardian parlor. Enormous pocket doors that slid out from a great curved arch were hideously caked with old paint, half the lovely etched panes cracked or missing. The tall and fanciful ceiling with its chipped plaster rosettes and cracked bracket moldings was like the top of a wedding cake that had been gnawed away by rats.

*A house. That's what he wanted to tell me. Thank goodness, it wasn't any bad news.*

Sylvie felt weak, almost light-headed with relief. Then she began thinking of what it would take – both in money and aggravation – to make this old wreck of a place habitable, and she grew concerned for Nikos. He wasn't such a young man, after all, past sixty now.

Sylvie looked back at him, standing now under an archway amid chunks of fallen plaster and a pile of broken vinyl floor tiles. But he appeared as sturdy as he'd been thirty years ago. A bit heavier around the middle, but certainly not soft. Hair thick as ever, too, only gray now, crisp as iron filings.

He'd taken off his jacket, and had it slung over one shoulder, a rolled-up blueprint tucked under his other arm. Head reared back as he took in the room, the glow of some future vision on his face.

It had been a while since she'd seen such a glittering in his black eyes. All through lunch, like a kid bursting with a secret, giving her those odd looks and then ordering that bottle of champagne. Well, no wonder her head was floating away. Weren't they both a little tipsy?

'I think it . . . it has possibilities,' she said at last, fumbling to avoid saying the wrong thing.

Nikos turned his dark gaze on her, and gave a booming laugh that echoed in the decrepit vacant chamber. 'Bullshit. You hate it. What a lousy liar you are, Sylvie. You look as if you just bit into something tasting very bad.'

'Well, it *is* going to take a lot of work.' She felt embarrassed. But why should she? 'Oh, Nikos, you aren't serious about buying this, are you? I mean . . . well, the location is good. So close to Gramercy Park and only five blocks from your office. But just *look* at it. It's a wonder it hasn't been condemned. And how big did you say it is?'

'Three stories besides this one. Come, take a look?' Before she could answer, he was taking her arm, guiding her up another steep, curving, and – Sylvie thought with alarm – quite perilously rickety staircase.

It *was* perilous, she decided, feeling certain stairs sway from their weight, and creak like a ship's mast in a high wind. And boards over the risers were missing here and there. If she were less vigilant, she could so easily fall, maybe sprain an ankle. There was a sharp, unpleasant smell, too, like rotten juniper berries. Panting as she neared the top, she saw a dark shape skate out of the shadows and streak across the landing. Her heart lurched. Then she saw it was only a cat. So that's why the place stank so.

On the third floor Nikos was taking her through a large, airy room with a discolored marble fireplace, probably a bedroom. At the soot-streaked window, looking sharply to the left, Sylvie could just make out green grass with lovely flowerbeds and neat gravel paths. Young women pushing baby carriages, and people on the benches, books open in their laps, splashed in leafy sunlight.

Suddenly, oh yes, she *could* see the possibilities here. A staggering amount of work, but in the end . . .

Sylvie turned away from the window, and there was Nikos, crouching over the floor, unrolling the plans, anchoring each corner with a chunk of chimney brick.

'You see . . . here and here . . . this is where I knock out the partitions, make big rooms, more sunlight. And look, here, no more tiny kitchen. I put in a big one. On Greene Street this morning, I saw an old butcher's trestle, enormous, and it could be perfect for right along this wall. But this door, I am not sure about this. I think perhaps it should be here . . .'

350

Before she quite realized what she was doing, Sylvie was kneeling beside him, caught up in his enthusiasm. Michel would probably throw a fit if he saw what she was doing to the classic eggshell linen suit he had designed for her; and Sylvie saw that there was already a black streak on her pale, biscuit-colored silk blouse. But so what? She was having fun.

Sylvie, inhaling the acrid, fruity smell of the blueprint, followed Nikos's blunt finger as it moved from room to room with decisive, jabbing strokes.

'No,' she interrupted him, 'I don't think you should put a door there. It looks cluttered. Why not open up this whole south wall, put in French windows? Make this space by the garden into a sun porch. You see, there's plenty of room for a dining room over here, instead.'

'Yes . . . I think maybe you are right.' He screwed up his eyes, as if trying to visualize the effect. 'And what about here? I should make a pantry, no? I think perhaps it's too small for a breakfast room.'

'No, not at all, if you take out this wall of cabinets. You see, you have enough room here to create an island in the center. Much more efficient, I think. A counter you can use on both sides, with cupboard space below. And a place to hang spectacular copper pots overhead.'

Nikos rocked back on his heels, and stared at her. 'Amazing! Sylvie, you always surprise me. How did you manage to hide your light under a barrel for so long?'

'A bushel,' she corrected him with a laugh. 'And never mind about me. How are *you* going to accomplish all this? You've never renovated an old house. It can be much more difficult than building a new one from the ground up.' She remembered years ago when they'd first bought the house in Deal, a century-old white elephant – but even so, not anywhere near as decrepit as this – and all the weekends she'd spent overseeing plasterers, carpenters, painters.

'With your help,' he answered without hesitation.

'Me? What do I know about it?'

'You've just shown me. And—' he held out his hand,

palm up, cutting off any further argument, 'you have an eye for beauty. This house is female, I can feel it, can't you? It needs a woman's touch.'

'Oh, Nikos . . .' Sylvie looked into his black eyes and saw that he was completely serious. She was both flattered and dismayed. 'You're the most impossible man I've ever known.'

'You find it impossible to say no then?' He grinned.

'I just don't know . . .'

'Think about it. Please.'

Then he caught her chin in his square calloused hands – she could smell the blueprint ink on his fingers, feel the grit of plaster dust along her jaw, which he was holding – and he kissed her.

Feeling the warm shock of his mouth against hers, Sylvie thought, *Dear God*, I'm *the one who's gone mad. Thirty years ago he kissed me like this. But now? This can't be happening. We're just old friends. We're way past this kind of nonsense.*

But she found herself surrendering to the sensations, which were both wonderful and overwhelming. And she felt warm, much too warm, as if the June sunshine spilling in through the window were focused on her, burning her the way she used to burn her name into pieces of wood with a magnifying glass when she was a child.

How long since she had felt this way? Years, oh years.

*Dear Lord, what made me think I was too old?*

Had he waited all this time, until he thought she was ready?

She drew back, thought she saw the answer in his eyes. Yes, he had waited a long time. They were so different now from the reckless fools who had clutched at each other in shame, so long ago. It had taken them time, yes, many years to learn to respect and like each other. To know each other as two people, two friends.

Now with one kiss, he had reminded her she was still a woman, and he a man. His eyes told her, *I am here, if you want me, if you're ready*.

352

*Not yet*, she answered him silently, *but maybe soon. Yes, I think it could be very soon.*

Sylvie drew back, feeling slightly chilled. The oblong of sunlight they had been kneeling in had crept all the way to the wall, leaving them in shadow.

A huge cat leaped out of nowhere, and stood frozen inside the doorway, glaring at them, dirty white fur on end, tail twitching. Sylvie, startled, let out a small cry.

'It's all right,' Nikos soothed, 'he is hungry, that is all. He is wondering if we have food for him.'

'He looks as if he'd like to eat *us*.'

Then the cat was gone, melting into the shadows.

Nikos rose, extending a hand to help her up. 'Come, my dear Sylvie. I shall take you home where no wild cats will eat you. Then I will say goodbye. I will be in Boston on business until next Monday. Perhaps when I return we will have dinner?'

'Yes, I think that can be arranged. At any rate,' she said as she rescued the blueprints, rolling them and tucking them under her arm, 'it'll give me a chance to go over these.'

He grinned, a flash of white teeth against the seamed leather of his face. She felt her heart turn liquid once again, and the old longing grow warm and heavy as an unborn child in her belly.

Sylvie, her hand tucked firmly in Nikos's warm, solid grasp, thought, *Oh dear, what in heaven's name am I getting into?*

353

# 19

Max Griffin sipped his coffee, and looked out at the Thames, gleaming like blackened, tarnished silver in the morning sun. A real bonus, this sunshine. Usually it drizzled nonstop here in London. He was having his favorite breakfast at the Savoy, enjoying his favorite view. So why did he feel so damned rotten? Hung over, as if he'd put away too much claret last night. Only he hadn't tasted more than a drop.

It had to be Rose. What else? Yesterday, they'd been hip to hip for hours in the airplane, then arriving in London, they'd ducked into that jammed Chelsea restaurant for dinner, taking the only table that was left, a tiny corner booth where they were practically on top of each other. All evening, smelling her perfume, feeling the warm breath of her laughter, seeing the sparkle in her eyes.

Last night, he'd wanted to reach across and take her hand, so badly. How close she'd been, her thigh pushed up against his in the narrow booth, her arm brushing him as she gestured. And yet they might as well have been back in the office. Which was exactly where he should have left her. Strictly business? Hell, who was he kidding?

Well, too late now. He'd just have to make the best of it. It'd be only three days. Less, if the uptight Brit lawyer would only accept the absurdly overgenerous settlement he'd been authorized to offer.

Max gazed down on Victoria Park, a strip of green lawn pocketed with flowerbeds, and seamed with neat stone paths. Below it, the Embankment was clogged with rush-hour traffic, while on the sidewalk secretaries and clerks walked briskly without appearing to rush, tightly furled umbrellas swinging at their sides, clocking their pace like pendulums.

God bless the Brits, he thought. The sun shining. Sky as clear as a newborn baby's conscience. And not one without his brolly. Many wore hats, too, and carried raincoats folded neatly over one arm.

*Playing it safe*, he thought. *But then, aren't we all?*

Max saw that door in his mind. The door that connected his suite to the room next door. Painted a pastel blue, inset panels, forged brass hardware, and no lock or key. Just a huge brass bolt, which he or anyone easily could slide back. And yet last night for a full hour he had stood there, hands sweating, pulse pounding, unable even to knock, much less unlatch the bolt. Wanting so to walk through that door, take Rose in his arms, and tell her what he'd been feeling for so long: that he was obsessed by her, that he wanted her desperately, that he loved her dearly.

And if he had dared? How would she have reacted? Shocked at first probably. Then overflowing with sympathy. Poor old Max. She was fond of him. She'd let him down real easy. Like an old dog who has to be kindly put out of its misery by a caring owner.

Yeah, she might even invite him into bed, out of gratitude, feeling she owed it to him. Christ, to have her that way . . . it would be a hundred times worse than not having her at all.

'Ready to order, sir?' A brisk voice broke into his thoughts.

Max blinked up at a waiter in a spotless white jacket and black bow tie, crisp damask towel folded over his arm. His face utterly impassive, brown hair pasted to his skull, flat and shiny as an otter's pelt.

'Not just yet,' he answered. 'I'm waiting for someone. She should be down any minute.'

'Very good, sir.' The waiter vanished as if into thin air.

Max gazed about at the other breakfasters. Seated by the sun-filled windows, immaculately tailored City of London types sawing at their eggs and kippers. A pair of shapeless middle-aged women, wearing tweeds, no makeup, and sensible shoes, probably two titled women, sipping tea and nibbling on brioches. Like a scene from *Masterpiece Theatre*. He had to look hard for the flaws, the outtakes. A trolley parked haphazardly by a pillar stacked with dirty plates and pulp-flecked juice glasses nested in silver servers full of melting ice. A fly buzzing about the basket of brioches on his table. A large coffee-colored stain on the carpet.

Turning toward the vast room's interior, he caught sight of a dark-haired woman making her way past the white latticed gazebo in the center, where at high tea a pianist played softly. Tall, leggy, voluptuous, she moved with the unstudied grace of a woman who is unaware of her own beauty. Max, transfixed, felt something flare inside him, as if he'd just drunk his entire cup of coffee in one scalding gulp.

*God almighty, six years, and I still get hard like a teenager seeing her walk into a room.*

He watched her wind her way toward his table, a Caravaggio in a room full of Sargents, olive-coppery skin aglow, wild black hair tumbled about her shoulders. As if to offset her exotic lushness, she was wearing a straight tweed skirt, a plain white silk blouse, open at the throat, with a single strand of pearls. He remembered giving her those pearls, nestled inside a Mark Cross briefcase, the day she passed her bar exams. Strange, how she wore that earring, though. Just one, like a pirate. For years now, always that single teardrop ruby dangling from her right ear. Her birthstone, she had told him. She said it brought her luck.

Spotting him, she broke into a smile. 'Hi!' She gave a little wave from twenty feet away, and Max saw a dozen heads turn and stare. Even the proper Brits, Max noted with amusement, knew a good thing when they saw it.

Rose slid into the chair opposite his. Her cheeks were flushed, and she was breathing hard, as if she'd been in too much of a hurry to wait for the elevator – which in this stately old hotel moved from floor to floor like an aged family retainer – and had run all the way downstairs. Her scent was like a gust of fresh air from a garden window hastily flung open.

'Sorry I'm late. I was dead to the world. Jet lag, I guess. You should have knocked on my door before you came down.'

God, if she'd only known how close he'd come last night to doing a lot more than just knocking.

'I figured you needed the rest,' he told her. 'Besides, we have plenty of time. The meeting with Rathbone isn't until eleven. It seems his client feels it's essential to sleep in even later than a certain New York lady lawyer I know.'

Rose smiled. 'Thanks. But just for the record, I was up half the night getting my notes organized. My God, the amount of papers generated by one half-assed remark! Say, is that coffee still hot? I'd love some. Been waiting long?'

'Just got here, as a matter of fact. I was enjoying the view.' He signaled the waiter. 'And never mind the coffee, I'll order you some tea. You're obliged to drink tea at least once your first time in London, preferably at the Savoy. It's the law. They stamp it on your passport.'

'Must be their way of getting back at us for the Boston tea party.' She laughed, but in her eyes he caught the same old shadow, some deep sadness in her eyes. A familiar helplessness swept over him. Six years now, a long time. Would she ever trust him enough to open up to him about it?

He watched her gaze wander past him, as she leaned forward on both elbows, cupping her chin in her palms, taking it all in – the spectacular view, the Cinerama of the Thames. Max, watching the light play across her face, and a slow childlike wonder dawn in her huge dark eyes, wanted to touch her so badly he found himself almost trembling.

Then his mother popped into his head, saying with one of her cynical snorts, *No fool like an old fool*. And he felt

357

his heart drop, suddenly, as if a trapdoor had swung down in his chest. Dumb, dumb, how could he have ever imagined . . .?

Get involved with a married man, why should she? And one twenty years older to boot.

*Fella, you are way off the wall*, a weary inner voice mocked. *She doesn't give a shit whether you are married or not. To her, you're a friend, a kindly boss, a dear old father figure, the kindly aging mentor. A cross between Edmund Gwen and Fredric March.*

*And one of these days she'll get married. Even if she never gets over the bastard who put that dark look in her eyes. She's thirty-one – hell, she's overdue. She'll want kids before it's too late.*

He imagined her pregnant, huge with child, carrying their child, *his* child.

Then he felt disgusted with himself. Lord, how long would he go on torturing himself this way?

'Beautiful, isn't it?' he interrupted her rapturous contemplation of the landscape.

Rose turned from the window, dropping her hands into her lap. 'Oh, Max, it's heaven! I've never been anywhere like this—' she ducked her head in a sheepish laugh, 'well, if you want to know the truth, I've never been anywhere at all. Not outside of New York, that is. London is . . . oh, it's like a fairy tale. I half-expect to see Peter Pan fly past.'

'Aptly put.' He smiled, recalling that their opponent in today's legal matter, Devon Clarke, had played Peter Pan here in London. She was said to be famous for it, like Mary Martin in New York. And famous for a few other things besides.

Like hopping into bed with every male in the company, from the lighting technician to Captain Hook.

How ironic, he thought, that it was Devon Clarke's infidelities that had brought them here.

If her ex-husband had only come to Max *before* he'd turned in his manuscript, hanging all the dirty lingerie out to air, Max would have banged some sense into his head and made him cut those tidbits. But Jonathon Booth, it was clear now, had been just as bent on revenging himself on Devon for cuckolding him, and so blatantly, as she was now on punishing him. Quite amazing, she'd refused even to discuss settling out of court. She'd been demanding the whole dog and pony show.

Then last week, that desperate call from Jonathon. Devon, it seemed, was finally willing to talk, but only if Jonathon's lawyer flew to London to negotiate . . . at Jonathon's expense, of course.

Rose had written all the pleadings on the case, and had done the research, so he had asked her to come along. And he also was playing a hunch. Rose had a peculiar talent for getting at a problem sideways, like a crab. In this case, that talent might make all the difference.

Max observed that a flush had crept into Rose's cheeks, outlining the high spoon-shaped curve of her cheekbones. Then she laughed. 'Peter Pan? Oh God, I just remembered that part in Jon's book, when he found her in bed with Lady Hemphill's sixteen-year-old twin sons. God, how weird!'

'Of course we know she wasn't doing it for fun.' Max made himself keep a very straight face. 'She's a method actress. She was just studying her part, trying to . . . how did she put it? Oh yes . . . "transmogrify" herself into the soul of a teenage boy.'

Rose chuckled, then said, 'She sounds interesting, this Devon Clarke. Believe it or not, I'm actually looking forward to this meeting. Are you sure she'll be there?'

'Yes, and she'll probably be wearing sequins and bells. I think she's enjoying all this. Good publicity for her new show. She's in a revival of *Blithe Spirit*. At first the Haymarket was half empty, and now I hear she's selling out every night.'

To the waiter who had materialized at their table, he ordered, 'Tea for the lady.'

'Max, I don't know. Do you think I'll be able to hold my own with a woman like that?'

'You're forgetting, you're the intrepid one. Remember, that little sportscar ride, you nearly breaking both our necks to prove that damn thing wasn't safe? I promise you, Devon Clarke won't be half as tricky. Or nearly as dangerous.' He passed her the napkin-covered basket in front of him. 'Brioche?'

'Thanks. I'm starved.' She helped herself to a pastry. 'Speaking of cyclones, human or otherwise, you were right, you know, what you did. Did I ever tell you? How much I admired you for risking your job the way.'

Max fell silent, remembering. The meeting with Graydon Wilkes, chairman of Pace Auto, two days after that hair-raising ride. Max had bluntly accused him of withholding vital information, and just as bluntly informed him of what the consequences would be if such information should ever become public.

'You'll have so many lawsuits on your hands you won't know which way to turn,' he'd told Wilkes. 'You'll spawn a whole new breed of ambulance chasers – lawyers who specialize in suing Pace Auto, like the ones who handle nothing but asbestos or DES suits. They'll take you to the cleaners. Ream you. You'll be lucky to be left with the skin of your back.'

Wilkes had turned as gray as his sharkskin suit. Then he had given Max a look of such hatred, Max had been sure he was about to be fired. In fact, he would have quit, walked out the door, if Wilkes hadn't, after an interminable minute, dropped his eyes and said, 'All right. Let's do a recall.'

Max remembered how high he'd been flying, and he felt some of that now, seeing the way Rose was looking at him, proud and pleased. 'No, you never told me,' he said.

Rose frowned, her eyes turning dark, pensive.

Now Max felt deflated, as if he were falling, tumbling to earth like a broken kite.

'A lot was happening at the time . . .,' he began, adding hesitantly, 'It was right after you . . . when you were so sick.'

360

'Oh. Yes . . . of course.' She looked away, but not before he caught that ghost hurt in her eyes.

Dammit, why wouldn't she talk about it? Wasn't six years long enough?

Six years. His thoughts went reeling back to those weeks Rose had been ill, feverish for several days, then so weak she could hardly get out of bed. No, the truth was, she hadn't *wanted* to get up. After a while, she had grown so thin it had frightened him, seeing the cadaverous hollows in her face, the sunken brackets of her collarbone. So every day he made time to visit her, on his lunch hour or after work. He would bring her food, tempting her with stuffed squabs, hot spinach pie, crusty fresh bread from Balducci's one day, spicy Szechuan take-out the next. He'd ply her with magazines, paperback novels, and finally, when she began to show some interest in getting better, a stack of paperwork from the office. Slowly, slowly, she had inched her way back to the land of the living.

Max knew what had caused it; he knew about Brian. He had pieced the story together from the little Rose had divulged, but mostly from the media coverage – after the story in the *News* there had been pieces in *Newsweek*, a photo story in *Life*, even a spot on the *Today* show. They were America's favorite sweethearts for a week or so.

But Rose never spoke of Brian after that first week. She suffered, he knew. It was in her eyes. God, those eyes. They haunted him, even when he wasn't with her. And heaven only knew what was in her heart, her poor heart that had been ravaged so.

Oddly, after that, she became harder, stronger, more . . . brilliant somehow. A diamond chiseled and faceted by tragedy. First, nonstop studying for her bachelor's degree. Then law school, the same single-minded energy electing her to the *Law Review* at Columbia. He and his partners hadn't done her any favor when they took her back, as an associate. If anything, it was the other way around.

361

The arrival of the tea broke Max's reverie.

He felt his gloom lifting, turning to amusement, watching Rose take it all in, eyes wide. The tall domed Sheffield teapot, the silver tea strainer that fit over the mouth of the cup, the bowl heaped with glistening brown lumps of Demerara, the white china pitcher filled with steaming water, the creamer brimming with foamy milk.

She stared at the array of paraphernalia on the white damask tablecloth. 'I don't know where to start. Are you sure they don't offer a course in this?'

The childlike perplexity on her face reminded him so of Monkey he felt a pang of homesickness for his daughter. He thought of how she had watched him pack for this trip, perched on the edge of the quilted bedspread – all legs and skinny arms and russet hair down to the middle of her back – solemnly following the progression of shirts, ties, socks he was folding into his suitcase. This had been their ritual before every trip, since she was a baby. In the old days, when he finished packing, he would stand there, hands on hips, lips pursed, and say, 'Hmmm, seems to me I've forgotten something. I wonder what.' Then Monkey would pounce into the open suitcase, all giggles. 'Me!' she would cry. 'Me, Daddy!' But this time she hadn't picked up on her cue. When he spoke the ritual words, 'I wonder what?' she had simply rolled her eyes and said with majestic disdain, 'Oh, Daddy, I'm *way* too old for that.'

Fifteen. Oh Christ, where had the time gone? He was frightened by the ease with which people you love could slip away. He mustn't let that happen with Rose. No, he must keep her . . . as a friend, if not a lover.

Max picked up the thick white china pitcher.

'Here, let me show you.' And in the same instant he thought ruefully, *Henry Higgins, you stupid old fart, don't you know when to quit?* 'Milk first, like so. Now you strain the tea through this. Careful, only halfway. It's very strong, that's what the hot water is for, to dilute it. Now sugar if you like. Voilà!'

He watched Rose take a first, tentative sip. 'Not bad.

362

But all this fuss over a cup of tea, it's no wonder they lost the war against us.'

'Drink up.' Max glanced again at his watch. 'The Brits haven't lost yet . . . not until we see the whites of Devon Clarke's eyes,' he joked.

Max shifted impatiently in the leather wing chair. It was twenty past one, and the Gray's Inn office of Adams Rathbone, Esq., had begun to feel like a sauna. They were no closer to a settlement than they'd been two and a half hours ago. He felt as if he were in a tedious drawing-room play, where characters cleverly sniped at one another, but nothing ever really happened.

Even this office, he thought, looked like a stage set. All cluttered with Victorian gimcrack – horsehair sofa laden with cushions, an antique needlepoint bellpull by the door, a scrimshaw tusk mounted over the fireplace. There was even a chair off in the corner piled high with books (probably just for effect). So Dickensian it hurt, right down to the coal fire in the grate – never mind it was a good seventy degrees outside.

Devon Clarke, the star of their little show, was sitting center stage, perched on one plump arm of the sofa, her tiny feet just skimming the badly worn Oriental carpet. A tiny woman well in her fifties, she reminded Max of a parakeet, with her leathery pink skin and pointy features, her bright green dress and the flimsy blue scarf knotted at her throat.

Directly across from her, behind a huge ornately carved desk, sat her caricature of a solicitor, a heavyset, balding gentleman, replete with waistcoat, gold watch chain, and a suffocatingly tight collar.

Max's client, Booth, had authorized him to offer up to fifty thousand pounds to get her off his back. But Devon Clarke seemed interested only in emoting. So far she'd lamented her way through eight or so versions of the Book of Job, with That Beast, Jonathon Booth, as the fiendish cause of all her affliction.

363

'. . . Would you like to know the real reason why he wrote that so-called book, that piece of muck of his?' she was asking now, lighting up her hundredth or so cigarette.

'I wonder—' Max was determined to remain statesmanlike, 'if such speculations can really help our business here.'

'Because I refused,' she continued as if Max hadn't spoken, 'to star in his play. I told him what I thought of it, too – a fat lot of self-indulgent nonsense. And boring, boring, boring!'

Max cleared his throat. Enough. This time he was going to nail her down, get this so-called negotiation off the ground.

'Miss Clarke, my client and I deeply regret the distress you've suffered. And Jonathon, believe it or not, is eager to make amends. In fact, he feels it would be in your best interest, as well as his, to—'

'My best interest?' Devon interrupted with a hard, bright laugh. '*My* best interest? Oh, pardon me, but that's rich. That's positively *priceless*. May I tell you how that wretched beast, your client, behaved on our honeymoon? Our *honeymoon*, for Christ's sake. We were in Majorca, and I was so sick, I had this beastly stomach virus. And where was he? With his suffering bride? No, not a bit of it. Not for five bleeding minutes. Sickness, he says, declaiming like some over-the-hill Hamlet, depresses him. Well I say, sod him!'

Max glanced over at Rose, seated in a rickety antique corner chair close to the fire. Now she was rising, looking vaguely sheepish. What could she be up to?

'I'm sorry to interrupt,' she said. 'But I was wondering, Miss Clarke, if you might show me to the, uh, Ladies. This place is kind of a warren, and I'm awful at directions, I'm afraid I'd just get lost . . .'

Max had to strain a bit not to laugh. Rose could find her way across the Himalayas in a blizzard. She was the only woman he knew who didn't get disoriented in Bloomingdale's.

*What's she up to?* he wondered.

The two women finally returned, looking oddly conspiratorial. What the hell was going on? Even Rathbone looked wary.

Out of the blue, the actress demurely turned to Max, and said, 'You were saying before, about some sort of settlement? Well, who knows, perhaps Jonathon really is doing the right thing. This whole matter has been such an ordeal, frightful really. And I'd just as soon not prolong the agony any longer . . .,

Max looked at Rose, and she shot him a glowing look of triumph.

'. . . In fact,' she simpered, 'I'm feeling a bit of a migraine. So I shall leave you two to conclude things with Arthur.' She turned to her solicitor. 'Arthur, darling, *don't* be a bore and keep these nice people waiting here all afternoon. They have made a generous offer, and I have accepted.'

A flutter of chiffon, a slipstream of Chanel N° 5, and Devon Clarke was gone.

Max, feeling euphoric, as well as slightly puzzled, could hardly believe his luck. Lourdes didn't have much over this.

In the back of a cab, headed back to the hotel, Max turned to Rose. 'How—'

'Simple,' Rose explained smugly. 'As soon as I got her alone, I told her I agreed with her. Men *are* such beasts. Then I suggested that maybe she was wasting her time suing Jonathon when the best revenge of all was right in front of her nose.'

'And what, may I ask, is that?' asked Max, amused.

'Writing her own autobiography, of course. I mean, listening to all those stories, anyone could see she's just bursting to tell the whole world everything she's ever done, with special emphasis on the beastly Booth. All I did was sort of nudge her in the right direction.'

'You're amazing, do you know that?' Max wanted to kiss her, badly.

Then, not knowing how it had happened, he *was* kissing

365

her. And it was just like his fantasies, Rose responding to him, mouth soft, willing, her arms cool and silky about his neck.

But in a moment, less than a moment it seemed, she was pulling away with a breathy, embarrassed little laugh, and the fantasy dissolved.

'Oh, Max, I know how you feel. I feel a little crazy myself just now. Such a strange morning. But let's not get *too* carried away.'

Max felt a little sick to his stomach. *She must be thinking I'm just another middle-aged married man off on a trip, looking for a little quick one on the side. Oh Christ . . .*

If only it were that simple. But what he wanted was more, so much *more* . . . and, then, not so much after all. He wanted Rose. That simple. And that complicated.

To reach out at night and feel her beside him. To see her across from him at breakfast not just today, but every day. He imagined her swaddled in his old terry robe, hair frayed from sleep, sipping coffee from a mug, scattering toast crumbs over the oak table in his kitchen.

Then he remembered his father at Edgemore Beach, looking like a boiled potato in baggy blue swim trunks, making a show of ogling the pretty girls as they passed by in their two-piece bathing suits. And his mother, pretending to be jealous, swatting him with the bottle of suntan lotion.

*No fool like an old fool,* she used to tease, as if the very idea of baggy old Sam Griffin and one of those girls were the *real* joke.

*No fool like an old fool.* And that's what Mom would say about me now too. And if she knew how much I want Rose, she'd probably laugh. And she'd be right.

Now he was no longer the golden boy, pride of the Griffins, Harvard scholarship winner, corporate tiger, promoted to senior partner in an astonishing ten years. No, now he was just middle-aged Max Griffin, growing soft like his pop, ogler of pretty girls. And old fool.

To try and salvage his pride, he said, 'Don't worry,' his

arm about her shoulders, casually though, as if he hadn't noticed it was still there. 'You're a damned attractive woman, Rose, but I like you too much to let anything get in the way.'

Rose, he could see, was immensely relieved. She laughed and said, 'Oh, Max, I *do* love you.'

Jesus . . . the words he'd longed for. He'd imagined her saying them a thousand times. But not like this, not tossed off the way she'd say it about a favorite dress or a delicious meal.

Max, feeling as if he'd been punched in the gut, stared out the window at the Strand skimming past, and saw that it had begun to rain.

## 20

'Do I really look OK? I'm not overdressed, am I?'

Rose fussed with her sleeve. Probably silly, she thought, going overboard with this dress. But what did she know about this kind of party? How was she supposed to know what people like these would be wearing? At least Cinderella had a fairy godmother to wave a magic wand over her; she'd just have to wing it.

'Stop worrying,' Max was reassuring her. 'The dress is wonderful. There won't be another woman at the party who'll look half as glamorous.'

Rose looked over at him. Max was seated on the deep-peach sofa in front of the fireplace (a marble *fireplace* in her bedroom, she still couldn't get over it). *He* looked totally at ease in his dinner jacket – and why not? This was Max's world – all of it – chic London, the Savoy Hotel. Her gaze swept about the room, done in whispers of pink and cream and blue, the delicate little bow-legged French tables and chairs, the huge bed covered in a rose satin quilt aged to the soft nappy sheen of velvet. Yes, Max belonged. But where did she fit in?

'But that's just what I'm worried about,' she moaned. Why couldn't he understand? She didn't want people staring at her. She just wanted to blend in. Rupert Everest, Jonathon Booth's publisher over here, was related to the royal family. She'd read about a party of his once in *Time*, Mick Jagger drinking champagne from Julie Christie's slipper. What could she say to such people?

Rose stepped over to the bathroom door to look in the full-length mirror. The moment of truth.

She stood perfectly still, no twirling about to check

herself from different angles or to see if her hem was straight in back. The woman in the mirror wasn't *her* at all – no, couldn't be. Because the real Rose Santini was still that gawky kid from Avenue K and Ocean Avenue, in her navy and white school uniform and oxfords. And this tall, slender, and sophisticated-looking woman in high heels, hair swept up with glittering combs, was . . . was . . . well, *beautiful*.

In the afternoon, Max had taken her shopping at Liberty's on Regent Street. Thick oak paneling on the walls, intricately carved banisters adorning the staircases, antique armchairs and settees upholstered in a glorious peacock design, which Liberty, Max explained to her, had made famous. Rose imagined she had died and gone to shopper's heaven. Caught up by the enchantment of the place, she'd splurged on a Burberry raincoat and matching cashmere scarf . . . and this dress.

Max was right, it *was* wonderful. Inspired by Renaissance design, it was fashioned from rubbed velvet an almost incandescent deep violet that dropped straight to just above her knees, then flared into narrow pleats – like the petals of a flower – each pleat opening on to a panel of pale mauve antique lace. The sleeves were of the same mauve lace, full and gathered at the shoulder and elbow, tightly fitted along the forearms and tapering to a V at the wrist.

Dark, vengeful triumph rose from some deep locked place inside her. *If you could see me now, my dear faithful Brian, would you be sorry you left me? Would you want me back?*

That *News* article, she was seeing it again, and all the others that had come after – the *Life* spread, those dramatic shots of the rescue, and the wedding, than a close-up of the two of them, Brian and his wife, curled together on the sofa of their Murray Hill apartment; and another of Brian at his typewriter – he was writing a novel about his experiences in Vietnam, the caption had said.

Rose had torn them all to shreds, all those pages and

pictures, but they were burned into her memory nonetheless. Her mind turned to it again and again the way her tongue might seek out an aching tooth. And each time, the same question going round and round, an endless unanswerable riddle: *Why? Why, Brian?*

She remembered again, how she had wanted to stay in bed for ever, hide away in her dark apartment for the rest of her life.

But after three black weeks, she had awoken one morning feeling ravenous, and wanting to get up, get out. But even after a huge, hearty breakfast she could barely make it to the door, she was so weak.

The next day she made it out, and then down the stairs, clutching the banister tightly. As she crept along like an old lady the three blocks to Washington Square, it came to her, a kind of epiphany: each additional step she took was proof. She could not be beaten. She was *somebody*. And someday Brian would see that, too. Someday he would realize his mistake. And he would regret it.

She remembered growing stronger in other ways too. Learning to ignore her grandmother's hectoring phone calls, Nonnie's demands that she visit, call more often, write at least. By the time Rose had finished her bachelor's at NYU, she felt as if she'd logged a million miles between this new life and her old one on Avenue K.

Mother of God, even now Rose couldn't imagine how she'd managed to get herself through those grueling exams, and her note – a misnomer if there ever was one – for the *Law Review*.

Her torts midterm had been a killer. A case for which she'd had to prepare a mock brief. God, how could she ever forget *Lambert* v *Western Securities?* She had sweated over it for weeks, knocking herself out checking facts, researching precedents, poring over sections and subsections of the Securities and Exchange Act. And Professor Hughes was the toughest, most demanding teacher at NYU, a campus legend. It was rumored he never gave anything higher than a C +, but Rose had been determined.

370

Her diligence would win him over, she was sure; he would have to award her an A.

And when she received her paper back, marked C – , oh, how devastated she'd been! Professor Hughes had scribbled across the bottom: 'Your arguments, though carefully researched, would stand little chance of convincing a jury.'

All that night, driven by fury, she'd attacked the floors of her apartment with mop and vacuum, and cleaned out every closet, every cupboard and drawer. By morning the place shone, and she was exhausted. But she had an idea, a way that might make Hughes reconsider her grade.

She'd gone to him the next day with her proposal: If she staged a mock trial here in class, and could win over the 'jury,' would he re-evaluate her paper?

Hughes had stared at her so long, and so hard, his eyes the blue of case-hardened steel, that Rose had felt her boldness shrivel.

Then he had smiled, a hairline fissure in the stony implacability of his face. 'You may be very foolish, Miss Santini,' he said. 'But you have nerve. I admire nerve. All right then, you have a bargain.'

The day of the trial, she had been almost paralyzed with nervousness. But sheer force of will – the will to prove herself, to Brian, to the world, that she was *somebody*, damn it – had forced her in front of the auditorium, and all those people.

At first she had had trouble making herself heard by those in the back rows, then, like a storm gathering strength, she grew less timid, forgetting her nervousness as she was caught up by the gale force of her convictions. Western Securities, she argued, could not be held accountable for an escrow account fraud scheme its president, now dead, had masterminded – and benefited from – all on his own. There had been no 'intentional misconduct'; therefore Rule 10-b of the Securities and Exchange Act was invalid.

One by one, she saw the bored, cynical expressions of

371

the jurors drop away, replaced first by curiosity, and gradually, genuine interest.

When, at the end, the jury returned with a verdict in her favor, the entire auditorium had surged to their feet and cheered her.

Afterward, glowing, she had gone to Hughes. Now he would give her an A, no question. But on her paper, the C – had been changed only to a B – . 'I still don't agree with you, or the jury,' he had written, 'but I applaud your mettle.' At first she'd felt crushed, cheated, then she realized – yes, she really had won. She had succeeded in bending the formidable Hughes, and the B had put her over the top. She would graduate summa cum laude, top ten per cent of her class. And more importantly, she knew now that in life she could accomplish anything, however frightening or risky, anything at all she set her mind to.

But didn't she owe a good part of her success to Max, as well? Without him to bolster and coach her, without his badgering, scolding, cheering, she probably could never have made it.

She turned to him now – *oh my dear, loyal friend* – and forced a bright smile, feeling the old anger at Brian drain away.

'You look, as the British would say, very dashing,' she said. He was wearing a black dinner jacket with a black satin collar and a maroon cummerbund in the peacock design he'd bought at Liberty's. She had never seen him look so handsome, elegant even, his rumpled brown hair neatly combed, his eyes the blue of Wedgwood china sparkling in a face ruddy with firelight. 'You remind me of Nick Charles.'

Max laughed, rising from the sofa. Three long strides and he was beside her, fastening the top hook of her dress in back, fingers warm against her neck, causing her scalp to tingle, making her feel deliciously taken care of. Darling Max. The most wonderful friend in the world.

A little slip-up, that was all – him kissing her in the taxi yesterday. Both of them, in their excitement over the settlement, forgetting for an instant who they each were.

*Yes,* a small voice in the back of her mind whispered, *but that's not what you thought then, was it? When he was kissing you, you felt . . . well, you enjoyed it, didn't you? And you were sure he meant it . . .*

And seeing him tonight, how distinguished he looked, and, yes – *admit it, why don't you?* – downright sexy, she felt that same flicker, and wondered, *How would he kiss me in bed?*

Rose caught herself, feeling ashamed and disturbed. What an idiot she was! Max was probably just as embarrassed by that kiss in the taxi as she had been. And what if he *had* wanted to make love to her? He was married, so it would be just a fling. And afterwards they would feel uncomfortable around each another, unsure where they stood. No, she treasured Max far too much to let that happen.

'You're too young to remember *The Thin Man,*' Rose heard Max's voice against her ear, light and bemused, blowing her confused thoughts away like so much dandelion fluff. 'Besides, where's the mystery?'

'I have one for you. Maybe you can tell me why, if both of us put our shoes outside our doors last night, only yours came back polished?'

'Elementary, my dear. The Brits may tolerate a woman on the throne, but to polish her shoes would be going too far.'

'I have an answer to that.' Smiling, Rose bent down, wrenched off one of the high-heeled pumps she'd polished herself, and angled it as hard as she could across the room at the heavy brass-handled door.

It landed dead center with a satisfying thump, and she immediately felt better. Not only about the party, but about everything.

She turned to Max with a triumphant look. 'Shall we go then?'

He offered her his arm, still smiling, blue eyes dancing. 'Delighted, Cinderella.'

373

Leaning on Max, Rose hobbled over to retrieve her shoe, wondering how on earth Cinderella had managed on the run going down stairs and wearing one glass slipper.

*Because anything is possible in fairy tales . . . even Happily Ever After . . .*

At the door, Max helped her on with her new raincoat. As she flicked the lights out, she glanced out the bay window that curved between heavy tapestry drapes. Old-fashioned street lamps wreathed in fairy rings of mist. The faint yellow glimmers of barge lights drifting up the Thames. She imagined she heard the clopping of hooves, the creak of carriage wheels. A magic coach come to spirit her off into the night.

And suddenly Rose felt happy, happier than she'd felt in years. This *was* a fairy tale. London . . . a beautiful-people party . . . this dress. Something out of another time. A place where it was safe to dream.

The cabdriver had a time locating Rupert Everest's house. The townhouses on Cheyne Walk stood well back from King's Road, and in the dark, the leafy branches of huge old trees obscured their grimy facades, making the numbers nearly impossible to read.

Rose peered at her watch, barely making out the faintly glowing numerals. Late. Nearly an hour! Well, maybe it wouldn't matter what she was wearing after all. By the time they got there the party might be over.

Max, as usual, remained unruffled. Rose felt his hand on her arm, giving it a gentle squeeze. 'Don't worry. It'll be such a crush, Rupert won't notice. He's promoting some new author – an American, I think – and he's probably invited the whole BBC, every gossip columnist on Fleet Street, and some rock stars for local color. He always does. When Jonathon was doing his publicity stint, Rupert rented the Aldwych Theatre, and held the party right up there on stage.' He winked. 'Even invited Devon Clarke.'

The squeal of brakes, a sudden lurch throwing both of

374

them almost out of their seats, and then the cabbie was cranking to a stop at the curb by a pair of tall harp-shaped wrought-iron gates.

'This 'ere oughta be it,' he announced grudgingly.

Rose, emerging from the cab, peered up into the mist-blurred darkness, and saw a pair of winged cherubs, one perched atop each gatepost, so delicately wrought they appeared on the verge of flight.

She stepped through a pair of high carved doors into a marble-floored vestibule the size of a studio apartment, flanked by twin arched alcoves filled with roses, dozens and dozens of them bursting from enormous urns, their effect dazzling, all crimson on one wall, pure white on the other. She felt moist, a bit suffocated by the heavy, perfumed air. Through the double glass doors that opened on to the hallway, she saw a wide staircase curving upward, and heard the hum of mingled voices drifting down from above.

Their coats dissolved into the arms of a maid straight out of a thirties movie, black uniform, ruffled organza apron and cap. Then a small elegant man in a plum-colored smoking jacket materialized from the top of the staircase, descending to greet them.

Max tightened his hand on her elbow, and whispered, 'He's a little eccentric. Charming, though.'

'*Wonderful* to see you . . . I'm thrilled you could make it,' their host gushed. Rose thought, amused, *He doesn't have the slightest idea who we are*. But the effusiveness of his greeting made up for the lapse of memory. Now Rupert's gaze swept over Rose's dress, and he clasped his hands – tiny and wrinkled like an infant's – in front of his chest, as if in prayer. 'You look luscious, my dear. Wherever did you find that dress? No, don't tell. I'm terrible at keeping secrets, and every woman at this party will want to know. Let's go upstairs, shall we? I want you to meet our guest of honor.'

'A famous writer, didn't you say?' Max managed to get in.

375

Rupert leaned close, so close Rose could see the faintest line of kohl around each of his jade-green eyes. 'His first novel actually, but I dare say he will become famous rather quickly. Quite a coup for me, too. In fact, a little birdie whispered in my ear that someone at the *Times* will be writing him up as the literary find of the decade. Sort of Hemingwayesque, you see, the man actually was shooting at people in Vietnam. The title is some sort of military jargon, I believe, *Double Eagle*. Perhaps you've already read it?'

Rose felt her heart stop, as if a fist had closed around it, and a terrible coldness begin to spread slowly down from her collarbone.

*Brian's* book, of God, oh yes . . .

She remembered the shock of seeing it on display in the Doubleday bookstore on Fifth Avenue. She had picked it up and stared at the glossy dust-jacket photograph of the man she had loved so dearly, for so long, feeling as if she had been struck clean through her center.

Rose wanted to scream, to grab this little raspberry of a man by the shoulders, and shake that silly grin off his face. *You don't know him, you don't know anything about me either, so how dare you mix in our lives like this?*

Then abruptly her anger was gone, and this house, everything around her, suddenly turned gray, flat and gray and far away. She felt immensely tired, her head floating miles above a body thick and useless as a stump.

*Please, God*, Rose thought, *I can't go through it again . . . don't let this be happening . . .*

'Rose?' A sharp voice broke through the buzzing static in her ears. 'Rose . . . are you all right?'

*Max*, she thought, clinging to that voice as if to a lifeline. *Thank God for Max*.

The gray shifted, and Rose found herself looking at Max, seeing a man built like an ex-prizefighter, going gray and a little soft around the edges, but oh, so wonderfully *there*, a man you could count on, always.

'I'm fine,' she heard herself say, cool as ice water. 'Just

tired. Jet lag. I guess it caught up with me all at once.'

'Why don't you have a little lie-down, my dear?' Their host, too, was being kind and solicitous. 'There are plenty of bedrooms upstairs where you won't be disturbed . . . quite frankly, you *do* look a bit Madame Tussaud.'

'I'm fine,' Rose repeated, more firmly. 'Really.'

Then she caught sight of herself in the long ebony and chrome Art Deco mirror at the bottom of the stairs, and sucked in her breath. God, she *did* look pale.

Then, as if in a dream, Rose was climbing the stairs, no, more like *floating*, because oddly her feet didn't seem attached to her body.

She found herself smiling and nodding graciously to the elegantly dressed people she passed. *Here I am, and isn't it funny, because I'm not really here, I'm just pretending to be.*

Then an enormous room at the top, a sweep of dazzling white ceiling and white walls, startling shapes and colors springing out at her – crimson dragons writhing on a black lacquered Chinese cabinet, a huge Mondrian canvas of yellow and red squares, mirrors that were reflection upon reflection, whole galaxies of tuxedoed men and sequined ladies streaming off into infinity.

And suddenly there he was, standing by the vast window that stretched ceiling to floor, his back to her, lean and slightly stooped, his face – the face that had haunted her sleep night after night – shimmering ghostlike in the darkened glass, and nothing else, no-one else existed.

*Brian* . . .

Rose felt as if the champagne she'd just swallowed had suddenly turned to acid. It was burning its way down her throat, tearing away at her stomach.

She found herself remembering the first man she'd slept with after Brian. One of her NYU professors, a short, heavyset man with thick dark hair and a beard like fur, who didn't look a thing like Brian except for his glasses – the same tortoise-rims Brian wore when he read. And she'd gone to bed with him for that. His eye-glasses.

377

He took her out for some beer and pizza, discoursing on Proust nonstop, and then she'd gone back to his apartment, climbed between his sour-smelling sheets, and let him make love to her. And she hadn't felt a thing except sorrow.

There had been other men since then, a few, men she had liked, flirted with, men whose bodies she'd enjoyed. But no-one she'd loved, no-one she'd have shed a tear over, no one who could have ruined her life as Brian had.

Oh God.

How could she go over there now? Talk to him, act as if all this were perfectly normal, just a bit surprising, two old friends bumping into each another in a strange place—

But somehow, she *was* walking over, breaking away from Max and walking toward Brian through air thick as water. The sounds around her were all distorted, as if she were under water. The conversation dulled to a low hum, but the clink of ice in someone's tumbler sounded to her like the violent shattering of glass.

Then she was facing him, putting her hand out – a hand belonging not to her, but the creature from the wax museum that she had just become. She saw the shock registering in his face. An instant of naked pain. Then he was the same man he had been a minute ago.

*Lean and hungry*. The words popped into her head. A cliché from a pulp novel. But it described Brian all the same. The face she had carried in her heart like a cameo all these years, only its angles sharper, hair longer, curling over the collar of his brown corduroy jacket, a shadowing of premature gray at the temples. Those silver eyes, which had seemed so startlingly lit from within, now like mirrors in which she saw only herself reflected.

'Hello, Brian,' she greeted him.

'My God, I don't believe it . . . Rose!' The glass in his hand slipped, and with a quick jerky motion he caught it, beads of amber liquid spattering on to the white carpet. That gave her a moment to swim to the surface, catch her breath before she heard him exclaim, 'You're the last person on earth I expected to see here!'

She gave a brittle, sparkling laugh that hurt in her own

378

ears. 'Well, me too. I mean, you're the last person *I* expected to see. How *are* you?'

'Good. Better than ever. I wrote a book. Even managed to get it published and sell a few copies. Mr Everest here is giving it quite a send-off in England.'

He was smiling, and it was such a false, strained smile, Rose wanted to kick it in just as she'd wanted to kick in those posters of him on cardboard propped up in the bookstores. Phrases floated through her head, snatches of reviews she'd read.

*. . . the debut of a powerful new novelist . . .*

*. . . more raw power than THE NAKED AND THE DEAD, more poignant than ALL QUIET ON THE WESTERN FRONT . . .*

*. . . DOUBLE EAGLE is the real-life code name for a military operation in Vietnam . . . but it is also the symbol of its hero's disillusionment with his own country. Don't read this book unless you're prepared to have your heart broken, and how you think of modern warfare forever changed . . .*

She had read it, wanting to hate it, and had been so moved she had cried for hours after finishing it.

Rose wanted to cry now, too. Hot tears threatening to betray her were gathering at the back of her throat. She imagined tiny hairline cracks fanning out from the corners of her brittle smile.

And then, she heard Brian saying, 'Rose, I want you to meet my wife . . .'

Incredible, but there she was. *She was standing beside him all along, and I just didn't see her.*

Now, suddenly Brian's wife was the only person in the room.

'. . . Rachel . . .'

Rose thought with a stab, *She's beautiful. I didn't expect her to be so beautiful.*

Tiny and slender, a good head and a half shorter than Brian, but there was nothing doll-like about this woman. She radiated strength, a sense of purpose. It was in her eyes, bright and blue as pilot flames, and in the tiny muscles that leaped under her skin as she angled herself forward slightly, smiling, to shake Rose's hand.

Slim fingers tightened about hers in a crisp, surprisingly hard clasp. Everything about Rachel was crisp, bright, hot, crackling with intensity. And different. Somehow, she was like no other woman in the room. Everywhere, beads and bangles and sequins sewed on to tie-dyed silk, and here was *this* woman in a crisp oyster linen suit as clean and simple as a thank you note written on a single sheet of expensive stationery. Her hair was the pale amber of good brandy, and she wore it parted in the center, falling in loose waves to the small of her back, oddly free spirited.

Rose, smiling, shaking her hand, couldn't take her eyes off the slim gold band on the third finger of Rachel's left hand. She wanted to rip it off. It didn't belong there.

*It's mine. I should be the one wearing it. Brian should be my husband, not yours.*

The tears rose, hot and suffocating, and suddenly Rose knew she couldn't stand here being polite a second longer. She broke away, and fled, pushing her way through the crowd – *go to hell, all of you, I don't care what you think* – down the stairs.

A long hallway, a door in back, and suddenly Rose found herself in a garden. A garden as old as the house, dark and silent as a well. Brick walls blanketed in English ivy, a moss-grown fountain guarded over by a headless stone cupid.

Quiet, except for the sound of water dripping off leaves on to the brick patio, a hollow and somehow heartless sound.

Rose sank down on a damp stone bench, and saw that she was still holding her empty champagne glass. Like a character suffering a bitter joke at the end of a Noel Coward play. She started to laugh, but the laughter turned into something else, emerging from her throat as a sob.

She lifted her empty glass to the headless cupid. 'Here's to us, Bri. May we rest in peace.'

380

# 21

'Rose . . . I'm sorry.'

Behind her, Brian's voice, soft, and somehow shocking in the stillness. Rose felt her skin pull tight with goose-flesh. Her heart racing in giant uneven bounds, she jerked around to face him.

'Sorry for what?' she asked bitterly. 'Sorry you came here tonight? Sorry I had the bad taste to say hello? Or just sorry you dumped me without a word all those years ago? You know something, Brian, it's true what they say, that one picture is worth a thousand words. You have *no* idea just how true—' She trailed off brokenly.

She stared at him, searching his face for what she hoped to find. Hurt. Pain. *Dear God, let him feel at least one tiny sliver of all I've suffered*. But when she saw, in the watery light that filtered down from the upstairs windows, how pale he was, almost shockingly white, how drawn and miserable he looked, she wanted only to go to him, throw her arms around him and comfort him.

And in that instant Rose knew why it was she would never be free of him. Because she couldn't decide whether to love him or hate him. God, why did he have to make it so hard? Why couldn't hating him be a simple thing?

'It wasn't like that,' he said with profound sadness. 'And I'm not sorry you came tonight. Rose . . . I . . . I've thought about calling you, so many times. But—' He spread his hands in a gesture of helplessness that said everything and nothing.

Rose was aware of her hands clenching, nails digging into her palms. Her breath raking her throat in hot, dry gasps. Mother of God, *why* did she have to go through this all over again?

But she knew, deep inside her, that though she wanted to run away, she could not. This somehow was her destiny, as if she and Brian had both been on a track, coming from opposite ends, and this meeting was the inevitable collision.

'If I'd known you were going to be here tonight,' she said, 'I wouldn't have come.' She brought her clenched hands to her face, so cold they were like lumps of ice. 'Oh God, Brian, why? *Why* did you do it? All these years . . . I just wish I'd known. That's what killed me. Not knowing why. *Why did you marry her?*'

A long pause, and Brian said gently, 'It wasn't because I didn't love you, Rose. I want you to know that. If it would have made a difference, I . . . well, I did try to see you when I got back, but you . . .'

'I hung up on you, right? About a dozen times if I remember. Do you think that changes anything? Do you honestly, Brian? Jesus, was I supposed to meet you somewhere for lunch, listen to your lousy explanations, let you tidy it all up into a neat little farewell package? So long, it's been nice knowing you, and by the way do you want that corned beef sandwich with mustard or sauerkraut?' She was weeping now. 'We were better than that, weren't we, Brian? We were *better* than just a couple of kids from Brooklyn screwing up on the roof.'

'Rose . . . Rosie . . .' He put his hands out toward her, as if he wanted to console her, but didn't know how. Those long hands, so pale in the darkness they seemed almost incandescent. She had loved them so dearly, and they had known her so tenderly, intimately. 'I still wish there was some way to explain. It just . . . what I wanted you to know . . . it wasn't simple. It wasn't one decision, one day when I decided this was going to happen, this was how it was going to be.'

Rose watched Brian's hands drop to his sides. He sagged on to the bench, staring sightlessly into the darkness. She thought helplessly, *Oh Jesus, he breaks my heart just looking at him.* Older, thinner, those bones jumping right out of his face like the stone ridges of a mountain, and – *I still can't believe it* – that gray at his temples.

'A lot of people, they'll try to tell you what it was like over there, in Nam,' he began, haltingly. 'But no-one, not me or anyone else, could ever make you *believe* it really happened that way. It was like . . . well, like *there*, the war, the jungle, was the only thing there was or ever had been, and nothing else was real. Not home or my family or even you. All of you . . . imagining what you were doing . . . it was like watching one of those old black and white TV shows where the reception is all snowy and you know, even while you're buying it, all those dumb lines, you *know* they're only actors getting paid to act as if they give a shit about each other. It didn't matter how many times I *told* myself you were waiting for me, that you loved me, it just never . . . seemed real. Then, when you didn't write . . .'

Rose felt as if he'd driven a knife into her heart. 'Your letters. The ones Nonnie kept from me. Oh God. Didn't you get my—'

'I got your letter. They forwarded it to me at the base. But not until after I was discharged. After Rachel and I . . .' He trailed off. 'So you see how it was.'

'Are you asking me to forgive you, Brian? Are you honestly asking me to believe you married *her* because you thought I'd stopped loving you?'

He turned his face up to her, and she saw that tears stood in his eyes. 'I don't know anymore, Rose. It's been such a long time. I honestly don't know anymore what I thought, exactly, at the time. I do know how I felt, and that it probably had nothing to do with you or what was real. Then . . . after I was wounded . . . it got worse, that feeling. It was as if I'd been asleep and had just woken up, and everything that had happened before that was just dreams. Some of those dreams I barely remembered.'

'Like me?'

'No I remembered you, Rose. You just . . . you were make-believe. The only thing real was that hospital, that bed I was lying in, the godawful pain. And Rachel. She saved my life, Rose. She . . . she was *real*.'

Rose thought, *This is real, too, the way I feel now. And I hate him for doing this, for trying to making me understand. For telling me all this, hurting me even more.*

But a part of her *did* understand. He had been far away from home, and something terrible had happened . . . and it was that *something* which had taken their lives and blown them apart.

She understood too, now, after all these years, that Brian hadn't meant to hurt her. But then, hadn't she known that all along – down in the deepest part of her heart where forgiveness lay buried?

Rose *saw* in his face that he was telling the truth, as best as he knew it. His tear-filled eyes caught the light, and for an instant they shone bright and sharp as broken glass.

A final truth of her own dawned in her, too: that she loved him, even now, and that she would go on loving him no matter what.

'Brian . . .' She choked.

Suddenly her knees felt weak. She sank on to the bench beside him, burying her hot face against the worn ribs of his corduroy jacket, clutching him the way she had, as a child, clutched at wonderful things in dreams, feeling that if she could just hang on hard enough, she would still have them when she awoke . . .

Rose felt his arms go around her, gently, as if he were comforting a lost child, and with a sick heart she found herself remembering all the times he'd held her like this. As if these were the roles they had been born into, and would carry all their lives.

'Kiss me, Bri,' she cried, pulling back a little way and twisting her face up to meet his. 'Don't do this to me. Don't make me ask. Just . . . for God's sake . . . *kiss me*.'

'Rose, I can't . . .'

Damn him. She would *make* him kiss her. She had to

384

know if there was some part of him, however deep down, that still loved her.

Then Rose was tightening her arms around his neck, dragging him toward her as if she were drowning and he'd swum out to rescue her. God . . . oh God . . . how many times had she ached for this? Dreamed of him coming to her this way? *Please, Brian, please let me have just this one thing . . . this one kiss . . .*

Then he *was* kissing her, opening his mouth, fierce and sweet, hungry for her, a strangled moan in his throat. *You see . . . oh Brian . . . you do love me . . .*

But something was wrong. He was pulling away, forcibly wrenching her from him, his fingers digging painfully into her shoulders.

'No!' he cried. 'No . . . I can't. We can't. Rose, those things I just told you. They're all true. But that was a long time ago. I love Rachel. She's my wife. This . . . this shouldn't have happened. I'm sorry.'

'Sorry?' Weak laughter bubbled up in her. Sorry was for when you stepped on someone's toe, or when you knocked over a lamp. Not for when you crushed some-one's entire world.

Then Brian was rising, towering over her with an expression of infinite sadness. And she wanted to scream at him, tear at his face. *Don't feel sorry for me, you bastard. I don't want your pity.*

'I really *am* sorry, Rose.'

There was nothing left to say. He was walking away, taking with him everything she had ever wanted.

Oh God, it hurt, it *hurt* so damn much . . .

Rose, crying out with rage and pain, snatched up the empty champagne glass that stood on the end of the bench to hurl it at him, to hurt him just as much as he had hurt her.

But somehow, instead, her hand convulsed about the glass. There was a snapping sound, and a savage, blos-soming pain. Rose looked down and saw blood, dark and thick, and wicked thorns of glass sticking up from her

385

palm. *God, what have I done? What have I done?*

Rose sat there, clutching her wrist, staring in hyp-notized horror as the blood spread, formed a lake in the cup of her palm, spilling down her wrist and spattering on to her lap, staining the beautiful rubbed velvet gown.

'Rose . . . oh Jesus, what . . .' Brian. Hadn't he gone? No. Because here he was, right here beside her, holding her, cradling her injured hand, bright drops of blood staining the front of his white shirt like tiny red flowers.

'It looks deep,' he was saying, voice choked. 'You may need stitches. Oh God, Rose . . .' Then he was crying, all hunched over, an awful sound, like some animal in pain, a sound not meant for human ears.

A feeling of twisted triumph came over her. For Rose knew then, in some part of her mind that floated free from the pain, that he was hers. That whatever happened, how-ever they hurt themselves, or each other, Brian would always be hers.

As Brian led her upstairs, her bloody hand wrapped in his handkerchief, Rose felt oddly detached. She thought: *None of this is really happening to me. I'm watching a movie of myself.* One of those BBC dramas they show on *Masterpiece Theatre.*

The crowd grew still, and moved back in waves, as if it had been rehearsed that way. *The parting of the Red Sea, Take One,* she thought, part of her now hearing an imagin-ary laugh track.

The stark, tidy room seemed to come apart, then rearrange itself in a bizarre collage. Little things jumped out at her, jarring, distorted. A cigarette burned down to a tube of ash in the hand of a tall blond woman who stood watching her, frozen in horror. A white Persian cat snaking its way stealthily among the forest of legs. A pattern of overlapping wet rings on the surface of the glass coffee table, like ripples on a pond.

Then, like a mirage appearing out of nowhere, there she was. Rachel. Shouldering her way through the crowd,

386

striding forward, seeming to rip right through the haze of red . . . everything blue now, the blue of her eyes, the blue of dreams and smoke and vanished promises . . .

*My twin,* Rose thought, *yes, that what you are. My Siamese twin. You don't know me. But I've lived with you for years. Tied to you. Hating you. Wondering why he chose you instead of me . . .*

'Let me help you,' Rachel was saying, coolly. Rose couldn't believe what she was hearing. But then those slim strong fingers were clasping her wrist. 'I'm a doctor.'

*This* is *a movie,* Rose told herself. *Things like this don't happen in real life.*

Rose drew away, shrinking from Rachel's touch, hating her gentleness, her competence, more than if she had been rough, hurtful. 'No . . . no . . . I'll be OK. It's . . . I don't think it's deep . . . thank you, but I'll manage—'

'Don't be silly.' Rachel took hold of her wrist again, firmly, an adult shepherding a stubborn child across a dangerous street. 'You're still bleeding. It must be deep. How did it happen?' Her eyes cut away to Brian. Just for an instant, but Rose saw the question mark in them.

She felt again that stealthy glow of triumph that had come over her in the garden. This time she did not draw away. A compelling fascination took hold of her. Suddenly, she wanted to know this woman. And getting close to her might be a little like getting inside of Brian, mightn't it? Seeing Rachel through Brian's eyes, maybe finding out what in her had made him fall in love with her.

*Know thy enemy.* Isn't that what the Bible said? Maybe she could discover Rachel's weaknesses. Places where a wedge might be driven in.

'A champagne glass,' she said. 'It broke in my hand. I must have been holding it too tightly.'

'Let me see.' Rachel started to unwrap the bloody handkerchief, then glanced up, her steel-blue gaze taking in the rubbernecking crowd. 'Not here. In the bathroom.'

Rose felt herself being propelled forward, a steadying hand on her elbow. She looked up, saw a familiar figure

387

burst from the crowd. Max. He looked disheveled, upset.

'Rose. I've been looking everywhere for you. Are you—' He stopped, stared, and his stolid face seemed to crumple, turn old before her eyes. Softly, he said, 'Oh Rose, oh baby.'

Immediately, Rose felt better, a great glassy wave of calm sweeping over her. Max was here. Max would stop these crazy red thoughts flapping inside her head. Max would make her sane again.

'Max . . . I'm OK,' she said, meaning it. 'Just a little accident. Wait for me. I'll be a few minutes. Then please . . . please just take me back to the hotel.'

'I'll wait,' Max said, and in that instant Rose caught something in his voice, his eyes, that made her wonder if . . .

Then Rupert Everest, wringing his hands, was ushering her into a bathroom, an Art Deco fantasy. Black marble tiles and flamingo-pink porcelain, a huge sunken tub with fixtures in the shape of bronze water nymphs. Mirrors on every wall, shaded in soft pink light, multiplying every angle, turning it into a fun show.

Rose sank down on the cushioned chair beside a glass etagere filled with French bath salts.

Rachel shut the door.

They were alone.

Rose, for just an instant, felt as if reality were holding its breath, leaving her – the two of them – in a sort of surreal vacuum. A place where nothing . . . and everything . . . made sense.

Like this feeling she had that, somehow, she'd seen Rachel before. It couldn't have been that news photo. So blurry, and her face mostly hidden behind Brian. No, it was something more. Something truly *familiar* . . . that was what was so creepy about it. Rachel reminded her of someone she knew well . . . only she couldn't think who. The image kept slipping away just when she thought she had it.

*Just my imagination*, she told herself.

388

Rachel slid back one of the mirror panels over the sink, and rummaged inside for first-aid supplies. Then she knelt on the thick pink rug in front of Rose, and peeled back the handkerchief, examining the wound: a long gash running diagonally across her palm like a sneering mouth, but no more than a fraction of an inch deep.

Rose felt relieved. It wasn't as bad as she had thought. Even the pain had subsided to a dull throbbing ache. She stared at the top of Rachel's head, at the pale pink line of scalp that looked as if it had been drawn with a ruler, at the waves of shimmering amber hair falling over her face. She thought about taking the Art Deco statuette of a discus thrower that stood on the marble counter, and bringing it down hard against that perfect pink line.

Then as Rachel drew a long sliver of glass from the wound with a pair of tweezers, she flinched. Fresh waves of pain blotted out her sinful thoughts.

Rachel glanced up, grimacing in sympathy.

'Ouch. Bet that hurts. But you won't need stitches. I'll just clean you up, and put a bandage around it.'

'Thank you,' Rose gasped. 'Really, I feel so stupid about the whole thing. It was such a stupid accident.'

'Accidents happen. It wasn't your fault.' But again, that question mark flashing in her eyes. *What happened between you and Brian out there?* Rose read in her clouded gaze.

*I'll let you figure that out for yourself*, Rose answered silently.

She remained quiet, watching Rachel swab the cut with sharp-smelling antiseptic, then wrap it in gauze. Secretly admiring the graceful, efficient movement of her hands, Rose imagined those hands on Brian's body, making love to him, dancing over him with butterfly touches . . .

*Stop. Stop it right now*, she commanded. *This is crazy. You're acting craz—*

Rachel, standing now, was turning the tap on to wash her hands. 'Leave the bandage on for a day or two.' Her voice rose over the running water. Now she was drying her hands on one of the fluffy pink towels lined up on the towel rack, now turning back to Rose. Her gaze dropped, and she shook her head. 'A shame about the dress, though. It's lovely. I hope it's not ruined.'

Her dress? She hadn't thought about it, and now she felt a twinge of dismay. Well, it could be cleaned. If only her life could be restored to her as easily, the life she would have had with Brian . . .

But that was like wishing Vietnam had never happened. Or the fire that killed her mother.

Rose, overcome, began to gasp with soundless, helpless sobs, leaning her forehead against the cool marble tiles.

'Look,' Rachel was saying, her voice helpful, professional, 'you've had a shock. Go back to your hotel, take a couple of aspirin, get some rest.'

Rose, struggling to contain her emotion, focused on Rachel through the tears standing in her eyes. 'Brian didn't tell me,' she said, 'where you're staying. Your hotel. So I can send you a check for your services.'

Rachel stiffened. 'That won't be necessary,' she said. 'I wouldn't think of charging a friend. Of Brian's,' she added quickly. Too quickly, followed by a deep flush that fanned up her neck, turning her creamy pink skin an ugly mottled red.

Rose felt a twist of satisfaction in the pit of her stomach. Good. So she had an Achilles' heel after all. And it was, as she'd suspected, Brian.

'I owe you then,' Rose said.

Rachel stopped at the door, and turned to give her a long look. And Rose thought, *We are in a Fellini picture*, seeing Rachel reflected in the pink mirrors, over and over, a dozen Rachels lined up like dominoes, tiny and golden with eyes like blue forget-me-nots. Once again, too, Rose had the eerie feeling she knew that face from somewhere else . . .

'You don't owe me anything,' Rachel said, a thin smile pasted in place. 'Consider us even.'

*Not yet*, Rose thought, her bitterness a cold thing now, *not as long as you have Brian*.

390

## 22

Rachel checked her panties again, just to be sure.

No blood.

A wave of exhilarating relief swept over her as she sat huddled on the toilet in the tiny washroom at the back of the clinic.

*Four days,* she thought. And her period was almost *never* late. Still, it was too soon to let herself get excited.

Except she *was* excited. Hands shaking. Stomach fluttering. As she stood, pulling her panties up, smoothing her corduroy skirt, her knees felt a little rubbery. She flushed, then reached under her thin cotton blouse to adjust her bra. It had grown tight over the past few days, uncomfortably so; and her breasts felt heavy and tender, nipples sore.

*All the signs are there.*

Now, as she washed her hands in the rust-stained sink, Rachel could no longer contain her hope. Just suppose she *were* pregnant. After all these years. There was always that one in a thousand chance. She had seen a patient just the other day, a woman who'd been trying for years, and had finally given up, thought she was in menopause. Now, at forty-seven, pregnant with her first. A fluke. But they did happen.

*Please, God*, she prayed, *let it be happening to me. To us. To Brian and me*.

She thought of those painful fertility tests. The last time she'd even taken the morphine. And what did they prove, other than what she already knew? And how many years now, taking her temperature every morning, marking it on a curve chart, like a laboratory rat? And those thousands of trips to the bathroom, checking for suspicious stains.

Feeling her breasts for tenderness. Hoping against hope. Praying.

And always, in the end, nothing.

But what made it so awful, so much worse than just her own disappointment, was knowing she'd lied. She'd let Brian go believing there was no reason why they couldn't have a child. If he knew—

*Six years*, she thought. After six years, she had not yet found exactly the right moment to tell him. Her fault, of course. Brian could not have been more tender, more understanding. She *knew* he would understand if she told him, but still she could not bring herself to say the words. And the longer she kept it from him, the worse it became, a betrayal all its own.

But, oh, those first years had been so good, she hadn't had the heart to spoil a single day, a single minute. Back in New York, finishing her OB residency at Beth Israel – and Brian, working like a madman on his novel – they had had so little time that each hour together had become precious.

She recalled one snowy evening, dragging home after thirty-six hours on call . . . and suddenly, in the cab, remembering Carnegie Hall, that the tickets for the Rubenstein concert were for that night. They had both been looking forward to it for weeks – a night of heavenly music, then dinner at the Russian Tea Room. But then . . . all she wanted, ached for, was a hot bath, a night luxuriating in bed. Yet how could she let Brian down? He'd been so patient with her beastly hours, never complaining, never making her feel guilty. She owed him this.

But when she had arrived home, Brian, scrubbed and splendid in his best suit and tie, had taken a long look at her, and said, 'I can't compete with the Russian Tea Room on blintzes, but I make a pretty mean omelette. How about us staying home tonight, and I'll throw something together?'

'Oh, Brian—' she had been close to tears with exhaustion and relief, 'what about the concert? I know how much you wanted to go . . .'

'There'll be other nights. Carnegie Hall isn't going to collapse tomorrow. But it looks like you are. Anyway,' he said and grinned, that wonderful lopsided grin that warmed her so, 'you're a lot more fun to look at than old Rubenstein. And we can always put a record on.'

And so she had taken a long hot bath while Brian made dinner, then listened to Brahms while they ate. Afterwards, he led her into the bedroom, and slowly, carefully undressed her. He licked her breasts, and the tender hollow between them, leaving the moist imprint of his lips in a trail along her belly. He threw off his own clothes, and pulled her down on the mattress.

'Now for dessert,' he murmured, grinning wickedly.

He entered her, and she was swept along the groundswell of his passion . . . and her own, building swiftly, lifting her from her exhaustion, making her cry out, arch her spine to take in all of him she possibly could.

Drifting asleep in his arms, she had felt such bliss . . . to think she was married to this wonderful man, that she had a whole lifetime of nights like this. And maybe someday, a miracle would happen and she would get pregnant – the specialists said it wasn't impossible, just unlikely. It could be happening right now, at this very moment . . . a baby . . . Brian's baby . . . then everything would really be perfect . . .

*God, when was the last time we made love?* she wondered now, as she stood at the sink drying her hands. Weeks ago. That night he'd woken her from a sound sleep, with his caresses, his need was so great.

But she would make it up to him, soon – as soon as she could clear a few days, they would go away somewhere romantic, Antigua maybe. And this place was worth a few sacrifices, wasn't it? Her own clinic, where she could somehow make up for, maybe even forget, the death she'd lived with in Nam, a place where poor women could get good prenatal care. God, it had been so hard, fighting through the red tape – lawyers, recommendations, interviews on interviews, mountains of applications and forms – just for their pittance of HEW funding. Then so hard, too, to find another doctor like herself, to wait for Kay to complete her nurse-midwife training, to find a suitable space.

She recalled opening day here at the East Side Women's Health Center. The cheerful yellow paint just barely dry on the walls of what had been for sixty years a hardware store, the vinyl tile floor gleaming with new wax. And the waiting room – with its slightly lumpy second-hand couches, hanging plants, baskets of bright plastic toys – all day not a single person coming in the door, the place as deserted as a subway station at three in the morning.

And then Kay's inspiration, a coffee maker. They stuck a big sign on the window, in English and Spanish: FREE COFFEE AND DOUGHNUTS. Three women showed up that day. Shy, dark-haired ladies with lowered eyes and tentative smiles, balancing plump babies on their hips. By the end of the week, the waiting room was overflowing.

Now, after a year and a half, it was all coming together. These proud, strong-willed women had begun to trust her. She delivered their babies, listened to their problems, helped whenever and however she could. Of *course* she wanted to be with Brian more, but these people here, they so *needed* her. They were like her children in a way.

The doorknob rattled, breaking into her thoughts. 'Rachel, are you in there?' Nancy Kandinsky called. 'I'm on my way out. I know you are, too, but I think you should see this one. She asked for you. Lila Rodriguez. She . . . well, you'll see for yourself.

Rachel sighed. It was after seven. She ached to go home. To feel Brian's welcoming arms about her. She wouldn't tell him what she suspected, hoped, not yet, not until she was sure. They'd both been disappointed too many times. But, oh, just to *be* with him.

Then she remembered. Brian was speaking at the Veterans' Administration tonight. So many requests for lectures, appearances on TV, and radio talk shows since his book, she couldn't keep track. One thing was for sure, he wouldn't be home until late. The third night this week she'd be crawling into bed without his long, warm body to cuddle next to.

*And he doesn't have to make all these speeches, go out all these nights. Could it be he's tired of waiting? For me, for a child? And if I can't give him that, isn't it possible he might go looking somewhere else?*

She remembered something else. The party two months ago in London. Rose. Beautiful, dark, with those haunted eyes. *And the way those eyes looked at Brian.* A cold sliver of fear wedged itself into Rachel's heart.

She pushed the thought out of her mind.

*If I'm pregnant, everything will change. We'll be all right. We'll be a family.*

*Tomorrow,* she promised herself. *I'll leave early, make dinner for a change. Something scrumptious, to go with champagne and candlelight, the whole bit. And later, when we make love, it'll feel like the first time.*

'Tell Mrs Rodriguez I'll be with her in a minute,' she called through the door to Nancy.

'OK. I'm off. See you in the morning.'

Rachel, emerging from the bathroom, caught a flash of carrot-red hair disappearing down the narrow corridor that led to the examining room up front. Nancy never walked. Everything she did was on the run.

Now Rachel was hurrying too, unearthing Lila's chart from the jammed file cabinet in her cubbyhole of an office, shouldering her way into the examining room.

Lila was slumped on the folding chair in the corner, beneath the iron-barred window that overlooked an alleyway. Tiny except for her enormous belly. Her face ghastly. Lumpy and bruised, like a rubber Halloween mask. Eyes swollen up to the size of doorknobs.

*Next time he'll kill her*, Rachel thought, horrified, fury sweeping through her.

She sucked her breath in, and struggled to remain impassive. Why did this woman let her husband beat her? She even *protected* the bastard, last time saying she had hurt herself falling down the stairs. Like hell.

'Señora,' she asked, gently taking hold of a hand that felt horribly limp and clammy. 'Dígame que pasó.'

Lila shook her head, greasy black strands falling over her waxen forehead. 'Mi niño? Está bien? Está bien mi niño?' She cradled her arms protectively about her pregnant belly.

'Let's take a look. I'll be very gentle, I promise.'

Rachel got her up on the examining table, and lifted her skirt. No vaginal bleeding, thank goodness. But there was a huge bruise just below her rib cage that worried Rachel. It might indicate trauma. The amniotic fluid would have to be tested for meconium.

'Your baby is probably fine, but I'd like to put you in the hospital overnight,' Rachel told her. 'Just to be sure. Entiendes, señora?'

Lila understood. At the word 'hospital' her face had gone from waxy yellow to gray, and her eyes rolled back in her head. She's scared, Rachel thought, more frightened of the hospital than of going home to the man who beat her.

Lila shook her head, then eased herself off the examining table, moving with exaggerated care, like a very old woman balancing a crate of eggs.

'No,' she said with a stubborn wariness. 'No hospital. They take my baby.'

She was already at the door, tugging at the buttons on her ratty pink sweater, before Rachel could stop her. 'Mrs Rodriguez, please, listen. What happened before, when you had the miscarriage, that was different . . .'

But again Lila was shaking her head, politely, but firmly. 'Gracias, Doctor. Gracias . . . pero no.'

Rachel wanted to run after her, grab her by the shoulders and shake her. Don't you know what you're risking? Do you have any idea how many women would give anything for just one baby? One chance to be pregnant?

But it wouldn't do any good. Lila wouldn't understand. And she'd stop coming to the clinic altogether. Wasn't half a doctor better than none?

396

Rachel, simmering down, went through the connecting door to her office, and fished among the folders on her desk, quickly finding the one she was looking for, SAUCEDO, ALMA. On her way home she'd stop at the hospital and check on Alma. Here, at least, was something she could do.

Kay stuck her curly head through the door. 'I'm headed out. Can I get you anything before I go? Sandwich, coffee, a transfusion? You look beat, Rache.'

'I'll relax once I get out of here. This time of night, I may even get a seat on the subway.' She dipped into an ashtray overflowing with rubber bands, paper clips, pencil stubs, and fished out a subway token. She tossed it at Kay. 'Here. Have one on me. By the way, have we gotten the results back on Alma Saucedo's blood work-up?'

'Not yet. Tomorrow morning, if I have to squeeze it out of them with fire tongs. You know those creeps at the lab – promises, promises. Want me to tell them it's an emergency?' Kay looked tired, dark circles under her eyes, a bit thinner.

'Tomorrow morning will be fine,' Rachel decided. ' 'Night, Kay. And listen . . . take care, hear?'

Minutes later, Rachel was locking up – two locks, dead bolt, double-padlocked accordion gate – then making her way up the no-man's-land of East Fourteenth Street. The sidewalk a wasteland, literally, dog turds, broken bottles, overflowing trash cans, vandalized phone booths. The very air somehow rotten. Graffiti scrawled on the walls – VIVA LA RAZA! CHICO LOVES ROXY! DEATH TO THE PIGS! And blasting from every window, it seemed, the relentless, hammering beat of Latin music.

It used to put her on edge. She remembered how at first she felt as if she were an astronaut setting foot on a strange and dangerous planet. Or Margaret Mead among the aborigines. What were they thinking as they watched her from their windows – was she just another uptown do-gooder in their eyes, did they only want to steal her purse?

But now she thought with a smile, *This is my planet*. She

waved to a woman sitting on a grungy stoop with a stroller parked beside it. Anita Gonzalez. Seven months ago, she'd delivered that baby now in the stroller. A difficult pregnancy, she remembered. And at the end of it a little shrimp of a thing, all black hair and not much else. But now he looked big, healthy, popping right out of his clothes. Rachel's heart lifted.

The wail of an ambulance siren broke through her thoughts.

Soon she found herself at the entrance of a huge, ugly brick building. Spray-painted red letters alongside the big glass doors read: MARIO GET FUCKED. Someone had also pried off most of the brass letters that once had spelled ST BARTHOLOMEW'S HOSPITAL. What was left was ST BAR, and then a red F scrawled beside it. ST BARF.

Rachel rode the creaky elevator to the sixth floor, jammed between a sleepy-eyed intern and a cleaning lady with an enormous laundry cart piled high with dirty sheets.

Alma Saucedo was in Ward C, the bed closest to the door. Asleep. Her face like a lovely ivory cameo, dark hair fanning across the pillow. *Only sixteen*, Rachel thought. *She should be studying for a history exam, dating boys, going to parties, not having a baby*.

Rachel remembered how her heart had gone out to Alma the first time she had shown up at the clinic. A shy, pretty girl wearing a navy-blue school jumper that had grown too tight. After the examination, which showed her to be about four months pregnant, the whole tearful story came tumbling out. Her first boyfriend. He'd said he loved her. And he *promised* nothing would happen. Now he wanted nothing to do with her. She didn't want the baby, either, but her parents would not allow an abortion. They were Catholics, and killing it would be a mortal sin.

Now, four months later, it looked as if this baby might be killing Alma.

Rachel glanced at the chart. Blood pressure up from this morning: 140 over 110. Edema unchanged despite the magnesium sulfate. Alma was getting lactated Ringer's solution, but her urine output was way down. *Damn. I'll have to induce soon if she doesn't improve. I could lose them both, Alma and the baby. Tomorrow morning, as soon as I see those blood results . . .*

'Doctor Rosenthal! Oh, I'm so glad you came!'

Rachel, startled, saw Alma was awake. She looked upset. Tears welling in her sleep-puffy brown eyes, then running down her cheeks.

Rachel sat down on the edge of the bed, taking Alma's hand. 'Feeling pretty rotten, huh?'

'That man,' she whispered, so low Rachel had to bend close to hear. 'Please . . . don't let him touch me again.'

Had Alma been dreaming? 'What man?' Rachel asked.

'A doctor, I don't know his name. Tall and . . . well, some girls would say, good-looking.' She screwed up her face; clearly, she didn't share that opinion. 'He came with a bunch of doctors, just a little while ago . . .'

Rachel nodded. 'Evening rounds. It's routine.'

'No, no.' Alma shook her head. 'He . . . he wasn't like the other doctors. Not just . . . you know, examining me. He was so *cold*. Like I was something for sale in a store. The way he *touched* me. I felt so—' She buried her face in her hands, and spoke through her fingers, a hollow choked sound. 'He didn't even ask. He just pushed my legs apart and . . . and . . . in front of *everyone* . . . with that metal thing . . . all the time talking about me as if I wasn't there . . . oh God, I wanted to *die*.'

Rachel felt anger like a coal burning in the pit of her stomach. *Bastard. I'd like to string him up by his thumbs, whoever he is. Better yet, turn a sadistic proctologist loose on him.*

It was a subtle war she fought every day, against the insensitive doctors who treated patients with as much concern as the cadavers they dissected in medical school. Less, even.

Especially here, on the labor and delivery ward. The general assumption among the intern and resident staff

399

seemed to be that any woman who got herself pregnant deserved to have her privates on display like apples and bananas on a grocer's shelf.

*I'll speak to Dr Townsend about it*, she thought. *His mind wanders, but his heart's in the right place. Let him do one last bit of good here before he retires.*

Then she caught herself, remembering that Harry Townsend *had* retired. There had been a party, which she hadn't been able to attend. But who had taken his place? She recalled hearing several names mentioned as possibilities, no-one she knew. And hadn't there been talk of luring over some big shot from Presbyterian?

She gave Alma's hand a gentle squeeze, then handed her a tissue from the box on the enamel nightstand. The crack in Rachel's heart widened as she watched Alma dutifully honk into the tissue. Was this how a mother felt? Wanting to give comfort, but helpless to do much more than dole out Kleenex?

*A mother. Dear Lord, that's exactly what I'll be if I'm pregnant.*

Her heart leapt for one wild moment.

*If, if, if . . .*

If only she knew for sure.

Rachel took a deep breath. 'Look, Alma, I know what you're going through. Everything feels uncomfortable right now, and the last thing you want is a lot of doctors poking at you. But believe me, the only reason you're here is so we can help you, and your baby. Now, try and get some sleep. I'll be back with you first thing in the morning.'

Alma nodded, then snatched her hand, gripping it hard, as she was about to go. 'Promise me, Doctor Rosenthal. *Promise* me no-one else will deliver my baby. I don't want anyone but you.'

Rachel paused, torn. How could she make such a promise? Nine chances out of ten, she *would* deliver Alma's baby. But what if something happened, if she were detained . . .

Rachel opened her mouth to reassure Alma, tell her

400

there were other doctors who were good, maybe better. But the look of raw, anguished appeal on Alma's face stopped her. To diminish Alma's confidence now, when she needed it the most, might do the girl more harm than a promise that might not be kept.

'I promise,' she said.

She saw light showing under the door marked CHIEF OF OBSTETRICS AND GYNECOLOGY. Well, whoever had replaced Harry, he was a go-getter, staying this late.

Rachel knocked lightly.

'Come in,' a voice called distractedly.

Rachel pushed open the door, and stepped in, eager to meet his replacement.

She saw a head bent over the desk, tousled blond hair gleaming in the hard circle of light cast by a tensor lamp, a pair of muscular forearms resting against an open folder, shirtsleeves rolled to the elbow. Then the head lifted, and Rachel found herself staring into a pair of weary green eyes.

Rachel blinked, thinking she must be overtired, imagining things. After all these years . . . oh dear God, *him*.

David Sloane. A little older, a fair bit heavier, and still handsome . . . but not pleasantly so. There were sags under his eyes, and an unhealthy bloated look to his face. Rather than aging gracefully, naturally, he appeared to be spoiling, like a fallen fruit left to rot.

She went cold for an instant, as if all the blood had been drained from her. Another David flashed across the screen of her memory, a younger one in a white jacket, holding a curette in his trembling hand.

But she quickly wiped away that image. Ancient history, she told herself. Now that they were both in the same field, sooner of later their paths were bound to cross.

*Awkward situation, but I'll just have to make the best of it.*

She watched him push out of Townsend's ancient swivel

401

chair, and rise to greet her. 'Well, hello there.' He switched on a smile as bright as a spotlight.

Rachel put out her hand, forced a smile, feeling oddly detached, as if she were standing outside herself, a puppeteer pulling strings, making her mouth move.

'Hello, David. It's been a while, hasn't it? Last I heard, you were at Presbyterian. There was a rumor they were considering someone from there, but I never dreamed it was you.'

'Last I heard—' he tossed the ball back at her, '*you* were off in the jungle somewhere playing Dr Schweitzer. Well, it's nice to see you made it back in one piece. You look wonderful, Rachel.'

'So do you.'

Not true at all, she thought. He looks awful, like a caricature of his old pretty-boy self. Like Dean Martin on talk shows, baggy-eyed and boozy, but ever the charming playboy. God, how could she ever have thought she was in love with this man?

'I'd invite you to sit down,' he said, 'but as you can see . . .' He gestured toward the half-filled cardboard cartons by the door. Messy stacks of books and folders were piled on every chair except his own. 'I'm in the midst of cleaning house. Harry Townsend was quite a pack rat. Saved everything from matchbooks to twenty-year-old autopsy reports. Ran the department pretty much the same slipshod way. So it looks like I'm going to have my work cut out for me here.'

'Well, St Bart's is not exactly Presbyterian. But I've been around a while, my clinic is in the neighborhood, so if I can help with anything . . .'

*Won't hurt to brown-nose a little. Stay on his good side. He could just as easily make it rough for me here.*

'Tell you what,' he said, switching on again that klieg-light grin, 'I was just getting ready to cash it in for the night. Why don't we duck out for a quick drink somewhere? Give us a chance to catch up. Kick around any ideas you might have for airing out this morgue. What do you say?'

*No*, Rachel thought. *The last place I'd want to be is with David in some bar, shooting the breeze.*

But then, on the other hand, if she refused . . . well, he might take it the wrong way. And the ugly fact was, she could not afford to alienate him. She was not on staff here, only surgical privileges. And privileges could be revoked. Besides, how much could it hurt?

'Love to,' she lied, 'but I really will have to make it a quick one. I was expected home an hour ago.'

Already he was reaching for his jacket – suede, very expensive, hip – and hooking it one-fingered over his shoulder, as if he were James Dean. Rachel felt tempted to laugh.

'Home to hubby?' There was a snide edge lurking behind that smile, but she'd already decided to be diplomatic even if it killed her.

She arranged her face into what she hoped was a pleasant expression. 'As a matter of fact, yes. And you? Married?'

'Who me? No, not yet. I still like playing it loose. A wife would just get fed up with me. Know what I mean?' He took her arm, guiding her out the door, and she had to struggle with herself to keep from snatching it away. 'So, yeah, I guess you could say I lucked out that way. I guess I must prefer hard labor to life imprisonment.' He chuckled a little at his own joke.

Rachel shriveled inside. She saw the light glint off something bright around his neck. A gold chain. Oh God, had she really agreed to have a drink with this creep?

There was something else, too, besides his macho humor, nagging at the back of her mind. Yes, something to do with Presbyterian. Her old friend Celia Kramer, an OB nurse on staff there, had mentioned something about David a while back. Some sort of scandal? But what? Oh well, it would come to her eventually.

She flashed the brightest smile she could muster. 'Well, I guess we can't all be lucky.'

*

403

'Just where is this place you're taking me?' Rachel asked, her stomach tightening as their cab turned down yet another narrow Village street.

She was wishing now she had not let him talk her out of Gordo's, the bar across the street from St Bart's. It was seedy, the TV sometimes got too loud, but she knew a lot of the regulars there.

'A quiet place,' David answered, 'where we can talk. I get all the local color I can stomach at St Bartholomew's. Don't worry, we're almost there.'

*Worried? Why should I worry? We're just two colleagues going out for a drink after work. Sure, we dated once upon a time. And you knocked me up, but . . .*

The cab was stopping, David paying the driver, getting out. A nice neighborhood, she saw. Trees, a row of old brick houses with freshly painted trim, a nicely dressed couple out walking their dog. Houses, but no bars . . .

'David . . .' She turned back toward the cab, but a pair of transvestites in evening gowns were already climbing into it.

'I wanted to show off my new place,' David explained a little sheepishly. 'Just moved in last month. I really scored, even if it is a walk-up. Come on, don't look like that, it's only two flights. And it's quiet, we can talk.'

She felt reluctant, though she couldn't exactly say why. 'OK, but really I can only stay a few minutes.'

More than an hour later, Rachel sat wedged in a corner of David's white leather sofa, her drink resting on one knee, forming a damp circle on the blue corduroy of her skirt. Twice she had already told him she had to leave, and each time David had insisted she stay and have just one more drink.

She hasn't finished even one, but David, she observed, was now on his third tumbler of Scotch.

The way he looked, that glazed expression, and the way he was sitting, sideways on the couch facing her, one leg tucked up on the cushions, an arm hooked over the back, it was all wrong somehow. Yes, he looked . . . as if he planned on settling in with her for the evening.

This apartment, all wrong too. Like a sample room in Bloomingdale's, all done in shades of biscuit and oyster, the furniture all hard right angles, somehow soulless. David probably didn't even know that etching on the opposite wall was an Icart. Some decorator probably had just picked it out to go with the table underneath.

David was talking about Presbyterian now, and she tried to concentrate on what he was saying, but her mind kept wandering. *Brian should be on his way home now*, she thought, *if he isn't there already. God, I wish I were home with him*.

Now David's voice was rising, petulant about something. Rachel tensed, her mind tuning in to him.

'. . . Yeah, sounds weird, but it's true. My Princeton degree didn't mean two shits at that place. You come from the wrong side of the tracks, and they don't want you in their club. It's all very genteel, they pretend that you can, then they snub you in little ways . . . like always calling you by your full first name while *they* all have nicknames for each other . . . and somehow there's never an extra chair for you at their table in the cafeteria. And then those bastards set me up. I worked the hardest, a perfect record, too. I *deserved* Chief of OB. I was the best, far and away, no question.'

He was breathing heavily, face flushed. Rachel sensed that he might be on the verge of really losing his cool. She put her drink down on the coffee table, and started to get up.

'I'd love to hear the whole story sometime, David, but I really have to—'

His hand shot out, gripping her wrist like an iron manacle.

'Don't go yet . . . please, you haven't told me anything about you, what it was like over there in Vietnam. And you haven't even finished your drink.'

David was trying to turn on the charm again, but it was slipping, like a mask coming loose. For some absurd reason

405

she thought of Lon Chaney, the Phantom of the Opera. And suddenly she didn't want to see what was underneath, didn't want to *know* what was behind those bloodshot eyes, his manic grin.

*He's not letting go of my wrist. He's not –*

She sank down, her legs suddenly weak, rubbery. She rubbed her wrist, which prickled a little. But David couldn't have *meant* anything. No, she was only *imagining* he might be dangerous. She was being silly. She'd come here to talk to him, about St Bart's, about Alma Saucedo. And, well, that's what she'd do.

Then, when he calmed down, *then* she would get up, go over to the door, walk down the two flights, hail a cab . . .

Ten more minutes tops, she promised herself. Then home.

'David, I'd like your advice about a patient of mine.' She began angling herself casually to be in line with the door. Then she gave him a run-down on Alma's condition. 'I don't like the idea of starting her on Pitocin. The baby's chances of survival would be less than fifty per cent. On the other hand, if I wait . . .'

'First day on the job I went over every department in the place.' David seemed to pull himself together. 'Pediatrics is a joke, the others not much better. You're talking fifty per cent on the *curve*. I'd say forty, maybe a whole lot less, if you factor in a substandard Pediatrics ICU, and a sixteen-year-old nullip who's probably been living off potato chips and Coca-Cola the past eight months.'

'That's pretty pessimistic. I won't argue that these are hardly the best circumstances, but Alma's a bright girl. Straight A's in school. She's very aware of what's going on, she's been very careful.'

'If she'd been a little more careful, may she wouldn't have gotten pregnant in the first place.'

Rachel felt as if she'd been struck. David was looking straight at her. Glaring at her. Oh God, she had not been imagining. He *was* out to get her.

She just sat there, paralyzed, watching David drain the

406

two fingers of Scotch left in his glass in one long gulp.

'Examined her myself,' he went on, 'couple two-three hours before you popped up out of the blue. She didn't look like she'd win a prize doing the tango, but I wouldn't rush into anything if I were you. Give her a day or two before you zap her with Pit.'

*So you were the one*, she thought. *I might have known. Still king of the assholes*.

Rachel abruptly rose, bumping her knee on the coffee table. Her drink skittered away, leaving a wet skid mark along the polished blond surface. Pain shot through her leg. Shit. She'd have a bruise. But she didn't care. Right now, all she wanted was to get out, get away from here.

'Thanks for the drink,' she said. 'I really have to run. Listen, don't get up, I'll find my way out.'

But he *was* getting up, moving with clumsy purpose, blocking her exit a few feet from the door. Rachel's heart began to beat very fast, and her stomach did a slow, sickening cartwheel.

'What's your big hurry?'

She saw that he was flushed, the veins standing out in his neck, eyes narrowed.

'Seven years, goddamn it, I don't see you in seven years, and all of a sudden you're burning rubber to get to the door. I ask you, is that any way to treat an old friend?'

'Look, David, let's not spoil things. It was great seeing you again, but like I said—'

'You got someone besides hubby waiting for you? A kid or two maybe?'

'No kids.' Even speaking those words hurt. Goddamn it, she didn't need him of all people to remind her.

'You know, it's funny, because I always thought you'd make a great mother,' he went on, slouching back against the door. 'Take my own mother, for instance. Wouldn't let anything stand in the way of me and my pop. Not even when he was beating the holy crap out of me. Now *that's* togetherness for you. My old man and I, we were just like that.' He held up two fingers, pressed together. His hand, she saw, was trembling. 'But I don't hold it against him, and you know why? 'Cause she was the one. Selfish bitch. Nothing ever good enough for her. Always wanting things *her* way. She drove him to it. She just popped the fucking clutch and drove him right into that six-pack every night. And if little Davey happened to be in the way, well, that was just too damn bad.'

'David, stop it.' She was scared now, her stomach in a tight knot. He didn't even sound like himself anymore. Older, coarser . . . the voice of a bitter man in janitor's overalls, not the David she'd known, the charismatic young resident in a crisp white coat.

'Hey . . . I'm just getting started. You know, seven years is a long time. A lot of thoughts come to a man in seven years. Like I never realized before how much you remind me of my old lady.'

His eyes, hard and fiery, fixed on her. Rachel felt a chill dart up her spine.

'David, you're getting yourself all worked up. Look, why don't you just try and relax, sleep it off. We'll talk in the morning.'

She took a tentative step backwards, toward the door.

He shot forward, grabbing her by the shoulders, roughly, fingers gouging. A scream stuck somewhere below her Adam's apple, but she couldn't get it out. She couldn't move. She was frozen, as if in a nightmare.

His face inches from hers, the booze stink of his breath enveloping her like some noxious mist, now she was seeing what was under the mask. She was dealing with a *madman*.

'No!' he roared. 'We'll talk now. *Now!*'

'You're crazy,' she said.

She struggled to free herself, but he swung her around, slamming her against the wall, *pinning* her there. She heard something slither past her ear, crash into her. A Roman candle exploded inside her head. A fountain of red sparks. She tasted blood. She'd bit herself. She felt like the time she'd fallen off her bicycle speeding down a hill when

408

she was eight, numb, disoriented, even a little foolish. This couldn't be happening to her. This couldn't—

David brought his mouth down hard against hers.

*Oh dear God, no . . . NO . . .*

She felt his tongue, rough as sandpaper, thrusting into her mouth. Hurting her. She tasted blood. God . . . oh God . . .

'Feels good, doesn't it, babe?' he panted. 'Yeah, oh yeah, I remember when you used to *scream* for it. You want it now, don't you? You want me to fuck you now just like the old days, make you scream. Isn't that why you came here?'

She felt a hot rush of adrenaline spiraling through her. Now she was angry. She wanted to kill him.

'You bastard!' she screamed, lashing out with both fists, wildly, blindly. She connected in a solid, bone-thumping hit that sent a jarring bolt through her arm. Good . . . oh good.

He brought his forearms up, shielding his face to ward off her blows. And she saw, horrified, that his teeth were all bloody, and there was blood drooling out of the corner of his mouth . . .

She bolted for the door, scrabbled wildly for the door-knob. She felt as if she were struggling to move under-water, the air heavy, her limbs like lead.

*I'm never going to make it. I'm never going to get out of here.*

Then she found the latch below the doorknob, turned it, heard it click. The door was opening now. Thank God. Oh, thank—

From behind, Rachel felt something jerk her, and suddenly the room was tilting, walls and floor spinning end over end. Then everything went gray and slick. She tried to think what was happening, but it was all somehow out of reach.

'Bitch.' A voice crashed into her skull. 'I'll give you what you've been asking for.'

Her head seemed to be clearing now, and she felt a fiery

ache in her neck, as if she had been skewered by a hot poker.

And she saw.

David. Kneeling over her. Frantically unbuckling his belt, yanking at the zipper on his pants. *Oh God. No. Please* . . .

She felt as if she'd gone mad. All those years had gotten swallowed up somehow. And she was lying on a table in a deserted doctor's office, hearing the rain pelting the windows, seeing the grotesque white mask of David's handsome face framed between her hiked-up knees . . .

David was jerking at her legs now, forcing them apart, forcing her out of that long-ago nightmare into the nightmare of now.

'No! *No! Stop it!*' She found her voice.

She heard something rip. Her skirt, he was tugging it out of the way. Then his weight against her, crushing, suffocating. She couldn't breathe. Air, she needed air. Something soft and damp pushed between her legs.

'Bitch. You fucking bitch. I want to hear you *scream.*'

She felt his whole weight heave against her.

But the thing he was pushing against her remained limp.

In a single, wild instant, Rachel understood. She'd been reprieved. *He can't rape me. He can't get it up*. Hysterical laughter clawed at her gut. She clamped her teeth down hard to keep it in. *Maybe he can't rape me, but he could still hurt me*.

But then David was collapsing. Rolling off her, letting the air come back into her lungs in a good clean rush. And she knew that it was over, as if a taut line had just snapped in two.

Rachel, sitting up, experienced a disoriented moment, as if she were looking at a surrealist painting. A Dalí portrayal of a disheveled, once-handsome man, lying on his back on an oyster carpet amid the melting ice cubes of an overturned drink.

He was weeping, tears trickling out the corners of his eyes, dribbling down into his fashionably long sideburns.

His chest jerking up and down, making an awful, dry hacking sound.

'Can't,' he sobbed, barely coherent, 'can't do it . . . not you . . . not anyone . . . seven years . . . oh Jesus . . . what did you do? What in fucking Christ's name did you do to me that night?' His fiery eyes were fixed on her, wet and glittering with malice. 'Should've killed you, not the kid . . . *I should have killed you.*'

Rachel staggered to her feet. He was sick . . . a sick animal . . . she wouldn't listen.

She made it to the door. This time is opened, easily, swinging out as if guided by an electric eye.

Careful now. The stairs. One step at a time. She pressed her hands against her ears to shut out a voice that was following her; but she couldn't. It seemed to be inside her head, shrieking, *'I'll get you. Somehow. I'll pay you back for what you did to me.'*

Outside, blessedly, she saw a cab with its roof light on.

Once into the back seat, the sobs came, wave after wave.

'Lady, you OK?' the cabbie rasped.

'No,' she moaned.

'Someone hurt you? You want the cops?'

'No, no.'

'Hey, lady, I'm sorry, but I gotta make a living. So where to?'

She gave him her address. Yes, Brian. Just Brian, no-one else. *I need him. Oh God, how I need him.*

Her whole body shook, heaving with sobs, dry hurting ones that seemed hacked from her middle somehow, and then it hit her. *I can't. I can't . . . how can I tell him? If I tell him about tonight, then I have to tell him everything. The abortion, everything, how all these years I've been lying to him.*

She felt herself grow cold all over.

She thought of poor, beaten-up Lila Rodriguez. *So this is why she doesn't fight back. Not fear. Shame. The way I feel now. Dirty. Guilty. As if I deserved what he did to me.*

411

But then she remembered.

There could be a way out of this. There was a chance. She might be pregnant. And then Brian would be so happy. He wouldn't care about the past. She shut her eyes, and imagined him in Central Park proudly pushing one of those big, shiny English carriages, and then gently, ever so gently, him nudging aside the soft blankets inside for those who paused to peek.

But as hard as she tried to picture it, Rachel could not summon a picture of that imaginary baby's face.

Then she sensed a dampness between her legs. A small, insistent cramp in her lower abdomen. She thought, *Oh God, no . . . please . . . no.*

But there could be no mistaking it. Her period.

Music from the radio drifted into the back seat. Bobbie Gentry singing in a smoky voice about the night Billy Joe McAllister jumped off the Tallahatchi Bridge.

Staring out at the blur of headlights, flashing traffic signals, the lighted store windows along Madison Avenue with their haughty, stiffly posed mannequins, Rachel wished she, too, could jump off a bridge.

## 23

Brian looked out at his audience. A hundred or so, he judged offhand. Mostly veterans, a few wives, seated in gray metal folding chairs. Hard faces. Frustrated, angry, weary faces. Faces whose stony expressions said: *There ain't nothing bad that I ain't already seen.*

He straightened, shuffled his index cards. What could they expect from him? Hope? Hope that he somehow might have a key, a cure to whatever was messing up their lives?

Brian felt himself sweating under his denim jacket. *How can I help them?* he asked himself. *I don't even know what's messing up my own life, Rachel and me.*

So many people wanted to hear what he had to say. Nam vets mostly. Men who couldn't find the right words, who needed a voice. A grunt like them who would speak out, tell it like it was. Someone to remind them that what they'd gone through wasn't the end of everything, that there was still good to be had in this world.

*All this flap about Watergate now,* he thought, *the hearings, everyone speculating. Will Nixon confess? It's like the whole country has amnesia. They've forgotten Vietnam ever happened. Dirt swept under the rug. And these men who'd served in combat, just a bunch of unwelcome reminders.*

'When I was growing up,' he began, stepping out from behind the podium, leaning up against it on one elbow, 'the kids in my neighborhood knew every four-letter word in the English language. Spanish, Italian, and Yiddish ones, too. And when we weren't shouting them at each other, we were marking them on the sides of buildings.

413

But there was one dirty word we didn't know. It hadn't been invented back then.' He paused, waiting for the last rustle to die down. Then into the stillness he said: 'Vietnam.'

'Damn straight!' someone yelled from the audience.

Brian smiled. 'You guys know what I'm talking about,' he went on. 'It's a word no-one wants to hear, right? You mention Nam, and they look away. Or they get mad, accuse you of murdering women and babies over there. They say we had no business being there in the first place.' He paused, saw several men nodding. 'So you learn to keep your mouth shut, bottle it up. Maybe they even got you feeling like you're a bad guy. And then you say to yourselves, "Hey, man, that ain't fair. I fought for my country. I'm supposed to be a hero!" He waited a beat, then brought his fist down with a hollow thud on the podium. 'Well, *forget* about being a hero. I'm here to tell you we aren't heroes. We aren't bad guys either. Just men. Men who did what they thought they were supposed to do, and got kicked in the ass for it . . .'

Half an hour later, Brian could see that those hard faces in the audience had cracked. Here and there men were weeping silently, tears running down their scarred faces. The applause gathered slowly, breaking in an angry, almost violent wave of acknowledgement.

*I'm lucky. I wrote about it, got it out of my system. Didn't even care at the time if anyone would ever read it.*

If he could compare the writing of *Double Eagle* to any other experience, Brian thought, it would be like having malaria. The words burning in him like a fever, leaving him at the end of the day exhausted, limp, drenched with sweat. That it had a proper ending, emerged in a form resembling a novel, was thanks to Rachel. She'd read each page as it rolled off the typewriter, offered suggestions, solace, helped shape the hot, angry explosion of words into a real story.

He remembered those days and nights of her residency, when she would arrive home, exhausted, yet somehow still have the energy to go over the pages he'd written that day. He could see her in his mind, a picture precise as a snapshot, Rachel in the plaid seat-sprung sofa in his den, typewritten pages spread over her lap, a pencil clenched in her teeth. Like a kid in school, she absently chewed her pencils, wearing them down to the lead. Yeah, and she didn't look much older than that, with her hair braided, in the big old shirts – his castoffs – she wore over jeans. Seeing her like that, his heart would catch suddenly, squeezing the breath out of him.

Brian remembered other times, too – the three weeks on Fire Island every August, before she became too busy with the clinic. The two of them, racing along the tide line until they tumbled, breathless, on to the warm sand. Sweet slow kisses late at night by a driftwood fire. Making love on sandy sheets, their bodies stinging from too much sun.

*Rachel. God, we were good for each other, weren't we?*

Brian felt a pang. He'd been thinking of their happiness in the past tense.

No, that wasn't true. He loved her now as much as ever. It just wasn't the same. Back then, it was as if they had both inhabited one space, breathed in the same air . . . and now they were living in two separate spheres. He thought of the His and Hers towel set one of his cousins had sent as a wedding present. How they'd laughed at the time. Now it didn't seem so funny. *His and Hers.* Yeah, that just about said it all, didn't it?

Now the auditorium was emptying out, a handful lingering, reluctant to let go, men wanting to be freed of Vietnam, and at the same time wanting to recapture the kick-ass camaraderie they'd had over there, the kind of closeness they didn't get from their wives or with the guys down at the plant.

Snatches of conversation floated toward him as he descended from the speaker's platform.

'One hundred first? No kidding? Me too. Delta Company. You guys fragged our asses at Phu Bai, after Tet . . .'

'. . . dicking around on the ground. Shit, man, we were

415

up in the air taking all the flak. Ever been up in a Slick and had your fucking tail shot out from under you? . . .'

Brian suddenly wished they would all leave. He could feel a headache beginning to bore in at his temples. A dull throbbing in his sinuses. What he wanted most right now was to go home . . . and find Rachel waiting for him there. Fixing supper. Or just hanging out. Waiting for him to walk through the door and take her in his arms . . .

*Get off it, man. She won't be there. She's at the clinic or the hospital. Saving a life probably. And one thing you can be sure of, it ain't yours. You had your turn.*

Brian looked up, and saw a woman moving out from the shadow of the far right aisle. For a crazy split second, he thought it was Rachel. He felt a surge of happiness. She had gone out of her way to meet him. Wonderful. Fantastic.

Then he saw with a stab of disappointment it wasn't Rachel. Too tall. Too dark. And she was wearing a hat that partially shaded her face. Rachel never wore hats. She always said that hats were for tall women; short women looked like mushrooms in them.

This one was no mushroom. A willow, tall, graceful. He watched her as she wound her way around the knots of men, her white cotton skirt fluttering at her golden-skinned calves. Something familiar tugged at him . . .

The woman lifted her chin, and the brim of the hat tilted up. Brian caught sight of her face, and felt his breath suddenly leave him, as if he'd been given a hard whack ·across the chest with a baseball bat.

*Rose. Good Lord. What's she doing here?*

He watched her purposefully cut ahead of three men headed toward him, then she was stretching her hand out, long slim fingers wrapping about his, warm and surprisingly soft. She tipped her head back slightly, a shy smile peeking out from under the brim of her hat. Brian's discomfort was immediately lost in a rush of tenderness.

In his mind he saw a little girl standing alone in a school-yard, scabby knees sticking out from under a dress that was

416

too small, her face pinched with misery. He remembered taking her by the hand, and the smile she had given him then, a look of such radiance it had somehow turned that shy, ugly duckling of a kid into someone so beautiful his breath had gotten all choked up in his throat.

Brian felt that way now, as if he couldn't get enough air in his lungs. 'Rose. What on earth are you doing here?'

'That's a fine way to greet an old friend.' She laughed, and he was relieved to hear the easy ring to it. No, this was not going to be a replay of London. 'I came to see you, of course. Well, to *hear* you, anyway. I wasn't sure I'd make it to the front with all these people. But I'm glad I did. I want to tell you, you were wonderful up there. I always knew you could write, but that . . . well, you really knocked me out.' She sounded sincere.

Suddenly he was very glad she was here. 'Listen, can you wait a few minutes? There are some guys here I still have to talk to. Then what do you say we grab a cup of coffee somewhere? There's a diner up at the corner.'

She hesitated, and for an instant her smile wavered and the light flickered out in her eyes. Then she answered, 'I could use some coffee, actually. I'm working on a brief. I'll probably be at it all night. In fact, I shouldn't even be here. I just couldn't resist when I read the notice in the paper. My place is only a few blocks from here.'

'Great. Give me five minutes.'

Brian turned back toward the group waiting for him by the podium, but a commotion at the far end of the auditorium, near the exit, caught his attention. Two men fighting. He caught the flash of a knife. Holy shit.

Brian felt his own anger rise. Damn. Didn't they *get* it? The war was *over*.

He lunged down the center aisle, half-aware of the milling crowd falling back, metal chairs skittering and clanging into one another. A knot of onlookers had formed around the scufflers, and he plowed into their midst, elbowing them aside. Inside the circle, Brian caught the blur of fists, contorted faces, a checked cowboy shirt torn at the sleeve. A skinny white man, he saw, was pummeling the shit out of a heavyset black.

'Fuck you, man!' cowboy shirt spat. 'I was there in sixty-eight, I saw action in Hue. I ain't no rear echelon motherfucker!'

'Hey, REMF,' the black man snarled, 'I lost a *leg* in the Tet offensive, so don't you be talkin' to *me* 'bout action.'

Brian noticed he was standing at an odd angle, one hip hitched higher than the other – a prosthesis. But, hell, he was game, no, *spoiling* for this.

Cowboy lunged forward, knife in hand, and Brian felt something in his brain click, his combat instincts snapping home like a chambered round. It was all there, just like Nam, the hot surge of adrenaline, the humming in his ears, the sudden loss of gravity.

Brian sprang at Cowboy, catching him by the wrist, locking his other arm behind his back. He heard a grunt of rage, and felt muscles and tendons strain and buck in his grasp . . . then abruptly go slack. The knife clattered to the floor.

Cowboy sagged, then crumpled. Brian caught him in a hard embrace, and felt his chest heave in a wrenched sob.

'It's OK, man,' Brian murmured. 'You don't have to prove anything. It's over. The war's over.'

Brian held him while he sobbed, and saw the others looking on, some with disdain, some in pity, most faces a mixture of both. *We aren't supposed to cry,* Brian thought, *but that's the trouble, isn't it? That's why we fight.*

But, damn it, what do you do when you don't know who or what your enemy is? he wondered, thinking of his marriage, wishing he could deflect whatever was wrong there as simply as he had this guy's knife.

Now Cowboy was drawing away with an embarrassed grunt, and shuffling off toward the exit with a couple of his buddies. The one-legged black man had disappeared.

'Take it easy!' Brian called after him. But Cowboy didn't look up.

Then Brian felt a gentle touch against his shoulder. He

turned, and there was Rose, her black eyes huge and luminous, her expression soft.

'I'd forgotten, how you used to break up all those fights out in the schoolyard,' she said. 'You haven't changed, Brian. One of these days, you're going to hurt yourself trying to keep somebody out of trouble.'

He shrugged. 'These guys . . . it's like they're walking hand grenades. It doesn't take much to pull their pins. They're not really out to hurt anyone.'

'But people get hurt . . . even when you don't mean for them to.' He thought he saw a shadow flit across her handsome face, then she ducked her head quickly, slipping her arm into his. 'Shall we get that coffee now? I think we could both use it.'

A short while later, sitting across from each another in a red vinyl booth at the City Diner on Twenty-third, Rose sipped her coffee, and said, 'I think I understand now . . . what you were talking about tonight . . . about how it is with a lot of these guys. A few months ago, I had a client. He'd killed a man for cutting him off on the Jersey Turnpike. All that rage over such a little thing. It didn't make sense to me then. Now it does.'

Brian had an urge to reach across the table and touch her hand, but he fought it. Steam rose from the white mug in front of her, making her face shimmer like a mirage.

'The anger is only part of it,' he said. 'There's also the guilt. You saw so many of your buddies die over there, and you wonder why *you* got the brass ring. What makes you so special. And when you keep coming up blank on that one, you begin to think maybe you aren't special at all, that maybe you *did* deserve to die.'

'Is that how you felt?'

'For a while. But I'm over it now. It helps a lot to talk about it. I got most of it out of my system when I wrote the book. Listen, you want something to eat with that? A burger, some pie? The blueberry's not bad.'

'No, thanks. I've seen the portions. Trucker size. It'd take me all night and a shovel just to get through one

419

piece.' She smiled, leaning forward slightly. 'Are you working on anything now? Another novel?'

'When I have the time. It's . . .' Brian hesitated. Should he tell her? The new book was based on his own boyhood, growing up in Brooklyn in the fifties. And she was so much a part of it. '. . . too soon to say what it's about. Right now there are more pages in the wastebasket than on my desk.'

'Oh, Brian . . .' She leaned across the table, smiling that radiant smile, lifting him two feet off the seat of the worn leatherette booth. '. . . I *am* happy for you. Really. I guess I also came tonight because I wanted the chance to tell you I'm sorry about what happened in London. It was . . . the shock of seeing you there. I wasn't expecting you. OK, I was angry, hurt, but it never stood in the way of my being proud of you. I always knew you would write a wonderful book someday.'

'You must have had a crystal ball. I wrote some pretty awful ones before this.'

She laughed. 'I remember. Still, bad as they were, you had a certain . . . well, flair. How many heroines get trampled by elephants, gored by a rhinoceros, strangled by a python, and still have energy left over to play badminton?'

'That wasn't as bad as the hero who came back to life in my murder mystery because I forgot I'd killed him in Chapter Two.'

'Face it, Bri. You weren't cut out to fill Mickey Spillane's shoes.'

She started to giggle. Then he caught the bug too, and nearly choked on his coffee. All at once Brian felt the years slip away. He thought of hot summer nights with Rose out on the fire escape, the smell of bagels wafting from the Hot Spot deli on Avenue J. The two of them munching on green grapes, and smoking Pop's Lucky Strikes. And Rose, showing him all those crazy card tricks. Christ, things had been a lot simpler back then. A time before Vietnam, when the thought of reaching thirty seemed as impossible as dying. He wanted this feeling to go on for ever.

'What about children, Bri? I know you always wanted a family . . .'

It was as if he'd been flying up in a swing, carving great swooping arcs in a crayon-blue sky, and suddenly the swing had been snatched out from under him.

'We're trying,' he said. 'No luck so far.'

'I'm sorry.'

'Don't be. It's not hopeless. Just damn frustrating. I wanted a big family. Now I'd settle for one.'

'Your wife . . . I've read about her clinic.' Rose tactfully changed the subject. 'It's wonderful, what she's doing for that neighborhood.'

'She's a dedicated woman.'

In some ways, he thought, Rachel and Rose were two of a kind. They both had a kind of inner fire, but in Rachel it was scattered in every direction. She was out to save the world. Rose's fire was slower, hotter, more focused.

Brian thought of that night in London, the way she'd looked at him. She was looking at him that way now, her dark eyes fixed on him, unwavering, with that quiet Mona Lisa smile he knew so well. Oh Christ, he wished she would stop . . . stop whatever it was that was making him feel something he shouldn't.

'That man, at the party,' he asked. 'Are you going to marry him?'

'Max?' She looked startled, and her cup wobbled as she brought it to her mouth. Some of it splashed on the back of her hand, and she quickly mopped it up with a napkin. Brian saw the jagged white scar creasing her palm, and winced inwardly. 'Now look what I've done. Don't you remember, Bri, how I was always falling off my bike and skinning my knees? Well, I haven't changed a bit. Just last week, I—'

'He's in love with you.'

Her cheeks flushed with color. 'Don't be ridiculous. Max is . . . well, Max. I couldn't get along without him,

421

but we're just . . . oh, this is silly, why are we discussing him?'

'Why not? Aren't you in love with him?'

'No, of course not. Anyway, Max is married.'

'Oh. I see.'

Her flush deepened, an angry mottled red. She dropped her eyes. 'No, you don't. We're not . . . it's not what you think. Max has been a wonderful friend. There was a time . . . a very bad time, after you . . . well, let's just say Max was there for me. I doubt I would have made it through law school, either, if it hadn't been for him.'

Brian thought, *Either you're a very bad liar, or a fool. I saw the way he was looking at you that night. I'd have had to be blind not to.*

It was clear, though, that whatever the truth was, she didn't want to know it. He had no right poking into her business, anyway.

'I'll bet you're a damn good lawyer,' he said. 'I'd like to see you in action one of these days.'

'Don't say that.' She smiled. 'You might get your wish. Max always says that lawyers are like morticians – we all need one sooner or later, but better later than sooner.'

'He sounds like a smart man, your Max. I'd like to meet him one of these days.'

'One of these days,' she echoed, tracing a pattern in the rings of moisture on the stained Formica tabletop.

Brian saw her profile reflected in the plate-glass window. There was something so brave and forlorn in that ghostly image, like a tintype he had of his great-grandmother, Mary Taighe McClanahan, who by the age of twenty had crossed an ocean and lost two babies.

Then Rose straightened, and glanced at her watch. 'Oh God. Look what time it is. I'll be up all night. And I have to be in court first thing in the morning.'

'Now I know why Perry Mason had those bags under his eyes.'

She laughed, and touched his hand briefly, a whisper of

warmth. 'It's been good seeing you like this again, Bri. I mean it. I want us to stay in touch.'

Brian thought, *I should stop this right now. She's still in love with me. I should put an end to it, tell her it's no use. It can't lead anywhere.*

But he couldn't bring himself to say those words. Instead, he felt a crazy, furtive urge to see her again.

'We'll have lunch. Soon. I'll call you.'

'Promise?' She rose to leave, lingering a moment, her eyes searching his.

'Promise, cross my heart, hope to die.'

Sitting there after she'd gone, he remembered the promise he'd made to her years ago. A promise he'd broken. He shouldn't do that to her now, all over again. But now, either way, he'd be hurting her.

*Do you still love her?* Whispered a hard, cool voice inside him.

Did he? The truth was, he didn't know. He would always love her, in one way. But was love ever that simple? One thing and not another? Defining how he felt about Rose would be like trying to cut a piece out of the sky.

Walking into his apartment on East Fifty-second Street, Brian was surprised to find it dark. It was nearly midnight.

'Rachel? You home?' he called softly, switching on the over-head light.

No answer.

The jumbled shadows of the living room assembled instantly into a bright, reassuring picture. *A good place,* Brian thought. He took it in with renewed appreciation, the rumpled chintz sofa with its fallout of plump embroidered cushions, an old pie safe with punched tin doors, a pine table beside it, piled now with bound galleys publishers wanted him to endorse, a sheaf of book reviews sent to him by his editor.

And that crazy Adirondack chair by the fireplace – they'd picked it up in Maine the first summer they were married. Brian smiled, remembering how, after poking

423

around in that old barn full of junk, sneezing and filthy, Rachel had stumbled upon it, nearly hidden behind a pile of rusty bedframes stacked against the wall. She had dragged it out, then walked around and around its hulking carved frame, examining its bear-claw feet and bear-head arms. Then she pronounced, 'It's the most hideously wonderful thing I've ever seen, and if we don't buy it I'm going to kick myself all the way home.' The old farmer who ran the store was no hick, no sir, he wouldn't take less than thirty dollars, practically a fortune in those days, and nearly their entire budget for the weekend. But Rachel had insisted, and they'd lugged it out to the car, roping it into the trunk. Driving home along the Interstate they'd argued about where it would go. Rachel wanted to make it the centerpiece of their living room; he'd thought it would be best hidden off in some dark corner. But when they'd finally gotten it home, and cleaned it up, yes, he'd seen how perfect it was. How unique and wonderful. One of a kind, like Rachel herself.

Brian had that funny little catch in his throat he sometimes got looking at old family snapshots. Pictures of his mother when she was young and slim, before her hair turned gray; pictures of his brothers perched on their tricycles.

*It got away from us somehow,* he thought.

Something brushed against his leg. He bent down and scooped a big yellow and white calico into his arms. 'Hello there, General Custer, holding down the fort for me, were you? Or just out looking for a late-night snack, you old freeloader.' General Custer began to purr loudly, a sound like a rusty bandsaw. Rachel's cat, really, but he was democratic about some things. He would let anyone feed him.

In the kitchen, Brian dug a foil-covered can of cat food from the back of the refrigerator, and forked the smelly mess into Custer's bowl by the radiator. He stood for a moment, looking out the window at the bright necklace of the Queensboro Bridge strung across the river, then noticed the asparagus fern in the basket on the windowsill. It looked yellow, brittle. He felt the soil with his finger. Bone dry.

He filled a water glass at the tap, and dumped it over the fern. This place was beginning to remind him of those apartments locked up for the summer, their occupants off in Nantucket or Fire Island. Except it wasn't summer; it was only April. And they weren't on vacation. He couldn't remember the last time they'd taken even a weekend off.

It even smelled closed up, dry and musty, like a blanket taken out of mothballs.

But now he smelled something else. Smoke. Cigarette smoke. A little alarm tripped inside his head. Rachel used to smoke, but she'd quit years ago.

Brian followed the smell down the hall. He found Rachel curled in the big padded maple rocker by the bed. It was dark in here too, the sodium arc lamps on the street below casting a purplish black-light glow over the room. Brian saw that she wasn't asleep . . . but then she wasn't quite awake, either. The cigarette in her hand was burned down to the filter, and there were ashes scattered over the crocheted afghan lumped about her knees. She was staring off into space, her face white and oddly still, and there was a look on it that caused a rash of goosebumps to crawl up the backs of his arms.

The face of battle fatigue, he recalled.

'Rachel!' he called softly, almost whispering her name. 'Honey?'

He'd never seen her like this. Christ, what had happened?

Then, as if he were a hypnotist and had clapped his hands, she blinked, losing that blank zonked-out expression, and turned to face him.

'Hi,' she said.

Brian went over, dropped a kiss on her forehead. Her hair was damp, as if she'd just washed it. 'I didn't think you were home. You didn't answer.'

'I didn't hear you. Sorry.'

425

Gently, he plucked the smoldering filter from her limp hand, and carried it into the bathroom, flushing it down the toilet. There were no ashtrays in here, only the ones in the living room that they kept for company.

He came back, and sat down on the bed, covered by an Amish quilt they'd picked up in Pennsylvania years ago. In the corner, by the foot of the bed, was an old Shaker cradle. Brian tried to bring back the image of a sleeping baby he'd had when he bought it, that first summer after they'd decided to start trying. But the image wouldn't come. All he saw was the accumulation of odds and ends piled inside it now – old magazines, books he'd started reading but hadn't finished, a pair of Rocksport hiking boots in need of resoling.

'Want to talk about it?' he asked.

She gave a thin, colorless smile. 'Not really. If you don't mind.'

He *did* mind. He felt anger knotting his gut, and his voice tightening as he said, 'OK. We'll skip over the "How was your day, honey?" When did you start smoking again?'

'I haven't. I just felt like having a cigarette. Please, Bri, let's not argue. I'm not up to it tonight.'

She looked like hell, he thought. OK, he wouldn't press. She'd get around to telling him what was wrong. Eventually.

He waited, letting the silence wash over him, listening to the soft whirr of the electric clock on the nightstand, the distant sounds of traffic.

'My period started,' she said at last.

The words dropped like large flat stones into a still lake. He felt his hands curl into fists, a slow anger seeping through him.

Not fair, he thought. Fourteen-year-olds get knocked up in the seats of Chevys their first time. And look at Ma. Seven kids. So why not Rachel? Yeah, a blockage in her tubes. But all those treatments, all that planning, rushing home to make love when her temperature rose. Propping

426

her hips up with a pillow to hold in the precious sperm.

And all for what?

Not Rachel's fault. Not his. Just one of those things. So why did he feel this way? Bitter, angry . . . *cheated* somehow. It hurt to be with her, made him feel raw. He wanted to lash out at her, blame her for other things, being so busy, so caught up in her work he hardly saw her until they tumbled into bed, went through the mechanics of making love.

Right now he hated her for being so goddamn *stoic*. Why didn't she cry, scream, knock a bloody hole in the wall? At least it would be out in the open. Not this great, silent, brooding thing. The Loch Ness monster lurking below the surface of their lives.

Brian stared at the cradle in the corner, tears burning his eyes. He couldn't bear it any longer. He would get rid of it in the morning. Just so he didn't have to go on being reminded.

And then suddenly he felt guilty. Here I am feeling sorry for myself, resenting her. Rachel, Jesus, this has to be much harder on her than it is on me.

'I'm sorry,' he said.

'Me too. This time, I really thought—' She bit her lip. 'Never mind.'

*Talk to me,* he willed. *Jesus, can't you even* talk *about it.*

'Rachel,' he began, tentatively. 'Have you thought any more about what we talked about? About—'

'No,' she cut him off. 'And I don't want to think about it now. I'm not ready to adopt, Bri.'

'We could put in our application. It takes years. In the meantime . . .'

She stiffened, pushing the blanket from her lap, standing up. 'I'm sorry. I can't. Not now. Maybe someday.'

He grabbed her shoulders, gripping her so tightly he could feel her bones beneath the thin fabric of skin and muscle. 'When? You won't even *talk* about it, for Chrissakes!'

'Why does it have to be now? Why can't it be next week, tomorrow even?'

His head was thudding now, a rushing sound in his ears.

'Because, don't you see, our life is nothing *but* tomorrows. Tomorrow you'll take some time off from the clinic. Tomorrow we'll talk. I'm sick of hearing about tomorrow. What happened to today?'

He was trembling, feeling himself almost dangerously out of control.

'*Talk* to me,' he pleaded, pulling her to him, pressing his lips to her forehead. 'Tell me what you're feeling. Tell me to go to hell. Anything. But please, Rachel, don't shut me out.'

Once when he was young, a bird had flown into his room and knocked itself unconscious against the window trying to escape. He had cupped it in his hands, felt it stir to life, warm, quivering, unbearably fragile. That was how Rachel felt now, trembling in his arms.

He ached for her in her pain. But he felt his own frustration even more acutely. He wanted to shake her. *Make* her answer.

Suddenly she tensed, wrenching away. She stared at him for a long moment, her face working, struggling with an anguish that appeared too great for words.

'Brian . . . there's something I . . .' She paused, her face working dreadfully. 'Tonight after I left the hospital . . . a man . . . he attacked me . . .'

Rachel hurt, oh God . . . and all this time he'd been needling her. Brian felt a hot surge of rage. *The bastard. I'll kill him, I'll smash him if he hurt her, oh Christ on the cross* . . . He caught her in his arms, holding her tightly. 'Christ, oh baby, are you OK? Did he hurt you?'

'He . . .' She drew away, and brought a trembling hand to her cheek, as if to make sure she was still there, all in one piece. Then in a strangled whisper, she said, 'No . . . not really. He knocked me down, that's all. I'm OK . . . just kind of shook up.'

'Why didn't you tell me when I first walked in? Jesus, Rachel, the things I said! Why didn't you stop me?'

'I don't know . . . God, I don't know. I was so scared when it happened. He pushed me down, but I got away. Then I just felt so relieved . . . I didn't want to talk about it . . . or even *think* about it.'

'Did you see him? Did you see his face?'

Rachel dropped her eyes, and he could feel a shudder pass through her. 'It was . . . dark,' she muttered. 'No, I didn't see his face.'

'What about the police? Did you report it?'

'I didn't call the police. Brian, I told you, there was nothing to report. He didn't hurt me, and I didn't see his face. Please . . . oh please . . . can't we just forget about it? I don't want to talk about it any more.' Her voice cracked.

Brian saw the white desperation in her face, and felt something hard and frozen inside him give way, like snow crumbling off a mountain ridge. She had never, not in all the years they'd been together, pleaded with him this way. She always seemed so strong . . . so capable. And now he was seeing all those layers of steel stripped back; for the first time he was seeing her naked and vulnerable.

Suddenly he wanted to protect her, heal her somehow. And he wanted to kill whoever had done this.

He drew her gently down on the bed, and held her until her breathing grew quiet, and his arm turned numb. And still he didn't change his position, until he was certain she was fast asleep, and wouldn't wake if he moved. Then, lying on his back, he let his own tears come, sliding silent and hot down his temples, into his hair.

Jesus, if anything had happened to her . . . if she really *had* been hurt. *I don't know what I'd do without her*.

'I love you, baby,' he whispered, turning his head so he could see her. In the amber glow of the street light, her profile stood out against the pillow like a cameo's. He watched a vein throbbing in her smooth temple, and was filled with tenderness.

What had happened to them? Why had she found it so hard to tell him about this? In the beginning, they had told each other everything . . . They had loved each other so much he had at times wondered if it was possible to love *too* much. It was as if his passion for her had somehow stripped away some necessary outer layer, a psychic skin he needed in order to survive. And so, perhaps they had both withdrawn just a bit. That was OK, that was natural.

But now . . .

Brian, smoothing his hand over the sweet curve of her cheek, thought, *We moved too far the other way . . .*

The irony was, he loved her as much as ever. Maybe more.

*But you loved Rose, too,* a sly voice whispered in his head, *and still you lost her.*

Rose . . .

Is loving someone enough? he wondered. Or is God like Stromboli, making us think we're in control of our fate while turning us all into jackasses?

Jesus, he wished he knew. He wished . . . he wished he could make it all turn out all right between them.

*If only she could have a baby,* our *baby.* He felt a stab of loss. He remembered each baby brother his mother had brought home from the hospital; how he and his brothers would all crowd at the window, looking down, watching Pop help Ma out of the cab, a fleecy blue bundle in her arms. Then the miracle of those tiny fingers and toes, and the sweet baby smell filling the whole apartment like the aroma of baking bread.

Brian wished he could talk about it with Rachel. But each time, she turned away, grew silent. Was it so hard for her?

Or – the bitter thought sneaked in – maybe she didn't want a baby as much as he did. Maybe that was the reason she clammed up. Did she care more about that damn clinic than having a family? Or maybe even than about him . . . ?

Brian pushed that thought away, suddenly afraid. If that was true, then what?

Carefully, so as not to disturb her, he rose from the bed, and covered Rachel with the afghan. Yes, let her sleep. She needed it badly. And tomorrow, they would start over. They would talk . . . yes, they would talk.

# 24

Rose yawned, staring at the papers spread out on her kitchen table. The paragraphs from the affidavit and from the Memorandum of Law were all blurred together. She was so tired she couldn't think any more, her mind soggy as that mess of coffee grounds in the sink. She would finish tomorrow, set her alarm, get up at the crack of dawn.

She glanced at the electric clock over the refrigerator. Two A.M. It *was* tomorrow. Mother of God. That left her four hours to sleep. An hour to shower, get dressed, gulp instant coffee, then lay out her argument before she was due in court.

*Who are you kidding?* a sharp voice cut through her drowsiness. *You wouldn't have slept anyway. You'd have lain in bed, staring up, thinking about Brian. Wondering when . . . or if . . . you were going to see him again. Praying it would be soon.*

The phone rang, piercing the stillness.

Rose jumped, thinking automatically, *Something bad.* Marie? Did Pete put her in the hospital this time? Hurt one of the kids? Or is it Nonnie? Clare calling again to say Nonnie was sick?

Then a sweet flash of hope. *Brian? Oh please, God.*

She lunged for the phone on the wall over the butcher-block counter.

'Rose?' a voice asked the instant she picked up. Familiar. Weary.

'Max!' she cried. An instant of disappointment, followed by alarm. Max had never called her this late before. 'What's wrong? Are you OK?'

432

A brief pause, then, 'I'm OK. Look, I'm sorry. I know it's late. Did I wake you?'

'Not a chance. I was working on the Metcalf case. Anyway, it wouldn't matter even if you had. Something's wrong. Or you wouldn't be calling at this hour.'

'This is crazy, I know . . . but can I come up? I'm at a phone booth on the corner.'

'Of course,' she said, not hesitating for even an instant. Max had never asked her for anything. After all he'd done for her.

She knew she wouldn't get to bed at all tonight, that she'd be dead tomorrow in court, and probably look it, too. But so what?

She hung up, noting with dismay that she was wearing her oldest, rattiest terry robe. Oh well, Max had seen her worse than this. Anyway, he wasn't coming up here for a tryst.

But the apartment – dear God – the first time Max would be seeing it, and it looked like Armageddon. She dashed out into the living room, scooping up old coffee mugs, scattered newspapers, clothes tossed over the backs of chairs. When was the last time she'd vacuumed? God knows. Weeks. Since the party Patsy threw when she got the part of Malka in the bus and truck crew of *Fiddler on the Roof*. Now Patsy was in Lexington, Kentucky, or was it Louisville? Either way, Rose had no-one to blame but herself.

She remembered how she'd fallen in love with this place, clutter and all, the first time she'd walked in. The top floor of a brownstone on Twenty-first and Tenth. And so sunny, like a greenhouse, all that light pouring in the tall windows, plants everywhere – hanging from curtain rods, sprouting in mayonnaise jars on windowsills, sitting in huge Mexican clay pots on the floor. The walls a crazy quilt of old playbills and movie posters. Big plump Moroccan leather cushions scattered across the floor in place of a sofa, a huge brass hookah in the corner like something out of *Alice in Wonderland*.

Patsy was an acquaintance of an acquaintance, a singer-dancer-actress. She'd been looking for a roommate to replace her last one, another actress, who'd moved to LA. Rose, feeling hemmed in by her cramped, dark studio on the Lower East Side, had moved in that very week. And now, with Patsy off on the road for a good year, she had the place all to herself.

*Max will see through all this mess, see how wonderful it is,* she told herself. *And he'll certainly understand why I'm too busy to do a lot of cleaning.*

She carried the gathered clothing into the bedroom, and dumped it in the middle of the bed – her wonderful bed, with its antique wrought-iron frame, painted white. The spread was exquisite, hand-woven mohair, the color of a desert sunset. She had spent a fortune on it at a crafts fair, imagining how Brian would love it. How good it would feel to be snuggled with him under its fleecy folds.

Now with a pang of longing, she thought: *Please, God, let Brian come to me. I've waited so long already.*

The shrilling of the door buzzer startled her. Max. She buzzed him in downstairs, and then hurried to unlatch the door.

In the hallway, she looked down and watched him slowly climbing the stairs. As he neared the landing, she saw that he looked pale, rumpled, his eyes bloodshot. His gray suit was badly creased, tie looped at an angle like a hangman's noose.

'Hi,' he said, giving her a crooked grin.

Rose was taken aback, a little horrified even. She had never seen him like this.

'Max, are you *drunk?*'

He met her gaze with an expression of exaggerated sobriety. 'As a matter of fact, no. I tried, I sincerely *tried* to get drunk – the bartender at PJ's can testify to that – but sorry to say, no cigar.'

Then she noticed he was carrying a small zippered overnight bag. 'Going somewhere?' she asked.

'You might say that.' He paused, and took a deep

434

breath. 'I moved out of the house. I was on my way down-town. There's a decent hotel near the office. But I guess I need a friend right now more than a place to sleep. Thanks for letting me come.'

'You know, I kept waiting for the right time to ask you over.' She smiled nervously. 'When things would let up at work. When I got the time to do a thorough cleaning. But it never seemed to happen.'

Stepping inside, his eyes sweeping about the living room, he said, 'Don't change a thing. It's perfect, just the way it is.'

Suddenly, she felt happy and relieved. Then she felt it sinking in; he'd just told her why he was here now. He'd moved out. Left his wife.

She should have been surprised. But she wasn't. Maybe because Max never talked about his marriage. Yes, she had sensed his melancholy, a sort of hidden despair underneath his brisk energy, his quick smile. And she had noticed things, little things – like the way Max unconsciously frowned when he was on the phone with his wife, sometimes pinching the bridge of his nose, as if his head ached. And how his face would light up when his daughter, Mandy, dropped by the office, but would seem tense, even a bit wary, when it was Bernice.

Rose, looking at him, felt the usual response spring to mind, *I'm sorry . . . maybe you can work it out . . . things always look better in the morning.*

But she could see that what Max needed most now was someone who would listen. Not a lot of platitudes. *I've known Max for how long? Years and years. And I know so little about him, really. What goes on inside him.*

Suddenly she wanted to be the kind of friend to Max that he'd been for her.

'Never mind a hotel,' she said. 'There's plenty of room here. You can have Patsy's room. And for heaven's sake, come *in*. Sit down. I'll make you a cup of coffee. You look as if you could use a whole pot.'

'I didn't mean . . . no, I couldn't do that.'

'My coffee isn't as bad as all that.'

435

'You know what I meant. It's sweet of you, Rose. But . . . oh hell, this is my problem. I have to handle it on my own.'

'For once in your life, Max Griffin,' she scolded, 'will you stop being Mr Tough Guy, and let someone help *you* for a change?'

He hesitated, but before he could get another word in, she was sailing past him into the kitchen.

'The back room to your left, you can leave your things in there,' she called over her shoulder. 'Turn on the light so you don't trip on the gym equipment. Patsy's an exercise freak. Keeps me in shape, too. One look at that torture chamber and I'm cured for ever of hot fudge sundae attacks.'

When she returned with the coffee, Max was seated on one of the hassocks, looking ungainly, out of place. Plopped on his rear with his knees sticking up in the air, ankles showing. He reminded her of a tourist in a strange country doing his damnedest to fit in. But she kept from smiling as she squatted beside him, and set the tray between them on the frayed Oriental rug.

'Ever use that thing?' Max asked, pointing at the hookah.

'Lord, no. I'm not even sure what it's for. Hash, I suppose.'

He looked thoughtful. 'I defended this kid for Possession once. Ounce of marijuana. Judge wanted to throw the book at him. I got it knocked down to a misdemeanor. Kid couldn't pay my fee, but he slipped something in my pocket as we were leaving the court-house. A marijuana cigarette, a joint. I brought it home, told Bernice we should smoke it, see what all the hoopla was about. You know what she said? She said she'd just as soon stick her head in the toilet.' A smile started, then faltered, and finally his whole face sagged with misery. 'You wake up one day, after almost twenty years, and realize, we're farther away from each another now even than before we met . . . oh Christ . . . if it weren't for Mandy . . .' He broke off, eyes glassy with unshed tears.

Rose took his hand. 'You don't have to talk about it, you know, unless you feel like it,' she said. 'It's not a requirement for being here.'

436

He looked at her, studying her face. Rose felt a light chill tiptoe up her spine, and remembered the rainy day in London he'd kissed her in the taxi.

She wished he would kiss her now.

*Crazy,* she thought, *I don't love Max . . . not that way.* But, oh, she ached to feel a man's arms about her, his breath hot against her neck, his naked body pressed against hers. It had been so long.

*Stop it,* she told herself, *it's Brian you want, not Max.*

Brian. Oh yes. Tonight, sitting across from him in that diner, she had wanted Brian more than she had ever wanted anything.

Rose felt a hot thickness in her throat. *Oh Jesus, don't let me cry,* she thought. *How selfish, and how unfair. Max didn't come here to console me.*

She poured the coffee into thick hand-turned ceramic mugs, and passed him one, wishing she could find exactly the right thing to say, or do, that would make his pain go away.

Max sat back, cradling his cup in both hands.

*Something is different about her,* he thought. *She's more alive than I've ever seen her. And so beautiful. Christ, she's glowing like . . .*

*Like a woman in love.*

He felt his heart catch inside his chest.

Had she met someone? *Had* she fallen in love?

The thought hurt, especially after what he'd gone through tonight. Saying goodbye to Monkey, who had sobbed, clung to him. The hardest thing he'd ever done. He ached as if part of his body had been physically torn away.

Sure, he knew it would be better in the end. He would see her often. They'd take trips together. He'd get an apartment in the city, a place where she could put her feet up on the sofa, have her friends over for pizza without being afraid if someone spilled Coke on the rug it would give her mother a heart attack. But still it hurt so goddamn much.

Tears stung his eyes like grains of sand. 'I'm sorry,' he

said. 'I'm not very good company right now.'

'Don't apologize.' He felt her hand on his shoulder, warm, comforting.

'It's funny, isn't it? For years, I've been trying to work up the courage to leave . . . and now I feel like such a coward. Like I'm abandoning Mandy. All those Judy Blume books she's always reading, all that teenage angst – well, now she'll be living it. A weekend daughter. God, I love her so much. It hurts to love someone that much.'

'I know.' Rose's dark eyes filled with pain. Then, she smiled. 'I think your daughter is very lucky. I would have given my soul to have had a father like you. Even part time.'

Max now felt the warmth of the coffee mug, as if it were stealing into his fingers, up his arms. Dear, wonderful Rose. She knew exactly the right thing to say.

If only . . .

*Stop it, no*. He'd come here for what she was offering – friendship, a little sympathy. And that's it.

Max pulled a handkerchief from his pocket. Neatly ironed, folded into a perfect triangle. Like a parting shot from Bernice.

He thought of Bernice sitting on the end of the bed watching him pack, dry-eyed, stiff-faced. She had asked only that he leave her a telephone number, 'in case of an emergency.'

With Bernice, every moment of life was an emergency. The straw that broke the camel's back was yesterday, coming home to find Monkey huddled in the bathtub, crying, her hair in wet tangles plastered to her back, the water cold and scummy. 'I'm dirty,' she'd choked. 'Mom says I'm dirty. And it won't wash off. I don't want anyone to touch me ever again.'

Max had felt sour panic rising in his throat. Jesus, was it a boy? Had some boy touched her, forced her to do something? And had Bernice found out about it? Was that what this was all about?

438

He had longed to scoop her up, wrap her up in a towel, as he had when she was little. But seeing her like that, hunched over her bony knees, shivering, miserable, he had known what she needed more than comfort was a little dignity. He brought her a towel, and held it stretched out so she could stand up without his seeing her full nakedness. At fifteen, she was so shy, so self-conscious about her body. And only when she was wrapped up did he hug her, and tell her that nothing could ever make him stop loving her, or think she was dirty.

When Monkey was calmer, he'd gone looking for Bernice.

He'd found her in the laundry room. Hair bound up in a scarf. Hands encased in huge yellow rubber gloves. Face grim. Stuffing clothes, sheets, pillowcases into the washing machine. A huge pile of laundry at her feet, more in the blue plastic basket on top of the dryer.

'What's wrong with Mandy?' he had cried, sick with worry, by now imagining even worse things than a boy her own age touching her – a pervert exposing himself perhaps, an older man coming on to her.

Bernice looked up at him, her face grim.

'She was sent home today with a note from the school nurse. Lice. She's *crawling* with lice.' Her mouth curled in disgust, and she backed away a step, as if she thought he, too, having touched Monkey, might be infected.

Max understood then. How Bernice must have humiliated Mandy, made her feel dirty, unloved. All because of something the poor kid couldn't even help.

He did something then that he'd never done, and never would again.

He slapped Bernice, full across the face.

He felt like a world-class jerk for having hit her. But he felt even more ashamed of all the years he'd wasted staying married to a woman he didn't love, who didn't love him.

He'd stayed with Bernice because of Monkey. Stupid. How he and Bernice felt about each other was hurting

Monkey. No, it was time to get out, salvage what he could for himself and his little girl.

So here he was.

Now panic was rising in him. What if he struck out all over again? What if now that he was free, he didn't stand a chance with Rose after all?

Where would he go from here? Would he become one of those pathetic middle-aged men who grow their sideburns long, buy trendy clothes, hang out in singles bars trying to pick up women half their age?

Then he looked at Rose, at her shining face.

She was the one, the only woman he wanted.

And if there was even the slightest chance, he would wait. However long it took.

Max began feeling calmer, stronger, better than he had all night.

'Thanks,' he said.

'For what? Letting you stay over?' She laughed. 'Tell you the truth, I've been a little lonely since Patsy went away. It'll be fun.'

'Just for a few days,' he reminded her. 'Until I line up something else.'

'Stay as long as you like.' She smiled at him. 'There's just one thing we'd better get straight. I'm not the neatest person in the world, as you've probably noticed. And I don't intend to change just because you're here.'

'Fine with me.' Better than fine. Wonderful.

'Now,' she said. 'I have a confession to make.'

'What's that?'

*She's actually blushing,* he thought.

'Well, since you mentioned it . . . Patsy gave me this joint before she left, sort of a going-away present. It's been sitting in my underwear drawer ever since. I've been too chicken to try it. You want to smoke it with me?'

Max grinned. 'What the hell. Why not?'

Max felt something heavy inside him, an iron weight on his heart, begin to lift. What was this, hope? It had been so long he'd almost forgotten the feeling. A hundred years.

440

Now he thought, *Maybe it isn't too late for me. Maybe I'm not too old to start over.*

A minute later, he was accepting the burning joint Rose was passing over to him, and, holding it to his lips, he drew in with a deep breath the thick, sweet, perfumey smoke.

441

# 25

A sudden blast of music tore through Rachel's head.

She came awake instantly, bolting upright in bed, a sour taste in her mouth. Then she saw. The clock radio. She had set it for six A.M. Now focusing on the glowing red digits, her eyes bleary. Nine-thirty? Oh God. Nancy and Kay would be getting anxious as hell at the clinic. She'd have to hurry, skip her shower, grab something to eat on the way.

Rachel banged the ON-OFF button with the heel of her hand, and Paul McCartney singing 'Rocky Raccoon' was instantly gone. She got out of bed. Her throat felt dry and raw, as if coated with fiberglass, and her temples thumped painfully.

Then the memory of last night came to her, and she sank back on to the mattress, legs weak, hot tears backing up in her throat.

David. Her period. The fight with Brian.

She had *wanted* to tell Brian. Everything. About David, how it was David who had attacked her, not some stranger. And she'd started to . . . but seeing Brian go white with rage . . . dear God, she'd imagined that anger turned on her, the shock and fury he would feel if he knew the whole truth. Why she couldn't get pregnant. And how she had kept it from him all these years. So she had lost her nerve, backed away . . .

Then she noticed Brian's side of the bed was cold, as if he'd left it hours ago. She vaguely remembered him putting her to bed last night, tucking a blanket around her. But where was he now?

'Brian?' she called.

No answer.

She snatched up his pillow, hugging it to her. A chilling thought struck her: if Brian ever left her, she'd wake up every morning to an empty bed.

*But he hasn't left me,* she reminded herself firmly. *He's only slipped out for a few minutes, to go for a walk, or jog, or to pick up something from the store. He didn't want to wake me, he probably figured I needed the extra sleep.*

Then she remembered. Of course. Brian always went out around this time for the morning paper, then he walked down to Levy's for a hot bagel. If she had spent more mornings at home with Brian, instead of always rushing off to the clinic, she'd have known that at once.

Rachel forced herself out of bed, feeling stiff and bruised. A heavy achiness that sent throbbing waves through her lower abdomen. Cramps. As bad as she could remember.

She ducked into the bathroom, and fumbled in the cupboard for a tampon. The box was almost empty, only two left. She had put off buying a new box. She'd been hoping so that she wouldn't need to. Now she thought, *I'm a fool. I'll never get pregnant. I should have told Brian. I should have given him that much. The truth.*

But now as the old misery was welling up in her, she steeled herself against it. *Enough,* she told herself. *You have a job to do, other people to think of besides yourself.*

Rachel scrubbed her face. Then, back in the bedroom, she threw on jeans, a loose sweater. On her way to the door, she moved slowly, cautiously. She still felt so shaky.

*A cup of coffee,* she thought. *Then I'm off. I'll stop at the hospital first, check on Alma. Make sure she's OK. But they would have called me if anything were really wrong.*

Rachel glanced at the phone on the antique schoolroom desk in the front hall, and her stomach did a ninety-degree drop.

Off the hook.

Last night came rushing back. Letting herself in, the

443

phone ringing and ringing while she fumbled with the keys. She'd dashed to get it, thinking it might be Brian. *Praying* it was Brian. But it had been David. His voice snarled with rage. *You fucking bitch . . . you think you can get away from me . . . I'll destroy you . . .*

She had slammed the phone down, then left it off the hook, terrified he might call again.

As Rachel drew closer, she could hear the disconnected phone's muted wailing. *Wah . . . wah . . . wah . . . wah.* Like a baby crying at the other end.

Carefully, as if it were made of glass and might shatter in her hand, she replaced the receiver.

She remembered the promise she'd made to Alma. Her heart bumped up into her throat.

What if something *had* gone wrong?

What if the hospital had tried to reach her and couldn't get through?

*Please, God,* she prayed, *let her be safe. Let the baby be safe.*

Minutes later, she was in a taxi, careening down Second Avenue toward St Bartholomew's.

'. . . eight centimeters. Ninety per cent effaced. And not a peep out of her the whole time. You'd better get in there fast. Looks like she's ready to let fly.'

Rachel, listening, staring at the stout black charge nurse behind the nurse's station, felt as if she had been picked up by a giant, then slammed down. Her thoughts and feelings jumbled, all out of whack.

Alma. In trouble. Bleeding. Fetal distress.

She pulled herself together, forcing her mind back on track.

'Who's with her?' Rachel asked.

'Dr Hardman. He's the resident on call. We *tried* to reach you.' Mavis's brown eyes narrowed, and a defensive tone crept into her voice. 'A number of times, matter of fact. 'Course we didn't *know* it was an emergency. All the girl would say was that she wanted to *talk* to you. She seemed upset, that was all. Didn't say she was hurtin'. So don't anybody go pointing a finger at me—' she snapped a file drawer shut, ' – as if I don't have my hands full without playing mind reader.'

Rachel, heart pounding, took off down the corridor, a fluorescent-lit corridor paved with ancient marbleized green linoleum that crackled beneath her running feet. No time for excuses. Later there'd be all the time in the world for blame and regrets.

She imagined Alma waking up in the middle of the night with labor pains. Terrified, wanting no-one but Dr Rosenthal to deliver her baby. Then, when they told her the doctor couldn't be reached, deciding she would wait. Not tell them that she was in labor . . .

Stupid, childish. But then, Alma *was* a child. A sweet, scared kid who'd wanted to believe her doctor was God.

*And I let her,* Rachel thought, heart aching. *I'm responsible.*

In Delivery Room One, Rachel found a young resident barking orders at a nurse. Hardman. One of the new crop, still wet behind the ears. His white face, glimmering with sweat, alarmed Rachel more than the sight of Alma spread-eagled on the table in lithotomy position, feet up in stirrups, huge belly draped in a sterile blue sheet. It told her he expected trouble. Big trouble.

'Readings?' Rachel asked. She wouldn't bother to scrub. It'd take too much time. From here she could see how much worse the edema had gotten. Alma's feet were swollen, the flesh around her ankles puffed up the size of cantaloupes.

'Not good,' Hardman said. 'Blood pressure one-eighty over one-twenty. I'm getting a tachy reading on the baby, too.'

'Water broken?' she asked, tugging on gloves.

'Just before you got here. I examined her. Head's engaged and ready to drop. Dr Rosenthal, if you're going to section her, I wouldn't wait.' Hardman might be inexperienced, Rachel thought, but he wasn't stupid.

Those were her choices. Vaginal delivery or section. The lady or the tiger. But in this case, behind either door she chose, a tiger lurked.

With Alma's blood pressure up so high, the strain of pushing a baby through the birth canal could cause her to burst a blood vessel. But a C-section, on statistics alone, meant an even greater risk.

Rachel stepped around to the other end of the table, to where Alma's face formed a bright red circle against the white sheet. Contorted with her contraction, dark eyes enormous and bulging. Hypertensive, all right. God in heaven, was she ever.

Then the contraction subsided, and Alma's lips stretched back in a grim, exhausted smile. Her lips were cracked, and the smile brought flecks of blood. She clutched Rachel's hand like someone drowning.

'I knew you'd come,' she panted. 'I waited.'

'You're almost there, kiddo.' Rachel squeezed her hand back, fighting the lump that had risen in her throat. 'Almost to home plate. The main thing is, don't be scared. Just think about the baby. Pretty soon you'll be holding him in your arms.'

'Her,' Alma corrected, 'It's gonna be a girl. I just *know* it. I'm going to name her – ooohhhh, Doctor, it *hurts*. It feels like I'm burning up down there.'

Rachel gestured the nurse over. 'Hold her up like this, almost sitting. That way she won't have to work so hard. You—' she shot a look at Hardman, ' – untie her feet.'

'But, Doctor, it's not proto—'

'I don't care whether it's protocol or not!' she hissed at him. 'Just do it!'

Hardman shot her a doubting look, but unbuckled the leather straps that bound Alma's feet to the heavy metal stirrups. He looked more frightened now than before, a dark half-moon of sweat staining the front of his green surgical cap.

If I were having a baby, Rachel thought, the last position I'd want to be in is flat on my back, feet strapped in stirrups. Easier on the mother this way. More natural.

Now she could sense Alma getting ready to push. Rachel positioned herself, took a good look at the cervix, saw that she was ready, then urged gently, 'OK, sweetie, push now. Give it all you've got.'

Alma screwed her face up and pushed, turning crimson with the effort, a ragged groan tearing from her throat.

The head was coming now, a circle of matted dark hair the size of a quarter, growing bigger, then receding. Rachel reached for the episiotomy scissors, waiting to see if Alma was going to tear. While at the same time listening to Hardman call out the pressure, which was climbing higher, higher. Rachel, anxious, scared, felt her heart beating in great leaping bounds, as if she herself were running a race.

*God, let me win this one,* she prayed.

Then the baby's shoulders presented, as if in answer to her prayer. 'She's in a hurry!' Rachel crowed, gently rotating the bunched shoulders in a forty-five-degree turn, cradling the baby's creamy little head with her other hand.

The rest of the infant came in a slippery rush. 'A boy!' Rachel shouted. She grabbed the cord clamps, clipped them on to the pulsing, turquoise-colored umbilical cord.

Alma was weeping, tears streaming down her face. 'A boy,' she echoed in soft wonderment. 'Can I hold him?'

'Of course you can. He's yours. You can even nurse him if you like.'

Rachel placed the tiny baby, still attached to the cord, in Alma's arms. His little raisin of a face nuzzled her breast, then found her nipple and began to suck.

A wave of sadness swept over Rachel. *I'll never have that. I'll never know what it's like.*

But she'd won the race, that's what counted. The baby was safe. Alma was OK.

She felt strong, jubilant, as if she'd climbed the Matterhorn and planted her flag on top.

A little while later, she was gulping lukewarm coffee in the doctors' lounge. Hardman rushed in, still in his wrinkled, sweat-stained greens. His face looked almost green, too. Before he opened his mouth she knew that something terrible had happened.

'It's Alma Saucedo. She passed out in Recovery. Won't come out of it. They're taking her up to OR now.'

Rachel lurched to her feet, heart leaping. *Dear God,* she thought. *What have I done?*

When she got home, sometime after ten P.M., Brian wasn't there. There was a note stuck to the refrigerator with a butterfly-shaped magnet:

Friend dropped by. We went out for a bite. Don't wait up.
P.S. I fed Custer.

Rachel sagged against the door, resting her forehead on the cool white enamel.

*Come home,* she willed him. *I need you. Now. Right now. I need you now, please. More than ever before.*

But how could she expect that of him? It wasn't fair. How many hundreds of nights had he waited here for her, alone in this apartment? How many times must he have needed her when she wasn't here?

She stared at the note. *A friend. But which friend. He didn't say. He could be anyone. Or she . . .*

This friend, it could be Rose.

Rachel shook off the suspicion. No, ridiculous. Brian was not seeing Rose.

*He loves me. He married me, not her.*

*Yes,* a cool inner voice answered, *but that was a lot of years ago. Suppose since then he's changed his mind? Suppose he regrets his choice?*

Rachel cranked on the faucet, hard, as if the rushing of the water could drown out these thoughts. She filled the kettle, and put it on the stove. A cup of tea would soothe her. Maybe some honey and lemon, the way Mama used to fix it when she was a little girl, sick in bed with a sore throat.

When was the last time she'd talked to Mama? A week,

more? Mama used to call practically every day. But of course lately she'd been so busy herself.

Rachel realized with a start that she missed her mother.

They differed in almost everything, how they lived, thought, dressed, behaved. But Mama was the one person she could count on always to love her, no matter what.

Rachel quickly dialed.

'Rachel!' Sylvie sounded surprised, and thrilled, as if Rachel were a long-lost friend calling from Nairobi. Had it been *that* long? 'Oh, darling, I'm so glad you caught me. I was just on my way out the door.'

'I won't keep you then.' Rachel felt disappointed. Then thought, *Selfish, expecting her to drop everything for me*.

'Don't be silly. It's just another one of those dreary fund-raisers. They won't discover the cure for cancer any sooner if I'm late. Anyway, I would have called you myself, but I've been running from morning to night. I was up at D and D all morning, then this afternoon—'

'D and D?'

'Designers and Decorators showrooms. On Third Avenue. The most wonderful wallpapers and fabrics and – darling, are you all right? You sound a little funny. Are you coming down with something?'

Rachel laughed. 'No. I'm just not used to the new you, that's all.'

'The new me?' Now Sylvie laughed. 'Heavens, that sounds so awful. Like one of these new, super-improved detergents. Have I changed that much?'

'You're—' Rachel struggled to find the right word, 'happier, I guess. Since you started doing this house for Nikos. But I'm glad for you. Honestly.' She was a little jealous, too. She yearned to feel as happy as her mother sounded.

'You don't sound as if you approve, somehow.' A pause. 'Is it Nikos? The fact that we're spending so much time together lately?'

'No, of course not. I like Nikos. You know that. He's

very sweet, and obviously crazy about you. Are you sleeping with him?'

'Rachel!' She heard the hiss of a sharply indrawn breath. Then another sound. Smaller, almost inaudible. The tiniest of chuckles. 'You never get tired of shocking me, do you? And the answer is no. Nikos and I are just friends.'

'Friends sleep together sometimes.'

'Honestly, I just . . . oh dear, there he is now. He's waiting for me downstairs. Did I tell you he was taking me? I have to run now. Was there something special you wanted to talk to me about?'

'No, Mama.' *Nothing special. Just everything.*

Rachel ached at that moment to be a little girl again, to crawl into her mother's lap, to rest her head against the sweet-smelling softness of Mama's chest.

'Well, then . . .'

'Goodbye, Mama. Have fun. Give Nikos a kiss for me.'

When she hung up, the tea kettle was whistling. Rachel snatched it off the burner, and poured some hot water in a mug. She rummaged for a tea bag in the cupboard. Everything smelled stale. When was the last time she'd gone shopping? Or cooked a dinner?

Rachel felt hungry, but she also felt too exhausted to cook anything. She carried her mug into the living room and flicked on the television. Same old thing. Excerpts of the Watergate hearings, which had been broadcast live earlier in the day. John Dean in his horn-rims earnestly leaning forward to speak into the microphone. His wife, Mo, seated behind him, elegant, stoic, her platinum hair screwed into a bun so tight it looked as if only that might be holding her together.

But how could Rachel feel sorry for Mo Dean, so beautiful, so obviously healthy? Even her suffering seemed somehow to have been designed to cast her in the spotlight, to tweak the viewer's heartstrings.

Rachel thought of Alma Saucedo. How many people would ever know or care about her plight? This very minute, lying in a coma upstairs in Neurology. A massive cerebral hemorrhage. She probably would never regain consciousness.

Or hold her baby.

Rachel's stomach tightened.

*My fault. I should never have made that stupid promise. I should have been stronger. Why in God's name did I do that?*

*God, if only Brian would come back,* she thought. *I want him so much. I need him.*

Rachel turned off the television, and went to the back of the apartment. Next to their bedroom was the extra room Brian used as an office. The room they'd planned to use as a nursery. She would wait there until he got back. At least she would feel less alone, surrounded by his things.

She sank into the deep leather chair in front of Brian's desk, staring at his typewriter, an old Smith Corona manual he'd had since college. His lucky typewriter, he called it.

There was a page in it now, half-typed.

And a stack of pages in the metal basket beside the typewriter. His new novel. It looked as if it were about half-finished. How could that be? Hadn't he just started? Or was it just that she hadn't been paying attention?

She felt a pang, remembering how close she and Brian had been while he'd been working on *Double Eagle*. Each day, reading what he'd written, telling him what she thought was good, what seemed like extra words that ought to be cut. Crying with him when the memories raked too close to the bone. Laughing at humor so black no-one who hadn't been there would understand.

So where had all that closeness gone? There had to be at least some of it left, hadn't there?

Rachel then rolled the page out of the typewriter and began to read.

*. . . dark, but he found the ladder, his palms meeting the metal rungs still warm from the sun, which had*

451

*gone down hours ago. There was no moon, but he
could see well enough with all the lighted windows
above and below him. In fact, damned if he couldn't
see all the way to Coney Island, lit up like a Christmas
tree. Laura was waiting, up there in the fort they had
built together when they were kids. The two Luckies
he'd swiped from his father's steel lunch bucket were
nestled in the front pocket of his shirt. One for each of
them. He thought of how it would be. Laura beside
him, her shoulder snuggled against his, her bare legs
stretching out from under a too-small dress, long and
darkly golden as maple syrup. He felt hot, even with the
breeze blowing cool against his neck. And angry with
himself all of a sudden. Maybe it was time he stopped
meeting her up here. Now that he was close enough to
fourteen to suspect that Laura's mouth was made for
more than shooting off wisecracks and smoking Pop's
Luckies . . .*

Rachel let the page drop. She felt cold, as if a hole had
been opened somewhere inside her, and all her blood were
draining out.

*Rose. He's writing this book about* her.

*Why didn't he tell me?*

What did it mean?

Rachel began to shiver. She was afraid. She wondered if
maybe she was even more afraid now than she'd been in
Vietnam.

452

# Part Three

*You may break, you may shatter the vase, if you will,*
*But the scent of roses will hang round it still.*

Thomas Moore

# Part Three

— Thomas Mann

# 26

'No, that one's too dark. Too formal. Now this . . .'
Sylvie selected a wallpaper sample and held it up against
the sheetrock. 'There, you see how it picks up the light
from outside? You almost feel as if you're inside a van
Gogh.'

'Yes,' Nikos nodded thoughtfully. 'I think you are
right. Once again. But you must give me credit for one
thing – knowing what this house needed most.' He turned
to her, smiling, his dark eyes gleaming. 'You.'

Sylvie felt his hand, warm and heavy, on the back of her
neck.

The swatch of William Morris paper with its bright
mustard sunflowers slipped from her fingers and fluttered
to the floor. How quiet it was. The painter's crew had all
gone home, and the late afternoon light filled the room
with a glow like dark wild honey. The ladders propped by
the window cast long, rippling trails of shadow across the
canvas dropcloths on the floor. Outside, she could hear
pigeons murmuring in the rain gutter.

Sylvie, a little frightened, her heart beating fast,
thought, *What shall I do? I want him. But am I ready
to take everything that goes with it? Love, perhaps even
marriage?*

*No. Maybe.*

*No, I don't know. I can't think. Not when he's touching
me like this.*

Warmth spread from Nikos's hand, down her spine,
filling her with slow, warm waves of desire. Dear God,
how wonderful to feel this way again. After so many
years.

455

Sylvie shivered, watching motes of dust eddy within the slanting bars of yellow sunlight. Then she felt a tiny gray speck of dread.

If Nikos knew the truth about Rose, would he still want her? If he knew how she'd lied, denied him what he'd wanted perhaps more than anything?

And her own life? Did she want it to change? All those years, trying to do what was right, what was expected. Now she was doing just as she pleased . . . and it felt nice.

She drew away slightly.

'Wicker,' she said. 'That's how I'd furnish this room. Like a garden, with white wicker furniture, cover the cushions in one of those splashy Japanese fabrics . . . and over there by the window, a basket of dried flowers . . .'

But Nikos wasn't listening, she could see. He was massaging her shoulders now, loosening the knotted muscles with deep, circular strokes of his thumbs.

'Nikos . . .,' she protested weakly, 'you're not paying attention. You hired me to—'

'You're too thin, Sylvie,' he interrupted. 'I can feel your bones. Like a starling.'

'A sparrow,' she corrected with a nervous laugh.

'Do you want me to stop?'

'Yes . . . no . . . oh, it *does* feel good. But, Nikos, I thought you wanted to go over these samples with me. I can tell you what I think will work best, but you have to make the final choice. It's your house, after all.'

'I like what you like.'

His hands moved down the slope of her shoulders, caressing her arms, bare in her short-sleeved summer blouse. She felt a sharp prickling of gooseflesh.

'Nikos . . . this will take *forever* if you don't cooperate.'

'I have been very selfish, keeping you from your other work, no?'

'Other work?'

'Running a bank is not work?' He smiled, the seams in his leathery brown face deepening.

Sylvie understood. He was not joking. Replaying his

456

words in her mind, she seemed to step out of herself, and see herself as Nikos probably saw her. A woman growing stronger with age, rather than weaker. A woman who now had more than the faded remnants of youthful prettiness. A woman with a good head, who was finally learning how to use it.

Yes, the bank *was* her responsibility. Not the way it had been with Gerald. But still, these days when she walked into a board meeting, there was no more clearing of throats, shifting of eyes. The men greeted her with respect, met her gaze directly, listened to her ideas.

God, the fears she had clung to for so many years, like that lumpy old baby blanket that Rachel, until she was two, had dragged everywhere. And now, for the first time in fifty-eight years, Sylvie felt free.

Letting herself fall in love with Nikos could only spoil it all.

'Nikos . . .' Now he was kissing her neck, his lips whispering over her skin, sending delicious shivers through her. Sylvie, sighing, relaxed against him, leaning into the safe cove of his muscular arms and broad chest. She felt so weak. She couldn't stop herself from wanting him.

'I warn you,' he murmured, 'I am a jealous man.'

'And just who is it you're jealous of? Mr Caswell at the bank? He's eighty, but I hear he's pretty spry. And there's Neal, who does my hair, but I suspect he'd prefer it if I were a boy . . .'

'No, no, no. It. This house.' He chuckled softly against her ear. 'You care for it more than for me, I am afraid.'

She considered this. 'You know, I *do* love this house. But not the way you think. It's what I'm *doing* that I love. It's like being an artist in a way, isn't it? This house is a blank canvas. Nikos, do you know something? I always wanted to be a painter. All that time I spent as a kid wandering around in museums. Poor Mama, she had big hopes for me, too. We couldn't afford meat, but she bought me sketchbooks and a watercolor set. And, oh dear, was I terrible. My horses all came out looking like dogs.'

'One might say the same of Picasso's.'

Sylvie swiveled to face him, tilting her chin back so that she was looking directly into his dark eyes. 'I have you to thank, Nikos. For showing me what I *am* good at. If it weren't for you . . .'

'You would have discovered it yourself in time,' he finished for her. 'You are a remarkable woman, Sylvie. You lacked only one thing . . . faith in yourself.'

'Oh, Nikos . . .'

He kissed her, slowly, lightly, with the gentle care of an old friend. Then his kiss deepened, a lover's kiss. Impatient. His strong fingers catching in her hair, pulling it loose from its pins. Sylvie felt it tumbling in a warm flood about her shoulders.

She was caught, achingly, between the desire to hold him, and the desire to run.

Nikos murmured, 'Shall we christen it, my darling Sylvie, this house you love? Here? Now?'

Sylvie knew then what she wanted.

*This,* she thought.

*Exactly as you say. Here. Now. This particular moment, no looking back, or looking ahead. The sun slanting just so. Your lips, your fingertips like brush-strokes against my skin. A painting. Eternal.*

Sylvie took a step back, and slowly began undressing. Blouse first. Six pearl buttons, one for every year it had been since she'd lain with a man, felt a man's hard flesh against hers. Now the skirt. Oh, her fingers were shaking so! Careful not to catch the zipper in the seam. Slip next. Panties. Thank goodness she'd always taken the trouble to buy good ones. Real silk, with lace trim.

Last, she took off her necklace, bracelet, earrings, placing each piece on the dusty windowsill.

And, finally, her ring – an exquisite marquise diamond surrounded by sapphires, at least two hundred years old – the ring Gerald had placed on her finger when they were married.

There. Oh lovely, the sunshine on her naked body, like a

458

giant invisible hand cradling her in its palm. She felt . . . oh, sixteen . . . a young girl on the brink of womanhood.

*Fool. You're past fifty. Wrinkled, and all skin and bones . . . didn't he say so himself? Doesn't he see the purple veins in your legs, the gray in your hair? How can he want you?*

Sylvie stared at Nikos. He had stripped off his khaki slacks and chambray work shirt, and stood naked in the dying sunlight. She saw that he had aged, too, the hair matting his chest, gray, the great slabs of his muscles sliding toward their inevitable decline. *Like an old graying tiger,* she thought. But seeing him like this only made her want him more. And, there, oh dear God, just *look* how he wanted her.

Then he was leading her toward a stack of fresh drop-cloths in the corner of the room. *I'll remember this, always,* Sylvie thought. Each little thing. The roughness of the canvas against my bare skin. The smell of new paint. The cooing of the pigeons outside.

And this man: the light sheen of sweat on his strong brown shoulders. The good earthy smell of him, like new-mown grass, like bread just out of the oven. And, oh, the solidness of him.

She felt him enter her, and the sweetness of the sensation was like coming home after an interminable absence. Her eyes flooded with tears. Over Nikos's shoulder, her blurred gaze caught a flash of sudden brilliance. A last ray of sunlight striking the diamond of her wedding ring on the sill, throwing off a dazzling prism, a bouquet of colors.

*Please understand, my darling Gerald. It's not that I love Nikos more than I loved you . . . not that at all . . . it's me. I am finally beginning to know the person you loved. The woman Nikos loves now . . .*

Then Sylvie cried out. 'Nikos!'

His mouth pressed open against her temple, hot breath spilling through her hair, and she was thirteen again, floating in the deep claw-footed tub that stood in her

459

mother's kitchen, letting the warm water eddy deliciously along her scalp, and down, flowing into other, secret tributaries, the tender nipples of her budding breasts, the soft tendrils of hair waving like seagrass between her thighs.

Nikos filled them all, her secret places . . . Oh God, was there ever such a feeling as this?

Lovely. Sweet.

*Oh Nikos . . . yes . . . yes . . .*

Then it was over, and she lay in his arms, feeling the cool air on her sweat-sticky limbs, and the quick hot pulse of his breath gradually begin to slow.

Nikos squeezed her once, very hard, the muscles in his arms compressing, hard as bricks. And he whispered in her ear in a husky voice, 'Marry me, Sylvie.'

Sylvie felt the beautiful thing they had wrought spring apart, like pearls scattering from a broken necklace.

Why, oh why did everything have to be so complicated?

*I'm afraid,* she thought. *When there's someone to cling to, I'll cling. And I'll grow weak again, like roses unable to stand free, once trained to a trellis.*

'I can't,' she said, easing away, sitting up. The cool air rushed at her. She shivered.

He stared at her, his face puddled in shadow, black eyes pricked with stars. His mouth a wound. 'But why?'

'My daughter . . . ,' she began. Then let the sentence die. What had she been about to say? That it wouldn't be fair to Rachel?

But it wasn't that.

Sylvie brought her hand up, stroked his cheek, sand-papery with the end of the day. And felt her tears come, hard tears, stinging her eyes, driving a spike through her throat.

*I can't marry him. But there is one thing I must do. I must tell him. About Rose. Too long, I've kept it from him.*

Thirty-two years, she'd kept this secret. And now she would have to trust him. He deserved that much, didn't he?

He might hate her, he probably would . . . but at least he'd know . . . and perhaps he could see Rose, from a distance of course . . . learn more about her . . .

He would have to understand, though, how disastrous it would be to approach Rose, to risk having her learn the truth.

But he would see that, wouldn't he? He was intelligent, and sensitive.

'Nikos, my darling, there's something I must tell you . . . something I should have told you a long time ago,' she began, feeling strangely out of breath. 'About my daughter. Our daughter.'

Nikos sat up, his face suddenly tense, alert.

'*Our* daughter,' he breathed. 'Yes, I have always known it was so. Rachel looks nothing like me – she is fair and lovely like you, Sylvie. But in my heart, I have felt she is mine. Oh, my dearest Sylvie, you have no idea how good it is to hear the truth.'

'Not Rachel,' she corrected him.

Nikos was staring at her as if she'd gone mad.

For one brief instant Sylvie thought she *had* gone mad. Why else would she feel this way, as if she were shrinking, growing smaller and smaller?

'Who, then?' he asked in a ragged whisper.

'Her name is Rose.'

Then she told him. Everything. How desperate, how frightened she'd been. That grimy hospital, the fire. The frantic decision that had turned her life into a terrible deception. The years and years of aching and longing to hold her child, even just see her.

Finishing her tale, Sylvie felt beaten, as if she had had to live it all over again, only worse, because now she had to face her crime mirrored in Nikos's incredulous black eyes.

Would he hate her?

Maybe better if he did. Better than more lying, deceiving.

And could he hate her any more than over the years she had hated herself?

Suddenly the room had grown cold; the rich sunlight

461

had retreated, faded into the gray sheetrock. She tried to stand, but her legs were trembling so badly they wouldn't support her. Her vision blurred, like staring through a rain-swept windshield, the room rushing at her.

And now the most incredible thing.

She felt Nikos pulling at her, pulling her against him, his great arms wrapping about her.

His chest heaving, his face wet with tears.

'Oh, Sylvie . . . my poor Sylvie . . .'

*It's like a miracle,* she thought, astonished and grateful.

His words seemed to lift her, and she felt the huge weight of her misery rising, a chunk of it tearing free. He understood. He forgave her. And if he could do that, why then, perhaps she too could begin to forgive herself a little.

Then Nikos, in a voice that seemed to rise from the bottom of the deepest well, said, 'Thank God, thank God. My child. My own daughter. We'll find her, Sylvie. We'll tell her together. It's not too late . . .'

No, *no,* he had misunderstood.

What he was saying . . . it was impossible.

She had to tell him . . . but she couldn't speak. She felt unbearably fragile, as if, with the slightest movement, she might fly apart in a thousand pieces. She wanted to shout, beat at him with her fists. But she couldn't move, couldn't breathe. She could only stare at Nikos in helpless, anguished appeal.

But no, not Nikos's fault, *hers.*

God help her, *she* had given him the power to destroy her, to destroy both her daughters.

462

# 27

The boy in the leather bomber jacket glared across the desk at Rachel.

'Aay, just who d'you think you are? You're telling me about *my* old lady? That's *my* kid she's havin'. So you can just knock off with the Marcus Welby roo-tine. I can take care of Tina just fine.'

'Like hell you can,' Rachel snapped, then sat back in her swivel chair, startled and unnerved.

She told herself, *Stop it, you're supposed to be in control.* Firm but helpful, and focused only on her patient.

But for weeks now Rachel had felt as if she were on a tightrope. Tense, anxious. Jumping at every little thing.

*Well, I* am *on a tightrope,* she reminded herself. *David out to get me, blaming me for Alma, turning everyone at St Bart's against me.*

Yes, that was it. This kid reminded her of David, though they looked nothing alike. Something in his callousness, his utter disregard for his girlfriend's well-being.

Now he was straightening from his slouched position, rising in a gunslinger's wary stance. His black hair falling over his acne-pitted forehead in thick, greasy strands.

Rachel shot to her feet, facing him, nerves humming.

'Look,' she said, 'this is no time to play macho man. Your girlfriend came to see me because she's in trouble. Big trouble. She could lose the baby. So I want you to be straight with me. Are you two doing drugs?'

'No way . . .' His eyes slid away from hers, and he licked his lips.

'I saw the marks on her arms. She said they were old. But they didn't look old to me. what do you say, Angel?'

'I *tol'* you, lady. Tina and me, we don't do drugs.'

Rachel sidled around her desk in its cramped space between the wall and filing cabinet. She came to a stop directly in front of Angel, close enough to smell the rancid odor of cigarettes and stale sweat that clung to him.

'I don't believe you,' she said, staring him down, trying to force him to meet her eyes.

'Well, *fuck* you, then!' A mist of warm spittle struck her face. Angel's features contorted in fury. 'It ain't none of your fuckin' business anyhow!' He advanced on her, eyes narrowing. 'This is *my* turf, lady. You come down here thinkin' you gonna show us spics how it's done. Well, we don't *need* your help.' He grinned as if something as close to profound as he would ever get had suddenly occurred to him. A grin like a broken bottle, the teeth in front crooked and discolored. He took another step until she could feel his breath on her, then reached up, drew one dirty fingernail down her cheek with menacing tenderness. 'Know what I think? I think you're jealous of all those ladies with the big bellies. Yeah. I bet you don't have no man, or no kids neither. You want me to knock you up the way I knocked up Tina?'

Something snapped in Rachel. She was aware only of a high, swift humming in her ears. A film of red washing across her field of vision.

She grabbed a wire basket full of yesterday's mail and flung it in Angel's acne-ravaged face.

Then stepped backwards, horrified at what she'd done.

Angel froze. A letter written on thick blue stationery that had been folded in half had come to roost on one of his shoulders. A snowfall of white carbon flimsies floated gently downward, settling in drifts about the scuffed toes of his motorcycle boots. He wore a look of stupid surprise, eyes glittering with stunned tears.

Rachel stared at him, trembling, her heart banging inside her chest.

*He wouldn't have hurt me,* she thought. *He was just acting tough. Why did I flip out like that?*

464

She watched him whirl, and stalk away, stopping only long enough to flip her the bird before slamming the door. The diploma on the wall crashed to the floor.

Rachel slumped over the desk, and buried her face in her hands. She felt sick to her stomach. *Jesus. You really blew it.*

Suddenly, she knew what really was hurting her. Alma Saucedo. She didn't want that to happen again, another fragile, sick teenager, another potential tragedy.

She thought of her last visit to Alma, seeing the lifeless creature who had once been a pretty, pregnant teenager. Still no improvement, and it had been three months. Her eyes shut. Her thin chest pumping mechanically, the only sounds the thump-wheeze of the respirator, the soft beeping of the cardiac monitor above the bed.

Rachel had fought the urge to kneel at her bed, beg her forgiveness. Yet, going back over it all, step by step, she knew, given the same circumstances, she'd have done all the same things. She had failed Alma only in making a promise she could not keep.

But apologies wouldn't help Alma now.

Besides, it was more than Alma. It was David, too. Guerrilla warfare, sneak attacks, but never an enemy in sight. Her lab reports mysteriously gone. The cold shoulder from nurses who used to be so friendly. Minimal cooperation, but not one bit more, from the residents. And then, David, who put the freeze on whenever she came into sight. Who behind her back was mucking things up for her, then making her look like an idiot when she didn't know what the hell was going on with her own patients.

She had to find a way to stop him. Stand up to David, get him off her back. She needed to tell Brian how he'd tried to rape her. And why.

But as she imagined herself doing it, she began to break into an icy sweat.

*What's wrong with me? I can handle this. I've always believed I could handle anything.*

But lately she felt as if her control were slipping away. Small problems she'd coped with easily now seemed to pull her down like some powerful undertow. Daily, she fought the tide, bucking against it, swimming with all her might. By midafternoon she was exhausted, ready to give up.

Rachel kneeled on the bright Ecuadorian rug in front of her desk and began scooping papers back into the basket. Her hands, she noticed, disgusted with herself, were trembling.

She felt a rush of air as the door swung open, footsteps. She tensed.

'Let me help with that.'

No, only Kay, thank God.

Her friend crouched beside her, scooping up the rest of the litter with a single broad sweep of her stubby hands.

'Good aim, lousy ammunition,' Kay said, rocking back on her heels, a squat, curly-haired gnome in black Chinese pajama pants and white lab coat. Her brown eyes behind their round lenses focused on Rachel. 'I heard the whole thing. You should have hit him with this.' She jumped to her feet, grabbed a paperweight from the desk – a geode, sparkling with amethyst crystals.

'I should have kept my cool, that's what I should have done,' Rachel answered, miserable. 'I feel like a jerk.'

'You're doing it again.' Kay's eyes narrowed.

'What?'

'Beating up on yourself. You're a doctor. Does that mean you always have to be wonderful? You also happen to be a human being. And that entitles you to lose your cool once in a while.' Kay sighed, looking down at the sparkling rock cradled in her hand. 'You know, sometimes I think we never left the front lines. It's just a different war.'

Rachel began straightening the mess of papers. 'Well, I feel like I'm losing this one.'

Kay slipped an arm about her shoulders, and Rachel caught a whiff of patchouli oil. 'Not by a long shot, kiddo.

466

A battle here and there maybe. Listen, I've got the perfect strategy. Take some time off. Grab your gorgeous husband and go off somewhere, one of those quaint inns with stone fireplaces, a four-poster bed. You know, the whole Norman Rockwell scene.'

If only it were that simple, Rachel thought.

'I can't,' she said.

'Why not? Nancy and I can hold the fort down for a few days.'

'It's not fair. You two haven't had a vacation either.'

'Someone's gotta be first. Anyway, if I had a husband – never mind one as sexy as yours – I'd want to stoke the fire once in a while. Never let it be said I stood in the way of life, liberty, and the pursuit of great sex.'

'Thanks, Kay. I'll think about it.'

Kay grinned. 'For an OB, you know surprisingly little about the birds and the bees. It takes more than just "thinking about it," my dear.'

Rachel, grateful to Kay for lifting her spirits, laughed, and thought, *Well, why not?*

To forget, even for a little while, the waiting room full of women with huge bellies, children clinging to their skirts, forget the lunch meeting with HEW to discuss new funding, forget about Alma Saucedo . . .

And most of all, forget about David Sloane.

She watched Kay get up, walk over to the tiny sink wedged in the corner by the window, where a coffee maker and hot plate were set up. Kay rummaged in a shoebox containing a jumble of loose tea bags, packets of sugar and Sweet'n Low, individually wrapped toothpicks, plastic envelopes of duck sauce left over from Chinese take-out. She fished out a foil packet marked *Lipton's,* and tossed it over to Rachel.

'Instant chicken soup,' she said. 'Just add advice, and stir.'

Rachel stiffened, sensing what was coming. 'Why do I get the feeling this is going to hurt?'

'Rachel.' Kay was confronting her, serious now.

'You've got to stop. It's killing you. Sloane is a maniac. But don't you see? You're helping him. It's *your* silence, and he's using it against you.' She paused. 'I didn't want to tell you this, but there's talk among the nurses that Sloane is trying to get your privileges revoked.'

Rachel felt as if she'd been struck. 'The bastard.'

'He should be thrown in jail for what he did to you,' Kay went on, furious. 'And if you hadn't made me promise to keep this a secret I'd march over there right now and announce it over the PA.'

'It's not David I'm afraid of,' Rachel said, 'it's Brian. If he knew . . .' A knock at the door caused her to break off.

It was their secretary, Gloria Fuentes. She looked nervous, standing there, twirling a strand of her long dark hair round her index finger.

'There's someone here, Doctor Rosenthal,' Gloria said. 'A man. He has something for you. It's important, he says.'

A salesman probably, from one of the drug companies, she thought. They all think everything they're peddling is going to save the world.

'All right,' she said and sighed. 'Show him in.'

He was very fat. You could see a bit of his undershirt between the straining buttons of his drip-dry shirt. And he wore a yarmulke, embroidered in gold with the name 'Dave.' Not a salesman, she thought. Maybe from some poor yeshiva, wanting a donation.

'You Dr Rosenthal?' he asked with a heavy Brooklyn accent.

She nodded.

He handed her a long thin envelope, then turned and disappeared through the door.

Rachel was suddenly afraid. What was in this envelope? She felt an urge to tear it up unopened, flush it down the toilet in a million tiny pieces.

But she opened it.

Her eyes skipped across the oddly typed document. County of New York. State of New York. Hector and

468

Bonita Saucedo, Plaintiffs, vs Dr Rachel Rosenthal, Defendant.

Alma's parents were suing her for malpractice.

Rachel felt dizzy, a terrible hot ache fanning up through her rib cage.

She squeezed her eyes shut, and saw pinpricks of light across the insides of her eyelids.

*David,* she thought. *It's him. He's behind this. I know it. He's got to be.*

*And he won't stop, he won't let up until it's over, until he's got me flat on my back, just like before.*

*So he can cut the life out of me all over again.*

## 28

The case of *Tyler v Krupnik* was unusual, all right. Rose had suspected it would be when last Thursday Bernie Stendahl had given her the file with a broad wink, along with the red-flag words, 'Have fun.'

Now, ushering Shimon Krupnik into her tiny office off the conference room, Rose wondered how on earth she was going to deal with this guy. Krupnik looked like someone out of a time machine, a visitor from a nineteenth-century ghetto. Eighty degrees outside, and he was wearing a long, black double-breasted overcoat, and a heavy black felt hat. His face was pale, his eyes molelike, behind thick rimless spectacles, as if he had lived all his life in a tunnel. Two long curls spiraled from each temple, and a moth-eaten-looking black beard only partly obscured his pasty cheeks. *Holy Jesus,* she thought, *what do I say to him?*

She extended her hand. 'It's so nice to meet you, Mr Krupnik. Mr Stendahl sends his apologies. He couldn't be here, I'm afraid.'

*Something's wrong,* she thought, feeling uneasy. Krupnik was standing there, staring at her hand as if she were holding out a dead snake.

He mumbled something like 'My pleasure,' but still didn't take her hand.

Then she remembered. A Jewish friend had once told her. Hasidic men don't touch women other than their wives. Ever.

Warmth rose in her cheeks, and she quickly dropped her hand, smoothing her skirt with it, as if she hadn't noticed. She asked, 'Can I get you a cup of coffee?'

He shook his head, and she caught the slight startled

uplift of his eyebrows. Then she realized. Of course. Unclean cups, not kosher. *Good Lord, I've hardly begun . . . and already two strikes.*

'Why don't you have a seat,' she said, pointing to the loveseat covered in faded green velveteen that matched the rows of leather spines lining the bookshelves above it.

Rose, watching him settle stiffly on the corner of one couch cushion, found herself remembering the Hasidic Jews she used to see as a child. Otherworldly men hurrying along Avenue J, black coats flapping, staring straight ahead, avoiding the eyes of any female. Once, passing a group of them, Nonnie had poked Rose and hissed furiously, 'They wear those hats to hide their horns. It's the mark of the devil. To remind us they killed our Lord Jesus Christ, killed Him in cold blood like He was a dog.'

This was the first time she'd ever spoken to a Hasid, and she was nervous. She wished Max were there. He'd know what to say.

Thinking of Max somehow calmed her. She pictured him uncorking a bottle of chilled Chardonnay at the end of a day, knowing exactly what she needed. Even music. Vivaldi, John Renbourne, Cat Stevens if her nerves were ragged; the Moody Blues, Led Zeppelin, Beethoven's Ninth, if she felt like a pick-me-up.

Two days, he'd said. And now it was two months. He'd been looking at apartments, but none of them seemed right. And the truth was, she was getting used to having him around. No, more than that, she *liked* it.

Rose, forcing her attention back to her client, looked down at the file in front of her.

Krupnik was accused of attacking Tyler, who operated a news kiosk under the Kings Highway BMT trestle. Tyler claimed to police that Krupnik, enraged at seeing a Zionist newspaper displayed – the Satmyr sect, it seemed, was violently opposed to Zionism on the grounds that God Himself had not designated Israel as the Holy Land – demanded Tyler remove it. Tyler refused, at which point Krupnik allegedly knocked Tyler to the ground, and hit him repeatedly. Bystanders gave chase, apprehending a man believed to be the perpetrator. Tyler identified him as such.

Krupnik denied everything. He'd been a block away from that kiosk, locking up his print shop. People rushed at him, grabbing him from behind. The red stains on his hands were red ink, not blood. Nevertheless, he was arrested. But charges were dismissed for insufficient evidence. No eyewitnesses other than Tyler could swear that Krupnik was the perpetrator.

Tyler then filed a civil suit, demanding three hundred thousand dollars in damages.

'Will I have to testify?' Krupnik blurted, his long white fingers twisting nervously together in his lap.

Rose smiled at him, hoping to put him at ease. Maybe he wasn't too different at that, she thought. Everyone was nervous facing a judge and jury.

'Not necessarily,' she told him. 'We have witnesses. But it would help. Aside from the facts of the case itself, a jury will want to know what sort of person you are, what kind of life you lead.' She paused, remembering Nonnie's horrible remark, and how suspicious, even fearful, people were of anyone different. 'Mr Krupnik, are you married?'

He blinked twice, his fingers twisting more relentlessly than ever. 'I live with my mother.'

'How old are you, Mr Krupnik?'

'Forty-three next month, the Holy One willing.'

'Any hobbies? You know, like bird-watching or, say, photography?'

He didn't answer, just stared at her incredulously.

*OK,* she thought, *dumb of me to ask.* But charity work, maybe. Selling raffles for muscular dystrophy, or reading books to the blind. That would impress a jury.

'Let me put it this way, Mr Krupnik, what do you do with your free time?'

'I study the Talmud.' This time he didn't hesitate. 'I read the Torah, the Five Books of Moses. I go to shul.' His tone was one of innocent arrogance. Was there anything else of any real importance? it asked.

472

Rose was getting worried. *If I don't think of something else,* she despaired, *the jury* will *start believing he's got a pair of horns under that hat.*

But what?

Then she remembered. A case she'd read about years ago. A black man on trial for rape. And in a courtroom packed with black faces, the victim, a white woman, had not been able to pick out the defendant.

'I have an idea,' Rose said, growing excited. 'It's a long shot, but it could work.'

'Yeah? So?'

'When was the last time you saw Mr Tyler?' she asked. 'The last time you were actually face to face with him?'

Krupnik thought a moment, his brows drawn together. 'Last October, it was. In court. Since then, only through the lawyers.'

Rose smiled. *Better and better,* she thought.

'Mr Krupnik, how many of your friends and acquaintances do you think you could gather together for the trial? I'll need at least twenty-five, more if possible.'

Krupnik stared at her, mystified. Then she told him of her plan, and a smile transformed his pale, solemn face, giving it the soft radiance of a burning candle.

'*Alevai,*' he exclaimed softly. 'I'll get them, sure. A hundred if you like. More, even.'

Ten days later, Rose stood on the steps of State Supreme Court in Foley Square and watched a private yellow bus pull up. Forty or so men in long black coats, black hats, black beards, and dangling forelocks filed out.

When the Hasidim had all seated themselves quietly in the courtroom, Rose addressed the bench. 'Your Honor, I have a rather unusual request. In lieu of an opening statement, I'd like to call upon Mr Tyler.'

Judge Henry, a black man with a snow-white Afro, frowned, and Rose's heart sank. If he refused . . .

'You'll have to be a bit more specific, Miss Santini. What exactly do you have in mind?'

'I'd like to have Mr Tyler identify my client, Mr Krupnik.'

473

There was a stir, and when Rose looked over she saw the bored-looking jurors straightening, coming alive. Good. Now, please, if only it worked.

The judge nodded, and she saw that he, too, was intrigued. Sure, who wouldn't prefer a bit of theater to one more barrage of words? Only the plaintiff, stiff and red-faced as he mounted the stand, looked outraged. He also looked as if he might have tossed back a few shots of eighty proof before showing up here.

'Mr Tyler,' she said coolly, 'can you identify the man who attacked you on the evening of October the twenty-first? Is he in this courtroom?'

'Well, of course I can,' he said. He pointed a stubby finger at the bearded black-garbed man seated at the defense counsel's table.

'Will you please stand up, Mr Krupnik?' Rose called out.

There was a hushed moment as all eyes turned to the man seated serenely at the counsel table.

Then Rose watched as, from the crowded spectators' bench two rows behind, Shimon Krupnik rose, slowly, majestically, the curls bobbing at his ears giving the scene an unexpected touch of whimsy. He broke into a grin.

Rose felt a surge of triumph. And she thought: *If only Brian could have been here. Seen this. Better than any of those card tricks I used to show him when we were kids.*

Ten minutes later, after her opponent's harangue and the judge's grinning dismissal, she was making her way to the back of the courtroom, feeling ten feet tall, a queen bestowing blessings, smiling at a cluster of Hasidim who nodded in appreciation as she passed, not minding for once the jostling of the courthouse hangers-on crowding the doorway.

Then she glimpsed a silver-haired man stepping forward, taking her elbow, steering her through the tall paneled door as he opened it for her.

Pausing in the corridor outside to thank him, she saw that he was older than she would have guessed from his firm touch. Over sixty. But still handsome, virile, in a darkly foreign way. His suit looked expensive, though he

474

carried his jacket slung over one shoulder, and the sleeves of his crisp white shirt rolled up, showing thick forearms matted with dark hair.

What was remarkable, she thought, was the way he was staring at her. *Studying* her almost, as if she were a painting in a museum, or a rare form of wildlife.

Abruptly, startling her, he'd grasped her hand in a firm, warm clasp.

'May I congratulate you, Miss Santini.' His voice was deep, and carried a faint accent she couldn't place. 'That was quite a performance. I was most impressed.'

'Thank you,' she said and laughed. 'It was a gamble. I could just as easily have ended up looking like the world's biggest fool.'

'No.' He shook his head, smiling. 'Never that.'

Why was he *staring* at her like that? He was making her nervous.

'I don't believe I know you,' she said, withdrawing her hand.

'Nikos Alexandros,' he introduced himself.

'Have we met before? I'm afraid I don't recall . . .'

A look of sadness that was almost pain crossed his face, and he said, 'I wish it were so . . . but, no.' Then, with a ghost of a smile, he added, 'Goodbye, Rose. And good luck. I hope we will meet again.'

It didn't strike her until she was outside, descending the wide stone steps of the courthouse. *He called me Rose. Strange. How did he know my first name?*

The puzzle glanced like a skipping stone across the surface of her mind, then sank.

As Rose hurried along the crowded sidewalk, scanning the late afternoon frenzy of Centre Street for a taxi with its overhead light on, she thought of the evening ahead.

A good bottle of wine, dinner with Max. Why not make it a celebration? Wear that white silk jersey I bought at Bloomingdale's last week. And flowers. Heavenly smelling lilacs for every room.

Out of the corner of her eye, she noticed three men turn

475

to stare as she dashed for the taxi that had swerved over to the curb twenty yards ahead. Flinging her briefcase into the back seat and climbing in after it, she smiled, thinking how she'd changed. Not so long ago she would have thought those men were staring because something was wrong with her, a stain on her skirt, a run in her stocking. Now she knew it was because they found her attractive.

And for the first time, she *felt* attractive. Even pretty. Last night after dinner she and Max had listened to some old Glenn Miller records they'd bought at a flea market last Sunday. Then Max showed her how to do the Lindy, his broad hands clasping her firmly about the waist, spinning her, dipping her, finally tumbling her on to the sofa, sweaty, hot, out of breath, giggling like a teenager. Rose couldn't think when she'd last had so much fun, or felt so happy. How natural then, this morning when she went to her closet to pick out what to wear, that she should push aside the businesslike, earth-colored suits she usually wore, and choose something bright, feminine, this pretty paisley skirt and pale blue silk blouse.

Rose gave the driver her address, and settled back, trying to find a comfortable spot on the caved-in seat. She couldn't wait to get home.

'Moo-shu pork.' Rose passed Max a carton, then peered into another. 'And I can't even begin to guess what's in this one. Looks like what was left of poor Mrs Lindquist's cat after the garbage truck ran over it.'

'Pressed duck,' Max replied. 'It was on special.' He pulled a bottle from the bag. 'This too. I thought we should celebrate a little.'

Rose peered at the label. 'Perrier-Jouet! Oh, Max, even *I* know how expensive that is. You shouldn't have.'

'A bonus. For today.' He wrapped the bottle in a dishtowel, and began easing out the cork. 'I don't think that P.T. Barnum could have done you one better.'

Rose felt a flush of warmth, and thought, *I want him to be proud of me. I owe him so much.*

476

She watched him pull the cork free with a discreet pop, and pour foaming champagne into two long-stemmed glasses. He'd just come from the shower, face rosy, hair damp, curling over the back of his collar like a kid's. Bare-chested and barefoot, wearing only a pair of soft, faded jeans. He looked leaner, younger somehow, and not just because he'd lost weight. It was . . . as if he'd gotten brighter somehow. Like all the lights being switched on in a room that had been half-lit.

She wondered suddenly if that was how other women must see him. Vital, handsome, sexy. She felt a prick of envy at the thought of Max kissing some beautiful, sexy client – say, a woman coming in for a divorce.

*And soon he'll be leaving,* she thought.

She didn't want him to go, Rose realized with a rush of sadness. The apartment would seem so empty without him. She'd miss evenings like this one, fixing dinner, discussing the day over a glass of wine. They had a routine, like a married couple in some ways. Taking the subway to work together, and sometimes home, too. But if one worked late, the other got dinner. She took a shower in the morning. He took his at night. They even took turns with the laundry.

Everything a couple did, except go to bed together.

Last night, dancing with Max, feeling deliciously warm and sexy in his arms, she'd thought briefly, *Why not?* They were friends, they liked each other. And it had been so long . . . so very long. Wasn't this the Age of Aquarius, Free Love, no-strings-attached sex?

But going to bed with Max would risk ruining her one wonderful friendship. And for what? Any day now Max would be moving out, meeting other women, maybe even falling in love.

*And I'll be here still, dreaming about Brian, lonelier than ever. No. Leave it alone. Better this way.*

Rose took a sip from the foaming glass Max thrust in her hand. 'Mmm. Nice.'

'Don't let it go to your head.'

477

'What? The champagne or winning the dismissal?'

'Champagne. Knowing you, I'll bet you skipped lunch.'

'Too excited to eat, I guess. Anyway, I promise not to be a cheap drunk. I couldn't. Not at a dollar a sip.'

He clinked his glass against hers. 'Here's to all your future victories, may they be many and . . . oh, shit, excuse me, the duck. I stuck it under the broiler to heat it up.' Smoke curled up from the corners of the oven, and Rose smelled something that reminded her unpleasantly of the refineries along the Jersey Turnpike. Max lunged for it, wrenched the door open, and yanked out a pan containing the charred remains of their pressed duck. He stared down at it mournfully.

'Never mind,' Rose said. 'I wasn't hungry anyway. I'll be more than satisfied with the moo-shu.'

Rose drank her wine, and poured herself another one. A pleasant glow was seeping through her, as if warm bath-water were circulating in her veins instead of blood. Her head felt very light, and she seemed to be moving in slow motion, an eternity elapsing between the time she reached for her glass and her fingers closed about its sticky stem.

*OK, so I'm a little drunk. But it's nice. Can't remember the last time I got high. Years and years. Brian and I? Yes. Up on the roof. That jug of Red Mountain. Well, here's to you, Brian, and the lady you're drinking with now . . .*

A sharp pain, like a sliver of glass, wedged itself into her heart, and her throat constricted as she was swallowing. Bubbles rushed up her nose, bringing tears to her eyes.

Rose gasped and began coughing uncontrollably. Max thumped her on the back. Finally it was over. She looked up at him, saw the concern in his face, and suddenly she was winding her arms about him, pressing her cheek to the solid warmth of his bare chest.

'If you were trying to get me drunk, it worked,' she muttered. 'Promise me one thing. If I pass out, will you put me to bed?'

'Sure. What are friends for?'

His hand came to rest on the top of her head, lightly,

478

smoothing over the curve of her skull. Rose shivered, feeling the brush of his fingers through her hair, along the back of her neck. Nice. So nice to be touched . . .

Abruptly, Max pulled away. He moved over to the sink, and cranked the water on. Rose watched it shoot up in a dirty geyser as it hit the blackened pan the duck had been in, splattering the countertop with greasy droplets.

'Max?' she called.

Something was wrong. He was moving in a tight, jerky way, as if he were angry. The muscles in his shoulders bunched up. Then he turned, and she saw. Heat crawled into her cheeks. She felt stupid, clumsy.

Max wanted her.

Of course. He hadn't been with a woman . . . at least not that she knew of . . . for months. How could she have been so thoughtless? Slopping around mornings in her pajamas. Hardly stopping to think when she dashed out to get the phone, half-dressed. And now . . . God, what must he think of her?

A locker-room word from high school popped into her head. Cock tease. Crude, but descriptive. It struck her as ridiculous, and funny too, thinking of Rose Santini as that, an overgrown cock tease.

She felt a giggle work its way up her throat, and bit down hard on her lip. 'Oh, Max,' she said and sighed. 'Let's go to bed. Right now. Never mind about dinner. I may be drunk, but not so drunk I don't know what's good for me.'

Rose got up a little unsteadily, and went to him. She looped her arms around his neck.

'Rose . . .,' he began, his voice hoarse.

'I know what I'm doing, if that's what you're thinking,' she said, smiling a little. 'I won't be sorry in the morning. As long as we're still friends. OK?'

He nodded, and his Adam's apple worked. Then with a groan, he pulled her to him, kissing her. Deeply. With so much hunger, Rose felt, quite suddenly, as if she'd been plucked inside out, her head spinning. Dear God. Who would have guessed? Max . . .

479

*Wonderful, oh God, how wonderful,* she thought as he undressed her in the bedroom. Kneeling to pull her socks off last, kissing her feet as he did so, running his tongue softly along the arch. Then turning her over on to her stomach on the big brass bed, and doing the same to the backs of her knees, and the tender crescents of flesh under each buttock.

Rose shivered with pleasure, each sensation a new and unexpected gift to be unwrapped slowly, savored. A box of fine chocolates to be nibbled one by one. What heaven, to make such love without being in love, without the *Sturm und Drang.*

Gently, he urged her on to her back, his head moving down between her legs.

*Oh dear God . . .*

She was coming. Swiftly, uncontrollably, like tumbling over and over down a hot, slippery sand dune. Her legs twined about his chest, fingers buried in his hair. *Jesus . . . sweet Jesus . . . Max . . . how did you know to do this wonderful thing?*

And when it was over, she was left gasping, glowing, hungry for more. 'Inside me,' she moaned. 'Hurry.'

Even better like this. Better than the silvery trills he created with this tongue. Solid, deep. Hips arching, falling, the muscular power in his arms and legs flowing into her like an electric charge. So different from Brian, long and loose-limbed. The difference between a long-distance runner and a prizefighter.

*No,* she told herself, *don't think about Brian. It's not fair. Not fair. Even if you're not in love with Max. You have no right bringing Brian into this.*

Max's breath was coming faster, coming in hard little gusts against her ear.

'Rose . . . I can't hold . . . oh Christ . . .'

'Yes, Max, *yes.*'

She felt him shoot forth, and she was carried along too. Her body singing with the exquisite pleasure of it. Again and again and again . . .

Afterwards, she collapsed, unable to move, her heart galloping in her chest. Wrapped in the warm slippery cocoon of sweat created by their bodies. Listening to the gradual slowing of Max's breath against her ear.

'My God, Max, my God,' she whispered, stunned.

And in that instant, she felt a piercing sadness. She wished so that she were in love with him.

Hours later, sleepy, sated, Rose snuggled close to Max, thinking how even after lovemaking she liked having him in her bed. Other men she'd slept with in the past, she had enjoyed, but then after a while she had started to feel restless, impatient for them to go so she could reclaim her solitary bed. But with Max, she felt cozy, in no hurry for him to leave her side.

She was on the verge of drifting off to sleep when she heard him remark casually, 'I got a call today from Stu Miller at Prudential. One of his policyholders is being sued . . . a doctor, someone you know, in fact . . . Rachel Rosenthal.'

Rose felt as if he'd dumped a bucket of icy water over her, every nerve shocked awake, her heart racing. Rachel . . . Brian's wife . . .

She rolled on to her back, avoiding Max's eyes. She didn't want Max to guess her feelings; they were too private, too painful.

'Is that so?' She forced a yawn. 'Too bad. What's it about?'

'Don't know all the details yet. I'm having a meeting with Stu about it tomorrow morning. He wants me to handle it. Thought you might like to join me. Should be interesting.'

Dammit, why was Max doing this to her? He had to know how difficult it would be.

'I don't know,' she said, careful to keep her voice neutral. 'I'll have to check my calendar.'

But her mind was racing, leaping ahead. In her imagination, she was already placing herself at that meeting. Seeing Rachel, and maybe Brian – would Brian be there, too?

481

Rachel would be upset, and Brian with his arm around her, consoling her. *God, no, how could I stand that? After everything I've already been through?*

No, dammit, feeling sorry for Rachel wasn't on her agenda.

But then suddenly she was imagining it a different way. Couldn't she merely *pretend* to feel sorry for Rachel, to want to help her? And maybe in the end she really could help, with Max so tied up these days on that Boston Corp case. And then how noble she would seem! How forgiving!

And wouldn't Brian be grateful? Oh yes. She could see it now . . . how they might get together, for coffee or lunch . . . united in the same cause. At first they would talk only of Rachel. But later, the talk would turn to other things . . . they would laugh together, remembering when they had loved each other . . . .

It struck Rose with stunning force: a link. Yes, that's what it would be. A link between her and Brian.

But Max? What would she tell him? This was some kind of test, had to be. Max was too damn sharp, he never missed a thing. He had to suspect what this might mean to her. Damn him, he was holding this out to her like bait. If she showed up at that meeting tomorrow, he'd know she was still interested in Brian somehow.

But why should he care? That's what she didn't understand. Rose turned it over in her mind. Well, OK, she'd take the bait . . . but on her own terms, not his.

Slowly, she rolled over to face Max, charged, crackling with excitement, as if she could stay up all night and not feel the least bit tired.

'Never mind my calendar,' she told him, 'I'll make room.'

## 29

Rachel shifted impatiently on the low-slung white couch in
the lawyers' waiting room. For the third or fourth time she
looked at her watch. Almost eleven, and the appointment
was for ten-thirty. If only she could spring up, and walk
right out of here.

The place was super-air-conditioned, cold as Antarc-
tica, but nonetheless she was perspiring. Her armpits
soggy, her pantyhose sticking to the backs of her thighs.
So long since she'd even worn pantyhose, much less a
business suit. And God, why had she dressed up? Who
was she trying to impress?

*Five more minutes,* she told herself. *Then I'll make
some excuse to the receptionist, and duck out. I probably
have a screw loose, coming here in the first place. Of all
people, Rose Santini as my lawyer!*

When the insurance agent first told her the name, she'd
laughed out loud, couldn't help it. God, the irony of
it. Fate, like a hand pushing at her from behind, shoving
her in Rose's direction. God, why Rose, of all people?
Of all the thousands of lawyers in this city, why
*her?*

Was that why she'd come? Curiosity? No, it was more
than that, something stronger. Rachel had had to come, to
see her, to know her. This woman Brian once had loved . . .
and might still.

One visit, she'd told herself in the taxi on her way over.
That was all. After all, the appointment had already been
made. She would just see Rose, talk to her, then insist
Prudential find her another lawyer.

But coming here like a spy, Jesus, how sneaky. She felt a

little ashamed. And foolish, too. What could she possibly hope to accomplish?

She stood up, and strode across the thick oat-colored carpet to the long wood and chrome desk in the corner. A young tanned receptionist with a mane of streaky blond hair and long red fingernails looked up from her IBM Selectric.

'Shouldn't be too much longer,' the young woman told her, offering a twinkly smile.

'It's just . . . well, I'm afraid I can't wait any longer,' Rachel told her. 'You see, I have to be back at—'

Rachel heard the click of a door opening, and felt a rush of cool air against the backs of her sticky legs. Then a voice, low and musical.

'I'm sorry. I had an overseas call. I hope I haven't kept you waiting too long.'

Rachel turned, and found herself facing a tall woman who stood in the doorway that connected the reception area to the inner offices.

Rose.

Rachel, staring into those dark, proud eyes, felt a jolt of recognition. She took in the mass of black curls caught up with silver combs. The plain black cotton shift and color-ful scarf draped artistically about Rose's angular shoulders, the hammered gold bracelet clasped about her dusky-skinned right forearm just below the elbow. And – how odd – a *single* earring, like a pirate's. A ruby in the shape of a teardrop, set in gold, which dangled from her left ear, winking and shimmering in the fluorescent lights that shone from the ceiling.

A cold gust of fear swept through Rachel, and she thought, *She's beautiful, stunning. Why didn't I see it, that night in London? No wonder Brian can't forget her.*

She felt dwarfed beside Rose, diminished somehow. Even in her best summer suit, a Galanos, raw silk woven into a cloud of sienna hues. But she herself was limp, like a plant someone forgot to water, listless. Her hair caught back haphazardly with a rubber band, her face pale with-

out makeup, dark circles under her eyes from all the sleep-
less nights since the summons.

*Go now,* she told herself. *Make an excuse, say anything.
You have no business staying here.*

'I understand,' Rachel said, 'but I *do* have to be back at
the clinic. Look, this is probably a mistake, my coming
here. Maybe it would be best if I—'

'You're in trouble, and you need help,' Rose broke in,
her dark eyes fixed on Rachel. There seemed to be no
sympathy in her voice, no resentment either. Just stating a
fact. 'Why don't you come inside, and we'll talk about it.
Then you can leave if you like. No obligation.'

Rose smiled, and her dark face seemed to glow like
some strangely beautiful icon.

'I told you once I owed you a favor,' she added, 'and I
meant it.'

Rachel, disarmed and a bit dismayed, too, found herself smiling back, thinking, *This woman should hate me.
Why is she doing this?*

'All right,' she said.

Rose came forward, extending her hand. Long cool
fingers that gripped Rachel's hand firmly, then slid away
like water. Rachel caught a faint fragrance, sweet, earthy,
like winter pears ripening on a windowsill.

'My office is a bit crowded at the moment,' Rose said.
'Papers everywhere. I'm preparing for a case. We can use
Max Griffin's office. Would you like some coffee or tea?'

'Tea would be nice.'

'Tea for Mrs McClanahan, Nancy,' Rose called to the
receptionist. Rachel was struck that she'd used her married name, and not 'Dr Rosenthal.'

Rachel followed Rose through a maze of paneled corridors, to a corner office overlooking the East River. Except
for the view, she felt as if she'd stepped into the house
she'd grown up in. A palatial antique Oriental carpet, a
Victorian gaslight chandelier, Dutch marquetry chairs
upholstered in worn velvet. An antique desk piled high
with papers and manila folders. A glass-fronted bookcase

485

filled with leatherbound volumes tooled in gilt. Lovely, she thought. And intimidating as hell.

Rose gestured toward what looked like a Duncan Phyfe settee. 'Please, sit down.'

Rachel, sinking down on the stiff seat, watched Rose settle in a chair across from her, carved at the top – she was struck by the irony of it – with a dove bearing an olive branch in its beak.

There was an awkward silence. Then Rose said, 'It might be easier if we skipped the small talk, don't you think, Mrs McClanahan?'

Rachel couldn't help but admire her directness.

'Yes, that would be easier,' she said. 'But please call me Rachel. Everyone does.'

Rose seemed to consider this, weigh it, while sun, filtering through the loosely woven drapes, fell across her in a ripply golden haze.

'All right then. Rachel.' She picked up a yellow legal pad from the table in front of her, and balanced it on her knees. 'I've gone over the paperwork Prudential sent over, and I'll be very direct with you. I believe you did everything within your power to give Alma Saucedo the best care you possibly could. And a jury will probably believe that, too. But nonetheless that very same jury *could* easily vote against you.'

Rachel felt her heart begin to thump, thudding hard against her chest. But that was impossible. She'd be ruined, the clinic destroyed. HEW would yank their funding – hadn't Sandy Boyle warned her of just this kind of thing at their last meeting? – and her privileges at St Bart's would be revoked, too. Everything she'd slaved for wiped out, all the women who needed her, who *trusted* her, they'd have no-one.

'In a situation like this,' Rose went on, 'the sympathy of the jury naturally lies with the victim – in this case, a sixteen-year-old girl who is brain dead, a vegetable for life. Survived by an infant requiring highly expensive care. So, OK, you know we're talking big bucks. The question in their eyes isn't necessarily going to be who, if anyone, is guilty, but who pays? The already overburdened parents of Alma Saucedo, or the rich insurance company?'

'I see.' Rachel felt strangely disconnected, as if she were on automatic pilot, listening and speaking normally, while her mind careened over the catastrophes that lay ahead.

'Do you? I wonder. Most people can't get rid of the idea when they walk into a courtroom, that it's a question of guilt or innocence.'

Rachel gathered herself, and answered, 'I don't believe it's ever that clear-cut in medicine. You always leave a patient feeling you should have done more.'

'Is that how you feel about Alma Saucedo?'

'Yes.'

'The question is, *Could* you have done more?'

'I wasn't sure at first, while it was all happening,' Rachel answered, determined to be truthful. 'But later, when I went over it step by step . . .' She straightened against the unyielding sofa. 'The answer is no, I could not have done more. Under the circumstances, which were far from optimal, I took what I felt was the safest course. I don't think any other doctor could have acted more responsibly.'

Rose's black eyes fixed on her with an intensity that made the back of her neck go tight with gooseflesh.

The thought surfaced out of nowhere. *She and I, we're here to see something through, aren't we? Not just this damned lawsuit.*

She had felt it the very first time she met Rose. This odd sense of helplessness – as if she and Rose both had somehow been thrown against each other by some quirk of fate.

Both in love with the same man.

And, strange, too, wasn't it, that of all the law firms in lower Manhattan, the one that represented her insurance company just happened to be this one, Rose's?

Rose felt it too, Rachel was sure, the two of them sizing each other up like two gunslingers about to face off for the draw.

*What does she want from me?* Rachel wondered. *She*

*doesn't have to be here. She could have turned this case over to someone else in the firm. But she didn't.*

Why?

The eerie tension broke when Rose bent and scribbled something on the legal pad she held in her lap.

Rose looked up. 'I talked to Stu Miller this afternoon. The Saucedos have rejected the settlement Prudential offered them. Two hundred thousand. According to Stu, yesterday they had tentatively agreed to it, but today they said they'd changed their minds.'

Rachel felt sudden, jarring anger. David. He was behind all this. She could feel him clawing at her. The poor Saucedos, they had a right to their sorrow and their anger. But David, what he was doing . . . it was hateful, *evil.*

And then she began feeling terrified, desperate. How could she fight David alone? If she told the truth, about why he was doing this, it would be the end of her marriage. If she kept quiet, it would be the end of her career. No matter which way she turned he'd destroy her.

'Where do I go from here?' Rachel asked, feeling trapped.

Rose looked at her directly, and spoke firmly. 'To court. With me as your attorney.'

Rachel stared at her, then blurted the question that had hung between them from the beginning.

'Why? Why *you* of all people?'

Rose was silent, and Rachel felt the space between them charged as if with static electricity.

Then Rose's mouth twisted up in a strange, lopsided smile.

'Let's just say I like to pay my debts.' She paused, and added, 'I can't make any promises. Except one. I'll fight for you. I'll do everything within my power to win this case. And who knows?' Her smile widened. 'I just may pull it off.'

Looking at her, at her dark flashing eyes, Rachel struggled to understand.

*Is she doing this for me . . . or for herself? Is she using me to get back at Brian? Or, God forbid, to get closer to him?*

488

Rachel felt as if she'd just swallowed a rock. Then she thought, *If that's true, if she's doing this for herself, then she'll fight harder than anyone else would. And I need that. I need every bit of help I can get.*

A knock on the door.

Rachel jumped a little, yanked from her thoughts. But it was only the blond receptionist with her tea, a steaming mug with the dangling string of a Twining's tea bag.

She took the mug, and sipped the scalding liquid. Tears pricked her eyes with the pain of it. She brought the mug down, cradled in both hands, glad for the warmth in the glacial air conditioning.

'All right. Say I agree. What now?' Rachel asked.

'We gather all the medical records and any other relevant evidence. Depositions from everyone involved. Can you think of anyone who might testify against you? Another doctor, a nurse?'

Rachel thought of Bruce Hardman, the young resident who had helped deliver Alma's baby. His white, frightened face, the patches of sweat staining his surgical greens. Relieved, probably, that no-one was pointing the finger at him.

The thought of David flashed across her mind, too, but she didn't dare mention him. Besides, she recalled, he had advised her to wait, not to induce labor. And he wasn't around when she delivered Alma's baby. So what evidence could he have?

'No. No-one I can think of.'

Rose scribbled something on the legal pad in her lap. 'We'll talk more about that later. We may not even go to trial. Prudential still wants to try to settle. I have a meeting scheduled with the Saucedos' lawyer for Monday. After that I'll have a better sense of where we're headed.'

For so many years now, Rachel had fought her own battles. Now could she just sit back, and let someone else fight for her?

The one person in the world besides David who had reason to hate her.

Yet, oddly, she felt that she could trust Rose.

*She'll fight for me if it means fighting for Brian.*

And if it should ever come to a contest between her and Rose, what then? Which of them would win?

In the end, who would Brian choose?

She remembered her father taking her on the subway when she was very little. Mama would have had a fit if she'd known; but Daddy wanted her upbringing to encompass even the unpleasant aspects of life. 'If the meek ever inherit the earth,' he had told her, gripping her hand as they descended into the IRT one hot Friday afternoon, 'it will only be because the mighty have given up inhabiting all but a tiny portion of it.'

She remembered the crowds impatiently waiting to push through the turnstiles; then after Daddy had dropped the token in, being propelled on to the jammed concrete platform, where she stood staring into the blackened throat of the tunnel, feeling the hot smelly air of an approaching train on her face. Daddy had turned his back for a moment to read the map on the wall, and she had crept closer to the tracks, until she was looking straight down at the rails. A train skidded toward the platform, shrieking, blue sparks shooting up from its wheels. And in that instant, she had thought, *I could jump. Right now. I could jump on to the track and it will be the biggest thing I've ever done.*

Rachel felt that way now. As if she were drawing too close to something that might be deadly, but was also irresistible. *I will know the truth . . . if he still loves her. Even if it may kill me.*

'Why don't we have lunch on Monday, then, after my meeting with their lawyer?' Rose suggested, rising.

Rachel placed her unfinished tea on the low table in front of her, and stood up. 'Yes, good. That would be a good idea.'

'The Odeon, twelve-thirty or so?'

'Fine. I'll be there.'

She was halfway to the door, where a secretary waited

to show her out, when Rose called out, 'Oh, and give my love to Brian.'

Rachel paused a moment, feeling a little sick, and started to turn, then decided she wouldn't, she just *couldn't* look into Rose's face, let Rose see how afraid she was of losing the man they both loved.

The hospital elevator was taking for ever to reach the sixth floor.

Rachel punched the button again, knowing it would do no good. The elevators at St Bart's, like everything else, were prehistoric. She could hear its creaking cables, its slow ratchety climb. She looked up, watching the strip of numbers over the door light up, one by one, as the elevator stopped at each floor. Four, five, next would be hers. And then, incredibly, it reversed, starting down again.

Damn. Damn it to hell. Everything else here was conspiring against her, why not the elevators?'

'Shit,' she swore out loud. A tall, reed-thin nurse, passing by, slowed and turned. Rachel recognized her, Jane Sackman, and started to greet her. She didn't know Jane very well, but liked her. A nurse who always seemed to manage a genuine smile. But Jane's gaze slid away from hers, and Rachel's 'Hi' stuck in her throat. She watched Jane quicken her step, hurrying past.

What was going on around here? She'd been getting evasive looks like this all day. Or was she just being paranoid?

Seeing Alma just now, up in ICU, hooked up to a respirator, catheterized, corpselike, God, it shook her up more each time. Rachel's knees felt weak, wrists floppy. And her mouth was sour from coffee, strong and bitter.

Finally the elevator doors wheezed open, and she ducked inside. Thank goodness, she was finally going home. Brian would be waiting. They'd sip some sherry, nibble on Brie and Rye-Krisp. Then they were going to an opening at that new gallery on Spring Street, then on to dinner with Brian's agent and his wife. The evening ahead shimmered in her imagination like an oasis in the desert. An evening with people she loved, people who loved her. She wouldn't think about anything else. Not Alma. Not Rose. Not—

'Hello, Rachel.'

She turned. David. She hadn't seen the face, only the white coat. Oh Christ.

And they were alone.

The doors banged shut behind her, the elevator jerked a little as it began its descent. Rachel felt her stomach roll out from under her, her skin pull tight.

David was grinning, a cold triumphant grin. He reminded her of how she used to feel watching hunters driving home with bloody deer roped to their bumpers. Under the fluorescent glare, he seemed almost unreal, the knife edges of his tan slacks, the white jacket gleaming with starch, the hair so immaculately sculpted. As perfect as if he'd been cut from a magazine ad, or one of those doctors on TV proclaiming the wonders of some cold remedy . . . except for the eyes – bloodshot whites and the cold Arctic green of his pupils.

Those eyes were fixed on her now, and she shivered. Turning her back to him, she thumbed the button marked MAIN though it was already lit, hoping to God he would leave her be if she ignored him.

*Damn* this old crate. She'd be trapped in here for ever. She thumbed the button once again.

'You can run all you like. But it won't help.' David spoke softly, almost caressingly. 'I've recommended to the Board that your privileges be revoked.'

She whirled around, furious. 'On what grounds?'

'Criminal negligence. My God, did you really think you'd get away with it? That kid and her baby. You might as well have tried to murder her.'

Rachel stood there, stunned. Some part of her had an urge to laugh. This wasn't really happening – David, saying those things, like lines from some hack melodrama.

But she knew the hollow punched-out feeling in her stomach was real.

The elevator jerked to a stop, doors bumping open.

David brushed past, immaculate, serene, pausing only long enough to cast her a thin smile, like a cold slice of moon glittering in a winter sky.

'It's a long way to hell, Rachel, and you're not even halfway there.'

Rachel, watching him walk away, was shaking so badly she could hardly stand. She was terrified.

Of herself.

She had wanted to kill him. If she'd had a gun in her hand at that moment, she would have pulled the trigger.

# 30

Rose and Max dined on flaky pan bread and tandoori chicken at an Indian restaurant on Lexington and Twenty-eighth, then strolled over to Fifth. It was a hot night, made even hotter by the spicy curry that kept sending up smoke signals from Rose's stomach. She felt uncomfortably warm, sticky, even in her coolest cotton blouse and seersucker skirt. The baked-in heat of the sidewalk seeping up through the thin soles of her sandals seeming to slow her, as if she were trudging across the salt flats of Death Valley.

She wanted to be home, first a cold shower, then naked with Max under the lazily spinning ceiling fan in the bedroom they now shared. She thought of how he would make love to her, slowly, with infinite tenderness. She felt herself go soft in the knees, and between her legs, just imagining.

All at once, though, she felt afraid, confused.

*How?* How can I want Max that way? Isn't it Brian I love?

And Max, what does he want from me?

A little warmth, she supposed, after so many years of a cold marriage. A friendly face to wake up next to in the morning, someone to encourage him, reassure him that there was, indeed, life after divorce.

And afterwards, when he moved on, what then? Would they be just friends again? Could they really go back to what they'd had? Rose felt a surge of loneliness.

She reached for his hand, and felt reassured. His fingers wrapped tightly about hers.

'We're here,' he said.

'Where?' She hadn't been watching the street signs, just following him in a sort of daze. Now she looked up, saw a limitless expanse of gray granite with mammoth Art Deco trimmings. The Empire State Building.

'Come on,' Max said, 'I'll take you to the top. There's a nice breeze up there.'

'Isn't it too late? The Observation Deck will be closed.'

Max winked. 'Don't worry, I have my connections.'

Minutes later they were in an elevator, rocketing up.

'Old friend of my father's,' Max explained, telling her about the elderly janitor who'd unlocked this elevator for them. 'Pop got Moe his job here. And the guy's been here on the same night shift practically since the place was built. He knows it probably better than he knows his own wife and kids.'

The elevator doors slid open, and they stepped out. The King Kong T-shirts, Big Apple mugs, and Yankee pennants opposite them in the window of the darkened souvenir shop looked forlorn.

He led her down a short flight of stairs, through a glass door, and then they were outside, a cool breeze whipping past the high plexiglass shield, tugging at her hair, her skirt. Rose felt as if she'd been plunged into an invisible river and was being caught up in the cool momentum of its current.

She leaned out as far as she could, breathless at the sight of Manhattan strung out below like a great jeweled web. She had been up here only once before, on a school field trip, but never at night. The gritty city was transformed into something magical. Gone were the hot, dirty sidewalks, the angry pushing crowds, the jangling traffic sounds. She felt as if she were being given a gift, an exquisite Cartier necklace presented to her in an equally splendid velvet box.

She turned, and caught Max's gaze. He was watching her, not the view. His clear blue eyes were fixed on her, a small smile on his lips. Rose thought, *You wonderful man. You knew. You wanted to surprise me.*

'Thank you,' she told him.

495

'My father used to take me up here at night,' Max said, slipping an arm about her shoulders, his bulk a warm cove she slipped into easily. 'He'd hold me up, and I'd feel as big as King Kong. And he'd say, "See that, Maxie. You're on top of the world! And it's all yours. All you gotta do is grab on to it." '

'Well, in a way you did, didn't you?'

Max dropped his head slightly and was silent, his face in shadow. She felt as if he had slipped away somehow, and she touched his arm, wanting to follow wherever it was he had gone.

Was he thinking about his daughter? The divorce papers had been drawn up, so Mandy had to know he wasn't ever coming home. That had to have been tough for Max to explain.

Max looked up, smiled, his expression so sad she wanted to hug him, tell him everything would be all right. But she couldn't promise that. Who knew better than she how mercurial life could be?

'It's funny,' he said. 'I used to think Pop had it figured right. That's what life really was all about, success and making lots of money. He thought so, because he never had either. And what you don't have is always more important to you than what you do have. But I know better now. I don't have to be on top of the Empire State to grab on to life. No, not when it's here. Right next to me.'

He turned, staring straight at her, and the lights from below caught his face, stunning her, as if she had been groping through a tunnel, and had emerged suddenly into blinding daylight.

She understood. It all became clear. What he was saying, the way he was looking at her.

*Dear sweet Jesus, he's in love with me.*

How long? she wondered. How long had he loved her, and she too deaf, dumb, and blind to see it?

Looking at him now, at the clear love shining from his face, the sad knowing look in his eyes, she realized with an

496

exquisite, nearly heart-stopping pang that probably it had been a long time. Longer than they'd been lovers. Maybe for years.

Rose saw it all now. His many kindnesses, each one like a tiny pearl, small and inconsequential by itself, but strung together, one after another, they had multiplied into a beautiful and precious necklace wound about her throat. He had given her the greatest gift of all, the kind that asked nothing in return.

Tears filled her eyes.

'I'm sorry,' she whispered. *Wrong thing to say, all wrong.* But it was all she could think of.

'Don't be.' He brushed her cheek with his knuckle, his touch so light it might have been the wind.

'I didn't realize.'

'I know.'

'Oh, Max . . . I wish . . .' she broke off, not knowing what to say, only what she felt. That it was hopeless.

He stroked her hair, gently, rhythmically, as if she were a child in need of comforting. She thought she could hear his heart beating, pounding like a hammer.

'I know,' he said. 'You're in love with Brian.'

'Yes.'

'Even though he's married.'

'Yes.'

'Is that why you're handling his wife's case? Because of Brian?'

'Partly.' She shrugged. 'Yes.' But there was more, too, and she wanted to tell him. 'This might sound strange, but . . . I like her. She's straight, and so incredibly dedicated.'

'And Brian? Is he still in love with you?'

'Brian? I don't think it's as simple as yes or no. I've known him for ever. We're part of each other, in a way. So there's a piece of Brian that's always belonged to me, and always will. But he's confused right now. He has to sort things out for himself. When he has, I'll know.'

'And you're prepared to wait?'

'Yes.'

She hated hurting Max, but she told him the truth. 'As long as I have to. As long as it takes.'

'I see,' he said softly.

Rose had watched a ten-story apartment building being demolished once, and she still remembered the sight of it collapsing, not exploding like a bomb, but folding in on itself, floor by floor, with an odd sort of grace, like an ancient dowager attempting a curtsey. Max reminded her of that now. Folding in on himself, the planes of his face shifting, caving like sections of wall. She wanted to reach out, stop him from hurting.

But all she could do was put her arms around him, while a strong wind tore at her as if it meant to carry her away. The only thing that seemed to anchor her to the concrete floor was the huge, aching weight of her heart.

'Max,' she murmured. 'Oh, Max, I wish it could be you. More than anything in the world.'

Max wanted her. She could feel it as she held him.

And the funny thing was, she wanted him, too. She longed to give him what she could, even if it wasn't enough. Wasn't a little love better than none at all?

Suddenly, Max was kissing her, and she was kissing him back. Hard, bruising kisses, not like the gentle love-making those other times. Desperate kisses that spoke of endings rather than beginnings. With a groan, Max sank to his knees, pressing his face into the furrow where the wind molded her skirt to her thighs. His fingers digging into her buttocks, his breath heating her through the thin fabric.

Rose arched against him, her head back, letting the wind ride over her face and stream through her hair.

Max was reaching under her skirt, tugging at her panties, his nails scraping her thighs. And dear God, she was helping him.

Now her panties were balled in her fist, a scrap of lace, a whisper of silk – she'd bought them at Lord & Taylor's after that first night they had spent together – and she tossed them into the wind, watching a strong gust catch at the silvery slip of fabric, sending it up over the partition in a long swooping arc. Then sailing out over the dark canyons and glittering avenues below like some fantastic bird.

She turned back to Max, riding her skirt up over her naked thighs, and whispered, 'Yes, take me.'

## 31

Sylvie lay beside Nikos in the dark, aching, exhausted. It
was the first time they had made love in her bed. The bed
she had shared with Gerald.

He'd been a little rough, not like the other times. And so
quick, hardly caressing her, as if he wanted it to be over,
get it out of the way.

Was he angry with her?

She listened to the labored flow of his breathing, feeling
her own heart wind down little by little. The hot darkness
felt almost smothering. She groped for Nikos's hand
across the tangle of sheets, and felt a flood of relief as his
fingers closed about hers.

Sylvie went back over the evening in her mind. A superb
dinner at Caravelle with a spectacular bottle of Château
Ausone to celebrate the house, finished at last. She'd
wanted tonight to be special, each detail perfect, exquisite,
down to her dress, soft green Burmese silk, the leaves of a
Monet water lily. It matched her eyes, and the emeralds in
her ears. Yet Nikos hardly seemed to notice. He had been
polite, but distracted, his mind on other things. And now
this heavy silence. What was he thinking?

She squeezed his hand, hoping for a response.

Yet she already knew. In her heart she dreaded his
words. It had been building between them for three weeks,
since she had told him about Rose. Nikos had been quieter,
more pensive, but she'd sensed his turmoil.

'I saw her,' Nikos said. 'Rose.'

Sylvie felt her chest grow tight, her lungs constrict, as if
she were sipping air through a straw.

*I should never have told him,* she thought. *I should have*

*kept the secret. What good could I ever have thought would*
*come of my telling him?*

'She is beautiful. And smart,' Nikos went on, his voice ragged. 'If you only knew . . . if you could see her, Sylvie, my God, our *daughter*.'

Sylvie, unable to bear the huge pressing weight on her chest, pulled herself up. She kicked off the sheets that clung to her ankles, and swung her legs over the side of the mattress.

Her legs were rubbery as she crossed the carpet, snatching her dressing gown from the needlepoint bench in front of the vanity. She pulled it on too quickly, hearing something rip in one sleeve. As if it mattered, as if anything mattered now.

She sank down on the Récamier daybed, its worn velvet cushions folding about her, seeming to hide her, bury her.

The tall French windows were open, a lukewarm breeze lifting the skirts of the parted lace curtains. In the moonlight, Sylvie could make out the shapes of her roses, but no colors, as if she were looking at a black and white photograph. The Shot Silk that had climbed up past the wrought-iron balcony railing, its huge blossoms peeking through the harp-shaped balustrades. And the Blue Nile, pale against the ivy blanketing the south wall.

*Oh, keep them safe,* she prayed. *My daughters. Keep them from harm. Punish me, not them.*

'For thirty-two years I've wanted nothing more than to know my real daughter,' she said softly into the perfumed night. 'Oh, Nikos, you don't know, you can't imagine! Your own little girl – to know she's out there somewhere, in trouble perhaps, or unhappy, and you can't help her. You can't hold her in your arms and make everything all right. I've dreamed so often of that . . . dear God, to *hold* her . . . just for a moment. To ask her forgiveness. What I would give for that!' She held her arms out. 'All this, everything . . .'

She turned toward the dark silhouette sitting up in bed, the pain in her heart so great she thought she might die. 'Even you, my darling Nikos.'

Now he was rising, shadowy, now stepping into the silver light, solid and glowing as he crossed to where she sat. He crouched at her side, taking her cold hands in his.

'I am sorry, my Sylvie. For all you have suffered. I do not blame you. You must never think that. I only wish . . .' His voice broke, and his eyes glinted in the moon-struck darkness. 'I wish I had known, years ago. Our child, *my child*, raised by strangers . . . it hurts to think of it . . . and if I had known, things would have been so different. Sylvie, Sylvie – why didn't you tell me before?'

He *did* blame her. And he had a right to. Could she really have expected him to feel any differently?

Tears slid down her cheeks and splashed on her clenched knuckles. 'There was never a time,' she said, 'when . . . when it seemed . . . possible to tell you. First, there was Gerald to think of. I would not have hurt him for the world. And you . . . well, you were part of the past then. I didn't know where you were, what had happened to you. And then when we met again . . .' She took a deep shuddery breath. 'I only told you because it didn't seem fair . . . your not knowing . . . even if it *was* too late.'

'Too late?' His eyes were fixed on her, only she couldn't see his eyes at all, just the pinpoints of light reflected in them like distant stars. 'No. I do not believe it is too late.'

Sylvie's heart thundered in her ears. Dear God, what did he mean? What could he be *thinking?*

Then Nikos said, 'I have watched her. Followed her like a spy. I know where she works, where she lives. I even pretended to run into her so I could speak to her. She is like you in some ways, I think. Clever and proud. And such fire! But she seldom smiles. I wonder if she is happy.'

'And you think it's me who's caused her unhappiness? Us? Oh, Nikos, don't you see? It would be so much worse for her if she knew! She would hate me. I abandoned her, gave her away to strangers. Took another child in her place.'

'But you didn't forget her. You made sure she was taken care of. That she had money.'

502

'*Money*,' she spat. 'How easy for me, and how cowardly, a phony bank account her father had supposedly opened for her before he was killed. As if any amount of money could have compensated for what I did!'

A cloud slipped over the moon, and the garden full of roses suddenly was eclipsed in shadow.

How many times can a heart break? she wondered.

'I saw her once,' she told him. 'When she was a little girl. I waited for her outside her school. I wanted . . . as you did . . . merely to see her, know that she was well. At least that was what I told myself. And then when I finally saw her . . . well, it was that precise moment when I realized what a terrible mistake I had made. I was overwhelmed. I had to touch her, to be near her. My own baby. The child I had carried inside me. Oh, don't mistake me. I could never regret Rachel, loving her, raising her as my own. And if I hadn't made that terrible choice in the beginning I would never have known Rachel. I wouldn't have loved her.'

Nikos gripped her shoulders. She could feel his calloused fingertips digging into her, bruising her through the silk of her dressing gown.

'It's not too late, Sylvie. Rose has a right to the truth. Then to decide for herself how she feels.'

Sylvie felt as if the room were coming apart in great jagged pieces, falling on her, cutting her.

'NO!'

She pushed him away, struggled to her feet.

'I can't!' she cried. 'Don't you see? However wrong the choice was, I cannot turn back now. I have Rachel to think of now, and she's so much more mine after all these years than Rose. I love her just as if she were my own flesh and blood. Think what it would be like for her. To learn I had stolen her from her real family, pretended to be her mother. Oh, Nikos, *think*.'

He rose, and stood beside her. The black stars of his eyes were hot on her face, but she couldn't seem to pull away from his gaze. *Rose's eyes,* she observed with a little shock. Those same eyes – huge and sad and somehow hungry – had looked up at her that day in the schoolyard when she had placed her earring in her startled child's small hand.

'I meant what I said,' Nikos replied, sounding sad and far away. 'I do not blame you. I think you have punished yourself enough. We each have our choices, and who but God can truly say what is right and what is wrong? Perhaps it is selfish of me, wanting a grown woman, a stranger, to be the little girl I never had. But the wish is so strong. It is stronger than I am. You say you have made this choice. I don't know. Often we just find ourselves walking in a certain direction. We don't know why. And then we look up one day, and we are there.' He was silent a moment, as if struggling for control, then his voice broke free. 'I *need* her, Sylvie.' Each word rang out like a gunshot. 'You have a daughter. I have nothing. Give me Rose. *Give me back my daughter.*'

She felt half-dead, some part of her surely killed, but she knew she had to answer. 'And if I refuse?' she asked in a ragged whisper.

Nikos stared at her, not moving, naked in the moonlight, his muscular arms hanging limply at his sides. Then he said, 'Then I will do what I must.'

Sylvie felt as if a crack had opened in the pit of her stomach, and a great coldness were welling up from it, seeping through her, numbing her.

She saw everything in her mind as if looking into a shattered mirror. Her life, her daughters' lives coming apart, crumbling into tiny sharp splinters.

Oh dear God, what had she done?

Sylvie threw her arm up over her face, as if to ward off a blow. She'd thought nothing could be more terrible than the lie she had carried inside her all these years. But there *was* something worse, far worse.

The truth.

## 32

Rachel watched her mother set the cake down on the table. Three layers high, glazed with black chocolate, it perched on a froth of white doilies atop Grandmother Rosenthal's Wedgwood cake plate with the sterling rim.

'Surprise!' Sylvie cried, beaming. 'You didn't think I'd forget, did you?'

Rachel stared, bewildered, then felt stricken with guilt. *My God, my anniversary, and I forgot. We forgot. So that's why Mama invited us to dinner tonight.*

She stared at the cake, wishing it would disappear, hating Mama for reminding her how her marriage had gone wrong, and hating Mama for her graciousness, which all Rachel's life had seemed to point out the gulf between the two of them.

The memory came rushing back, those awful piano lessons after school, tinkling out 'Mary Had a Little Lamb' and 'Farmer in the Dell' over and over until Rachel thought she would die. But Mama never got tired of listening, even singing along or tapping a foot. Rachel first used to think she was just being nice and motherly, but after a while, Rachel realized Mama actually *liked* hearing her thump out those mind-numbing tunes. Her little girl was supposed to be like herself, gentle, sweet-tempered, a lover of the finer things in life, music, art, flowers. But Rachel, as she grew, saw herself very differently.

'Mama, you shouldn't have. It's . . .' Rachel trailed off, defeated by her mother's good intentions. 'You just shouldn't have, that's all.'

Sylvie smiled at Rachel, and lowered the porcelain-handled cake knife in her hand. 'I know, dear. I *wanted* to.' She smiled, looking more ethereal than ever, her skin pale as soap against a scoop-necked cranberry silk blouse, her carefully arranged hair brushed with wings of silver. Graciously, she added, 'You've been under so much pressure with this dreadful lawsuit, I didn't think you'd have the time or energy to make a fuss over your anniversary. But that's what mothers are for, isn't it?'

Rachel felt a pang. Would she ever be a mother? Not bloody likely.

She looked over at Brian, seated in the Chippendale chair beside hers, wearing a faded shirt and worn cords. His informality felt like a breath of fresh air in this dining room with its symmetrically arranged sconces, dark paneling, and stiffly draped curtains. He was wearing his hair longer these days, fanning just over the back of his collar. She noted the gray in it, but it looked good on him, comfortable. He had grown into himself, she realized, rounded at the corners like the covers of a well-read book, his lanky frame filled out, the angles of his face softened.

His eyes met hers, then cut away too quickly. A pain ripped through her chest.

*I love you,* she wanted to say to him. *I love you so much. Can't you see that? We don't need hearts and flowers and cakes. From the very beginning we weren't ordinary.*

Then Rachel suddenly felt flat, defeated.

'Just a sliver for me,' she told Sylvie. 'I ate so much dinner, I don't know if I can manage another bite.'

Sylvie cut a generous slice, and passed it to Rachel. 'You're too thin. You *should* eat.'

Rachel smiled. 'Look who's talking. If I'm too thin, Mama, it's only because I take after you.'

She watched Sylvie flush, her eyes take on an added sparkle. Sylvie gave a tinkly laugh. 'Well . . . maybe. It's funny, but I had lunch with Evelyn Gold the other day, and she's put on so much weight. She's big as a horse! And, well, I know it wasn't very nice of me, she's my dearest friend after all . . . but I couldn't help feeling just the tiniest bit smug.'

'I thought the Golds were living in Florida,' Rachel remarked.

'Why, yes. They're just up for a week or so, visiting Mason.'

Rachel perked up. Mason! God, she hadn't seen him in ages. Let's see . . . it had to be a couple of years. She should call him; would do her good to see Mason again.

Breaking the brief silence, Sylvie asked, 'By the way, have they set a date yet?'

'Date?' Rachel felt confused, then realized Mama was talking about the trial. The last thing in the world she wanted to think about now. But she supposed Mama had a right to know. 'Not yet,' she answered. 'My lawyer says it may take a while. Snowing, she calls it. That's what attorneys do these days, snow each other with so much paperwork that maybe one of them gets buried in the avalanche.'

'She? Your attorney is a woman?' Nikos leaned toward her. Rachel turned her attention toward Nikos. He looked more somber than usual. Dressed in a dark three-piece suit, Nikos seemed older, too. And he'd been much quieter than usual all throughout dinner, his speech careful and measured. Could he and Mama be having problems?

Rachel hoped not. Nikos was so good for Sylvie. These past few years, Mama seemed to have bloomed, like one of her own roses. Color in her cheeks, a sparkle in her eyes. Rachel was sure they were sleeping together. And wasn't it wonderful that Mama had Nikos to take care of her?

Yet how silly to think of Mama that way, as some kind of virgin, someone in need of looking after. Mama, after all, had proved she was perfectly capable of looking after herself.

'Yes, a woman,' Rachel told Nikos, adding with a laugh, 'we do rise above being nurses and secretaries now and then.'

Nikos smiled. 'Yes, of course, I didn't mean . . . it's just that your mother has told me so little about this unfortunate situation.'

'My fault,' Rachel said. 'I've been keeping her in the

507

dark as much as possible.' She turned to Sylvie. 'I didn't want to upset you any more than necessary, Mama.'

Something flashed in Sylvie's misty green eyes, turning them hard and brilliant. Rachel drew back, a bit startled, uncertain.

'There's no need to keep anything from me,' Sylvie said. Her voice was soft, gracious as always, but with a vein of steel. 'I won't fall apart. I've dealt with a lot worse.'

Rachel again felt ashamed. Of course. When Daddy died. Mama had been strong then, stronger than Rachel ever thought she could be.

Then Brian reached for her hand under the table and squeezed it, and Rachel felt moved to tears. How long since he had touched her this way, spontaneously, without awkwardness?

'I'm sorry, Mama. I just . . . I haven't felt much like talking about it. To anyone, as a matter of fact.'

'There isn't much to tell at this point,' Brian volunteered. 'The usual pretrial stuff, what they call discovery. Rose has been taking depositions. She—'

'Rose? Her name is Rose?' Sylvie interrupted, her shoulders stiffening, her voice sharp. She sat immobile, knife poised, flame points of reflected candlelight leaping on the silver blade.

Brian shot her an odd look. 'Rose Santini,' he said.

The name seemed to echo in the now unnatural stillness of the room.

Sylvie just sat there, eyes wide, face drained of color. Why should her name mean anything to Mama? Rachel wondered. Why on earth was she *staring* like that?

The knife slipped from Sylvie's hand with a muffled chink, scattering black crumbs across the snowy damask. Sylvie sat clutching her chest, swaying slightly, her face blanching.

Rachel rushed to her side, alarmed.

'Mama! What's wrong?'

Sylvie shook her head. Her mouth fell open, then

508

snapped shut, then opened again, as if she were struggling for breath. Her hands tightened on the edge of the table, knuckles white.

Now Nikos was at her side.

Sylvie waved him away, her hand fluttering in midair like a wounded bird. 'Nothing . . . nothing,' she whispered. 'I'll be all right. Something I ate. Just a bit light-headed at the moment. I . . . I think I'd better lie down. Will you please excuse me? No, Nikos, you stay. Rachel will help me upstairs.'

Rachel slipped an arm about her mother, surprised, shocked even, at her thinness. Could she truly be ill? *I've been so caught up in my own problems,* Rachel thought, *chances are I wouldn't even have noticed.*

The possibility of losing her mother hit her like a blow in the stomach. She couldn't imagine life without Mama, her gentleness, even Mama's rose-colored view of the world, so pleasantly sheltered and old-fashioned, so different from hers.

Upstairs in the quiet of what had been her parents' bedroom, Rachel heard only the ticking of the carriage clock atop the highboy. Slowly, she looked around her. She remembered, as a child, tiptoeing through this room, with its pastel carpet and polished antique furniture, the delicate vases and Staffordshire dogs arranged on spindly tables. Holding herself in, not even breathing too hard, for fear of breaking something. Now she saw how lovely it was. How it reflected Mama, beautiful, serene, an island apart from the rest of the world.

*Nothing bad can happen in this room,* she told herself.

Rachel gazed down at Sylvie, thin and pale under lace-trimmed Porthault sheets. Rachel had found some Valium in the bathroom medicine cabinet, and given her one. She was almost asleep.

If only Mama weren't so horribly white. In the soft pink light from the lamp on the nightstand, Rachel could see the dark, bruised-looking circles under Sylvie's closed eyelids.

She settled carefully on the edge of the bed, concentrating on the gentle rise and fall of her mother's chest.

Rachel thought with a pang of Alma Saucedo, the times she had sat there like this, keeping vigil. Except that Alma, wasted and almost unrecognizable now, would never wake up.

Mama *is fine*, she told herself. *She's just tired*. Decorating that house for Nikos, running all over the place, looking for just the right piece of carpet, the best price for walnut floor tiles. Like a child, caught up totally in the thrill of something new, not having any idea at all when to slow down or quit.

Still, just to be on the safe side, she'd insist Mama call her own doctor in the morning. Go in for a thorough checkup. Mama had probably been putting it off for years.

Suddenly a hand darted out from beneath the coverlet. Cold fingers convulsed about Rachel's wrist. Good God. Mama! What—

Sylvie's eyes were open, fixed on her, wide and glazed as a sleepwalker's.

Rachel's heart bumped up into her throat.

'My daughter . . .,' Sylvie whispered, sounding odd, her eyes staring, unfocused. 'Where is my daughter?'

'I'm right here, Mama.' Rachel made her voice brisk, sensible, to disguise how panicked she felt. Was Mama feeling disoriented, or was it something more?

Then Mama seemed to right herself, her eyes blinking into focus. 'Rachel. Yes.' She smiled, a smile of such deep sadness it was as if a veil had been lifted, revealing to Rachel fully the secret soul she had before only glimpsed in her mother. 'I want you to know. I've never regretted—' She broke off, her eyes drifting shut.

'Regretted what, Mama?'

There was a long silence, and Rachel thought – no, hoped – that Mama was finally asleep. She had the strangest feeling, like the goosebumps that rose on the back of her neck when she was walking down a dark street and heard footsteps behind her, that whatever Mama had been about to tell her, she would be better off not hearing.

Then Sylvie's eyes fluttered open.

'You,' she spoke softly but distinctly into the rose-shaded darkness. 'I've never regretted you.'

Rachel felt oddly relieved. Not a confession, after all, no more than she'd known all along.

'Oh, Mama, don't you think I know that? I couldn't ask for a more loving mother.'

The corners of Sylvie's mouth appeared to turn up ever so slightly, a wisp of a smile. 'Oh my baby . . .'

Then Sylvie let her eyes fall shut, and seemed to drift off. Moments later, Rachel heard the sound of steady, even breathing. Her mother was asleep.

Rachel bent close, and kissed Mama's cheek. Cool dry skin like silk, a sweet powdery scent. She waited, vigilant, for several more minutes, until she was certain Mama was fast asleep.

But then, as Rachel was slowly rising to leave, she heard Sylvie mumble something in her sleep. Rachel froze.

Then she quickly told herself, *I'm imagining what I just heard. I'm tired too. Tired of keeping my head above water. Tired of David's threats, and Brian's distance. Of course I imagined it. Or perhaps she was just muttering something about one of her flowers.*

*Why else would Mama call for Rose?*

Rachel was lost. And she felt perfectly ridiculous – she, a born New Yorker, lost in Grand Central! She glanced at her watch. Damn, she'd be late . . .

She hurried back along the cavernous tunnel, which had proved to be yet another dead end. Then, rounding a bend, she saw it – the Oyster Bar. Relief swept through her as she pushed her way through the door.

Scanning the large, bustling dining area, she spotted someone who vaguely resembled Mason. Hastily, she threaded her way past waiters whisking platters heaped with oysters and clams on the half shell. Outside, the streets were baking, but down in this great room of gleaming wood and brass, it was blissfully cool and pleasantly fishy-smelling, like a giant sea cave.

As she got closer, she found herself breaking into a grin. Yes, it *was* Mason, and look at him! Gone, the ponytail and clunky Jesus sandals. His curly brown hair looked neatly trimmed, even if his sideburns were on the long side. He was wearing a crisp-looking jacket and tie. Was this the Legal Aid look, or had he gotten tired of being a hippie? It had been so long. They'd exchanged a few cards at holiday times, and a postcard now and then, but it had to have been more than a couple of years.

She caught Mason's eye, and he waved.

Reaching him, she ducked down to kiss his cheek before scooting into the chair opposite him. 'Mason! God, it's great to see you! Sorry I'm late. My cab got stuck behind a double-parked moving van, so I walked the last six blocks, and then would you believe it? I got lost here in the station.' They both laughed, while she settled back, scrutinizing his face. It was thinner now, tiny lines radiating from the corners of his merry brown eyes. 'Lord! It's been ages. You look wonderful. But what happened to all the hair?'

'A sacrifice to the great god of capitalism.' Mason heaved a mock sigh. 'You know, back in frontier times there really was a wall on Wall Street, built to keep the Indians out. Well, I'm back inside the fort now, fighting off corporate raiders.'

'What happened to the downtrodden, and Justice?'

He shrugged, tugging his madras tie loose, leaning back in his chair. 'Nothing dramatic . . . I just got real, as they say. Found out most of the people I was trying to help didn't like me, and I wasn't too crazy about them either. One kid put it rather eloquently, I think – this nineteen-year-old punk, second-time offender, up for breaking and entering – he said, pardon me, but these were his exact words, "You ain't doin' this for me, man, you doin' it for yourself. So you can go home at night and shit vanilla ice cream." '

'Oh, Mason, *I* know.' Rachel couldn't help but laugh. 'It's just like that for me sometimes . . . at the clinic.'

'But you're sticking with it.' Mason raised his glass in a salute. 'You always were stubborn as hell. Say, how about a drink?'

'Sure, but it's on me. Remember, I'm the one who invited you.' She ordered Campari and soda. She felt more relaxed, better than she had in a while. 'And your family . . . how's the brood?'

'Oh, you should see Shan . . . took to the burbs like a duck to water. She loves it – even the overflowing septic tank doesn't faze her. And the kids, well, they're all over the place, having a ball. Right now we have one of those inflatable plastic pools set up on the back lawn, and the three of them splash around in it all day long. We got them a dog, a golden retriever named Drake – and he loves the water too.'

Rachel smiled at the image of Mason, who used to dunk her in his parents' pool, now a full-blown adult, taking out the garbage, mowing the lawn, driving his kids to nursery school. And she felt a pang of envy. Three kids . . . it wasn't fair. Couldn't God give her just one?

Now Mason was dropping his eyes, staring into his glass. 'Rachel, I heard . . . about the malpractice suit. Jesus, what a crummy break.'

Her Campari came, and she was glad to be distracted. She took her time squeezing the wedge of lime. She sipped her drink. It tasted like mouthwash to her. Nothing tasted right these days, even the lousy cigarettes she had begun smoking again. She heard trains rumbling below, and the noise seemed to vibrate in her stomach.

She felt as if she were up on a tightrope, and any minute she might fall. The easiest thing right now would be to tip over, unload on Mason. But, she vowed silently, she wasn't going to do that.

Rachel shrugged. 'OB has a higher rate of malpractice suits than any other specialty.'

'Damn, I wish I could do something to help you, Rache.

But the firm I'm with now, we're so specialized, we don't know from nothing about that kind of law. But I might be able to recommend someone, if you're not satisfied with who you've got. Who is your attorney?'

'Rose Santini. With Stendahl and Cooper.'

'Santini, Santini, yeah, I read a little piece about her in the *Law Journal*. Name should be Houdini, not Santini. You hear about this case of hers, with the Hassidim?'

'No, I don't think so.'

'She was defending a guy, a Hassid, accused of aggravated assault, so she brings in a whole busload of these guys, black beards and black coats, and Santini asks the plaintiff to pick out her client. So naturally he picks wrong, and Santini gets a dismissal.'

Rachel felt her spirits lift, and a smile tug at the corners of her mouth. Not that her case would be so easy. But she could imagine Rose pulling off some spectacular sleight of hand like that. Rose was damn clever . . . and she didn't shrink from taking risks.

But Rose could destroy her, too, and so easily.

In some dark corner of her mind, a voice whispered, *And wouldn't that be convenient for Rose then? If she told Brian everything about David, wouldn't he naturally turn to her, his oldest, dearest friend, for advice, for comfort even? How perfect, how very cozy.*

And yet somehow, Rachel trusted Rose. Working with her so closely, she saw what Brian must have loved about her, her vulnerability beneath that fiery spiritedness, a warmth and gentleness.

'She is good,' Rachel said. 'I like her.' All true . . . in spite of Rachel's fears, jealousy. 'There is one problem, though. She's Brian's ex-girlfriend. Small world, huh?'

Mason whistled, silently shaking his head. 'That's a kicker all right. You figure she's still got the hots for him?'

'Maybe.' She shrugged, feeling a little sick, and wishing they could change the subject.

'Well, I don't know, if it was Shan's ex, I think I'd want to fix it so he'd get sent to the slammer.'

514

'I thought you two weren't the possessive types.'

'Oh yeah, that was great, thinking we were so cool. Until a couple of months after we were married I found out that Shan and Buzz had gone skinny-dipping out at the pond while I was picking up a few things in town. She swore it was perfectly innocent, and I believed her, but that didn't stop me from seeing red.' He chuckled at himself. 'And now look at me, Mr Maplewood Drive. I'm beginning to remind myself more and more of the old man.'

'How are your folks? I heard they're staying with you.'

'Just for a couple of weeks. Then it's back to Palm Beach. They're living there full time now. They sold the house in Harrison after Pop retired. Now he puts in his eighteen holes every day, and Mom spends her time playing bridge and organizing Hadassah benefits. They're both brown as Naugahyde sofas. Shan and I, we fly the kids down to see them as often as we can. Pop can't get over our Dylan . . . a two-year-old who's absolutely nuts for peas, spinach, brussels sprouts. Anything Gold Star freezes, that kid eats.' Mason was shaking his head, but Rachel could see the pride and love in his face. 'How about your mom? How's she getting along?'

'She's fine. She's having an affair.'

Mason's eyebrows shot up. 'No kidding? Well, good for her. She going to get serious with this guy? Or is she just having a good time?'

'I don't know. It seems pretty serious, but my mom hasn't mentioned anything about marriage. She's different since Dad died. Not so nervous, and happier, too, I think. And you wouldn't believe how she's taken charge over at the bank. My mama, the big boss! It's just . . . well, it takes some getting used to. Mason, do you think it's our parents, really, who've changed? Or is it us? Have *we* changed?'

'Both, I think. But listen, here's a scary thought. You and I are about the same ages now that our folks were when you and I were kids dunking each other in the pool.'

515

'God, has it been that long?'

'Yeah, it has.' He gave a short laugh, and tossed back the rest of his drink. 'You know, I even like driving my station wagon.'

Rachel, feeling oddly tender, reached for his hand. She needed a friend, and he was the oldest one she had. 'Mason. I'm scared. Of this trial coming up. Of getting older. Of . . . oh, a lot of things.'

Mason squeezed her hand. 'Join the club, kiddo. Some days I look in the mirror, and who do I see looking back at me? Ward Cleaver, that's who. Listen, the day I stop taking at least a few *pro bono* cases, and buy a condo in Florida, shoot me, will you?'

'I'll do better,' Rachel said and laughed. 'I'll draft you to work in my clinic. Defending junkies will seem like a breeze after a couple of weeks.'

Mason smiled. 'Deal.'

The waiter was standing there now, ready to take their orders, and Rachel suddenly felt ravenous. So life did go on. And, damn it, she would too. And if the ocean was getting rough, well, she'd just have to swim harder, that's all.

'Oysters,' she told the waiter. 'The biggest plate you've got.'

# 33

Max slipped in through the double doors at the back of the courtroom as the clerk was taking jury attendance.

The court was crowded, its long oak benches filled. On the sides people were standing against the paneled walls, and in the back he saw a few jostling to get a better view. Damn those idiot reporters, Max thought. Yesterday, the very first day, the case had made page three of the *Post*: DEBUTANTE DOCTOR ACCUSED IN TEEN MOM'S TRAGEDY, with a big photo overlay of Alma, lying unconscious surrounded by life-support machines, and alongside it, a cameo shot of her baby. *Saucedo* v. *Rosenthal* was being turned into a circus. This crowd made Max think of a school of hyenas, grubbing around the remains of an abandoned carcass.

Soon Rose would be in the spotlight. And she'd have to be good, or the media would tear her to shreds. But what was he getting himself all wrought up for? Rose *was* good. But then so was Sal Di Fazio, for all his oily histrionics. Max watched him now, pacing back and forth at the front of the courtroom like an overheated actor, beaming at the crowd as if they'd all bought expensive tickets to see him.

Max, peering through the crowd, spotted Rose at the defendant's table, shuffling through her briefcase. She was wearing a suit he'd never seen before, cobalt blue, with a demure ivory blouse open at the neck, showing the delectable golden-skinned column of her throat. She bent down just then to retrieve a paper that had slipped to the floor, her electric dark curls fanning out, obscuring her face, the pearls he had given her swinging away from her throat, catching the light just so. His heart did a slow ninety-degree turn.

He thought about the call last week from Gary Enfield in Los Angeles. Gary, telling him about Bruce Oldsen's triple bypass and how it had nudged Bruce into early retirement, then dropping his bomb, asking Max to come and take over the litigation department out there in Century City.

Max, his mind whirling, had told Gary he'd think it over. Which he'd been doing.

Totting up all the reasons it could never work. Balancing those with all the why nots.

Now, gazing at Rose, he thought, *How can I leave you? How can I let go of even the part of you I have?*

First it had been the separation from Mandy he couldn't bear to think of. But ironically it was Monkey herself who solved that problem.

'Cool, Dad,' she had said when he broached the subject over a sundae at Rumpelmayer's. She'd turned her spoon over, and licked off a blob of fudge sauce. 'I could really get into spending my vacations out there. Wow! California. Cyndi says the guys out there are really boss. Would we get a house near the beach?'

And so it had been settled, Monkey in tight jeans and Styx sweatshirt, prattling on about boys, reminding Max that in a few more years she would be eighteen, old enough to live where she wanted. She might even decide to go to college near him.

But with Rose there'd be no future, no summer vacations, no second chance. Watching her now he felt helplessly drawn to her. While there was any chance with her at all, how could he walk away?

Was it four months since he'd moved into the Beekman Place sublet? Four whole months of sleeping alone, of coming home to an empty apartment. Of fantasizing each morning when he stumbled into the bathroom, still half-asleep, that he'd find Rose's stockings drying on the shower rod. And each night when he unlocked his front door, dreaming that she'd be waiting for him in the living room, waiting to wrap her arms around him and tell him

518

about something funny that had happened to her on the way home. Max felt a hollow ache in his gut.

Other women? He thought of the last time, a few weeks ago, the pretty little blonde who managed the Lawyers Association on Vesey Street. A disaster. He hadn't been able to get it up. Finally, out of pity probably, she had taken him in her mouth. Afterwards, when she'd gone into her bathroom to wash him out, he'd lain there on her waterbed and cried. He had felt disgusted with himself, sick with missing Rose.

*Come on, stop this,* he commanded himself. *You're a big boy.*

He forced himself to pay attention to the trial, to turn his gaze on Rose's client. The doctor was holding herself very straight, hands clasped in front of her. Her butterscotch-brown hair, ending above the small of her back, shone as if it had been brushed one hundred strokes. It was held back on either side with a tortoise-shell comb. She wore a simple, well-cut suit of sand-colored linen, with a peach silk blouse. No makeup except for the palest pink lipstick. She looked young and small and frightened, despite the firm set of her chin and the steely expression of determination in her eyes.

*Strike one,* Max thought, growing worried. That jury wants Marcus Welby, someone they wouldn't hesitate to trust if right there in the jury box they should happen to have a heart attack. not a wisp of a girl who scarcely looks old enough to have graduated from medical school.

At the plaintiff's table sat a woman who could only have been Alma Saucedo's mother. Forty or so, overweight, wearing a cheap flowered dress that was pulled tightly across her plump back, showing the indented outline of her bra. An enormous black patent-leather handbag perched in her lap, her hands nervously twisting and untwisting its frayed straps.

*Strike two,* Max groaned inwardly.

The clerk, in a loud monotone, announced, 'Court is in session. Continued trial, *Saucedo* v. *Rosenthal*.' The jury

519

filed into the box. 'Let the record indicate all jurors are present and all attorneys are present.'

The hum of voices, the shuffling of shoes on the wooden floor, the rustle of coats being removed gradually died away. Only the soft hissing of the old-fashioned steam radiators, and the creaking of footsteps in the hallway outside could still be heard.

'Good morning, ladies, gentlemen,' greeted Judge Weintraub from the bench. A fair man, if a bit long in the tooth. Almost completely bald. Bad heart. He'd be retiring soon. 'Mr Di Fazio?'

Di Fazio, who had taken the chair beside his client, now jerked to his feet – like a marionette, Max thought.

'Your Honor,' Di Fazio intoned in a voice tinged with a bit of the Bronx, 'I would like to call to the stand Dr David Sloane.'

Max followed the collective gaze of the courtroom, watching as a tall, good-looking man rose from a bench near the front and strode to the stand. He wore a smartly tailored navy pinstriped suit – cut in the new Edwardian style – and a broad tie. His sideburns were long, widening into a fashionable wedge, but perfectly barbered. Max suspected the guy drove a Corvette, and listened to Mantovani on a tape deck. But, Jesus, he looked impressive: just the kind of doctor you'd want for your heart attack . . . or to give testimony in a malpractice suit. As long as he was on your side, of course.

'Good *morning*, Dr Sloane.' Di Fazio twinkled. As if it weren't thirty degrees and raining like hell outside. The worst November Max could recall in an age.

'Good morning,' Sloane lobbed back pleasantly.

'Doctor, are you a physician duly licensed to practice medicine in New York?'

'I am.'

'Would you give your educational background toward becoming a doctor?'

'I attended and graduated from Princeton, did graduate work in microbiology at Johns Hopkins, then studied medicine at Columbia, The College of Physicians and Surgeons. I interned at Good Shepherd in Brooklyn, and I was selected there to be Chief Resident in Obstetrics and Gynecology.'

Di Fazio leaned up against the witness stand, one hand shoved in his front pocket, as if he and Sloane were two old pals shooting the shit across the backyard fence.

'And are you a member of any specialty societies, Doctor?'

'Yes. I'm a diplomate of the American College of Surgeons, a member of the American College of Obstetricians and Gynecologists, a member of the International College of Surgeons, a member of the New York Gynecological Society.'

*Too smug. Good. The jury will pick up on that,* Max thought.

'And are you now affiliated with a hospital in the metropolitan area?' Di Fazio questioned.

'Yes, I am. I'm Chief of Obstetrics at St Bartholomew's.'

'And how long have you held that position, Doctor?'

'Six months. Before that I was on staff at Presbyterian.'

'Do you recall a patient who was admitted to St Bartholomew's on July fifteenth of this year, a young woman named Alma Saucedo?'

'As a matter of fact, I do. Very well.' He frowned slightly.

'Doctor, we heard testimony yesterday from Emma Dupre, who was the charge nurse on duty the night Miss Saucedo was admitted.' Di Fazio ambled over to his table, and fished a document from his open briefcase. 'Now, I'd like to hand to you Alma's hospital record, initialed by Mrs Dupre, which is Plaintiff's Exhibit Number Two in evidence. Have you seen this before, Dr Sloane?'

'Indeed I have.' He glanced over it, and returned it to the attorney. His every motion and gesture looked plainly as if they'd all been rehearsed. 'Those are my notations at the bottom of the first page. I examined Miss Saucedo on the evening of July sixteenth.'

'Can you tell us what you found when you examined the patient, Doctor?'

David Sloane appeared to be thinking, head bowed slightly, his long graceful hands clasped lightly in his lap, almost as if he were praying.

When he lifted his head finally, his green eyes troubled but clear, the effect on the crowd was electric. Murmurs rose, bodies leaned forward, expectant. Now, at last, after three days of dry testimony, they were going to get the real soap opera.

'Miss Saucedo,' he said finally, 'was in her eighth month of pregnancy. I found her to be hypertense, and showing severe signs of edema – that is, her retention of bodily fluids was very high. In other words, highly toxic.'

'So, in your opinion, she presented a risk?'

'Toxemia isn't unusual in pregnant women, especially in the final months. But yes, left untreated, it can lead to dangerous complications for both mother and child.'

'Did you prescribe anything for the patient?'

'No.'

'Oh? Can you tell us why not, Doctor?'

'She wasn't my patient. The attending physician in this case was Dr Rosenthal.' David leveled his cool gaze at Rachel.

Max could have sworn, even from this distance, he saw her shudder. The color drained from her face, the skin under her huge blue eyes seeming to take on a faint, violet tinge.

His gaze cut away to Rose. She sat very erect, chin up, shoulders thrown back, ready for battle. Good girl.

Di Fazio was grinning. A man clearly unused to smiling, his thick lips stretching to cover bad teeth.

'But you *did* have an opinion concerning the treatment being given to Miss Saucedo, did you not?'

'Yes.'

'And what was your opinion at the time, Doctor? Did you agree with Dr Rosenthal's diagnosis in this case?'

'No. I did not. Not then, and not now.'

Max saw Rachel's body jerk a little, as if she'd been slapped. She turned to Rose, shaking her head, mouthing a silent no.

'Oh? And did you share this opinion with her at the time?'

'I did. In fact, we discussed it at some length. I recommended to her that she do a caesarean section without delay. I felt the risk of premature delivery to the child was outweighed by an even greater risk to the mother. I quite distinctly remember warning Dr Rosenthal that Miss Saucedo was in danger of an embolism . . . or worse.'

Max glanced over at the jurors. This was something new. Something damning. There was a moment of deep silence punctuated only by a few rattling coughs and the hissing of the radiator.

Rachel seemed to sway slightly in her chair, as if she might faint, and suddenly a man seated directly behind her was on his feet, moving around to her side. A man in a tweed jacket with elbow patches. Tall, angular, loose-limbed, he seemed not so much to rise as unfold. Max thought of a young Gary Cooper.

Max recognized him. The same face he'd seen in magazines, talk show interviews, and later on the dust jacket of his book. And there was Rupert Everest's party in London. How could he ever forget Brian McClanahan?

The man Rose was in love with.

He felt short of breath. He needed to sit down.

Whatever Brian felt for Rose, he realized, would not affect his own fate. Not one iota. Rose loved this man. And it hardly mattered that he wouldn't – or couldn't – love her back.

Brian, too, seemed torn; his arm was about his wife's shoulders, but his eyes were on Rose, beseeching her. Was it help he wanted, or understanding?

*Time to move on,* Max told himself, feeling older, and so very sad.

At least in California the sun would be shining.

Max glanced at his Rolex. Quarter past already. He'd have to hustle. *Good luck, Rose. Good luck and goodbye,* he wished her silently as he slipped out into the corridor. He felt as if he'd come to the end of a long journey, glad in one way to put his feet up at last, and at the same time profoundly sad that it was over.

## 34

'He's lying,' Rachel said.

Rose watched her light a cigarette, and slump back in her chair. She looked gray with exhaustion, and so tense, as if a touch might shatter her. They were seated in the bailiff's room. The judge had called for a ninety-minute lunch recess.

Rose, pacing, furious, stopped and glared at Rachel.

'Either that, or *you* are.'

*What a damn idiot I've been,* she cursed herself. *Believing she's told me everything. She deliberately concealed that conversation with Sloane. God only knows what else she's kept hidden.*

Rachel shrugged. 'Does it matter?'

Rose brought her fist crashing down on the table, knocking over an empty Styrofoam coffee cup, a flimsy metal ashtray. Ashes and lipstick-stained butts spilled over the wood surface. Rachel flinched, but only slightly.

'You're damn right it matters! Yours isn't the only ass on the line. Imagine how I felt, sitting there, listening to Sal Di Fazio's hired gun fill me in on what my own client should have told me. You purposely kept me in the dark!'

Rachel just sat there, staring at a large framed photograph of President Ford on the opposite wall. Smoke drifted from her cigarette in an elongated question mark. Rose felt so helpless, frustrated. If only Rachel would yell back.

But this strange new apathy of Rachel's, how could she fight against it? Jesus, what was going on with her?

Rose thought back over the past few months, the long sessions in her office, their countless phone conversations, the endless cups of coffee they'd downed. And through it all, Rachel, with her two-fisted energy, her anger, fueling them both. Rose had come, reluctantly, to admire this woman she had considered her enemy. She had started wanting to help Rachel only as a way of getting to Brian. But now, surprising herself, she wanted to help Rachel for her own sake.

She sat down opposite Rachel, calmer now. She would *make* Rachel talk to her, tell her everything about this creep Sloane and anything else she might have been concealing . . . for both their sakes.

Rose took a deep breath.

'All right. Let's assume he *is* lying. Why? What's in it for him?'

'I don't know.' Rachel's voice, flat, dead, might have been a recorded message over the telephone.

But something in her face, a flicker of her eyelids, a muscle leaping in her clenched jaw, gave her away. *She's lying,* Rose thought.

Rose leaned forward, palms flat against the table.

'OK. Let's try it another way. Why don't you give me your version. Did you ever discuss Alma Saucedo with Dr Sloane?'

'Yes.'

'Did he make a recommendation?'

'Yes.'

'What?'

'He advised me to wait. He said there was probably more risk in inducing her labor prematurely.' She stubbed out her cigarette in the ashtray with a jerky, impatient gesture. 'I didn't bring it up because there didn't seem to be any point.'

'Do you think he's protecting himself?' Rose asked. 'Is that why he lied . . . to cover his own ass?'

But Rose didn't think so. Sloane was too smooth. Too deliberate.

'Maybe. How should I know? Look, is this really necessary? You know now. There isn't anything else to tell.'

'I think there is.'

526

Rachel turned, ever so slowly, swiveling her head toward Rose with the small careful movements of an invalid. Her blue eyes squinted against the smoke that rose and spread in a hazy stratus.

*I can see now why Brian fell in love with her,* Rose thought. *She's as stubborn as he is. I'll bet she fought like hell to save his life back in Vietnam.*

'David Sloane would like to see me drawn and quartered,' Rachel said. *'That's* why.'

'Any particular reason?'

Rachel was silent.

Rose felt hot frustration welling up in her, spilling over.

'Dammit! Just what the hell kind of game are you playing here? How do you think it's going to look when we go back in there and I make a fool of myself during cross-examination?'

'That's the thing you really care about, isn't it?' Rachel said, her voice rising. 'Your reputation, how *you're* going to look. What does it matter what happens to me?' Her eyes glittered with anger. 'Well, I can't say I'm surprised. I knew what I was getting into. Maybe that's why I agreed to hire you. Tired of secrets. Tired of bumping around in the dark. I guess maybe what this really is about is – Brian.'

'I guess maybe it is,' Rose acknowledged softly, feeling strangely elated. Maybe now it would all come out. Was that what they'd both been after from the beginning? 'I've always needed to know. Why he married you instead of me. Why he stopped loving me.'

'Are you so sure of that?' One side of Rachel's mouth twisted down in a bitter smile.

'I've done my best on this case,' Rose said. 'I want you to know that. Whatever I felt about you, I've done my best.'

'I know that. But now, tell me one thing. Are you still in love with Brian?'

OK. She had asked it, finally. And with those words Rose felt some of the bitterness that had been acting on her like a slow poison all these years drain away.

527

'Yes,' she said.

Rachel blinked hard.

'I guess I knew that, too,' Rachel said quietly, her face frozen. 'All right then. You've been honest with me. I'll tell you about David Sloane. You might as well know. There's a kind of justice in it, I can see that now. Because if I hadn't lied to Brian in the first place, he might very well have married you instead.'

'I don't understand.'

Rose felt as if the room had suddenly been tilted off balance. *Dear God in heaven, what is she saying?*

Rachel appeared calm, only her eyes glowed with a light so intense, so naked, it hurt to look into them. Rose felt slightly sick, shivery, as if she were coming down with a fever.

'You will,' Rachel said softly. 'When I explain. When I tell you how David Sloane and I murdered our child.'

Brian, she saw, was waiting. Rose spotted him in a banquette near the back, where the coats were hung. The bar was crowded, smoky. From a back room drifted the low, velvet lament of a saxophone. She waved to him, but he didn't see her. He was staring into space, a nearly empty glass of beer on the table in front of him.

She inched past the noisy hedge of people crammed along the bar. The dense sour odor of beer hovered like a mist, and the faces reflected in the long mirror above the bar shimmered in the smoky air.

She felt guilty, almost like a criminal, as if everyone here knew, and they were staring at her, accusing her. And what if, in the end, Brian didn't really want her after all? Each step sent a hot glassy sheet of terror through her. Her heart was thundering, drowning out the bar sounds.

Rose tossed her head back, clenching her jaw, reminding herself, *I'm only taking what's mine, what was always mine. Brian belongs to me.*

So close now. After waiting so long.

Almost within reach.

It was the moment she'd been waiting for, praying for, dreaming of, for seven long years. And now it was here.

*We'll be together,* she thought, *just like we planned all those years ago. We'll buy a house in some quiet neighborhood, maybe on Long Island or in Westchester. I know what he needs, a wife who will put him first, him ahead of everything and everyone. Then, in a year or two, a baby. Brian's baby. Something I could give him.*

The hazy bar, the raincoat she was wearing, and now the ripple of piano keys joining the crooning saxophone reminded her of her favorite old movie, *Casablanca*. Except for the ending – she had always hated the ending, the part where Bogie walks off into the mist, leaving Ingrid behind. Now matter how many times she saw it, she always yearned for Bogie to take Bergman in his arms and tell her that nothing mattered more than their being together.

Well, now she would rewrite that ending, have it her way.

Rose took her coat off, and slid in across from him. Her throat was so thick with emotion, she was afraid for a moment she wouldn't be able to speak.

Then Brian looked up from his beer, his deep gray eyes expectant.

'I was afraid you wouldn't be here,' she said.

He looked surprised. 'I told you I would.' He smiled. 'Would you like something to drink? A beer? I'm afraid that's about all this place has to offer. Their idea of a mixed drink is a boilermaker. I only chose it because it's right around the corner.'

'It really doesn't matter.' She felt a tiny stab of impatience. Did he think she *cared* where they were? 'I don't want anything to drink.'

He shrugged, finishing his beer in one swallow. She saw the long stubbled slide of his throat as he threw his head back. She wanted to touch him, hold him, kiss every part of him. How sad he seemed, older somehow than the last time she'd sat across from him at a table like this one, lines fanning out from the corners of his eyes.

529

'Brian . . .' She reached out, felt his long fingers curl about hers, warm and slightly moist.

*What will you say when I tell you? That your wife has been lying to you all these years? That she'll never have your child? Will you come to me then?*

'. . . I'm glad you're here,' she finished. 'I wanted to talk to you . . . about something. About Rachel.'

Brian's shoulders sagged, and the light seemed to go out in his eyes.

'You know then.'

'What?'

He was silent a moment. Then, 'She's left me.'

Rose felt a wild joy filling her, expanding her. Brian was free, *free*. It was all so easy. Rachel had done it all for them.

'*She* left you? Did she say why?'

'She didn't have to. It's been coming a long time now. We . . .' His throat worked, and tears stood in his eyes. 'Look, I don't want to dump all this on you. It's got nothing to do with the trial. It started a while back . . . I don't know when or how. God, I wish I did.'

Seeing the hopeless despair on Brian's face, Rose felt her elation drain away.

She felt as if she were sinking. He's upset because of the shock, she reassured herself. He'll get over it. Someday, he'll look back on this and see it as good fortune in disguise.

Especially once she told him the truth about Rachel.

'Brian, there's something you should know . . .' Rose broke off, suddenly unsure.

She was remembering the bravery of Rachel's confession. If she'd cried, moaned in self-pity, telling Brian now would be easier. But all Rachel had asked was that she listen, not judge. With those naked blazing eyes of hers, she'd asked for understanding, not forgiveness.

Rose grew annoyed with herself.

*Tell him now. This is your chance. Their marriage is over anyway. You didn't have anything to do with that. You're only taking what was yours in the first place.*

530

But Brian wasn't even paying attention, she realized. He was staring into space again, far away from anything she had to say. She wanted to snatch him by the collar, shake him, *make* him see her, be with her.

Then she sat back, a little shocked at herself. She had imagined drumrolls and violins, lightning bolts, glorious fireworks. And here they were . . . in a crummy bar on Third Avenue . . . drinking beer . . . lost in their separate thoughts. Brian wanting consolation. She wanting promises of love.

*We're like* – oh God, it hurt her just to *think* a thing like that might be possible – *strangers. Can it be? Is it possible I've changed so much, that we've become such different people from those we were before the war?*

Suddenly, as the music changed, she found herself thinking about Max. How empty the apartment seemed since he had moved out. How only last night she had reached out across the cold expanse of bed and he wasn't there. How she missed the stupidest things, his razor and toothbrush on the bathroom sink, his papers scattered across the coffee table.

Oh God, what was wrong with her? Brian was all she wanted, all she had ever needed. And now was her chance.

But something stopped her. Was it recognizing the loneliness in his face? Yes, she'd felt it too, that emptiness, like a deserted city street at four in the morning with the cold wind whipping. Oh, yes . . .

*I felt that way after Max left.*

Then the words were spilling out of her. But not the things she had come here to say.

'I don't want to play five-cent psychiatrist here or anything,' she began gently. 'But I've seen this before . . . whatever problems you might have been having . . . a thing like this, a trial, your life laid open to a courtroom full of strangers . . . it has a funny effect on people. On marriages. Don't come to any conclusions right away, that's all I'm saying. Give it time.'

'When will it be over, this damn trial?'

531

'A day or two more at the most, I'm hoping. I've asked Judge Weintraub for a recess until Monday. There are a few loose ends I need to check into.' *Dr Sloane, for instance. I have a feeling he's not exactly kosher, over and above what Rachel has told me.*

Brian hung his head for a moment, and when he lifted it, his eyes were rimmed with red. He smiled then, a gentle, sad smile.

Rose felt her heart break a little, and she remembered a time when he had grieved for *her*. Yes, that awful day when she was thirteen, playing the part of Mary Magdalene in the school's Easter play. All those hateful boys throwing their papier-mâché stones straight at her breasts – her big cow breasts – smirking so only she, not the audience, could see. Oh, how humiliated she'd been! But she couldn't let them know. And then, afterwards, there was Brian, finding her backstage, all the suffering she had felt written there in his face. His arms wrapping about her, folding her stiff, proud body into his embrace.

Looking at him now, Rose saw how little he had changed, really, that same compassion was undimmed. She stared at his hand on the table, his long fingers curled around his glass, a faint ink stain on his thumb, and she imagined him reaching for her, stroking her face.

'It's like Vietnam,' Brian was saying. 'You know why we lost the war? I'll tell you. It had nothing to do with Tricky Dick. Or Kent State. Or the CIA. It was because we couldn't *see* what we were fighting. Not just Charlie. Not just the guys in black pajamas planting pongee sticks and claymores – what I'm talking about is not knowing what the hell we were supposed to be fighting for. The enemy wasn't the Viet Cong after all, it was *us*. That's what killed us. We didn't know what we were fighting for, and it kept us running around in circles instead.

'And that's what's killing Rachel. Not knowing who the enemy is. The Saucedos? Di Fazio? I don't think so. I think it's her . . . *us*. There's something wrong with the two of us, something missing. I used to think it was the child we didn't have, but now I know it's more than that. We both need something we can hang on to. Something solid. But, Christ, it's just not there any more. It used to be. Maybe it still is . . . somewhere . . . and we're just not looking hard enough.'

*Or maybe you chose the wrong woman in the first place,* Rose thought.

But the bitterness was less strong than it used to be. She felt something else mixed in with it now, something that rinsed through her, sweet and clear as a mountain spring.

Forgiveness.

*I loved you, Brian. I loved you enough to die for you. But I couldn't have saved you, not as Rachel did. And now I understand. How the winds of change can blow. How events can be bigger, stronger than we are. And even how you can love more than one person, each love with its own subtle shadings, one maybe stronger but not necessarily canceling out the other.*

She had been chasing the proverbial rainbow. A part of Brian had loved her, and always would love her. Just as a grown person loves his happy memories of childhood. Barefoot summers and Orange Ne-Hi and a ten-cent ride on the subway to Coney Island. A love so poignant because, she sensed, there was no going back to it.

'I wonder how it would have turned out for us. If you'd married me instead,' Rose said. There was a time when she couldn't have said those words, it would have hurt too much.

Brian smiled, some of the sadness lifting from his face. 'We'd be making mistakes, just like everybody else. We'd be squabbling over who left the toothpaste uncapped, and which movie to go see. And, yeah, there'd probably be times when we'd wish we'd married other people.'

'But we'd have been happy.'

'Yeah. Probably.' His hand tightened about hers, and his gaze met hers, clear and untroubled, for a brief moment. 'But, Rose, we didn't have a monopoly on happiness. You loved me partly because you felt so alone. And

533

you were so damn *proud*. If you'd let others in . . .'

'I didn't want anyone else.'

'It's tough, Rose, being the only one responsible for another person's happiness. No-one should ever be the *only* one.'

Tears stung her eyes, but she forced a smile. 'You didn't do so badly.'

He shook his head, looking pleased. 'I never thought I'd hear you say that.'

'For a long time, I couldn't have. It hurt too much, remembering those days. But I guess I've changed. We both have. I guess I'd rather remember the good things than throw them all out with the bad.' She cocked her head, remembering. 'Do you still have that Saint Christopher's medal I gave you?'

'No, but it saved my life. In Nam.' Haltingly, he told her his version of the rescue Rose had read about in the newspapers.

'I'm glad you told me.' She withdrew her hand to brush the wetness from her eyes. 'All those months, I felt so frustrated, not being able to reach you. In a way, this sort of evens the score.'

'What score?'

'Rachel and you. For years, I've been jealous as hell over the fact that she saved your life. It was something I would have done for you a hundred times over . . . only I never got the chance.'

*But you have the chance now,* she told herself.

'Rose . . . if it makes any difference,' he told her, haltingly, 'I *did* love you. I . . . I still do, in a way.'

'I know,' she said.

They exchanged a long, tender look. She understood exactly what he meant . . . because she felt the same way. They loved who they'd each been, and who they might have been . . . not who they were now.

'Do you love Rachel?' Rose asked, breaking the long silence.

534

'Yes. I'm not sure I knew how much until these past few days.'

He looked at her, and she saw nothing but honesty in those fine gray eyes that seemed to open straight off his heart. There had never been anything but honesty in Brian.

*I could tell him how she lied, I could bring him to his knees, but that isn't what I want, is it? No, not any more.*

Rose sat back, marveling at how little pain she felt. She had come to the end with Brian, and there was only bittersweet nostalgia.

'Go after her,' she told him with sudden urgency. 'If you really mean that, then go after her, tell her you love her no matter what she's done, or will ever do.'

'As simple as that?'

'No. It's never simple. I'm not saying that.' An image of Max filled her mind, free at last of Brian's shadow. An image keen as a beautiful keepsake she had given away, not realizing its value.

*Oh, Max, why didn't I see?*

'You have to try,' she finished lamely, unable to convey all that she was feeling.

'Rose, there's something else . . . I've hated myself for a long time for what happened with us.'

'Don't,' she said, and she meant it. She squeezed his hand once, then let go. 'You were right, what you said before. If we had gotten married . . . well, maybe I wasn't ready then for anything less than perfect. Like that fort up on the roof. Our own little world. But it wasn't real, was it? It was just made up. Like those stories you used to write.'

'Rose . . . what I felt for you, that was real.'

'I know. I know that now.' She slid sideways, and stood up. 'I have to go now, Bri. There's something important I forgot to do.' *I just hope it's not too late.*

He rose, and awkwardly put out his hand. 'Goodbye, Rose.'

Ignoring his hand, she kissed him lightly on the cheek, feeling a knot in the back of her throat. 'Goodbye. And good luck. I hope everything works out for you. You know, it's funny, but in spite of everything, I still believe in happy endings.'

Rose turned back into the crowded bar, trailed by the lonesome trill of a saxophone, and said a silent prayer that Max would be home when she called.

# 35

The judge brought his gavel down with a perfunctory thunk that sent a shudder through Rachel. She felt so tense, the muscles in her back and shoulders locked in place, as if the slightest movement would snap her in two like a dry twig.

*God, let this be over soon.*

She had handled worse, far worse, in Vietnam. Broken, bleeding men. Dying babies. But she had been strong then, knowing what to do, and doing it. Here she felt powerless to help even herself, her future in other people's hands.

'Continued trial, Saucedo versus Rosenthal . . .,' the clerk called out loudly for the benefit of the stenographer bent over her little machine, tapping away at it like some manic overgrown insect.

The preliminaries observed, jury attendance taken.

And now the show begins, Rachel thought, glancing about, seeing the faces around her sharpen with attention, hearing the din fade away. She fingered the charm hanging from the chain about her neck – a tiny gold caduceus, symbol of the physician. Kay had given it to her at the start of the trial.

'I almost got you a Star of David,' she'd said. 'But I chose this instead. I figured you'd need reminding – so OK you're not God, you're a doctor . . . but a damn good one.'

She wished Kay were here now. But Rachel had insisted, despite Kay's protestations, that she stay at the clinic. There was too much to do, and they were short-staffed as it was.

Though after this trial, there might not be a clinic, she reminded herself bitterly.

Well, it wouldn't go on much longer. Whatever the

outcome, the agony would soon be over. Then there was life to be faced without Brian, and she'd have to find a way to deal with that. But at least the secrets, the lies, would be finished.

A strange exhausted relief stole over her.

*It's in Rose's hands now. The perfect weapon. She can save me and destroy me in one stroke. Reveal everything about David and me, save me from his lies . . . and damn me with my own.*

She looked over at Rose, rising from her chair, tall and somehow invincible. She seemed to dominate the courtroom, a blaze of determination. She wore a blouse of deep crimson, tweed skirt, black leather boots. A crucifix at her throat, with pearls looped below. That odd, lone ruby earring. Her dark hair riding her shoulders like a thundercloud.

*She's different. Stronger. Something's happened to her. Brian? Has she been with Brian?*

Rachel imagined them together, Rose and Brian. Intertwined in bed, touching, kissing, loving each other without barriers, without secrets. She felt as if her heart had been sliced open.

She missed Brian, more than she would ever have thought possible. She had not seen him in two days, except here in the courtroom. They had not spoken. Not since she'd gone to stay with Mama. She had left him a note, asked that he not try to contact her, at least not for a little while.

He would know why soon enough.

She willed herself not to turn around, not to search for his dear, familiar face. But she could feel his presence. Warming her, supporting her. Despite everything, he would give her his loyalty.

But soon he'd know how she'd lied to him. What then?

Her life was in Rose's hands now. Everything depended on Rose. Why had she confided in Rose? Why put a loaded gun in the hands of the one person who had the most to gain by destroying her?

*Because I'm tired,* she thought, *exhausted from lying.* So exhausted she felt ill.

Suddenly she couldn't bear the thought of everyone knowing, Brian, Mama, all these bloodthirsty strangers. Her secret – how she had forced David to abort his own child – dragged into the light like some grotesque insect from under a rock. People would never understand, they'd see it as her monstrous revenge, something vile and depraved. And how could she explain it, make people believe that what she'd wanted was something decent, something her conscience could live with?

*Don't do it,* she pleaded silently, watching Rose approach the bench, the white-haired judge lean toward her. *Oh, please, don't.*

'Your Honor, I wish to cross-examine Mr Di Fazio's last witness, Dr Sloane,' Rose said, her voice ringing out, clear and confident.

Judge Weintraub cleared his throat, nodded, crepe-paper eyelids drooping. 'You may proceed, Counsel.'

Rachel stared down at her hands, clenched tightly in her lap. No. She wouldn't look at him. Wouldn't give him the satisfaction . . .

A rustle of cool air passing alongside her, that could only be David. She caught a trace of something sweet-smelling, cloying. His aftershave. Her stomach twisted.

Then her gaze was drawn upward, in spite of herself, as if by a reverse gravity. She met his eyes for an instant, and as if she had touched an exposed live wire, an ugly shock kicked through her. His eyes were utterly cold, devoid of all emotion. The eyes of a department store mannequin.

Rachel watched him take the stand in what looked like a custom-tailored gray suit, French-cuffed shirt, and Gucci loafers. An impressive-looking man, a formidable witness.

A smooth liar.

Anger made her sit up straighter, tilt her chin back the tiniest bit. *I can't fight you the way I'd like to,* she told him mentally, *but I'll be damned if I'll give you the satisfaction of thinking you've beaten me down.*

She fixed her eyes now on Rose, standing relaxed and poised before the witness stand, a sheaf of papers in one hand. Did she *feel* as confident as she looked?

'Dr Sloane,' Rose began pleasantly, 'I'm going to ask you questions, and I'm going to ask you to keep your voice up and project, if you will, in the direction of the jury so we can all hear your answers.'

'Happy to,' David replied, smiling a little.

'Doctor, you testified on Friday that before you accepted the position of Chief of Obstetrics at St Bartholomew's, you were on staff at—' she consulted the sheaf of papers in her hands ' – Presbyterian Hospital. Is that correct?'

'Yes, it is.'

'And before that?'

'I was in private practice for a short time.'

'I see.' She consulted her papers once again. 'I don't believe that was mentioned when you were questioned by Mr Di Fazio. Perhaps it slipped your mind, Doctor. Would you tell us, please, when and where that was?'

A tiny frown had appeared to mar the celluloid perfection of David's demeanor. 'Certainly. It was in Westbury, Connecticut. I was in group practice there with two other doctors. Let's see, that would have been from the fall of seventy-one to the spring of seventy-three.'

'A rather short time, wouldn't you say?'

He shrugged. 'Private practice isn't for everyone. I prefer the challenge of a city hospital.'

'Doctor, do you recall a patient under your care at that time – a woman by the name of Sarah Potts?'

He hesitated an instant, then, 'Yes, of course.'

'Can you describe her condition?'

'She was pregnant.'

'Did you deliver Mrs Pott's baby, Doctor?'

'No.'

'Could you tell us – and please do speak up, Doctor, so all the members of the jury can hear – *why* you didn't.'

540

Rose's admonition for David to speak up had just the opposite effect, clearly the effect Rose had desired, Rachel observed. David's voice dropped, seemed to stumble a bit even.

'She miscarried in her fifth month. Naturally, I did everything I could, but she was—'

'You don't have to explain, Doctor. Just answer the question.'

'Doctor, do you recall a patient you examined on January seventeenth of 1971. A patient by the name of Edna Robbins?'

'Let's see now . . .' He hesitated, appearing uncertain.

'Let the record indicate I'm showing the witness a medical chart, Mrs Robbins's. Doctor, do you recognize your handwriting?'

'My handwriting.' David frowned a little, studying the paper in his hands. 'Ah yes, Mrs Robbins. It comes back to me now. An unusual case.'

'Unusual in what way? Could you describe for the jury Mrs Robbins's condition at the time you first saw her?'

'She'd been referred to me by her family practitioner for infertility. She and her husband had been trying to have a baby for years without success.'

'And what treatment, if any, did you prescribe?'

'I ordered the usual tests to begin with. A sperm test for her husband, which showed a normal count. Then a tubal X ray for Mrs Robbins . . .'

'And was this tubal X ray administered by a licensed radiologist?'

'Naturally.'

'And what were the results of that test, Doctor?'

'I . . .' David faltered.

'Isn't it true, Doctor, that Mrs Robbins was indeed pregnant, without knowing it, at the time that test was administered?'

'I . . . yes, it's coming back to me now. So unfortunate . . .'

'Why unfortunate?'

541

'Well, you see, they inject a dye . . . and it would have automatically aborted the pregnancy.'

'But couldn't such a dreadful mistake have been avoided?'

'Mrs Robbins *came* to me because she and her husband had been trying for a child for more than five years.' David sounded irritated, and he was beginning to look a little flushed, too.

'But isn't there a test, Doctor, a *simple* urine test for determining pregnancy in a woman?'

'Yes.'

'And did you administer that test to Mrs Robbins?'

'No.' The word came out tight, clipped. 'What happened was a fluke, one in a million, it . . .'

And now, descending like a hammer stroke, 'Doctor, isn't it true you were *asked* by your associates to leave their practice? That they felt you had a drinking problem that was affecting your performance?'

The Saucedos' attorney, Mr Di Fazio – a little toad of a man, Rachel thought, eyeing him with revulsion – hopped up, face pink.

'Your Honor, I object. This is entirely out of line! Doctor Sloane isn't the one on trial here.'

Rose, unruffled, turned toward the bench, saying, 'I am only attempting to establish the credentials of this witness, since his testimony is so vital to my client.'

The judge turned to Rose. 'Unless you're prepared to substantiate this, Counsel, I'm going to have to ask you to desist from this particular line of questioning,' he admonished.

'Very well, Your Honor, I'll withdraw the question, since Dr Rausch could not be here today.'

Rachel was aware of a stirring behind her, voices murmuring. Jurors who, a moment ago, had looked bored were leaning forward in their chairs, eyes sharp, attentive. Something big was happening, she sensed. Something that made the room seem to crackle with electricity, and caused her scalp to tighten.

Judge Weintraub, frowning, seemingly annoyed, rapped his gavel several times in quick succession.

Rose hesitated, bowing her head slightly, a small smile fixed on her lips. She toyed with the crucifix around her neck.

'Let's move ahead, shall we, Dr Sloane,' she continued, 'to when you were on staff at Presbyterian, following your . . . ah, shall we say, *disenchantment* with group practice in Connecticut. Isn't it true, Dr Sloane, that you were *asked* to leave Presbyterian as well?'

'Certainly not,' David said just a hair too loudly. 'I resigned.'

The very tip of his tongue, the tiniest sliver of glistening pink, edged out, sliding over his lips.

'Perhaps you'd care to enlighten us, Dr Sloane, about the circumstances which led up to your . . . ah, resignation.'

'I'm not sure I know which circumstances you're referring to.' David was leaning forward now, his frown deepening, his hands forming a steeple under his chin. 'I was offered the position of Chief of Obstetrics at St Bartholomew's, and I took it. It's as simple as that.' He managed a smile that was somehow less convincing, less confident than before. 'I'm sorry to disappoint you, but I'm afraid there's no mystery.'

'But isn't it true that with your present position at St Bartholomew's you took a cut in pay?'

'I don't know why my salary should be of any concern here.' He spoke through gritted teeth, and Rachel watched him redden, his composure slipping another notch. 'I had reasons . . . good reasons . . . St Bartholomew's was a challenge . . . the OB department in need of proper management.'

'Dr Sloane, isn't it true you were *asked* to resign from Presbyterian, that your colleagues had threatened to take you before the board of medical ethics if you refused to cooperate?'

'That's a lie!' David erupted, his handsome face fracturing for an instant into something ugly, mean. Then

543

he caught himself, and smoothed his face with one long elegant hand, regaining his composure. Lowering his voice, he volunteered, 'There were people . . . colleagues . . . who were jealous, didn't want to see me promoted. I was the best, you see . . .'

*Something is happening*, Rachel thought, a tiny blade of hope forcing its way up through her depression. *Dear Lord, look at him, he is losing his cool.*

'The best at what, Doctor? Tell us what you were best at.'

'Objection!' Di Fazio roared. 'Counsel is badgering the witness!'

'Overruled.'

Rose turned back to David. 'Doctor, do you remember a delivery you attended in February of 1974, when you were still at Presbyterian? A woman named Katherine Cantrell, in her seventh month of pregnancy?' Her voice was soft, almost seductive.

'Katherine Cantrell,' he echoed dully. 'Yes.'

'Was it a normal delivery?'

'No . . . let me see . . . her labor was premature. And there were . . . difficulties.'

'You delivered Mrs Cantrell's baby by caesarean section. Is that correct, Dr Sloane?'

'Yes.'

'And afterwards, you performed an emergency hysterectomy? Please correct me if I'm mistaken, Dr Sloane.'

'Yes . . . yes,' David answered, sounding impatient, wary. 'But what has that got to do with—'

'Doctor,' Rose cut in, her voice soft, almost velvety, yet each word somehow distinct, sharp as nails, 'was Mrs Cantrell's baby born healthy?' He stopped, staring ahead vacantly. Then said, 'It was premature. There were complications. It . . . didn't survive more than a few hours.'

'It? You mean you don't even remember the infant's sex, whether it was a boy or a girl?'

'I . . . no, I don't seem to recall.'

'Let me fresh your memory then, Doctor.' She didn't

544

look at her notes this time, but stared straight at the witness. 'Lynda Ann Cantrell, weighing three pounds, six ounces, at the age of two hours and forty-two minutes, died on February the nineteenth, at three-thirty A.M.'

The hush fell over the court.

Then Rose continued softly, 'I hope this won't sound simple-minded, Doctor, but is it true that after a hysterectomy a woman is unable to bear children?'

'That is correct.'

'To be more specific, Mrs Cantrell will never have another child?'

'That's correct.'

'And was this Mrs Cantrell's first baby . . . her *only* baby?'

'I . . . yes, I believe so.'

'You believe so? You mean you aren't sure?'

'It . . . it was some time ago.'

'But, surely, even the busiest doctor would remember such a terrible tragedy. Surely he would remember it as well, if not better, than a casual comment, made months ago, merely in *conversation* about another doctor's patient.' She paused. 'Dr Sloane, isn't it true you were intoxicated at the time you performed a caesarean section, then a subsequent hysterectomy on Katherine Cantrell? That the physician who was assisting you, Dr Roland Church, issued a complaint to that effect to his superior?'

Rachel watched Di Fazio start to rise, open his mouth to object, but he was too late. David was on his feet, lunging forward, hands splayed against the wooden barrier in front of the witness stand.

'Lies! All lies! Church . . . that bastard . . . he wanted the promotion for himself . . .'

'Your Honor, I'd like to move for a ten-minute recess.' Di Fazio was on his feet, sweating profusely, wheedling now. 'My witness is clearly upset by all this unsubstantiated innuendo. Miss Santini seems to think, by pointing the finger in another direction, that she can cover up the wrongdoing of the defendant.'

545

It was coming back to Rachel now, the gossip she'd heard. She'd run into Janet Needham some months ago – Janet was now specializing in neonatology at Presbyterian – and she *had* alluded to rumors about David's drinking, come to think of it. But Rachel hadn't taken it too seriously. As far as she knew, David had always avoided liquor, because of his father.

She felt the muscles in her shoulders and back cramping, sending a sharp ache up the back of her neck. She knew she ought to be relieved. David had said nothing about *her*, the two of them . . . and yet Rose had nonetheless managed to place his sterling reputation in doubt.

But what Rachel felt was angry. Why should David be let off the hook now? He was obviously guilty, so why wasn't *he* on trial?

Rachel felt something building inside her, rising up like a bubble from the queasy tension in her stomach. Pushing up her throat, inexorably, even while she struggled to control it.

Then bursting forth, a shocking sound in the silence of the courtroom.

She began to giggle helplessly.

Now David was staring at her, his face seeming to swell, turning an ugly bloated scarlet.

Then she was remembering something else, years and years ago, a Sunday when she and David had been strolling in Central Park, David nearly tripping on a crack in the asphalt, his arms flinging out, pinwheeling madly, the expression on his face almost comical. Catching himself just in time. Standing nearby, there'd been a kid, ten or eleven, who'd started to laugh, hands cupped over his mouth. And David had stridden over, out of breath, enraged, grabbing the kid by the front of his T-shirt, nearly lifting him off his feet. 'Don't laugh,' David had hissed. 'Don't *ever* laugh at me.'

*And now he must think* I'm laughing at him. Making fun of him.

Rachel watched, still giggling, as he grew pop-eyed, and a muscle in his cheek began to twitch.

Then, incredibly, others began to laugh softly, and Rachel remembered how infectious giggles could be, especially when you were trying hard to control them.

It was too much for David.

Now his mouth was working, twisting, making him ugly somehow. Breathing heavily, David leveled a wavering finger at Rachel.

'Bitch! It was you. All your fault. Everything.' Even his voice had changed, coarse and rasping. 'I'll get you for this. I'll make you suffer. *Fucking bitch!*'

The silence in the courtroom was absolute. A moment of suspended animation so perfect it was almost a vacuum.

Then all hell broke loose.

Di Fazio rushed to the stand, struggling to subdue his witness.

Mrs Saucedo, in a kelly-green pantsuit, began jabbering excitedly in Spanish to the woman behind her, probably a relative.

The calm of the jury box disintegrated, men and women – blacks, Hispanics, whites – suddenly all talking at once.

Other voices, speaking rapid-fire Spanish, joined the babble.

*I have to get out of here. Now. Right now.*

Rachel stood up, felt the blood rushing from her head, leaving only white noise, like the snowy static that fills a TV screen after the station has switched off for the night. She felt as if she were traveling backward through a tunnel at a very rapid speed. She thought dreamily, *I'm going to faint, aren't I?*

The last thing she remembered was the crashing sound of a gavel.

Rose watched Rachel fold in on herself, begin to crumple. Rose started toward her, but by the time she reached

Rachel, there were half a dozen people clustered about her.

A stocky silver-haired man had his arm about Rachel's shoulders, supporting her. Rose, drawing closer, recognized him as the man who had spoken to her once before, who had congratulated her in the corridor after she had won the Krupnik case. Oddly, since then, she had run into him several times outside the courthouse.

A Greek name. Alexandros, wasn't it?'

What was he doing here?

Then Rose stopped, arrested by the sight of a woman rising in consternation from a bench in the very back of the courtroom. A woman, straw-slim and graceful, dressed in a cashmere suit, a heathery blend of cerulean and lavender and misty blue. And underneath, a wisp of silk blouse showing, soft as a cloud. Gloves, too, and a hat that shaded most of her face. An older woman, but still quite beautiful. You could see that, just in the way she moved.

As the woman came closer, Rose felt her heart quicken. *I know that face. Where? Where have I seen her before?*

Then the woman reached distractedly to straighten her hat, brushing her ear, where a tiny diamond earring glittered.

It came to Rose, suddenly, wondrously. *It's her.*

Rose unconsciously fingered the ruby teardrop in her right ear. She felt as if she were in some kind of absurdist play in which all points, past, present, and future, had converged on this one stage.

*No, I'm imagining things. It can't be.*

Then the woman was pausing, midway up the aisle, her gaze locking with Rose's. Eyes that were huge and bright with tears, the color of sea water, set in a face as fine and webbed as old Meissen china. Eyes filled with a mute and terrible anguish.

And with that one glance, Rose felt reality abruptly end, the long and gritty sidewalk that had brought her to this place, this moment. She had stepped off the curb into a dream.

*Who are you? What do you want from me?*

Then the moment was gone. The woman became suddenly brisk, angling her way toward the group clustered by the table, her slender gloved hands reaching out, forming a beautiful blue bower about the pale statue that was Rachel.

With shock, Rose heard Rachel cry out, 'Mama!'

# 36

Letting himself in, Brian immediately caught sight of Rachel, curled in the Adirondack chair by the fireplace. He stopped, his hand still on the doorknob, a stunned joy spreading through him.

'Rachel.'

His heart leaping now, Had she come back, then? Was that what she had been waiting to tell him?

She looked up at him and smiled. Yet her expression was so sad, her blue eyes bright with unshed tears.

Brian felt his joy fade, his gut wrench. What was she going to say?

*Dear Christ, if she's come to tell me it's over, for good, I don't think I could stand that. I've been missing her so damn much. I need her.*

'Brian. Hi.'

Her voice seemed to unlock him, pull him in from the door. He walked toward her, slowly, eyes fixed on her. He imagined himself a photographer. One who had spent endless hours frustrated by imperfect angles, murky light, awkward poses, and then suddenly saw everything come perfectly together. The table lamp giving off the perfect amount of light, a muted sepia shade, rounding out the woman curled in the chair with soft shadows, painting her in soft pinks and golds and greens.

All he stood to lose, it was so clear to him now.

Brian felt as if a cold finger were touching his heart.

When had she ever looked so young? Or so beautiful. Almost like a teenager, in jeans and one of his old shirts, her bare feet tucked up underneath her, hugging her knees to her chest. Her dark gold hair looked freshly washed, spilling over her shoulders, damp and still glittering with moisture.

He saw now how vulnerable she was under that tough facade. He had expected her always to be strong, to be able to manage anything. And maybe the anger he'd felt toward her had been frustration that she didn't really need him. He had wanted so many times to gather her into his arms, the frightened little girl he'd always suspected was inside her somewhere – the girl he saw before him now – just the way he'd used to do with Rose.

He ached now to touch Rachel, hold her, but something held him back. As if she might break apart, or worse, draw away from him, pull back into her shell.

No, he'd let her set the pace, choose the moment to say what she'd come here to say.

'It's over,' she said.

His blood seemed to turn to ice water.

But she smiled faintly.

And then he understood. She meant the trial. Oh Jesus, of course.

He hadn't seen her since yesterday, that unbelievable scene in the courtroom, people crowding around her, cutting him off from her. He had yearned to scoop her up in his arms, carry her right back here where she'd be safe, where together they could begin again. But he had stopped, afraid she would resent his intrusion. And – even more stupidly – he had felt angry. *She* should make the first move, he thought. She had hurt him. Leaving like that, with only a note stuck up on the refrigerator.

And now, with the trial over, she'd had a chance to think things over, and decided it was hopeless for them to go on.

'The lawyers met this morning,' she said. 'The Saucedos have agreed to settle.'

Brian, sitting down on the sofa opposite Rachel, felt a stiffness in his limbs, as if he were folding the blades of his old Swiss army knife. And he felt cold, so cold.

But still he forced his attention to what she was saying.

He *was* glad the trial was over. But not surprised, after what happened yesterday. That bastard, Sloane. Why hadn't Rachel ever told him Sloane had it in for her?

'You don't look too happy about it,' he said.

She stared at the painting over the mantel, a watercolor of huge sea turtles swimming underwater. Brian remembered when Rachel had found it, in a little gallery on Grove Street, and how she'd fallen in love with it on the spot. *Don't you see,* she had explained, *what a miracle it is, how graceful they are underwater, those creatures who are so clumsy on land?*

Rachel was like those turtles, in a way. Swimming with powerful strokes in waters where she was familiar, dangerous waters other people would drown in, saving lives, even risking her own when necessary. But faltering, unsure, when it came to opening her heart and trusting someone, trusting him.

'The insurance company's offer,' she finally said, 'it was a lot lower than the one they made before. Just a token, really. And the Saucedos . . . they were so grateful to have it, to have anything . . . oh God, Brian, it was so . . . *pathetic.*'

'You shouldn't feel responsible,' he told her. 'It wasn't your fault.'

She shrugged. 'Who is responsible for anyone when it comes right down to it? No, I don't think it was my fault, what happened to Alma. But I've told the bank to release some of the money my father left in trust for me. I want Alma's family to have it. I don't feel I *owe* them anything, but I *want* to do this. For that baby. For Alma's son.'

Rachel looked at him, and he saw some of her old fire kindle in her eyes. He thought of the courageous doctor who had gone out on a limb for him, just one more grunt chewed up and spat out by the war, but she – who knows why – had believed in him, and had cheated death. And it was *that* passion of hers to save and heal that had made him fall in love with her. A medicine of the heart.

Could he reject that now?

And the blame for all their troubles, he had a share in that. *I wanted it for myself, all that passion, that burning light, I was jealous.*

'Rachel . . .' He started to say 'I love you,' but the words seemed to freeze in his throat. It was hard to get past that stony look on her face.

'We have to talk, Brian. About us.' She unfolded her legs. and stood up. She walked over to the fireplace, started to reach for the pack of cigarettes on the mantel, then changed her mind, and pushed them away almost savagely. She turned to Brian, face tilted up, jaw cocked, eyes blazing.

He felt chilled, knowing this was how she looked when facing a hard task, all steel and fire, clenched with grim purpose.

Brian instinctively jumped to his feet, put his hands out in front of him. 'Wait. Listen. Before you say anything else. I want you to know . . . I'm sorry.'

'*You're* sorry.' She was staring at him, shocked. Then she blinked, and he saw that her lashes were studded with tears. 'Oh, I see, because of Rose, you mean.'

'Rose?'

'You're still in love with her, aren't you?'

Brian had a sudden urge to laugh. Rose? She thought he was having an affair with Rose. Oh Jesus, where could she have gotten such an idea – from Rose?

'How on earth—' he began.

'Your book,' she cut in, 'I read some of it. About her.' All at once her steely composure seemed to crumple. 'You don't have to explain. Brian. In a way I understand. I . . . I don't blame you.'

'You *don't* understand,' he shouted, angry that she was hurting herself, and for no reason. 'I wrote that about a time in my life. That time has passed. Just because I can recall how I felt then doesn't mean I feel that way now.'

'How do you feel now? No, wait, don't answer that.' She folded her arms over her chest, gripping both elbows tightly. She kept her head down, addressing the hooked

553

rug at her feet. 'I have something to say first. Something I should have told you a long time ago, before we were married. I was afraid then. I was afraid if I told you, you would stop loving me. And now I'm even more afraid. Because . . . oh God, this is so hard . . .' She stopped, seemed to struggle with herself, her face so pale it seemed almost transparent. 'Because I've been lying to you all these years. I let you think something that wasn't true. I let you believe there was no real reason why we couldn't have a child.'

Rachel felt as if she were tumbling down a gentle hillside. A spiraling light-headedness, a rush of blood to her face. A good feeling, a feeling of letting go, breaking free of this heavy weight she'd worn on her heart for so long.

For one wild, elated instant she flew up in the air, totally free. She'd done it. And she couldn't stop now even if she wanted to.

And then Brian, she saw, was staring at her, shocked, bewildered.

'I don't understand,' he said.

Once again, Rachel grew heavy and afraid.

*No, I can't turn back now,* she thought, filling with panic. *I've made it this far, I have to tell him the rest. Even if he curses me, hates me, that would be better than this . . . this wall between us. This awful invisible barrier.*

Oh, she wanted him back so badly, seeing him standing there, so familiar, so unbearably dear. Staring at her with those deep eyes, the first part of him she had fallen in love with. She could almost feel the heat of his body. She wanted to reach out, wrap herself in all that warmth. Lose herself in him.

But not if she had to lie to him.

She jerked her head up, and held his gaze. *Be brave,* she told herself.

'You probably wondered, yesterday in court—' Rachel stumbled ahead, slowly, as if learning to walk again after an illness, groping for words, 'why David Sloane hates me

554

so much, why he wanted to hurt me. You see, he and I . . . we were lovers. A long time ago. During my internship. I got pregnant, and he . . . well, he wanted me to have an abortion. But I couldn't. Not his way, cold, like having a tooth pulled, as if it didn't matter. And so . . . I . . . I made *him* do it, the abortion. That's why he hates me. And that's why . . . I was sick, you see so sick afterwards . . . and they said . . . oh God . . . the X rays . . . they said I would probably never have a child . . . a chance in a thousand . . . ' She broke off, stepping backward, feeling the cold edge of the marble mantel against her back. She felt as if she were shrinking, huddling to ward off the awful pain inside her. 'Now you know. Why you should have married Rose instead. Why there's no point in going on from here.'

She felt tears rising in her, but she held them back. She had no right to cry, feel sorry for herself. This was *her* doing. And right now she was making Brian look like when he was wounded in Vietnam, pale as death, shocky, pupils dilated.

*Oh, my love, I wish I could go back, change what happened, start all over. How different our lives might have been! But I can't. What's done is done. And I accept that. All I ask is that you not hate me too much, that you try to understand.*

But Brian wasn't saying anything, he just stood there staring at her, with those eyes that seemed to reflect a whole universe.

She felt lost, floating, weightless. Free of her lie at long last . . . but, oh God, so alone.

*Go now,* she told herself. *Go before you start begging him to forgive you, to take you back.*

Rachel turned away, and started for the door. She felt as if she were walking through water, slowly, with a strange weightless grace.

*Don't look back,* she told herself.

'Rachel. Wait.'

She stopped, turned, and saw through a film of tears his

blurred shape rushing toward her. A tiny bead of hope rose in her.

She pushed it away. He wanted to say goodbye, that was all. To wish her luck perhaps. That was Brian, always gracious, even in the worst of times. A true gentleman.

Oh God, why wouldn't he just let her go? She couldn't bear the thought of them parting like tennis partners shaking hands after a match.

Then suddenly Brian was crushing her in his arms, knocking the wind out of her.

Rachel's heart took flight with a startled burst.

Oh Lord, was this really happening, Brian's arms around her? Oh, the miracle of him, his strong hard body and his bones, so blessedly solid, as if she'd been drowning and now he was dragging her on to some wonderful shore.

'Rachel,' he murmured, his voice choked with tears. 'You idiot. How could you ever think I would stop loving you? And all this time I thought it was me, that you'd stopped loving *me*.'

He was crying, they were both crying. She tasted salt when she kissed him.

'Brian,' she whispered, 'oh, Brian . . . can you ever forgive me?'

She waited, hearing sounds she had not noticed a few minutes ago, the ticking of a clock, Custer purring on the end of the sofa, the hissing of the radiator.

Then she heard Brian say, 'I already have.'

Rachel, delirious, wanted it to go on and on, this marvelous soaring feeling, but there was still something she had to know, something too important to be left for later.

She pulled away slightly, needing to see his face when he told her.

'Am I enough for you, Brian? Just me? Without a child?'

The light in his eyes was clear, achingly bright, shining with love.

'You are enough,' he said.

*

556

Rose, walking quickly, saw the open door at the end of the east corridor. Max's office. There was a light on.

She broke into a run, her heart slapping against her rib cage.

*Oh, let him be there,* she prayed, *oh please.*

All weekend she'd been chasing Max. First, phoning him at his apartment, over and over. Letting it ring and ring and ring. And this morning, the frustration, having to hold herself in, somehow to get through the meeting at Di Fazio's, before she could let herself think of Max.

And now finally, *finally,* she would be able to see him. Not yet lunchtime, he should still be in his office. *Please* . . .

She stopped in the open doorway, her heart, too, seeming to come to a standstill.

Max was crouched in front of the oak cabinet behind his desk, unloading files into a carton. 'Max, what on earth is going on?'

He glanced up, giving her a sheepish smile. 'Well, I guess it looks like I'm moving.'

Some kind of joke, of course. And not a funny one.

Rose scanned the office, saw how empty it looked, his desktop swept clean, cartons stacked over by the glass-front bookcase.

Oh, Mother of God, he was not joking.

Rose felt as if she had run for miles and miles . . . only to cross the finish line too late. Hot, aching all over, blood pounding. She wanted to lie down, somewhere dark and cool, away from the pain in her chest, from this nightmare, from the awful sight of Max packing his things in that box.

*This isn't happening. I'll walk out of here, and when I walk back in again, everything will be just as it was. Exactly the same as before.*

'What *is* this? Max? For God's sake, *tell me.*'

'I tried to call you last night,' he said. 'Your line was busy. I was going to tell you. I'm sorry you had to be surprised this way.'

'That's funny, that's really funny, because I tried to call

557

you last night. I tried calling you all weekend as a matter of fact.'

Who could she have been talking to when Max called? Oh, of course, Clare, calling from Syracuse, babbling, so upset she could hardly talk straight. Nonnie. Another stroke, a minor one, but still worrisome. So Rose had had to spend half an hour calming her down, all the while wanting to hang up, so the line could be free in case Max called.

And he *had* called . . . but only to tell her goodbye.

Jesus. The irony of it struck her, and Rose started to laugh and cry at the same time.

Max looked up at her, smiling, a bewildered expression on his face. 'Want to let me in on it?'

'Oh, Max, you look so funny squatting down there. Like . . . like . . . oh, I don't know . . . like I caught you with your hand in the cookie jar, or something.' Tears squeezed from the corners of her eyes, and wet her temples.

Then he was rising, his face red and hot-looking, gazing at her with such a woebegone expression that her laughter abruptly stopped.

'I'm taking over the litigation department in LA,' he explained. 'It all happened kind of suddenly, and you were so caught up in that trial . . . I didn't want to throw you this until . . .'

'Is it what you want, Max, is this really what you want?'

Max shrugged, almost grinned, the ghost of a grin. 'It's a great opportunity. And Mandy loves it out there. I'll have her summers, school vacations, that kind of thing. I took her out with me to look around last weekend. We even got in some pool time.' He rolled up the sleeve of his shirt, showing a forearm toasted golden brown. 'Look, you believe it? In the middle of November. Yeah, there's worse places to be than California.'

God, Max really *was* leaving. And for good.

Rose felt as if the floor – with its parquet floor and Oriental rug – had unhinged suddenly like a trapdoor, dropping her into black space.

Max, her staunch, never-failing pillar of support. The one friend she had counted on completely. She had taken him for granted, like the good air she breathed, always there.

And now . . . She wanted to say, *Max, don't go. I need you. I want you.*

But the words wouldn't come. She'd just be making a fool of herself . . . embarrassing them both. Max had already left her. That was clear. In his mind and heart he'd already put three thousand miles between them. He'd been traveling those miles probably from the minute he walked out her door four months ago, when she had not done one thing to stop him.

*It's too late.* The terrible realization sank home like a blow.

'When?' she asked.

'A week. I'd prefer more time to finish up things here, but Gary says it's a broken rudder out there.' He spread his hands in a helpless gesture. 'So here I am, trying to clean up twenty-three years. I don't suppose you'd care to give me a hand.'

Rose made a sound in her throat, a sob she just barely managed to hold back. She ducked her head, so he wouldn't see the pain in her face. Then she pasted a phony smile on, and spoke in a bright, congratulatory tone.

'Love to, but I have an appointment. I'm in kind of a rush. But, hey, listen, if you're not too busy, we'll have lunch or something before you go, OK? Champagne and everything.'

'Sure thing.' Max was on his knees again, digging into the bottom drawer of a file cabinet. He waved a manila file absently in her direction. 'I'll check and clear a date soon as I can find my calendar under all this rubble.'

Rose paused, taking in the scene, memorizing it, grainy with the early afternoon light that sifted in through the venetian blinds. Max's bent head, the hump of his broad back pulling the back of his shirt taut across the shoulders. One wrinkled tail had worked out over the waistband of his gray slacks, and she remembered him once saying, when they were in the shower together, that he was 'built like an old buffalo.'

She thought of that now. A buffalo. Somewhere she'd read that the Plains Indians, if caught in a blizzard while out hunting, kept from freezing by killing a buffalo, then cutting open its belly and crawling inside until the storm had passed. And that's what she'd done with Max, wasn't it? She'd used him to stay warm.

What else should she have expected? That he'd be here, waiting with open arms for her for ever? No. She had hurt him. And he had done what any sane person would do.

And now it was too late.

She had imagined herself unwinding with Max over a glass of wine at the end of the day, the way they used to. She, telling him everything about the trial; how it had climaxed, the settlement meeting this morning, And the thing that had been puzzling her, haunting her all night long, the weird coincidence of her long-ago guardian angel turning out to be *Rachel's mother*.

If only they could go home now, uncork that bottle of wine, take it to bed with them, then after they'd made love, as she lay in his arms, they would talk about everything, just like before. Only it usually had been *her* talking, asking advice . . . and Max listening, hadn't it?

Now suddenly there was so much she wanted to know about Max. But there wasn't time. She'd lost her chance.

Rose, feeling tears coming, turned away, and slipped out the door.

# 37

'The Lord will open to them the gate of paradise, and they will return to that homeland where there is no death, but only lasting joy . . .'

Rose listened to the young priest's words, her eyes dry as she watched him place a wooden cross on top of the simple white-painted coffin.

*Lasting joy?* she echoed in her mind. *Well, I hope so. God knows Nonnie took no joy in living. Let her get what she can out of death.*

She was surprised at how little emotion she felt. *I'm not sorry she's dead, how could I be? But I'm not glad, either.*

And, really, wasn't this what Nonnie had been toiling toward, all those First Fridays and Sunday masses, the endless rosaries and confessions, accumulating points for admission to heaven as if life itself was not much more than a giant bingo game?

Thank God, at least, it had been quick. A series of tiny strokes following Clare's call last week, and then Nonnie had slipped away in the middle of the night. Everyone had been spared, Nonnie most of all, the nightmare that would have followed if she'd lived. Bedridden, her mind gone, an oversized infant to be fed, changed, washed, diapered.

Rose glanced over at Marie, seated beside her on the wooden pew. Thinner than ever, and older, yet oddly dignified, holding herself straight, face flinty as an Indian-head nickel, wearing a ratty navy coat with a bit of torn lining drooping from one sleeve.

Rose felt the same old pity and irritation rise up inside her. *Look at her, still as aloof as a cat.* Marie would seldom chat on the phone, and she'd always come up with some excuse to turn down Rose's invitations to lunch, to dinner, a night out on the town. Rose was tired of always being the one to make the effort, so she hadn't seen Marie in a year or more. And now, here they were . . . God, what a rotten reason for getting together.

She felt rotten, too. Weary, a heaviness in her bones. *Tomorrow,* she reminded herself. *Tomorrow Max leaves for California.*

The thought was like one of Nonnie's knitting needles piercing into her heart.

God, she missed him already, and the pain of it kept getting worse. How stupid she'd been, how blind. And why, she agonized, why is it that the things that matter most, we get so close, we don't see them?

So different from the way she had felt about Brian. Max had never been pure and shining, enthroned on an altar in her heart, an icon. No, he was something that was *lived in.* Like a house full of nicks and jumble and worn chair arms, and more wonderful than any immaculate palace.

*I'm going to start crying any minute now – that would be funny, wouldn't it? Everyone thinking I was crying for Nonnie?*

No, not even poor Nonnie deserved that, tears at her funeral shed for someone else.

Rose forced her attention back to the priest. Old Father Donahue had retired, she'd heard. So this cherub-faced kid – why, he looked hardly older than an altar boy! – had to be his replacement. Strange, Holy Martyrs without wizened little Father Donahue in his green and white vestments.

And instead of Donahue's mumbling drone, this bright and youthful voice ringing out over the mostly empty pews.

'Oh God, you are my God whom I seek; for you my flesh pines and my soul thirsts like the earth, parched, lifeless and without water . . .'

Yes, lifeless, that's how she felt without Max.

'. . . You are my help, and in the shadow of your wings

562

I shout for joy. My soul clings fast to you; your right hand upholds me.'

A soft burbling sound now, *someone* was crying.

Rose looked beyond Marie, hard-eyed and stony-faced, to where Clare sat, head bowed, her face hidden by the flowing gray wings of her wimple. Clare reminded her of a feather pillow, soft and shapeless, plumped there on the bench. If only she would stop *crying*, for heaven's sake. As if Nonnie's dying hadn't been a blessing, really.

'She went just like that—' Rose heard Clare mutter weepily to Marie, 'like a light going off. Oh, I feel so terrible. So . . . so responsible.'

'Why should you feel responsible?' Marie whispered back impatiently. 'It's not as if *you* killed her.'

Rose watched Clare's round, tear-swollen face go still with shock at the very *idea*.

For an instant, Rose almost felt sorry for Clare. Then she remembered it hadn't been Clare who had cared for Nonnie these last years, but the orderlies and nurse's aides in a Catholic nursing home. Clare had done little more for Nonnie than she had in the past. Except to pray, of course. Clare was a real pro at praying.

At last, the service was over, the young fresh-faced priest making the sign of the cross over Nonnie's coffin. *My God,* Rose thought, *he didn't even* know *her*.

She felt a shiver run through her. The sudden horrible notion came over her that Nonnie wasn't really dead, that inside that coffin, she lay grinning, waiting to spring out at them like some ghoulish jack-in-the-box.

Then Rose realized Marie was fussing with her coat, reaching for her purse.

'I have to get back,' she said. 'The baby-sitter could only promise me an hour.'

'You're not coming out to the cemetery?' Clare asked, her doughy face seeming to sag.

'To watch somebody shovel dirt over her?' Marie shrugged. 'No, thanks.' Then she softened the tiniest bit, giving Clare's hand an absent pat. 'Look, I really do have to get back. Missy's sick, and Bobby was looking a little peakish this morning.' One corner of her thin mouth twisted up. 'Like they say, 'Life goes on,' you know?'

Rose saw that Clare had turned from Marie to her now, her expression beseeching.

Rose stiffened, thinking, *I can't stand any more of this.* But then she thought, *Is it fair, leaving Clare to deal with these mourners alone? Mrs Slatsky, and that bunch of old crones from the auxilliary.*

*Yes, that's what I would have done before – the so-called proper thing – in the days when I used to be a doormat. But that has changed. I have changed.*

And, mostly, she had Max to thank for that.

'I'm going back with Marie,' Rose found herself saying. 'Why don't you go on alone to the cemetery, Clare.' Kindly, she added, 'I think that's what Nonnie would have wanted, don't you?'

Anyway, there was something she had to talk about with Marie. Alone. Something Marie might be able to help her with.

Rachel's mother – yes, Sylvie was her name. It could be that Marie knew something.

Rachel touched her ear. *And if she does know something, then maybe I can figure out why Sylvie Rosenthal gave me this earring all those years ago.*

Marie's apartment hadn't changed. The same gloomy cave of a living room, with its stale nicotine smell. The same motel-style furniture, but shabbier now than it used to be. The playpen was gone, and a hockey stick was propped in the corner by the TV, a nude and contorted Barbie doll on the rug.

'Just set that on the floor, and have a seat,' Marie said, pointing to the overflowing laundry basket on a Laz-y-Boy recliner criss-crossed with friction tape. 'By the way, Bobby went nuts over that Atari game you sent him for his birthday. Can't pry him away from it.'

'I know. He sent me a nice thank you note. He's a great

564

kid, Marie. They all are. You're doing a good job raising them.'

The sound of television filtered in from the bedroom off the living room. All three of Marie's kids were in there, clustered around Missy's sickbed, watching 'The Mod Squad.' Rose promised herself she would spend some time with each of them before she left, and Bobby was old enough to stay over with her in the city sometimes. She would suggest it to Marie . . .

'Jesus,' Marie was now saying, 'you're getting to sound almost as holier-than-thou as Sister Clare. That what being a bigshot lawyer does to you?'

Before Rose could take offense, Marie had slumped on to the couch, all the starch seeming to have gone out of her. She lit a cigarette, and peered up at Rose through the smoke.

'Oh, hell, don't pay any attention to me,' Marie said and sighed. 'I just get so damn stir-crazy rattling around here all by myself with the kids off at school. It turns you mean after a while.'

'Where's Pete?' Rose asked.

'Pete!' Marie snorted. 'He left. Moved out. A couple weeks ago. Didn't I tell you? Oh well, good riddance as far as I'm concerned.'

'But . . . what . . .' Rose stopped herself, thought better of asking, *What are you living off of then? At least while Pete was around you had his unemployment check.*

The chilly look in Marie's eyes didn't invite any sisterly concern.

'Can I get you something? Coffee?' Marie asked.

'No, don't bother . . . please. I can't stay long anyway.' Rose took a deep breath. 'Marie, I came to ask you . . . about . . . about something Nonnie said a long time ago. About our mother . . . how she might have . . . well, that I might not have the same father as you and Clare.'

Marie was staring at her as if she'd lost her marbles. 'You serious? What do you care what that old bat said? She was always stirring up trouble. I don't care if she *is*

565

dead, it's the truth, ain't it? She liked making us squirm. Anyway, what difference does it make now?'

'I just want to know, that's all. I thought maybe . . . well, that maybe you knew something. That Nonnie might have told you—'

Marie's eyes cut away from hers, and all of a sudden she seemed tense as an alleycat. 'I *told* you. I don't know any more than you do.' She sounded irritated. 'Now, why don't you just forget about it?'

But Rose couldn't stop. This thing was eating away at her, and she knew it wasn't her imagination. Sylvie Rosenthal. Seeing her in that courtroom, seeing that flicker of recognition in her eyes. She *knew* something. And Rose was certain it had to do with her real father. Not the smiling sailor in the silver-framed photograph, Nonnie's son, Marie and Clare's father, but the man from whose seed she had sprung, someone dark and different-looking, so that she'd been set apart from her sisters from the day she was born.

'If another man was my father, then he must have had family, right?' She pushed on, desperate. 'A wife maybe? A sister? And this wife or sister, she might have known. About me. She might have wanted to see me . . .'

Marie rose abruptly, clutching at the throat of her dress. 'I told you I don't know anything about that! You're dreamin', that's all. You're just dreamin'.' She busied herself with the laundry basket, yanking an undershirt from the tangled pile and folding it in one savage motion. 'Look, I've got a lot to do. So if you're leavin' anyway, don't let me keep you.'

Rose felt a surge of angry frustration. Marie was lying, she *had* to be. Rose was sure of it. Marie *was* hiding something.

Rose leaned forward in her chair, grasping the plastic rim of the laundry basket, forcing Marie to look at her.

'For God's sake. Marie.'

'I *told* you. I—'

'I know what you said, but I think you do know

566

something. Oh, Marie, don't do this to me. All my life I've felt different, an outcast in my own family, and now *you're* turning against me.'

Rose jumped to her feet. She was trembling, furious with her sister, and at the same time aching with need.

'I have to know—' Rose choked, searching for the right words, 'who I am. Don't you see? I . . . I'm not asking for anything else. If my real father has a family, I won't bother anyone, I don't want to stir up trouble. *I just want to know.*'

Now Marie was glaring at her, feverish color staining her pale, sharp-boned cheeks.

Then Marie collapsed on to the sofa, and burst into tears.

Rose stared, stunned. She somehow couldn't move or speak. She couldn't remember ever seeing her sister cry.

When Marie lifted her face, her eyes were red-rimmed and puffy. She rose wearily, and said, 'Wait. There is something.'

Rose watched Marie shuffle out of the room, her heart beating faster than it should have been. She remembered that story, 'The Monkey's Paw,' all about how wishes can come true in the most hideous ways.

She was sweating, afraid.

Marie was back a minute later with something in her hand, a small blue book. A savings passbook, Rose saw. Marie thrust it at her, quickly, as if she had to get rid of it.

Rose opened it, and saw the name typed inside: *Rose Angelina Santini.*

The original deposit was twenty-five thousand dollars, dated September 15, 1945. But then there were pages and pages of withdrawals, years and years of them, a hundred dollars, fifty, seventy-five. In the very last column, the balance showed seven hundred forty-two dollars remaining.

She looked up at Marie. What was this?

Her sister's eyes slunk away.

'It's yours, all right,' Marie confessed, her voice low

with shame. 'I found it in Nonnie's things along with those letters of Brian's. She must've had it a lot longer, I figured, 'cause the postmark on the letter was—'

'What letter?' Rose interrupted, a slow heat building inside her head, pounding in her temples.

'The letter that was in the envelope with the bank book. It was dated a couple of months after our dad died. From some lawyer. It just said that someone had opened this account in your name – it doesn't say who, just that he wished to remain anonymous.'

'And Nonnie—'

'The way I look at it, she must have figured something was rotten in Denmark. I mean, why would some perfect stranger have given you all that money? She must have had suspicions all along about Dad not being your real father, and this just clinched it.'

'But you didn't tell me. You kept it.'

'Yeah, I kept it.' Marie met her gaze finally, squinting a little as if it hurt her to do so. 'Every day I'd tell myself it was just for a little while, I was just holding on to it for you. Then Pete got fired down at the hardware store, and we were so broke, and I told myself if I borrowed just a little, a hundred dollars to tide us over, it wouldn't matter 'cause I'd pay it back soon as Pete cashed his unemployment check. It was easy, *too* easy. At the bank, I told them I was you. I had this old library card of yours, and the letter addressed to you, and I knew all the family names. After that—' she shrugged, 'it just seemed like one thing after another. Bobby having his tonsils out. Gabe with his adenoids. And Pete, in and out of jobs faster than a Times Square hooker, with the bills rolling in, and overdue notices. I kept borrowing, telling myself I was going to pay it back someday . . . and then when you got to be a fancy lawyer and all, I changed my tune, told myself you didn't really need the money as much as I did, that it was unfair in the first place for you to have gotten it all. But I guess that doesn't change what I did. And for whatever it's worth, I hate myself. You couldn't hate me anymore than I already hate myself.'

Rose felt stunned, too shocked to think or speak.

Anger rose in her, thick and choking. *Damn it. How could Marie have lied to me? All these years. If she needed the money, all she had to do was ask. I would have given it to her, all of it.*

Then Rose saw the way her sister was stiffening, squaring her shoulders, lifting her chin. Tears glittered in her eyes, but now they were hard, defiant tears.

Her anger faded as suddenly as it had come. She understood. Marie's pride was all she had left. For her to have to ask for money would have been worse than lying. Worse than stealing, than anything.

Rose, overtaken by emotion – pity, relief, love – went over and put her arms around Marie.

'I don't care about the money, Marie. Keep it all. But don't you see what this means? He *did* care. Whoever my real father was. *Somebody* cared.'

*Yes, somebody,* she thought, *but who? Who is he? And how is he connected to Sylvie Rosenthal?*

# 38

Sylvie, sighing, closed the ledger. It had been Gerald's once, but now the spidery script that filled its lined pages was hers. She smoothed her palm over its worn calfskin cover. It had once been bright maroon and was now the color of port. In faded gold letters tooled across the top, it read: ACCOUNTS.

Monies received, monies paid. Each monthly column of figures nicely balancing out. All in order. All debts paid.

*All except one*, she thought.

The largest, most important one.

*You're a fool*, she told herself. *You should never have gone to that courtroom. Didn't Rachel tell you not to go? Why couldn't you listen to her?*

Remembering Rose, her Rose – and how magnificent she had been, saving Rachel – Sylvie felt the old regret welling in her, but accompanied now by a new, sharper pain.

*I've seen what you have made of your life, my daughter. And I am proud. You are beautiful and brilliant, just as Nikos said you were. And I was wrong to deny you. Even having Rachel, having her love, can never make up for that.*

Last night, when Nikos told her he had decided he would not reveal her secret to Rose, she'd been so relieved. She had felt like someone from the Bible, delivered from a deadly plague by the hand of God.

And then, when he said he still wanted to marry her, more than ever now, she'd been moved to tears.

Now, alone, with her thoughts, Sylvie wondered if she should say yes.

*I do love him*, she thought, *but do I really want to marry him?*

Sylvie gazed for a long moment at the portrait of herself over the fireplace, her likeness, yes, but someone altogether different, really. She was no longer that timid woman who had once come secretly to Nikos in his basement room, but someone who could be herself, openly, without embarrassment or regrets.

It was only her heart that hadn't changed. Her heart, which had never stopped grieving for Rose . . .

Sylvie suddenly felt very tired. She brought her forehead to rest against the ledger, its leather so smooth and burnished from handling it seemed almost to have the patina of living flesh.

Alone, she could almost enjoy her weariness, let it settle in with her like an old friend. She could put her head down in the middle of the day, and there was no one to cluck over her, ask if she was ill.

*How strange life is*, Sylvie thought. *After Gerald died, how I hated being alone, sitting down to a breakfast table set for one, the whole day stretching out ahead of me like the loneliest road in the world.*

But now she found she liked it, her solitary breakfast, sometimes on a tray in bed, making her feel pampered, luxurious, with the *Daily News* or 'Good Morning, America' for a bit of the world. Writing all the checks, her *own* money, no-one raising an eyebrow if she splurged on another pair of irresistible shoes, or a new dress from the designer floor at Saks.

But most of all, she loved depending on no-one but herself. What a luxury that was! And how good to feel strong enough now to do so much!

Sylvie recalled a day at Nikos's house, less than a month ago. She was there alone, poring through fabric swatches, when upstairs a pipe burst, water gushing as if from a spring right out into the center parlor. She had panicked, too overwhelmed to think what to do. But then she had rushed to the basement, found the main cut-off valve, called the plumber's emergency number, and even mopped up the water before it could seriously damage the ceiling below.

But if Nikos had been there, he'd have taken care of everything, and she would have felt weak and quite useless. And she would have *wanted* him to do it all. That was what was so awful. She was strong. But was she strong enough to resist letting a man take charge? And not just a broken pipe either, but of everything, of her whole life?

Yet Nikos, God bless him, he needed her.

*I have Rachel, at least*, Sylvie thought, *but Nikos has no-one. No, it's even worse than that, a daughter he yearns to love but cannot.*

*Oh God, forgive me, all those years I was so afraid of Gerald's finding out. But it was Nikos I was really hurting.*

Could she ever be forgiven? By Rachel, by Nikos, by Rose? God, how she longed for it!

Sylvie lifted her head. Somewhere in the silence of the house a clock was chiming. Why was it so quiet? Bridget's day off. Only Manuel, out in the yard raking up the dead leaves in the rose garden.

The weatherman had promised snow. And it did look that way. Outside the window, the sky looked still and somehow swollen; soon her rosebushes might be blanketed under a white quilt of snow, vanished like a dream.

But not gone, not really. Under the snow and beneath the frozen soil, some lovely green would be secretly hibernating. And in the spring, there'd be a miracle, and everything would bloom again.

*And so it goes*, she thought. *Something dies, but it's never really all gone. In our hearts, there's always a little piece left. And it can bloom again.*

The front-door buzzer pierced the silence, startling her. And for no reason at all, her heart began beating quickly.

She felt frightened of answering the door.

But even while inwardly she hesitated, her footsteps carried her across Gerald's office, out into the hallway, her heels clacking on the marble-tiled foyer. And without even pressing the intercom to see who was there, she pulled open the heavy walnut door.

Sylvie had not asked, because in her heart she must have known somehow who it was. Even before she'd swung the door fully back, and glimpsed the tall, olive-skinned girl in the Burberry raincoat poised on the front steps, the first snowflakes swirling down, catching in her dark hair like petals, Sylvie knew.

Standing in the doorway, rooted to the spot, she felt her heart leap, smashing against her chest.

'Rose,' she breathed.

## 39

Rose stepped inside, bringing a gust of cold air with her. Sylvie felt the young woman's huge dark eyes fixing on her with the same bewildered curiosity as the last time they had actually stood face to face, that wintry day in a Brooklyn schoolyard.

Sylvie, almost overcome with an irrepressible longing, had to fight to keep from clasping her daughter to her bosom.

Instead, Sylvie just stared at Rose, watching the snow-flakes turn to water, dripping off her raincoat on to the black and white marble tiles. A shiver ran lightly up her spine.

'How did you know my name?' Rose asked.

Sylvie took a step backward, and her hand found her throat, found the little buttons marching up the neck of her red cashmere cardigan. She caught hold of the top one, twisting, feeling it begin to tear free of its threads.

'I . . .,' she began, but her voice caught in her throat. She wanted to cry out the truth.

But it was as if her voice, her throat, her lungs all had frozen, and the cold was spreading now in waves, numbing her, turning her to ice.

*I am your mother. I gave birth to you, then gave you away. But how, how can I ever tell you such a thing?*

'We haven't, I suppose, actually been introduced, but Rachel has told me all about you,' said Sylvie, feeling spineless, and hating herself for it. 'Please, won't you come in? You must be half-frozen. They say we may have six inches by the time it's over. Amazing, isn't it? In November? Here, why don't you give me your coat? Then we can go up to the parlor and talk. You've come about Rachel, haven't you?'

Her chatter seemed to come out of nowhere, someone else's voice sliding past her frozen lips.

Rose seemed to falter, her expression hesitant and uncertain. She allowed Sylvie to take her coat. Under it, Sylvie saw, she was wearing a simple navy wool skirt and a white sweater. She looked so much like that solemn little girl, dressed in her school uniform, whose image Sylvie had carried like an invisible locket in her heart for more than twenty years. She couldn't go on with this dreadful pretense, no, not a moment longer.

'Coffee? Or do you drink tea?' But, oh dear God, she *could*. She was doing it. 'I myself prefer tea. Camomile tea. It's very soothing to the nerves, they say.' As she led the way upstairs, Sylvie kept up the chatter. 'Please, sit down. Anywhere.' She indicated the coziest chair, the plump chintz loveseat beside the fireplace. 'You didn't say. Coffee or tea?'

'Tea, please, if it's no bother.'

'No bother at all. It's my housekeeper's day off, though, so I'll just pop into the kitchen myself. I won't be a minute.'

Sylvie felt a great relief at just getting out of the room, at not having to look into those eyes, Nikos's eyes. Accusing her. Blaming her. *Rose can't know who I am, but she senses things. Deep down she must remember . . .*

In the kitchen, waiting for the kettle to boil, Sylvie clung to the edge of the counter, her arms and shoulders aching. She felt dizzy, and the cold seeped through her body with a constant, burning pain.

When the tea was ready and she'd stayed away as long as she decently could, she carried the tray up, listening to the chinking of the Wedgwood cups trembling in their saucers, willing herself to stay steady.

'Here we are,' she said brightly, settling the tray on the low rosewood table in front of the settee. 'Do you take lemon?'

Rose nodded. 'Yes, please.'

'Now then,' Sylvie said, handing Rose the delicate flower-painted cup brimming with steaming tea, 'is there something I can help you with? Something concerning Rachel?'

'I . . . not really . . . it's just . . .' Rose shifted uncomfortably in her chair, her eyes darting about the room as if she didn't really know why she was there. Then her dark gaze fell on Sylvie again, and Sylvie felt herself begin to shiver helplessly, terrified that Rose was now peering right through the window of her pretenses, seeing right into her dark secret.

'I didn't come about Rachel, actually. I . . . well, it all seems a little silly now that I'm actually here . . . but the thing is, yesterday, in court, I thought I recognized you. I was sure of it, in fact.' Rose reached up under her cloud of dark hair and pulled something from her ear.

Sylvie flinched. *Dear God, oh dear God, the earring I gave her. She kept it. All these years.* She stared at the earring, cringing inside, as if it contained some deadly poison that might harm her.

Now Rose was holding it out, a ruby in the shape of a teardrop that dangled from a diamond stud. It twinkled bright and hot as blood in her outstretched palm.

'A lady gave it to me when I was a little girl, just nine years old,' Rose explained. 'A lady who looked like you. Almost exactly like you, as a matter of fact. Of course it was a long time ago, but I remember her so well . . . You . . . this woman . . . took this earring from her own ear, and just handed it to me, without saying a word. Well, you can't imagine how shocked I was . . . it was as if . . . as if a fairy godmother had appeared out of nowhere and waved a magic wand over me. Only she ran off without ever telling me why, or who she was. I was hoping maybe you could help me. I thought you might somehow know why . . .' She trailed off, staring at Sylvie as she refastened the earring.

Now those black eyes were burning her, just as Nikos's had, burning right through her. And Sylvie could feel

576

layers and layers of her pretense peeling back like so many coats of old paint. *She knows. She remembers me. Dear God, let the lies stop. Let me tell her the truth.*

She couldn't, though. The truth felt too huge, a great boulder that would choke her if she tried to push it out.

And now another truth struck her: *I've kept the secret so long it's a part of me, like my own living flesh. Cutting it out would be like killing some part of me.*

'I wish I could help you, my dear,' she lied once again, hating herself more than she ever thought she could, 'but I'm afraid I don't know this woman. You say I remind you of her? Well, I know what that's like. I met a woman once, and it nearly drove me crazy, she looked so familiar, and I couldn't think why. I never did figure it out. Oh dear, your tea has gotten cold. Let me pour you a fresh cup.'

Rose replaced her cup in its saucer with a decisive click. 'No . . . thank you.' She seemed very agitated. 'I . . . I have to go. I apologize for taking your time. For barging in on you like this. But, you see, I thought . . . I was so sure . . .'

'Please, don't apologize. I'm delighted you came. I wanted to thank you anyway. For helping Rachel. You were marvelous.'

On her way down the staircase, Sylvie prayed that Rose wouldn't notice how badly she was shaking, how false and tinny her words surely had sounded.

And then she saw, as they reached the bottom, the look in Rose's black eyes. *You lied*, those eyes said. *I don't know why. But I know that much.*

Sylvie thought of the ruby earring that matched Rose's. And she remembered how, years ago, she had pulled out a loose brick in the garden wall, and hidden the earring behind it. *Like a seed*, she thought now, *one not planted in the earth, one that will never grow*.

Right then, she wanted to lie down on the cold tile floor and die.

# 40

Rose, watching Sylvie go to the closet for her coat, felt an urge to grab her and shake her. Her one chance to find out the truth, maybe her only chance, and it was slipping away. In a moment it would be gone.

*She knows something*, Rose thought, *but, dammit, she won't tell me. She seems afraid. But why? Who could she be afraid of?*

And then, glancing about as she waited for her coat, Rose looked into an open doorway – the room looked like a man's study: worn leather chairs, an antique map, and huge 1920s posters of great operas framed on the walls. Over the fireplace, with its massive brass lion's-head andirons, hung an oil painting of a young woman in a blue chiffon dress, hands resting in her lap. Pale as she was, she seemed to glow with warmth and life, as if she might step right down into the room.

Rose, intrigued, drew closer, crossing the threshold. Stopping before the fireplace, she stared up at the portrait, at the willowy green-eyed woman with hair like watered silk. Then she noticed something else, a bit of red shining below her ear, a ruby set in gold, and shaped like a teardrop. The artist had painted it with such skill it actually seemed to sparkle.

Rose felt dizzy, her heart leaping with quick, shallow beats, like a stone skipping over the surface of a pond. *It's her . . . my guardian angel.*

'This was my husband's study,' Sylvie's voice fluted behind her. She sounded anxious, flustered. 'All his books, his record collection . . . he loved opera, you see . . .'

Rose forced herself to turn and face Sylvie, who stood near the doorway. Bunched in her arms was Rose's coat. There was something odd, Rose observed, about the way she was holding it, clutching it to herself, almost as if it were a child.

'It *was* you.' Rose barely managed to squeeze out the words; all the air seemed to have been sucked out of her.

She had known it, of course . . . but this . . . actually *seeing* it . . . that earring. A perfect match. God, what was happening?

She felt the blood rise inside her head like a great wave, crashing, roaring in her ears.

She watched Sylvie take a step backward, then wobble, her delicate ankle turning under her so that she stumbled, and had to catch hold of a side table to steady herself. Rose's coat fell from her arms, splaying out on the Oriental carpet.

Then Sylvie was straightening herself, slowly, cautiously, like someone very aged, or very ill. Perfectly still, erect, she looked like a marble statue, illuminated by the hazy gray light that glowed between the heavy drapes.

Rose took a step forward, feeling chilled, as if she had been treading water in a lake and now had swum into a cold spot. She felt her skin shrink with gooseflesh, and a vein in her neck begin to pulse wildly.

Rose, not aware of what she was doing, suddenly realized that she had brought her hand up, and was fingering her ruby earring.

She saw Sylvie flinch, as if she'd been struck.

'Who *are* you?' Rose whispered.

Sylvie stared at her for a long time. She stood as if frozen, her eyes unblinking, like a wild animal caught in the headlights of an onrushing car.

Then she said: 'I am your mother.'

Her voice seemed to carry an echo, as if she were speaking inside a tunnel.

What did she mean? Rose felt stupid. Sylvie seemed to be saying something to her, something important, but it

579

was as if she were speaking Chinese. Mother? How could this woman be her mother? No. Impossible. She must have heard wrong.

'I don't understand,' Rose said. It was hard to speak. Her lips felt frozen, her face too.' I don't . . . my mother . . . my mother is dead . . .'

'Yes. Angie, she died. But not your real mother. Me, *I* carried you, here.' She pressed a pale hand to her belly. 'I gave birth to you. You, so dark . . . all that black hair, eyes like jet buttons . . . but I wanted you . . . oh yes, I wanted you. But Gerald, he would have known then that I'd loved another man . . . and I knew he would hate me, divorce me.' Sylvie was trembling, her words spinning out wildly, disconnected from the pale contorted oval of her face. 'Then the fire . . . there was a fire that night . . . and, God forgive me, I took Angie's baby instead of my own. Instead of you.' She covered her face with her hands, her thin shoulders hunched beneath her red cardigan.

'Rachel,' Rose breathed.

Then in a flash, it came to her . . . that nagging feeling she always had around Rachel . . . Rachel always reminding her of someone, but who? Who? And now, oh sweet baby Jesus . . . *right there in front of my eyes all along, only I just couldn't see it . . .*

Marie. God, yes.

Rachel, golden-brown hair, hot blue eyes, petite, just like Marie. A younger, prettier Marie.

Rose felt a strange lightness, as if someone were lifting her up, and she was weightless, floating in the air. This wasn't real . . . this couldn't be happening . . .

*This woman, Sylvie Rosenthal. My real mother.* No, that couldn't be.

And yet . . . at the same time she felt it must somehow be true. Somewhere, in some hidden part of her, she must always have known it. The way in dreams you know things, things that otherwise you have no way of knowing.

Then she felt as if she were coming apart inside, like

580

fragments of colored glass in a kaleidoscope, whirling and scattering. But her center remained still and cold. A rime of fury settled like frost around her heart.

*My mother is not dead. She didn't die in that fire . . . she just walked away . . . left me to strangers . . . oh God . . . she LEFT ME . . .*

'I regretted it,' Sylvie said, dropping her hands and showing her drawn, tortured face. 'As soon as I did it, I was sorry . . . I wanted to go back, tell them it was a mistake. But I couldn't. I didn't see any other way.'

'And my father? Who is my father?'

'Nikos Alexandros. He was my lover. I didn't tell him . . . but he knows now. And he wants you . . . more than anything. He would have wanted you then too. But . . . I was so confused, you see, and so afraid. Wrong. I know that now. So wrong to give you up. There hasn't been a single day all these years that I haven't hated myself for this.'

'But you could have come back for me . . . when I was one, or five, or seven.' The coldness gripping her heart was spreading, numbing her fingers, her toes. Outside, she could see, the snow falling faster, harder, swirling against the windowpanes with a sizzling sound. 'And when you came to my school. Why? Why didn't you tell me then?'

'I just wanted to see you. Just once . . . see how you were. What you looked like.' Sylvie's voice cracked a little, and she brought a trembling hand to her ear, remembering. 'And then I couldn't let you go without . . . without something of me.'

'But what about *me?*' Rose cried, taking another step forward, her knees buckling a little. 'You had Rachel, you didn't need anything from *me.*'

'No . . . no, you don't understand . . . *I wanted you.* But it was too late by then. Far too late.' Reflections of the falling snow flitted across Sylvie's thin white face. 'How could I have told you then? You would have run away. You wouldn't have believed me. You wouldn't have wanted me.'

'But you're wrong. I did want you. I *needed* you . . . or someone . . . anyone to love me.' Rose stared at Sylvie, watching her grow even paler. She remembered that day, the cold wind whipping at her thin coat, the shock of her unexpected gift – a ruby earring, like a drop of sacred blood in her palm, like the scourge of Jesus. Oh yes, how she remembered. 'What if you had claimed me then? Was it Rachel that stopped you? What would have happened to her?'

Sylvie jerked upright, as if there were invisible wires attached to her, pulling her spine erect, lifting her head high. Her face worked with the tears she was holding back.

'I won't lie to you,' Sylvie said. 'I've lied enough. I love Rachel as if she were my own. I could no more have given her up than if . . .'

Rose felt something within her snap. She sprang forward – in her new weightlessness she seemed to clear the room in a single giant step – gripping Sylvie's shoulders, her thumbs digging into the soft flesh below the delicate bow of Sylvie's collarbone. She could smell Sylvie's perfume, a light flowery scent, sweet, filling her with equal measures of desperate longing and rage.

'*If what?* Than if she were your own child? Is that what you were going to say? *Is it?*'

Sylvie made no attempt to pull away. She stood there, arms limp, her huge green eyes burning.

Slowly, Sylvie shook her head, and the movement dislodged a tear. It rolled down her cheek, dropping off her chin, splashing hot on to Rose's wrist.

Then it was Sylvie holding her, cradling her face between her hands . . . her fingers cold, shocking Rose with their coldness. For an eternal moment they stood that way, joined, silent. The only sound was the thundering of Rose's heart.

'All these years . . .' Sylvie's tremulous voice shattered the stillness. 'To touch you . . . oh, just to touch you . . . like this . . . my child . . . my daughter . . .'

582

Rose wrenched away, a wave of fury rolling up from her gut, dull red blossoming inside her skull.

'No!' she screamed. '*No!* You didn't want me then . . . you never wanted me . . . you *left* me there like . . . like I was a dog or a kitten. All my life, I've felt like I wasn't a part of my family. Or anybody's. My own grandmother, she hated me. She saw how different I was . . . she thought it was *my* mother, Angie, who'd been sleeping around. She blamed me for her son's death. And you thought a lousy bank account could make up for that? Oh yes, I know about that, too. It had to be you. But even then you didn't have the guts to show your name.'

'I couldn't. But I wanted you to have something . . .'

'You gave me nothing! No, less than nothing. That day at my school, you were like some beautiful dream, you gave me hope. But it was a false hope. Useless. Like this earring. Did you ever stop to think how useless a single earring is? Worse than that . . . it's a reminder of what isn't there.'

Sylvie pressed a hand to her heart, grimacing as if she were in terrible pain. Her face was wet. 'I am sorry . . . so sorry,' she choked. 'I didn't mean . . . I never wanted to hurt you . . .'

'How could you hurt me? I didn't know you.' Rose felt a salty taste on the back of her tongue; any minute now, she might start to cry.

Rose stooped to snatch her coat from the floor. Blood rushed to her face. Pinpricks of light danced before her eyes, blinding her for a moment. Then her vision cleared, and she started toward the door.

'Goodbye . . . *Mother.*'

'Wait! You can't go. Not now . . . not until . . . wait, oh please!'

Sylvie's voice, calling her back, was like an echo inside Rose's head. An echo of another time. She could feel, as she had on that long-ago day, her arms and legs growing heavier, slowing her until she couldn't move. And like that winter day in the schoolyard, she found herself turning,

583

hopelessly snared by the urgency of that voice.

*Stupid. Get out of here!* But she stood there, hating her own weakness. Even now she was longing for what she could never have. A mother's love. It was too late for that. If only Sylvie had told her sooner . . . if only she had loved her more than Rachel.

'I have something for you,' Sylvie said. 'Wait.'

Rose wanted to run . . . but something held her fast, the sight of Sylvie, so pale and silvery she seemed to shimmer, the look of absolute torment in her face.

Now it was Sylvie who was running . . . dashing across the room, then suddenly, shockingly, flinging open the French doors behind the heavy drapes. Rose felt a gust of icy air, and saw snowflakes swirling, catching in the velvet folds of the drapes.

Rose, shivering, stared into the swirling whiteness beyond the open windows. A garden, she saw. A garden under all that whiteness. Skeletal bushes. Trees, with snow pillowing in the crooks of their limbs. A tangle of vines on the far brick wall.

Sylvie was plunging into that whiteness now, mindless of the cold, not bothering to grab a coat, or even an extra sweater. Rose watched Sylvie struggling, half-slipping on the steps leading down, her high heels gouging deep holes in the snow that covered the patio.

*Holy Mother of God . . . what is she doing?*

'Sylvie!' Rose called.

But the wind seemed to snatch up her voice, and toss it away.

Throwing her coat around her, she started after Sylvie, the cold closing around her, biting, snowflakes pelting her cheeks, her lips, like cold grains of sand.

'Sylvie!' she screamed, forging across the slippery patio. 'What are you doing? You'll freeze!'

But Sylvie didn't seem to hear her . . . or didn't care. Squinting against the swirl of snow, she was feeling her way along the brick wall. And now, with her bare hands, clawing at one of the bricks.

584

Rose, drawing near, saw that Sylvie's hands were blue with cold, her fingernails broken, clotted with snow and crumbled mortar. Her thin back heaved as she frantically scrapped and tugged. Scarlet patches stood out against the blue-white of her face.

'Sylvie, for God's sake!' Rose dropped to her knees in the snow beside her mother, half-sobbing, desperate to make her stop. She could not bear another moment of this . . . seeing Sylvie like this . . . blue with cold, broken and weeping . . . clawing at the wall.

Rose pulled her coat more tightly about her, the cold like sharp pins pricking her legs, her hands. What was Sylvie searching for here?

The brick Sylvie was tugging gave suddenly in a small burst of red chips and dirt. Then Sylvie was reaching into the gaping hole, pulling out something folded inside a dirty piece of plastic. 'See! It's here!' she sobbed in triumph.

She tore off the plastic, and there, nested inside a scrap of rotting velvet, lay the earring. The ruby earring that matched the one in Rose's ear. Sparkling, unblemished, as if Sylvie had unfastened it from her own ear just moments before.

'Here.' Sylvie held it out to her, just as she had so many years before. But now her hand was thin and dirty, and it wore no elegant glove.

Rose felt her heart tumble, over and over, as if down a sleep slope.

*Mother* . . .

She could feel herself reaching out . . . reaching to take the earring.

No guardian angel now, this woman kneeling before her was someone real . . . and someone who wanted something from her as well . . .

Did she have something to offer? And could she let herself forgive?

Before she knew the answer, Rose was taking Sylvie's hand. She felt Sylvie's stiff fingers curling about hers, tightening, the ruby earring like a sharp thorn gouging into her palm.

*I don't know you*, Rose thought, *but I want to. I want to try.*

'Let's go inside,' she said softly.

# 41

Rose sat at her window, staring out. She realized she must have been that way for some time, and now noticed that it was dark and still snowing hard; under each yellow cone of street-lamp light a small blizzard of flakes. Below, the sidewalk was carpeted with white, and furrowed down the center with footsteps. This new snow, covering up the dirt and rubbish, seemed to transform the city into a fresh white canvas, a new surface on which a wonderful painting might appear. *And me? Will my life be different now? Better maybe?*

How stiff she felt. How long had she been sitting here? Hours maybe. Since leaving Sylvie's, she seemed to have lost all track of time.

She thought of that whole long afternoon she had spent in the big house on Riverside Drive, thawing out under a soft mohair blanket, curled on the sofa in front of a flickering fire. Sipping smooth port wine, and talking . . . talking, telling Sylvie everything she could remember about her whole life. Remembering aloud how Nonnie, year after year, had taunted and belittled her, Rose had felt more anger burst forth than she had thought she harbored. But what also came out strongly was her love for Marie, and yes, even for Clare. And she'd told Sylvie all about Brian, how for so long she had both loved and hated him, and hated Rachel too.

Sylvie had been relentless, no, almost hungry, with her questions; and Rose had gradually felt herself let go of the last vestiges of her resentment as she talked and talked, feeling lighter, freer, until her voice began to give out.

And then she had sagged back into the sofa cushions, too tired to say more.

For a long then, they'd both remained silent. Rose heard only the crackling of the fire, the sound of snow hissing against the windows. For a wonderful moment, she let herself fantasize about what it would have been like to grow up in this house. In her mind, she made herself small, small enough to crawl into Sylvie's warm lap, and lean against her soft bosom.

Then Sylvie leaned across to her, and took her hand. 'There is something I must say, my dear.' The solemnity of Sylvie's tone caused Rose to stiffen – whatever it was, she didn't want to hear. 'I don't expect you to understand, but I hope you'll at least try.' Sylvie paused, but now the silence was somehow threatening. *What is it? What do you want from me?*

'It's about Rachel,' Sylvie continued, averting her eyes, staring into the fire.

Rose felt her resentment once again flare. Dammit, this was *her* day! Rachel had had her mother all her life, plus every other luxury imaginable. Why was Sylvie ruining her one day of the life Rachel had enjoyed for ever?

'What about Rachel?' she asked, hearing the anger that had crept into her voice.

'Oh, Rose, don't you see! How all this could only hurt her, if she were to find out that I wasn't her real mother?' Sylvie sighed deeply, closing her eyes for an moment, as if she were in pain. 'Yet how can I ask you to lie for me? I have no right to, I know. I've already forced you to make such terrible sacrifices. But please, I beg you, before you do or say anything, you must think carefully, weigh the consequences. So you . . . don't end up punishing Rachel for my crime against you, for what I've done.'

'So then we never tell Rachel. She goes on living her myth, and where do *I* fit in?' Rose had demanded, feeling cheated, like a child who had just been handed a gift, exquisitely wrapped, then had it snatched away before she even could open it.

588

Sylvie squeezed her hand. 'Oh, Rose. Not God, not anyone can give back what I've taken from you. Certainly Rachel can't. So you and I . . . we have to try and start from here. From now, this minute, this day. As friends. And what we feel, what we know, will not change if we refrain from saying everything out loud.'

*Lies, lies, and more lies*, she felt tempted to snap at her. But something – she wasn't sure what – held Rose back. She hadn't said no, or yes, just that she'd think about it. Wearily, she had embraced Sylvie, memorizing the feel of Sylvie's delicate bones under the soft cashmere sweater, the faint, sweet scent of her perfume. Then Rose had left, a part of her wondering if she would see Sylvie again, if all this had really happened.

But now . . . sitting here, going over and over it in her mind, Rose could see the rightness in Sylvie's plea. What crime had Rachel committed? And hadn't she already suffered enough, with the trial? No, it wouldn't be right.

Still, part of her – the hurt child crouching deep in her heart – wanted to hurt Rachel too, punish her somehow for all the good things she'd had, for the love that should have belonged to her. And that same part of her, Rose knew, would go on resenting Rachel for the rest of her life.

But Rose wanted Sylvie too, what she was offering – her friendship, perhaps one day real closeness, even love. And she could not drag all this into the open, wound Rachel terribly, and then expect Sylvie's unqualified love. They could not begin that way.

A gust of wind rattled the window. Rose looked down, and saw a lone figure hurrying along the snowy sidewalk, hunched over, clutching his overcoat at the neck. The man looked so forlorn, cut off from the world, snow dusting his shoulders; and then she thought of herself, so alone here.

Suddenly she longed for Max, for his arms about her, holding her, squeezing her to him, for his smell, warm and tweedy and vaguely musky. She felt a pang. Tonight he was leaving for Los Angeles. Probably gone already.

589

*Stupid,* a voice inside her sneered, *Max isn't leaving you. It's you who gave him his walking papers.*

*That day I found him cleaning out his office, why didn't I tell him then that I loved him? I could have. Was it my damn stupid pride?*

Or was it something else altogether? Had she been afraid to get close to Max? What if Max hurt her the way Brian had?

*But I don't want to be alone anymore.* The thought came to her, clear and bright as a chime.

For so long she had felt lonely, set apart somehow, but now she didn't want that. She wanted Max. She wanted him more than Sylvie, more than anything.

Maybe . . . maybe she could still catch him.

Rose felt her heart leap. She jumped up, and dashed into the kitchen. Eight o'clock, she saw. He was taking the redeye, so there might still be time.

Rose grabbed the phone, dialed. *Please . . . please be there, Max.*

Damn, he wasn't picking up. She waited, letting it ring and ring and ring. She wanted to kick something, punch the wall. It wasn't fair. Tears rose, her throat swelled, choking her almost.

His plane, she remembered, wasn't leaving until ten. He had sent a memo around the office with his complete itinerary, in case anyone needed to reach him. United, JFK, ten P.M., each one of those words was engraved in her mind. In this weather, he'd probably be delayed, so if she hurried, she just might make it.

Now she was at her closet, tugging on her snow boots, throwing on her heavy coat, fumbling with the buttons. *Look at me! I'm shivering already, and I haven't even gotten out the door!*

Somehow, she was able to grab a cab almost immediately. But on the Long Island Expressway, traffic was slowed almost to a standstill. She cursed the snow, and the trucks bullying their way ahead of everyone, and the commuters clogging up the road who should have known better

590

than to go out in this weather. Christ almighty, at this rate she would *never* get there. She peered at her watch. Nine now. He might be boarding soon. God, she had to tell him. Please. She could not let him go without that . . . she *couldn't* . . .

*Please, Max . . . please be there.*

After a dozen bumper-to-bumper traffic jams, they reached the United terminal. On the approach ramp cars were double and triple parked. Inside, mobs of people, engulfing the ticket counters, packing every seat in the waiting area and camping on the floor, thronging the walkway toward the gates, ramming her with their luggage. Dozens of flights had been cancelled.

*God, please . . . let Max's be one of them.*

She scanned the departure board, quickly spotting it, Flight 351, Los Angeles, 10:05, Gate 12. According to her watch, that still gave her six minutes.

Rose, her heart pounding in her throat, blood beating at her temples, ran, dodging her way through the crowds, nearly crashing into a huge black man lugging an enormous suitcase, almost knocking over a child. The gate numbers gradually grew higher, four, now six, seven, nine . . .

Twelve. Gate twelve. Her lungs bursting, she dashed past the counter, into the lounge. The door leading to the airplane was closed. But maybe she could still get through . . . maybe . . .

Then Rose saw. Through the huge plate-glass window, red lights blinking, a dark gliding hulk.

Max's plane. Taxiing away from the gate.

Her whole body grew heavy, her legs seeming to sink into the floor, her heart an iron weight.

*Max . . . oh Max . . .*

# 42

Max jammed his gloved hand against the door buzzer for
the second time. Christ, what did he expect? She had to be
dead asleep. It was hardly light, not even six.

He should just go, get moving. It was stupid coming
here. No point in it. He had a plane to catch.

Max could feel the cold of the snow-crusted stoop
creeping up through his soles. His hands were numb. During the night it had stopped snowing; too cold for snow. It
had to be well below freezing. His breath, pluming out,
made white clouds in the still, gray air.

Finally, after pressing the buzzer a third time, it hit him.
Rose was not going to answer. She was not. Maybe she
wasn't even there. He felt his heart sink. Turning to go, he
picked up his suit-case.

Trudging down the snow-mounded steps, he remembered. God, he still had the keys. For days, he'd been meaning to give them back, but somehow he always forgot.

He dug a hand into his pocket, and pulled out the key
ring. Yes, still there. Rose's keys. He felt a surge of joy he
knew was ridiculous.

In a minute, he was upstairs, turning the key, feeling the
dead-bolt slide back, then, slowly, gently he was opening
the door. He lowered his suitcase soundlessly just inside
the door.

Max stood there, his heart surging up into his throat.
*Shmuck, who are you kidding? You didn't come up here
to say goodbye. You're still hoping, aren't you?*

Christ, why couldn't he ever learn? How many times
did Lucy have to snatch the football out from under
Charlie Brown before he wised up?

No, this was ridiculous.

But still, how could he go off without at least saying goodbye?

True, if the weather hadn't been so lousy, if Monkey hadn't begged him to take a later plane, he'd have been in Beverly Hills by now.

But this flight wasn't for another two hours. So he'd thought, *Why not?*

Max tiptoed across the living room. Morning light, reflecting off the snow piled around the window frames, made everything seem brighter, far later than six in the morning. He noticed a jumble of clothing on a chair, a coat, a pair of boots askew on the floor nearby. She must have come in late, too late to bother hanging her coat up. Could she have been on a date? Some guy? He felt a little sick – Christ, she might not be alone in that bedroom. His breath left him suddenly, as if it had been sucked out of him.

Softly, he edged into her bedroom. Dim light leaked in through the venetian blinds, dividing the room into hazy bars, glimmering dully off the brass knobs of the bed. He looked down at the figure under the rumpled quilt. *Alone, yes, thank God.* He felt a sweet rush of air enter his lungs.

He gazed at Rose, asleep, the rise and fall of her chest barely disturbing the quilt. Her face divided into two halves, light and dark, her hair a black cloud against the pillow. God, she was beautiful. His heart broke a little, and his eyes filled with tears.

'Rose.' He touched her hand. 'Rose, wake up.'

*Just let me say goodbye, and I promise I'll be out of your life.*

Tomorrow, this time, he'd be navigating the Santa Monica Freeway. Seventy degrees out there, Gary had told him over the phone just last night. In fucking November. Seventy degrees! *I'll take you down to Venice,* he'd said, *you won't believe your eyes. Girls in bikinis roller-skating down the sidewalk. Max, out here, you'll have it made in the shade.*

593

Yeah, Max thought, along with all those other pathetic guys, shirts open to their navels, gold medallions around their throats, chasing girls half their age.

*But what if all I want is right here?*

*But she don't want you, Max old boy. So you better head on out before you make a complete ass of yourself.*

No, just one quick goodbye. *Got to do it. It's the lawyer in me. Everything has to have a beginning, middle, and end. Closure.*

*Sure, we'll probably exchange Christmas cards for a few years, and maybe I'll poke my head in her office to say hello when I'm in town. Hell, she'll probably get married one of these days and invite me to the wedding. But this is where I get off, last stop, jury in.*

'Rose,' he murmured again, staring down at her, memorizing her face. She was sleeping so soundly he didn't have the heart to really wake her. She looked all done in, poor kid.

OK, probably better this way . . . to leave before she even knew he'd been here.

'Goodbye. I'll miss you,' Max whispered under his breath.

He felt as helpless as he had those long-ago nights standing watch over his daughter's crib – Jesus, he could have watched Monkey sleep for hours, she was that sweet to look at – knowing that no matter how badly he wanted to protect her, to shield her inside the bulletproof vessel of his love, the time would come when she would walk out into the world and leave him standing back there on the curb.

His heart slipped in his chest, and tears stung his eyes. 'Yeah . . . well.' He dropped a kiss on her slack mouth. 'See you around, kiddo.'

He was at the bedroom door when he heard Rose croak, 'Max? That you?'

He turned back, his heart leaping. 'It's me. Sorry if I scared you.'

Now she was bolting upright, wide awake, her huge

dark eyes fixed on him in amazement. 'Max, what are you doing *here?* You're supposed to be in LA.!'

'Mandy was worried about me flying in such lousy weather, so I told her I'd wait until it cleared. And now I'm on my way to the airport. Just stopped in to say goodbye . . . and leave you these.' He slid the keys off his ring, and dropped them on the dresser with a muffled click. 'Don't get up. I only have a minute.' He forced a smile. 'California, here I come, as the song goes. Hey . . . hey, what's this? What's with the waterworks?'

Suddenly, Rose, in a rumpled blue flannel nightgown, was leaping from the bed, with that wild clock-sprung hair sticking out all over her head and tears running down her cheeks. And now she was blocking the door, hands on hips.

'You can't go. I won't let you.'

Max stared at her, stunned.

'Rose, what are you talking about?'

'You heard me, Max Griffin! You're not going anywhere, not without me, you're not!' Flags of stung red stood out on her cheeks, and her eyes glittered.

A kernel of hope broke open inside him, and sent out a pale, searching tendril. Max found he could move then, and he was crossing the room in two strides, grabbing her by the shoulders.

'Rose, are you crazy?'

'You heard me. I'm going with you.'

'Are you dreaming? What the hell do you want to go to California for?'

'Grapefruit.'

'Rose . . . you're not making—'

'Smog. Hot tubs. Freeways. Ronald Reagan . . .'

'Have you gone completely—'

'You.'

'What did you say?'

'You.' She was smiling. 'I love you, Max. I can't stay if you're not going to be here.'

Now the hope was blossoming in him, full blown,

595

incredulous. 'I think I'm the one who's dreaming now.'

'I loved you from the beginning, I think, only I just didn't know it. Then when I thought it was too late, when you told me you were moving to LA . . . oh Max, *is* it too late?'

'Did you mean that, about coming out with me?'

She grinned, but he could see that the corners of her mouth were trembling. 'I hear hot tubs do wonders for your sex life. I also happen to love grapefruit.'

Max stared at her, feeling as if the floor had been yanked out from underneath him, and he were tumbling in midair. And now landing with a bone-jarring thud. Jesus, oh Jesus, he had been down twenty years of bad road, and here she was suddenly, a mirage shimmering on the horizon, promising coolness and sweet water and an end to the loneliness.

God, could he trust this?

A memory floated up from his subconscious. Sixteen years old, and wanting so bad to own a car that he spent every day of a summer working the bag-packing line of the Jersey cement plant. Coming home each day in a pall of dust, eyes on fire, a gritty taste of cement dust in his mouth that wouldn't wash out even when he brushed his teeth until his gums were bleeding. And then finally, come September, when he'd had four hundred saved, the car. Oh, Jesus, that shit-kicking *car*. A 1941 puke-green Oldsmobile Eighty-Eight. Rust-eaten and hung together with old coat-hangers. His mother cried when he brought it home and parked it in the driveway. But it ran, goddamn it. Wouldn't have stood up in the Indy 500, but it *ran*. On a gallon of spit for every gallon of regular. Christ, he'd loved that car. Better than the brand-new Thunderbird he'd bought after law school, and all the cars he'd owned since. Now he thought he understood why, in spite of all its flaws, he'd loved it so.

Because he hadn't just bought it, he'd *dreamed* it. He had conjured it up, like some demented teenage Ali Baba, out of cement dust and wishful thinking. And he had known, then and for ever, sitting behind the sun-cracked steering wheel of that Olds, that if you wanted it bad enough, dreamed *hard* enough, anything was possible.

Max blinked, bringing Rose into sudden, dazzling focus, and it was as if he were seeing a tiny universe of sorts, the delicate blue veins tracing her temples, each glistening coil of hair, the specks of clear light in her dark eyes, making them shine.

He brought his hand to her face, palm up, not touching her but close enough to feel her heat. Rose leaned into his palm, closing her eyes, and the silken feel of her skin over the hard curve of cheekbone made him feel as if he were turning cartwheels on new grass, leaving him breathless, dizzy, heartstruck. No mirage, he told himself. No, she, like himself, was just another weary traveler come home.

'One condition,' he said, his throat rusty with emotion.

'Shoot,' she murmured.

'Marry me.'

Her eyes flew open. A slow smile spreading across her face. 'I do. I mean, I will. Yes. Does that answer your question or do you want me to go on?'

'Yeah,' he said. 'But keep going. I like hearing it anyway.'

She threw her head back, laughing, arms stretching up, up, her throat arching, her electric hair falling away from her ears and neck.

And that's when he noticed – the earrings. *Two* of them, identical, shaped like tiny teardrops, sparkling in each of her ears.

# Epilogue

Sylvie sank into the deep chair by the fireplace, and luxuriated a moment in its soft velvet. She kicked off her pumps, and let her head fall against the plump backrest. Through the etched glass panels of the parlor pocket doors, she could see shadows wavering – the caterer's people clearing away empty glasses, ashtrays, plates.

She felt tired, but it was a *good* tired. Like arranging roses in her best Waterford vase after a hard morning of pulling weeds in the hot sun.

*They loved it. Everyone. What Nikos has done with this old wreck of a house. What I have done. A miracle, they said.*

Drifting up the stairs, she could hear the faint tinkle of the women's laughter, the deep rolling bell of Nikos's voice bidding the last of the guests good-night. And sounds from the kitchen directly below, too, the singsong patter of Jamaican patois, the tap running, dishes clattering.

Sylvie propped her stockinged feet on the needlepoint foot rest. She felt a twinge of sheepishness now to think how shamelessly she had basked in the evening's praise, worn it about her like a crown of laurel leaves.

But then, why not? She *did* deserve it.

Sylvie looked about the parlor, soft in the rosy light of the dying fire, and saw it in its splendid completeness as if for the first time – without the invasive memories of cracked walls, sagging ceiling, lumber and paint buckets. A slow, wondering pride crept through, made her feel lifted up.

*Grand, yes. And intimate, too. The best of both worlds.*

How right she'd been to choose this light color to offset the mahogany moldings about the doors and windows, a William Morris design in the palest silver; and for the ceiling, with its garlands of plaster rosettes, soft pastel colors. And instead of the heavy funereal velvet, she'd picked drapes of a soft lemony weave, with the sheerest of liners, designed to drink in the sunlight. And, here and there, bright accents. A red-lacquered Chinese tea cabinet, a striking Louis Quinze gilt pier mirror between the two tall windows, a Georgia O'Keeffe lily over the fireplace.

*I created this. Something to be proud of. Oh, Mama, I wish you could see this . . .*

In the tall pier mirror, Sylvie caught the shimmery amber reflection of a slender woman wearing a crèpe gown the color of Blue Nile roses, her pale hair caught up with two antique silver combs. There was a look of deep calm in the woman's wide, sea-green eyes.

She gazed at this image of herself, feeling distanced, as if she were seeing a portrait someone had painted of her. And she was struck by the woman's dignity, her air of self-possession.

'You've made up your mind, haven't you?' she whispered to herself, breathing in the scent of perfume and cigarettes which still lingered.

Yes. Finally. She knew how she wanted to spend the rest of her life. Nikos was growing impatient. She had put him off too long. Now he deserved an answer, though it hurt so to think of what she'd be sacrificing.

*But for every choice there is a price. And who knows that better than I?*

She thought of that long-ago night, the choking smoke, terror, searing flames, and how after claiming the sheet-wrapped bundle in her arms as her own, she'd had to live with that choice. But, thank God, it wasn't so painful anymore. She had found her child, her Rose. She had held her true daughter in her arms. And she would never let herself be separated from Rose, not completely, not even with Rose in California. She would visit often. She'd flown out once already. And there would be the wedding, this summer. Other times, too.

Nikos had visited Rose too, just two weeks ago. He'd brought home snapshots, and told her everything, every detail of their reunion, what they'd talked about, what they'd done together.

Sylvie finally could look ahead of her, instead of looking back. She could go on, devote more energy to her work.

She thought of the place in Murray Hill she'd bought last month, a wreck . . . in worse condition even than this house had been.

Now she was spending her days tramping through rubble-strewn rooms, sweet-talking Building Department inspectors, counting deliveries of tile and lumber, haggling with contractors. But eventually the raw work would be done, and she could begin the part she loved best – the finishing touches, the lovely details. Each room like a blank canvas awaiting her brush.

The excitement of it! A cup of coffee first thing, then off to D and D for wallpaper samples and fabric swatches, to the Bowery for lighting fixtures, or to a huge warehouse she knew of in Red Hook, full of dusty architectural remnants – mantels, stained-glass windows, ancient paint-encrusted doors.

Then, at the end of the day, her reward, a hot bath, a glass of sherry, a quiet dinner. And best of all, Nikos. Friend, lover, partner. He would make a wonderful husband, too. If only—

Sylvie started at the sound of the heavy pocket doors rolling back on their tracks.

'You look so relaxed, I thought you were asleep.' Nikos's voice, low and husky, stole up behind her. Then she felt the warm brush of his lips against the nape of her neck. 'Darling Sylvie. You were the belle of the ball tonight.'

He came around and sat across from her in the wing chair. He looked so handsome in his tuxedo, Sylvie thought, yet distant somehow, like some distinguished senator chairing a fund-raising banquet.

Nikos leaned back heavily, pushing his fingers through his hair, then unbuttoning his jacket, tugging at his bow tie and studs. She watched as his throat, broad and brown, appeared in the gap of his undone collar. Now he looked like hers again, a man of earth and fire.

'I think I had one too many glasses of champagne,' she said and laughed. 'The only bell I know about is the one ringing in my head, I'm afraid.'

'Well, then, I shall have to put you to bed,' he said and smiled, points of reflected firelight leaping in his black eyes.

Sylvie felt something tighten in her chest. 'No . . . not tonight, darling . . . I should get home. I have to be up at the crack of dawn tomorrow. The architect at eight-thirty, then over to Phillip's. There's a Tiffany transom I have my eye on. It would be perfect for the Murray Hill house.'

'Sylvie . . .' Nikos was leaning forward, his elbows braced on his knees, his blunt weathered hands forming a steeple upon which his chin rested. He looked troubled. 'I may not be the most educated man, but I know an excuse when I hear one. And you have been running away from me all week . . . is there something you wish to tell me?'

Sylvie stared into the dying fire, and felt sadness well up in her. She heard the soft ticking of rain against the windowpanes. Spring rain always seemed the coldest to her. Why was that?

An old memory swam up. She'd been trudging to school in her yellow hooded rain slicker and red rubber boots. Halfway there, accidentally she stepped into a big puddle, her boots filling with water, her feet feeling all slushy and cold. She had sat down on the curb and peeled the boots off – shoes and socks, too. But then, she couldn't undo the wet laces to put the shoes back on. So she just sat there, crying, until a man came along and called Mama from a phone booth.

She thought: *I've spent most of my life feeling weak and*

*stupid, waiting for some man to come and rescue me.*

No more. She'd stand on her own.

'I can't marry you, Nikos,' she said softly. 'I won't put you off any longer. It wouldn't be fair.'

Nikos seemed frozen, as if this time she were looking at a photograph of him, sitting there, tie askew, chin resting on the steeple of his fingers, his eyes like two holes burned in his leathery face.

'It's ironic in a way,' she went on, seeing him double now, her eyes filling with tears, 'because it was you who helped me see that I could survive on my own. I never would have if it hadn't been for you. But now I like having them ask my opinion at the bank. I like knowing that if the roof caved in, I wouldn't panic, I would handle it. I like being . . . in charge.'

'I don't want your submission,' Nikos said, his hands opening in supplication.' Only your love.'

'You have that, my dear. Always.'

'Then, *why?*'

'Because . . .' she thought, forming her words carefully, '. . . I know myself too well. Each day I would grow a little more dependent on you, a little more afraid to try things on my own. It's not your fault, Nikos. It's just the way I am. And perhaps that's my greatest strength . . . to be able to see my own weaknesses.'

'Oh, Sylvie.' She saw there now were tears in his eyes, too. 'It is *I* who am weak. I don't know how I could survive without you.'

'You don't have to,' she said. 'I only meant I couldn't marry you. But that doesn't mean we have to stop seeing each other, does it?'

'Perhaps not.' He sighed, leaning back. 'But I would always be pulling in that direction. I want a wife, Sylvie. I miss being married. I'm growing old . . . too old to chase about, not knowing which bed I'm waking up in, yours or mine. I want *you*. All the time, not just here and there.'

Sylvie felt a tug at her heart, but not as strong a pull as she'd feared. 'Oh, Nikos, there is nothing wrong with what you want. And I wish I could give it to you. If it was just a . . . a matter of handing it over, I would do it gladly. In fact, you have my heart already . . . but I cannot give you more than that.'

There was silence, and Sylvie heard a sudden noise, like a sigh. She looked over, and saw that the embers in the fireplace had fallen in on themselves, and a swarm of sparks was spiraling up the chimney.

She felt calm, strangely. As if this decision had been a steep hill she had finished climbing, and now she could rest for a bit.

After waiting a long while for him to say something more, she decided to take a chance, and stretched out her hand to where he sat.

For an awful moment her hand seemed to hang in mid-air, heavy and cold.

Would he push her away? Be angry at her? *Oh please, God, don't let him be angry. I love him, and I still need him in so many ways . . .*

Then, blessedly, she felt Nikos's strong warm fingers curling about hers; and now he was rising, pulling her to her feet.

'You think you have conquered me, do you, my head-strong Sylvie?' He was frowning, but his eyes were tender.

'Beaten you? Oh, Nikos, please don't think of it that way. I only meant that if I married you, I wouldn't remain the woman you love now.'

'You are wrong. I will love you always, in whatever guise. And I do not give up so easily, as you well know. Not when I am truly determined.'

'But, Nikos.' Sylvie smiled. 'You *already* have me.'

'Forever?'

'For tonight, tomorrow, the day after, and the day after that, and—'

'I see. Well, then, we shall start now. With tonight. Will you stay with me tonight?'

She saw through Nikos's strategy, and smiled. Oh well, it wouldn't hurt to give in just a *little*, would it?

Then he was rising, pulling her to her feet, and into his arms, his hard bulk warming her, his stiff shirt collar tickling her neck. Sylvie smiled to herself, her heart beating much too quickly. Oh yes, she understood now. All the tomorrows Nikos would string together, on and on.

'Well . . . I suppose I *could* cancel that architect tomorrow morning,' she said. She would let him think he'd won, when really she had already decided.

'And in the morning,' he murmured, 'you must stay for breakfast. I need your advice about something. That little patch of ground out in back, I've been thinking about planting roses there . . .'

THE END

**AN EQUAL CHANCE**
*by* Brenda Clarke

She was married at eighteen to an American G.I. and, when she finally arrived in America she found her new husband had vanished – decamped ahead of her, not wanting the responsibility of a wife. She was stranded in New York and couldn't afford her passage home again. The only job she could get was as a waitress in the Last Chance Saloon, a rough diner with an even rougher clientele. Desperate, she took it.

It was the beginning of Harriet Chance-Canossa-Contarini-Cavendish-Georgiadis-Wingfield, one of the richest women in the world.

But as her great empire grew, as her wealth increased, as other men took the place of the husband who had abandoned her, she never forgot the secret so carefully concealed from those about her – the identity of the child she had left behind her in England so many years before.

0 552 13230 6

# THE NAKED HEART
*by* Jacqueline Briskin

Their friendship began in the Paris of 1941 – a Paris held in the double grip of an icy winter and the Nazi occupation. But for Gilberte – the daughter of aristocratic French parents – and Anne, vibrant, generous and American, it was the beginning of a life-time of friendship, betrayal, love and hate. It was the time that they both fell in love with Quentin Dejong, handsome, brave, and a member of the Resistance – Quent, who was to prove the catalyst in both their lives.

As the frightening shadow of the Gestapo moved closer, touching first Anne, then Gilberte, their lifetime pattern was set. Gilberte, whose experiences turned her into a survivor, a collaborator, and a cold ruthless planner, was to become obsessed with seeking vengeance. Anne – forced to grow up almost overnight – made a daring escape over the Alps and then waited for Quent to come back to her.

It was not until the Liberation that the three met again – and by then the terrible secrets of the past began to dominate their lives and the lives of those who loved them.

0 552 13395 7